A CYBERPUNK ADVENTURE

I0718532

ARTEM: REVENANT

>>>BOOK ONE<<<

JEZ CAJIAO

Copyright © 2023 by R J Cajiao

Published through MAH Publishings Ltd

Audio production was handled by Christopher Boucher and Jessica Threet in collaboration with Podium Publishing LLC

Editing by Michelle Dunbar

Editing by Faith Williams

Cover by Marko Drazic

Typography by May Dawney Designs

Formatting and additional editing by Emily Godhand

All rights reserved. This book or any portion thereof may not be reproduced in any manner whatsoever without the express written permission of the author/publisher except for the use of brief quotations in a book review.

This is a work of fiction, all characters, places, spells, realities and secrets of the Upper and Lower Realms are entirely my own work, and if they offend you, it's not intentional. Probably.

TABLE OF CONTENTS

THANKS!

Hey everyone! Well, that's another bloody book written and released, it seems amazing and insane that I get paid to do this, as crazy as I am, and as wonderful as you all are, frankly you make it happen.

Thank you. Seriously, I started writing as a form of therapy, due to severe damage to my lungs in a job I did. I went from being very fit and active, to unable to cut the grass without having to sit down.

Writing for me was a last ditch hope to keep from going crazy, as well as spending the rest of my life dealing with asshole clients in IT that didn't understand that laminating their password and login details to their laptop was a bad idea.

Seriously. Some of them worked in government. *Shakes head*

But I digress, SO…thank you. Thank you all, my wonderful readers, my fellow authors, for giving me such amazing worlds to explore when I relax. Thank you to my team, first and always, my wife, Chrissy. She keeps me more or less sane, supplied with bacon sandwiches and Redbull, and occasionally peels me off the ceiling.

Thank you to my boys, Max and Xander. I love you, you crazy little buggers, so much. Thank you for making each and every day a wonder (and no thanks are due to the vomiting bug that you brought home, that'll be giving me nightmares for years to come).

To Geneva, partner to Chrissy and I in Legion, who's working tirelessly around the clock to keep things going and to develop the business!

To Kristen, for doing a million side jobs, and running after us all, to Michelle, Faith and Matthew, all editors extraordinaire, tweaking my madness and telling me the difference between a gamma tokamak and a Black Corium rod!

To Emily, for polishing the turd! To May for straightening and fixing, and of course, to Marko for his amazing Cover-art.

To Eddie of Zealot Miniatures, and Alb the Extraordinary, and amazing digital artist, who'll be responsible for some of the madness you'll be seeing soon. Thank you both for your patience with me.

To my Betas! You buggers are fantastic, and I appreciate you all, Scott, Richard, Spencer, Neil, Shawn, Chris, Kat and Keith, and Ben! Seriously, you catch so many little details, so thank you!

Lastly to a few of my team that rarely get a shoutout, not because they're not insanely deserving, but because it's generally not a good idea to feed the trolls…

To Paul, Zac, Jay and while not really a troll, more of a right hand and troll-hunter, to BJ.

Thank you guys, you really keep me cheerful. Plethora. (It means a lot.)

Now there's three people I've not mentioned yet, and that's deliberate. They're alternately responsible for driving me mad, and for making me laugh my arse off, keeping me sane, and making sure the horizon of madness is many miles behind me, all at once.

To Kev, Lars and Dawn, my fellow authors of Artem, may you always receive that which you deserve! HA! Seriously though, its been an experience…lets never do it again, okay? Love you guys!

We're almost done, I promise…To Chris and Jess, you guys have done an amazing job with the audio, thank you both for your effort and your care!

Lastly, to you. You the reader, sat there, reading these words, as I speak to you from the distant past. As I sit here now, typing, I'm feeling seriously thankful to YOU, you make all of this possible, you help me to feed my kids, and hide in my office when they shit everywhere, and I need to pretend I'm too busy to help clean up.

THANK YOU!

Love to you all,

-Jez
22/05/2023

PROLOGUE

Hanson scrabbled to his feet for what felt like the thousandth time. His hands and knees were shredded and bloody, his breath rasping in his throat as he fought down tears and panted, trying to suck in more of the foul-tasting air.

The whisper-thin *whirr* of the lung mods filtering the air was lost beneath his ragged, panicked breathing. Above it all, barely audible over his hammering heart—which must be echoing off the walls by now—was the shuffle and clank of the specters as they closed on him again.

"No…" He whimpered, shaking his head and turning, hands desperately slapping the walls as he searched in the darkness for the way out.

He'd been mad, he must have been, agreeing to this! It wasn't an initiation—sending people after the specters—it was madness!

A brief flare of light illuminated in his vision as the Keystone picked up a signal from overhead, and suddenly a woman stood by his side, glowing with health and overt sexual promise.

"Hey, handsome, come visit me at…"

"Fuck!" he half screamed, before waving his hand through the advert, his demand enough to cut off the image, but not before his shriek had drawn even more attention.

"Oh, gods…" He whined, shaking his head and swallowing hard, unable to understand how he'd been so fucking stupid to get into this situation. There wasn't a better option…he knew that, but there *had* to be…there had to be a better option than…than *this*!

"You want a mod?" Jacker had asked him and the other three what felt like an eternity ago. He'd been sitting at the table in the chop shop somewhere that was probably a dozen levels higher by now.

"Listen. Ya'll want into *our* shit, 'cos we gots the best mods. Ain't nobody fuckin' with the Reapers. But you?" He shook his head. "Ya need to earn it! Ah mean, seriously? Look at cha—not a real soldier among ya!" Jacker had scoffed, picking at his teeth with a fingernail, before shrugging, as if already giving up on them all.

Hanson and the others had shared a look, at once on the same side—*we're all in this together*—and simultaneously looking for an advantage over the others, each one a competitor for the promised place in the Reapers street gang.

Hanson remembered his stomach quailing at the thought of what was to come, but he'd had no choice. He'd stood straighter, sneering at the others, trying his best to project confidence and determination, despite his lack of mods and his malnourished, weak body.

If he wanted to live? If he wanted to survive long enough to climb up the ladder out of the worst of the slums, he needed someone to watch his back. He needed to not be prey. He needed to be a *predator*.

The only way to do that in this city? Mods.

"Ain't nobody gonna risk primo chrome on you, not 'til you prove yourself." Jacker had nodded to the bench on the left, and the collection of hammers, knives, pipes, and a single, shitty old handgun laid on it. "Go on, pick whatcha want. Ya take it down into the dark, an' ya bring me back somethin'. If it's good? Maybe ya get to keep it. Hell, mebbie ah'll even fit it maself."

There'd been a scramble for the gun. The lucky shit who'd gotten it laughed at the others down the barrel as he'd threatened them with it.

Jacker laughed at him. "Only three slugs in 'der. Better make 'em count, boy," he'd sneered.

The asshole with the gun went pale as he realized the target he'd just drawn on his own back. No longer was it a room full of individuals going down into the undercity. Now it was him…against them all.

The first thing that he'd done when they all got pushed into the undercity—the abandoned thousands of miles of tunnels, old metros, and lost passages under the living, breathing skin of Artem—was to put the gun to the head of the nearest of them. He took her knife, and ordered the rest to find him a mod, or he'd kill them, one by one.

They'd set off as a group, all of them watching one another's backs, an uneasy alliance struck without words.

Him first, then we see.

That had been the deal they silently agreed to, and they'd stuck to it, climbing deeper and deeper. All of them in their filthy work overalls, the literal shit and worse of the undercity clinging to them as they clambered here and there, avoiding collapses and sealed-off sections.

Occasionally, rich fucks—or corpo scum—would seal off sections of the undercity, holding back the nightmares that lived down there long enough to make solid, defensible areas, then move in and set up factories.

Some made food, growing the various "schmeats" in great vats, flavoring them and selling them off in vending machines and restaurants alike.

Others set up literal mind-fucking hellholes. Places that, for minimum wage, the poor jacked in, and people got to ride along on their nerves as shit happened to them.

If they were lucky enough to have a skill? A dancer, for example? They would dance to the music, and people born without rhythm could "ride" them and enjoy it as well, either live or a memory core.

For the vast majority, though? It wasn't so noble.

For those with fuck all "marketable" skills, it was down to three tracks: violence, fucking, or "experiences."

The orcs and half-orcs ruled in the violence tracks. Anyone who faced off against them got beaten to the point of death daily, and they were only lucky it was virtual, not real.

If you were ugly? Well, that's fucking out of the window, unless you were unlucky enough to be in certain "specialty taste" groups.

That left "experience"' for the vast majority. That or advertising, acting the part of backgrounds in whatever new shit the corpos wanted people in.

Basically, rich fucks jacked in to feel people's terror, pain, and more as they were loaded into full reach-around VR, feeling everything from the cold of being abandoned to die on a mountaintop, to being dropped out of an arcology window to plummet to their deaths.

That this was all that was left to a load of people to earn their creds, and that they still wondered why people hated them, said all that anyone needed to know about the government and their corpo masters.

Hanson and the others kept going, stumbling along long-lost train tracks, climbing through access hatches that seemed like nothing, until, on the other side, they found rotting, rusted ladders that vanished beyond the range of their shitty dark-vision goggles.

Rats and worse crawled around down here. The occasional dried smear of blood marked the death of something small and defenseless when a predator found them.

Through it all, the four crept, trying to make no noise as they hunted, half in utter terror, watery bowels and all, and the other half in desperate hope, praying to the gods of blood and chrome that they'd find a broken-down specter dead by the side of the passage.

Hanson had heard that up north, and 'round the center of the city, nobody actually believed in the specters, that they thought they were a myth.

He *wished* that was true.

Living this close to the outer edge, he and his sister crammed into a tiny one-bed apartment literally against the outer defensive wall, he'd seen them.

They all had.

The unquiet dead, shuffling along the streets, driven mad by their own mods, viruses that had torn through their firewalls and shredded their neural state. It erased their minds, breaking down what they'd been and leaving behind an unthinking, dead shell driven by hunger and need.

They were a cautionary tale to any gangbanger, as it was almost always their kind that ended up like this. Mod the wrong gear, chip something that was too high for you, something that was past your capabilities?

Or worse, use 'nites that were already corrupted to bond the mod? That got you *this*.

They saw the old ones sometimes, specters reduced to bone and metal, long dead and forced back into a terrible imitation of life, prowling the streets, hunting for 'nites—nanites that were pure and functional—or worse.

They were men and women who had modded themselves beyond their capacity to control them, mods that were too powerful or too corrupt for the user.

They'd been driven by a hunger, though—a hunger to mod themselves—and that lived on after death, the most basic drive brought back by whatever dark magic roamed the stack.

They hunted the living, tearing mods and flesh free with equal determination, ramming them into place, more often than not without any 'nites to form the bond between the user and the mod. The mod would sit there, an ocular enhancement rammed deep into the decaying skull of the specter, never again to be activated.

Never again, that was, unless some dumbass fool killed the specter and stripped it of its parts.

Some would still be good, uncorrupted. All they needed was to be cleaned, and a fresh set of good 'nites. That was the secret; fresh, *pure* 'nites could form a bond between anything, healing the flesh around the implant, bonding it to the user's nervous system.

The risk was in chipping a shitty mod, one that was corrupted, or trying to use 'nites that weren't pure.

That or, you know, trying to fucking harvest the fucking mod in the first place.

They'd searched for hours, doing loops though more and more of the collapsed and deeper areas, desperate to find something, anything, and to get back out without stirring up a swarm.

It'd not ended well. They'd turned a corner, exhausted, batteries low on all their gear, and one of them had walked straight into a specter. It'd been asleep, or on battery-saving mode or whatever they did, swaying on its feet, not even seeing the world around them, until they'd knocked it over.

It'd hit another in line, staggering it, and it'd slashed at the first with a bladed arm, waking more. In seconds, it'd spread; fury and hunger, as well as a desperate demand for the tech they all carried, raced through the specters as they woke to the hunt.

Hanson hadn't even been the first to run. The fucker with the gun had fired off a single shot, hitting an ocular mod and sending a ricochet deeper into the tunnel. It'd woke them all, driving the few still in hibernation into a frenzy as they fell on the nearest poor asshole.

Then they'd rushed the rest of them, and Hanson and the others had run, splitting up as they frantically searched for the correct tunnels, the ladders and stairwells to the levels above, and the way out of the undercity.

Now, though, the tunnel he'd been following ended against a sloppily built brick wall covered in dim, spreading mold. Hanson skidded to a disbelieving halt, his mouth falling open in horror.

He squinted as he frantically searched, losing skin and fingernails to the wall as he pounded his fists against it, hunting for a way through.

"No...no...fuck me no!" He whimpered. The clanking and clicking of the swarm got louder behind him, never far away. They'd been chasing him for how long now? A day? Two?

His goggles were broken, flickering in and out as the power cell ran low and the connectors failed. The left lens was missing, the right spiderwebbed with cracks that sent bright pulses of light searing through his eye then guttered out, making it almost impossible to see where he was going.

He'd get a half second of an image, then blackness, then a surge of light that blinded him, giving him the choice between a horrific migraine or utter blindness.

"A ladder..." he cried. "I just need a *ladder*..." He spun around, squinting up at the roof of the tunnel, but finding nothing.

His weapon was lost, the pry bar left somewhere behind him in the warren of tunnels. *This should have been the way out! This should have been...*

They all looked *alike*, dripping water and oil, fungus and dead bodies, torn flesh and...and...*the cracks*!

He spun, having seen one only a few seconds before, and he panted, trying to make it out in the darkness of the old tunnel.

There!

It was a few meters ahead of the bend that he hid around, and the oncoming figures had to be nearing it. He sprinted for it, desperate to reach it before he was spotted. Fractured tiles, once part of a mosaic that gave directions in the distant past, hung shattered around the fracture, along with cobwebs and dirt. His breath whistled as he pushed himself to reach it before he was seen.

There were cracks in all the tunnel walls. Sometimes they were ways through from one tunnel to another, or out into a long buried and forgotten building. Businesses that had failed, or were lost when the nearby wall failed and monsters roamed until the army took them down. Hell, some were just cracks.

Shen had tried one, and it'd collapsed as she pushed through. Masses of stone and metal fell, pinning her. They'd all run, abandoning her as she screamed and begged for help. The specters barely slowed to feast on the fallen before giving chase again.

Well, it was Hanson's only chance now, and he ran to the side of the tunnel, dropping into filthy knee-deep water and mud, splashing frantically as he went to his hands and knees. The water rose, going up to his chest as he forced his way into the crack.

It was narrow. Hell, he could barely fit into the crack *sideways*, but he shoved and wriggled, gritting his teeth and ignoring the hisses of indignation as *something* made its displeasure known.

Searing pain erupted from a bite to his shoulder, small but damn! He twisted and rammed his shoulder into the rock, dragging it as he moved deeper, feeling the crack and crumple of little bones or maybe carapace.

Whatever had bitten him paid for it, but that pain! It was like someone had injected white-hot lead into him…But the fear of what had bitten him and the diseases it probably had was just another tiny ember beside the burning bonfire of his terror.

Seconds passed as he pushed as deep as he could, before he froze in disbelief. The pulsing light of his optics showed that there was nothing in the solid rock ahead but narrowing cracks, and twisting to look back out…

Movement.

Stumbling movement as bodies passed, the silence broken only by the clicks and whirrs of old mods.

Outgassing could be heard distantly as nearby pressure valves were released, and Hanson covered his mouth, staying as still as possible.

He'd heard about the pressure blow-off valves from down deeper, how they released into the tunnels; hell, he'd seen the constant mists on the lower levels of the slum, rising through grates to hide the wet, night-darkened streets of Artem.

Here, though?

It might just be his chance.

The specters used a combination of electromagnetism and heat vision to hunt, or so he'd been told. Well, the valves were blow-offs from the reactors under the city, and the gas was hot, hot enough to cook you, if you stood too close.

He might have a chance! If he was lucky? The outgassing would hide him yet!

The jets released in the distance; the pressure changed in the tunnel as thousands of cubic feet of gasses were forced into the area. Distant squeals sounded as something living was caught too close to a valve and cooked.

The air filled with the hot metallic taste of copper and more, as something nearby had its blood blasted over the walls.

The swarm stood still, their optics whited out by the approaching clouds as more and more vapor was released, until the final valve, a dozen meters away, opened. Hanson fought not to scream as the temperature leapt upward with terrifying speed.

The clatter of collapsing bodies, the splash as something fell into the water outside his hiding hole…then the bleed off was over, as suddenly as it began.

He bit his lip, holding on. His skin was burning, but death literally stood outside. As the tunnel returned to a more manageable temperature, not to mention silence, Hanson sagged.

Minutes became hours as he stayed where he was, pressed against the back of the crack in the tunnel. Sounds filtered down from the city and distantly from the factories.

Hours slowly blurred, one running into another. At first, he fought against his bodily needs, but gave in when it became too much, adding more filth to the water he hid in, trying to contain the terror and shame.

His legs cramped and then went numb. Pain flowed through him from the contorted position he was in, but he forced himself to silence. The choice was that, or death.

The pain in his shoulder slowly died away, dulling, and he allowed himself a tiny spark of hope, as first one, then another of the swarm sunk back into hibernation.

Eventually, sounds rose distantly: a gunshot, then screams and two more shots. More screams. It was enough, though, as Hanson saw the effect the noises had on the swarm.

They weren't overly concerned with the shots—just another regular sound of the city. But the screams? As soon as they rang out, the swarm awoke again, shuffling and clanking as they staggered around, some falling over, struggling back to their feet as they joined the hunt.

Inside of a minute, the last of them had hurried past. After two more, the sounds of their passage faded into the distant roar of the city.

He forced himself out, moving as slowly as he could, waiting on his goggles and searching the dead end, and finding…nothing.

It was abandoned.

They'd gone!

He sagged, still half hidden in the crack in the tunnel wall and up to his chest in water, before slowly hauling himself out. His legs were cramped and numb, making him drag them along the ground more than walk, forcing him to use his arms to "walk."

The bottom of the filthy pool—it was too big to be a puddle, nearly a half a meter deep and dozens wide—was covered in mud and debris, and shattered stone. He struggled to keep his head above the water as his hands probed the muck ahead of him.

He felt little stones and broken glass under his fingers, whimpering as blood bloomed into the stagnant waters and then…metal attached to flesh!

He panicked, eyes widening in the darkness as he jerked his hand back, splashing and gasping, coughing as he went under, before frantically trying to be silent, spitting water and fuck knew what else out.

He was horrified, expecting to be attacked at any second as he forced his legs to work. More splashes rose as Hanson pushed himself to his feet, almost falling and stumbling to the edge of the water and out as his cramp-riddled legs twitched and sagged, almost dropping him to the ground.

He backed up against the far wall. His eyes darted from side to side, looking for a way out. *Did he run back down the other tunnel? Was it too soon? Were the specters just around the corner?*

His eyes locked on the water and stared fixedly, unable to look away as the ripples across the surface of the water shivered and danced, waiting, as the goggle's optics flickered and rebooted.

Seconds passed, and yet…nothing.

Nothing left the water.

Glancing around to make sure there was nothing nearby, Hanson grabbed a large rock, ready to use it as a weapon, before slowly inching closer.

It couldn't be, could it?

His luck wasn't that good, right?

Slipping into the water, and reaching out with one foot, slowly feeling around, he found it after a few seconds, and kicked it, before jerking back, rock raised high, ready.

Nothing.

Crouching this time, the rock held awkwardly in his left hand, he reached out, fumbling around with his right.

There.

Fingers met soaked cloth, then soft flesh underneath. Unresponsive flesh. Moving his hand around slowly, he recognized a leg, then a foot, and he knew what he had to do.

He didn't have long, and this was a chance like no other!

He set the rock down, seized the leg with both hands, and pulled, dragging the body of a bigger woman free of the pool, grabbing the rock again as soon as she was out.

He could barely make her out, the way his goggles flared and died, but…she wasn't old. She'd not been down here that long, either. Judging from the state of her flesh, she'd been killed finally by the steam valve.

Her clothes were shredded, and her head was caved in on one side, presumably what had finished her second life as she was fired off the grating over the valve and into the wall or ceiling. But the mods?

She had three! Three mods that he could see!

Her right hand was entirely cyber. Her chestplate was under her tattered clothes, meaning she'd had armoring done at the very least…maybe more? Organelle replacement?

The right leg was a full mod as well!

Hanson hugged himself, shaking in disbelief and shock. *This was insane!*

He didn't know what had happened to her, not to drive her down here and turn her into a specter. *A hack maybe?* He shook his head. It didn't matter.

None of it did.

She'd only been down here a few days or weeks. Her skin was still softish, and it hadn't rotted. That meant there was probably no real contamination to the mods. Hell, she'd been literally steam-cleaned for him!

He let loose a giggle, then clapped his hands over his mouth, afraid. *No. He had to think.*

Someone like this wouldn't have come down here without weapons, without gear.

Searching her body, he found ammo, two grenades, and a small knife, but that was it. The gun could be anywhere. The holster on her hip was ripped and full of mud, and even after a few minutes of desperate and careful searching, it wasn't in the water.

It was infuriating that his goggles were so fucked. There could be a gun anywhere here, just out of sight, and he couldn't find it! She didn't even have a set of goggles on her!

He snarled, forcing her eyelids open, then digging in with the blade, shaking as he felt metal under the blade.

Ocular implants! He nodded and set to work, the blade a literal lifesaver as he removed her head whole, stripping her of mods as best he could.

The chest piece was locked down tight—he'd need the proper gear to take that—and she was too heavy, even after taking her flesh leg and arms off. He snarled at how selfish the bitch had been. *She deserved this!*

He rolled up her cybernetic leg, the hand, and her head in a makeshift rucksack from her clothes, leaving the rest of the body there.

Bitch hadn't even had anything in her pockets.

Stumbling to his feet, Hanson sneered and kicked the scattered remains of the woman, then stifled a laugh, shaking as he set off, stumbling along, keeping as quiet as he could.

An hour…an hour more of wandering around it took, climbing two ladders and a—

He was sweating, he realized.

Damn, he was hot!

The tunnels had been cool when they'd come down, but now? It must have been the damn venting, making the tunnels *insanely* hot.

Two more turns in the tunnel, creeping along, and there…He froze, fear rising.

Just ahead was another specter, halfway down the next cross-tunnel, and right next to them—literally a meter or two behind them, as they swayed drunkenly, staring away into the distance—was the ladder he'd been searching for, marked with Jacker's skull and crossed wrenches.

Hanson paused, waiting, then set the parts down oh so slowly, dragging the leg free and holding it by the ankle, sneaking up…step by step…and wham!

The specter collapsed, its neck breaking like a twig. The sound echoed around the tunnel.

Hanson stifled a scream, almost dropping the leg. *His fucking shoulder!* He'd jarred it, and the entire area around the bite suddenly felt insanely itchy. He tried reaching around to it, but just as his hand was about to touch it…the body before him moved.

The leg was up and swinging before he thought about it. The rest of the bundle clattered to the ground. The cybernetic limb arced over and over, pounding down into the twitching specter, its cheap level-one mods clacking as it tried to get back up.

He panted and cursed, swinging hard and fast. Sweat rolled down his face and body; sparks flew as metal met metal, smashing the bones of its skull in, before he sagged, staring at it, his rage spent.

Distant screams shocked him out of his fugue, and he jerked around, searching the tunnel.

He moved quickly, gathering up the head and hand, then hurried back, staring down at the old broken thing on the floor, and pausing.

Could he strip it?

He'd be a legend, that's for sure. There were a good five or six mods on it—cheap ones, tier one, old and damaged—but if they could fix them? He'd never heard of anyone looting so much!

He'd start off with loads of mods! Hell, maybe he could sell the gang some?

A noise farther down the tunnel made him flinch. "Fuck it," he whispered. Better to get out of the tunnels first. He could always come back, right? *Get these mods chipped, and then come back, bring some actual weapons, and hunt the fuckers down!*

He'd be someone then!

Struggling up the ladder, barely able to carry it all, and trying to ignore the liquids that were running out of the head and onto his chest, Hanson grinned. Even the flare of the light and the sudden blindness that followed wasn't enough to ruin his beautiful fantasies.

When he reached the top of the ladder, he braced himself and keyed the code in that Jacker had given him: 80085. Stupid using a code rather than "knocking" on it with his Keystone, but the old fart had laughed when he gave them it, insisting. He'd even made them repeat it back again and again. And now, as he punched the softly glowing numbers on the grimy keypad, each one flaring as it was hit, the readout flashed…

He blinked, confused. *Had it almost made a word?*

It was gone just as fast, and the hatch slid open, making him sag with relief, before climbing higher.

The next stage, he'd been warned, might take awhile, but he could rest, sit on the hatch below, once it was closed, locking down.

He repeated the code, and it flashed red.

Locked.

He tried the lower pad as well, to see if it opened it back up, and it didn't.

He was locked in.

"Just in case we're asleep, and you bring back friends." Jacker had explained there was an alarm on it, and that he'd come to the hatch as soon as he could with medics and backup.

A handful of minutes later, a small screen in the wall flickered to life. Hanson squinted, covering his eyes at the bright light as he saw Jacker's face.

"What ya want?" came the gruff question. "Ya run and hide? Ya ain't getting back in here unless—" Jacker cut off as Hanson wearily lifted the leg to show him, getting a grudging grunt, then a clearly forced smile. "Well, that's diff'rent, boy! Ah'm comin'."

Hanson sagged against the rungs of the ladder, not trusting the hatch to hold him. He panted in relief, wrung out. The adrenaline crash now that he knew he was safe made him shake constantly, and even here, the heat was insane.

He couldn't stop shaking. His left hand quivered, like it was going to go into cramp. And the shoulder? It was itching like crazy!

If he dared to let go of the ladder for even a second, he'd have writhed the skin off. He didn't, though, as a sudden cold hit him, making him shiver like his balls had been dipped in nitrous.

The hatch above him slid open with a whoosh. A bright light of a flashlight shone down on him, even as two gun barrels made themselves clear as well.

Hanson flinched from the sudden combination, and almost fell off the ladder, before catching himself and clinging to it desperately.

"What's up with him?" a gruff, deeper voice grated, and Jacker shrugged.

"Who cares, boss?" he replied. "Hey, kid, the mods! Whatcha got?"

"A…a leg…" he mumbled, teeth chattering. "An…d a head…"

"Two?" Jacker squinted. "You look like shit, kid…What's up?"

"Cold," he mumbled, flinching as another flashlight was turned on and shone over his face and upper body. "S-so cold…"

"Yeah," the second figure said after a few seconds, shifting around and pointing his flashlight at Hanson's face, making him squint and shield his eyes. "Real cold today…"

"Cold? It's—" Jacker muttered, only to shut up as the other figure cut him off.

"Pass up the mods, then we'll help you up, kid…Handsome, right?"

"Han…Hanson," he corrected wearily, suddenly barely able to cling to the ladder. "There's another…a specter down…there." He fumbled, passing the leg up, seeing the chrome and black lacquered leg clearly for the first time as it was grabbed and tugged free of his hands.

"Military grade. Tier three or higher. Nice." The second voice grunted. "Fetch a nice set of creds, that."

"What else ya got?" Jacker asked, and for the first time, Hanson felt something other than relief. "C'mon, boy, hand it up."

"I…" he mumbled, shaking, and fumbling the hand free, only to drop it. The clang of the metal hand hitting the hatch rang out in the tight space.

"Fuckin' fool!" Jacker snapped. "Get it! An' gimme that head!"

"I…" Hanson tried to speak, before hissing as a sudden jolt of pain tore through him. His left shoulder spasmed. "Help!" He whimpered, shaking his head, as he tried to climb up, managing two rungs before he came to an abrupt stop. "I need help!"

"Gimme the fuckin' head!" Jacker growled, the barrel of the gun that was jammed against the broken glass of his goggles all that Hanson could see suddenly. "Last chance, fool!"

Hanson passed the head up, his hand shaking so badly he nearly dropped it, and it was torn free, passed up to the other figure, as the barrel was pushed harder against his face.

"Now the hand, and anythin' else you got!"

"You said…you would let me join!" he forced out, as his world came crashing down around him.

"Gimme the hand, fool, or I swear ah'll shoot ya in the fuckin' face!" Jacker snarled.

It was all suddenly clear to Hanson, as he clambered down to the bottom of the tube, reaching out with a shaking hand to pick up the gleaming black metal hand, pressing it to his chest and struggling back up the ladder.

"That's it…Shit, mil-tech as well. What you think she had in her?" the second voice asked as he passed the hand over. "Hey, asshole! She have anything else?"

"Chest…" He coughed, nodding, and climbed back up, forcing a smile as he reached the last few rungs, only to be stopped by Jacker's gun again.

"Go get it," he ordered, and Hanson shook his head.

"I can't…" He whimpered. "I'm hurt, and…"

"You want into the gang? You want this shit? You need to *earn* it, motherfucker."

"Please," he whispered. "My shoulder…"

The other figure was there in a second. A scanner held out a bright light as he was examined, before a snort of disgust.

"Draukka."

"Spiders? And you brought them here?" Jacker snarled, jamming the gun into his goggles, shattering the last of the glass and making Hanson scream as it cut into him.

He grabbed at his eye, or tried to. His right hand made it, but the left spasmed and fell to his side, twisting as something wet poured down his back, making him shake uncontrollably.

"Close it and get rid of him! Shit, fuckin' draukka!"

"You dumb fuck!"

Jacker kicked him in the chest, driving him back down into the tube.

He fell, hitting the bottom hatch with a crash and a splat as something burst below him.

His right eye full of glass, blood leaking from the shredded flesh, Hanson whimpered, looking up. Barely able to focus, he saw the disgusted and furious face of a massive orc standing next to Jacker. Their flashlights blinked off, and they dragged a barrel close…then Jacker poured something down atop him.

It splashed and stung, covering him and making him scream as he recognized the smell.

Korn syrup, it smelled like, but its clear golden hue sparkled as the grains suspended in it caught the light. That made the difference between the syrup and what this was, really clear.

Korn *fuel*.

"No…no, please!" he cried out. "I did it! I did what you asked!"

"Dumb fuck," the orc growled. "Even if you'd not brought draukka back here, you think I'd waste good nites on you? You were always just a rat! We send dozens like you down every day!"

The awful certainty that he was going to die rose as Hanson saw the grin on Jacker's face. The rest of the barrel was dropped in toward him; the hatch below him opened up just as the container slammed into his stomach.

Hanson fell, arms windmilling and legs thrashing until he landed on the old railway tracks below with a crunch of breaking bones.

His scream cut off. The sound became a wheeze as broken ribs punctured his lungs. His left arm flopped weakly, but uncontrollably, before his face. He stared in horror, seeing the tiny bump that crept along under the skin of his left forearm.

"Drau...kka..." he whispered in shock, finally recognizing the burrowing spider as something from the tales. They laid their eggs in you, and they ate as they grew, numbing your body as they spread, consuming everything.

"Ple...ase..." he managed, staring up at the distant light overhead, as the orc casually thumbed something to life and tossed it down to him, even as the hatch closed and darkness fell.

The incendiary grenade landed on the barrel and bounced, flying off to the side and rolling several feet into the darkness before activating.

A sudden vivid magnesium flare of light lit the tunnel, bathing the broken form of Hanson in reflected brightness...as well as the silent, clanking forms of the specters that closed on him.

"No...NOOOOOOO!" he screamed, as claws and hands, hooks and tattered bone tore into him, tearing gobbets free, even as the incendiary set light to some of the figures.

They would bump into others; the flames spread until they finally met the home-made rocket fuel. It filled the tunnel with a ferocious fire that killed everything, making the building above shake, driving the gang out for several hours as they waited to see whether it'd collapse or not.

All of that came as little consolation to Hanson, though, his last sight being of glass teeth and mechanical mandibles opening wide to close over his face.

CHAPTER ONE

"Three minutes to drop."

I blinked, shocked out of my post-fight adrenaline crash. The messages I'd been scrolling mindlessly through froze as I tried to make sense of the words.

"Repeat?" I snapped, banishing the messages plugin and bringing up my full HUD, the titan that was my APS suit surrounding me.

"Two minutes fifty to drop," the uncaring voice of the distant helo pilot came back, and I snarled.

"You fucking said that! We're on RTB. What the fuck do you mean, 'drop'?"

"Return to base has been canceled. Rerouting to new target. Retrieval mission," the voice came back. "Now, I'm actually busy, grunt, so if that's all?"

"Are you fucking kidding me?" I growled as the commlink closed without waiting for a response, and I quickly pulled up the team tacnet. "Red Team, sound off!"

"Red Two." Barnes in the deployment bay to my left responded hesitantly, new to the team, and the limited expected life span of an APS operator.

"Red Three." Fergie to my right responded flatly. The wall of the deployment container between us creaked as he shifted his massive armored bulk.

"Red Four." Scott yawned, sounding like he'd just woken up, and was still trying to figure out what planet he was on.

"Red Five," Richie called out, the comm tech already sounding distracted as he no doubt searched for data.

"Red Six," Sync, our sharpshooter, behind and to my left called.

"We're being dropped in…T-minus two-thirty. No clue where, no clue why, just got that it's a retrieval mission. Richie?"

"Working, boss," he replied, and I nodded, unseen, in my suit.

"Right. Check your ammo, people. Check your batteries. We've got two minutes. If you didn't plug in on pickup, do it now. Even a single point might make the difference. No need to spend our creds on fresh backup cells."

"Working on it, but…" Barnes growled.

"Boss, we've got Blue Team incoming as well. They set off an hour ago," Richie interrupted, the annoyance clear in his voice.

An hour ago. A fucking *hour*.

"What's the op?" I stifled my need to comm Captain Tyrannus and call him a shit-useless pig-fucker. He'd no doubt forgotten to hit us about the change because he was too busy ass-tonguing some corpo.

There was no point. All that would happen was Tyrannus would lie that he'd sent us the deets, blame it on us, and I'd get another fine for fucking up his Zen or some shit.

"Corpo retrieval job. Satellite crashed near here…and then the signal moved to an old factory complex. Looks like specters or scavs."

"Let's hope it's scavengers." I sighed. "Okay, people, you know what to do. Break the drain at T-minus thirty seconds. Lock in and get ready. We got maps of the target?"

"Here." Richie grunted, as we all received a datapacket, team comms allowing the image through automatically.

This time, it wasn't some busty hooker or similar, instead being a fairly recent aerial shot of the site.

We were originally somewhere far to the west of Artem. Hell, I'd not even paid attention beyond that we were far enough out that backup beyond the onboard drones we had was fuckin' unlikely, making it possible that the enemy weren't raiding, but were instead setting up a trap to capture us for our suits.

It'd not been the case, thank the gods. Instead, some damn tech had been found, some remnant of the old world, buried in a forgotten lab. We'd caught them as they left, taking down their transport and retrieving their kit, not to mention a few nice bits of loot.

We were in line for a bonus, a nice one, despite Tyrannus's attempts to divert most of it to himself for his "leadership."

That was the way life was for an APS operator. Out here, in the lawless lands between the cities, we brought order. Sometimes we'd be dropped to retrieve old world tech; sometimes it'd be a security gig, or a counter to another city. Sometimes we were deployed as judge, jury, and executioners, taking down scavs that hit merchants and more.

This time hadn't been a bad one, thankfully.

There'd still been a nasty firefight, and Richie in Red Five had serious damage to his left leg's servos, as well as most of us being at less than half ammo. Energy weapons were low as well. Typical.

Goddamn flyboys didn't like the team recharging our batteries from their toys, so we'd gotten into the habit of not even asking to plug them in.

Now we'd pay for it, with only a few minutes' additional charge on the suits.

The site was a few miles into the no-man's-zone of the southwestern plains, dry and dusty, about as lifeless as everywhere else these days. The old factories were built around a vast collection of the old solar cells, long since trashed by the frequent storms.

The buildings were grey stone, dusty, dark inside, and looped on all sides by shattered windows. It looked utterly dead, like there'd not been another soul here for at least a century. So, yeah, perfect for scavs or specters.

"We need a scan of the site," I told Richie, who clicked his mike, letting me know he was already talking. "Right. While he sorts that, people, we've got a retrieval mission. No clue what yet, but someone wants it badly enough to 'encourage' the army to send us *and* Blue Team. That means it's expensive. It's probably more valuable than all of us put together, and therefore breakable. No heavy weapons, no EMP, no frags, not till we know what we're hunting."

"You take all the fun out of life, you know that?" Sync, Red Six, sighed, and I snorted.

"Nope. Just means we get to watch Scott dance again," I corrected.

"Ah, man, bait again?" Scott groaned.

"Hey, you chose a melee specialist's role. What the hell did you think was going to happen?" Fergie—Red Three—responded, clearly amused. "At least you get to fuck shit up. I'm heavy weapons on an op with no heavy shit allowed."

"No scans allowed either." Richie came back, dropping into the chat to the sound of groaning and swearing from the rest of the team. "Corpo's worried we'll warn someone, and they'll damage the target."

"Any ID on it yet?"

"Classified."

"Well, that's just *great,*" Scott grumbled. "We're risking our lives for something, but we can't be trusted to know what it is—how the fuck does that work?"

"It's a black cylinder about eight inches across, twenty long. It'll fuck up our comms when we get too close, due to the retrieval signal it gives off," Richie told us all seriously. "That's the official line. Which smells to me. It sounds like a Black Corium Rod to me, which is all sorts of bad news."

"Starting with radioactive." I growled. "Any gear to contain it?"

"Blue Team is bringing it," he confirmed, and I groaned under my breath.

"Be right back. One minute to drop," I snapped into the tacnet, before changing the channel and routing through Richie's gear, rather than the helo's, requesting a link with the base. I knew this was pointless, I *knew* it, but I couldn't help myself.

It connected after a few seconds, defensive AIs approving me and passing the commlink through to Tyrannus's office, where it was refused.

"Motherfucker!" I snarled, pinging him again and again, until he answered.

"What is it?" Tyrannous sneered eventually. "I'm busy here, Red. You need your hand holding again?"

"What the hell is this op?" I asked through gritted teeth, knowing damn well this was going to cost me. But sending a half-kitted team after a radioactive bounty in the badlands was fucking insane.

"Retrieval," he replied unconcernedly. "I take it you didn't bother to read the mission report?"

"I did," I growled, flicking the "disengage" for the physical connections to the helo on autopilot as I spoke. Data cables, power connections, and more clicked and slid free, retreating into the rear wall of the deployment container as I stood, facing the bay wall before me. "There was fuck all about this mission on it. 'Counter Raider,' it said, and it's date- and time-stamped."

I made that last bit clear, a bit unsubtle to point out that I had a copy of the mission report that hadn't been updated, and that if we were fucked on this mission, I'd make sure it stuck to him too. The floor gave its warning shudder, by now so familiar it barely registered as I lifted my feet from it; the restraint harness held me in place and took my armored weight.

"There was an update sent," he replied after a few seconds. "Maybe you didn't get it. You need to connect to your own comms, not use the helo-net. You know what they're…"

"I am." The bay doors before me opened outward, retracting up and into the helo walls even as the section under me slid back, and the wall across from me lifted up and out. "I'm on full comms right goddamn now."

Night air flashed past beneath me, empty, and far below, I could make out the blur of dead ground and cracked asphalt. Rusting hulks of cars tore past, long dead on the old highways, passed now only by tumbleweed and the ghosts of the past.

"Well…maybe it got delayed?" Tyrannus tried again.

I snorted as the helo banked suddenly, killing its forward momentum, flaring its engines and rearing back. My team and I triggered the release as one, restraining bolts in the harness not just releasing us, but adding a pressurized jet of gas to literally shove us out of the bay.

"I need to know what we're grabbing!" I shouted into the commlink, plunging through the air, rifle held close to my chest, even as I triggered the secondary systems of the suit automatically. "Is it dangerous?"

The air whipped past me. Green and amber lights around the inside of my HUD made the condition of my suit clear. My secondaries—the hardpoints on either shoulder of my suit—were showing as amber for the right arm, and green for the left.

My ammunition reserve was at half, triggering the amber warning, but the connection was stable and no kinks in the delivery system. The shield on the left upper arm showed green, at seventy-two percent battery capacity.

The remaining two backplate hardpoints were set for mission critical gear on my model, so after retrieving the tech from the last job, and having that removed on return to the helo, I felt a little weird, the usual storage mass removed and my balance subtly off.

"It's fine, just a container," Tyrannus lied.

I barely heard him over the boom as I crashed into the ground, knees bending as I took the impact in my three-meter-tall war machine. We set off running. The rest of the squad fell in around me, even as Scott picked up speed, taking the lead.

"Fast in, fast out!" I snapped through the tacnet, switching channels. "Richie, get us a scan going and a target!"

"As you're busy…" I heard, as I switched back to the secure line. As I opened my mouth to reply, the commlink disconnected.

"MOTHERFUCKER!" I roared, realizing he'd been waiting for the opportunity.

"Tacnet," Richie warned me, the commlink returning automatically to the open connection.

"I'm gonna…" I growled, shaking my head as I muted myself, swallowing what I was going to say. They'd keep a transcript of this, like they did everything else. A recording of me screaming about how I was going to ram my rifle up Tyrannus's ass and pull the trigger as I used it to fuck him into the next life possibly wouldn't help my career.

I'd been scanning the area on autopilot. Radar pings drew sections clearly and others…*Well.*

The results weren't good. That, as much as the fear of what the hell that desk jockey asshole had gotten us into, forced me into professional mode at a sobering speed.

"I'm getting blank returns," I said grimly. The walls of the factory reflected the scans straight back, revealing nothing of the interior.

"Same."

"I've got Blue Team incoming. Ninety seconds and they'll be here. But the dead zone is blocking my scans as well," Richie said.

"What's causing it?" I asked.

"Most likely a jammer. High-powered and recent tech, or we'd have cut through it, combined with solid steel and lead mix in the walls."

"Steel?"

"Reinforcement. Probably why the building's still standing."

"Scavs?"

"Possible. No specters, that's for sure. Any specter finding something like this would have tried to integrate it, breaking it, or would have ran outta juice feeding on it."

"What?" Barnes asked, making me snort and shake my head. "Seriously, guys, come on!" he begged.

"Goddamn noob." Scott snorted, even as Richie started to explain.

"Scavs, or scavengers, loot the old world—and the new when they can. They're always on the search for tech they can sell, so if this is a scav base? They might have a signal jammer to help hide them. It'd take a lot of power, though, so they'd have to run it sparingly, or it'd not be worth it. Cost as much as they could possibly save."

"If it was scavs? We'd be on a judgment run, check for crimes they're committing and execute as needed. This isn't that…or not as far as we know," Fergie rumbled.

"Or it's specters," Sync added. "They'd not care about the power cost. Not like they're going to be selling it. All specters care about is adding more powerful mods into their rotting bodies."

"Could a specter do this?" Barnes asked. "I mean, they're dead, right? Brain-dead bodies that are being puppeted around by their mods, viruses and more running them?"

"Survive a month with the team, and you'll know the answer," Scott said laconically. "We hit them at least once a week these days."

"Red Actual, this is Blue Actual, incoming on your nine."

A fresh connection popped up, and I accepted it, nodding in relief, even though he couldn't see me.

"Good to have you, Blue," I replied. "You know more than us about this clusterfuck, I hope?"

"Retrieval," Blue One, Jon, said. "Something from an old spy satellite. It's radioactive as fuck, so we're stuck with these…Wait, where's your retrieval sleeve?"

"You got me on visual?" I asked.

"Yeah, we're closing in. Got a good helo team—they jacked me to their kit. You got some kind of new retrieval system?"

"Try again." I snorted, my disgust evident.

"They didn't give you a sleeve for it?" He groaned, clearly not surprised.

"Bingo bongo. Five minutes ago, I was falling asleep on my way back to base, no clue we were even being dropped," I growled. "We hit a raider team, got minor damage, and we're low on ammo. Nobody even told us we were coming here until we hit the three-minute marker."

"*Fuck.* To think we thought we had it bad. Okay, you secure, we'll retrieve. Fifty-fifty?"

"Argh…fuck it. Deal," I agreed, sighing, then switching the channel. "Okay, people, we're switching roles. We'll secure the zone. Blue retrieves it; we split the bonus fifty-fifty."

"What?" Fergie groaned. "We do all the work and…"

"It's radioactive as fuck. We carry it, we're spending the next week on anti-radiation meds and scrubbing our suits. You want that?"

"So they get half our bonus for landing and picking it up?"

"Yeah, basically," I snapped. "Unless you want to spend the week shitting through the eye of a needle and scrubbing?"

"Not to mention losing our active-duty bonus and any other missions," Richie pointed out. "Because surely you don't think that 'someone' is going to admit they fucked up and take the hit for us not being active in their paycheck instead?"

"Not a chance," Sync growled. A chorus of assent echoed around as we all reflected that there was no chance Tyrannus would own up to his fuckup.

"Movement!" Fergie called, cutting off the chatter. He picked up speed, as a pair of specters staggered out of the broken factory doors ahead.

"Tracking movement," Sync replied, sending an image of the second factory upper floors on the tacnet. There'd been definite heads moving there, but too fast and blurred to make out more than humanoid.

"In and secure the area," I ordered after a second's hesitation. "Scott, take them down, full speed."

"Oh, yeah!" Scott whooped, his "blitzkrieg" build picking up speed as he powered ahead. The rest of us fell in behind him. Blue Team's helo flared to the left in a small space between several buildings, rather than on the outskirts and making them run in, as ours had.

"Damn." Fergie grunted into the tacnet, aware that Blue would be able to hear us now, deploying as they were. "How'd you guys get a flyboy who actually helps?"

"Just lucky!" came a laugh from Blue Two.

"Yeah, well, breaching!" Scott laughed. The pair of specters finally staggered toward him, arms grasping.

They looked like stick men, or the zombies I'd seen on old entertainment reels: Bones stuck out everywhere. Hollow eyes, long since blind to all, but hunger-locked onto us.

They were a mess, clothes reduced to rags, stumbling through the dust and debris of the old world. Their mods whirred and creaked, optical mods locked onto the fast approaching-Scott, teeth clacking in terrible hunger at the leaking light of electromagnetism that we all emitted.

I'd seen the world through their eyes once. We all had. A hacker a few years back had somehow remoted into a specter—nobody knew how—and recorded it, controlling it as he guided it along corridors deep in the undercity, surrounded by similar shuffling monstrosities.

Corpos had labeled it propaganda, but the only one who was surprised when the hacker puppeted it out into the street to stand with him, as he tried to show it was mindless and safe…was him.

It'd hesitated only a second before falling on him and ripping his ocular implant free. It tried to replace its desiccated old fleshy system with it, before trying for another local, one of the crowd who had been watching.

The one good thing about Artem came out then, and it was basically that its citizens were *not* to be fucked with. Everything from a bright-pink custom handbag-sized grazer to a cannon that should have been used for orbital clearance was pulled out and discharged.

The fucker had no chance.

Neither, now, did these two.

Scott didn't use his rifle or plasma blade, not his cluster bombs nor his shield and electro-discharge knuckles. He'd slapped his rifle to his back, the mag-plates locking it down, and simply reached out, grabbing them both by the head.

Twisting and pulling, he ran in the opposite direction to the one they'd been headed in; they fell like stick figures, heads torn free with mechanized strength. What was left collapsed to the ground as he crushed, then tossed the heads away. For a few seconds, leg mods kicked where flesh laid still, and cybernetic hands opened and closed. Their fucked-up nanites had no clue that it was all over, but for them, at least, the fight certainly was.

We raced into the building behind Scott. The clatter of our boots crashing on the steel rang out. The whoosh of Blue's transport helo flashed overhead as it took off, and the instant cutoff of Blue Team from the tacnet made me snarl.

Definitely something in the walls. Then: "Richie!"

"Yeah, boss?"

"Relay drone out. I want to be able to call for backup."

"Done," he agreed, skidding to a halt, lifting his left arm and firing one of his precious relay drones.

It was small, barely four centimeters on a side, and square, but when it hit the ceiling by the open door, the monomolecular bonding field powered up, sealing it into the frame. Camo blended it in, just in case.

It'd take some serious effort to remove that now, and as soon as the link was established, Blue was back in the tacnet, closing on the entrance.

"Helo, you read me?" I asked, pinging the circling bugger high overhead.

"This is Helo-7. Confirm readiness for extraction. Over."

"Negative," I replied. "Comm check."

"Comms good," came the uninterested reply. "Be aware, Red Team, we have fuel for forty-seven minutes on station, then we bug out."

"That better be a bad joke, Helo-7."

"Not smiling here, Red Team. Forty-six minutes and counting."

I cut the line, growling as I directed my attention back to the crumbling building around us. We ran past rusting hulks of ancient mechanisms and vast towers of scaffolding, most long since collapsed and laid shattered across the ground, still surrounded with abandoned machines.

"Mech assembly," Richie said in recognition and wonder. "It's an old mech assembly plant. Has to be!"

"What?" I gestured to the team to hold up, ducking down around a series of fallen frames, as we scanned the interior for movement.

"Old world mechs were like ours, but they used them for everything from construction to mining, not just war. They were all constantly trying to steal each other's secrets. That's why the damn walls are like they are!"

"And the roof?" I asked, squinting up.

"Reinforced and probably lead-lined to stop signals…Damn," Richie said, sending us all a close-up shot of a section of sagging roof where the water had been getting in. "Keep shots clear of there, people. That starts coming down and we're all fucked. It'll take a week to dig you out."

"That means you, Three," I said.

"Hey!" Fergie responded, pretending to be hurt, although we could all hear the smile in his voice. Not only was he physically the largest at damn near six foot seven, but as our heavy weapons specialist, his APS had been built to take seriously big fucking guns.

Everything from area denial smart drones, bombardment cannons and gamma cannons to missile or rotary fléchettes launchers could be mounted to his massive frame. Even now, the ground shook as he stomped past; the twin shoulder-mounted rail guns he'd chosen today—armor killers—tracked his vision, locking in on the slightest threat.

There were similar but smaller versions for mine and the blitzkrieg models to carry, but his? Easily twice the size of ours.

Where Richie—Five—was an expert with comms and all forms of tech, Fergie was the bear of the team: massive, a heart of gold, and a temper that could drive him to beat the face of God in.

"You getting anything now that we're inside?" I asked Richie, and he nodded, as the first pings started up.

"Looks like a scav base," he repeated. "I'm seeing multiple recent tracks of boots, too many and too regular in routes to be specters."

"Tracks? What if it's raiders? Man, we've not got the ammo for this shit—" came the whine before I cut him off.

"Can it, Barnes," I snapped. "You earn the right to bitch on my team."

"How we looking?" Blue One skidded to a halt across from us, ducking down behind a fallen mass of rusty metal as he peered into the darkness of the factory.

"Scav base," I advised, bringing him up to date quickly.

"What's the play?"

"Couple of specters roaming the outside, most likely drawn by the tech we're here for. Betting there'll be more around. But there's booted tracks…"

"Tracks?" Blue One asked.

"Here." Richie sent, and a second later, we all saw what had caught his eye: multiple sets of tracks trodden through the dirt and dust, patrolling what looked like a regular perimeter.

"Recon drone out," I ordered, hearing Blue One order his team the same a second later.

Rich, in Red Five—the traditional slot for the tech in any team—lifted his left arm, the suit not even shaking as the larger recon drone unfolded its repulsors and took off.

Where the relay drones were four centimeters on a side—cubes that the suit carried three of as standard—the recon drone was their far bigger cousin. Half a meter long, with four small repulsors that folded down, locking into the left arm of the comms loadout, and with a small turret for defense, it could operate autonomously as needed, its RI—restricted intelligence—able to follow simple commands.

Right now, though, Richie broadcast the feed on the tacnet. A small window popped in to the bottom right in my HUD, making it possible to see it or to ignore it as I needed.

"Blue? Want to take the lead?" I asked, seeing the second image flashing up as an option, and he nodded.

"Blue Team, advance!" he called out, and they were up and running. The six of them raced forward as we spread out, watching all sides and behind, ready for anything as we followed.

"Richie, check out the upper floor. Sync, what'd you see outside?" I asked, rifle sweeping as we moved forward, expecting to be hit.

"Movement up above, but too fast to make out. Angle was shit, even on replay," Sync responded, her words clipped and precise as she walked backward behind us, watching our backs.

"No scavs gonna fight us," Barnes interrupted. "I mean, come on, they're *scavengers*! We're the APS Corps! They'd not stand a chance!"

"Barnes…" I said slowly as my radar, and that of others in the team, flickered, the jamming clearly being reinforced.

"Yeah, boss?" he replied. A confident grin would be on his stupid face, I knew.

"Shut the fuck up. The adults are talking."

"Boss…" Richie interrupted.

"Yeah?"

"Switch to heat vision," he whispered.

I did, trusting him implicitly, before stumbling.

"Oh, fuck…BLUE, FALL BACK NOW!"

CHAPTER TWO

I screamed the warning into the tacnet, as a dozen areas I could see around me, never mind how many more must be hidden inside the factory, suddenly showed up as the telltale dark blue of coolant pods.

"What?" Blue barked into the tacnet, confused, but going with it. "Blue Team, break!"

The team, running forward as one, broke apart, darting left and right, skidding and sprinting for cover, even as the coolant pods triggered.

On all sides, the upper dome of renovated, previously recessed turrets broke free. Their delicate electronics filled the air with tracking data as they triggered, homing in on us.

"Take them down!" I roared, my rifle locking on as I opened fire, a three-round burst sufficient to shred the old turret as it tried to acquire its first target.

All around us, they went active, and they were heavy models, clearly intended to defend the mech assembly plant against incoming enemy mech.

We were in the latest and greatest personal armored suits that could be built…but yeah, built by the lowest bidders. That meant that although we were generations ahead of these turrets, we were far from impervious.

The turrets had been designed to take down assault mechs, and the chatter of heavy fire roared out from the left. Three locked onto Fergie.

"Fuck youuuu!" Fergie roared, our heavy weapons specialist clearly "forgetting" the minor rule about no heavy ordnance as his twin rail cannons opened up.

The air filled with the clatter and chatter of heavy and light machine guns, the crack of supersonic rounds from rail guns, and the sizzle of atomized shit from the lasers and grazers.

I slid to a halt behind a mass of fallen scaffolding, using it as cover even as I fired again and again, pivoting my aim left and right, taking out turret after turret.

Where I'd seen a dozen or more earlier, now more were going active, and the fuckers were everywhere! Lasers joined the ancient slug throwers. Turrets chewed the rubble and scaffolding I crouched behind. I swore, hearing shouting as scavs raced to join in as well.

Grenades and old-style slug throwers, chemical rockets screamed through the air and more.

Fragments of stone and rusted metal showered me, and I snarled, returning fire over the top, using the camera on the massive rifle—sized for use by a three-meter-tall APS unit—while I searched for a more defensible spot.

This was the best I was gonna get, I guessed, as I figured out flanking paths. The mass behind me shifted, and I froze, thinking it was about to collapse.

The recon drone flashed overhead a second later, then exploded as it was shot out of the air by at least five separate sources.

"Boss, *move!*" Sync screamed.

A crack rang out. A supersonic round flashed past me to smash into something out of sight.

I was up and running as soon as she said it, sprinting. Cameras on the back of my APS showed an image of something that had been buried *under* the mass of rubble beginning to tear its way free.

Staggering, I cursed as my shield dropped. The blue aura flared red as it went from just under seventy, to fifty, to thirty. I dove right, hitting the ground and rolling, coming to my feet and sighting in on the heavy turret that had been pounding me.

I fired a three-round burst. The high-powered armor-piercing slugs tore the old turret apart. But even as I did that, my eyes widened at the form that shredded its way free of the rubble and scaffolding.

We'd been *badly* fucked by Tyrannus with this one.

They were scavs, all right. Nobody else had the skills, nor the insanity to do what they'd done, and certainly not the sheer fucking brass balls. But now?

"Richie!" I bellowed, firing again and again, as I shifted from target to target.

"That's why they took the Corium, boss. It's a fucking power source!"

"What the hell is that thing?" Blue One shouted over the roar of gunfire.

"It's a mech!" Richie replied quickly. "Overlord or nemesis class, and they found it. They've probably been rebuilding it for years, and shot down the satellite to loot the power core!"

"Weaknesses?" he asked after a few seconds, their own tech keeping noticeably fucking quiet.

"No shields—it's why they were scrapped—heavy weapons, but slow to turn, easily targeted from the air, so…"

"Get outside!" I ordered. "Everyone, fall back!"

"Turrets first or we'll be chewed up!" Sync called.

I cursed, agreeing and opening fire on another and another as I corrected my order. "Turrets first."

"Weapons?" Blue One called over the gunfire.

"Didn't see," Richie snapped. "I literally saw enough of the torso to ID it, and they blew the drone."

"How big?"

"Assault mech," Blue Five said, clearly reading specs as we took out as many turrets as possible, getting ready to run. "Fifteen meters at the shoulder. Original recommended loadout has it with shoulder-mounted LRAMS, Gatling cannon, and a flamethrower for trench clearance."

"LRAMS?" Barnes asked, and Richie took pity on him.

"Long Range Artillery Missile System. Basically, it's a launcher on its back. Fires the missile like it's out of a cannon, then the missile activates, autocorrects and steers. Think rail gun, but a missile instead of a slug."

"Well, that's not fucking happy making!" Barnes grunted, and I stifled a laugh as Fergie spoke up.

"Speak for yourself. I wants me one!"

I shook my head at the mad bastard. He'd try to fire it offhand as well…and probably succeed, knowing him.

"Scott," I called, seeing the mech was still struggling to free itself.

"Yeah, boss?"

"You think you could take that down?"

"If you keep the turrets off my back, hell yes," Scott replied.

I turned to ping Blue One, opening a private command line.

"You think?"

"Sacrifice play?" Blue One's voice made it clear he didn't like it.

"No. We back them, you send Blue Four as well."

"I..." He hesitated, then swore, before switching to the tacnet. "Blue Four, don't let that Red asshole have all the fun—get in there!"

"Sir!" Blue Four agreed.

Scott burst out of cover, and we all stood, opening fire over and over, switching from target to target.

"Sync!" I barked. "Vanish. Get the high ground and end these fucks!"

"Moving!" came the agreement, as her camo-plates powered up, the multi-ton APS vanishing in a heat haze.

"Go!" Blue One, and his Six, vanished as well, as he and Blue Two joined me, even as a good dozen new signals appeared. The jammer was clearly running out of power.

"Threes, I don't like this building—get rid of it!" I ordered, no longer bothering to go through Blue One.

"Sir!" Blue Three acknowledged, as Fergie, Red Three, whooped and planted his feet.

The heavy weapons build for the APS wasn't just in the upgraded servos and the enhanced armoring and musculature to handle weapons that used to be carried by ships, tanks, and mechs. To handle the recoil, their legs and boots were entirely different than the other models, and they made that clear now. Stabilization platforms locked down; additional shielding came online as their secondary power cells activated. Barnes backed up without having to be told; connectors snaked from his backplate to Fergie's, sharing the load and forming the soldier/heavy symbiote.

Rounds slammed into Fergie's shield, now extending automatically over Barnes, and powered by the combination of both Fergie and Barnes's cores. It barely flickered, while the rail guns fired over and over.

Barnes laughed, a crazed sound that was barely this side of madness, as he fired, and we all understood.

"You want some?" he cried out. "You do? Fuck yeah!" Where the rest of us were mobile, ducking in and out of cover, Barnes and Fergie had to stay where they were. Any movement would break the connection.

Where Fergie was heavily armored, and could take a pounding, Barnes was in a standard soldier build, like mine, but without a command mod.

That meant that as much as he was a kid, as green as that fucker was, if he stayed in place and survived this? He'd earned his place in the team. Stepping up like that took balls, and doing it without being ordered to? Well, it spoke volumes.

He hammered away at anything that wasn't us, and the turrets were being replaced by the scavs.

They were asshole mercs and thieves in a mixture of heavy armor, ex-military surplus, and the kinda brand-new next-level shit that corpos swore they'd never sell outside of to the government.

Which meant every fucker had them.

Missiles and gear designed for the sole reason of taking down APS teams started to pop up, and I swore as my shoulder-mounted replenishment system, mounted on my right arm hardpoint, went dry.

I changed to the locked-in mag, armor-piercing punching holes in my targets as I called to Richie.

"Get those helos on station!" I barked. "I want the back half of this building leveled!"

"Got it!" Richie grunted, switching channels as we all shifted and fired.

"Bringing the *pain!*" Fergie bellowed as both gamma cannons went active at once. The eye-searing green light of a grazer—a gamma-ray laser—lit the factory, and enemy screams filled the air.

Lasers could cut steel, slugs could deform it and even punch through, fléchettes could tear through and shred, but only the gamma cannon could render a living form to mush through six inches of steel.

The cannons' boom rang out over and over. Each hit, even if the target hid behind cover, was a kill, and we cursed as the mech struggled out from under the mass of fallen steel.

They'd clearly left some of the crap above it hoping to keep it hidden, and although they must have expected a response, they'd must not have been anticipating it for a while yet.

If not, they'd have had it clear and ready to go. Systems were coming online, but others were failing. The left arm was working, the right totally dead; automated turrets on the outside of the hips opened fire, as the Fours leapt on it. Scott had a plasma blade out and active; Blue had a power-axe, a massive thing that crackled with energy as he swung it at the right arm of the mech, just as it started to jerk, coming to life.

Scott hacked through the hip turret on his side, then staggered, vanishing in a bloom of fire, hit by something on the far side of the mech. He reappeared, lurching, wreathed in flames.

"Motherfuckers!" he screamed, bracing himself and leaping out of sight behind the mech, as Blue's axe sliced into the right arm, severing sections.

The mech sagged, then braced itself and rose. The sheer fucking insanity of a fifteen-meter-tall assault mech towering over the three-meter APS teams made my asshole clench and stomach twist.

"Richie, where the *fuck*—"

"They won't fire!" He cut me off, even as Scott's camera flashed up on my HUD, clearly being fed to me directly and deliberately.

I focused on it as I ducked back down, searching the image, seeing…"Scott!" I barked. "Fall back!"

"Can't!" he bellowed. "Too many…sorry…"

The feed cut off as an explosion rang out. The entire factory shook as I replayed the last seconds of Scott's fight, including the mech staggering and falling to its knees.

The area behind the mech, and where Scott had been seconds before, vanished in a huge fireball. Entire sections of walls, the floor, and upper and lower levels were shredded in an instant.

The mech was sent careening and support beams flew in all directions.

At least half the scavs were wiped out, maybe more, as flames and worse filled the air. Shrapnel reduced unshielded bodies to mince as Scott's markers flatlined in my vision.

The mad bastard was a martial arts genius, ducking and weaving, his fists, feet, and blade as lethal in the APS as Fergie was with his cannons. But in the last seconds, I saw what he—and the bastard scavs had—done.

They'd had a massive stockpile of weapons behind the mech, buried under something, and had been bringing them up from a basement floor below.

Dozens of the scavs had been there, with three of them hefting a latest model AROC—Armored Recovery Ordnance Control—and pointing it at Scott. In that last second, he'd seen the lock-on and flung his blade into the piled-high explosive, knowing exactly what would happen.

"*SCOTT!*" Fergie roared, pummeling the massive mech repeatedly as it hit Blue Four with a backhand, sending him staggering, then pummeling him with turret and scav fire.

His shields failed. Shots slammed into him and sent him reeling, until the mech's Gatling cannon spun up, the damn thing still trying—and failing—to get to its feet.

The fire cut Blue Four's armor apart like a hot knife through butter, as we all focused fire on it.

Fergie screamed at the loss of Scott even as rail guns punched holes through the assault mech's outer armor. The gamma cannons had little effect, thanks to some property of the design.

I snarled as I connected to Richie's comms kit and onward. Even with the jammer down, the walls here were too thick for a clear signal, and I needed this to be clear.

"Helo-7! This is a direct order. I want the north side of this factory fucking *vaporized*!" I bellowed, cutting off the ongoing argument between Richie and the pilot.

"Negative!" Helo-7 bit back. "Captain Tyrannus has refused authorization. Feel free to take it up with him."

"Richie!" I snapped, cutting the link to the helo, and grunting as Richie replied.

"Patching in Operations Control. Captain Tyrannus is…he's refused the link, redirected to…fuck! Redirected to corporate liaison!"

"What the fuck?" I grunted, dismayed and in shock. Yeah, this was a corpo gig; they'd paid for us to be assigned here on "recovery"—no doubt greasing that fucker Tyrannus's palm to make it happen—but this was an army mission! The request for reinforcements had nothing to do with…

"M-Corp Liaison, please state your request," came the bored voice of the liaison.

"Request?" I snarled. "This is Red One, Harry Kabutt. We're under heavy fire on *your* retrieval op, and the helo—"

"Acknowledged and identity confirmed. Sergeant Kabutt, your request for orbital bombardment is denied—"

"What the fuck do you mean, denied? We're surrounded here!" I roared, barely able to hear the operator on the other end. "And *orbital*? I want the fucking helos to—"

"As the sponsoring corporation, M-Corp has enforced a maximum threshold on investment for this operation, as we're paying for everything from fuel to ammunition. Until the target is physically confirmed in the containment sleeve, M-Corp will not authorize any additional expenditure."

"You…I…"

"Is that all, Sergeant Kabutt?" the liaison asked coldly. "I'm a very busy man."

"We've lost two APS already!" I barked. "We'll lose more—hell, we might lose the entire team!"

"That has been factored into the mission evaluation. Insurance premiums have already kicked in, and the loss of the APS will be covered. Orbital bombardment and helo Hellfire munitions, however, are an entirely different class of expenditure. If you want M-Corp to assist you, finish the mission."

"Are you fucking—"

"Have a nice day," the liaison sneered.

"Commlink is blocked, boss," Richie growled. "Tyrannus has blocked us too."

"I'll kill them all. With my own two…MOTHERFUCKERS!" I roared, standing up and firing the last shots from the mag, sending scavs flipping and falling, before dropping it out and switching to incendiary.

"New plan!" I snarled into the tacnet. "Drown them in their own blood!"

"So…no backup then?" Blue One asked me on the command channel.

"We're not worth the extra investment," I hissed.

"Insurance kicked in as soon as we lost the Fours, didn't it?"

"Yeah."

"Well, that's fucked my week."

"Same. So, fuck it…might as well kiss the bonus goodbye," I joked blackly.

The mech finally rose again, towering over us all. Fergie forcibly overrode and disconnected from Barnes, reaching back and shoving him away with one smoking cannon.

"What the…" Barnes gasped, stunned, not expecting Blue One and me to run left and right, firing over and over, punching holes in the massive mech…before the Gatling cannon screamed out again and tore Fergie apart.

The line of fire jerked to the right, slicing Blue Two and Three apart, their twinned and boosted shield still popping under the onslaught.

"Boss!" Sync cried desperately.

"*What?*" I screamed, rifle clicking empty again. I ejected the mag and tore a fresh one, my last but one, and slammed it home, not even looking to see what it was.

"The pilot's a scav!"

"So?"

"Link me!" she demanded, and I did it, trusting her.

The scav pilot's voice was full of hatred and glee. "Surrend—"

"I've got your family under my eye," Sync cut him off flatly. "Thirty-seven women and children, with three fighters watching over them…" A single shot rang out. "Two fighters…" Another shot. "One…"

"Power it down, or she launches the area denial drone. Full summary judgment," I cut in grimly.

"You…you'll kill them all anyway." His voice changed to disbelief and desperation. "Hold fire!" he bellowed into a separate link. The fight slowly petered out, as Blue One did the same, the link shared live on my side.

"You attacked us. We came for the core, and we've nothing to lose. One more of my people die, and she launches. We all lose."

"Or…?"

"Or you power down the mech, you drop your weapons, and we judge you. *Combatants* only. We win, we retrieve the core, and we didn't see your women and children, and they stay hidden until we leave."

"They'll be killed in days," he snarled. "Raiders, hunters, monsters…"

"They'd have a chance," I countered. "Better than they have now."

"You wouldn't," he bluffed. The commlink expanded to show a tired, scruffy man in filthy overalls, head wired into the mech on the right side, hair hanging down his face on the left. "You'd not kill…"

A second image popped up, as Sync connected her scope to the commlink, zooming in on the face of an older woman, one who was looking around fearfully, before reaching for the gun of a fallen fighter.

"She touches that weapon, she's a combatant," Sync warned him.

The woman's fingers curled around the grip of the rifle, lifting it and turning…then she vanished in a bloom of blood. The scope dialed back out, before zooming in on another, a young man—a boy, really…maybe twelve or thirteen— as he reached for another gun.

"Sooner or later, we'll get to one you care about." I hated that Sync had done it, but knew that it needed to be done. I'd been on fucking hundreds of judgment runs, hitting scav bases, caravans and more, after they'd raided merchants or tried to steal from the recovery teams.

That's what we were now. We were the law to the lawless; we brought judgment on these fucks when they attacked the innocent. I didn't like it much, but the value of a life in these days? Nothing compared to what it had been in the old world.

The wilds and those who lived in them understood force; they understood consequences. Fuck with Artem and its people? The APS came out and judged you. That was all the law that existed out here now.

"You fucking corpo scum! You goddamn monsters! We just want to be free! Is that too much to—"

"Bang," Sync said coldly, moving to the next target.

"*Stop!*" he begged. "Look, you leave, back up and run, I'll let you g—"

"Not without the core," I snapped. "Not without our people."

"You can't win," he warned us, shaking his head. "If you kill them all, you die and—"

"You know why nobody ever talks about taking down a full APS squad?" I bluffed. "*Orbital strike*. We die, *you all die*."

"Bullshit."

"How certain are you?" I asked, sensing a string to pull. "You've got a choice. We all die—you, me, your families, everyone. *Or* just you and any soldiers we've seen." I stressed that last part, and I saw the wild look in his eyes. "We win, or you lose. No other way this plays out."

Seconds passed before he cut the connection abruptly, and I cursed, ready to open fire…until the mech sagged. Pressurized gasses vented around the massive hulk as it powered down.

The pilot stepped out, raising his hands into the air, glaring at us in hatred, and I raised my rifle, sighting down it.

"This is for my team, you fuck," I growled, and shot him in the head, painting the mech's interior red. "Guilty!"

CHAPTER THREE

It'd taken three hours to strip the Corium out of the mech. Helo-7 and Helo-11—Blue's transport—had stayed on station, landing and cycling down to save power, rather than leave when they realized the threat was gone and the possible bonuses to capturing an intact assault mech.

I'd refused the comm requests from Tyrannus, noting the ever more frantic tone of them. I leap-frogged him entirely, feeding the entire affair to Major Marcial, recordings and all.

Admittedly, they'd been subtly edited on the fly by Richie, removing the women and kids and making it sound like we'd been bluffing and had never seen them, just guessing they were there somewhere.

The major had taken one look, had seen the AROC and apparently decided that the request from M-Corp hadn't come through the correct channels, and had denied it, locking the entire thing down to his office and him alone as classified.

That made this a military op again, even if the corpos were going apeshit about losing their tech. It probably meant they'd originally cut the major out of the deal, and he would no doubt change his mind once he was getting his beak wet instead of Tyrannus. But hey, that's the way the world worked.

I'd lost good soldiers today, good friends, all because of the almighty credit, and I still had nine more months left in my contract. Tyrannus would fuck me as hard as he could, but getting the major happy with me and my team limited that in turn.

There were recovery teams inbound, specialists to examine the site, talk of recovering possible old world tech, and so Sync had been given the job of liaison with the women and children.

Not because she was a woman—hell, she was the most vicious of all of us. No, it was because Richie had already jacked her suit and wiped her recordings, making it look as if she'd been hit with an advanced hack. As such, she was off the record and could give them the heads-up, as well as checking to make sure there were no wanted targets among them.

They'd buried themselves in some safe room they had prepared but hadn't had the time to reach before now, and we piled scrap against the door—they had a secret exit, apparently—to hide it. We did that rather than break the deal and kill them all, as the site was going to get checked over more thoroughly.

I knelt on the floor next to the remains of Scott and Fergie, jacked into my friend's suit, downloading all the recordings and personal details before he was sealed to be shipped.

I'd already wiped Fergie. No way some fucker in Reclamation was getting access to his memories and selling them, we'd all vowed, and that was the deal in the APS division.

Just like we hid the dodgy porn from those with families, we stripped away anything that made them look like anything less than the gods of war they had been. Then our tech heads and the fallen's friends would scrub the footage, providing a sanitized, and yet awesome reel of their loved one's final fight.

Even if they'd been struck down with the shits, or their knob dropped off from cock-rot, what their families saw was a final footage of them saving us all, a warrior-titan they could be proud of.

That was the deal we all made.

Right now, though, I was staring at the AROC that Scott had seen, and the recording of the readouts that were playing over his suit as he decided to blow the fuck outta himself, taking millions of creds of explosives and gear with him.

The AROC device that was locked onto him had been dragged into position. That much was clear by the marks behind it.

They'd not been ready for us, and that was the only saving grace. These were insanely top-shelf kit, like I'd only ever seen *one* out of the container, and that'd been on a recording.

As soon as I'd told Major Marcial what it was, and that a bunch random scavs had one? That was when he'd decided to "review" the corpo request. I'd been ordered to provide all recordings of the kit to him and only him, and to erase the originals.

That'd made hiding our shit easier, as we had official codes to let us erase shit, but that they'd had one of these machines at all was terrifying me now.

An AROC was a last-chance device, one that was deployed to fry and remotely take over an APS if the soldier went on a rampage. It was designed to be used only after everything else had been tried, as the sheer pulse of power that was needed?

It'd kill the soldier every time.

Then, the suit rebooted into remote mode. They'd be able to control the APS and send him after us, to force us to fight our own people and their mech, and while we were dealing with that, they'd have been locking on and frying more of us, if they had the power.

If they'd had the chance to get ready for our arrival, or if there'd only been one team sent rather than two? It could have worked.

They could have captured a full APS team of suits, and our bodies would have been locked inside to do the dance for them all.

These were stupidly hard to get hold of. Like, insanely so. We had one back at the armory—*one*. It was under lock and key and required two senior techs to unlock the housing to retrieve it.

There were literally millions of creds of gear laid around in the APS and its armaments all day, every day, but the AROC needed DNA fucking verification to release it.

The big four corpos were permitted one each. *One.* I was betting the fact that seeing one out in the field would result in some fucker's balls being nailed to the wall. After all, if it'd been a raider team, here to capture our suits?

They'd have them now.

All the cities knew the basics of the armored suits. They were scaled-down mechs, heavily armed, that's all, and each design had its own strengths and weaknesses.

Each of the twelve cities had their own versions of our APS. Some stronger, some higher tech, some weaker and breaking all the time.

That was why our suits were always retrieved. They couldn't be used by another, not without insane investment in terms of new nanites—too much integration with the nanites and the individual operator. Instead, the suits needed to be simply smelted down. If we died in action, we were included with the suit. Our impurities were rendered into the next generation of the suits that would replace us.

It was morbid, but also, it was kind of cool, knowing that we were walking out to the fight with our brothers and sisters literally around us in our armor.

Alternatively, once we retired, if we'd taken the option to buy out our suit—at a cost of half our wages, bonuses, and bounties for the *entirety* of enlistment—we were fitted with trackers and a hardpoint on the backplate was taken up with a permanent, shaped explosive charge.

If we flatlined, or the suit stopped broadcasting verified telemetry, it fired, turning us and the interior of our suit into a puddle of glowing metal and impurities, which would be collected by the army.

Of course, we could not pay the fee, and leave our suit to be melted when we retired. Most didn't, after all, as the massive cost over the years of service was insane. But for those of us who dreamed of climbing the ladder as a merc?

It was no choice at all.

All the cities had a version of the APS, and the various spies and shitbirds spent half their time trying to get hold of their models, and making sure they didn't get ours. And the very best method to get our suits? It was undoubtably an AROC.

All that meant that some fucker was in for a world of hurt when the investigation was done. But for now, the fallout meant that Tyrannus was suddenly being investigated while the major took a direct hand.

That meant he got no bonuses, which was the only consolation in an otherwise shitty day.

The salvage from a working assault mech alone was going to be well over a million credits, and although we'd not get that, the few tens of thousands extra each we'd get was damn good money for just doing our job. Plus whatever the deal the major struck with the corpos, and our successful mission before this?

Overall, it meant that when I left the corps, I had a nice cushion to start replacing and upgrading my mods to seriously high spec.

Fergie and I had joined together, only a few months apart; Scott a year later, and Richie two after that. Sync had been with the team nearly as long as Richie, and we'd all planned to go merc together.

Our papers were in, Fergie and mine. Scott's were due to go in soon—it was a year's notice to retire at the end of the ten years and they'd not accept it early—and we'd expected to be cleaning up on contracts, getting ready to hit the major leagues as a merc squad once Scott, Rich, and Sync were finally free and the team was back together.

As a full team—we'd have replaced or done without Barnes; he was a dipshit and had only recently joined us anyway, despite his bravery, nine and a half years he had left on his service—we'd have been able to take on seriously high-end contracts.

Corpo bodyguard jobs as a team? We'd have been living in the skyscrapers in the middle of the city, earning insane creds and living the dream.

Now I was kneeling next to my friends, their armor torn apart, loaded on recovery sleds, ready to be sealed away and rendered down.

I forced the tears away, blowing out a long, shuddering breath as the connections released. The [WIPE CONFIRMED] message printed across my HUD.

I hesitated, images of the pair running through my mind. The laughter, the jokes, the *team*. They were my brothers in chrome and titanium, and I lost a part of me when I lost them.

I was empty inside, now, and I felt the flickering flames of the rage I was carefully not acknowledging.

I couldn't afford to do anything, not yet. I carefully blocked that line of thought as well, as a new connection request from Tyrannus flashed up.

We were still in an active combat zone, until I or Jon marked it as clear, and so we got comm requests, even from higher, rather than direct connections. It was simply because an idiot in an office demanding an ammo expenditure report in the middle of a firefight tended to result in expensive replacements being needed, be those team members, additional fire, or the dipshit themselves.

That cost creds, and so common sense remarkably prevailed.

Sooner or later, though, I'd have to accept it.

I sighed, reached out, and laid a hand each on Fergie and Scott's shoulders, and squeezed once, feeling the reassuring solidity of their armor, and the terrible ache that came from knowing that they might be inside still, but they had gone where I couldn't follow.

I triggered both sleds, closing my eyes as the straps and sheeting rose, concealing the bodies from my view, as a call request blinked frantically again.

"Captain Tyrannus," I greeted through gritted teeth, accepting the connection finally as I turned away, and the harried and furious face of the arrogant little fuck bloomed before me. "Apologies for going to Major Marcial, rather than to you direct, sir. But I couldn't get a connection to you for some reason, and the use of an AROC in the field required immediate response and reporting by Section 16:27 of the regs."

He stared at me, mouth flapping as he tried to counter—Richie had provided the regs detail, and I knew the fucker before me would have never even read them—as I forced a smile.

Gods, it sickened me, having to pretend respect for this scumbag, but I damn well knew this was being recorded and would be used against me at some point. Better to get it all out now and force him to respond.

I knew, and *he* knew, the slimy fucker, that he'd deliberately been away from his desk at the worst point, so that if anything went wrong—and it had—the worst that could be pinned on him was that he was in the toilet or something.

"I…was ill," he forced out through blatantly gritted teeth. "Unavoidable."

"Of course, sir. As a result, I had to go to Major Marcial, and he's waiting for an update from me."

"Give him the update, by all means. Then you'll repeat it, word for word, to me. In fact, I want your combat logs. Send them direct to—"

"I'm *sorry,* Captain," I lied. "The major directed all combat logs are to be sent direct to him and only him. I'll make him aware of your demand, however." I smiled again. "Sorry, *sir.* I have to go."

I cut the connection. The forced smile poured off my face, as I huffed out a breath, controlling and burying my emotions, and requested a connection to the major.

Ten minutes later and it was all done. Combat logs were sent, along with Richie's reports on the assault mech, and the viability of the site. My non-too-subtle hints about Tyrannus meant we were ordered—the major knew the game better than we did; I'd barely needed to explain—to report to the major directly and exclusively should we have any concerns about the AROC or any suspicions about it.

Included in that was that we were forbidden to discuss the AROC or any details of the fight with anyone beyond the official line.

We were given permission to make the death reel for Fergie and Scott's family and friends, but it was to be vetted by the major and his team.

Once the line was cut, I reached out to Tyrannus, and took great pleasure in "apologizing" to him and informing him that because of the major's direct orders, we were now forbidden from discussing the mission with him at all, repeating that all records had been locked to the major and his team, and we'd see him when we got back.

I even included a hint that I was to remain in direct contact with the major, just to make sure he backed the fuck up. But I saw in his eyes that he'd already gotten the message.

Whatever happened between us, it'd not be anywhere that anyone could find and officially trace.

That was fine by me.

He was due to get out a few months after I was. Chatter on who was getting free was always rife, but as a non-combat, back-office shit-stain, he'd be leaving with a pension, not an APS.

Out in the real world, he'd end up busily slurping on a corpo dick, while I was stomping on throats.

We'd found our natural level after all, it seemed.

"All done?" Jon, Blue One, stepped up. His own sleds were loaded, and he linked to my suit, enabling me to confirm that his logs were wiped.

Now I held the only "full" copy of the fight that hadn't been sent to higher.

"All done," I agreed. "Higher have been updated. Orders stand—no discussing the AROC or anything else, the mission is sealed, death reels to be done, but handed to the major's team for confirmation before release."

"Let's hope they don't fuck them up then." He sighed. "Damn, what a clusterfuck."

"You're telling me," I growled, shaking my head at the recovery pile.

The scavs weren't hard to take down. They were only scavengers, after all—most of them, anyway—wearing atmo gear, layers of cloth and armor that was more leather and composites than titanium and steel.

They *looked* impressive, and probably badass to people they found out in the wilds, but a round from one of our rifles could take down an old world tank. A direct hit on a scav? They were toast. The sheer force made sure of that every time.

They had no chance, which made that they'd had an AROC even crazier.

Someone had been bankrolling them. Someone had to have been giving them information and the AROC at least, and that meant that that someone was expecting to have to fight APS operators.

Maybe it even meant that some stupid fuck out there had planned to get their hands on us, and that the mech—although powerful and valuable—wasn't the real prize.

Hell, had we known it was here? With the right loadout, it'd have been taken down easily enough by Fergie alone.

We stripped the scene, and when the recovery teams arrived, we handed it over with a palpable sense of relief. The trip back to base, with our friends in cold storage and the surviving members of the team back in our deployment pods—there was nowhere else in the helo for us, after all—was going to be a shitty flight.

A few hours ago, we'd been on our way back to base, knowing that we were getting a decent bonus, one that'd be spent on leave in the bars and whorehouses next to the barracks most likely, partying as a team.

Now the heart of the team was gone.

We'd get replacements assigned, but they'd never take Fergie and Scott's place, not really. And with only a matter of months left? I didn't give a shit about integrating some new assholes beyond enough to keep the rest of us alive.

All in all, I was in a foul mood sitting in my suit, swaying gently aboard the helo, staring unseeing at the blinking cursor on the report I'd zoned out while writing, when the commlink activated.

"Boss?"

"Yeah, Richie?" I coughed, blinking away tears again.

"You know that drone I tagged the site with?"

"The one by the entrance?" I struggled to remember. "When we needed the relay link?"

"Yeah…turns out I forgot to de-activate it."

"Uh-huh," I agreed, both of us knowing damn well he'd not "forgotten" anything.

"Well…they just cleared the caved-in section. The one that Scott did, I mean, not the scaffolding."

"Uh-huh."

"And…"

"Richie, do I need to pull the fucking words out with a plier?" I growled. "What the hell did they find?"

"No clue," he admitted. "They've been bringing out heavy weapons for the last ten minutes, though, like current mil-spec shit, and nobody seemed bothered."

"What?"

"Then they found something else."

"And?"

"And the recovery team went apeshit. Full black-site lockdown protocols. Cut the connection to the relay drone."

"Well, fuck. Any ideas?"

"Nope, but they, uh, they might have found the drone, boss. Sorry."

"Great," I growled. "Leave it with me. You weren't doing anything wrong," I assured him, the pair of us knowing damn well he was.

"Thanks, boss."

I cut the connection, pausing before I called the major to bullshit an excuse, and thought about it. Really *thought*.

This didn't make sense.

That there was an AROC was insane, and the corps would be going apeshit over that, but the site was open and working, getting cleared through, and no corpo asshole was going to get away with hiding anything that was found there now, but…

"*Incoming!*" the pilot screamed into the local net, twisting the helo sharply, as the world filled with fire, light, and noise.

CHAPTER FOUR

I blinked muzzily. The HUD before me flickered unsteadily as it rebooted, for a minute showing me the reflection of the inside of my armor, before it shifted and lit up again, this time bringing me back to the full three-hundred-and-sixty-degree field of vision I was used to.

Not that I could see much of anything. I was pressed into the corner of the deployment pod, literally the corner before me an inch or less away, with more of it fallen atop me.

I shifted. The camera view from the feeds on my shoulders and the back of my head showed me a collapsed stanchion lying across me, having punched through the pod next to me.

"Ferg—" I started to call, before cutting myself off. It'd come straight through his bay. Even if he'd been alive? He'd not be now.

I snarled, reaching out, bracing myself and pushing, tearing sections of fallen helo off me. Sparks flared and cascaded across my armor as I shook myself.

"Red Team!" I bellowed into the local tacnet. "Sound off!"

"Red…Two…" came a weak cry, along with a cough that sounded like he was drowning.

"Fuck!" I snarled, ripping the last of the structural support off and turning to the wall between us. "Scanner!" I barked, falling back on the old "shout it as you want it" that we were taught in training.

It was stupid, I'd not done that in years, but today was just one of those fucking days.

The scanner booted, sending a ping out that gave me first an image of the section I was in and part of the next one, the debris that was through it and more. And a second higher, and then a lower ping sounded, as a dozen different mapping systems activated.

If they'd not had a jammer back there, they'd never have snuck up on us. But that was the joy of war: one side invented something, the other countered it, on and on until the guy with the hammer and knife showed up and fucked everyone's Tuesday up.

As it was, an image was steadily building of the surrounding bays, and I was damn glad I'd not gone with my first instinct and punched through the wall.

Barnes was laid pressed up against the bulkhead, right where I'd have started punching. And considering the post that was rammed through his stomach, that'd have really ruined his afternoon.

I drew my blade, a vibrating wonder that could carve steel like butter, and I flicked the activation, sinking it into the separating wall a few inches above his head, carving my way upward.

Three slices—up, across, and then looping down to link up with the first one—and I punched it, sending the dividing wall flying away from us.

"Richie...Sync?" I called, as I sheathed the knife and grabbed the cut sections, bending them out even as I looked at Barnes.

"Sync here..." came the crackling connection, dropping in and out. "I have Richie. Unresponsive, injured."

"Thank fuck." I groaned, before wincing at the state of Barnes. "Damn, boy, you couldn't do it by halves, could you?"

"Hey, boss," Barnes whispered. "H-how do I look?"

"Like a pit beast ate you up and shit you out." I grunted, shaking my head in the suit. "You able to move?"

"I think my back's broken. Spinal tap connection feels wrong, like it's dropping in and out."

"Remember your training," I ordered him, while frantically trying to remember mine. "If your spinal tap is damaged, what do we do?"

"Activate medical suite, which I've done, then assess location of damage, attempt a reroute," he quoted.

"So...?" I checked the image of the local area and winced. We were in the remains of the helo all right, but damn.

The rest of the helo was just...*gone*.

"Sync, where the hell are you?" I asked on directed singular engagement mode, as I scanned the kid.

"Uh...comms work, internal systems work, scanning and linkup...no movement, though," Barnes interrupted, and I switched back to him.

"That's good. So the spinal Cs are good. You're breathing, and your chest works okay, so the early T grades are fine as well. Internals?"

"Numb," he admitted. "I can move my fingers and arms *in* the suit, but no response from the suit's arms."

"So you've got a break in the T5 to T12 range. Solution?"

"Reroute to the higher T?" he asked.

I nodded in approval. A video link to him showed him my face, even as I pretended not to see the paleness of his skin, nor the steadily dropping vital signs.

"That's it, son. Reroute motor controls to the higher connection. You're increasing the risk of damage to the nerves and spine, that's why there's a set limit on connections at each point, but they can fix that once we're back at base."

"Aye, sir," he breathed, already working to reroute.

"Good man. I need to check on the others. Back soon," I promised, getting a nod and a wan smile, before I shifted his connection back to verbal only, and reconnected to Sync.

"What was that?" I asked. "Sync? You there?"

Silence.

Utter fucking silence.

I didn't like that, and I kicked my way out of the remains of the bay, before swearing furiously as I realized where we were.

The impact had come when we were passing through the Fingers.

The Fingers of God was a section of the mountain range to the northwest of Artem, a mass of high, solid rock spires, ranging from a dozen meters to half a kilometer or more thick, and kilometers high.

Nobody knew what kind of weapon had been deployed to shred a mountain range like that, but the fact it wasn't all radioactive had kept conspiracy theorist nutjobs busy for years.

Some areas were literally glowing, all day and night, and others? Less radiation than I usually got from a soda.

The world around me was aflame while also being seemingly a blizzard of snow and sleet, just to make my life more interesting. The helo had been sheared apart by whatever hit it. The entire back section of the helo was just fucking missing, and the front?

Helo pilots—probably because they were useless fucks in every other aspect of their lives—always had to fly *through* the damn Fingers, rather than *over*, risking everyone's lives for shits and giggles.

Whatever had happened, had happened as we wove through them, and with the heavy damage to the superstructure, we'd then crashed into a fucking Finger, tearing the rest of the craft apart.

The pilot might have been a useless cowardly fuck, but he, and anyone else aboard and who wasn't in an APS, was dead now, and it was more by sheer luck that I was alive.

Sync wasn't responding. Neither was Richie when I tried him. I swore, seeing on my HUD that my long-range comms, usually used to link to a satellite and then onward, were down, with a reading flashing that there'd been damage to the antenna.

I moved on, clambering up and out of the helo wreckage, and moved to the edge, looking over the side.

I was at least half a kilometer up, right on the edge of a cliff, and the wind blasted snow around me, making it damn near impossible to see anything.

*What the hell had the helo pilot been thinking, flying in the Fingers in this? He'd probably hit the fucking side himself and...*I hesitated, replaying the last seconds. The wonder of the suit's tech once again made my goddamn life easier.

"*Incoming...*" he'd screamed, and he'd sounded terrified. Yeah, he could have meant that we were about to crash, and to have used a phrase that he knew we'd respond to instantly, but...

But my gut swore that was bullshit.

"Barnes, you okay?" I was getting a very bad feeling about this.

"I'm here, boss," he replied.

"How you doing?"

"Medical kit has stopped the bleed. Estimated six hours to full recovery. I...had to use the large medikit. Sorry, boss."

"It's fine. I'd rather we had to replace the nanites and lose the bonus than you," I assured him. "Although, I'm going to higher ground. I lost contact with Sync and Richie. Helo crew is dead."

"My comms are fucked. Maybe it's the storm?"

"Maybe," I agreed grudgingly. "Hold tight, kid. I'm going higher."

I started up the side, then hesitated, and moved back, reaching one of the recovery sleds. I triggered the open and swallowed hard.

The crash hadn't been kind to my friends. The blood that coated the inside of the container covered the jack ports as well, and I wiped it clear, before taking Scott's secondary battery, and ejecting the damaged ammo feed on my right shoulder.

I attached the battery to the hardpoint as I moved back out of the wreckage. The symbols came online as my suit tested the connection integrity and power cycled the battery, confirming its load.

My available power went from thirty-six percent to seventy, and I nodded. Scott would have been furious with me if I'd not taken it, when it could help me stay alive.

The climb across the side of the Finger to the highest point only took a few minutes, but when I got there, I swore.

I was in the middle of them, literally, with at least three days' run back to Artem by land, and that wasn't counting going around the fucking cove.

I shook myself, turning back, and froze, dropping down and triggering my stealth systems on instinct.

The standard APS came with a limited stealth suite. It was limited in *my* model anyway, as a command module took the place of the secondary kit needed, not to mention lacking the full plate upgrade for the photo-reflective panels.

But the kit I had was good enough, considering I was crouching on a mountainside, surrounded by blasted rock and ancient shattered metal and debris, in a snowstorm.

It was only by sheer fucking luck and a break in the clouds that I'd seen the drone at all.

It was a shark—that was what we called them, regardless of their official designation. They were fast, vicious, and used to tear your opponents a new asshole. The shark flitted across the Fingers, moving from one to another, clearly searching for something.

"Hey…oss!" came the sudden relieved voice of Barnes, through a mass of static and dropped words. "I've…a conn…on to the…satellite. Uplink's…stable. Relaying…location and…"

The shark spun, light blazing to life as they locked onto something down the mountainside I couldn't see, even as I frantically tried to establish a secure link.

"Barnes!" I screamed. "Kill it! Kill the link!"

"You…?" I got through a wall of static, before the night lit up.

Two missiles screamed out of recessed pinions on the shark, slamming into the wreckage I could no longer see below me.

The site exploded, the entire side of the Finger going up, and I threw myself down again. The stealth field I'd not thought to deactivate was all that kept me alive as the shark tore past, vanishing in the storm. I laid there, cursing myself for my cowardice, for my stupidity, for all of it.

I'd not even thought to take my rifle—hell, I didn't even know where it was— but I'd not *looked*, and that was unforgivable in an operator. Never mind that it was a fucking shark, never mind that my chances of taking down an armored assassination drone in a snowstorm were less than me going for a random piss and finding I'd magically gained three inches and my balls were now champagne flavored for her pleasure—it was still an *unforgivable* fuckup.

I hesitated, torn between staying hidden and alive but a fucking coward, or checking on my teammate.

I forced myself to stay still for a few more seconds, before moving, my determination outdoing my fear. I crawled as fast as I could. Losing my antenna suddenly seemed like an insane intervention from one of the gods.

There had to be one whose offering cup I'd not pissed in at some point, and maybe that was what was paying off now.

I kept going, knowing, damn well *knowing* that there wasn't a cat in hell's chance of anyone surviving, but needing to see it for myself.

A minute later, I got my answer. I stared down from a ridge at the devastation. Nothing could have survived it…nothing. The shark had used Hellfires, I guessed.

Insanely hot, high explosive, and monomolecular fléchettes. The same kind that the helo would have been carrying, the same kind that I'd wanted them to use on the factory.

If anyone scanned the debris later on? It'd pass a quick and dirty inspection, written up as a helo pilot error, then a Hellfire detonating on impact.

Full team lost…too bad, so sad.

Well, that was bullshit, because I was still here. I was still fucking alive, and I'd find whoever did this. I'd find them and I'd fucking murder them, each and every one.

For now, though? Sync had cut the connection; she'd been alive, and she had Richie with her. I'd only heard the one strike—two missiles, but that was it.

Knowing that sneaky fuck Sync, she'd have Richie hidden away somewhere safe by now, and no matter what happened, the APS Corps wouldn't just shrug at the loss of us…Blue Team!

Fuck's sake, where was Blue?

They'd been with us, hadn't they? Behind our helo…

No, they'd been ordered off, sent somewhere else. I vaguely remembered a message telling us we'd get a beer later, when they got back. Now it was obvious.

They'd been sent away to separate us. I'd confirmed that all trace of the recordings we had were deleted…a copy was sent to the major, but beyond that there was only one other copy.

Mine, a physical recording locked into my suit.

Was I the target? Clearly someone thought we had something, on the recordings or that I or one of my team had seen personally. Or maybe they'd done it after finding the drone and that we'd been watching the shit found at the site? No. That was ridiculous. Richie had only just been caught and seconds later, we were down.

No, they had to have been ready, waiting and planning to do this already. I stayed there frozen for long minutes, my mind racing, until I swore. The warning on the secondary battery flashed that it was almost depleted.

It was almost dead, and although my own was good still at thirty-six, the additional battery being drained first, it wouldn't last that long if I kept using it.

The drain from active camo on my shitty systems was too great, and I was in a fucking snowstorm anyway. Our suits were designed to be stealthy, so fuck it. Without the antenna, I'd register as slightly warmer metal than the mountain's average, sure, but a hundred meters below me was a fire and flaming wreckage.

I'd probably pass a basic scan.

I cut the camo, staying still and letting myself vanish under the snow as my mind raced.

However they spun this, the corps would send a recovery team, usually a few dozen suits plus a couple of helos, as well as grunts to do the actual shlepping around of the crap that needed to be collected.

No chance they'd all be in on it. No, this read like it was a hit, something to shut us down.

Something had been found in the base, and it wasn't even under *lockdown* until then. Just a standard recovery situation. Something there had changed everything, and I was going to goddamn find out what. There were too many unknowns, too many assholes, and too little people being shot in the face by me for my tastes.

One of those I could fix sharpish, though, and I'd start with Tyrannus.

I was exhausted, physically from the fight, mentally from all the shit that was going on, and emotionally from…from losing my best friends.

No way I was making good decisions right now, and regardless, there was nothing I could do. Richie and Sync had their nanite medikits, so unless they were dead by drone already, which there was nothing I could do anything about, they'd probably recover.

They'd be doing what I was: hiding and waiting. Best to make the most of it.

I let my head fall into the snow, stretched out as I was, and barely stayed awake long enough to deploy a scanner. It was a low-level one, optical only, but if Richie and Sync came looking, I wanted to know about it.

Then I let the darkness take me, lost on the mountainside, my friends' remains still glowing hot far below.

CHAPTER FIVE

When I awoke, it was with a pounding headache, a taste like a cat had shit in my mouth, and a steady beeping as the suit pulsed audio and visual cues to wake me up.

I focused groggily, the flashing lights of the HUD tamping down to normal, as I saw the stealthy movements below.

It took a few seconds to make sense of them. Snow was still falling, and we were high enough in the mountains that we got as much low clouds passing over the ground as we did them passing above.

After a minute, though, it resolved.

Footprints appeared. Whoever was making them moved, pausing and waiting for the footprint to fill in, before making the next.

It was slow going, but they were in full stealth. The only person I could see being up here, in full stealth, and moving that carefully?

I locked a tight beam onto the figure and whispered as I "knocked" on her suit for the connection.

"Sync?"

"Fuck's sake," came the response. As the request was approved, Sync's image appeared in my HUD. "You owe me what it's going to cost to have my armor cleaned."

"Shit yourself again, huh?" I replied, unable to help myself.

"We're in a suit that's so cutting-edge that we don't know half the shit it can do yet. Most of the really high-end tech is locked down and restricted until it's been approved for the battlefield, and yet we still get a fucking tube rammed up our asses without so much as a drink bought first, and it's held in place with tape. Tape I'm allergic to," she snarled.

"Thanks for that mental image." I sighed. "Where's Richie?"

"Hidden in a cave. Barnes?"

"Toast." I shook my head. "I left him in the wreckage to rest and climbed up high. He got his commlink working and connected to a satellite. Next thing I know, a shark is Hellfiring him into the next life."

"Damn."

"Yeah. My antenna was trashed, or I'd have been hit as well."

"Mine's offline. Richie locked it down."

"He okay?"

"Broken pelvis. Swears it's from all the action he had last leave."

"Lying bastard." I grunted. "He gets less action than Fergie, and Fergie's both ginger *and* dead."

"Fuck's sake, boss. He's only been gone a few hours!" Sync snapped, and I bit back on my response, hanging my head in shame. "Be realistic—if there's another life after this one, Fergie's already knee-deep somewhere."

I snorted, knowing she was trying.

"Fine, let's get to Richie, then we can plot a fucking murder."

"You don't think it's accidental then?" she quipped.

"Yeah, in the same way that Kevski's marriage broke up because he tripped and his dick 'fell' into his wife's sister. Total accident."

"I remember the mimed demonstration of him trying to 'help her up.'" Sync sighed. "And Tyrannus walked in, first day in charge, only to see that."

"Wonder if that's where it all went wrong?" I muttered, pushing up and out of the snow, shaking it off my back, then moving to start the climb down.

For a second, the hairs on the back of my neck rose. I couldn't afford to use the active camo, nor could I climb down without turning my back to Sync.

I trusted her—she'd been one of us for years—but...*someone* had arranged all of this, and for a second, I doubted her. Then I remembered all the times she could have killed me, and I shook it off. Paranoia was a useful tool, it kept you sharp, but there was a limit, a point where it fucked you up.

I'd need to watch that.

By the time I reached Sync, she'd deactivated her camo, and to my relief, she was both armed and ready. We hugged briefly. The incongruity of two of the feared APS operators, massive machines of death, hugging it out made us laugh, before she led me back down the mountain.

Forty minutes later, and we were with Richie in a sheltered cave, taking turns to exit our suits, stretch, wash with handfuls of compacted snow—a refreshing and yet terrible experience—and then reentering, locking the suit up tight and shivering as we recovered.

"What's the plan, boss?" Richie asked after we'd eaten some emergency rations, and I shook my head.

"Honestly, I don't know," I admitted. "How'd you both survive, anyway?"

"Something hit Scott's bay," Richie said. "It detonated. Next thing I know, I'm falling, smashed through a tree, then landed on a rocky outcropping. A spike, you know? I think it's done permanent damage to my sex life."

"Your right hand will forgive you, I'm sure." Sync snorted. "I landed a little farther off, hit a snowdrift, and when I dug myself out, I found him."

"Dragged me into the drift, then laid on me." He forced a grin. "Told you I was irresistible, even broken."

"I have active camo and a secondary battery designed to use it," she grumbled. "Unlike you idiots, I can use it properly. It made sense."

"Irresistible," Richie said again, then sighed. "It's a curse that's followed me all my life."

"Anyway, what's the play here, boss?" Sync gnawed on a bit of dehydrated schmeat. "Gods, I hate these shitty rations..."

"As I said, I don't know. Some fucker has it out for us. They sent a shark to take down the helo—that's a serious cred loss for the corps, even without all of us—then Hellfires to make sure that we were down. Someone seriously doesn't want us reporting shit, but not sure who."

"Tyrannus. Has to be," Richie said flatly. "He lost his bonus, and got slapped down hard from above. Probably fucked any chance of him getting any juicy corpo job when he gets out without serious creds changing hands. He'd do it."

"He would," I agreed. "He's enough of an asshole he would, I've no doubt. The point is, though, *could* he do it? I'm not so sure. Hell, I don't think the major could either. Too many moving parts, and too many chances to go wrong, with too short notice to seal it up tight."

"Maybe he saw the chance and ran with it?" Sync suggested. "What about the corpo scumbag?"

"Could do it. Again, the question is why?"

"Hide the AROC," Richie suggested.

"Then why send us there when they weren't ready? If it was M-Corp fucking us over, trying to get our suits or make the corps expand or whatever, they'd have been ready. Think about how it could have gone. We walk in and they're ready for us? Just send the teams in separate, space out the helos? We land, spread out to search and get hit with the AROC; we're dead and the suits are theirs. They wait for Blue to arrive, do the same again—take the helos down, bug out with whatever escape plan they had in place."

"They'd have had both teams easy enough." Sync nodded. "Hell, the mech wasn't even ready."

"If that'd been ready, hidden and loaded? It could have taken us out like it did Fergie, cut us all in half if they weren't after the APS. Can't have been the corpos that did it…or at least not M-Corp."

"I still hate those shifty fucks," Sync muttered, and I nodded.

"Everyone does."

"Their credits spend well though." Richie sighed. "Look, we can figure out who and why later. What do we do right now?"

"SARS will be on their way, and there's no chance that they'll leave the area before they know what's happened," I pointed out. "Search and Rescue Squad are like fucking dogs with a bone. They'll tear the mountain apart looking for us, and they'll be running full record all the way. Nobody can make us vanish then. We wait for them to arrive, walk out, and boom."

"It'll be boom, all right," Sync snapped. "They took out the helo, they sent a shark with Hellfires—you think they'll just shrug and say 'Ah well, maybe next time'?"

"Nope, but whatever they do with SARS there will be recorded. Nobody gets to hide shit when there's that many people involved. It'll come out, because some turd will want to make their name by sharing it with the world."

"So, not for the sake of truth and righteousness?" Richie snorted. "Nah, don't answer that. It's always some hack who 'wants the world to just be safe and fair' and all that crap. The next thing you know, they're doing tooth-gel adverts and starring in pornos with brand-new horse cocks grafted on."

"You've got real issues, Richie, you know that?" Sync sighed.

"Exactly, and yeah, he does," I agreed with her. "So we wait for SARS or whoever comes. I walk out first…we see if I get hit with an orbital or whatever. You fuckers stay hidden. Maybe we bury the entrance here…fuck my armor up a bit, make it look like I crashed outside. Draw them in nice and close. Then, if something happens, I've got you fuckers backing me up."

"I don't like it," the others said, almost as one.

"You think I do?" I countered. "I get to stand out there and wave my dick around, see if anyone shoots it."

"Maybe we're all being paranoid," Sync said after a few seconds, and we both glared at her.

"You hit your head or something?" Richie asked her, and I snorted.

"No. Some fucker is out to get us, that's sure as shit. I mean we're thinking that SARS might be in on it. For that to happen, SARS as a whole would be compromised. Who'd bother? Just pay an armorer to fuck our kit up on the way out, put a virus in the latest updates, shut our suits down when we walk in. That'd take a single guy, maybe two or three to do the code, that's it. A whole SARS team, as well as the headquarters' operators watching over it? The captain and the major? For what?"

"You got a point?" I asked.

"I think it's an opportunist. Like the scavs…what if they hit a depot and it got hushed up? They grabbed the AROC and then they sent the shark as well; some gang funded them and they got all pissy? Look, hitting us in a snowstorm when some dickhead pilot's playing with the Fingers? That's easily hidden. As far as anyone's concerned, we crashed and the Hellfires went off. Maybe they pay off someone high up to read the SARS report and close it, no fuss…that's doable.

"As it is, though, we *survived*. We go back to the base? They'll come after us again. We're the only witnesses. They can't afford to let us live."

"So what do we do?" I rubbed my chin in thought. The confines of the suit made even that movement awkward, let alone eating and drinking.

"We go rogue," Sync said softly. "Come on, guys, don't tell me you've not considered it. Just walking the fuck out, heading back to Artem, vanishing into the mess? Richie, you can hack anything—you could sort us new identities easily enough. We hit a gang, wipe them out…that's disposable income. We use their IDs, start again."

"The trackers?" Rich asked, his voice making it clear he was considering it.

"In the suits?" she asked. "Kill it."

"Wait, that's a point. Our suit trackers—why didn't they use them to find us?"

"Storm around the Fingers will block it. There's a shitload of electrical and magnetic debris here. Once the storm is over? Sure, they'll activate them, and boom. But I can kill them, I think," Richie said.

"Do it, and wipe these conversations," I ordered him. "I don't need a fucking missile interrupting us."

"Sir," he responded automatically, reaching out with both arms. Filaments extended from recesses to jack into our suits physically. His role as the team's tech granted him access to shit we didn't see or need. "Working on it, but thanks to the codes from the major, I've erased the recordings now, and taken the system offline. We can talk freely."

"Right." I sighed. "So, they think we're dead, and we what? Walk away? You think nobody's going to notice three unregistered APS suits rocking up to the West Gate?"

"No way they'd let us in," Rich said firmly. "The suits would be reported miles out. We'd have helos inbound in minutes if we're not on the list of merc operators."

"So what do we do?" Sync snarled. "We just go back to the base? Wait and see when someone's going to wipe us out? It's not happening! You're all right…" She looked at me. "You've got what? Ten months left?"

"Nine," I corrected.

"Nine months…you play up you don't know what happened, maybe no memory of the whole mission, and they might leave you alone, not worth the risk. No way all three of us can pull that off. No, we try that shit, and we're dead." She shook her head. "We've got four *years* in the corps yet. That's a hundred missions easy. A hundred chances to fuck with us, if a knife in the dark doesn't do it for us."

"So what, we run off and live in the wilds?" I shook my head. "They'll soon hear about a set of suits roaming around. Not to mention batteries. Where the hell we gonna get recharges? Food, water, ammo?"

"The scavs manage it."

"They're scavs. They've got entire communities out there. We're city, and worse, we're judgment. They'll hunt us for fun without the suits, and with them? Hell, we'll have the other cities hunting us in a few days!"

"What if we sleep?" Richie asked suddenly.

"What?" I asked, confused.

"What if we sleep?" he repeated. "Seriously, think about it. Sync and I, we trigger the emergency cryo function. I trick it into thinking we're injured. All the failsafes go online, and it locks us into a coma, drops our body temps into cryosleep. You come back for us, get us registered with a merc company. You can get our suit details easily enough."

"And what, I just leave you here?" I asked, aghast. "Frozen in a fucking cave? Ready for some scav to find and strip?"

"Yeah, basically," he replied, grinning as he thought about it more. "Look, Sync was right—one of us, a sole survivor, injured, confused? It looks like the pilots crashed and you were thrown clear. You claim no memory of the mission, they tell you whatever bullshit they like—you know they will. You just agree, keep your head down, stay off the grid, make no fucking waves, nothing. Then you leave."

"And you two just sleep it all away?" I asked, disbelieving what I was hearing.

"Shit, yes. Look, you find out that it's a genuine fuckup, and there's no threat? Great, you come back for us, wake us up. We all get bollocked, maybe a year or two added on, but that's it. We *live*. If they cover it up and sell you a bullshit story? You know they'd have killed us, and you know who to fucking hunt. You get out? Follow the original plan."

"Join a merc company," I said softly, nodding slowly. "Get my suit registered, get all the shit we need, then get a hacker to get us a mission up here, just me on the way out, pick you up, bring you back."

"New identities, suits licensed…we're out of here in, what? A year? Year and a half tops. Give you six months in a normal merc outfit and you'll be running it, especially in a suit."

"We'll need to replace the mil-spec mods. They take them back."

"So, two years. Tell me you've not been saving to replace them anyway."

"You know I have," I muttered.

"So six months as a standard merc, shit detail, pay off the carvers to upgrade you, then you get into the leadership once you're back in your suit. I know a hacker—he can sort this shit for us. Once you're plugged in, he'll sort trackers and authorizations. As far as the local police know? We've finished our service. We're all legit."

"You trust him?" I asked skeptically.

"Hell, no." Richie scoffed. "But he loves credits, and if he has the chance to earn real scratch? He'll take it, and he'll not dare fuck us over. Armored Personnel Suit operators, remember? A hacker pisses us off, he ends up as a smear on the floor."

"How, though?" I muttered a minute later, actually thinking about it. "How do we convince them I wasn't just hiding and..."

"That's the bit you're not gonna like, boss," Richie said apologetically. "You want to do this?"

"No, but it's the best chance we've got, and this storm isn't going to last much longer. They'll send drones in soon. Hell, they might be outside already..." I shook my head. "It's not like I've got a better plan."

"Then you need to be fucked up, and badly, and we need to time this so it looks like you've been laid there in the snow, fucked up for a while..."

Silence fell, and I cursed, seeing exactly what he was getting at.

"We need to bury the entrance as well," I pointed out. "If you're outside..."

Grim nods were shared, and Richie disconnected from our suits, straightening up.

"Last chance to change your mind, boss. We've got no time, so either come up with something fast or..."

"I..." I sighed. "Fuck. I've got nothing," I admitted. "You sure you're going to be okay in here for a year or more?"

"Be safer than you'll be out there," he assured me. "I'll do you a datapacket, one that I'll hide, like seriously hide, better than those pornos you watch and we all pretend aren't obvious in the team tacnet."

"I...How?" I asked, choosing not to respond to that.

"Data log. I'll encode it, lock it right down. You take it to my man, he'll know how to unlock it. Nobody outside of a high-tier AI will be able to besides him."

"I'll bury us," Sync said softly, shaking her head. "I don't like this, but you're right. It's our best chance. You sort the logs, I'll get the cave entrance ready, then fuck him up. He covers us over, and then..."

"Then we get to have a nap." Richie grinned. "Hey, look on the upside. We no longer have to put up with those dickhead officers."

"Yeah, if we live and don't end up in a military jail."

"Or stripped by scavs when you're asleep, and I'm shot in the head when I open my door," I pointed out, getting grim chuckles.

"Well, what will be, will be," Richie quoted, reaching out and laying a hand on my armored shoulder. "You've got this, boss."

"I do, but do you?" I asked. We all knew the cryosleep was an emergency deal. It'd freeze them, all right, but if their batteries gave out before I got back for them? It'd not be pretty.

"I'll make it work," he assured me, before grinning. "You remember, boss, this data? It'll be the only way to find us. You can't have the location on anything else. And the Fingers give off weird signals at the best of times—radioactive as fuck, so that'll block any scanners. You lose this, we're stuck here till the batteries die, and we rot."

"How do I find it?" I swallowed hard, not liking the way this was going.

"You get in your suit, and you ask for it. Simple. The suit tracks everything that you are, remember? If someone's forcing you to ask, it'll never give it up. It'll detect duress, so you ask only when you're *really* ready."

"And if I lose my suit?"

"Yeah, don't do that," Richie said quickly, shaking his head. "Like, seriously, don't lose your suit."

"Nine months." I sighed, clapping him on the shoulder. "Nine months till discharge. Six months on the merc list, doing shitty jobs, build my rep. Then, as soon as I can afford the rest of my mods, I'll be back for you, and I'll bring the hacker."

"And a medic," Richie recommended, glancing toward the mouth of the cave where Sync was already stacking rocks. "Seriously, if you're much more than a year? We'll need one, regardless. More than a year in cryo without the proper prep, and we're gonna be fucked up. But a little medical magic and some nanites? We'll recover."

"A year," I promised. "I'll be back within a year. Somehow, I'll make it happen."

"That'd be good, boss," Richie said on a private link. "Seriously, the longer we're down? The more risk of memory loss. The nanites will rebuild the cells fine. As long as we're alive? They can bring us back given enough time, but cell damage in the brain? It's the memories and more that'll be lost, and those are what make us, *us*."

"I know. I'll make it. I've got most of what I need for the mods as it is. A few jobs—hell, a few decent bonuses between now and then? I'll be done."

"Yeah, well, give it a few months before you come for us after you get out, okay? Just in case."

"Don't come too soon, don't come too late, eh?"

"Not the first time you've been told that, is it." He grinned. "Okay, boss. Go help Sync. I'll get this ready."

I clapped him on the shoulder again and moved to the entrance to the cave, grabbing a large rock and heaving it into place.

"So…snow's still pretty heavy," I commented.

"Yeah."

"So…might be awhile before the storm blows itself out," I tried again.

"Yeah."

"You want to talk about it?"

"Not really."

"Sync…"

She stopped, spinning to face me. "Just don't, okay?" she begged. "I've lost two of us today, and now you're going. We're going to fucking sleep, and we might never wake up…"

"This wasn't my idea—"

"My idea was to run!" she snapped.

"We'd die. Even if we could hide the suits, the scavs left us alone, and the monsters and shit didn't find us, we'd die of starvation and fucking dehydration, not to mention radiation."

"We'd die together," she muttered. "Not slipping away in my fucking sleep."

"I'd rather go in my sleep," I admitted.

"Not me. Just the thought…Why'd you think I don't sleep well?"

"Because you're a paranoid psycho?"

"Well, yeah, all right, but besides that," she offered with a forced chuckle.

"It'll be all right, Sync, you know it will," I assured her. Both of us knew I was lying.

The next fifteen minutes were spent in hard labor, digging massive boulders out and piling them over the entrance to the cave, then burying it in snow, until it was almost all hidden.

"Time to get inside," I told her, and she nodded.

"You know you need to look really fucked up for this to work, right?" she said, and I nodded. "And to make sure they don't look here too closely."

"Just not my face or my dick, all right? I need a reason to live."

"It'd be a service to women everywhere," she joked softly, before shaking her head. "But no. Best way?"

"Yeah?"

"If I shoot you or cut you, they might analyze it. Better it's impact, and weather."

"So…" I groaned, knowing what was coming. "The cliff?"

"Yeah, boss. Sorry, and…we need the power. So, as you're not gonna need it, if we could siphon your batteries?"

"Get in there," I growled, nodding to the cave before sighing, and stopping her with a hand on her shoulder. The wind screamed around us; snow whipping back and forth made it impossible to see much beyond a few feet. "You're right, and I'll miss you, okay? Look after that idiot?"

"I always do." She nodded.

She moved in, and we worked to bury the entrance, her on the inside and me on the outer, dragging a sheet of old steel from fuck knows what or when, across part of the entrance, and laying it over and under more stones and fractured shale.

When there was only a small space left, I reached my left hand in awkwardly, and I felt the connections locking in. I approved the battery drain, watching as it fell, siphoned off to Sync's suit.

Twenty minutes later, the connection retracted and was replaced by Richie, as a datapacket was fed through to my suit, vanishing without a trace as quickly as it appeared.

"I'm going to set a general system wipe for fifteen minutes on your suit," he told me. "It's top level only, personal stuff. It's all backed up, like Fergie's and Scott's stuff, and ours, now that I think about it. But it'll read like the system was damaged and did a reboot. Your main bond and synergy will be fine. It's just so nobody finds us doing this in the system memory and comes looking."

"Fifteen minutes." I nodded that I understood.

"When it happens, the suit will power down, like full offline mode, then reboot. Be ready to hit the lock. You don't want it opening automatically and not being able to close it again…"

"I'll make sure I'm in place," I said, not looking forward to it.

"How will you do it?" he asked, and I snorted.

"There's a cliff to the left, three hundred meters. Provided I survive the fall, I'll be believably far enough away from the crash, and you both."

"You'll survive. Impact resistant, remember? Just make sure you don't tense. Stay loose, relaxed, and yeah, be ready—it's gonna suck."

"I know."

"Hey, SARS is good, though, right? They'll find you?"

"I damn well hope so," I muttered, gripping his hand once in farewell, then moving back, trying—and failing—to not feel like I was abandoning my friends.

Once they were covered, I got moving. The external battery on my suit drained utterly, and my internal went on emergency backup. I grabbed a rock as I walked, smashing the external battery free, so that nobody could tell that the power had been siphoned away, and getting ready for what was coming.

The impacts would mess my suit up—and me—pretty badly, but as far as the fall was, I'd have a good chance of surviving it.

I kept telling myself that the suits were made with this kinda shit in mind, and that I needed to do it. But the truth was, when I finally made it to the cliff edge, across a narrow divide from where the now frozen wreckage of the helo was buried, I was fucking *terrified.*

Electrical bursts, bright blue and white, flared all around me, some blanketed by the flurries of storm and the clouds, others seemingly right before me as the centuries-long buried masses of metal attracted them.

I shuffled up to the edge, standing right on it, watching the wind and driven snow whipping around literally right before and under me. I took a deep breath.

The counter ticked down. *4...3...2...*

I'd always felt that stupid urge when on a high ledge or wherever, to just step off, to let myself tumble free, and today? Right when that self-destructive impulse would be at its most useful?

Totally gone.

1...

The suit lights flickered and died, plunging me into darkness deeper than that of a corpo's soul, and my suit powered down. I heard the various fans and more slowing. A steady, distant buffeting of the wind outside my suit was the only evidence that the outside world still existed.

For long seconds I stood there in silence, waiting for the wind to tip me out, as memories of my team came thick and fast.

I saw Fergie and Scott, Barnes and the others. I saw their smiles and heard their laughter, and my blood *boiled.* They were dead, or had their lives ruined, altered forever, by some corpo scumbag trying to make an extra few creds.

They'd never face justice, not for what they'd really done, and the destruction their greed had caused, and I knew it. No. What was worse was that looking back? I should have seen it coming. Yeah, fine, I couldn't have foreseen all of it, but that Blue had been split off? That Richie was watching the base and that the stupid fucking pilots had taken us through the Fingers?

If I'd paid a little more attention, instead of being so trusting? I could have saved them. If I'd questioned the pilots on the way back, I'd have known more. I could have prepared. I could have looked up data on the target site, and maybe figured out what we were chasing.

All of it was there, and I could have done something about some of it at least.

The APS were supposed to judge the wasteland. We were supposed to bring the law to the lawless, to enforce the little civilization that we managed to cling to, onto the fucks out there. Now others, people who thought they were above the laws, had turned on us.

No. The guilty paid for their crimes. They had to, or what was the point?

We'd planned to go merc from the APS, sure, but we'd always be ready to dispense judgment. We'd protect the innocent, and we'd fucking bring judgment to the guilty.

We could be mercs and do that still; we'd just be picky fucking ones, that's all. This couldn't be allowed to stand. The guilty had to pay.

My heart grew colder and colder as I reforged myself in the fires of my own blame. I used the pain of the loss of my friends to drag up images, and to stare at them, to see them, and then to look at Richie and Sync, knowing that their lives were truly in my hands.

I couldn't afford to be a trusting fool. Never again. Trust and mercy got me into this clusterfuck. No, I needed to be hard. Like so many others from the shittier areas of the city, I'd learned to be a bastard when I was crossed, to stab first and to ask questions never. But now?

The army had taught me right from wrong; it had taught me honor, and that until someone picked up a weapon, they were classed as innocent…But when they did touch a weapon, they weren't innocent anymore. They became a threat, even if they weren't yet guilty.

Now I was going to have to be even harder.

Tyrannus would be out soon as well. I had until then to get myself in check, start getting whatever kit I needed, and to get things in place.

I needed to be ready. Four months he'd be on the watch list for, like me and any other who was on release from the forces. If I waited until he was off the list? No doubt he'd be in some cushy corpo compound.

No, I needed to get things moving, and fast. Maybe hit him and question the fucker by taking a few days' leave? I needed to be hard, I needed to be merciless, and I needed to get this right the first time. If I didn't? Then I was failing the only family I'd ever known, and I wasn't doing that.

They trained us to be questioners, as well as the rest. They taught us that once we left the base, we were the arbiters of justice. If we had to, we did whatever was needed.

Well—I'd do whatever needed to be done, and I'd make fucking sure that Richie and Sync were out of this and safe, even if I had to burn my soul to ash in the process.

I stood there for several long seconds, breathing coming faster and faster, nerving myself up to this…before rocking myself forward, the sensation of movement slow to come.

I fell outward, tumbling into the stormy night air.

CHAPTER SIX

Everything was silent for what seemed like the longest time as I fell, the arms and legs of the suit insanely heavy and unresponsive.

Only my inner ear told me I was falling—only, that is, until I hit the first outcropping.

I'd been trying my best to stay relaxed, knowing damn well that if I was tense, it'd hurt more. But, fuck me, I failed.

That first impact, despite me being literally locked in place and surrounded by cushioning and padding, felt like I'd been hit by a truck. The spinning of my inner ear went haywire as I flipped over and over, crashing into snow-covered rocks, buried debris, and worse.

I'd have had no chance of surviving this without the suit, I knew, but as I picked up speed, ramming through semi-solid things I guessed to be trees or something, the suit's backup systems finally started to boot.

Vision came first. The screens all around me flickered, then cut out as cameras were smashed. My head yanked to one side then the other, as I rolled and crashed.

Bio-monitor warnings flashed up, information and recommendations that I should avoid "further head trauma" and other *oh so helpful* recommendations.

My shield attempted to activate. My internal emergency battery diverted power as the RI system saw something coming that it didn't like...and it popped like a soap bubble.

My internal power, already on the emergency backups, triggered warnings, and the suit tried to open, automatic releases activating...and I frantically gripped the emergency handles, countering it.

This was one of the worst parts of all of this: I crashed into something solid, and even the padding that restrained me wasn't enough. Blood burst from my nose to paint the inside in a lovely shade of claret.

The few remaining cameras that piped in the outside world cut off as the emergency power dropped even further. I was left in utter blackness again, this time without the solace that I might be able to force the suit to open for me.

More impacts came and went. The world flashed and vanished in rapid succession as I was knocked unconscious, and my own internal upgrades shocked me back to wakefulness.

Another impact, a bigger one, smashed into something solid. The joints of the suit were designed not to extend past normal human limits, but hoo-boy that failed.

I screamed as my left arm suddenly stopped dead, locked in place, and my entire armored body twisted and spun around it.

The metal buckled; the bones broke as something gave way. I screamed, as behind the stunning and horrific feeling of the arm bending, the pain rose up.

Then I was moving again, my left arm numb, the hand…I didn't know if it was still there. It wasn't responding, and I dimly remembered a conversation with Fergie when he replaced his hands. Between the new ones being attached and his "original" ones being removed, there'd been a hack on the block the chop shop was in. He'd ended up sitting there, hands gone and connectors waiting for the new ones, for nine hours.

He'd sworn he could feel his hands still, and now…I was suddenly filled with the terror that it might not just be my hand.

I could have lost half my body by now, and would I know?

The pain…I'd been knocked out a dozen times at least. Who knew how much damage had been done, and…and I could feel the cold.

There was a leak in the suit somewhere! A leak, one that would steadily drop my body temp on a fucking frozen mountainside? I panicked, before another impact jolted me out of it. I bit down hard, forcing myself to relax, to stick the brain in neutral and just…be.

Two more minor impacts, and a sensation of sliding. A bang, as I apparently slid into something solid. Then…nothing. I tried to move, to lift my arms, to…the pain was horrific.

It was as if my body had been waiting, daring me to move, and now that I'd done it? I gritted my teeth, frantic to stop the scream that bubbled up in me.

Heat and cold warred on my left arm, and I knew instinctively that it was my hot blood and the outside world getting to know each other.

I was trapped here now, unless the corps found me, and I needed to just stop. There was nothing I could do, not anymore.

Minutes passed as I forced myself to stay as still as possible. The cold leeched away at me; shivers became shudders. Distant sounds convinced me that the SARS team was arriving…and then silence falling again and again.

The very worst part, undoubtably, for me at least, was the terror that all APS soldiers learned to bury, but never fully escaped.

The suits were marvels of technology, but they also induced crippling claustrophobia. The knowledge that once the batteries were dead, that once all power was gone, there was no way to get out, short of someone else physically cutting you out?

Knowing that you'd be all alone in the dark, unable to move, to see, to hear?

The suits, designed as they were as counters to chemical, biological, and radioactive weaponry, were utterly sealed—or mine had been, at least.

Sensory deprivation tanks had been a thing in the old world, apparently, where people would pay credits to be utterly alone, all sound, motion, and more taken away.

When it was a choice? It still seemed weird. But when a suit broke down? It was utterly terrifying. You never knew what was happening outside. There could be a dozen tech types all digging away to get you out, or nobody.

The fight might have been lost, and you were about to be cut out of the armor by some asshole and killed. Or you might have been forgotten entirely.

There was an emergency air tank, and I was already sucking on it, I damn well knew. That gave me twenty-four hours. But after that? I was fucked.

Thus the terror as I dealt with the fact I'd forced the suit to stay closed, against its automatic response to open on power failure.

Outside, I'd have died instantly with most of those impacts, and even if I hadn't, I'd certainly freeze to death. But as it was now? If and when SARS finally came looking, I was seriously *fucked*.

The heat from my injuries would show on scanners. Life sign scanners should get me, and the suits were made of specific types of metal, so the scanners should be able to pick me up anywhere, but…but we were in the fucking Fingers!

Minutes became hours, and I laid there, my own implants kicking in, activating to administer emergency drugs, to control my heart rate, to cut off circulation to the left arm.

I saw messages from my internal system RI flash up: warnings on blood toxicity, blood pressure, declining core temperature, drug and chemical levels, nutrients, all of it.

I saw them all slide slowly from yellow, to amber, to orange, and then red.

Laid there, the cold slowly stealing up and into my suit, my limited internal, personal HUD flickered and dimmed as the world slid away.

Hours passed.

The damage to my suit must have been enough to let a little air in, but not much, as I guessed sometime later that my twenty-four hours of air should have long since expired, and yet…

Music.

Distant music seeped through to me, and I felt something shake nearby. I coughed, tasting blood and shivering, suddenly aware of the cold, as warmth washed over me.

Fergie came and sat by my side, and I blinked, staring up at the red-bearded giant, watching him as he settled himself to my right on that stupid little red stool he loved so much. His bloody ridiculous bass was cradled in his arms, and he started to play. Scott picked up the tune, and the two of them happily sang, even as I stared numbly.

Sync joined in next, and I jerked, shaking my head, knowing this was all kinds of wrong.

Her voice was high, melodic, and…*Sync had never sung before, had she?*

She didn't like to sing, but…but she was there…

I stared at Fergie, the steady rhythm of his fingers as they danced across the strings. Something was burning suddenly, and something jerked me sideways.

Pain flared; my armor jerked again. Someone was dragging me. I looked down at my feet, seeing the mech from earlier.

It had hold of me, and it was dragging me somewhere.

I tried to move, to reach out, but nothing worked. Pain from my left arm, and, and…something held my body in place, forcing me to stay still.

I saw them as I looked down, the ghosts of those I'd killed. Hundreds, maybe thousands of them, and they held me tight. I opened my mouth to say something, only to see Scott shake his head.

Richie stood next to him, in his armor, but…his chestplate was missing, and he stared out of the cavity, mouth twisted in a dark grin, frozen blood glued to his lips and chin.

"We don't get to rest, not yet," he told me.

"It's time," Sync called, her voice changing, deepening. "It's time to go back…Are you ready?"

"Wha…?"

"Are you ready!" she screamed at me suddenly, appearing right before me, her face literally inches away. Her dark eyes swallowed up the world. "It's gonna hurt! But it's the only way!"

"Hurt…?" I mumbled, totally confused, before pain, so much fucking pain!

My chest felt like all my ribs had broken at once, literally, from just above my hips, as Fergie and Scott, Richie and Sync, the helo pilots and Barnes—all of them were there—kicked me as hard as they could. Voices warbled in and out as they screamed about me killing them all.

I'd failed them.

It was all my fault and…

Their voices were lost in a roar of sirens. Something was screamed by others, and then a chattering bark I recognized: a rotary cannon on full rock and roll, the whoosh of rockets and chaff launchers…

Sudden cold flooded me, followed by a bright light, as my armor was ripped open. I flinched as a shadow reached in toward me, screaming something garbled through external speakers, the strobing lights of a helo on station overhead as darting, fast-moving shapes erupted in fire, tumbling free to crash into the surrounding mountainside.

The figure over me leaned in, stabbed a tube into my chest and triggered it, making me scream in pain.

Seconds passed as they hooked up power leads, then triggered restraining bolts, freeing me of the armor's embrace, naked beyond my under suit and exposed to the terrible temperatures of the Fingers, as the world came back into focus.

SARS.

The SARS team was here, and they were under attack. A blur of sharks flashed past. Missiles tore free of rails, streaming through the night sky, barely visible in the swirling blizzard, only to be cut apart by the defensive systems.

Chaff illuminated the night; phosphorus flares triggered and bathed the world in insane, eye-searing brightness. Pain roared through me as bones were popped back into place. The SARS medic had hit me with an emergency trauma pack of nanites.

It was the good shit, I knew instinctively, as my mind was forcibly blasted free of fog. Everything slammed into close proximity, as the medic screamed at me over the wind and gunfire.

"Survivors?!"

"I don't know!" I screamed back, shaking my head, even as the left shoulder sections of my armor finally responded, the explosive bolts blowing.

The right arm was released, and I looked to the left, swallowing hard. The armor was fucked, as was the flesh inside.

Multiple breaks, bleeding, and frostbite had combined to change healthy skin into a mass of black, grey, and purple. Dried, frozen blood was everywhere, as were something that looked like maggots despite the subzero temperatures, and I bit down on the revulsion that rose in me.

"It's trapped!" the medic shouted. "Look away!"

I did as I was ordered, seeing the bright glow of a plasma blade, and knowing what was coming.

This was no chop shop where the arm would be locked down, then my body prepared for its removal.

This was a mountainside. The arm infected and the twisted mess of metal that was holding me in place? It all needed to go.

The plasma blade fell, and for a second, I felt nothing, just a strange sensation of being shifted, almost dragged by the sawing motion of the blade on the armor…and then the pain blocks failed, and I screamed.

Another form appeared, leaning over me, moving fast and pinning me down. Another emergency battery was plugged in, and a blanket of reflective foil was pressed against my chest.

Heat, welcome and shocking, flooded my overloaded brain.

More streams of fire, intermittently mingled with tracers, roared out, and a second SARS helo roared past. The downdraft made the world vanish in white.

"Get him ready to move!" someone bellowed. "No time to gradually warm him—we can't stay!"

"Got it!" the first voice called, lifting his blade free, killing it and stowing it away. "Thermite grenades on the armor?"

"No…headquarters wants it as intact as possible. And it'll help hold him together—we'll winch him up in it. Then we toast the hillside, leave any scrap!"

"Wha…" I mumbled, my words torn from my lips before they could form fully.

"Connect him up!" the second figure yelled, passing some cables to the first, going to work himself on my right side.

It felt like I blinked, like the world skipped, an old record player that someone had been playing when a mech stomped past…and then I was dangling in the remains of my armor, being drawn upward into the belly of the SARS helo, the other two on either side of me riding cables of their own.

Blink.

The inside of the helo, a transport bay, sirens still flashing, shouting…Blood sprayed out of my side suddenly, as someone did something, more pain and additional injectors being hurried in and jabbed into place as they stripped me out of my armor.

Blink.

A ceiling, cracks and intermittent lights, warmth from a containment field. The subtle warping of space around me telling me that I was in an emergency sled, a combination of two medics on either side of me, and a handful of massive armored figures running alongside.

Blink.

"The hell happened! We were diverted and some fuckers took them out! Me and mine want…" Jon, Blue One, was roaring into the grim face of a corpo suit, sneer intact even as he stared up at the massive APS operator.

Blink.

Darkness. Dim lights around a hospital room. The beep and flash of machines. Pressurized systems forcing fluids into me as my eyes rolled, trying to make sense of the world.

Blink.

A nurse, kind eyes, smiling down at me, professional, as she checked something…and removed a connection, lifting something as my vision clicked off on the left, my right eye seeing a camera system being disconnected and lifted clear.

Blink.

"Worth the investment?" a bored officer was saying. "Look at him. He's barely got a few months left before his discharge goes through. Just spend the bare minimum. Clone graft for those parts that are covered by the insurance. The rest? Tier-one mods only. And don't bother replacing his suit mods. He's got, what? Seven months left?"

"Nearly nine, sir," a nurse replied, making notes.

"Whatever." The suit sneered. "The cost for the suit mods, not to mention the rebuild to get him up to standard spec, is far more than he's worth for that time. Give him an early severance package. Standard military buyout. Sign him out and get him off the base as soon as it's done. And get me the list of replacements for Red Team. I want…"

Blink.

I sagged, barely able to keep my head up. The cocktail of drugs they'd pumped me full of made my head spin as they questioned me, going over a laundry list of forms that, every time I asked what they were, changed.

Blink.

"Choice, though, of course you can refuse our generous offer, and you'll be permitted to stay on base until the end of your enlistment period. Due to the limited roles you are currently suitable for, you'd be charged for your accommodation, meals, and medical supplies."

"Choice?" I mumbled, stunned.

"You sign the waiver of rights, you accept the replacement mods package as full and final payment against the injuries sustained in the accident…"

"We were att—"

"You sign that you understand that *all* injuries sustained in the *accident* occurred on the way back to base, meaning you were in transport at the time and as such were not covered by Section 37:1 [a] of the APS war frame code." He glared at me. "I won't make this offer again, soldier."

"A minute, if you will?" an unknown voice said, and the suit glared at someone outside my limited vision, before sighing and dumping a pad on the table to my side.

"Fine, you get him to sign it. You get him on board, or you get him moved into the reserve block. I'm not wasting any more time on this." The corpo scumbag stood, smoothing his slate-grey suit, glasses already displaying rolling text as he started to do something else, heading for the door.

He started a call before the door even closed properly.

"His kind are all the same." Major Marcial sighed, moving into sight and standing over me. "You there, Kabutt? Operator?"

"Sir…" I slurred, right hand twitching as I started to salute.

"Ah, no!" He cursed as my hand caught on something and pain reared its head again.

Minutes passed before I could focus. When I finally could, the major was sitting by my side, a cigar almost burnt to the butt.

"You back?" he asked, and I nodded slowly. "Good. Look, son, we're literally out of time, and you need to make a decision. We've talked about the situation at the base, and the attack, but…Kabutt? You there?"

I'd zoned out again, staring at the glowing tip of his cigar, mesmerized, and I jerked back to wakefulness.

"Sorry…sir…" I whispered.

"Fucking medics! Drugging you up to the eyeballs!" He cursed. "You're gonna have a nightmare of a time kicking that addiction after this, never mind the rest of the shit you'll be dealing with…Fuck. I'll make them include a full wipe, get you off them, but it's gonna leave you feeling rough. Be ready for that. Okay, look, do you remember us talking? The attack? The AROC? Anything?"

"I reported it…" I muttered, blinking owlishly.

"Yes!" He nodded quickly. "You reported it to me. You cut out that little shit Tyrannus and his corpo friends, and you started off the bug hunt."

"Bug hunt, sir?" I managed to get out.

"Let's just say there's a lot more of our corporate 'friends' making requests than there should be, and a lot of good men and women are paying the price. Your 'accident' was due to two of them playing games. I've tried to fill you in a few times, but you've been in no fit state. All I can say right now is that there are measures being taken. That, though, brings us to this next point.

"The corpos and their friends need us to be quiet about this, publicly at least, and your injuries are the most obvious reminders of what happened. Now, you'd put in your retirement papers already, and due to the injuries you've got? Well. It's a simple decision for the credit crunchers.

"Pay you off, give you cheap tier-one mods in place of the damaged systems, and give you your remaining nine months' pay up front, boot you out, move on." He snorted, shaking his head in disgust. "Never mind that you're a hell of an operator who was badly injured thanks to their games and fuckups. They only see the bottom line. Well, that suits us just fine."

"How…sir?" I grunted, forcing myself up a little from where I'd been slumping down the bed.

"If you accept their offer—and I'll make them add a few credits to the pile— you'll be out of the army now, rather than in nine months. You'll be out of the loop, and no longer considered a target, partly because, and let's be honest here, you're broken. I might even get them to remove the watch on you early, or not place it at all."

"Wow…thanks, sir," I mumbled, glancing down at my missing left arm, and the dozens of cables and connectors that were feeding into me.

"Don't take it to heart." He smiled. "You lost friends out there…you remember?"

"My team," I growled.

"You want some payback?" he asked curiously.

"Fuck, yeah."

"Then this is how you get it. The corpos have been involving themselves in the army, much more than they're allowed to, and now that it's come to light? Some of my investigators had leads to follow. Twelve hours later, and they've all fucking vanished. Others, well, they couldn't find anything. Besides their new cred balances, that is."

"Bought…and…paid…for…" I whispered, the world spinning again.

"Exactly. The thing is, though, I lost some damn good people, the honest ones, and all I'm left with is those bought and paid for corpo types."

"And…?"

"And I want answers."

"Just…answers?"

"No," he admitted, his voice dropping. "I want blood as well. Fucking oceans of it."

"And what's…my choice…sir?" I forced out, focusing on him again.

"You refuse the payout, get tier-two mods, maybe—most likely clone vat replacements—and no mil-spec mods installed. Come the end of your term, you're given a bill for the time you've been in the hospital and in reserve housing, and then you get booted out onto the street, probably broke."

"Or?"

"Or you accept their offer. You're out of here tonight, after they get you in for basic mod-one implants. You spend the next few days and weeks healing up, and then you work for me."

"Doing what?"

"What you do best, Sergeant. You evaluate, you judge, and you kill everyone who so much as looks at you sideways."

CHAPTER SEVEN

I signed it.

Not that there was much of a choice. I got a bit extra from the settlement, not much, but a basic apartment prepaid for a month to get me on my feet. Most people would call it shitty, but for a soldier fresh out of the army?

I didn't give two fucks. All I needed was a rack to recover in.

The major couldn't be seen giving me anything—there'd be a trail for most things—but he said he'd make sure my suit was fixed up, ready for when I was recovered enough to use it.

He couldn't do anything about my mods, though, and I was coldly furious as I laid back, closing my eyes and swallowing hard, before I nodded my agreement to the shit that was being demonstrated on the screen.

The damaged kit they needed to take out to put these in was better quality, even trashed, than what was going in, not to mention more functional than the new gear. Literally.

Mods came in five tiers: trash, basic, professional, elite, and artisan. Professional was what it said on the tin, mil-spec and the standard for operators of high-tech gear like the APS.

For me to get back to the level that I could integrate with my APS, I'd need replacement-specific mods that were pro level, or tier three. They weren't officially supposed to be publicly available, not the gear that would interface with *my* suit certainly, but there were a hell of a lot of different sets of equipment that ran on spinal taps. Drone swarms, helo pilots, high-level racers, and basically anyone who operated a mech of any caliber needed them, after all.

There was a work-around though, as APS mercs were insanely popular with the corpo types.

That meant that with a little specialist calibration, and a replacement tier-three spinal mod, I'd be back in the game.

The gear they were fitting me with right now? It was *trash*, basically, or most of it was. The mil-spec specialist mods I had—the command and control gear, special linkages into the command net—all had to be removed. That was standard on leaving the forces. What was normal, though, was that we'd get the equivalent civilian kit installed at cost. After all, we'd had our bodies altered to fit them in, and they couldn't really rip half our brains and spines out and just leave us on the doorstep.

Thanks to the fact I was so broken, and they wanted me out of the door? I was getting full-range cybernetic replacements. Rather than wait for a clone replacement and then the days to weeks of therapy needed with that, I was being rebuilt right now.

It was literally fully cybernetic from the shoulder down to and including the hand, which sure as shit wasn't cheap but the entire thing was a goddamn tier-*one* mod. Not a three, like the rest of my gear had been, and the shit it was replacing. No, it was a fucking *one*.

The only reason I'd accepted it—beyond a lack of any realistic options—was the ease of replacement for the future. As this was being done by army augmenters, the connective systems, where the mod joined my body, were being done professionally, meaning that when I could afford it, I'd have a much easier time installing replacement third-tier equipment.

All cybernetics and mods required nanites to function. Most worked on a day-to-day basis through chemical interactions as I understood it—an ex-girlfriend had tried to explain it all once and I'd not cared, seeing only the glory of the chrome.

What they needed, though, were nanites, and they had to be pure grade.

Nanites formed the interface between the body and the mod, tying one into the other flawlessly, and providing the systems that allowed the arm to convert the chemical and potential energy into electrical to move.

They enabled the actual "feeling" of the mod as our own limb, letting metal fingers pick up a tomato without crushing it, or vibrate at just the right frequency to "get the job done" with a partner.

The more nanites you needed? The more expensive the mod, and the more powerful. A good interface, like I had, meant that the tier-one arm could be replaced easily and cheaply, like the spinal replacement could. The basic organelles that were being prepped to replace my fucked-up liver, spleen, and half of my goddamn guts were something I was feeling a bit more accepting about, but every time I saw that arm…

I had a civilian-grade, tier-one brain mod as well. My mil-spec grade-three allowed for faster target acquisition and detection, and allowed me to tie into the military subnet. The standard mod?

I'd be able to access the entertainment packages that all civilians got access to at school age, from the standard Keystone mod everyone got, and with the specialist brain mod, I'd have access to basic identification and recognition software, as well as a housing for my RI.

The only reason I was being left that was that otherwise I'd have a literal hole in my head, so, yeah. They gave me the entry-level brain upgrade.

Mods came with a slot, as standard. Tier-one mods like mine had a single slot, and although all of my others were left empty, and they'd stay that way—no sense on wasting money on something I'd be replacing sharpish—at least my brain had my RI plugged into it.

Richie was going to be disabling sections of his and Sync's…hell, he would have done them by now, and the pair of them should be deep in cryosleep.

The organelles that were being brought in to replace my damaged organs— the corpos and their army cred-counting counterparts had halted any replacement or healing of my injuries beyond enough that I was kept alive, until they got my signature; they'd wanted confirmation of cost, so I'd been in pain and delirious on drugs since I'd been recovered—were something most of us wouldn't invest in. It wasn't because they weren't good; they could make a massive difference. After all, the human body was pretty old in design terms.

We'd evolved past needing things like the fuckin' appendix, and replacing half of our organs with synthetic, higher-grade versions took up less space and made us more efficient at the same time.

Food was processed better; we could last longer between meals and drinks and so on. It meant that, overall, I was more limited than I had been.

There wasn't much of a choice, though, considering the damage that had been done.

The mortal body, and the mind especially, could only handle so many individual mods. After a certain point—which was different for each person—we tended to break down, becoming mad, dead, or specters.

So, even though I knew the organelles were necessary, even though I knew that I goddamn needed them, and that I'd actually be physically more efficient, more resistant to poisons and all that shit…I wasn't happy about it.

It limited the work I could have done later, and adding in the full left arm, the brain, the cyberspace access in the back of my skull…I just wasn't sure how many I could handle further down the line. Lose a leg? I might be fucked.

Right now, though, it was time.

I nodded to the surgeon, as he settled the mask over my face. The various bits of kit in the room that were to be put in were wheeled in, and I fixed the arm with a glare.

Time to get this over with.

The surgeon set the arm up on my left side. Other medical staff came in and looked over the details. Tubes of active pure nanites arrived and were trayed up, ready for injection.

That fucking arm.

I couldn't help but stare at it, literally the most basic of all the models I'd ever seen: a single post from the shoulder to elbow, a multi-way orb joint, then a single post to the hand, that—thank fuck—actually looked like a hand, not a hook or a claw.

It was also bright polished *silver*.

I was going to look like a pure chrome believer, one of those nutters who bought the very cheapest and first mods they could afford, going down to the road to "integration with the machine" as their pamphlets and crap declared was holy.

I wasn't gonna be able to sneak up on shit. I wasn't…

"Okay, Sergeant Kabutt, I'd like you to count backward from ten for me, please."

"Ten. Nine. Eight. Seven…Six……F…ive……"

The world slid sideways as I fought to keep my eyelids open. The surgeon moving in close and examining me, the gentle hum of the staff's conversations dopplered away as I sank into the world of dreams.

Hours passed, presumably, but eventually the sound of conversation woke me again, as I blinked blearily.

Light.

A bright light moved around me, and I turned my head slowly to focus on it. I winced. The pain of still healing injuries made me jerk, which caused me even more pain.

*What the hell was…*I froze as it all crashed back on me, as for the first time in ages, I could think without the goddamn drugs fogging my brain.

I jerked my left arm up and over. A clatter echoed as the table brace that had been holding it in place fell over.

Steel.

I stared at the shittiest arm I'd ever seen in my fucking life, and it was attached to *me*.

Lips drew back from my teeth in a furious snarl before I even knew what I was doing. I ran through a basic checklist with my RI, something I'd done so many times that it was instinctual now, but the resultant screen? Fuck.

Identification: Harry Kabutt				
Species: Human		**Bonus**: None		
Mod Capacity: 19		**Mod Capacity in use**: 6		
Stat	**Current Points**	**Description**	**Mods**	**Quality**
Dexterity	11	Governs agility and movement	Left Arm Mod: (DEX 6)	Trash
Mental Power	10	Governs swiftness and fortitude of the mind	Brain Mod: 1 Cost: 1	Trash
Perception	11	Governs an individual's senses and connection to the world around them	Brain Mod: 1 Cost: 1 (PER 5)	Trash
Strength	10	Governs physical strength and damage dealt	Left Arm Mod: 1 Cost: 1 (STR 11)	Trash
Toughness	9	Governs the body and internal fortitude	Basic Organelles: 3 Cost: 3	Basic

My RI was basic. Hell, it was dependent on the system it was jacked into, so right now it was literally dumb as fuck. But *seriously*? Mods usually granted a bonus to the user, or an ability, such as tracking, remote reference and appraisal, integrated weapons and more. Mine?

I pulled up the specs and snarled.

Cranial Capacity Upgrade	Tier: One
The Wilmat Corporation 300 model cranial upgrade comes complete with RI storage and integration capacity (RI and storage chip not included) as well as unbelievable tracking and pattern recognition as standard! (For warranty details, please submit form 376[t] through correct channels. No responsibility will be accepted by Wilmat for issues arising from this or any modification unless the original user submits them personally.) Perception: 5	
Durability: 91/100	**Cost**: 2

The brain mod was terrible and Wilmat was a byword for low-level mods. Hell, it was brand-new and implanted by a military surgeon, and the durability was already ninety-one out of a hundred? That wasn't good, probably some shitty quality control on the relays or something, but that was hardly a surprise.

They wouldn't accept any responsibility for issues? What a surprise there as well. That the original user had to apply personally, not a third party? Not their lawyer—if they could afford one—but them personally? Motherfuckers.

Everyone knew a brain mod that went bad meant you were fast-tracking yourself to life as a specter, so they might just as well have included a picture of them pointing and fucking laughing.

That it had a perception level of five? Fucking FIVE? I'd have to focus on someone's face for several seconds before my RI could bring up the name. Hell, I'd have to go back to actually learning fucking names the old-fashioned way, and that was a ballache.

I pulled up the arm specs and continued to swear.

Left Arm	Tier: One
This entry-level Cybernex left arm is a fantastic model at an unbelievable price. Sturdy, reliable, and solid, the Cybernex 2701 comes with a limited two-year warranty. (Please register your arm to gain access to warranty upgrade offers.) Dexterity: 6 Strength: 11	
Durability: 88/100	**Cost**: 1

The arm was the same. Read "utter shit" instead of "entry level" and it made more sense. Basically, the arm was slow to react. I focused on it, moving the fingers and running through a full range of movement tests, like I would each time I entered my APS.

Yeah, its specific dexterity rating was a six; my own was an overall ten, which meant, simply, that it was slower than my natural arm had been. It was also stronger, which was something at least, an eleven to my natural ten, so not huge, but considering that was my overall?

It encompassed things like my having strong legs, and a strong back. That the arm was an eleven individually? If I grabbed onto someone, they'd have to be strong to get loose.

That is, if I could fucking catch them.

I couldn't even upgrade the arm.

Usually you could augment the mod, so I could swap out the shoulder and elbow joints to increase speed, or replace the hand with the Santos version, making it faster, or give myself claws or an inbuilt weapon.

Not this model.

It was literally trash tier.

I'd be replacing it and damn soon.

Looking over the organelles, well, I dismissed them straightaway. They were functional, biomechanical, and efficient—nothing special but nothing wrong. I'd been a bit luckier there, because it was a system that was replaced every so often for grunts on the frontline, foot soldiers rather than the corps, so I'd gotten what looked like their standard package, and basic ones, so tier-two rather than one.

I kept my mouth shut, attributing that to a bit of good fortune, or the major intervening, rather than anything else. Best to keep quiet; I'd been told they'd be trash, after all.

Now I'd not need to replace them, just leave them as they were.

No, the real issue was the spinal tap.

Spinal Reinforcement	**Tier:** One
The Wilmat 4596 Spinal Reinforcement mod is a direct replacement to the original biological, physical spine, meshing cybernetic know-how with cutting-edge neural integration tissue, and all for an unbelievable price!	
Please Note: Support for this model was withdrawn due to internal quality issues in the last quarter. Details included: [Redacted].	
Warranty: [Void]	
Toughness: 5	
Durability: 97/100	**Cost:** 1

That the military had put a model in me that was cheap was to be expected. The military was always cheap. That they'd used a model that was fucking withdrawn from the market?

That the details were fucking redacted, and the warranty void *before* it'd even been installed? I had the equivalent of a glass spine, one that would break if I made any kind of a mistake. And that, of course, was the most expensive fucking part to replace.

I was left with two choices: replace the spine with a mid-level reinforcement model, a tier-two most likely—I'd never be able to afford higher than a three for a while, and even that would clear me out—just so I had a functional fucking spine, and then replace it with a specialist spinal tap model when I could afford it.

That would cost a fortune. I'd be buying a spinal mod—one of the most expensive mods to get—and then replacing it only a few months later with one that was geared toward being able to drive my APS. But it was that, or just keep this shitty one until I could go straight to the full spinal tap, and risk it crapping out on me at any point.

Hell, my bank balance wasn't great anyway. Half my wage went toward paying off the APS. You take off accommodation, food and drinks, then recreational drugs and hookers? Basic costs of living, and I was down to barely saving a handful of credits a month.

My bonus, though…

I pulled up the balance in my account, seeing the overlay that hovered over my bonus section from the last two missions, and for a long few seconds, I wanted to end it all.

<u>Bonuses reclaimed</u>

Reason: Excessive expenditure on mission, requiring replacement of APS and Helo line items.

Approved: *Cpt. A. Tyrannus*

I glared at it, horrified, disgusted, and furious all in one.

Not only had they taken my bonus off me for the last mission, and the one they'd sent me on before it, but they'd drained my fucking account of *all* the bonuses I'd earned in the last quarter!

I stared at it.

<u>First Olympic Bank</u>

Credit balance: 147c

I scanned the details, row after row of ins and outs, as that little fuck Tyrannus billed me the absolute maximum for utterly everything.

I had a hundred and forty-seven credits left.

That was it.

I'd spent more than that on nights out, for fuck's sake, never mind dates.

That was *after* the payments from the military—after my eight months' advanced payments and discharge payments.

The door opened, and a nurse stepped in, seeing me laid there, blinking in disbelief as I opened and closed my metal arm reflexively.

"You're awake!" She smiled, moving in closer. "That's a relief, sir. I was sent to wake you, or get authorization for the bed for another day."

"Authorization?" I mumbled, then coughed, clearing my throat, forcing myself to sit upright and look around. "What do you mean?"

"The army paid for your transport here two days ago, sir, along with covering the cost for a full cleanse and nutrient paste, but the paid-for time expires in thirty-seven minutes. Do you need to stay another day, or should I have a porter help you pack up your belongings?"

"How…how much?" I asked, trying to make sense of everything.

"Three hundred credits a day, sir, for the room, two hundred for the cleanse, and…"

"I'll leave." I tried to get off the bed and frantically grabbed for a nearby brace when my legs gave way below me. I crashed to the floor instead, when my fucking new arm didn't respond in time.

"Here we go…" She grunted, looping my arm over her shoulders and helping me up, smiling sadly. "Sorry, I should have phrased that better…"

"What?"

"You've got thirty-seven minutes before they charge you, but you can take a few minutes to recover first?" She tried again, and I nodded, blowing out a long breath as she helped me to sit.

"What happened?" I wondered aloud.

"You came in with a lot of work done. Accident?"

"Army." I shrugged. "It…yeah." I corrected what I was going to say and nodded. "An accident on the way back from a mission."

"You've had a lot of work done, and while you'll recover, it'll take time. You need to give yourself that time," she told me seriously. "Push through it too fast? You'll end up back here, and not out of choice."

"Where am I?" I forced a smile as I arced my back and shifted my legs slowly.

"Recovery Clinic Twenty-Seven, South Laviathon." She glanced around the room. "Look, you've not got much, and if you ask for a porter to help you gather your gear and help you to leave, it's thirty credits. Can I help you? You'll have to be quick."

"Please."

I knew what she was doing.

Helping me out got me out of the room quickly. I'd owe her a tip at the least, and then she got something rather than the porters and anyone else getting nothing, as the clinic administrators probably pocketed it.

She'd no doubt get a bonus for getting me out of the room on time without having to call for someone to drag me out. I'd been unconscious, after all.

Regardless, the help to dress was appreciated, as was gathering my gear, what little of it there was. A shoulder bag contained it all: a change of clothes, which I struggled into, my tactical knife and its sheath, my handgun—thank the gods of blood and chrome for small mercies, someone had sent that out with me—a box of ammunition, and my toiletries.

That was it.

Hell, I knew I had an apartment paid for, for the month, and I vaguely remembered seeing that I had a load of messages when I'd logged into cyberspace when I was in the military hospital, but I couldn't remember where or…

I queried the RI, getting a lagging response that included an image of a tower block, a locator designation, floor number and door code, and I grunted.

At least I'd not imagined that. I had somewhere to lay down.

Before I knew it, I was being helped to stand, and to take a few steps, followed by more, then down a corridor and I was standing at the checkout desk, bracing myself as I waited for the asshole before me—who smelled like he'd never heard of a cleanse, let alone deodorant or soap—to goddamn move.

Once he was done, I shuffled forward, bracing myself on the desk, and had my RI offer up my ident.

"Room twelve." The older matronly woman behind the desk grunted, scanning details. "Paid for in full, and a medication scrip as well. Confirm, please."

A request popped up, a knock on my Keystone, and I acknowledged, seeing the request for my ident on a form that was displayed.

What does it say? I sent it to my RI, before gritting my teeth and canceling the request. Considering what it had to work with, it'd take forever to scan and evaluate the damn thing.

I dismissed the form, my ident attached, seeing it was a general "you left us healthy and can't sue us for anything" kind of crap.

I accepted the digital scrip that was offered and staggered to the dispenser, a cylinder in one corner of the room. The nurse who'd helped me out of the room and along to here made sure I got a seat—these dispensers were always slow— and I flashed the seven credits I had to spare to her, knocking on her Keystone in the same way that the counter staff had reached out to mine.

She accepted it, her face lighting up at the credit transfer request…and darkening when she saw it was only for seven creds.

Fuck knew what she'd been expecting, but she took it and strode off, not even bothering to thank me or pretend any more.

I grabbed the pill bottle when it clattered into the tray at the bottom. My RI highlighted the ident and made it flash in my vision, so I knew it was mine.

I still barely got to it before another guy, scruffy with a grey beard that sprayed out in all directions, tried to grab it, and we glared at each other, before he snarled and backed up.

I stumbled across the floor toward the exit. The double doors slid open soundlessly as litter was blown past. I gritted my teeth, each footstep as I headed for the doors slightly steadier than the last.

Then that was it: I was discharged, free to make my own decisions, to start my new life…and I was in fuck all state to do any of it.

Staggering out of the doors of the clinic, blinking blearily in the bright sunlight and flinching at the roar of passing traffic, I stood there for several long seconds. The screams and the laughter, the assault on the senses that came from every goddamn billboard trying to advertise direct to you…

The fucking brain mod!

Something about it, about all the work I'd had done, had reset the privacy filters! The goddamn settings I'd applied on my Aug-World account! For a few seconds, I was subjected to a full-on audio, visual, and olfactory assault, not to mention a tickle as some impossibly beautiful woman appeared on my right, stroking a hand down my cheek, and a man on the other side.

More figures appeared, as whatever advertising system that had locked onto me tracked my responses, trying to get a read for my tastes, to "better serve you" and all that bullshit.

It was too much, and I ordered the RI to block it all, maximum privacy mode. I turned as it worked, processing its way through the command as I searched for a little respite, a place to gather myself for a few seconds…

Suddenly, I was staggering, slamming into the ground, head reeling. The vaguely remembered conversation about the full drug detox fucking me up even more replayed as...as I saw running feet vanishing, and realized that my fucking bag was gone from my shoulder.

I barely caught sight of the bastard—that same grey-bearded guy—running into the road, weaving between traffic, my own bag vanishing into his larger one.

Motherfucker had just *mugged* me!

CHAPTER EIGHT

I forced myself to my feet, legs moving like I'd shit myself. The goddamn spinal work made me slow as I adjusted on the fly, left arm dragging. But something that'd been missing since the flight roared up from deep inside.

Mugging…*me*?

Who the utter *fuck* did he think he was?

I forced myself to move faster. The grey hair vanished under a tattered blue baseball cap, as he crossed the last lane of four ahead of me, dodging into the streaming crowd that rolled left and right, even as I furiously started out into the traffic.

Normally, I'd have dodged easily. Hell, "normally," I'd have kicked his ass when he tried to rob me and moved on with my life. But as it was? Cars and bikes, as well as automated transports and cabs, screamed and honked at me. Warnings blared on the sidewalk advertisements, telling me that I was committing a felony, and to cross at approved places only.

They'd not triggered for that grey-haired old fuck—he'd been fast enough. But for me? The fines were already knocking on my Keystone.

I ignored them, locking onto him and ordering my RI to track the fucker.

It might be hamstrung by the kit it was operating in, it might be running on bare-bones and no longer have access to mil-spec data, but this? This was something it could do all day.

Target Acquired

The rising thrum of adrenaline banished the last of the confusion as I hurried across the last lanes. All that other shit could wait as I dodged into the streaming mass of people, not one of them bothering to look up from their own lives. None of them seemed to notice the squeal of brakes and honk of horns starting and then stopping again.

With the RI tracking that bastard, and me being unable to up and catch him, as slow as I was—I was walking as though that lump of shit I'd felt earlier was liquefying and dripping now—I used the time to fix my screwed-up Aug-World settings.

The vast majority of Aug-World I couldn't deal with right then, not willing to let the reality around me be brushed and polished until I wandered in a corporate dream. The distant stares everyone I passed made it clear that they were using it all the time.

For some, it was something they couldn't live without now; the literal shit on the streets, the bums, the goblins, and the dead, all of those inconvenient little details that the corpos wanted rid of? All of them were gone in an instant if you let the Keystone and Aug-World do it.

You'd be walking through a calm and virtual paradise, if that was your thing, or along a cliff with the sea crashing nearby. You could pick any reality you wanted, change the people around you into demons, angels, make them all fucking naked—with certain unofficial mods, you could even scan them all as they approached and get simulated "99 percent accurate" images—and more.

Aug-World was a fucking cesspit designed to do one of two things: force you to be a good little corpo drone, or strip you of anything it could if you wouldn't conform.

The slight advantage it had, and that I was grimly activating and shutting down all the pop-up shite from, was the overlay.

It was literally the bare-bones augmentation of reality all around us, adding in street identities, making things like crossings, emergency incoming vehicles, and my own weapons and personal details visible again to me, while blocking any attempts at changing reality and hiding stuff.

When I'd woken in the clinic, that'd been another reason I'd been so confused, I realized now; when they'd installed the new kit, it'd wiped my old settings. I'd kept the recordings, so I didn't really care, but the clinic must have been operating a dampening field of some kind, so when I left it? Boom.

That was also what that fuck ahead of me must have been waiting for, meaning this probably wasn't an opportunist; he probably hit the place several times a day.

I pushed through the current of people, swimming upstream against the majority of corpo drones. I drew ever closer through the mass of people, unable to make much headway on him, but slowly and surely getting control of my limbs again, until after twenty minutes, I was down to a dozen meters from him.

I took the right turn at the end of the block, hesitating. The fucker had vanished. The RI plotted possible escape vectors, plastering them across my vision.

Three flashed green, and I made my choice. He could have made the second and third locations, but it'd have required a sudden sprint, but here? A narrow cut between buildings to my right, a chain-link fence was flapping free at the bottom, as well as scuffs on the ground—all clear indications someone had recently struggled through.

I hurried over to it. Packing crates had been layered across the entrance to obstruct the view, and I grunted, getting a familiar itch between my shoulder blades. I was being watched.

I grinned savagely and grabbed the chain-link, hauling it up as I ducked down, dragging my knife free of my right ankle as I did, flipping the blade up and concealing it along the inside of my wrist.

Standing on the far side, I strode forward, weaving between packaging crates and piled crap. I passed plastic sheeting that ran from one side of the narrow alley to the other, noting barrels complete with basic filtration pumps to clean the water that sat at the end of them.

I ducked under another low sheet and straightened, suddenly surrounded by boxes that faced inward, their interiors shadowed, hiding who knew what.

Only down an alley off a side street, and already I was in a little camp, one of the millions of homeless shanties that filled the city.

I was also out of reach of the city net. A blocker activated as my RI flashed up a warning signal in the corner of my vision, and low chuckles and laughter rose around me. Clearly it was intended to prevent me calling for help…and seeing the way this was set up? Yeah, I felt entirely fucking vindicated about what I was intending to do here.

Judgment. It was time to make the world a better place.

"Shoulda let it go…" The grey-haired old fuck sneered, stepping out from behind a box ahead of me, as others moved out into plain sight.

"You stole my shit," I said coldly.

"You corpo types steal from us every day," another snapped to my left.

I glanced at him.

"Are you fucking blind?" I snarled. "Army; APS operator, discharged on medical fucking grounds, *this morning.*"

"Shame that…" The greybeard shrugged. "Nice gun, though…This'll get a good price." He pulled my handgun out and hefted it, his scruffy fingers curling around the grip and a finger resting on the trigger.

"You're not man enough to touch a gun like that." I shook my head, well aware that two others had slunk out from the boxes behind me and were closing on me.

"You think it takes a man to hold a gun?" an unfamiliar voice asked angrily, as a woman limped out of the darkness to my right, straightening as she ducked out from under some sheeting. The rusty chrome of her skull plate reflected cracked lights from a neon light overhead.

She lifted a rifle—not a bad one, either—and aimed it at my stomach.

"If it takes a man to handle that, no wonder a woman's got the biggest one here…" She grinned, and I snorted.

"Sister, I've fought with women who'd snap any of you fuckers like toothpicks. I said *he's* not man enough to touch *my* gun."

"Oh?" Greybeard chortled. "Why's that then?"

"Because." I smiled. "It's gene-locked."

I focused on the gun and sent a command to my RI. It was a simple one, but oh so effective: *Terminate.*

His eyes flared open in horror, looking to the gun, even as the woman shrieked to him to drop it.

It was too late.

It was *way* too late for that.

"Judgment!" I growled.

Two hundred fifty amps of electricity released from the twin electrodes embedded in the grip and nestled against his palm, killing the fucker almost instantly. I was already moving, as his friends stared at him in horror and his greasy hair burst into flames.

I'd sensed as much as I heard the pair "sneaking" up behind me, or trying to, and rather than wait for them, I simply stepped back, flicking the blade I'd concealed along the inside of my wrist into an overhand grip, the point down, and stabbed it into the stomach of the figure on the right.

The one on the left?

Well, I didn't trust the left arm yet, not really, and certainly not to stop anything like a weapon, but what it could do?

It could grip, and crush.

I swung it down, aiming for center mass, and unfortunately for the guy on my left, he was taller than average. A *lot* taller.

My robotic hand caught on his crotch; the fingers closed like a vise, crushing the metal components of the filthy button-up fly…and the flesh concealed behind it.

I dragged the one on my right around in front of me, using the blade as a handle, then left it buried in their stomach, grabbing Lefty's gun as he dropped it, squealing like a stuck pig.

The woman opened fire. The rifle got off three rounds before she stopped, having realized she had shot my knife victim in the back. She hesitated, holding her fire, and I didn't.

Snaking my hand around the figure that was even now slumping in death, stabbed in the gut and shot in the back three times, I opened fire, missing twice, but taking her in the chest with the third and fourth slugs.

She staggered, then snarled, opening fire again, and this time I moved, twisting Dickless around to drive him backward before me, forcing her to shoot him, even as the remaining two people on the far side of "Mr. Crispy" finally started to move.

I hit her again, seeing the sparking of an embedded chestplate, and adjusted aim, hitting her in the right thigh before the gun clicked empty. I rushed forward, half carrying the fucker by his crushed dick, as she unloaded into his back.

One of Crispy's friends opened fire. A single slug hit my metallic left shoulder and jarred me, but did fuck all else. I threw my victim at the riflewoman, taking them both down before I leapt on her.

The only reason I was still alive was the narrow confines of the alley, and the fact these assholes were clearly used to mugging idiots and innocents, for all that they were rarer than virgins in a whorehouse.

My metal arm was slow, but what it lacked in speed, maneuverability, and, well, fucking *everything*, it made up for it in being a mass of fucking steel with a vise grip.

I grabbed her rifle barrel with my right hand and yanked it aside, slapping my left over her face and ordering the fingers to close.

I saw the look of panic, the horror in her eyes, and she released the rifle and reached up to grip the fingers.

She was strong, surprisingly so, considering that she was evidently living in a slum. But what she wasn't, was *smart*.

The reason the army trained people the way they did, over and over, constantly repeating actions, was to instill muscle memory, so that when something happened, you didn't respond the "natural" way.

The "natural" reaction to my hand, a hand that might be able to crush bone closing over your face, was to try to stop it. To grab the fingers, to stop them from crushing your skull.

It wasn't the logical thing, though.

If you used logic, then fingers that *can* crush the bone of your skull aren't going to be stopped by your own flesh-and-blood fingers, but that didn't mean that you wouldn't try.

As a soldier, though, and one trained to fight against heavily modded and often armored opponents, I responded differently.

I yanked the rifle up and around, training it on her friends and firing two quick, three-round bursts, killing one and making the other dive for cover, before ramming the rifle against her sternum and firing again.

She'd clearly had some reinforcing done, significant subdermal armoring, but she'd either had it done a long time ago and it'd degraded, or it'd been damaged already, because the second close-range round penetrated, as did the third. I angled it up and fired again. The shots ricocheted around inside the armored cavity, making damn sure she was down.

I released her face—the hand wasn't powerful enough to crush bone, after all, but I bet it'd damn well come close, and it'd hurt—and I shook that hand, splattering her with blood, before staggering slightly as I twisted wrong.

Fucking back!

I snarled, then went hunting, finding the last of them dragging himself across the ground. A trail of blood that led to him was a nice surprise, considering I'd thought I'd missed.

"Please..." He whimpered, and I paused, looking down at him. He was bleeding heavily from the right thigh, probably an artery nicked, judging from the amount of blood, and I nodded, crouching down next to him, rifle pointed at him, and making damn sure I could see his hands.

"Sure," I agreed, sending him a "knock."

He blinked, then hissed in understanding, glaring at me.

"Hey, you fuckers mugged and were planning on killing me. Pay up."

"I'm broke..." he started, and as I shrugged and started to stand up, he went on. "Fuck's sake! You think we'd be here if we had creds!"

"I think you've been robbing assholes for kicks and shit, so you've either got creds stashed, or you've got a stash of gear you ripped. Hand them over, or I leave you here. How long you think you'll last? If you can close the wound? Maybe you'll survive. Thing is, though, you'd have to let go of it first, find something to seal it...You let go? You've got maybe thirty seconds."

"Kit..." he hissed through gritted teeth, nodding to a pile of discarded plastic packaging and sheets.

I staggered over, cursing the spinal mod, and kicked it aside, seeing a grate in the wall hidden behind it all. I smiled at him, before crouching to the right-hand side of it and reaching in with my metal arm. I grabbed the cover and yanked it sideways, hearing his scream as he tried to move out of the way, while I kept the steel on my side pressed tight against the wall.

I was totally unsurprised when a blast went off. A braced shotgun firing a mass of buckshot tore the packing crates apart to the left, barely missing him as he rolled aside. My maniacal smile mushroomed at the growing fury and fear on his face.

Reaching inside, I found a handful of things: a medikit—small and blatantly stolen from some corpo's purse, from the classy design—a handful of credit-chips, and three boxes of ammo—two were rifle, one was for a handgun, and not my caliber...*of course.*

That didn't matter at this point, though.

I straightened, taking them all, and grabbed my bag from the floor next to Mr. Crispy. I took my handgun, and its holster, shrugging into it, before securing the gun.

"Must be getting old," I muttered. "Going out with a gun I couldn't reach." I quickly searched Crispy, finding nothing of any real value beyond an old-style lighter, and I took that, flicking it and seeing that it did, in fact, still work.

"Hey!" the guy cried, and I looked over at him in question. "Help!" He practically wept, his face grey, half laid in a puddle of blood and piss.

"You want help?" I saw the desperate nod he gave me, and I smiled, standing up, and walked over to him, holding the medikit where he could see it. I knocked on his Keystone again. "Credits. You know what this is worth."

There was a second of us staring at each other; I got a link, and twenty-six credits slid from him to me.

"Thanks."

Then I shot him in the face.

The fucking asshole had tried to rob me, tried to kill me, and he'd tried to get me with a trap—what the hell did he think I was going to do after all that?

He was guilty and fucking deserved to pay the price.

Idiot.

I searched him roughly, finding nothing of interest, and moved to his friends, gathering up the guns as I went. Most of them were crap. There were two more credit-chips, which I quickly drained, pressing their thumbs against the back and moving from corpse to corpse until they activated.

Once that was done, I was a grand total of seventy-eight credits richer, including the asshole who'd so kindly transferred his personal stash to me.

Two hundred and ten credits to my name.

What a fortune indeed.

I searched around a little more, conscious of the gunfire drawing attention, but also conscious that the little gang wouldn't have been acting the way they were if they thought there would be a visit from the enforcers.

I found nothing else of any real value, and remembering at the last minute about the shotgun in the stash, I pulled that out, stuffing it, three handguns, and the rifle into my shoulder bag, the grips and stock of the rifle and shotgun sticking out.

After wiping the blood from my hand and upending a bottle of what smelled like clear grain whisky over my left arm to clean it, I gathered up my bag and headed back out into the city.

Just another cold-ass murderous psychopath in a city full of them.

CHAPTER NINE

The trip to my new apartment was a slightly less violent one. As much as I'd tried to clean off, the fight had left a few stains on my clothes, especially from the guy I'd stabbed. Surprisingly, even in this city, there were few people who saw a man in blood-soaked clothes stomping the streets with a bag full of guns over his shoulder and decided to fuck with him.

The enforcers, of course, took note, pulling in alongside me as I trudged along, looking me up and down, before getting out of their transport and making me stop for a "wellness check."

They searched my bag, one of them unsubtly pocketing the two credit-chips they found there—empty; scum like these being exactly why I'd already cleared them—and asked me some shitty questions about the state I was in.

"Just got discharged today from the army," I answered flatly, giving them no reason to say anything. "Someone was hurt outside the recovery clinic; I helped him in. That's it."

"That's where the blood's from?" one queried, looking me over.

"Yup."

"Why'd you help?"

"Just helping a fellow man in need."

"You one of those religious nutters?"

"Nope."

"Why all the guns?"

"You seen this fucking city?"

"Fair."

"You broke any laws?" the second asked suddenly, speaking for the first time, now that he was finished searching me for "contraband" and having pocketed another cred-chip, presumably having some way to unlock them.

"No."

"You sure?"

"Davy, you dumbass," the other one groaned, looking at me as if to say *What can you do?* "Come on, if he has, he's not gonna come out with it, is he?"

"He might…"

"He won't."

"Look, guys, you about done? I got discharged this morning. I really need to sleep, and I need my pills."

"These pills?" Davy dug through my bag and held up the container. "What's in them? These drugs?"

"Yeah. You see my name on them? You see that they're sealed?"

"Yeah, so?"

"So there's nothing in there but what it says on the scrip. You think I'm smart enough to forge a seal like that?"

We all looked at the iridescent seal that ran in a loop around the top. Then they looked at me, and he spat after a few seconds.

"Probably not," he admitted.

"Exactly. Look, I'm not looking for trouble, and I'm not being a dick. I just want to take my pills, get some sleep, and figure out my life, right?" I entreated the slightly less thick one.

"You live here?" he asked, and I shrugged.

"Army paid for a month for me to sort my life out, so I guess so?"

"Right." He grunted. "Well, nobody with any money or clue would live here by choice. Behave yourself, citizen."

"Yeah," I growled. "Will do, thanks." I forced as close to a smile as I could manage, noting that the other one made no move to give me back the credit-chips.

They turned and sauntered back to their transport, and for a long second I idly considered shooting them both in the back of the head. Not for any reason, not really, just that the enforcers were always like that.

Fucking dickheads from birth to death, corrupt as the night was dark, and those who weren't? Well, they soon ended up floating in the river.

Eventually I forced myself to remember that it wasn't my place, though. I...*we* brought the law to the wastes. We had no authority in the city. We had no place here, and even if the APS did? I was out of the army.

I'd take care of the guilty as I saw them now, but I'd never again be responsible in the way I'd led a squad in the wastes.

Corruption and city police forces went hand in hand, and the few who weren't thieves, who weren't bought and paid for, or who weren't on the take outright? They never lasted. The others couldn't afford to let the occasional good guy who wandered in by accident survive long.

They gave snakes a bad name, and made goblins look trustworthy.

I watched the illuminated golden sign as they pulled away: ACE, Artem City Enforcers. Beneath it, in golden letters, read the words "To protect our way of life," and I snorted again, shaking my head and picking my bag up.

Everyone knew what that sign meant. They protected *their* way of life. Fucking assholes.

I slowly made my way across the sidewalk to the apartment building, stepping inside out of the harsh sunlight, and breathing a sigh of relief, before snorting and spitting at the acrid stench that filled the air.

"Hey!" someone shouted. A short, wrinkled older woman shuffled forward, jabbing a cane at me. The stench got markedly worse the closer she got. "You clean that up, ya hear!"

"What?" I frowned and looked around. The foyer of the apartment block was black with filth, smeared mud and quite possibly shit up one wall, and mold covered the front of a vending machine, clawing its way up the inside between the glass and the light that proclaimed its "wonders."

I'd tasted the nasty as soon as I'd taken that breath, and spitting it out had been instinctual.

"Spittin'—it's a dis'gustin' habit! You clean that up, ya hear!" she snarled at me, before edging closer, shuffling sideways and peering up at me from between greasy locks. "You new here? You…you a hooker?"

"Yes, I'm new, and no, I'm not a hooker," I growled.

"You sure?" She flattened her hair down on one side and peered up at me suggestively. "Maybe I can change yer mind?"

"Uh…no." I moved around her and headed toward the elevator.

"No, you're not sure?" she tried, smiling hopefully.

I sighed, stabbing my finger at the button for the sixty-fifth floor, before turning back to her. I was going to be here a few days at least, and there was no need to take my foul mood out on this crazy old bat.

"I'm not a hooker, but thanks for the offer." I forced a smile.

"Well, can't blame a girl for tryin'." She sauntered off, kicking a pile of rubbish that was piled in one corner, and laughing when a voice rose in drunken complaint, then started to search them, expertly dodging a kick from the body.

I shook my head as the doors closed. I turned, looking around the piss and blood-stained interior of the elevator, waiting as the mag-lev slid me up the tower with reassuring speed.

Looking out over the city, I smiled as glass sections opened and the lower buildings fell away, shaking my head as for the first time in a long while, I was reminded that the city could be beautiful.

When you stripped away the corpo scumbags, the enforcers, the criminal gangs, and the assholes, what was left was the city herself. And when you looked? It took your breath away.

The harsh sunlight reflected off towers of glass and chrome; metal of all colors held a mind-blowing variety of projectors, and a riot of colors filled the air. Advertising slogans were too far away to see clearly, and so they projected images, perfect smiles and grassy fields, paradises of easy living and more.

Those, in turn, blurred into streams of colors when you saw them from somewhere like this, as nobody in their right mind would try to advertise to the people who lived here.

I distantly saw the homes of the mid-level wage slaves, crafters, high officers, and corpo starting slots. All the real "better than the rest of us" scumbags lived atop the towers, or in the slender elite megastructures that radiated power and wealth. But here and there?

We still existed.

Regular giant megastructures like the apartment block I stood in now were dotted around the city, restrictions on how many could be how close to each other, due to the immense weight of the structures. Rather than let us have actual homes in the nicer areas, we were jammed into these megaliths, half a kilometer on a side and a hundred stories high. Each floor housed nearly six thousand apartments, and fuck, they were horrible places compared to virtually anywhere else.

What those fuckers out there didn't care enough to see, though? Was that this was where the real city lived.

The lift had been hacked at some point by a juvenile motherfucker, as rather than the traditional chime on arrival at the destination, there was an amusing fart noise, ending with a subtle note whose suggestion was clear that trousers would need to be changed immediately.

I sighed and turned; the doors before me slid open slowly, as music rolled in, along with clouds of smoke from the half dozen gang members who stood about talking or sprawled on couches dragged near to the doors.

All conversation stopped as I strode out, and after a second, the sniggers started.

"Fuck, man, look at that arm!" One laughed.

"*She-et*...my gramma got better mods than this fool—she bin dead ten year!" another called, half laid back in a filthy old padded chair.

"What you doin' here, fool?" A third stepped forward, and I stifled a growl.

My instinctual reaction was to compare these street and tower thugs to the people I'd fought alongside and against for the last nine years.

They were utterly no threat in comparison.

My second was that they were certainly a threat to the innocent, and probably guilty of *something*.

But...I wasn't wearing an APS. I wasn't armed to the teeth with the latest and greatest the military could provide.

I wasn't surrounded by my squad, and last of all, I was still barely walking at this point. If I pissed these guys off? They'd slaughter me.

"I live here," I said coldly, knowing damn well that if I backed down, I was giving off a signal that I was prey. Do that? I was dead, and we all knew it.

The trick was not to be prey, and not to be a challenge they couldn't ignore. I couldn't cow them all the way I'd normally do it, so instead I needed to be a threat, but not one that was worth the effort.

"Nah, dog," another voice said, and I turned, seeing the characteristic tilted eyes and tipped ears of a half-elf as he strolled forward, a drawn sword laid across his shoulders. "This here's our place. No street trash like you allowed."

The space I'd come out into was a nexus of five corridors. Three were lit, one was blocked off by battered and broken-looking boards, warning signs plastered across them, and the fifth...

"I'll be here a month, tops," I said firmly, turning to walk in the opposite direction, reading the sign on the wall to the left, and following it.

"Hey asshole!" Elf-boy called out. "I didn't say you could leave!"

"Nope, you didn't," I agreed, as two more of the gang moved to intercept, closing ranks ahead of me.

"What's in the bag?" one of them asked, and I fixed him with a glare.

"You blind or just dumb?" I shrugged the bag. "It's full of fucking guns."

"Gimme."

"No."

The one on the right pulled a short plasma knife out and thumbed it to life. The sputtering glow, as it flared and the containment chamber struggled to maintain its form, bathed us all. "I said..."

"*I* said no," I repeated, whipping my personal gun out and resting the barrel against his forehead. His eyes widened slightly, the speed not being something he was ready for, as he went cross-eyed staring down the barrel, and I thumbed off the safety. "Anyone moves, and I kill him."

"Nah," an unknown voice rumbled.

I shifted slightly, looking toward the dim corridor. Every instinct told me that this was the power behind the gang.

"Nah, you won't kill him. You do that, and we kill you."

The idiot before me spoke up. "Yeah, fool! You—"

"Shut it, Jerry."

"Uh…yeah, boss. Sorry," the terminally stupid Jerry replied, swallowing in fear.

Although the barrel of my gun was still pressed to his forehead, I knew it wasn't me he was afraid of.

"That's a nice gun." The boss slowly moved out of the shadows.

I grit my teeth at what I could see in my peripheral vision.

Orc blood, I knew straightaway: the grey-green skin, the overdeveloped musculature, the jutting forward chin—all of it.

I'd fought with, alongside, and against orcs for years. They were some of the most dangerous opponents out there, and one of the most shit-upon races to make up the city.

Walk away from an orc like this? It would be a fight, no matter what.

"Yeah, personal piece." I lowered it from the idiot's temple, turning to him and holding it up, angled to the side so that he could get a clear look at it.

As I did it, I was insanely conscious that there was a spitting, flaring, and barely contained plasma projector masquerading as a blade right behind me, but…I had to show I was unafraid, or I was dead.

"Revolver?"

"Hurricane model." I nodded. "Custom upgrade with personal gene-ID and twelve-shot cylinder."

"Mind if I check it out?" he rumbled, striding closer.

I hesitated only a second, before flicking the safety back on and twisting it around, offering it to him grip first.

He took it, looking at the grip, nodding at the barely visible electrodes.

"High charge?"

I nodded. "Two hundred and fifty."

"Impressive." He grunted, hefting it experimentally, turning to point it straight at my face. His gang members laughed and hooted, while we stared at each other, looking for the slightest shift, the giveaway that would bathe the corridor in blood. And, to their surprise, he nodded slowly, grudgingly.

Then handed the gun back.

"Boss?" one of the monkeys asked, confused, and getting a glare from him.

"How long you say you'll be here?" the boss asked me instead of replying to the idiot.

"A month, probably less. Army paid for the month, regardless."

"Medical discharge?" He glanced me over, seeing the blatant fresh chrome, and I nodded. "A month. You have any issues here? You come see me in my office." He jerked his thumb back to the dim recess he'd been sprawled in with a few women; he nodded to me and turned, wandering back the way he'd come.

"Uh…will do," I muttered, before turning to the idiots who still blocked my way, seeing the shock on their faces. "So, you gonna fucking move?"

They practically fell over themselves getting out of the way.

I moved past them slowly, forced myself to walk at a steady, unhurried pace. All the while, my heart hammered and my legs shook. Adrenaline and a trained and experienced readiness for violence warred against exhaustion, the remnants of drugs, and the sheer overload of damage, stress, and changes that had been inflicted on my body and mind over the last few days.

I staggered along corridors, with only the occasional light to see by. The deeper into the tower I walked, the darker it got, as the windows got rarer and rarer. So did the working lights, with even the Aug-World connections dropping out.

By the time I found my apartment?

I was down to using the lighter that I'd stolen from that old grey-bearded fart, and I was damn thankful for it.

I "knocked" on the door through aug-space, offering my ident. After a brief second, it slid open, exposing a squalid room. It was barely big enough to hold my bed, two shitty built-in closets, a gun cabinet, a desk with a single chair, a transport crate with my gear from the barracks, and the bathroom, complete with a shower.

That was it, in a room I could almost touch opposite walls in at the same time.

It was tiny, it was shitty, and for the next month, it was all mine.

I forced myself into the shower, collapsing to sit on the floor in the tiny cubicle, chin resting on my knees and deep in thought, as much as I'd wanted to hit the sack.

I needed to process the shit I'd just done, and take a long hard look at who I was now. I'd been changed by the army—hell, that was obvious. We all were. But I'd been further trained and taught that if anyone crossed the line and was a danger to me, my team, or Artem's interests? The best response was summary judgment.

I hadn't always dealt with shit like that, and the constant cocktail of enhancement drugs the army provided had kept me purring along. But now?

Now I needed to figure out who I was. I wasn't APS anymore.

Did I have the right to judge? Did I have the need to? Could I just walk away? I'd regretted that Sync had started to execute the scavs combatants—they'd gone for the guns, which made them valid targets, but still—I needed to have a hard look at myself.

The more I thought about it, though? If I gave these fuckers an inch, they'd kill me. I'd known growing up before the army that if you turned your back on a threat, it'd stab you, and what'd changed?

Nothing really, I decided. Nothing at all. The only difference was that rather than being in a full suit of armor that kept me safe, and let me have the luxury of making mistakes, I was now exposed.

I had to strike first. I *had* to, or they would—and my friends would die in that cavern.

CHAPTER TEN

I woke slowly. The pills I'd been prescribed to help with the "adjustment period" kept me under all night and made me groggy as hell when I finally did wake. My RI pulsed flashing lights and slowly rising beeps in my ears, attempting to follow its normal routines despite the shit it was forced to work with.

I blinked, then coughed and rolled over, the gel-foam mattress feeling as if I'd spent the night on a rock.

Army beds were *supposed* to be bad. Hell, my rack in my quarters had been cursed almost every damn day of my enlistment, and yet…I'd have killed for it over this shitty bed any day of the week.

I sat up, turning and planting my feet on the floor, sitting on the edge of the bed and blinking around as I tried to boot my brain into gear.

My bag lay where I'd dumped it, my handgun still stuffed under my pillow, and the single transport crate for my personal gear the army had arranged to be brought still sat against the far wall.

I yawned and stood, swaying slightly as my spinal mod and arm seemed to take forever to come fully online. I growled to myself in disgust.

First thing I was doing—well, second thing, once I'd gotten dressed, sorted this shithole out, and checked my gear—was getting registered with one of the merc guilds.

I needed credits, and I needed them fast, to replace these shitty mods, and to get a decent, secure place to live. I was out of the army early; Richie and Sync were expecting at least a year in that shithole of a cave, and there was no way my friends were going to be left there for any longer than was absolutely necessary.

I'd be watched for the first four months; that was standard. Any soldier leaving the army was on watch for that period. After all, releasing a trained killer who'd spent years living under strict rules and hierarchy, into a total cesspit of threat and stress, with easy access to guns?

Best to keep an eye on us, make sure we weren't going off the rails.

The army trained us to deal with our problems permanently, and in the city? The biggest problems we were likely to face were the gangs—which nobody gave a shit about if we started exterminating—and the corpos, which everything was built around.

That meant that either the corpos could stop being utter fucking dickheads and making us all hate them with a passion, or they could monitor us, and have a hit squad sent if we displayed certain tendencies.

After the four months, if we'd not gone corpo hunting, or loaded up and gone psycho, we were cut loose.

Best to give it a few months after that, then go for them when I was sure that I wasn't being watched. And besides, the major would be in touch with a plan soon, hopefully.

A memory of him saying something about getting rid of the monitoring flared up, but I couldn't remember whether that was true or a fever dream, so I shook it off.

I took care of nature's needs, then started clearing around. The room was bare, the chair and table being the only things in the room that weren't mine. Hell, even the blanket and pillow were from my case.

Still, my shit was in the way, and I needed room to work out.

I made the bed, sorted through my belongings, finding everything there—surprisingly—including my boxes of ammo for the handgun.

The personal items, stupid things like a recording on a projector cube of Fergie and Scott with their band, playing their hearts out, all of us steaming drunk and partying, I sorted and put away.

The guns were next. I laid them on the little table along with my cleaning kit, and continued on.

Clothes were sorted through, not that I had many.

That was life in the military: you didn't keep much. Even as a sergeant, your room was subject to spot checks, and it was just damn easier to keep everything just so.

There was limited space in quarters, so you got in the habit of keeping a few personal items, and the rest all being digital. I had two outfits in here: one that I'd used for going out, and one that was literally for slumming around when I didn't want to be in regs. That unfortunately was it, though; they'd kept my goddamn military gear, everything from training tops to fucking underwear, all-weather gear and boots, all of it.

That pissed me off to an *insane* degree, because that wasn't usual. Hell, one of the few good things about serving was that you got all your gear. And it wasn't like they could reuse it.

Hell, you lost or damaged it beyond what the cred-counters decided was "reasonable" wear and tear? They charged you to replace it! Then they ended up selling whatever you didn't take when you left to a company that processed the material down for literally a handful of credits per ton.

That they'd not included my general army clothes with my personal gear? It was *deliberate*. Hell, it'd have taken more effort to arrange the disposal of them than chucking it all in my bag, so I knew it had to be intentional as well.

Tyrannus.

He'd stripped me of every fucking credit he possibly could, then he'd done this?

He was always on my shit list, but that fucker kept making sure he was staying up at its head. That the major was investigating the whole thing gave me hope. It gave me a little promise that I'd find out who was responsible later, and I'd hunt them the fuck down and kill them for Fergie, Scott, and the kid's deaths.

Ideally? Tyrannus was heavily involved, and he'd be booted out of the army. No protection, and he'd go running straight to his corpo friends, and then I'd be able to kill them all. But that was wishful thinking at this stage.

I shook those thoughts aside, forcing myself to process the rest of my stuff. Stupid little keepsakes, but they were mine, and each and every one had a memory attached.

I went through them all, then packed them away again, hanging my "good" clothes up, and dumping my clothes from yesterday into the sink in the bathroom, scrubbing the blood and shit from them, and hanging them to dry as best I could.

The transport box was stashed in another closets, and I set to work on the guns, stripping, cleaning, and servicing them, before coding the gun safe to my ident and locking the rifle and shotgun away in the gun cabinet with most of the ammo I had.

My handgun, and the shitty caliber handguns, I left on the desk, as finally I got to work.

The first thing you were supposed to do with any new mod was let it heal, sure, but the second was use the fucker. Even with nanites, and a pure batch, there would be differences between the original, flesh model you were born with, and the new shit.

Slight "calibration" issues that would slow you down.

I'd already experienced them to no end with just walking; trying to run had been a bastard, as were most movements.

The best way to overcome that, though, was to use them over and over again, and the best way I could do that was exercise.

I spent the next two hours doing a combination of push-ups, burpees, sit-ups, squats, lunges, jumps, and more. Continually dropping prone, rolling, and leaping to my feet was a pain in the ass. Although I felt little difference—save being exhausted—by the end of it. The RI ran the numbers while I lay there on the shitty bare floor, panting and sweat covered, and assured me that the delays between my nerve impulses were significantly down.

The first hour of that was painful. The second? As I moved from stance to stance, following my sword kata? Infuriating.

I had no sword, which was bad enough, but the way my arm, my legs, and basically *I* moved? It was juddery, slow, and clumsy, and I hated every second.

A few days of this? I should be back to running, jumping, and more like I'd always done before, and I'd damn well need to buy a sword, even if it was just a solid blade. The arm was going to be a problem as well. There was no way to cover that; it was slower than my old one, as well as frankly shit, so I needed that replaced ASAP.

As soon as I could, I'd swap out the spinal reinforcement for a spinal tap and the shitty tier-one brain mod as well. They'd not be cheap, though.

Best-case scenario, I'd be paying at least ten thousand per mod, probably closer to fifty. As I was right now? With two hundred and ten credits to my name, I was so far from where I needed to be it wasn't even funny.

The merc guilds wouldn't offer me anything like an actual contract without me being at an average mod tier of two, with at least a few higher-end weapons and some decent armor.

With no armor, a handful of guns—most of which were crap—and tier-one real mods—the organelles didn't really count—I'd be lucky to get a job clearing a basement of an infestation of rats.

Even goblin pest control jobs would laugh at me.

Fuck's sake.

This was going to be a long month.

I needed food and drinks for the month. I needed somewhere to live after that, and at the very least some fucking armor. Without that, the mercs wouldn't even take me on at the lowest level.

That left me a few choices, and none of them very good.

I forced myself to send a message to Tyrannus, *asking* when I wanted to fucking scream abuse at the little turd, for access to the reels of data recordings for Fergie, Scott, Richie, and Sync, as well as Barnes, though there would be a lot less of his stuff.

I'd lost that access with being booted out, and I hated that.

I needed to make their reels. It was going to suck, to be an emotionally crippling and horrible few days, made even worse by working with my shitty kit, but I needed to do it, to show their families what had happened.

That done, I forced myself to my feet, and into the shower, thankful that, at the very least, I'd bought some decent soaps and a nice towel at some point, so I had them now.

I reveled in the luxury of a long shower, ignoring the warnings that were sent to my ident about "excessive water usage" and stayed in the fucker until it cut off, before finally drying and getting dressed.

I had no clue what the weather was like outside, and considering that I only had two outfits? One of them was a "going out" shirt bright enough to be seen from orbit that Fergie had talked me into buying, and a pair of charcoal slacks with a bright-red streak down either hip.

That meant that I was down to a pair of black trousers with reinforced knees, more pockets than my goddamn army gear used to have, and a thin training-style top that left my shoulders and arms bare.

Usually that was good. I was fairly well-muscled, after all, but hey, *usually* I didn't have the cheapest, shittiest cybernetic arm replacing my own.

Fuckers.

My only coat was soaked from being covered in blood and recently washed, and I dismissed wearing that out of hand. I picked up my shoulder bag, full of the handguns, and I left my own gun on open display hanging under my arm in its holster, before heading for the door.

It was time to get my fucking life in order.

The corridor outside was as shitty and dark as it had been on the way in yesterday, and it took ten minutes to find my way to the lift I'd used yesterday.

Needless to say, when I was actually thinking the gang might be useful, if I could get them to answer a few questions, they were all elsewhere.

Dicks.

I grumbled a little, then sighed as the lift flowed down the floors at speed, making me stare out across the city at the heavy grey rainclouds that had settled in for the day.

Joy.

Reaching the ground floor, I strode out, passing the old bag who was now unconscious in a pile by the door. A stream of piss leaked from her to run to a nearby drain, adding that little extra ambiance the place really needed.

I walked out into the driving rain without stopping, picking up the pace and jogging across the uncovered sections to wait in line for the mag-train, letting two pass before paying my five credits and shuffling aboard with all the others.

One of the best things about the city was the prevalence of fast, affordable transport: two credits to anywhere in the outer city, or five credits for the day pass. That was on the outer ring. Admittedly, the inner ring was more expensive—more than double that—although the trains were a lot better. Fewer drunks passed out and drug-dealing going on, for a start.

The last ring was corpo and wage-slave territory only, and the likes of me needed a pass to even get access to their stations, never mind paying whatever the hell their trains cost to ride.

West Shamrik was my destination today, a neighborhood I'd grown up in. Although I'd lost touch with most of those I'd used to call friends, the few who didn't die or join the army—and then die—meant that I still had a few contacts.

Forty minutes later, most of it spent ignoring a couple of beggars who probably had more credits than I did, a goblin asking for work, and two shaven-headed monks telling everyone that mods were the route to hell, and I finally jogged down the old street that was my destination.

I ran, trying to stay under the rain deflectors where I could, and yet I was soaked when I finally opened the door to Gunther's Guns and Mil-tech Surplus.

I paused on entry. A powerful burst of memories hit me as I shook the rain off, seeing the miserable old fart behind the desk at the far end, staring at some ball game as usual.

"Buying or selling?" he called distractedly, before looking up and doing a double take. He took in the arm, the shitty clothes, and soaked appearance, as well as the fact I was alone. "Harry, that you, kid?" He shook his head in disbelief as he recognized me.

"Gunther." I nodded to him, walking over and dumping my bag on the floor with a wet splat, then stripping water off my arms and face.

"Damn, you look like shit," he whispered. His right eye—the cybernetic replacement—whirred as it tracked over me, no doubt evaluating and assessing me to within an inch of my life.

"Tell me about it," I growled, sitting on a stool he kept on my side of the desk.

Gunther's was old school, much like the man who ran it, selling all sorts of military surplus, from the shittiest rations for those that missed "the good old days" and wanted to reminisce, to under-the-counter mods and stolen gear.

I'd not seen him in years, and in taking the seat without asking, I knew I'd find out exactly how good my name was here in seconds.

Gunther *invited* people to sit, if there was a good bit of haggling to be done. Sitting without his permission generally got your prices doubled and locked you out of the good shit.

I'd been a "sitting" member of Gunther's customers for years before I joined the army, and when I was in the regular squads, I'd continued to do business with him, going so far as to "arrange" some "samples" to make their way to him for resale on several occasions.

He paused, glancing from me to the seat and back again, then nodded and reached under the table, pulling out an unmarked bottle of golden liquid and two glasses.

"You look like a man with a story to tell," he said simply, pouring for us both.

"Yeah…" I sighed, picking the offered glass up, saluting him, and hesitating. "To the dead," I toasted, and he nodded solemnly, lifting his own.

CHAPTER ELEVEN

By the time I made it back to the apartment, I was roaring drunk, dressed slightly better than I had been, and yeah, broke as fuck.

Gunther had sorted me out, as I'd hoped he would, and he'd looked out for himself as well, ripping me off well and truly. I staggered out of the lift, waving generally at the gang members as one of them tried saying something. Somehow, I made it down the corridor, through the darkness, and to my own apartment, only burning my fingers three times on the lighter.

I didn't remember much of the night before when I awoke the next morning, but the pounding hangover, the reek of cheap whisky, and…yeah, the bloody and battered knuckles told me I'd spent longer in West Shamrik than I should have.

I was half dressed, having evidently passed out drunk while trying to undress, and I'd apparently vomited at some point. I wrinkled my nose, looking at the congealed mess on the floor. With absolutely nothing else to use, I had to gather it all up with my hands and wash it away in the sink.

The apartment was by now in an even shittier condition than when I arrived, and stank to high heaven, but ten minutes of cleaning, followed by scrubbing the floor with my still sodden top from the recovery clinic—then flushing it away—meant the room was livable again.

I forced myself to go through the full two-hour workout, despite being desperate for a drink, some food, and a fucking shower. The water ration I'd used yesterday was three days' worth, and if I wanted to use the toilet and shower each day for the rest of the week, I was going to damn well need to be tactical about using it from now on.

Panting and covered in sweat, I lathered up and quickly rinsed off. The entire shower took less than a minute. The lease stipulated it'd charge by the "gallon used or time, whichever was the greater, and each minute of usage would be rounded up."

Basically, if I went to sixty-one seconds, I'd have two minutes' worth of water flow deducted from my tab. Assholes got you every which way they could.

Still, now clean, and feeling a little more human, I was ready for the day.

I had sixteen credits left to my name, but yesterday had been about more than seeing an old friend who bought and sold dodgy gear.

I'd sold him the three handguns—all trash tier, cheap and mass-produced—but for thirty credits a piece. That'd taken me to two hundred and ninety-five after my train ticket, and I'd gone on a spending spree.

A decent jacket—army surplus, as that was literally what he stocked, but not bad. A second pair of combat trousers, reinforced and in good condition. Two tops. A hip holster for my handgun, a back holster that would do for either the shotgun or the rifle. Some basic-as-fuck body armor—it'd been blatantly scavenged and repaired—gloves, some tactical goggles. And, just in case, a pair of flash-bangs.

It didn't seem much for the money, considering it was all secondhand, but I was now as comfortable as I could be. I could see in the dark thanks to the goggles, and I'd got a lead on a few quick credit jobs that I could do to scrape enough together to pay the entry fee to the cheapest of the merc guilds.

They, in turn, would pay the bare minimum for jobs. But considering the situation I was in? Bare minimum was something at least.

An hour later, I was dressed, armed, and getting both far less attention and slightly more respect, dressed back in army gear, armored and departing the train, only two stops along the line.

The area I was in was shitty, but I wasn't likely to get many jobs collecting on debts in nice places—not for a cut of the claim, anyway.

These were the kind of debts that got written off, and that people like Gunther bought for an absolute song, sending some muscle to collect anything that could be sold.

The location in question made me curse as soon as I saw it.

Thankfully, it wasn't some little old lady. Gunther knew me enough, and had some standards left himself, to refuse those kinds of debts.

The three gangbangers lounging outside the shuttered-up shop that was my target, smoking and jeering at the passing girls, weren't going to make this an easy call.

"What you want?" one asked, perking up as I approached, misunderstanding my reason for being there. "Skiff? Char? Got some angel dust as well, for the right price."

"Here to see Hector," I said calmly, as the other two rose from the shitty plastic chairs, moving to either side of me.

"Why?" The figure before me sniffed, scrubbing at his nose. The purplish glitter suggested that the angel dust he had wasn't likely to be as much as he had a few minutes earlier.

"He owes a debt."

"So?"

"So I'm here to get the creds," I replied flatly, seeing the way they moved, and the hands moving to guns.

"He don't owe you shit." The talkative one threw his shoulders back and widened his stance, resting his hand on the butt of a handgun. "So you turn around and fuck off, maybe we forget about this."

"This doesn't have to get nasty." My RI tracked the other two as they moved, projecting probable locations based on sound and the distance they could have traveled.

Fuck, the prediction was rough, though, considering the way it'd normally appear.

"You come onto our turf, you want my money? Oh, believe me fool, it does!" the fucker before me snarled.

"You Hector?" I asked, and he snorted.

"Nah, dog. I *own* Hector…"

"Own…" I glanced at him, at where his friends sat on the wall outside of "Hector's," a dilapidated shopfront that looked as if it'd closed down decades ago. But the traffic, and them?

"He's your chemist?" I asked, and the one before me smiled.

"He's workin' off his debt to me. He don't owe nobody else nuffin'."

"He owes me fifty credits." I grit my teeth when they laughed.

"Fifty creds?" the one before me hooted. "*Fifty* goddamn creds? Bitch, he owes me thirty K! You want fifty creds? I'll pay you to go fuck up some fools for that. Shit, fifty creds!"

"You about to get your ass kicked for less creds than I spend on getting my dick sucked, fool," the one to my right whispered, stepping in close, visibly relaxing and deciding that I was little threat. After all, who'd send anyone serious after such a pathetic debt?

I smiled, looking from the one directly ahead to the one to my right, locking their locations in, and then glanced at the one to my left.

"So, who wants to go first?" I felt the rising adrenaline, now that the situation had moved from "possible" into "definite" violence, and the old mad thrill.

"What?" Lefty grunted, as I struck.

My first target was the one to my right, a chop to the throat. No need to kill him outright—none of them had drawn a weapon…yet.

I hit hard, though, and with my training, he was out of the fight at the very least. He'd probably be fine with a little medical help, but that was as far as my goodwill went.

The one on my left, I grabbed, slamming my left hand down atop his right as he tried to draw his gun from the hip holster, holding it in place, even as I ripped my own gun out and paused, waiting.

The one in front, the mouthy one of the three, had tried to pull his gun free, but the iron sight had caught on something in his pants, making him almost castrate himself as he tried to rip it free.

In the time it took him to look up, he was staring down the barrel of my gun, Righty was coughing and wheezing on the floor, unable to breathe, and Lefty…*well.* I'd closed my metal hand over his flesh one, and he hissed in pain, trying to draw the gun still.

"Now…I came for Hector," I said softly. The people who'd been walking past on the sidewalk hurried to be anywhere else…but once they were what they judged to be a safe distance, they paused and watched curiously, most utterly unconcerned if some gangbangers got hurt.

After all, fewer gang members was good for everyone—less chance they'd pull a gun on someone innocent.

There was a handful of heartbeats as I waited, before Mouthy released his gun and lifted his hands.

"Fine, you want, what? Fifty creds? Here."

I acknowledged the knock. My RI located, reported to me, and blocked the crude attempt at the trace he activated as well as the money transfer.

"Ah-ah." I shook my head slowly. "That's not nice."

"Fuck nice," he growled. "You're a dead man walkin'."

"You tried to spike the transfer," I said. "You don't get to know who I am. You don't get to come after me. I came for a debt—it's paid. You want to live through this? You view it as a cost of employing Hector. We all walk away, and nobody gets hurt."

"Nah. I'll find you," he promised, eyes wide, pupils dilated, and I snorted. "I'll find you, and I'll f—"

"Fuck's sake, you know what? Fine! Whatever, you dumb motherfucker. Guilty." I sighed as I pulled the trigger, blowing his brains across the metal grates of the shop entrance, then rammed the barrel against the eye of the man on my left.

"What do you think?" I moved slowly so that he was between me and the door now, and so I could clearly see the third figure still on the floor, gasping, with a damaged trachea. "You think you'll be coming after me?"

"No…" he whispered, eyes wide. "Cost of doing business, right?"

"Good boy." I smiled. "Now you fucks just cost me ammo, and ruined my good mood. I'm going to let go of your hand. You're going to let go of the gun, and you're going to transfer me a hundred credits…"

"I've only got ten."

"Ten?"

"My girl…" He swallowed.

Not for the first time, I wished there was a way to check someone else's balance.

"Fine. Whatever, dickhead. Gimme." I felt the knock and nodded, accepting the transfer. As soon as I let go of his hand, he cradled it under his arm, and I pulled the handgun free, feeling by the weight that it was almost certainly empty.

"Goddammit," I growled. "Their guns, and credit-chips," I ordered, getting a shitty, badly modded gun that looked as if it were from some ancient war, a knife that would be slightly less use than harsh language, and a container full of drugs.

That I took, dumping them all in my bag, before gesturing to the door into the building, the one covered by their friend's brains.

"Now let's take your friends and go see Hector."

"Why?" he asked dumbly.

"Why?" I glared at him. "That fucker owes a debt!"

"But…" He shrugged, grabbing his friends at my direction and dragging them inside.

The shop had been stripped. Everything but the walls were gone. A mass of chemical equipment was spread across three tables, with a figure huddled in the far corner, trying to hide under a sleeping bag.

"You Hector?" I called, and a terrified pair of eyes peeked out over the top of the tattered fabric, before nodding frantically.

I sighed, glancing around the room, noting the utter lack of any creature comforts. Literally, his sleeping bag was laid on a tiled floor, and the only things in here, besides the chemistry equipment, were two glass door cabinets with shit growing in them under heat lamps.

"Get your ass up," I growled at him. I'd been planning to get the credits from him as well, so I didn't have to share the money I'd gotten outside, but yeah, that wasn't going to happen.

The state of Hector as he stood made it clear that he'd not been getting paid for his time. Hell, he'd apparently not been getting fed and watered, never mind paid.

He was a lanky elf, clearly one with a pharmaceutical bent to his mind, and he looked like he'd been here awhile. His pointed ears were…well, one looked fine. The other had been recently hacked into a rough rounded shape, presumably by these assholes, judging from how bloody and battered it was.

His skin was pale, grey almost, rather than the golden hue most of the posh fucks had, and his fingers were bloody, the nails chewed—hopefully by him.

His clothes were filthy. His blond-gold hair looked like straw. And his eyes? Shit, he'd been on the ragged edge for a while. I could see the tracks of tears in the dirt on his face, and I growled, seeing the state of him.

Seeing him was a distraction, though, and one that nearly cost me my life as Lefty lunged at me with a scalpel aimed at my throat. I went to bat it away, bringing the gun around, and cursed as my new arm moved far too slowly.

The scalpel darted around the arm, and buried itself in my side. Most of it was stopped by the armor. The tip was all that made it into me, but that fucking hurt, despite only being a flesh wound.

Not as much, admittedly, as the slug that tore through his chest and out of his back though, sending him staggering, and the second shot that took him in the head. As he fell, Hector screamed, promising me anything I wanted, and the guy whose trachea I'd damaged struggled to his feet, taking a bullet to the chest, then one to the head when he fell, just to be sure.

By this point, Hector was practically frothing at the mouth, shrieking and trying to hide under the bedding, as I searched the dead, swearing.

Nothing of any use.

A watch that was probably worth about a credit, clothes that were ruined by blood, guns I already had in my bag, and another two containers of drugs off the table.

Well, drugs weren't part of my remit. That was a city enforcers job, so fuck it. The chemist might be guilty of making drugs, but he was probably more guilty of being terminally fucking stupid than anything else.

Once that was all in my bag, and I could distantly hear the warbling siren of the enforcers that someone had presumably called, I turned to the elf, huddled in the corner.

"Hey…HEY!" I yelled, getting the eyes peeking out again. "You want to go to jail?"

"N…no?"

"Then run! Get out of here, you idiot!" I ordered him, not waiting to see whether he listened as I headed for the door.

I made it outside in a handful of steps, banging the flimsy door off the wall as I ran through it. The distant flashes reflected off a wall to the left, telling me which direction the fuckers were coming from. Knowing them, they'd have all scanners active when they arrived at the scene.

My guns might not draw much attention—this was Artem, after all—but the containers of drugs would. And, again, I had no authority to dispense judgment anymore.

I sprinted to the right, the crowd parting to make room for me. I put my gun away, taking the first alley on the right, then the second right as it came up.

Now heading back along the street, running parallel to the one I'd just left, I paused, dropping into a fast-food joint and ordering a bag of food randomly from the board.

It wasn't the food that was important; it was the bag, and these places always advertised with…yeah.

The figure behind the counter, a grey-faced, clearly miserable half-orc, went to hand me the food in a bright-white, logo-covered bag, then looked confused when I knocked on him, and transferred a credit.

"A big bag, mate," I requested.

He frowned and shrugged, handing over a second bag as requested, this one much larger.

I dumped my shoulder bag into it, putting the food on the top of it in the second bag, and turned my army coat inside out. The inside was black and looked a bit stupid. It wasn't intended to be reversible like this, but it wasn't a fashion statement.

Instead of a guy wearing all army gear and body armor, holding a gun with a backpack, running in one direction, I was now a guy in combat pants, which were common, a black jacket that was closed up, and a carrier bag full of takeout.

It'd not stand up to real scrutiny, but that wasn't the point.

The streets were full of hundreds of people at all hours, and I weaved in and out of them. Now, unless I passed a transport with its scanners going—unlikely, as high-powered scanners running constantly fucked with everyone's mods, and they'd get lynched—all I had to do was keep going, and get to the mag-train.

Twenty minutes after that, I sent Gunther a message with the details, and I was on my way to the next job, happily eating my takeout, feeling a little happier about the organelles as well, considering that replacing my organs with them meant the scalpel had literally missed everything besides a little fat and muscle.

It stung, but that was fucking life. I wondered whether Hector had made it out before the enforcers arrived. They'd have pinned that slaughter on him most likely, otherwise.

The least possible effort was about their style. But fuck it, I'd given him a chance and that was the best anyone could expect.

CHAPTER TWELVE

The next two jobs were shit as well. The first was supposedly just tracking…but it ended as beating the crap out of a thief. I had to chase the little shit through a crumbling and deserted factory to get back some stolen gear, and the entire time he was shouting abuse while his friends looked on and laughed.

I was getting a lot more practice with my mods, but I was lathered in sweat when I finally cornered the bastard and got my hands on him.

Next was a missing kid—finding him took all of the next three hours, and I got paid ten credits. He'd been stoned to fuck in a char den. It was a shitty place to be, literally. Char addicts tended to lose control of their bowels, so anyone who ran such a place made people wear giant diapers, which, in turn, made the whole thing that little bit more hilarious for the people I passed with the skinny little shit thrown over one shoulder.

Dumping him on his parents' front door resulted in them giving me a lecture, as if I were somehow to blame for the state of their son, who proceeded to drool and shit himself the entire time the mother complained.

I offered to "solve" their problems and got paid the ten credits, after none too subtly resting my hand on the butt of my handgun.

The fourth and final job of the day, for another measly thirty credits, was a bug hunt.

Some dumb fuck had bought a lanton as a *pet*. Gods alone knew why—they were ugly as sin and blind, spending their lives burrowing around underground, eating crops, and, when they got the chance, farmers as well.

This dumb fuck had apparently decided it made him "cool and interesting" to have such a weird pet. Then it'd tried to maul him, and had escaped into the nearby streets.

Considering that lantons were asexual, set up nests, then grew to over a meter in size, and liked to chew on certain specific and fucking expensive metals used in the power cables that ran everywhere in the city?

They were banned from the city and miles around on exactly the grounds that this dipshit was now worried about: that they'd get loose, breed, and be almost impossible to root out without doing massive damage to the local network and costing tens of thousands of credits in damages, not to mention the fines.

He tried to claim it'd be an easy job, and that he wanted it "set free" beyond the city walls, and was willing to pay five credits. The agreed upon price, with Gunther, was *thirty*. Well, one good turn deserves another, I decided, after turning to walk away, and forcing him to agree to the thirty.

I set it free, all right—free of this mortal fuckin' coil. No chance was I leaving it alive to breed.

Then I bagged up the corpse and took it back to him, slamming it down on his table, and pointed out the empty egg sacs.

"It's laid eggs already," I lied. "I'll need to report this, because it'd take me hours, maybe *days* to find all the eggs, and the enforcers will need to clear this whole area…"

"No!" he squeaked, panicked. "They'll blame me!"

"That's because it's your fuckin' fault!" I snapped, glaring at him, seeing the panic and disbelief that this was happening to him in his eyes.

"But…but…you could find them, right?"

"I could, maybe," I admitted. "But why the hell would I? You already tried to rip me off!"

"No!"

"Five fucking credits," I growled. "The deal was thirty, and you tried to lie and get me to do your dirty work for *five*?"

"I'll pay!" he promised, nodding. "I'll pay the thirty!"

"You're damn right you will!" I snarled. "The thirty that you'll pay me *right now* is for this fucker! You want me to find the others? You want me to crawl through the gutters and the underside of the fucking city, to risk specters and fuck knows what, crawling through shit for maybe days? You'll damn well pay me a fuckload more!"

"How…how much?" he whispered, licking his lips, clearly terrified and desperate.

"Four hundred!" I demanded, expecting to be bargained down to a lot less, but hey, I was scamming him anyway.

"Uh…uh…Okay? I've not got much now, but I'd owe you…"

"No," I said flatly, pointing at the full immersion rig in the corner of his room. "You want me to do this on a *promise* of payment? I'm taking that until you pay up."

"No!" He gasped. His pasty face went white as he shook his head, scraggly ponytail flapping and bouncing off his filthy clothes.

"Pay me my thirty, and I'm out of here." I put my right hand on my gun's grip to make my position exceedingly clear.

"You don't understand! That took years of saving to get! It's almost brand-new, three thousand credits!"

"How many eggs do you think were in that fucker?" I nodded at the corpse. "A hundred? Two? You get fined per beast, remember…fifty a pop, isn't it?" I shrugged.

"I don't have that…" he whispered. "I…I don't have the thirty, but I can get it! And another *hundred*! You kill them, make sure they're all dead, or, or just that nobody can trace them to me? I'll give you it!"

"You don't have the thirty?" I asked him slowly.

"N…no…"

"Three thousand you said?" I nodded, shoving him aside, and stomped across the floor to where his entertainment rig was plugged into the wall.

"Please!" He whimpered as I started to disconnect it from the wall.

"You want it back? You pay Gunther a hundred, plus whatever fees he puts on it." I unplugged it from the chair and folded the arms down. "That's for wasting my fucking time."

It was a standard entertainment rig—basically a glorified virtual reality package—but rather than your implants projecting it in your mind, this would physically touch you at the same time.

The matching upgrade to your implants would make the caress of the steel rollers feel like anything from a massage to a fucking hand job, and although, yeah, these kits were sold for gamers, they were primarily used for porn.

I disconnected the groin attachment and dumped it on the floor. I knew *exactly* what that was used for, and I didn't need the fucker pressed against me when I was carrying it.

With that disconnected, and the power leads and so on pulled, the entire form began to fold automatically.

It was designed to be laid over a bed or a long chair, ridged layers that you laid atop of, and a dozen small arms on the sides that moved to simulate pressure and impacts.

It was a hell of a kit, but looking around the room it was in?

He'd have done better spending the money on literally anything else.

His apartment wasn't much bigger than mine, and it was far dirtier and smellier, with discarded food containers, filthy piles of clothes and worse strewn about.

"Please!" he begged, and I turned to him, pausing.

"You want me to give up possibly days of my time, risk my life to pull you out of the shit. You put out a job that you couldn't afford to pay for, and you knew it. Now you want me to let you off? That about it?"

"But...I'll pay you back..." he promised, nodding. "You'll see..."

"You already tried to rip me off twice. I'm taking this, that's a given. You've got a choice, though."

"What?"

"Do you want me to take care of the eggs? Make sure they're all dead?"

"YES!"

"If I don't, you know this will cost you tens of thousands? That the enforcers will come for you? They'll take this. They'll not even take it against your debt—they'll just keep it, and you know that."

"I know."

"This is the deal. You get a week. I'll kill them all, make sure it's done, but this goes with me now. You'll pay Gunther four hundred credits, plus whatever he charges as a fee for holding this. You want it back? You want me to risk myself? That's how this happens. Otherwise, you just tried to rip me off, and wasted my time. This is going with me, regardless. This way, at least you know that the enforcers won't be coming for you, and you've got a week to buy this back."

"I..."

"Say you agree," I ordered him, and he swallowed hard, then nodded slowly.

"I agree."

"Good boy." I grunted, grabbing the transport box for the kit and sliding it in, sealing it up, and heading for the door.

"You can leave it here...while you hunt them..." he tried, and I glared at him.

"If I did that, you'd hide it," I pointed out, seeing the flinch in his eyes, the way he tried to conceal that he'd been planning exactly that. "Then, I'd kill you." I drew the handgun out of the holster slowly. "Do you really want to try to annoy me again?"

"No."

"Wise, that."

An hour later, Gunther was wrinkling his nose at the smell of me, while plugging in the rig, running diagnostic tests.

"You need to shower before you come to see me next time," he grumbled.

"You need to make sure these fuckers can afford to pay me before you take the job," I countered. "I'm stinking because I spent an hour in a fucking sewer hunting a goddamn lanton nest."

"You think you'll be able to find the eggs it laid?" he asked, squinting as he read the specs for the rig from his personal interface.

"I took the eggs out and squashed them." I shrugged. "I was going to try to get a bit more out of him after he tried to rip me on paying only five credits, but then finding he didn't even have the thirty? Nah. I gave him a week to pony up four hundred, plus whatever fees you charge for holding onto this and handling it."

"And you what? Want me to sell this when he can't afford it?" he asked, and I nodded. "Fair enough. Maybe get eight hundred creds, but most of my buyers won't be interested..." He paused, scratching his chin. "You need the credits, or you want barter?"

"Both," I said. "Give me a hundred now, and the rest against stock."

"It might take me months to sell this."

"It'll take you an hour. You said yourself it's worth eight hundred. Give me half, a hundred upfront and store credit for the rest. We both know you jack these prices up." I grinned.

"Ah, lad, if only you could bargain as hard as you fight." He shook his head. "I'll do it, but only because I know you need the money. You owe me, though."

"This for old time's sake?" I asked, and he snorted, shaking his head.

"You accept the deal?"

"Aye."

"Here." He knocked on my Keystone.

I approved the transfer. The hundred credits slid into my account as I nodded my thanks.

"Now that's done, and everyone's happy, I'll tell you the truth, lad. Yeah, you're right. I'll have this sold inside the hour. Already got a kid interested for nineteen hundred. So, take some advice—learn to bargain and what things are worth before you go looking to replace those mods, or you'll be in debt for the rest of your life."

"Nineteen...Fuck." I groaned. "You're bullshitting me, right?"

He grinned. "Nope."

"I'm keeping your share of the jobs," I grumbled, and he snorted.

"Oh no, whatever will I do? I'm losing, what? Thirty credits?" he responded sarcastically, shaking his head.

"Asshole."

"Amateur."

"And I'm taking a goddamn change of clothes. Army surplus, and you're giving me them free!"

"Fuck's sake, Harry." He sighed, tapping the release and folding the rig back up into its box. "Okay, look. That kid's almost certainly never gonna be able to buy this kit back, but hey. You gave him a week. You want me to hold it, or you want me to sell it on now?"

"You got a buyer already?" I asked, and he nodded.

"He just responded. Damn, that was fast, but hey. I'll give you the change of clothes, and you can leave that shit you're wearing here. I'll process it and dispose. In return, you deliver the kit for me on your way home, deal?"

"All right." I sighed, before standing again and moving through the store, searching. My new clothes were free, as he said, but he'd be pissed at me if I chose only the most expensive. Besides, in the real world, expensive didn't always equate to valuable.

The store was ten meters across, and thirty long, with racks on the side walls, suspended gear from the ceiling and concealing netting to add to the military ambiance.

Dotted around here and there were dozens of circular stands, holding everything from packs of grain and energy bars, to racks of different sized trousers and tops. Rows held boots in every size, and I moved quickly, grabbing a pair of combat boots, fresh gloves, reinforced trousers with additional armoring on the knees, thighs, and shins, and a temperature-regulating top.

I kept the body armor I'd already been wearing—it'd been under the jacket so it hadn't been fouled, thankfully—and the replacement jacket was plain black, additional armoring included here and there.

"Good choices." Gunther approved. "I should have set a limit on the cost..."

"Don't get greedy, you old fart." I grunted, laying them on the table and letting him check them over.

"Okay, so you've got three hundred in credit with me. What you looking for?"

"Decent glasses rather than these shitty goggles. I need to fucking see and upgrade my mod."

"Model?"

"Mil-spec. I need to augment my chip with them," I suggested, referring to my brain augment, and he snorted.

"That'd run you a lot more than your damn credit. You got tier one, right?"

"Yeah..."

"With your RI in there, that's gonna be taking up all its capacity, just about. Glasses that'd connect, and that your RI could spread out into, would run you about three thousand. If you're seriously looking at that as your next proper purchase? I'd say go full helm instead. You're looking at about five thousand, but it'd give you vision options, hide your ugly mug, and provide armoring."

"Yeah," I agreed ruefully. "I figured. I'm gonna be going full merc kit-out in the next month, get as much earned as I can, then I can start taking real jobs for real money."

"Well, you've got, what? A hundred and fifty?"

"Hundred and seventy-three. Train and lunch outta the day as well."

"Man, that's pathetic." He snorted. "Fine, I'll spot you fifty creds to get you to registration, but you owe me that...You sell me your loot for the next week—deal?"

"Deal." I forced a smile, hating that I was reduced to this, then cursing and reaching in my bag as I remembered something. "Fuck, I forgot all about this. I grabbed these from Hector…"

Laying the three boxes of drugs on the counter, I looked to Gunther hopefully, gritting my teeth when he opened them, then shook his head, sliding them back to me.

"Not something I can move. Not at any price that's worth the risk, anyway."

"Thanks anyway." I nodded to him, before using his facilities, washing and changing quickly. I dumped the filthy clothing in a bag on his desk, grabbed the boxed-up rig, and headed back out the door.

Two hours later, a trip into the north of the city to drop the rig off and one back to the apartment to find the gang, I went to the merc guild.

This time, fortunately the gang was "in," and I got curious looks as I arrived on the floor, before they ignored me again. I stepped out and turned directly to face the gang leader's shadowy nook.

He was there, sprawled on a large three-seater with a blonde woman—half-elf, judging from the ears—half draped across his lap.

He was in a conversation with another resident when I stepped up, and he waved me to wait, continuing like a king holding court.

"Sit there," one of the gangers ordered me, sneering.

"Fine." I forced myself to behave, sitting and waiting, as they talked, something about a debt being owed, and respect, before a handful of credits changed hands, and the resident moved off.

"So…you come looking for work?" the half-orc called, and I smiled, standing and striding forward. "You look like you're doing a bit better than when you first arrived."

"I'm not looking for work…" I started, before pausing. "At least, I don't think you'd have work I need. For the right price, though? I'll listen."

"Lookie here!" one of the gang called, laughing. "New boy thinks he's better than us, huh?"

"I think I'd kill most of you without even noticing," I corrected, shooting him a glance. "That's not why I'm here, though."

"So?" the half-orc asked curiously. "What do you want?"

"You think you can find me a buyer for this?" I took the first container of drugs out of my bag and handed it over.

He took it, cracked the lid, and looked it over, glancing at me.

"Where'd you get this?"

"Took it off a ganger who annoyed me."

"This all you got?"

"These two as well." I took them out and passed them over.

"That it?"

I nodded and he turned to the woman, who'd sat up and was suddenly much more interested. "What grade?" he asked her.

She opened each of the boxes, checking them with a finger dipped in, and rubbed across her lips for the angel dust. Her eyes lit with a bright-red artificial glow as she assessed them.

"Dust is third grade, not badly cut, but weak. The char is good…the skiff is trash," she said, before shuddering as the dust took hold. "Check that…" She gasped, blinking as the red faded, her natural blue returning. "Second grade. Took awhile to hit."

"I can move this," the half-orc grunted. "You getting more?"

"Wasn't planning on it," I admitted. "If we do a good price, though, any I come across I'll bring to you."

"I'll do thirty creds a box," he offered, then smiled as I glared at him, laying my right hand on my gun grip and reaching out to take the boxes back. "All right, thirty each for the angel. Char, I'll do fifteen each. Skiff? You can keep."

"One thirty-five?" I asked, hesitating. "Call it one fifty, and you can do whatever you want with the skiff."

"One forty."

"You have something to do with managing the floor?" I guessed, and he shrugged. "One forty, and you get me unlimited water rations."

"Unlimited?" His eyebrows crept upward.

"I like a long shower. For some reason, I keep coming back covered in other people's blood. It takes awhile to scrub off."

"Lots of blood?" he asked, and I shrugged. "What you do in the army?"

"APS operator."

"Shit, really?" he asked, as low whistles broke out around the group. "Guess you didn't invest, huh? Regretting that yet?"

"No, I did," I said with a forced smile. "When my mods are back up to speed? I'll be taking my armor back."

"Shit." He grunted again, looking at me with new eyes. "Why'd they stick you with that?" He nodded to my arm.

"Accident," I replied, not wanting to go into it. "That's why I'm here, but not for long."

"You registered with the mercs?"

"Heading there once we're done," I said, getting a nod from him.

"I'm Lucky." He paused, looking at me.

"Kabutt," I offered after a second, realizing it was his fucking *name*. "Harry Kabutt."

"You got a problem working with orcs, Kabutt?"

"Do I look like I've got a problem?" I quirked an eyebrow at him.

"I'm a half-breed…" He shrugged. "Most don't like full-bloods."

"I served with some. Damn brave."

"Fair enough." He grunted. "You need a good mod? You come to me, I'll send you to the right guy."

"An orc carver?" I asked, surprised, and he snorted.

"He doesn't need to do that shit himself. He provides the mods and he's got a few people in his team who fit them. Maybe you'll find a price better than the usual chop shops."

"I'll remember. And yeah, I'll need someone. So?"

"One forty and no lockout on the water." He smiled and knocked on my Keystone as his partner made the containers vanish.

"Pleasure doin' business." I nodded, taking the money and making a note of his ident just in case, before turning back to the lift. The gang moved out of my way quicker now, and without looking to the boss first.

The fear in their eyes made me feel a hell of a lot better.

CHAPTER THIRTEEN

The trip to the merc guild didn't take long, just under an hour of marching through the streets, watching the world. I could have gotten a cab, or hell, paid for the mag-train full-day ticket again, but I wanted to walk, to get a feel for the city, and to understand what had changed since I lived here.

The army barracks, like the rest of the military, were self-contained towns, or maybe tiny cities, considering that there were at least a hundred thousand living there, between the various squads, platoons, companies, and all the attendant hangers-on.

There were hookers, gear suppliers, bars and places to eat, entertainment and training, places to take a few days' leave, and places to run, to train, and to damn well live.

There were also the less useful hangers-on as well: thieves, rip-off merchants, and officers, not to mention the corpo types who lived in the middle ground.

Too important to associate with the likes of us, and too unimportant to live in the corpo wonderland that was the heart of the city.

It'd been ten years since I'd bothered with the rest of the city, and considering the army's rules about merc squads? Going to visit and scope the place out was likely to get serious punishment detail.

Nobody knew why, considering that most of us went to work there when we left the service anyway, if we survived, but that was just the way shit went.

I'd spent some time doing some rough background checks, knowing, goddamn *knowing* something about this guild was familiar. But for the life of me, I couldn't figure out what it was. I'd dug deeper, finding they'd gained a reputation for being more of a "no questions asked" outfit, and a lot of their higher earners were in the guild's management.

That meant that either they were rewarding the best of them, or they were taking all the juicy contracts for themselves.

That would be a problem, long-term, but for now? A no-questions-asked guild was definitely the way to go.

The merc guild Errant Mergers was at the end of a row of weapons and chop shops, clearly knowing their regular customers. There was also a massive whorehouse and a pair of bars, one of which was already rocking, considering the pair of women who staggered out into the street as I walked past.

Cheers and screams rose from behind me, and I turned, before finding a comfortable place to lean against the wall, watching the fight as it continued.

One was stripped to the waist—full upper body dermal armoring, so nothing "fun" to see—and the other was a full cyborg remodel, glossy black metal and plastic in place of skin, but the pair of them were beating the absolute shit outta each other.

The subdermal armor-wearing one was massive: boosted musculature, fists that looked like she could crush steel, and her head was a full chrome-dome. The skin was replaced with armoring, glowing red optics.

I winced as the glossy one slid past her punch, before driving a fist into her armpit.

There was a grunt from the bigger one, and I grinned, silently acknowledging that her opponent knew her stuff.

If that'd been armored properly, she could have lost her hand. But, the speed that the bigger one moved, and the mobility, suggested the armoring was incomplete.

A blow to the back of the knee, the back of the neck, the front of the throat, and another to the back of the opposite knee, and the giant went down. Two fast blows to the shoulders, numbing the arms, and a foot that flashed up high, then slammed down hard on her opponent's crown, and the fight was over.

I shook my head. The pair were heavily modded, literally tens of thousands, if not hundreds. And had the giantess managed to land a blow? It would have been all over. But as it was?

The glossy, much faster of the pair won on skill alone. I was impressed despite myself, and I smiled before heading off again. I rolled my neck as I tried to remember why the hell this merc guild stood out among all the other bottom feeders when I'd gone looking for the nearest with my RI.

Something to do with Richie, I was sure, but it just wouldn't come right now. I shrugged it off. Once I had a decent mod again, I'd be able to recall it perfectly. It wasn't important, though. Most of those who worked in the army had either dealt with or moonlighted with the guilds at one time or another.

I was an exception. As an army brat, I'd not done much, and those I'd dealt with obliquely with friends? They'd mostly changed hands or been renamed, bought out, or taken over in—very—hostile takeovers.

It meant I needed somewhere fresh, somewhere that didn't know me, and somewhere that, when I fucked off, it didn't matter. No long-term contracts, no background checks…I needed a shitty, dodgy guild, that was all, and these assholes ticked all those boxes.

The building was squat and wide, the front door bracketed on either side by a pair of orcs, glaring at anyone and everyone who came past.

"Ident," one snapped at me when I strode up, and I extended it, knocking on the reader he extended. His brow furrowed as he tried to read it.

Glancing at the other, and clearly smarter of the two, I quirked an eyebrow in question.

"You a member?" he asked, and I shook my head. "What you want?"

"To join." I waited as they looked me over, and the first one continued trying to read the screen.

"Go in. Second on right. Red desk." The other glanced at his companion and sighed.

I nodded my thanks and moved in, noting that the first guard still hadn't noticed I was moving. The mere thought of letting an orc do a mod on me? It was insane.

Some of them were smart, sure, but of all the races that made up the city, orcs were invariably the dumbest, most violent, and the ones most likely to be taken down by the enforcers if anything was happening.

Having a pair of them out front as guards?

It sent a message, all right—one that suggested the guild didn't have a fucking clue what it was doing.

The only people likely to attack a merc guild were other guilds, so the orcs would be taken down from a distance before they ever saw their opponents.

What the orcs would do, though, at the slightest provocation, was beat the shit out of people. So although having them on the door would intimidate regular citizens, it made anyone with a clue think twice about these amateurs.

That made the guild perfect for me.

Marching straight up to the red desk, and the bored-looking elf who sat behind it, polishing her nails, I offered my ident chip, this time unlocked to show my military service and status as an elite operator.

She went from uninterested, to confused, to wide-eyed in a handful of seconds, before glancing at me and then away, clearly searching for something to do to look busy as she sent messages.

"I need to register," I said after a few seconds of her frantically sorting through things on her screen.

She bobbed her head, forcing a quick smile.

"I'm…just looking for something, sir!" she assured me hurriedly, as others at the desks around the room got up, shuffling out of the room.

More and more vanished, including the handful of people who had been looking at the jobs boards at one end, or arguing over missions.

"You've got some fucking nerve!" a voice called out, and the elf behind the desk darted away as I turned and looked at the figures marching out of a pair of double doors at the other end of the hall.

"What?" I asked, confused and staring at the five men and a woman who marched out of the back rooms, guns at the ready.

"APS, eh?" their leader snarled, marching right up to me and shoving me, hard. "You think we'd forget? That we'd just forgive and move on, not fucking judge *you*?"

"What the fuck are you…?" I snapped back, staggering. Then I hesitated, as finally, *finally* the traitorous memory surfaced.

Richie, drunk, laughing his ass off as he talked about a job he'd done right before joining the APS. He was literally days away from a solid year in training, so he had gone off the rails, and he'd taken a load of "credits only, no questions" jobs.

One of them had been for a gang—some hacker had been pissed at another gang or something; I'd never paid that much attention—and they'd hired Richie to do a little "distracting." In pure Richie style, he'd blown half the apartment block up, and had shot the shit out of anyone who tried to get at him, killing a handful of their people.

So he'd claimed, anyway. The exact number changed regularly, from one or two, to fifteen, depending on the audience. He'd then hung around, taking potshots while holed up behind cover, having a great time.

He'd even released a canister of TRX-42 into their atmo, literally dosing a bunch of them on nasty psychedelics, making them see fuck knew what.

Worst of all, he'd done it all while off his head on some very good angel dust. After about a year and a half, when he'd been forced to actually come down and go clean by the APS Corps, not to mention going all in on his tech skills and joining my team, he'd finally seen the "minor details" he'd missed when taking the job.

It was a gang versus gang job, yeah, but he'd been identified by the gang, and he showed them how effective mercs could be. They reformed their gang as a merc company, after that, and got access to heavy weaponry. They also marked a vendetta against him. And yeah, that was why their logo was familiar.

We'd all been shown it and warned to stay the fuck away from anyone wearing that logo if we were alone and unarmed.

Then we'd been told that if we were ever alone, unarmed, or stupid enough to let them get the drop on an APS operator? We deserved what we'd get.

It was also probably why the guards were outside, I assumed. So no lunatics could rock up and toss in a gas grenade, then seal the doors and laugh their ass off.

"Well, shit!" I growled, before dodging to the side as he lunged at me with an electric shock baton extended. "Whoa! Stop it, you stupid fuck!"

"You're a dead man!" he screamed, practically frothing at the mouth. He swung for me again; the others spread out, guns leveled.

"It wasn't me, you stupid fucker!" I shouted, jumping back again. "I came to join up!"

"Bullshit!" He lunged again, this time flicking a knife around and trying to stab me with it.

I blocked, a backhand swipe, left to right with my right hand, grabbed the shock baton with my left—which was a mistake; that fucking stung despite it being a robotic hand—and I kicked him full force in the balls, dropping him with a wheeze, tossing the baton aside before freezing as the others pointed their guns at my head.

"Whoa," I repeated. "Look, I didn't do shit to you, none of you, all right? I heard about it, and figured you'd know what we were capable of, that's all."

"Oh, we know." The woman smiled coldly, her grazer rifle pointed unerringly at my face. "Drop the guns."

"Fuck's sake!" I shouted, exasperated. "It…"

"We know it wasn't you." Another of them stepped up to my left, and I looked at him, shocked and wondering why the hell they were like this then.

"Huh?" I asked, articulately.

"We just don't care!" The one who I'd kicked in the balls grunted as he climbed to his feet, limping in closer, before punching me in the face.

I staggered against the wall, bounced off, and raised my arms, reaching for a gun and ready to sell my life dearly, if that was all I had left, when someone plowed into me from the side, lifting me and driving me back into the wall.

I gasped, the air knocked out of me, and half fell onto the orc who'd just hit me. I blocked a punch, then another, then cried out as I was hit with a taser round, hissing in pain as I collapsed to the floor, jerking and spasming.

Hands ripped my gun free; a voice lifted in pleasure at the revolver, even as someone stomped on my crotch, then punched me in the face.

There was a brief respite from the pain when the charge finally expired. Then the next kick landed, and the world around me spun.

Others came fast and hard: kicks, punches, the butts of rifles, another taser round…It all blurred as they kicked the absolute fuck out of me. The orcs grunted as they put serious effort in, making me cry out as even with my body armor, my additional armoring on my clothing, and all my attempts to curl up and weather the storm failed.

"Judge this, motherfucker!" someone screamed, and a booted foot smashed into the side of my head, filling the world with light and pain.

They emptied my pockets of ammo and the medikit—the bastards—and laughed about it, before spitting on me, and going back to kicking.

The first of my ribs broke under the blows, and then quickly so did a second and a third. I tried to get my blade out of my boot, only to have a boot slam into my face and stars explode all around me.

More came, and then, after what seemed like hours, mercifully, it stopped.

I laid there, wheezing in pain and shock, and shuddering. Tides of agony rolled through me, before words, meaningless in my haze of pain, were exchanged overhead.

I was dragged across the floor, coughing, blood running free from dozens of wounds, only to hear a sound that I knew instinctively was seriously bad for me.

Laughter.

There were beeps—a keypad, my brain distantly registered—and then clunks as a lock disengaged, before I was unceremoniously tipped down into an air lock.

I crashed into the bottom. The hatch below me was solid metal and rang out as I hit. I laid there for long seconds, barely clinging to consciousness.

"He asleep, you think?" I heard from above, then more laughter. "This'll wake him up!"

Sudden wetness, warm and stinking, as someone overhead, to the amusement of their friends, pissed on me.

The last thing I heard from them, besides one of them commenting on how nice their "new gun" was, was a voice that called down to me.

"There's no open hatches in the area, but if you head a half kilometer to the north? You might find a way into the canning factory. That's your only chance."

"Wha…?" I whispered. Rage, fear, pain and horror fought in me, with the overwhelming disbelief that this had happened.

"Yeah, good luck, you judgy bastard…" he called to laughter. "Consider us even, you fuck!"

I looked up at him, only able to focus one eye, the other swollen shut.

He reached out to a pedestal and started to input a code.

I saw it, and the location of the air lock, the hatch—all of it made terrible sense.

They had the guild house over an entrance to the undercity, one of the abandoned ones, and they'd sealed it off. Now they were going to use it to dump their trash.

Laughter rang out as one of them said something; the figure overhead paused, letting someone else move in to look down at me. He grinned before pulling out a shitty handgun and emptying the magazine, save for one round.

Then he threw that down, hitting me in the side with it, before holding up my goddamn handgun and waggling it from side to side and making sure I could see that he had it.

"Thanks for the new toy!" he called down. "I always wanted one of these!"

I glared at him and focused before cursing. The battery in the grip was dead. I'd totally forgotten to charge it after the Mr. Crispy incident.

"Bye!" he called. More laughter rang out, and the hatch under me gave a sudden, ominous *clunk*.

I shifted, frantically looking around and seeing the rungs of a ladder right behind me. I twisted, reaching…and saw them retract into the wall, before the hatch below me slid open, and I fell with a scream into the blackness of the undercity.

CHAPTER FOURTEEN

I crashed into something soft with a grunt, the impact almost absorbed, before whatever it was shifted, letting loose a growl.

I rolled to the side, blind, falling off whatever it was, feeling leathery carapace and warm scales as I went. I hit the ground, left hand catching my weight for a second, and then my right hand came down…into a deep puddle.

I fell sideways, face-first into the water, gasping as I forced myself back up, struggling to get my body to react after the savage beating I'd taken. But at least my new arm still worked.

Dragging myself free of the water, I frantically dug through the pockets of my jacket, thankful that they'd been too busy kicking the shit out of me to search me properly.

The cheap goggles that I'd gotten from Gunther on my first visit were still there, and I struggled to pull them on, gouging a bleeding cut on my forehead with my steel fingers and making it worse.

I hissed in pain, but blinked frantically. The goggles adjusted, linking to my chip and…

And suddenly the tunnel was bathed in green light. The tail of something I didn't want to see the rest of vanished around the corner, out of sight.

I shook myself, quickly panning left and right, checking the entire area.

I was laid on what had once been train tracks, I guessed. The lip of a raised platform to my right blocked off most of the view in that direction, the ground ran off ahead of me to bend around to the right, and behind to bend out of sight to the left.

The ground was covered in a dozen centimeters, if not deeper, of old mud, filth and…and tattered, shredded clothing. I searched hurriedly, knowing the gun had come with me, and hissed in pain as I tried to move quicker.

I felt like I'd been hit by a truck. Hell, I probably looked like it too.

After a minute of looking, I found it. The old-fashioned slug thrower laid in a puddle, making me curse as I shook it, desperately emptying as much of the water and muck out as I could, before quickly checking the mechanism.

Searching around some more, I found an abandoned knife—a machete, more like—as opposed to the short blade I had on my ankle, and I felt a lot better with that in hand.

I also found a load of what could only be piles of shit scattered around. When I checked one of them, swallowing against the disgust that rose in me, I found it was liberally dotted with shards of bone and teeth.

Humanoid-looking teeth.

Those fucktards had been using this tunnel to dispose of their victims for a while, presumably people who they either owed money to, or who owed them money. But who knew, really.

It might have been the Girl Scouts who came to sell them cookies for all I cared. All I was sure about was that they should have fucking shot me in the head before dumping me.

One body or a hundred—I might have no authority here, but that wasn't going to change anything. I'd get them for this.

Whatever I'd landed on was clearly used to regular feeds from above, and for it to move away when I'd still been alive? I had to assume either it wasn't dangerous—which would normally equate to the same chance of survival down here as those Girl Scouts would have had in a bear's den—or it was easily startled, and it'd be back once it was hungry.

Deciding that was the most likely of the outcomes, I forced myself to my feet, and scrubbed my hands in the puddle, before limping across to the raised platform. I dragged myself up and onto it, collapsing, panting, when I finally got my entire body over.

I laid there for long minutes, gasping and waiting for the pain to subside some, staring at the ancient, corroded metal of the ceiling, and wondering where I could lay my hands on a fuckload of high explosive.

Both far too long after I made it onto the platform and far too soon for my body, I forced myself back to my feet, left arm pressed to my stomach. I hissed out a breath, seriously glad I'd been wearing so much body armor.

I should be dead, or at least unable to move, so many bones broken that my only option was to lie there until something got hungry.

Instead, I was up and moving. Yeah, I was in serious pain, but I was also able to look around, seeing a pair of exits from the platform. They were both unmarked, and I chose the nearest one at random, bracing myself against a tiled wall as I shuffled along. I had the machete gripped tightly in my right hand, the gun—which I seriously doubted would fire, and even if it would, would draw *way* too much attention—was stuffed into a pocket, ready for an emergency.

The walls were filthy, a combination of old mold that had climbed high and fungus that covered unidentified piles in the corners. They released clouds of spores when I pushed past, making me cough and hack to get them out of my lungs. I grimaced, noting some old, and not-so-old, blood smears here and there.

I tried to walk properly, but could barely stay upright, and left smears of my own blood along the wall as I went, adding ambiance for the next victim.

The corridor joined another, but of course, it led down, rather than up. An arched ceiling little higher than my head was covered in dangling old growths of fuck knew what. I continued along it, no thought beyond following it and hopefully getting out.

The tunnel dipped lower and lower, before splitting around a metal-covered gate. Massive padlocks and welds sealed steel over it from fuck knew how long ago. I leaned against the gate, squinting into the gaps, trying to figure it out, before finally nodding to myself.

A lift, presumably one that led to the lower floors and higher, considering the shaft that vanished in both directions. But someone had *really* not wanted this opening again.

I looked left and right, and having no reason for one over the other, picked left. If you were stuck in a maze, and kept choosing left, you'd eventually find your way out…or so I was told once.

It sounded like bullshit to me, but hey, it wasn't like I could file a complaint if it was wrong.

A handful of minutes passed in silence, beyond the occasional grunt and groan from me, or the sudden skittering of claws brushing against something nearby, before I found my first body.

It was in a bad way, having been shredded by dozens, if not hundreds, of tiny claws at some point. The remains, what little there were, were desiccated and broken, bones long since pulled this way and that as creatures foraged in the corpse.

I hissed in pain, crouching down and starting to search, little hope remaining. But I had to try. Most of the corpse was gone, eaten and broken, but whatever had feasted on them had no taste for metal.

A small chipset—no clue what it was, but about an inch across, with three tubes attached on the back, and spaces for connective tissue—was left behind.

I picked it up and pocketed it, searching the rest of the corpse. Aside from their standard neural jack at the back of the neck leading to the Keystone—which looked like something had gnawed it—I found nothing.

I left that, embedded as it was in the spine, and frankly worthless; I moved on again.

Corridors came and went, shuttered and sealed mostly, but the occasional one was clear. Now and then, I'd find signs that this corridor had been sealed as well in the distant past.

I passed more bodies, scattered and broken, the vast majority missing their mods. I gripped my machete tighter, barely able to stay on my feet, exhausted, still bleeding steadily and…

I blinked, suddenly realizing that I'd stopped. I'd reached the end of the tunnel, a solid grate welded in place over it, and I'd been staring at it for who knew how long.

Glancing around, I tried to decide where to go, then shook myself. I could barely focus, I was that tired. I made my way to the edge of the grate, sitting and pressing my back against it and the sloped wall of the tunnel, telling myself it was just for a few minutes.

Just a few minutes, while I caught my breath.

I didn't know how long I'd been out, head resting on my arms, drawn up tight around my knees, when the tugging sensation finally grew strong enough to register.

Blinking, I felt something tugging against my back, rhythmic, rough…

I twisted, pulling free and turning, then freezing at the growl of protest, and the blind eyes that stared back at me through the grate from inches away.

I frantically grabbed at my side, forcing myself to my feet and staring in horrified fascination as the specter shifted, pushing itself up as well, growling in anger at its interrupted meal.

Its face—no, its *chin*—was covered in red blood. I checked my side again, feeling the scabbed flesh that fucker had been licking through the grate.

I stared at it in shock, stunned by the knowledge that this thing had crept up on me, that it'd been *feeding* on me, lapping my blood up while I slept.

We stared at each other for long seconds. It reached up, fingers stroking down the grate, trying to get them through toward me…and I saw them.

The fingers of the left hand were tattered fragments of bone, the nails mostly missing, utterly fucked rotting meat. But the right?

They were filthy, but clearly synthetic, and I fixed on them, then the fucker that had been feeding on me.

Anger rose in me, anger that this shit-stain had dared to do such a thing. But also? Anger over everything that had been done to me. Everything that had happened over the last week or so.

I glanced at my metal arm, then his filthy one, and I nodded to myself slowly.

It was risky, insanely so, but I needed to get out of here. I needed to get back up top. And more than that? I needed to get credits. The underground was riddled with specters. In a city of a hundred million or so, all of whom were obsessed with mods, hundreds of new specters were created every day.

People who'd tried to cut corners, who'd trusted the wrong carver, or who'd been terminally unlucky in that they got a virus that was compatible with their mods, and that sparked just the wrong outcome.

All of it was possible, and it all led to a thriving undercity of creatures.

I'd heard the tales, growing up, of gangers who would buy the mods that could be harvested from specters, that they'd sell them to dodgy chop shops that asked no questions, and I gritted my teeth.

I'd never believed it, not really. Sure, there were rippers around, people who literally mugged and stripped people for their mods. To take healthy, intact mods? That was one thing. But to take the mods from a specter and put them in a normal, sane person?

I hesitated, then snarled to myself. I'd just had a lesson on how hard Artem treated those who let their guard down. It was time I looked out for myself instead. If I didn't get my ass in gear? No way that Richie and Sync would get out of their cave.

I glanced at the arm again and nodded.

Well, Lucky *had* said he'd put me in touch with a carver. I'd not want to turn up to a normal chop shop with a bag full of torn-out mods, but maybe an orc wouldn't give a shit?

Fuck knows, but one thing was for sure: if I came across more of these fuckers on the way out? I'd have to kill them anyway. Maybe it'd be worth the effort to strip them.

Either way, I was getting out of here.

The grate before me was solidly attached to the walls, made up of crisscrossing strips of steel, narrow enough that you could get a few fingers through, or, as that cheeky fuck had proved, a tongue.

I moved up close, staring through the grate and waiting, checking the width and wondering whether this fucker was dumb enough. It moved closer, so I crouched, drew my knife, and swapped it to my right hand, the machete in the left, then straightened, and moved even closer, staring into the milky-white rotting eyes of the specter.

Its skin was drawn tight, the lips pulled back to expose teeth that were split between gleaming anti-stain ceramic and blackened, rotting original.

The tongue was pinkish, the blood having soaked into it, and made it look slightly better. But half of it had been bitten off at some point, leaving a ragged section.

The overall look was of someone long dead, and not a recent body who'd gotten lost or was in the early stages, and they clearly wanted me.

We moved closer, the specter trying to worm its fingers through the gaps, even as it moved its face closer and closer.

I did the same, mimicking it and waiting.

Once we were eye to eye, literally with just the steel grate between us, inches away, I slowly lifted the blade and laid it point first against the middle of one of the gaps, waiting.

It shifted, watching the blade, clearly curious, but not aware enough to recognize it as a threat, then turned back to me as I leaned even closer.

It pressed against the grate, trying to force its tongue through this thicker section, and I moved.

The blade sank deep into one eye, digging through the decaying flesh and into the brain. It stiffened, and I shoved harder. Something scraped against the blade before it cracked, and the body just fell.

It collapsed like a puppet with its strings cut, fully dead at last, although I'd never understood entirely why, considering they were literally the dead being puppeted by their mods until the brain was destroyed. I mean, why still the brain?

Either way, I pulled the knife back and wiped it clean, before searching the grate more carefully. After a few seconds, I growled to myself. It was sealed too well. *Sod's Law.*

I set off back the way I'd come, limping, still in a hell of a lot of pain. But as I stretched out the muscles, forcing them to work, I found that although I was a mess of bruises, I probably wasn't quite as badly fucked up as I thought.

I had some broken ribs, definitely, and I was basically one big bruise from head to toe, but the more I moved, the less it hurt in most places.

A decent medikit had to go on the shopping list now. A medium dose of good nanites would have me fixed up and back to peak health by the time I'd slept the day away.

I tried connecting to Gunther, to the city net, and then finally to anyone, including the fucking enforcers. Yeah, too deep. No connection at all, and I growled as I came to the first grate that a way through had been forced open.

The entrance was down near the ground, bent into the corridor I was leaving, and I hissed with pain as I laid down on the floor and dragged myself through the gap, grunting as I climbed back to my feet on the far side.

This new tunnel was much like the rest: flat tiled floor, arched ceiling, and small, presumably once-white tiles that covered the walls. I hesitated, seeing a map at one point, a handful of meters into the new tunnel. But considering it helpfully didn't have so much as a "you are here" and nothing was marked clearly?

I moved on.

It ran for a few dozen meters, then split to the left and right. After sniffing the air, trying to locate any hint of a way to go, I thoroughly fucked my previously well-reasoned out plan of always going left by going right.

There was a reason. I wanted to find that corpse, after all, and considering the direction I'd gone, back away from the corpse, then right, then right again? I was heading back to what I hoped would be a parallel path.

It wasn't, of course.

It led to another grate across what I assumed had been another lift access, splitting left and right, and I took the right, finding a set of steps that led downward a minute or so later.

I winced with each step down, but soon passed another two bodies. These two had clearly fallen in combat, and I paused, searching them both.

A handgun with no rounds and after a few seconds of mentally arguing with myself, I pocketed an optical implant: a full-on, old-school eye mod that covered half the right side of the corpse's face.

The sounds that echoed around the stairwell as I removed it were horrific, and yet…judging from some of the bodies I'd seen already, there'd been far worse sounds in the past than the cracking of bones and the grunt of ripping free tech.

An hour passed. The bottom of the stairs led to a T junction, and I took a right, guessing I had a pattern by now, and after hitting a dead end, went back and took a left instead.

I passed bodies here and there, pausing to make sure of them before moving on if they were more or less intact, and searching them as I went.

Surprisingly, I found credit-chips, as well as things like watches, rings, and more on the corpses. But the lack of any viable weapons?

Someone had passed this way before me.

There was no way that a citizen of Artem walked around unarmed by choice. I could get occasional people being dropped by the merc assholes, and had I not landed on whatever lived in the tunnel? I'd have broken more bones and I'd probably not have gotten far, admittedly. But most?

I had to guess these were ordinary people who came down here for other reasons. Searching for loot, hiding maybe, or…

I searched the bodies I passed more carefully, not just for mods and weapons, but for how they died, and for those with missing mods, when they'd been removed.

More and more, now that I started to check, had been stripped post-death I guessed, and that pointed to others coming this way, looking for mods.

That gave me hope, lightening my step, right until I took the next corner and walked out into a sudden wide open underground station area with a dozen specters standing listlessly around one, much larger, fucking *armed*, and yeah, aware.

I'd just found a goddamn ghoul.

CHAPTER FIFTEEN

I staggered to a halt, freezing, staring open-mouthed in horror at the figures right before me, and they slowly turned to stare at me as well.

A dozen of them, all in various states of decay and collapse—bodies that ranged from perhaps days old, to decades and probably more—stood as if they'd found out their dog ran off with their partner and left them a fresh turd in their pillow as a goodbye, heads hung, shoulders slumped, and arms stilled by their sides.

Until the fucker in the middle made a sound. It was a click, sounding almost like a lock snicking closed, but ending in a hiss of static. At that noise, they all shifted, seeming to go active all at once, reaching for me.

I spun, running in the opposite direction, bypassing the way I'd come down with only a brief panicked glance. There was no way out that way, no way to the surface I'd seen.

The click sounded again, followed by a fucking *boom* from the shotgun. I cursed as the solid slug tore past my head. Every legend of the specters I'd ever heard rose in me, making my asshole clench in fear as I forced battered and bruised and exhausted limbs to carry me ever faster.

I knew there were different grades of specters. Everyone did. But anything beyond the mindless feeders? Insanely rare. Like, there were occasional outbreaks from them, or rumors and tales of them happening, but fuck me! I never expected to see a fucking *ghoul*.

The ghouls were their equivalent of soldiers, or if you believed the tales, they were what happened to a soldier who'd gone bad. Not just in the traditional mod-extreme and virus ways, but in the "fucked up and slaughtering civilians" way.

Ghouls had serious mods, usually combat ones, carried weapons and could use them, and tended to act as low-level leaders for the specters.

That itself was a serious source of argument. Most people didn't want to even accept that specters existed, for fuck's sake, and those who did?

They wanted to believe that *all* grades of specters were the same: brain-dead, puppeted by viruses written by evil hackers, and weaponized.

That something could command the others, that they could think to lead them, to use weapons and more? And that they could become these from any of the races? Humans, orcs, elves, goblins…any of us?

It was terrifying to a society built on modding itself.

I darted into the next opening in the station, emerging into an abandoned train tunnel, and dropped to the edge of the platform, skidding over the side to fall to the tracks below with a grunt.

I hissed in pain, forcing myself to keep moving. The lurching steps behind me grew in volume, and I ran again, left hand pressed tight to my side, right hand full of machete as I frantically searched for a way out.

The tunnel was huge, from way back when people had traveled across the city in vast numbers down here, and the trains were appropriately massive as well, meaning that the first emergency hatch I passed after only a hundred meters was fucking miles out of reach above me.

I cursed, staggering on and on. The tunnel twisted slowly left and then right, in great, slow arcs.

Some two hundred meters on, gasping for breath, I finally collapsed against the wall, unable to go on. My entire body screamed at me that I was fucked and needed to just stop and die, my broken ribs slowly doing more and more damage to me.

I'd passed a handful of bodies already, most of them torn asunder, literally shredded into separate parts, unrecognizable as humanoid beyond the occasional skull; bones had been broken apart, presumably to get at the marrow inside. But the figures that shuffled into view were terrible to behold.

They were a mix of old and new, but what they really were was *intact.* That might not sound terrifying when you considered the original horror of what they were—that they were the dead, or brain-dead at least.

But these weren't the barely upright figures I'd usually seen as specters. These were solid, most of them armored, integrated mods, and several still had…one of the front-runners wore military body armor. It was an Air Force rig— one of their perimeter guards, I mentally tagged him as. Although his gun was gone, his vest and uniform, tattered and torn, remained.

My heart raced, panic surging that his armoring and mods might give him more of an advantage over me. Then I focused in and realized that he was also gifting me a goddamn chance.

As part of his uniform—and he still had them attached—were the ammo pouches. Even at this distance, I could see they were full. It might not be ammo I could use in here, but it was likely that it was. And any chance was a better one than I'd had a minute ago.

He was third in line, and I could already see others stumbling out behind him.

"Okay, you want to play? Let's play," I muttered. The panic that had risen before, the ragged emotions I'd been dealing with for days, the edge of exhaustion and more, faded away under a layer of determination and professionalism.

I needed some time with him, to search him properly. So far, he and the rest of the first three had demonstrated they were the fastest of the pack, so that was fine.

What was needed was to kill the other two in the lead, slow him down, and take out the next nearest competitors. Then draw him away from the rest.

I could do this.

Checking quickly behind me, and seeing that the tunnel drew off into the distance to the limit of the goggle's range unimpeded, I nodded, and rather than waste any more time, started forward toward the incoming horde.

The first in line was an ex-corpo type, which made the entire thing much more palatable, considering the grey and filthy suit he wore. Hands reaching, he lunged at me, eyes glowing bright blue in the darkness; the chest looked too big and bulky for his frame, indicating subdermal armoring or a hidden removable kit.

I didn't care, slashing the machete left and right in a figure eight. He was left fingerless. And then a hard slash, left to right, removed the head, sending the corpse crashing to the floor, twitching.

The next in line was too close to repeat the move, as was my actual target, coming up behind him. I spun, hacking the arm almost off at the elbow with the machete, before twisting around, ducking and grabbing the remaining arm by the wrist, tugging her forward and flipping her over my shoulder, dirty-blonde hair streaming through the air.

She hit the ground hard, and I straightened, twisting the arm, and stomped on the side of her head while pulling, firmly.

I felt and heard the snap of the neck, but it was the machete chopping down into the skull that finished her off.

I wasn't as fast as I'd hoped, slowed by the wounds, and my target in the ammo vest plowed into me, fingers reaching and drawing long scratches down the side of my bloody, bruised, and swollen face.

He tried to bite me, teeth lunging for my throat, and I stabbed him in the stomach on instinct, before cursing and head-butting him to get some room.

The others were getting too close, and I shoved him backward. His foot caught on something and sent him sprawling, before he started to rise again.

I lunged forward and kicked him in the face, then hacked wildly at the next two that drew close, before turning and hobbling off, trying to open up some distance between them and me.

A hundred meters or so farther on, gasping with the pain of my wounds, I stopped again, bracing myself against the wall of the tunnel. They were still in sight, only a dozen meters back for the first of them. I forced myself to move again, stepping up and slapping the reaching hands aside, then beheading the first of them, grinning as I looked at the next. The ammo vest stood out. I had maybe six or seven meters from this one to the next; I ducked under the outstretched arm, the other having broken, apparently, in our fight before.

Stabbing upward, the tip of the machete sank into the underside of his chin…then the worst possible thing happened. It hit something hard as hell, and the goddamn blade snapped off at the hilt!

I froze, staring in horror, before its arm swung in and wrapped around me from behind, bear hugging me and dragging me in close to those flashing teeth.

I panicked, left arm braced against his chest, and I dropped the useless hilt, bracing the heel of my hand under the snapped-off blade base and shoving, even as I fought to break free of the bear hug.

Whatever augments or mods this fucker had before his death, his working arm was like a piston, slowly dragging me in closer and closer, and my own could barely keep us apart. Flashing "overload" warnings popped up in my vision. I snarled, grabbing the blade and cutting my fingers as I dragged it out, then angled it toward the back and shoved again.

Whatever internal work he'd had done, the blade scraped across something, then slid almost smoothly upward, punching into the brain via a gap, and he collapsed atop me, crashing us both to the ground.

I hissed in pain, desperately trying to roll free, only to find that the arm that had been around me was locked tight. The body atop me kept me in place, and I snarled in frustration, determined not to go out like this.

Bracing my knees against his stomach, I roared with the effort, pushing him back. But as soon as the ammo pouch was visible? I was in it.

The first pocket held rifle ammo, as did the second. The third was a handgun, fortunately, and I could feel something hard in the lower pocket as well.

That wasn't important, though, because I could damn well hear the fuckers closing on me. I fumbled the seals open, pulling a magazine free for a different model of handgun than the one I had—of course—and I had to waste time flicking free the individual rounds.

A face appeared over the shoulder of the body on me, and I focused and fired in one motion. The echoing retort of the gun in the tunnel made it abundantly clear that I was now even shorter of time than I'd thought I was.

The single shot I had, thoughtfully given to me by the asshole who stole my revolver, took my target in the right eye. He fell soundlessly, brain and bone decorating the tunnel behind him. The round sparked off the wall and vanished, as I frantically reloaded from the loose rounds.

Three I managed to get into place before the next appeared, and he took two shots. The first bounced off his chrome-plated skull as I swore in frustration.

Two more rounds into the gun, and the next three figures went down one at a time.

That was eight, or maybe nine? I didn't know. Fuck, it might have been seven. But I had a few seconds, and I used them well, reloading, getting shots off only as the figures closed the distance—two more, then a third going down.

I grinned, reaching for more…and found the cupboard was fucking bare.

The second magazine was for an incompatible handgun—not much of a problem, but it was the red iridescent strip around the tip of the bullets, marking them as high explosive, that was the issue.

The reason such bullets were marked was that they couldn't be used in regular handguns; they needed specific magazine and contact points.

The army was exceedingly particular on this, going so far as to demonstrate— using a cadaver with a shitty cybernetic hand—exactly what happened when you tried to use them in a regular handgun.

The detonation, the destruction of the gun, the hand holding it, and the remains of the body that had once held it?

It made an impression that stuck with you.

What also made an impression on me was the sound of footsteps.

I looked up, seeing the figure approaching out of the darkness at my goggle's maximum range. I cursed, struggling to get free; the arm behind my back still clicked away as it processed the last command it'd been given, and tried to crush me.

The ghoul walked slowly closer, a tactical shotgun lifted and pointed at my head, each step slow and methodical as it approached, then hesitated as I made no move to shoot the fucker.

I had no ammo, of course, and whatever was running the show behind its tactical goggles clearly realized that.

The shotgun slowly tracked to my right hand, locking in on the handgun clutched there in warning. I dropped it, only to have the ghoul kick the gun aside, before slowly circling me.

It clicked and hissed, the static sound rising and falling. But what was it doing? If it was trying to talk, trying to radio for fucking assistance, maybe to order a large pizza, or who knew what, it just wasn't clear.

What was clear? The feeling of something round pressed against my right kneecap. I'd braced my knees against the dead one's chest, trying to force it to release me, or to find the strength to get free.

Now one of them was pressed against something that felt suddenly familiar.

Three things came to mind instantly: a baseball, a stupid little container for gum that Scott was always buying, mainly because he could bounce the container off the walls to ricochet into the corner of our shared chill area back at base…

And a *very* specific kind of grenade.

I lifted my right hand slowly. The shotgun whipped back around to lock onto it, even as my left hand slid into the pocket, finding the grenade and slipping it free, dumping it into my crotch, then sliding up slowly.

The fixation it had with staring at my hand made it clear that even if it was more aware than its brethren, it still wasn't firing on all cylinders.

As soon as my right—flesh—hand was out of sight, I lifted the left, and instantly the shotgun tracked across. It froze, locked onto the hand, and I forced myself to breathe again. The sweep of the shotgun's barrel over my chest had made my asshole twitch like I'd been given bowel prep for a surgery, and it was about to go nuclear.

With the fucker fixated, though, I lifted the hand higher, moving it slowly back and forth, waving then lowering and slowly slipping from sight under the body that pinned me.

He shifted, tracking the arm, moving closer, and I grinned. My right hand closed on the grenade and felt the familiar ridges, as well as the thumbprint.

Activating it was as easy as breathing. The thumb plate, once triggered, would pop clear, storing the activation signature inside, as the use of a fucking EMP grenade in civilian areas was a serious fucking offense.

That this dead fool had one?

That spoke wonders as to how he'd ended up down here. Either he'd been hunting the dead as I sort of was now and it was a last-ditch backup, just in case, or he'd intended it for himself. Because using an EMP?

It wasn't something that most low-level mods would survive.

They'd need full nanite replacement packages.

Use it somewhere outside? Or in, just as a wild example, a corpo headquarters?

You were looking at millions, if not billions of credits of damage, not even counting the deaths and physical damage.

EMPs more powerful than the grenades, were seriously hard to get hold of outside of the military. And even there, they were watched more closely than a wandering priest who found their way into a preschool.

Either way, as I gently pressed my thumb to the activation plate, and I felt it shiver then disconnect, starting the five-second countdown, I smiled.

I'd been luckier than I had a right to be, finding one of these. My organelles weren't going to like me much—they were biomechanical, not electronic, so would survive with only their installation nanites wiped; my arm, though, was gonna be *fucked.*

I set a two-second shutdown to my goggles, hoping being offline they'd survive, and triggered an emergency deactivation protocol for my RI.

It might survive…My brain mod? My left arm? Nope.

This was gonna suck donkey dick.

The ghoul moved closer, shifting to line its shotgun up on my forehead, clearly tracking the sudden spike of activity in my nanites with whatever senses these fuckers used in place of normal eyes…and I grabbed the shotgun barrel with my left hand, yanking it sideways.

It fired, any sign of aggression enough to set it off. The explosion of the shotgun going off literally right next to me was enough to burst my left eardrum, and red-hot fléchettes smashed into the ground right next to me, ricocheting in all directions.

I dragged it hard to my left; the ghoul yanked it back and tried to free the shotgun barrel, fixated on it. My right hand came up. Counting down in my head—*three…two*—my goggles shut down, and I gritted my teeth, imagining the figure before me.

I sent the grenade flying like a fastball, aiming to hit it in the forehead. The sound rang out of it, hitting something…before detonating.

There was a bright flare of light as whatever magic the armament manufacturer stuffed into those fucking terrible little balls went off with three flashes. A visible pulse flooded the area, before vanishing, and then a crash nearby.

I heard the clatter of metal on metal, and I grunted as my arm dropped, dead. The constant distant thrum of activity and clatter of work that had been filtering through cracks and more in the walls?

Anything nearby shut down, and I heard distant shouting, making me curse as I tried to reboot my goggles, getting nothing, and then the same from my brain mod, my arm…nothing!

I forced myself to shove free of the fucker that'd had me pinned, its own arm that had given me so much trouble now dead. I searched my pockets until I found that damn lighter, and sparked it up.

The ghoul was dead, well and truly, as were any others nearby. But where I'd hoped to set it off and run? Nope. I was stuck down here. And if I found a way out into some factory or whatever down here that I'd just fucked with the EMP grenade?

I'd be absolutely fucked up by the workers I'd just screwed over.

The corpos wouldn't care that it wasn't the workers' fault; they'd refuse to pay them until they were working again. Meaning that anywhere from a few people to hundreds of families would be going hungry tonight.

I needed to get the fuck out of here, as I'd swapped being killed by a fucking ghoul for possibly being killed by angry factory workers. But first they'd have to fucking find me.

The EMP wouldn't have gone far, but anything in proximity would be fucked, so I needed to get moving and out of the area, get rid of the evidence that I'd triggered it—hopefully, before any more fucking specters wandered in.

I searched around quickly, finding some dry wood in a crevice off to one side, and I wrapped some torn cloth from one of the specter's clothes around it, before lighting my makeshift torch.

The difference from a tiny flare of a lighter to the bright flame of the torch was insane. I moved quickly, my left arm utterly useless and my RI not responding. And my spine?

Well, I was damn thankful I didn't have any attachments or spinal tap systems in any more, they'd need replacing for sure if I did. I knew that the actual signal was partially run through electronic methods as well, but as I could currently still move. I wasn't going to question my good fortune.

I guessed that having the body atop me and that section of my spine pressed hard against the ground might have protected it somewhat, but that was a guess.

I jammed the torch into the ground, using the armpit of a specter to hold it in place, and I got to work recovering the activation plate from the EMP grenade and searching the corpses.

I didn't have time for this shit—I *seriously* didn't have time for this—but I was fucked if I didn't do it. I was beaten to fuck, had my favorite gun stolen, my mods were fucked…

I'd not be able to get any work as a merc without working mods, and no factory work or anything like that either. So that meant that my options were find something that covered the costs of repairs at least, or end up on the streets, begging and thieving.

That or sell my soul to a gang.

If I did that? I'd never be free of them. And that was *if* a gang would take me.

The thought of Richie and Sync dying, their cryosleep failing and the pair of them simply never waking, rotting in their suits in a fucking cave, lost to everyone, all because of a bunch of dickhead mercs who'd jumped me for something Richie had done six goddamn years ago?

That it was all down to me being too slow to remember why the fucking sign had been so familiar?

That fed right back to the shitty mods I'd been saddled with and the general crapshoot that had become my life.

I gritted my teeth, working as quickly as I could.

I ignored the other bodies for now, focusing on the ghoul.

The shotgun was nice, a high-tech one as well. The ammo counter and palm ident reader were dead, but that meant that the weapon had unlocked automatically, and I quickly checked it out.

Seven rounds, five solid slugs and two…I couldn't make the writing out, not without my damn mod working in the flickering darkness, but I was betting either incendiary or bolo, considering the weight.

Incendiary was literally a massive "fuck you" to anything that you fired it at, the combination of a flamethrower and a shotgun to the face at the same time.

Fergie had summed it up once in his description of dealing with some fucker who'd been running mutated funnel-web spiders. They were augmented and enhanced to where a dedicated controller could control them, much like I could my suit, but remotely.

"Fucknoasaurus," he had said, dragged the normal clip out, and slotted a Devil's Asshole clip, turning the entire tunnel full of nightmares into a literal entrance to hell.

Bolo, on the other hand, was just evil:

two steel ball bearings connected with a short chain. When fired, they opened out and spun, creating a hell of a wound when they hit something.

In the distant past, shit like that had been used in cannons to take down enemy ship's masts. Now we used them on people who played their music too loud and ate with their mouths open in public.

Progress was wonderful.

Either way, I quickly loaded the shotgun with a slug, then one of the unknowns, and then spread out the rest, before loading the last unknown as the final shot, glad that the shotgun was a magazine-loading one rather than the old breech versions.

That done, I searched pockets, coming up with a single credit-chip that had somehow survived out of five. Even more luckily, his thumb was identifiable enough that it unlocked, and the hundred and seven credits were locked to my thumb instead as I took ownership of the chip.

Two grenades—both frag—went into my pockets, and I dragged the knife free, resolving to make the most of the chance. Ammo for the handgun was plentiful in his pockets and body armor, and for several seconds, I tried to remove his armor. It was better than mine, and we were both covered in filth and shit from down here...

It wasn't meant to be, though—there was too much damage to it. In the end, I settled for stripping it and filling my pockets.

I continued to search him, finding a handful of random bits: some ident-locked key, a trigger from another EMP grenade—making me even more curious about his path down to here—and a nice little gun cleaning kit in one long thigh pocket.

The real prizes, though, were his mods.

He'd had a chest piece embedded, heavily armored; right arm, definitely higher end than most. Hell, it had to be a tier three at a minimum. It was a full arm replacement—like mine—but Sod's Law, it was a right instead of a left.

I didn't know how I'd feel about using a recovered part, especially when it was recovered from a specter. Hell, I wasn't sure I could bring myself to do it, but...but it was a feasible way to seriously supercharge my upgrades for a much more reasonable cost.

I shook the thought away again, and got back to work checking him over.

Spinal mod—reinforcement, like mine, not a tap job like I'd need to get, unfortunately. Something in the skull, probably a high-end brain mod...I gritted my teeth and slammed the skull into the ground a few times, hoping to crack it like an egg. But the result?

It was nasty. In the end, I managed to crack it open and put the brain and eye mods into a pocket.

The mess, though—just horrible.

I moved on in a state of numbness, partly from the beatings, the exhaustion and, yeah, partly from the shit I was having to do in the dark now, all thanks to some fucks deciding that I'd make a good punching bag.

I moved onto the next, getting a hand and a heart pump, no clue what it was, but it looked well-made in the limited light I had, and I kept going.

The body that had been holding me in place had some serious mods—the right arm again, especially, but it'd looked mainly "normal," so rather than spend time checking it, and very conscious that other specters could be incoming, I simply hacked his off, roughly, and kept going.

All in all, I spent less than five minutes there, but it felt a lot longer, coming out with two right arms, a new back sheath for the shotgun, a new handgun—it was crap, but hey—two optical and one brain mod, a lower jaw mod, and a hand. I bundled them all up in the ghoul's chest mod.

It was shaped like a normal rib cage, with thick reinforcement for the organs, overlapping plates of armor, and then attachment points for internal replacement organs and more.

There were mods that I'd never seen before in there, when I'd opened the fucker up. I'd frozen, looking them over and hoping there wasn't a dead man's trigger on something; then I'd moved on.

If there had been, I'd have already been fucked, or he would have been. The chest was like an old-style knight's armor, shrunk down to fit under a skin graft, and damn it was impressive.

I stripped two more coats away, looping them under and around, tying the arms to each other and essentially making an insanely awkward bundle I could carry.

It was a fucking mess, but I was armed with a handgun with actual bullets now, as well as a spare. I had a new shotgun, and looking at it in the flickering torchlight, it was a good one. And last of all, I had some military-grade mods.

Yeah, they were salvage, but fuck it. They still had value.

I stumbled through the darkness, torch tied to my left arm, which dangled like a corpo without a dick-stiffener. The bundle, pressed tight to my chest, constantly slipped and shifted. I couldn't even carry my gun at the ready, thanks to all this shit, but still I went on.

I'd walked right into there, walked in with my eyes open and as innocent as a fucking lamb. I was an idiot, a complete fucking idiot who had almost cost Richie and Sync their best chance at life.

I wasn't doing that again, not ever. I needed to be harder, less trusting, and even more of a bastard. I needed to not give anyone a chance, not now. I was alone. I needed to act like it.

Every step I took, I repeated a promise to myself, each stumbling, limping footfall hammering it into my soul.

"I'll get revenge," I swore. "I'll judge them *all.*"

CHAPTER SIXTEEN

By the time I found a way out, it was late at night, and even by Artem standards, it was quiet, it being a few hours before dawn.

I was on the outskirts of an industrial zone. I'd spent several hours stumbling around in the dark, expecting at any second to be jumped or to walk into another specter nest, only to eventually find a steady stream of rainwater pouring in from an old drainage pipe.

Another hour of climbing the pipe, my back braced against one side, feet against the other, the package on my stomach, and a knife in hand, used frequently to clear away the various horrible fucking spiders and worse that called the drain home.

Eventually, though, I dragged myself out into the neon-lit night, staring around in shock at the steady banging, clattering, and screams of the city. Discarded packaging crates, plastic sheeting, and stolen metal surrounded me, making it clear I'd found another of the tens of thousands of homeless camps around the city.

The drain's grate had been damaged at some point, and cut away, probably to dump a body or something. But when I'd seen it above me, eventually, I'd almost given up.

Reaching it, almost falling as I tested it? Finding it was open? I'd almost wept with relief. Dragging myself up and out? It'd been harder than I could believe. The number of times I'd slipped and fallen, bracing myself and forcing my way back up? Un-fucking-believable.

I'd pushed the package out ahead of me. Only a minute later, I'd dragged myself out as well, catching two local bums arguing over whose it all was, knives drawn as they tried to take it.

My appearance was missed at first, until I raised the handgun and fired a slug into the air. The crack of the round made them flinch and drop low.

"Fuck off, or I'll kill you both," I growled.

One backed away immediately, plastering a fake smile across his face. The other licked her lips, glancing from the collection of obviously valuable mods, to the gun, and to her knife, then back again.

I counted to three, and just as I was about to shoot her in the knee, figuring she'd had her chance. She took a step back, then another. I lowered the gun, only to hear a non-too-stealthy footfall to my right.

A handful of seconds later, the man who'd backed away before crept out between two old packing crates, knife held low and ready…only to find the barrel of my gun roughly jammed into his eye socket.

He babbled out an apology, before turning and running, and I cursed him and the others peering around the various debris piles.

I grabbed the package, dragging it along the ground, gun ready, until I hit a main street, and the last of those who had been following me dropped away.

I sagged, bracing myself against the wall, before cursing as I realized two things. First, I'd been planning on calling a cab when I got to the ground level. I had the credit-chip, after all. It'd not been in use when I'd set the EMP off, so it had been fine, but I didn't have any way to actually *call* the fucking cab!

My mods were all down, even my goddamn Aug-World access. I gritted my teeth. A wave of frustration rolled through me as I tried to process everything.

I couldn't, physically or mentally, drag this load through the streets to my apartment. Hell, I didn't know where the fuck my apartment *was* from here!

Any enforcers who passed me—filthy, heavily armed, and dragging what was obviously half a fucking body—would arrest me on the spot. If I was lucky, anyway.

Most likely they'd look at it all, see it was expensive gear, and shoot me for resisting arrest or some bullshit, then take it themselves.

Any "honest" citizen—like there were any of them here—would probably report me as well.

I sagged, letting my back slide down the wall, slumping to the ground next to my loot, and stared at the neon lights overhead, thinking.

I needed to get my Aug-World access up. *With that? I could do anything else I needed to, but how the hell could I do that here?* I hissed in frustration, dismissing the people who staggered past, most of them steaming drunk. I kept thinking, until suddenly I blinked, actually seeing the advert I'd been blankly staring at for ages.

A *datadeck.* I'd not used one for literally years, and there the latest corpo-pushed model was in all its glory, a hundred meters high flashing as they advertised it. Some skinny dipshit jacked into it, hacking a firewall, then was showered with credits, knee-deep in hot men and women who clearly wanted to fuck them.

Typical corpo advert: buy this, get rich, get laid, yadda, yadda. I ignored all of that. The latest model that they were selling? Thousands of credits. And even if I had that to waste, I didn't need that shit.

What I needed, though, was a *basic* deck. The kind that kids learned to use while they were starting to unlock their cyberspace mod. Even these days, nobody was going to let a five-year-old loose on Aug-World.

They got their mods and they learned to use them, gradually getting more and more unlocked until they were adults.

In the meantime, they learned to manipulate their mods with basic decks, like those weirdos who hated mods did, and when they needed a new one? They sold the old ones to a merchant.

I forced myself to my feet, then started to search, staggering up and down three streets until I found one. A shitty buy-and-barter shop had its windows covered in grates, the door reinforced, and totally unsubtle cameras all around it, letting the staff watch out for dodgy fucks.

Clearly, I qualified. I tried the door of the twenty-four-hour shop, only to find it locked. An intercom came to life after a few seconds.

"What do you want?" a rough female voice husked.

"I need a deck," I replied flatly, dumping my burden by the door and rolling my shoulders, my left arm a dead weight. I snorted and stripped the home-made torch free, tossing it aside as I shook my head in bemusement.

"Yeah? You got credits?"

"Yeah," I replied, glaring at a lens through the reinforced glass, itself on the other side of the shutters. "How much for the deck?"

"How much you got?"

"Ten creds," I said grimly, knowing it wouldn't be enough. But if I said more? Whatever price I quoted, I'd be ripped off.

"Fuck off. You're wasting my time!" she snapped.

"Ten credits and this." I held the shitty handgun up to the lens.

"Put it in the drawer," she ordered. A drawer slid open before me, ready for me to deposit the gun.

"Get fucked. What's to stop you just taking it?"

"You want a deal? I need to examine the gun."

"You can see it just fine from there." I held it up and angled it from side to side.

"How do I know it works?"

"You want me to shoot your window?"

"Do it, and I'll come out and shoot you myself."

I smiled and waved the gun once more, before pocketing it and drawing the shotgun from over my shoulder.

"You try that, and I'll kill you and anyone in there." I showed the shotgun and its clearly heavy-duty build. "Your shitty security won't stop this, and we both know it. Ten credits, and the handgun for a basic deck, charged, and a connection jack."

"That's a lot you're asking for..." she muttered.

I snorted, staring at the lens, making it clear I knew that was bullshit.

It was a hell of a deal, and it wasn't me, as she was implying, getting the better out of this bargain. Even a shitty handgun she'd be able to sell for a hundred—more with ammo. And an old deck? If I'd been searching cyberspace for one, it'd have been twenty credits, maybe thirty, *delivered*.

Ten seconds of silence, and then a rifle barrel slid out of a port across from me, leveled at my stomach.

"Put the gun in the drawer, and the credit on the pad, then take the deck, no funny business," I was warned, and I grunted, tapping the credit-chip to the pad and checking the amount that showed up.

Fifteen credits.

"Want to try again?" I glared. "Military mods." I thrust my chin out, bluffing. "You shoot me, all it's gonna do is piss me off."

There was a long pause. The screen shifted to show ten credits. I released the payment, then put away the chip, and took the handgun out of my other pocket. I made the point of emptying the gun, daring them to say something, before putting it in the drawer, pocketing the bullets, the cable, and the datadeck and backing up with my gear.

The drawer slammed shut and the gun withdrew, making it clear the deal was done.

I dragged everything around the corner, sitting on the armor in the rain, ignoring the looks I was getting as the constant hammering washed the filth away…as well as a stream of old blood from my "seat."

I plugged the cable into the deck. My stomach dropped as the screen remained blank, before plugging the other end into the jack at the base of my neck.

It took a few seconds; then, mercifully, the screen lit. The old deck barely booted, but it was working.

Five minutes later, an automated cab pulled up, the trip back to my apartment already paid for.

I sat back, eyes flickering as the city outside streamed past, lost in a digital world as I assessed the damage. The pulse had been strong enough to wipe unshielded tech, but whatever calibration the grenade used, it'd barely gotten through my skin. I vaguely remembered being told that the human body was a shitty electrical conductor.

Fuck knows really, but what I did know was that my Keystone hadn't been totally fucked beyond redemption.

That was a relief.

No.

That was an understatement: everything that was me was on that fucker. Starting with my personal ident, which would have taken weeks, if not longer, as well as far too many credits to get a new one issued, to personal memories, recordings of my friends and me in battle and parties, to my fucking favorite porn.

Everything I'd done digitally for the last twenty-five years was on that thing, and it wasn't until I saw it flicker to life that I dared consider what I could have lost.

As it was? A new external connection—the jack doubled as a decent broadcast point, after all—and I would be back in business.

My RI was intact, but the brain mod was trashed. My left arm was utterly unresponsive, but that was expected. And the spinal reinforcement was down to sixty percent durability now.

Essentially, the hardware was good still, but the digital and connective parts were fucked.

I opened my eyes at a chime from the taxi sometime later, blinking and realizing I'd drifted off to sleep. Looking out, I saw the entrance to my apartment block through the driving rain to my right, and a flashing warning that the auto cab wouldn't release the door locks until I paid the additional thirty credit "fouling fee."

Glancing down and seeing the literal dried shit clinging to my clothes? I sighed and authorized the transfer, imagining the cab giving me a prissy little sniff of complaint as I dragged myself out, grabbing my bundle and slowly slogging across the sidewalk.

The foyer was the same as ever, in that it smelled like someone had died in there, and the crazy lady was laid in a chair she'd dragged in from somewhere, head thrown back, snoring loudly.

The trip up to my floor seemed to take forever. Three people got into the lift with me, before staring in disgust as they realized the awful smell was me.

One of them went to say something, only to be grabbed by another and quickly shushed.

I heard a snippet of conversation, muttered directions to *Look at what he's carrying…Is that a body…Part of one…Shut up! Just smile…*

The one who'd started to speak reached out and hammered the button for the next floor, despite them having requested one higher than mine before, and all three hurried off as soon as the doors opened.

I looked out, dully curious, and saw a much cleaner floor, with working lights, and I shook my head in disgust at my luck. The rest of the journey was alone. When the door opened onto my floor, the gang was there, music blaring, a good dozen dancing between me and my corridor.

I stepped out, getting a disgusted look from a figure that was wearing high heels and a hat, and that was it. They pointed at me, seeing the dirt, the filth, and that I was dragging something that left a mark on the ground, where she was trying to dance, and she opened her mouth.

Before she could get a word out, one of her friends—one I dimly recognized as the one who'd been draped across Lucky's lap and who'd confirmed the quality of the drugs—slapped a hand across her mouth and made room for me.

"Do you, like, need anything…?" she asked me.

I paused. Now that the gang "knew" me, the way they treated me had changed massively.

"A shower," I said, then sighed. "Then tell Lucky I need that introduction to his friend. I need repairs, and upgrades, as well as to sell some shit."

"Drugs?" another of the gang asked, one of the guys who'd been there earlier.

I snorted, nodding downward.

A handful of lights turned on and shone at my prize, before squeals of horror—obviously feigned, considering they were either gangbangers or there as dates with them—and questions rang out.

"Mil-spec, full chest and internals," I said as Lucky stomped up out of the crowd, looking from me to the pile in question.

"Do I want to know where you got it?" he asked, and I snorted. "I mean was it anyone I know?" he corrected. "You were registering with a merc outfit, weren't you? Shouldn't you be selling this there?"

"I'll be judging them all soon," I said flatly.

"I…" He paused, then snorted and shook his head. "Normally when someone says something like that about a merc outfit, we get ready to pick up their pieces."

"You want to try it?" I made it clear I knew what he was thinking. I was there, obviously wounded, surrounded by his people and with valuable loot. I was a hell of a temptation for him, like a goat wandering into a dragon's lair and head-butting it. "Seriously, you'll never get a better chance," I promised, my voice low and hard.

"I think…" he said slowly, "not."

"Good choice." I smiled. "I've had a bad day…I'd have taken it personally."

"What's he saying?" one of the dancers whispered, shocked, to a friend. "Does he know who he's talking to?" She was quickly shushed, while Lucky nodded to my gear.

"Need a hand?" he asked, and I hesitated, desperate to say yes. But showing weakness here would be terminal.

"I'll be fine, but I'll need to see that orc…"

"Oshbob." He nodded. "I'll reach out to him, see if he'll see you. When do you want to go?"

"What time is it?" I asked.

The silence deepened as everyone considered that I didn't have access to my systems.

"Just after five in the morning," he said eventually.

"Send someone to wake me around fourteen hundred hours," I said after a few seconds. "They can take me to see this Oshbob."

"I'll see to it." He vanished back into the crowd, as I started moving again.

Ten minutes later, I was in my room, the deck having helped to get me in my damn room, and I stood under the water in my shower, glorying in the steady warm trickle.

I'd once stayed in a corpo-style place, years ago, fresh to the army. I'd been seeing a girl and wanted to make a good impression. I'd paid for the full package, taking her away for the weekend, and damn had I got it, both from her and the hotel. Almost a year's wages on a single weekend, and although she'd not stayed once I couldn't spend like that regularly, the memories had.

Now, the water from my shower a steady trickle in place of the thunderous roar of that shower? I still loved every damn second.

That my left arm was utterly dead was annoying the shit out of me right now, but at least I had cleaning gel, and I was getting the shit off me.

The condition of the water when it'd first started had been disgusting, and by the time I finally crawled out of the shower, laying naked across the sheet on my small bed, I'd exhausted at least a month's worth of personal water allocation.

Thank fuck Lucky had been as good as his word.

I laid there, struggling to keep my eyes open, as I thought about everything that had happened, and I nodded slowly to myself.

I'd walked into the merc den as innocent as could be, and what had happened, had happened. I was a bastard at times, but I was straightforward and honest, mostly.

I gave everyone a chance, and then, when they betrayed my trust? I fucked them up. And *that* was the mistake I was making.

I was giving them a chance. You had to, it was drilled into us, in the APS. If they weren't armed? If they weren't a threat, and not a confirmed target, you let them be until they were.

Richie and Sync were where they were because of the choices of others, and I was here, fucked up for the same reason. If I didn't change the way I was acting and soon?

Next time I'd not survive, and then my friends were as good as dead. No, I wasn't risking them, not like this.

It was time to stop being such a pushover. It was time to make them all fucking bleed, before they did it to me.

CHAPTER SEVENTEEN

When I woke to the banging on my door sometime later, I pulled a pair of pants on, groaning as the bruises pulled, and was surprised to find it was Lucky himself waiting when I opened the door.

"So, you always make house calls?" I stood back, before making room for him to step in, turning my back and strolling to my meager closet, dressing quickly.

"I wanted to see what you have, and Oshbob…well, he's a bit of a legend," he admitted, glancing over at the kit.

I'd taken it in the shower with me before bed, taking a few minutes to hack away the flesh that I could now see more clearly, and to disconnect as much as I could.

It was still very clearly "used" with parts of its previous owner still attached, it seemed, but fuck it.

"Mil-spec?" Lucky asked, referring to my comments last night, and I nodded.

"Took it off a ghoul." I figured it would be evident enough to anyone who dealt in such things—half the flesh that was still attached was rotting, after all.

"No shit?" he asked, eyebrows rising. "A real one?"

"Yeah, took a corner too fast and there were a handful of specters," I said, before making my position clear. "Had to kill them all, but couldn't carry everything. If there's a market for it, though, and he can do some decent deals for me? I'll bring him more."

"What you got?" He gestured to the pile, and I shrugged.

"Couple of arms, internal mods, brain mods and optics, a hand…few things," I repeated. "You speak to Oshbob for me?"

"He knows we're coming." He shrugged. "Doesn't give a shit, though."

"What?"

"He gets orcs bringing him stuff all the time to strike deals, and he barely tolerates them. Hates you humans."

"Well, what the fuck's the point of going to him then?" I asked, exasperated, my anger sparking to life.

"I owe him a favor, and you owe me one." He smiled toothily. "He might do you a deal, or maybe—depending on what this is—I'll do *you* a deal."

I saw the readiness in his eyes. He'd clearly like to have me working with him by choice, especially after I'd demonstrated my ability to bring back interesting things he could turn a profit from. But I could see the other side as well.

If I wasn't going to "play nice"?

This little room would become a bloodbath.

"As long as I get my mods upgraded and replaced, and I get paid? I don't give two fucks if it's you or him who pays me. These mods?" I gestured to the pile. "Over three hundred thousand credits' worth," I bluffed, guessing all the way.

"At retail, maybe," he agreed, glancing at the pile then back to me. "I'm not buying from a proper chop shop though, am I? And even if I was? They're contaminated. They'll need to be cleaned and…"

"They need cleaning," I agreed. "But the 'nites? Already wiped."

"You think I'll just take your word?"

I snorted, before lifting my left arm. The servos whirred, but as soon as I let go, the arm swung back down, lifeless.

"EMP," I said firmly. "All their gear was exposed. If mine's fucked? Theirs is totally wiped."

"What makes you different than them?" he asked, and I smiled.

"I wasn't as close to the pulse, and I'm alive, beating heart and all that shit. The living flesh blocks the pulse. Rotting, dead flesh? Not so much."

It was bullshit, but I didn't care. I needed the credits and replacement parts, so although I'd not be taking parts from this Oshbob—he bought chopped-up specters, after all—I needed replacement nanites. Preferably I'd get a full rebuild.

"So, what is there?" he asked again, and I sighed.

Fully dressed, I finished putting my gear away, including the shotgun into the back sheath, and I moved across to the deck. Plugging it in and checking for model identification numbers on the first two mods I came to, I pulled up the specs on the separate spinal and the main chest armor with its attached sections.

Torso Integrated Armoring	**Tier**: Three
Orion Systems cybernetic subdermal Torso Integrated Armoring with integrated internal processing and [optional] hardened datadeck storage. This model offers five integrated expansion slots to upgrade user internals, including Bio-Mesh™ internal upgrades to replace organic lungs, synth-flesh layering to protect and prevent hemorrhaging, and bionic organelles to replace basic digestive tract and organs. [Optional] Hardened Datadeck storage is the standard for enhanced security delivery operatives. Toughness: 15 Strength: 12	
Durability: 86/100	**Cost**: 11

Spinal Reinforcement	**Tier**: Three
The Nexus 9700 Spinal Reinforcement mod is a significant upgrade over the original biological, physical spine, improving upon the organic in every way. The 9700 can take significantly more damage than a biological variant, and stores three additional emergency injection ampoules, ready to give you that much-needed boost in an emergency, or when someone *really* needs to learn their place! Warranty: [60 Months] Toughness: 11	
Durability: 86/100	**Cost**: 3

"Shit, a hardened datadeck!" I looked up from the specs I'd read off, seeing the way Lucky stiffened. "You got something to say?"

"I'm thinking data courier who got lost." He looked the datadeck over. "A high-end one."

"He was geared up with EMP grenades as well as standard, and a good bit of kit beyond it, including one of the arms…that one, I think, as well as optical and brain mod," I muttered, gesturing at one of the arms.

Lucky picked it up and examined it, clearly accessing something, before nodding. "Tier three, mil-spec," he agreed, before rubbing his chin and looking over the pile. "That one's tier two." He pointed to the other arm, before sorting through the rest.

"Tier three, tier one, tier one…" he muttered, and I glared at him.

"Fuck's sake, Lucky!" I grumbled. "Why the hell'd you have me do that look-up manually if you could have scanned it all?"

"I don't work for you, Kabutt," he snapped back, before forcing a smile as he looked over the lot as one pile. "Okay, so yeah, maybe two to two-fifty in retail, but selling it to Oshbob? Like I said, he hates humans."

"So?" I asked, sensing what was coming.

"So you need a partner, someone he *doesn't* hate."

"Or, you know, I could go to another chop shop."

"Maybe. But you're on my territory, and maybe there's a tax for this kinda shit."

"Maybe you try that shit, you'll need to be dragged out and burned," I warned him, and he nodded.

"Maybe," he agreed. "Of course, *maybe* you've only got one working arm, and I've got people outside the door, ready."

"You probably have." I nodded, forcing a smile. "But let's face it, you go down this route, it might be that I sell you it all for a great price, I go get myself fixed, then I pay you a private visit, you know, when you're sleeping and alone…"

"I don't sleep alone." He grinned. "You've seen my girls."

"Yeah, nice tits." I opened my mouth, then nodded. "And they're not just for fun, are they?" I said slowly. "They're bodyguards."

"Modded all the way up," he agreed. "You try surprising them when they're having fun? It'll not end well."

"You think fucking with an APS soldier will?" I suggested. "I get my armor back, and I could slaughter you all without raising a sweat."

"You've not got your armor, though," he pointed out. "You're on your own, mods are broken, and you could do with a friend, I think. How about this? I'll pay you for all of this, and I do you a good deal. Then you go get more?"

"I need a fucking rebuild," I growled at him. "You think I could go hunting like this?"

"And I know a chop shop that'll accept my view of you as an investment." He grinned. "You do a little job or two for me, maybe go find me some more gear, pay off my investment and…"

"You think I'm going into debt with a gang?" I snorted. "Are you fucking mad? You know what I am."

"Fine. You think you've got a choice?" he asked coldly, the "good buddy" veneer pouring off him like milk from a glass. "Listen, Kabutt, you're in a shitty position to be pissing on my offers. We all need friends, and it's not like I'd be asking for anything you're not willing to do."

"Oh, really?" I laughed sarcastically. "Fucking practically charity work, is it?"

"You'd be taking care of some business for the gang, that's all. None of these fuckers are innocents," he said flatly. "Look, let's lay it out on the table. Oshbob is the only one who'll buy this from you. Nobody else is gonna buy specter mods, and he'll give you half of what he'll give me." Lucky moved past me, sitting down on the end of my bed and glancing around. The frame creaked under him as he sneered at the state of the room.

"So?" I asked.

"So I'll pay you for this, here and now. Then I'll cover you for say, twenty grand at a chop shop I know, on top of the creds for this. That gets you fixed up and back out. You bring me a hundred grand's worth of parts, and you do six jobs for me? The slate's wiped clean."

I nearly refused him outright, opening my mouth to tell him to fuck right off, before closing it. A new thought occurred to me.

"How much?" I asked after a second's thought.

"For this?" He looked it over, pretending to consider it. "Twenty thousand."

"Try again."

"Oshbob won't give you that much…" Lucky started, and I shook my head, drawing the shotgun out and laying it across my knees, not pointed at him, but not exactly pointed away either.

"You want to lay it all on the table?" I asked him, and he nodded. "Well, that works for me too. Let's dispense with all the fucking bullshit. We do a deal here and now, or only one of us, and possibly neither, leaves this room." I said it calmly, but I also said it with my fingers around the grip to my shotgun.

"That's a two-handed weapon," he pointed out.

"Only to reload." I smiled. "I won't need a second shot."

"You will when my people come in after me."

"You'll still be fucked."

"So…let's hear your offer." He nodded.

"You want me to do six hits?"

"Three outright hits, three cleaning out of security," he admitted. "Two are people encroaching on my territory. You kill them, gangbangers, so no innocents, then you go on and raid their labs, capture their chemists and bring me what you find."

"So that's four of the six jobs." I had no issue with eliminating scumbags.

"Yeah, and the salvage is mine. I'll have my people standing by, ready to move in and secure it, so don't fuck with me and try to sell it."

"No to the salvage. You can have the drugs, though. The other two…?"

"One's an outright kill. Old fucker who pissed me off. Armed to the teeth, though—he'll be hard. Merc who hit a friend of mine on a contract, killed him when there was no need."

"Anyone in particular?"

"The merc or my friend?"

"The merc," I said flatly. "Did I even bother to learn any of your crew's names?"

"Fair enough. His handle is Stinger. He's known for the…"

"For the fléchettes he fires," I finished for him, shaking my head disgustedly. "He fires a modified dart that's custom made for him, from a fucking custom rifle. It's designed to go through *walls*. He's a legend of an *assassin*, not a merc, and you think I'll just stroll up and kill him as part of this shitty deal? There's a two hundred and fifty thousand cred bounty on him. Fuck knows where I'd even find him."

I knew who he was, because yeah, I'd kept an eye on the bounty lists, and I'd been considering going bounty hunting once I was out of the APS Corps regardless. But that was with a fucking *suit.*

"Bounty would be yours," he assured me.

"Fucking too right it would be. But you might as well name a corpo head and a fucking god while you're at it, because—"

"I know where he is."

"The fuck you do," I said. "If you did? You'd have tried claiming the bounty."

"I was going to sell the location. All I want is him dead and his gun."

"Why the gun?"

"He killed my friend with it."

"So?"

"So I want his fucking gun and his head!" Lucky snarled. "The last job—"

"You can fuck off with the rest of the jobs." I snorted. "You want me to do a hit on a fucking master assassin, and then stroll over and do over some drug dealers on your patch?"

"You saying you can't do it?" he asked. "That the APS Corps rep is bullshit?"

"Do you fucking see an APS suit here?" I asked, exasperated. "Seriously?"

"So, it's about the suit, not the soldier then?" He grinned.

I glared at him. That old argument—about at which end of the arm the true weapon was—reared its head in me.

"It's a suit," I said. "It's the operator who makes the difference."

"Then the operator should be able to do this." He spread his hands wide.

"This operator could. But I'd need a fuckload more than you're offering."

"You'd get the two hundred and fifty thousand bounty as well."

"Yeah." I snorted. "Provided I live long enough to claim it, and I actually survive going after him. He'll have traps."

"Drones too, and sentries," he agreed, making me snarl in frustration.

"Are you kidding me?" I shook my head. "Look, the very least I'd need, not including the equipment, is a new arm, tier two as a minimum, a new brain mod, tier *three*, and a replacement spine…" I jerked my thumb toward my back. "Those alone are going to be close on a hundred grand. Then I'd need some decent kit, and a fucking hacker."

"I know a hacker."

"I don't give a shit if you know the Santa Bunny and you're personally ass-fucking her. It'd do me no good without the rest!" I glared at him. "Then add on decent weapons. I'd need an arsenal—decent sniper rifle at the very least, a new assault rifle, probably a Nutronics 6500, a bio-suit, and armoring."

"So, a couple of hundred grand?"

I snorted. "Yeah, basically."

"So how do we get them?"

"What?"

"We agreed to lay it all on the table," Lucky said. "I've got forty-seven and a half thousand, and I could run up a tab with a chop shop I know for thirty thousand. That gives you seventy-seven thousand..."

"And a half," I added absently, before grimacing at the grin that appeared on his face.

"And a half," he agreed. "That's enough to get you some serious mods, or equipment."

"But not both," I pointed out.

"Not both, but that's life," he suggested. "I'll sell this to Oshbob, but I'll not get that much back, so I'd need more, a lot more to square my debt with the carver, never mind anything else."

"So?"

"So we're back to the deal." He shifted, rolling his shoulders and getting comfortable. "I give you those creds, you do the jobs for me...the hits. And when you're not on the job? You're in the undercity, hunting more of these fucks." He nodded to the remains of the ghoul. "Find me five more? Kitted like this? That's your hundred grand paid off. We're back in business. Each mod you bring me, I'll sell, and we split. We pay off our debt with the carver first, then it's fifty-fifty."

I pretended to consider it, really did for a few seconds. After all, he was right when it came to Oshbob. Few full-blooded orcs and humans got along that well; there were too many years of spilled blood between us. If I went to sell him gear? I'd be forced to accept a lowball offer. And even then, I might not walk out with my life. This dickhead, though?

Yeah, he was half-human, but he was half-orc as well. He'd get a better deal, all right. Add in that I was essentially getting someone plugged into the underworld as a partner.

If I refused? Yeah, one of us was probably dead. Or I take the deal, and we're back to consequences. First and foremost, I get fixed up, and I always had the option of judging and just slaughtering them if they crossed me later. Make him pay for it? Poetic justice, in my eyes.

The bounty, though—that changed a lot.

Two hundred and fifty thousand credits would cover all my rebuild to APS standard and beyond. Hell, I could get some tier four's in there possibly, and a master assassin would have some shit-hot mods of his own. Rip them?

The gang would be waiting; I knew that straightaway. As soon as I hit the assassin, they'd hit me. They'd not let that payday get away from them, so I'd need to be ready, but...I could use Lucky to get an "in" with the underworld. *Get ready, gear up, and when he came for me, maybe have drones in place? Take them all down? Maybe hire some mercs of my own for that hit?*

Either way, this option got me back in the game, and with the way things were going...? Fuck it. I was done with playing nice.

The short-term solution was a good one. I get fixed up, I hit these gangs, treat him like any bounty fixer—he's hiring me for the job, but I can't trust him. Wipe out those who have been fucking with him...they're gangs, after all—no innocents.

Hit them, wipe them out; he gets his gear. I do runs underground, clear out sections, see what I can find. Hell, with the right mods? I'll be back in the game properly. I don't have to fuck around with the low-level merc outfits, go straight to a medium one. Register and see if they've got any specter outbreak jobs, get paid for the same shit twice.

That made sense, yeah. There were always stories of merc guilds that made a living hunting and killing specters. If there's any truth to that, then as long as I strip the corpses as well, I'd be winning.

I'd have to split my time between the gang and the merc outfit, but I could do that. It wasn't as if I had a fucking girlfriend to fill my evenings.

"I'd need medikits," I said into the silence. "Three of them. You'd need to get them—and nanite based."

"Shit, you think I'm running a charity?" He grunted, sitting forward. "I'll give you one, and it's a small kit."

"Nanite?"

"Yeah."

"Gimme," I demanded, holding my hand out.

"So, we have a deal?" He smiled widely.

"We have a deal," I confirmed. "Seventy-seven and a half thousand credits, thirty-thou of them in credit at a genuine chop shop. No ripped mods. You get this shit, and I'll do the *five* jobs…two outright gang hits. *No innocents or the deal is off.* Then two of their chemists—take the guards down, and you can move in. You get their stuff, unless there's a decent gun or armor, as I'll need those."

"Then you go specter hunting, strip them as you go, bring me some good milspec shit for Oshbob. I split the creds with you, and you pay for your upgrades and gear. You survive long enough? I'll give you Stinger's address, and you kill him. That's it, our debt is paid." He smiled toothily as he said it.

"That's it," I agreed. "But we split whatever you find on that hardened datadeck."

"Not a chance," he replied, still smiling. "I'll have to go into debt to even get that cracked, and that's if the EMP didn't wipe it."

I paused for a few long seconds, before smiling. "Then you owe me four of your gangers to pick a fight."

"You want them to kill someone?" he asked, confused.

"No, I want them to pick a fight with some guards, merc guards specifically, as a distraction. Then they can fuck off."

"Will they live?"

"Maybe. Depends on them, really," I admitted.

He considered it, scratching at his chin as he squinted at the door, clearly thinking about his people.

"They don't have to be any in particular?" he asked. "I don't want to risk useful ones."

"Send your fucking stupidest. I don't give two fucks. They just need to be loud and get attention."

"It sounds like we've reached the point for this then…" Lucky frowned in concentration, before I grunted at the request that popped up for me.

<table>
<tr><th colspan="2" align="center">JOB</th></tr>
<tr><td colspan="2">

Kabutt will carry out five [5] contract hits for Lucky, including and limited to the following:
- 2 x Assassination hits
- 2 x Chemist lab raids
- 1 x Assassination and Bounty of [Stinger]

Supplemental:
- 1 x Recover 100,000 credits worth of Specter Mods

In exchange, Kabutt will receive:
- 47,500 x direct credit transfer
- 30,000 x store credit for Lion's Chop Shop
- ? x Additional bounties
- 4 x gang members will be dispatched to Kabutt's choice of location to act as a distraction.

</td></tr>
<tr><td align="center">Accept</td><td align="center">Refuse</td></tr>
</table>

"Whatever," I agreed, glancing over the details, uncaring. "Give me my goddamn credits and get out."

"We have a deal." He reached out one enormous fist, and I clenched my own, smacking his knuckles once, hard. "To show how generous and what a good friend I am, I'll even get you some decent furniture," he promised, looking around the room with a snort of disgust as he climbed to his feet.

CHAPTER EIGHTEEN

As soon as the credits were in my account, the address for the chop shop shared and the door was shut, I sagged backward, relieved.

That had been all I fucking needed, but…as much as I hated being railroaded into a deal? That dumb fuck had just given me pretty much everything I needed. Yeah, I'd have to risk my life to get the jobs done, but seriously?

I was going to have to risk it before all of this anyway.

All this meant was that I'd see more of the gang, and when they came to turn on me, I'd be ready for them. There was no way they'd let me claim that kill for Stinger. That bounty would be the end of the deal: Stinger died, then they'd hit me, so I needed to be ready for them.

The last thing he'd done before leaving was underarm toss the medikit at me, making me think he'd been expecting to give me it all along.

Catching it, I'd sighed in relief, totally ignoring his parting words and waving a hand at him in dismissal, triggering the charge on the kit.

It was an older—and cheaper—model, a small dose, but for what I needed? It would make a hell of a difference either way, despite it needing hours to get the job done properly.

I jammed the injector into my stomach, directly below the worst of the damage to my ribs, and hissed in pain. The icy-cold feeling of fresh nanites pouring into me gave me the creeps, as it always did.

Jerking the spent injector out, I tossed it aside, the expensive part of the kit now inside me, assessing the damage and getting to work.

Realistically, I could have held off on the medikit. The nanites that I'd need to be injected with later to bring whatever upgrades I got to life would have done some of the fixing on me, but better that I was in a good place before that.

I dressed quickly, putting my shotgun in the sheath and the shitty handgun on my hip, wearing the last set of moderately clean clothes I had, and set off for the chop shop.

It was an hour by mag-train and on foot—or three hours by cab, and ten times the cost—so that made it simple enough, although I was starving and the bruises that remained were aching like the devil had been at me.

By the time I turned onto the right street, entering the ground floor of a massive old "tech-u-like" store and heading straight down to the basement—ignoring the sales assistants, who in turn ignored me, staring around them in dull-eyed wonder—I was exhausted.

The chop shop was like any other I'd been to: half insanely high-end technology, and half a literal butcher's slaughterhouse, with bone saws and drills sitting in a bio-detergent bath, ready for their next victim.

"Welcome!" called an insanely cheerful voice from the far side of the room, and I jerked, having missed them in the gloom. "Sorry, friend. Didn't mean to scare you!" He walked out of the darkness and fixed me with a wide smile, as I glared at him, returning the handgun to the holster and trying to calm my racing heart.

"So…what can I do for you? A new arm? A new hip? Maybe a bionic upgrade?" he suggested, making a suggestive thrusting motion. "You know it makes sense…why just be human, when you could be—"

"Repairs or upgrades," I interrupted him. "Lucky sent me."

Those three words resulted in a massively marked difference in the atmosphere. The cheerful and bouncy nature vanished as his lip curled in disgust.

"Oh, he did, did he! Well, you can tell him from me that he pays or he can fuck himself!"

"He sent me here to get thirty thousand creds' worth of debt paid off," I growled.

"He's paying me thirty—" the carver started to ask, perking up, and I shook my head.

"No! He owes me!" I snapped. "I'm here for the work!"

"What!" he snarled, before gesturing at the chair. "You just…you sit. I'll be right back!" He stormed off, already booting his Keystone to call Lucky, I guessed, his voice rising as he left the room.

I threw myself into the chair and dragged the deck out of my pocket, plugging into my jack, and the other end into the chair attachment.

A menu popped up, asking me to approve access to my mods. That done— and when it could barely get a connection—I was met with a wall of possibilities.

I took a deep breath, and started at the top, both physically, and in importance.

Mod	Tier
Brain	One –Three
Brain mods are separated into three separate distinct designs: Augmentation, Enhancement, and Storage.	
Augmentation: Augmentation deals with augmenting what is already here, and your physical connection to it, including data-jacks, ancillary connectors, and improving your connection to the Aug-World all around us. We're offering sensory additions and even boosting your access to Aug-World—perfect for modders, hackers, and system designers, as well as all those who want a little more "bang" from the world.	
Expansion: Expansion refers to replacing what you have (to various degrees), everything from adjusting the brain to allow for additional cooling and processing power, to inter-synapse regulation and improved linkages. All things are possible! Want to be a brain in a jar? Fully dedicated to research? We know who you should speak to!	
Storage: Many functions that we take for granted these days in many of the roles we do are provided by the systems we integrate with. From additional data processing through datadecks to secondary bodies and more, all are controlled by dedicated levels of RI [Restricted Intelligences] or AI [Artificial Intelligences]. Where most store these in the relevant system, for the best coordination and results, a dedicated, personal assistant is required, and they in turn, require storage.	

I grunted, nodding as I mentally marked one of these as a definite purchase. There were a thousand, thousand variations, but the shop only had four in stock I could see, and after checking, I dismissed the three tier ones out of hand, pulling up the data on the single third tier available.

Brain Mod	**Tier**: Three
The Takemoto Cerebrau model is an excellent entry model into the realm of cerebral enhancement, providing an expanded storage capacity, capable of housing a Class 3 RI or Class 1 AI, additional processing power to run those facilities, *and* a full management suite.	
This model is primarily geared toward construction management, providing additional personnel tracking and evaluation enhancements, as well as space to download and store data recognition sets.	
Additional:	
New this year is the primary scanning and pattern acquisition mod, with free updates for the life of the user, provided the installation is carried out by a Registered Takemoto Flesh Carver.	
Warranty: [Void unless installed by Registered Takemoto Staff]	
Perception: 12	
Mental Power: 12	
Durability: 100/100	**Slot Cost**: 3
Availability: In stock	**Credit Cost**: 17,000

I tagged that straightaway, making sure no other fucker could come in and grab it, nor the carver decide that he wasn't doing good gear.

It wasn't just the text that sold it, although that was good; that it could run a class three RI was nice as well. My APS gear had restricted my RI to a class two, and this would give it plenty of space to roam and eventually I could upgrade it.

It was the video that it played as a demonstration.

It might be sold as a "construction" variant, but target acquisition, tracking of moving markers signifying people as the operator moved a construction mech around and the scanning upgrade?

Hell yes. It needed "data recognition sets" downloaded to it, but that was fine. Why download the specs for building mechanics and so on, when I could download guns, armor, and mods?

It was a case of the scanner would reference the data in the file, so if that file had rifles instead of wood types? No problem.

The management suite was nice as well. No use for it right now—I wasn't using smart weapons, nor was I likely to any time soon—and installing weapons controllers like the smart weapon guidance systems had always been in my suit in the past…it had a fuckload more space, after all.

I'd take it, though, and hell, maybe I'd even use the Aug-World shit for a change. I'd barely used it at all since getting out, and the military training in me wouldn't let me use most of its functions to their intended level. But still.

I could treat myself to a little R&R in my room with it later.

Moving on quickly, I had both a spinal and an arm replacement coming, and I needed them both.

I skipped the rest of the mods, not willing to tease myself with what I could have had, and paused on the left arms.

Seven variations, three used. I removed those straightaway. The durability made it clear, even if the fucking price didn't, that I didn't want them. They might be specter parts, after all.

The four remaining were tier one to three. The single tier three was seventy-nine thousand, nine hundred, and ninety-nine, and it was *nice.*

I stared for long seconds at the military-grade arm: the recessed forearm blade, the emergency nanite dispenser, the fucking electrified knuckles, and best of all, the hidden single-shot plasma shotgun in the hand.

Literally, the video showed it lifting as if in surrender, then the palm's padding split and the nozzle slid out, spitting a blast of plasma into an attacker's face.

I loved it.

I wanted it.

I closed the video and felt a little scream of complaint from my very soul.

"Later," I promised myself, going back to the tier twos with a sigh.

They were a massive step down from the three, but they were also a serious step up from the shit I had attached.

Looking from my arm to the one demonstrated before me? Hell yes, there was barely any comparison. This was a burger with all the trimmings compared to eating cardboard.

I sorted through the arms quickly, dismissing the others and settling on a mid-range, but seemingly solid model.

Left Arm Mod	Tier: Two
The Nemesis #1 left arm is an excellent introduction to the Nemesis series of full limb replacements. Although missing the more advanced options of its later models, it is both sturdy and quick.	
This standard model offers interlinked targeting (weapons system permitting) as well as enhanced strength and a single augmentation slot in the forearm for a tier 1-3 weapon or utility add-on.	
Warranty: [18 months]	
Strength: 14	

Durability: 100/100	Slot Cost: 2
Availability: In stock	Credit Cost: 6,999

I nodded to myself. This and the brain mod would be a hell of a change, and it came to twenty-five thousand. Well, a credit under, but fuck it. I had thirty thousand to spend here before looking at my gear, and I quickly brought up the spinal tap models, or I tried to.

None available.

Great! Spinal reinforcement?

Two choices: one was a tier one, and sixty percent durability. *Nope.* The tier two, though? It was…well, it was all right. Looking it over, I grunted, before adding it. It wasn't what I wanted, but after a few days, I already knew the one I had was destined for the scrap heap, and this one was made by the same people as the arm. As much as all the companies denied it publicly that there were any issues mixing and matching? Everyone knew that the best results came from modding using the same kit. There were always little "niggles" that showed up in twitches and tremors, or addled zoom functions and so on. Best to avoid it if I could.

Spinal Reinforcement	Tier: Two
The Nemesis #1 Spinal Reinforcement Mod is an excellent introduction to the Nemesis series of body replacement and improvements. Although missing the more advanced options of its later models, it is significantly improved over the standard biological issue.	
This spinal modification offers stability-enhancing internal bracing, enabling overloading with significantly lower chances of damage, as well as additional attachment points for internal bracing, armoring, or organ replacements.	
Warranty: [12 months]	
Toughness: 11	
Durability: 100/100	**Slot Cost:** 2
Availability: In stock	**Credit Cost:** 6,999

With that, I was up to a hair off thirty-two thousand, and that was fine; I still had over forty-seven thousand credits.

Decent armoring and weapons would strip me of that pretty fucking fast, but honestly, I needed one more mod, despite the risk of chipping too much shit in one go.

I needed at least one, if not both, of my eyes done.

I'd always avoided getting the eyes done in the past, despite the advantages, and only partly because mil-spec gear compensated. Literally, in an APS? I didn't need any shit beyond the spinal tap and brain mod, and that was to control the suit and to link into the command net.

The main reason, and I'd been open about this with my friends, was the absolute freak-out I'd had when I'd been new to the forces, and I'd gone to get my right eye chipped to give me night vision.

I'd been fine, understood everything mentally that was about to happen, and I'd even let them put the needles in to numb the area up. But the sight of the drill coming for me?

Sliding forward, unhurried, a serrated, circular drill bit that was going to literally carve the eyeball into shreds, my eyelid being slowly cranked back by the separators?

Nope.

Panic rose in me, and I'd been young enough and inexperienced with fear enough that I couldn't manage it. I'd freaked out totally, ripping gear off me, screaming.

It'd cost me nearly as much as the implant would have in the various drugs, the damaged equipment, and in shutting the fucking carver up, and I'd ended up having nightmares for years about it.

Now, though?

If I was going to do what I needed to, and to survive the undercity? A simple set of goggles, or indeed any equipment that could be taken from me, wasn't good enough.

I needed to able to fucking *see*.

I forced myself to open the section for ocular implants, and I moved through them slowly, swallowing reflexively against the sudden block stuck in my throat.

Mod	Tier
Eyes	One – Three
Ocular mods are separated into two separate distinct designs: Augmentation and Enhancement.	
Augmentation: Augmentation deals with augmenting what is already here, offering additional clarity, color corrections, and fixing damage.	
Expansion: Expansion refers to expanding beyond the current biological system, adding zoom functions, integration with external scopes, additional scanning facilities, heat vision, and more.	

I chose the enhancement drop-down, even knowing that they'd be replacing rather than "fixing" the eye, which freaked me out even more, before selecting Night Vision and Target Acquisition and Scanning Interface, figuring it'd only help me if both the eye and brain mod were compatible.

The single expansion option that came up made me swallow my steadily rising bile. It was a dual ocular full replacement—both my eyes, blended up like a fucking protein smoothie and removed, then brand-new ones being connected and slid in.

Fuck.

Ocular Mod	Tier: Three
The Suba Systems 2701 Ocular Expansion is one of the top-rated ocular tier-three mods available on the market, providing not only night vision, but zero-light vision out to 200m, movement and pattern recognition, and a 50m zoom facility included for a fantastic price!	
Perception: 12	
Durability: 100/100	**Slot Cost:** 3
Availability: In stock	**Credit Cost:** 29,999

With all of those, I was down to just over seventeen thousand. Hating the damage that was being done to my credit balance—I still needed goddamn guns and body armor, after all—I pulled up the medikits, knowing that a chop shop would have some.

Yeah, a decent selection there, ranging from the smallest range at two hundred credits, to a hundred thousand.

Snorting, I dismissed the top and bottom end, taking three for a thousand each, still classed as "small" medikits. They were tubes, slightly thicker and longer than my thumb, with a needle at one end that deployed into the damaged area.

Medikits themselves were generally available, but you couldn't get the nanites just anywhere. Once used, like credit-chips, the kit would be blank, and there were plenty of the poorest in society who crept around searching for them, taking them to chop shops and selling the empty dispenser back to them for a credit.

The chop shop kept them wherever until they were needed, and rather than using the nanites to ensure a full and correct bond between a customer and their new mod, they simply "filled" the medikit.

Sure, you could get specific tailored 'nites if you had the money, and they'd be much more effective, meaning you needed less of them to heal an injury and so on, but getting "blank" pure 'nites coded to you? That was something only corpos could afford.

I picked three of them, then dismissed the screen, settling back, listening for the first time to the argument I could just about hear going on in the next room.

"…the deal! I paid that back and…"

"…"

"…then tell him to go fuck himself. I'm not…"

"…"

"No!"

"…"

"No, fuck's sake, Lucky! Don't tell him that, all right?"

"…"

"We agreed!"

"…"

"…fuck's sake, you better!"

"…"

"Thirty thousand?! Fuck you! No way!"

"…"

"…shit, man, you think I care? I can't afford to restock for that! Fuck, look—no, *you* listen, Lucky! The parts? Yeah, I can do the parts, as long as you hold up your end. But the 'nites? It's all I've got! I can't restock, I can't work! I might as well close the doors and fuck off!"

"…"

"How much's he got?"

"…"

"…he better. Last time, Lucky. Seriously, you don't pay me by the end of the week? I won't be here. And that debt? I'll sell it."

"…"

"…you don't like it? Pay on time! We both owe him. You bury me? I'll take you down too!"

A handful of minutes passed, before the carver walked back into the room, forcing a smile, until he saw my face and that I was staring at him.

He clearly put two and two together, before sighing. "Guess I need to remember to take those kinda calls elsewhere, huh?"

"Probably a good idea," I agreed, and he snorted, grabbing one of those weird little kneeling cushioned stools, and dragging it over to my side.

He half sat, half knelt on it, somehow still looking comfy as he leaned back, arms folded. "So."

"So."

"You're in debt to them as well, huh?" he asked, getting a sharp nod in return. "You know what this is costing you?"

"The thirty k worth of mods?" I asked, getting a frown and a nod. "Yeah, I know, and I know the likely outcome."

"You think you can pay it off?"

"I can."

"No, seriously, you think you can pay this off? You can't. Once the gang gets its hooks into you, they don't let go."

"Five jobs, and a hundred grand's worth of salvage mods," I said flatly. "That's the deal, not that you need to know, but once that's done, I'm out."

"The hundred grand's worth of mods." He smiled crookedly. "You know who decides their worth?"

"We will between us," I said. "Lucky and me."

"Nope," he corrected. "Look, I don't need this shit, but take it from someone who knows—you'll be handing those mods in and they'll be checked by the syndicate. They decide what something's worth."

"The deal's between Lucky and me," I growled.

"Lucky works for Oshbob. Nobody fucks with the orc. If Oshbob says he owns your debt? He owns it."

"I've got a shotgun that'll say different," I assured him.

He shook his head slowly.

"Fine. Look, friend, last chance to back out. You get these parts into you, and they won't let you go." He gestured to the wall, where the used mods hung as demonstrations. The sealed and pristine new ones were still in special see-through containers behind locked doors, just like the nanites themselves in their storage cradles. "You ever wonder where most of the used parts come from?" He smiled sadly.

"I'm guessing not from people upgrading, the way you're looking at me."

"Nope. They're people who don't pay their debts. That's what's left of them. Just be sure that you want in. As long as you haven't taken their money yet…"

"I took credits already."

"Fuck." He sighed, rubbing at his eyes, clearly tired, before shaking his head and forcing a smile. "Well, guess there's no point in discussing it any further. We might as well get started. Thirty thousand in mods…"

"I've picked some out, and I'll pay the rest in credits."

"Really? Well, fuck, that's a relief." He perked up, sitting forward and squinting as he accessed the selection I'd made. "Nice, you've got some good kit there," he said a few seconds later. "What's wrong with your current loadout?"

"Besides it's mainly shit and tier one?" I forced a smile. "EMP."

"No shit?"

"Nope."

"Anything still work?" he asked, then shushed me when I went to answer, instead dragging a fixed scanner on a mobile arm across the room from behind the chair and starting to click away at things. "Right, settle back. I'm gonna assess your gear, see what we're working with. Then we talk. And if you can afford it, and run it, we get started, right?"

"Right." I sighed, settling back into the chair and trying to get comfortable, even as I tamped down my fear.

The chair was an old one, but well made, a cradle system that supported each limb or part separately, and held straps to make damn sure I stayed still during delicate proceedings.

As I stared upward, watching the solid arm with the scanner attached inch down my body, I forced myself to stay where I was, working from the top of my head down, picking out each individual muscle I could, tensing it and relaxing them one at a time.

I'd just gotten to my stomach, then the paddle cranked back out of view, and he grunted, pulling a screen around for me to look at.

"Your implants are fucked," he said without preamble. "Seriously, your arm? Battered, sure, but the nanites are totally dead. The spinal reinforcement is screwed. Does it work? Yeah, sort of. You're losing around a quarter of the impulse control from the T10 vertebrae down—you're having to force the signals through. Judging from the quality control on that model? I'm betting that it's always been shit?"

"Yeah, had to practically relearn to walk," I admitted, getting a nod from him.

"Thought so. Well, that needs replacing, and frankly, it's barely worth the cost of scrap. I'll give you fifty for it, and that's being generous. It's too fucked to reinstall."

"Done."

"Good man. Right, your organelles—they're intact, but about a third of their 'nites aren't responding. An influx of nanites when we reattach the new shit should deal with all of that, but get ready for some really nasty shits in the near future."

"Good to know, thanks."

"I'm serious. Avoid anything spicy, or you're gonna be praying to the gods of blood and chrome to end it all."

"I'll remember," I assured him, getting a long stare, before he shrugged and moved on.

"Whatever. Not my problem. So the organelles will survive, and so will you, but you might not want to. The arm is, well, it's shit. Fifty credits."

"Done."

"Next is the biggie. Brain mod. It's a Wilmat three hundred, basically the entry-level model for Wilmat, only sold as the three rather than the one, because nobody wants to buy a tier one that admits it's bargain basement stock. It's basically housing for an RI while not providing the processing power to use it. And yeah, the quote they use is 'unbelievable tracking and pattern recognition as standard' because, once you use it? You can't believe how shit it is."

"Yeah, believe me, I know."

"Well, the good news is your RI is intact. The mod is barely responding to pings, and I seriously doubt it's responding to you at all. I'll give you ten."

"Ten credits?" I asked flatly.

"Believe me, that's being fucking generous. What use do I have for it? Nobody will buy it. It's basically the shittiest mod on the market. Why you bought one is beyond me." He fixed me with a look, and I nodded, sighing.

"Fine. One condition, though."

"Go."

"You fix my goddamn Key," I said flatly. "The fucking EMP killed it and left me having to jack in using a cable."

"Yeah, don't worry," he said with a faint smile. "You'll be needing that anyway. I already factored it in with the ten-credit offer. So, all your mods to me for a hundred and ten, and your replacements, once the thirty thou is off, come to…nice." He broke off, having apparently just noticed the total. "Thirty thousand, nine hundred and ninety-seven credits."

I winced, doing the math and coming out with seventeen thousand, one hundred and twenty-five credits left.

That was a hell of a lot compared to what I'd had the last few days, but still, no armor, no new guns and…

"And three medikits," I added, and he smiled, adding them to the bottom of the list. *Fourteen fucking thousand. Ouch.*

I stood, stripping off and climbing back onto the chair at his direction as he fetched the medikits, setting them on the table to the side, each empty, but ready for the nanite infusion.

"Jack in and authorize the transfer and—"

"And you knock me out," I said. "No local nerve blocks. I need to be asleep for this."

"You're a trusting man then." He smiled, and I snorted, slotting the cable into my jack.

"No, not at all. But let's face it—you fuck me over? The gang fucks you over because they've lost their investment. I go to sleep, and while I don't like it, I wake up and everything's either fine or you're fucked up. It's not like you couldn't do something to me when you've got the nerve blocks in, or when you're working on my brain."

"Fair point," he agreed. "So…you ready to get chopped?"

"Never been more ready," I assured him grimly. The transfer went through, the knock on the shop's credit account smooth. "Rebuild me, carver. Make me better."

CHAPTER NINETEEN

I woke slowly, a feeling like a hot needle sliding out of my brain as the nerve block was removed. Suddenly, I was assaulted on all sides by the world again.

Screens flooded my vision as my RI rebooted, connections testing through the brain mod and out into my body. Data connection charts flashed up. Numbers that meant nothing scrolled across, and behind them? Data dumps from the various mods inundated me.

I lifted my arms slowly. The carver backed away quickly, a datapad in one hand, holding it up where I'd have to focus to see it, even as he held a veritable cannon down by his side, almost—but not quite—out of sight.

"Kabutt, you there? I need you to connect to the pad and read the verse for me," he ordered.

I nodded, clearing my throat and coughing before reaching out with a data request, then started to read. I glanced at it, then snorted, seeing what was going on and making a point of ignoring the tube of shining nanites that sat on a table next to me.

"On the breast of a woman called Gale was tattooed the price of her tail, and on her behind, for the sake of the blind, was the same information in braille," I read, then snorted. "Seriously?"

"Hey, you think a specter's gonna give a shit about that?" he replied, grinning, and put the pad down and picked the nanites up. "Seriously, anyone who's on the border of specter, even if they're not all the way gone yet? A container of pure nanites that close means they're not gonna be able to focus on anything."

Even as he spoke, he kept hold of the gun and moved the tube constantly, watching my eyes.

"There must be a better way to test for it."

He shrugged. "There's hundreds. Ask any carver and they've got their own, and there's the corpo methods as well. But seriously? The estimate is seven hundred specters created a day. Some merc outfits hunt them, handing their corpses in to the government for a bounty. If they weren't doing that? I don't want to imagine it."

"Well, whatever." I sighed. "Now, you mind?" I gestured to the gun, then up at myself, making it clear I wanted to test myself.

"Yeah, no worries." He smiled. "You've got half an hour, okay? After that, I'm charging you rent."

"Yeah, yeah." I waved him off, lifting my left arm and looking it over.

It was only a tier two, yeah, or "basic" as most people figured it, but Nemesis made good quality shit. The arm was matte black, made seemingly of steel, and with a hand that gleamed softly in the subdued lighting in here.

Three red lines ran from shoulder to elbow, then spiraled around the lower arm, ending at the wrist.

Turning it over, I noted the hatch on the inside of the wrist. I mentally ordered it to open, watching as the plate unlocked and slid up, letting me slide my fingers in and open it fully.

As it wasn't being used currently, the mod slot was simply empty, and just in case, I slid one of the three medikits on the table next to me into the gap. It fit, but rattled around, and a second later the carver was leaning in, offering me something that compressed like foam, but expanded to fill the space when I released it, cushioning the kit.

He shrugged, stepping back. "We use it to fill internals."

"I didn't get your name," I said after a few seconds of prodding at it, and he smiled.

"Lion."

"Lion?"

"Yeah, like the old cat." He smiled. "Parents were into the old world stuff, you know?"

"I'm Harry…"

"Kabutt," he finished. "I know…had to jack into your Key, remember? That's all fixed up as well, by the way."

"Thanks, man." I shook my head and looked around the room, stunned by the level of detail the eyes were giving me. "So, my eyes…"

"Yeah?"

"Ummm, my *old* eyes?"

"Here." He moved to the side and lifted a narrow tube.

I took it, staring in mixed revulsion and fascination at the bobbing orbs, suspended in fluid.

"I thought you blended them?" I asked slowly, staring in wonder.

"Nah. I know some do…mostly idiots, though. There's a market for them. People who can't afford a replacement, be that cybernetic or credit cost, they still go blind, you know? Fresh set of eyes like this? Twenty to forty credits, depending."

"That even cover your time?" I asked, and he shrugged.

"Not really, but that's why I became a carver. Lost my parents to a wall breach. Grandfather raised me, and he went blind. Nobody helped him. If I'd been able to at the time? Hell, we could have raised the credits for this. All it takes is a few chips and a literal hair's worth of nanites."

"So you keep the eyes you get in, put them in people for the cost of a few meals."

"A bit more than that," he admitted. "And organs and more as well. You'd be surprised how many gangbangers want to upgrade perfectly good organs. Once they're out and cleaned? A little suspension fluid and boom. Someone who had issues and couldn't afford the hospital is given another chance."

"Damn," I muttered, having never really thought about it before.

"So, you want them?" he asked.

"What?"

"The eyes." He nodded to the container I held. "We didn't strike a price for them, and considering the turnaround, I can't pay you for them. So either you take them—and I'll be charging you for the container and fluid if…"

"You can have them." I straightened up and handed them back. "It's fine."

"Thanks." He set them back on the side counter, and turned to me, hesitating before speaking. "Look, Kabutt, I know I was frustrated before, but I'd appreciate it if you didn't tell Lucky about our conversation?"

"You're fine," I assured him. "Besides, I need a chop shop I can trust anyway and…"

He handed me a small note on a piece of folded paper, pressing it into my hand and shaking his head as I opened my mouth to ask about it.

"Great!" he assured me. "I'd love the business, but you know, if you're okay to move along? I've got shit to do today."

"Yeah." I stood slowly, and let out a long breath as my legs took my weight happily.

The constant extra effort I'd had to put in to just damn walk before now was markedly absent, and although I staggered a little at first, it was because I'd pushed too hard, not because my legs were slow in reacting.

A few steps, and suddenly I was back, feeling so much better it was unreal. I moved my left arm; a tension in my shoulders, a level of stress I'd not even known was there until now, slipped away, as my arm reacted as quickly and easily, if not more so, than my right did.

I sighed, holding onto the note, and slipped it into a pocket of my pants, before dressing quickly.

A handful of minutes later, and I was outside, squinting around at the brightness before my eyes adjusted. The world suddenly dimmed as if I'd slipped a pair of shades on.

I grinned, and as I headed for the nearest station, I brought up my details, taking a deep breath as they registered.

Identification: Harry Kabutt				
Species: Human		**Bonus:** None		
Mod Capacity: 19		**Mod Capacity in use**: 13		
Stat	**Current Points**	**Description**	**Mods**	**Quality**
Dexterity	11	Governs agility and movement	Left Arm Mod: 2 Cost: 1 (Dex: 12)	Basic
Mental Power	10	Governs swiftness and fortitude of the mind	Brain Mod: 3 Cost: 2	Professional
Perception	11	Governs an individual's senses and connection to the world around them	Brain Mod: 3 Ocular Mod: 3 Cost: 4 (PER 12 + 14)	Basic
Strength	10	Governs physical strength and damage dealt	Left Arm Mod: 2 Cost: 1 (STR 14)	Basic
Toughness	9	Governs the body and internal fortitude	Basic Organelles: 3 Cost: 3 Spinal Reinforcement: 2 Cost: 2 Toughness: 11	Basic

"Damn," I whispered, seeing the difference in both my overall details and the individual. I was also at thirteen points of my predicted nineteen possible, though, seriously limiting my future mods. But that was fine. I'd survived till now with the shit I had.

Before I'd been mustered out, I'd had a full tier-three, top-of-the-range command module, costing me five points, and a full spinal tap, costing me another five. I'd not need to get that level again, but even if I did? Take off the five in use for the current spinal and brain, and I still had a single point. Hell, I'd probably just get cheaper-costing eyes and a lower-grade arm.

I'd be in armor most of the time, after all.

Regardless of all that shit, I continued to walk, zooming in on random things: a bit of trash blown along the sidewalk, a rat hiding in rubbish, a dead bum curled up in an alleyway I passed…the line on the ass of the girl ahead of me that showed her panties in a ridiculously sheer skirt, and…yup.

The lack of a similar line on the girl next to her, wearing the same outfit, and none of the underwear.

For a second, I checked her out, and her friend. Then I shook my head. I had no time for that. Despite the *much* more interested looks they were giving me than they would have been earlier, seeing the average mods, the shine of recent applications, and my heavily armed condition.

I wasn't that interested.

Besides, it wasn't like I could take them to my goddamn apartment.

I took a seat on the mag-train. The hum of its acceleration from stationary to high speed was all that I felt, until a questing finger touched something, and I remembered the paper Lion had given me.

I pulled it out, being subtle just in case, figuring he wanted to hide giving me it, so…The words I read didn't make sense at first, and then?

I crumpled the paper up into a tiny ball; then, just in case, popped it into my mouth and chewed. I didn't need to reread it. The message was simple enough.

> *Tracker installed. You're bugged. Sorry.*

I stared out of the window blankly, seeing nothing of the city as it rolled past, my mind ticking over. It couldn't be in my eyes, or brain. If that was the case and they could remote in and see everything? Giving me the note was pointless.

The spine? Yeah, probably, or attached to an organelle. The arm was fairly solid—putting it inside would risk too much, but alongside the spine, nice and safe? Or up under the lungs?

I accessed the RI, feeling a strange relief as it indicated readiness, and I fed it the parameters, much as I'd done for years.

A scan of my body had been included along with the warranty details to register the mods, and I pulled that up, telling the RI to search for unknown internal signals.

Nothing.

Not really a surprise. Although the signal would need to be reasonably powerful, most likely they'd not have it on unless there was a need. No, I was an *asset* to the gang now, and they were likely to have included more than just a tracker.

He'd not said it, but I was betting there was a bomb or something in there as well.

That was what I'd have done, at least.

Staring out of the window as the skyscrapers and slums, the arcologies and the megastructures rolled past over and over, I examined the situation from every side.

So, I was bugged. Probably also a bomb, because the gang didn't trust me. That was fine, because not only did I not trust them, but I was actively planning to fuck them over now.

Once this was done? I had no doubt that Lucky would try to kill me and collect the bounty on Stinger. That was also why that was my *last* job.

They wanted a return on their investment, after all.

So, logic time. They wanted to make their money back, and then some. They had a chance to make a serious pile of credits off me, if I could take down Stinger, so until then? As long as I was working my way down their list of jobs, they'd leave me alone.

That gave me time to figure this shit out.

Lion? He warned me when he didn't need to. I was betting that after the shit he said that he still hid the note. It meant either his shop was bugged, or someone was there, somewhere, watching us.

I couldn't see Lion letting them bug his shop, too many potential issues, but having someone hide there?

I'd never even considered searching for them, but logically, between taking the money and getting the tracker implanted, that was the point of most risk for Lucky.

I stood, rolling my shoulders and stretching, checking the shotgun in its sheath, and then my handgun, making it clear I was getting off, before moving to the doors. I glanced around, acting like I was just idly curious.

My RI, acting on the parameters I supplied it—armed, cheap clothing, multiple mods, and within thirty meters—picked out three potential targets.

Two were making a point of not looking in my direction, while standing to leave.

The third…well, he was out of it. A trail of drool ran from the corner of his mouth, his cheap suit barely fit him, and the hand cannon in its underarm holster was secured.

Add to that, the goggles he was wearing and the bulging erection?

He'd fallen asleep on the mag-train watching porn. He was both very memorable, and instantly dismissible, making it unlikely he was here for me.

He was either exactly what he seemed—an off-duty merc or bodyguard on his way somewhere and flat out—or he was a great deal more professional than the gangbangers could afford and was hiding it well.

I waited until the train stopped, got off, then started to check my pockets, as though I'd dropped something. The gangers got off as well, then jerked to a halt and headed back to the train as I darted back inside. As they boarded and the departure alarm rang out, I scooted off again, pretending to have found whatever I "left."

The gangers glared at me as the train pulled away, and I frowned at them, pretending confusion and not understanding what was going on. Best not to tip them off. For now, they just looked unlucky and dumb.

I changed platforms, two separate trains needed, then I was pulling up at Gunther's, parading through the door, heavily modded and with the credits burning a hole in my account.

CHAPTER TWENTY

Two hours later, I was marching up to the second merc outfit I'd been to this week, and this time I was both ready for a fight, and hopefully, far less likely to get one.

I'd brought Gunther up to date on everything that had happened, and I'd been weirdly touched when the old fart had sworn that if I needed him, if I was going back after those asshole mercs, the Errant Mergers, he'd be there.

It was kind, but honestly? Fuck no. Most of the mercs, I had no issue with. But the bosses and the guards? I was gonna fuck them all up. And as nice a guy as Gunther was, it'd be fifty-fifty he'd be dead in the first volley.

No, this time I asked for his help in a different way. He helped me narrow down the merc guilds that actually hunted specters, and we narrowed it further, searching by reported fatalities and bounties handed in, coming up with a single name that was most likely to take me showing up on their doorstep with a smile and arms thrown wide open.

The Vigilant Heart mercenary guild advertised that they took on the specters to "protect the city and its people."

They all did that. Admittedly, even for mercs, *"fuck you all, we just love credits"* was unlikely to be a motto, publicly at least—but these guys seemed serious about it.

They'd also suffered some serious losses recently, leading to them desperately recruiting experienced mercs to replace those lost, before they lost their contracts.

I'd paid Gunther back the fifty creds he'd lent me for the registration fee with the Errant assholes, and I'd bought some decent gear.

It felt a bit ridiculous, considering that every time I went to him I bought new gear, but this time, it was an order of magnitude better.

I started off logical: good boots, the soles electrically dampening and fitted with a stealth field that projected a noise-canceling effect. I'd seen them in practice before. Scouts wore them generally, and although they needed a dedicated battery, they weren't that expensive at fifteen hundred creds.

New pants, again. Armored, lots of pockets, and fucking waterproof as well as including a basic heating element—I was sick of being cold and wet—for another hundred and ten.

Two tops, both for under body armor, thin and heat regulating. Thirty credits a pop.

Body armor, this time a full upper body kit rather than just the chest, and that came in at a thousand.

A jacket, reflective layer underneath the outer one to deflect laser fire, reasonably non-flammable, waterproof, and with a "hard shell." Basically, it was a form of smart fabric: it bent, it was flexible, and on detecting an impact, it'd harden to a solid frame.

It'd not take many hits, and hell, close range from a heavy round? Little chance it'd stop it. But fléchettes or a normal slug thrower at range, or the rotting nails of specters?

It'd give me the time I needed to fuck them all up, well worth it at three thousand.

Tactical gloves and a gorget—a section of armor that was specifically designed for the throat—that was made of the same hard shell as the armor, the pair for five hundred each, and boom.

All I needed was the helmet.

I chose one that covered my whole face, a black gently curved arc that covered my head entirely, for two thousand. And it even gave me limited vision on all sides like I was used to in the APS. The gorget tucked into it. And with that, I was ready, save the guns.

I'd gone from fourteen thousand and change to around five and a half by now, and on general principles, I refused to buy a new handgun to replace my revolver.

I was getting that fucker back.

Instead, I got a new gun kit, a better one than I had before, trading in the one I'd looted against it, with most of the parts I'd need to fix my damn shotgun, and a new rifle.

The gun kit set me back two hundred, and the assault rifle? It was a slug thrower, but still a damn good one, made by Pinnacle Assault Systems. Cost me fifteen hundred. It came with three magazines, as well as a box of two hundred bullets for another four hundred credits.

I was down to three thousand and change after the three hundred credit was applied as well, but that was fine. The last things I picked out were a new vibro-blade at two hundred and fifty, a canteen, two frag grenades, and an expandable bag to carry any "salvage."

Two thousand, five hundred and eighty-seven credits left, and as I marched into the front door of the Vigilant Heart mercenary guild, the difference was insane.

Not only was I one of the few individuals in there who didn't look pissed, exhausted, or downright filthy, but I was also one of the best equipped.

My gear practically shone compared to theirs, and although shiny gear was certainly no demonstration of fitness, the fact that all my gear, although mismatched, was chosen to work together with the minimum of issues—the way my magazines, my frags, flash-bangs, handgun, rifle, and shotgun were all racked—made it clear I knew what I was doing.

To any professional, my gear "fit" at a glance, meaning that if needed, I could access all of it, as far as was realistically possible, including the vibro-blade on the reverse tactical grip on my chest. None of the various pockets, straps, or gear blocked access to another. And at even a cursory glimpse around the room before me?

I could see that easily three-quarters of the wannabe mercs in there hadn't learned yet that a magazine pinned in place by a gun strap might as well be back in the armory when you needed it in a firefight.

A quick look around the room told me all I needed to know. There were easily two dozen people, maybe more, hanging around, on uncomfortable seats, reading from job boards and with the glazed look of people using implants. They were mainly off to the left, while there were a collection of desks behind armoring on the right.

Between the two groups I mentally tagged as wannabes and staff were a few others, here and there.

Someone walked out of the back as I entered, holding up a job card, and called out in a loud voice that carried well over the low-level grumbling.

"I need a single melee specialist—no, I said a single one, not you two!" he snapped as a pair of half-orcs stood at the back. "Melee specialist," he repeated. "Hundred creds up front. Once the advance is paid off, you'll get…"

Shrugging and dismissing the recruiter, I strode up to the front desk, rifle on a sling, and removed my helmet, nodding to the woman behind it as she silently pinged me for my ident.

My RI responded at a thought from me, attaching my military records, and she glanced it over for a few seconds, before smiling warmly and directing me to take a seat to one side, as someone would be with me "shortly."

I did as I was asked, hand on my fucking rifle this time, and ready should it turn out that, maybe, just fucking maybe, Scott had slept with this entire merc company's wives or something.

Two minutes later, though, a tired-looking figure in dented but well-serviced body armor opened a door in the far wall and called out for me by name.

"Sergeant Kabutt?"

"Aye, sir," I responded automatically, standing at attention, and getting a grin from the man as I did it without thought.

"Good man. Get in here." He jerked his head at the room behind him.

I hurried across the room, passing a handful of others who had been waiting.

"I'm Julius," the man who'd called me in said by way of greeting, waving me to a comfy seat in what I instantly recognized as a ready room.

There were a dozen seats around the room, two desks set out for weapons maintenance, a couple of vending machines, and a whiteboard. Everything was covered in a low level of dirt, battered and scuffed, with an overflowing garbage bin, and a few people scattered around the room looking utterly exhausted, one even asleep.

Directly outside was the public view of the merc company, all calm and polished, professional. Although not high-end, clearly they spent a bit on appearances.

Back here? This was where the actual mercs hung out, getting briefed, recovering and shooting the shit.

"Good meeting you, sir." I nodded to Julius.

"So what brings you to us, Sarge?" He threw himself into a chair and picked up what looked to be a cold cup of coffee by the grimace he made when he sipped it.

"I need credits." I sat in a chair near him and cradled my rifle.

"Yeah, that's why we all do the job. But I mean why *us*, specifically. You're APS. Top guilds will take you and pay for the privilege. Hell, the Armed Brigade will give you a slot."

"You don't want me?" I lifted an eyebrow in question.

"Oh, no. We *want* you. We're just not sure if we can afford you, and certainly not whatever issues you're bringing."

"Issues?"

"Everyone has issues, Kabutt. You know that."

"I was mustered out after an accident—nothing to do with me—took down my transport. The cred-counters decided it was cheaper to pay me up and let me leave early, rather than replace the full range of mods that were broken, as I had papers in already," I explained. "That meant that they gave me shitty mods, and I need to upgrade them. I earn enough credits to pay for the proper mods again, and I can use my armor to earn real paydays."

"You've got your armor?" He sat up, staring. "You've paid it off?"

"It's being repaired. Major in charge of my mustering out said they'd fix it up then send it, so I've got a few months."

"Damn," he whispered, shaking his head. "For a second there, well, I thought we must have all been good little boys and girls." He settled back in the chair. Its plastic creaked under his armored weight as he scrubbed at his eyes with tired fingers.

"What's that?" I asked.

"I thought the gods of blood and chrome were giving me a fucking lifeline," he admitted, before sitting forward and forcing a smile. "Okay, look. You want to earn, and I desperately need mercs to do the damn job. Most won't fight specters, think that they'll catch whatever creates specters…"

"Can you?" I asked.

"Not as far as we know," he said. "Get taken by a ghoul? Who fucking knows. We've got unconfirmed reports of higher-class specters dragging people off, and then those same people returning as specters, but nothing proven. The simple truth is, more than ninety-nine percent of the specters you'll come across in any sweep are literally brain-dead.

"They'll wander in and out of the zones we cover, totally without aim, and they're not hard to take down. The issue comes when a ghoul or higher turns up. They control the others around them, and a random mass that we can easily deal with, provided we've got the ammo, is suddenly a tactical mess.

"We need to clean out nests as they form, and before they reach critical mass. Once that happens, they seem to spawn higher-class specters. This could be a coincidence. It might be that the specters are better at hiding than we are at finding them, and they come out when they think there's a decent size group to control. Or it might be that enough of the bastards together creates them…doubtful, but hey. We don't know. Studies are ongoing."

"Studies?" I asked, and he nodded.

"The Vigilant Heart works with several research groups. We provide escorts for their field trips, capture when they ask, and we bring them samples. If you join us, there's a standard bounty for any ghoul and it's tripled if you can bring it in alive."

"What's the bounty?"

"Ten thousand credits per ghoul, and it'll net you thirty thousand, if you can capture it. Like I say, tripled."

"Anything higher than that?" I asked. "Like, there's supposed to be higher than ghouls, right?"

"In the depths?" He shrugged. "In theory, yeah, there must be something above a ghoul. There's been sightings of some that are willing to make trades, asking for specific things, like transport containers of pure nanites. One that hit a chop shop a few years back was nicknamed a banshee, 'cos when it screamed, all the electrics in the area went fucking mental. Realistically, though? You see anything like that, you fucking run. I've lost entire teams in the depths the last few months, and yeah, that's why I'm desperate right now."

"Desperate, eh?"

"Desperate enough that I'm willing to be honest with you, because you could be either a great asset or a fucking waste of my time, and I've neither the time nor the energy to figure out which you are." He scrubbed at his face with one hand, then sighed. "*Look*, you get a chance to capture a ghoul? Great. Grab that fucker. We've brought a few in of late. It'll get you a decent payout, but that's split across the team. You kill standard specters? Each one is worth a hundred credits. Each, again split across the team. You go in with four others, you get twenty credits per confirmed kill.

"You all try to grab a ghoul? You'll probably lose a few people, and you'll be hit over and over again by specters as you try to extract them. I've seen it. Instead, you kill the fuckers, take down a swarm of specters with a team by your side, and you'll earn a fuckload more in the long-term. Trust me, unless the opportunity to take the ghoul is a guaranteed easy one? It's not worth it."

"So, you want me to grab them, but don't grab them?"

"I'd rather have a live team without a ghoul, or with a dead one, rather than a dead team who tried to grab one that was still functioning," he admitted. "We've had to turn down contracts this morning because we just can't cover those areas. That's not happened in years, and the specters are growing in numbers. Most mercs won't touch specter hunting. As I said before, they think they might catch something.

"That means that we're getting more and more nests popping up. They kill people or drag them off. Most of the time, they just leave the weak flesh bits, only interested in the mods, but hey. Still sucks for the one who's grabbed.

"Word spreads, and then those areas shut down. Factories fail and that's thousands of people out of work and starving. We're paid to go in and clear the area out, and we're doing that, but we can't be everywhere. We've lost teams, and now, rather than sweeping the area and keeping it at manageable levels, we're reduced to sending teams in to flatten nest after nest. It's much harder and more dangerous."

"And this is where you tell me how much extra you'll pay for me," I said flatly.

"And this is where we talk credits," he agreed. "You're a sergeant with a background in leading assault teams on fortified areas. With you leading a squad, much more likely we'll not suffer losses, or that they'll be manageable."

"You're giving me a squad?" I asked incredulously. "I just walked in the fucking door."

"And if I had a choice? No, I wouldn't be," he said. "But the simple truth is, if I give you a squad—of green recruits, to be clear—I don't have to give that squad two of my experienced people. I can give you one of them to watch over and assess you, and then I've got one more body here to rely on when the next nest pops up."

"How green?" I winced.

"You see those wannabes out there?"

I groaned.

"You're kidding me?"

"We get ten to twenty applicants a day. Even as things stand right now, we're refusing most of them. There's no point in doing it differently. If I send in thirty idiots to a fucking outbreak, chances are they'll shoot the good ones in the back, drop frags at the wrong point, or just plain run off with our guns."

"You give them guns?"

"The good but poor ones. Yeah, they're loans, but we salvage what we can down there as we go."

"Salvage…"

"As a squad, you get sixty percent of the value. Squad leader gets twenty; rest of the squad shares what's left. Four members? Ten percent each. Eight? They get five percent."

"I can do basic math." I grunted, shifting my rifle around and running my finger around the barrel, checking for dirt unthinkingly.

"Yeah, well, you were army after all…can't be too careful." He grinned.

"You a flyboy or something?" I asked, getting a glare.

"Fuck no, I had standards. Navy all the way."

"Standards in the navy? No wonder you left." I grinned. "What, didn't you want to cuddle with all the others?"

"Fucking army." He laughed. "Look, I'd happily point out the shit you ground pounders do to farm animals in training, but I don't have the time…"

"Farm animals?" I pretended to be excited. "Real ones? Where!"

"Exactly!" He grinned, before sighing and straightening. "Look, you want in? We need you, so yeah, great. You join us, and we'll make you a provisional squad leader. You'll do a few sweeps with a more experienced merc with you. I don't doubt you know your shit…" he said quickly, holding one hand up as I opened my mouth to speak. "But this isn't fighting humans—you're fighting specters. You done that much outside of an APS?"

"No, only a handful of times," I admitted.

"Exactly." He nodded. "You'll lead the squad, but we'll send…Hey, Reign!" he called to a body slumped across three seats at the back of the room, snoring in a seemingly deep sleep.

"Uh? Wassit?" An elf or thin human jerked upright, before falling off the chairs she'd apparently been sleeping on. She had blonde hair tied in a tight ponytail, and was presumably called Reign.

She sat up and wiped a hand across her mouth in about a second, a gun in one hand, staring around blearily as she surreptitiously scrubbed the drool off her other hand and on her plate carrier.

"You seen Pinot?" Julius asked her, and she blinked confusedly.

"I saw the inside of my eyelids," she said slowly. "But Pinot? He was heading for his rack."

"Damn."

"Why?"

"This is Kabutt." Julius introduced me. "New join. He's an APS sarge. Giving him a squad, but I need someone to ride herd."

"When?"

"Now?" he suggested.

I opened my mouth, about to refuse. I'd been planning to hit Lucky's first target, but after a second's hesitation I shut my mouth and shrugged. I could always do it later.

"I'm...—*yawn*—free." She covered her mouth with one hand, and I nodded to her as she looked me over.

"Appreciate it," Julius said with a smile. "I'm thinking the southeast quadrant, wall section five?"

"The bio-farms?" She stood, and I got a proper look at her.

Tall, *half*-elven, judging by the eyes and narrow build, and yeah, a massive sniper rifle. Elves had fantastic vision, naturals with ranged weapons, much as orcs were at fights where they could get up close and personal.

"Yeah, a sweep under there. They've been spotting a lot of movement and want a check over. I'd been putting them off, and honestly, I was going to just tell them to do it themselves. But hey, today's their lucky day."

"Sounds fun," she said sarcastically. "What squad are we taking?"

"A new one."

"New?"

"Green."

"Ah, fuck, boss, you didn't say that before!" she complained.

"Because you'd have been too busy," he said.

"I *was* busy."

"Sleeping."

"Three patrols in the last twelve hours," she pointed out. "One nest cleared out."

"And the reward for a job done well?" His tone made it clear this was a common comment.

"Is another goddamn job," she finished with a grumble, looking over at me. "Well then, Sarge? You coming?"

"Yeah." I stood as well, fist bumping when Julius offered me his knuckles.

"Welcome to the team," he said.

CHAPTER TWENTY-ONE

The actual registration details were trivial—literally a case of approving access to my ident, and my RI filled out the form for me. I checked it over, made a couple of corrections, as RIs were notorious for blind spots between minor details, and I approved it, pinging it across and getting a standard employment contract back, complete with penalties for collateral damage. I winced at that part.

The RI flagged a few lines; I got them clarified. Boom, the deal was done. And while I'd been doing that? Julius had called out to the room, informing the sixteen hopefuls milling about that there were spaces opening up.

They were told that they would be going on an evaluation mission, under an experienced soldier and guild evaluator, and that there would be limited numbers taken. Also, absolutely no responsibility would be taken for injuries, damages, or death sustained while trying out for the guild.

As he finished that, he turned to me and waved me forward, stepping back.

"Your team, your pick," he said simply.

"Fucker," I muttered, stepping up. "Coulda warned me."

"Where's the fun in that?" he whispered through a smile, and I glared at him.

"Right!" I barked, stepping forward and automatically falling into parade rest. "I am Sergeant Kabutt, Harry to my friends, and Sarge to you maggots! This here is Reign!" I nodded to her, and she gave them all a little wave, leaning against the wall to the left.

"Reign is *God* as far as you are concerned. I will lead you, but she will *evaluate* you and me equally. I, too, am joining the guild today, and believe me, I'd rather you all died than I got my boots dirty for nothing, so, this is how it'll work.

"*I* will direct and lead you. *You* will obey. *We* will kill any specters we see, rescue civilians, and return here. Reign will give us all an evaluation, and provided you pass her evaluation, you may be admitted into the guild. If, however, you fuck up *my* evaluation? I'll take you out back and shoot you myself. DO YOU GET ME?"

That last bit I barked at them, and among the sixteen, three called out automatically, "*We get you, SIR!*"

"You three!" I snapped. "Front and center."

The three shuffled forward, and I nodded, smiling despite myself. Two women and a man. The women seemed to be sisters, both half-orcs by the look of them. I remembered seeing them earlier. The man was a full-blooded human. All of them wore ragged but serviceable clothes, and carried standard-issue assault rifles, each with a handgun on their hip. And the two women had swords over their shoulders.

"Watch yourself with them," Julius whispered, turning his back on the group so that they couldn't see his lips and leaning in. "The sisters are lethal, but they're also fucking unstable. Get too worked up and they go off the rails. That's why they're here and not already in. Had a warning about the pair from the Noxious Ten."

"Who?"

"Another specter-hunting guild." He sighed. "They used to be in a team there, lost the rest of the team and they got booted out. Happened twice now, so nobody wants to work with them."

"And the man?"

"Not connected to the loss as near as I know. Lasted three months in the army, failed on physical training. Some genetic defect means he can't integrate with mods, so the army booted him, and he's been roaming guild to guild."

"I'll take you three," I called out. "The rest of you, dismissed."

"Fuck's sake, man. This is bullshit!" one of those not picked shouted out, waving his arms. "You some orc fucker? That it?"

I opened my mouth to respond, then saw the way one of the sisters looked to me for approval. I nodded, and she casually pivoted and punched him in the face.

Once.

He hit the floor, unconscious and as if his bones had been liquified, making me grin. A left hook like that I could respect.

"Okay, you three, this way," I ordered, leading them over to where I'd been with the reception staff, getting them into a line and ready. Each got hit with the various forms and so on while I moved to the side to speak to Reign and Julius.

"It'll be easier to work with a team that responds automatically to orders than it will to an untrained group," I explained, getting a nod from Reign and a shrug from Julius.

"I used to think that. Now I prefer experienced mercs to soldiers," he admitted. "That's my choice, though, so! Your patrol route should take about three hours. It's all underground, and while most of it is in the lower sections, floor by floor of the bio-farms, there's a few old tunnels that loop them, and you can clear them as well. Ideally? A small number to wipe out and you all get some experience in the tunnels."

"Got some of that," I muttered, before squinting at the three as they stood uncertainly. "Over here," I called, and they moved quickly, stopping before us. "Okay, we're going to be in the tunnels, so a standard sweep formation. But it's going to be darker than a corpo's soul in there. Goggles?"

"I've got some but…" the man, whose name turned out to be Hobbs said.

"But?"

"But they're a bit shit," he admitted. "Ten meters."

"Fuck." I grunted. "You two?"

"No goggles but scopes," one of the sisters said. The pair, clearly used to being mixed up as they were identical, had helmets with them, as well as their body armor, with a streak of paint down the middle of each. The one on my left introduced herself as Gessh, and had a streak of red from top to tail, and the one on the right, Luna, had blue in the same way.

Luna nodded, and I grunted.

"We'll need three pairs of goggles from the guild stores, and comm units," I said to Reign, who sighed and nodded, then flicked her gaze at their rifles in a blatant hint. "Uh…ammo. Tell me you've got plenty of…"

"Half a mag," Luna said.

"Each?" I asked, then winced at the look on her face. "And some ammo for each please, Reign. Hobbs?"

"I'm good."

"You're all carrying the same model rifles, and all here at the same time. Clearly you know each other, so…?"

"I've known her for years," Luna said cheerfully, nodding at Gessh, and I snorted.

"Yeah, all your life, right? Like sisters?"

"Damn, he's good," Gessh rumbled, before grinning as well.

"And you, Hobbs?" I asked.

"I joined the Noxious Ten a month ago," he said. "I've done four patrols, all no-shows. Then we hit a nest and it all went tits up. Only two of us survived and the team lead claimed all the loot for himself, including our shares, because 'I had to be rescued by him.'"

"Right?"

"There were three left," he spat. "We took down over a hundred. There was a ghoul leading them, and he just strolled in at the end, threw an EMP grenade and that was it, all over."

"Where was he during the fight?" I asked.

"Fuck knows. There were ten of us originally. He vanished, and they came in on all sides. And then, when it was all done, he turned up again."

"So?"

"So I quit. The bastard was blatantly hiding, thought I was dead when he claimed to be the only survivor, and he'd thrown in an EMP without checking. If the team had been alive? That'd have taken half of them down. He didn't even look."

"What did the Ten do?" Julius asked grimly.

"They said I could make a formal complaint, but I wasn't getting paid, so I took my gun and walked."

"We were leaving anyway," Gessh admitted. "We got in the shit and went…Look, we carry swords for a reason, okay? The fight goes nasty and it's in close…we're strong, so why not make the most of that?"

"What happened?"

"I killed one of our side." Luna hung her head. "I thought he was dead, piled on by a load of them, and I was swinging. It was a mess of teeth and claws and fucking implants. I just…I swung too hard and I never saw him. The assessment RI highlighted it, and I…I never even knew until afterward."

"We understand if you don't want us," Gessh said after a second, squaring her shoulders.

"Will you follow orders?" I asked, and they all nodded. "Then we're all here because we need to sort ourselves out."

"We ready?" Reign handed the goggles and bullets out: nine magazines, three for either of the girls, and three were offered to Hobbs. He shook his head, and I reached out and took them instead.

"I'm not turning down free ammo," I assured her, getting a knowing smile. "Shall we?" I nodded to the doorway, and Julius pinged me a map of the route, as well as a silent reminder that Reign would be watching, and evaluating, all of us.

Two and a half hours, three trains, and a long walk later, we eventually reached the patrol area. Reign was apparently well-known to one of the guards at the entrance to the bio-farm, who took a cursory glance at our idents before waving us through.

"Once you're all members in good standing, we get to bill transport costs to the client," Reign offered with a smile as we walked across the short distance to the main entrance.

I didn't care though, not about that at least.

"What the hell is that goddamn *smell*?" I stared around in shock. It was worse than that time the entire squad caught blue fever and we were quarantined in our barracks. Three days in a small space with all six of us shitting and throwing up every few minutes.

By the end of it, we'd all chipped in together and had the rooms fumigated and all soft furnishings—which there weren't many of; it was the army, after all— were burned unceremoniously.

"And that's how you spot a first-time visitor to the bio-farms!" Reign laughed. "You've got sensory input linked to your mods?"

"Yeah…"

"You should be able to adjust it. Here, use this." She sent me a compressed datapacket, and I eyed it dubiously. "Seriously, it's not a virus. Fuck's sake, I'm about to go hunting specters with you. Believe me, I want you at your best right now."

"Okay…" I agreed, but still, I had the RI assess the package.

> **Confirmed:**
> Datapacket contains adjustment commands to alter sensory input to new preset levels.

I squinted, then thought *fuck it*, and ran it, making sure I could undo it with a thought if need be.

The smell intensified, then shifted, lessening, before a sudden burning sensation and prickle in my nose that made me want to sneeze, and then…fresh baked bread and vanilla pods.

I hesitated, took a deep lungful, and relaxed.

"Damn. Hot damn," I said. "What a difference!"

"Nice, right?" she asked, and I nodded, before looking at the others, and the distress on their faces.

"I take it you've not got any brain mods?" I asked, getting shaken heads as my only response. "Fair enough." I sighed.

"Here, it's not as good, but it works." Reign passed out little pots that she'd picked up from a dispenser by the door. "Smear it below your nostrils. It's minty."

A handful of seconds and the others had done so, relaxing marginally as they did.

"Right, so once we're in here, we need to pass between the workers' sections first. There'll be people in here, not specters—or at least there better not be—so keep your weapons on safe. Once we're past there, we get a lift down to the first level, and the evaluation begins. Good luck, everyone," Reign said, and I nodded my thanks.

"Appreciate it," I said softly, and she smiled as she led the way, pausing for me to send our job ident to the door controller.

"Oh, believe me," she said firmly. "If possible? I'd love nothing more than for you to all get full marks and join us full-time. More teams mean more backup and a generally easier time for everyone." She turned to make sure I was listening before going on. "That said, Kabutt, I'd rather fail you all than put a team out in the field that hasn't got what it takes. You fuck up here? It's on you. You get a pass and then fuck up later? That's on me—that's my rep that's ruined, and maybe my ass that's left out hangin' in the wind."

"And it's such a nice ass too," Luna quipped, getting a glare from Reign.

"You often interrupt private conversations, recruit?" she snapped.

Luna swallowed hard.

"Sorry, Assessor. I assumed that if it was private, it'd have been on a single party sub-vocal."

"Never assume." Reign glowered at her. "And next time you reference my ass, it better be when you're holding a goddamn drink out."

"Uh…yes, sir," Luna replied, frowning.

Reign turned away. The assessor shot me a wink when she knew Luna couldn't see.

I hid a smile, already liking Reign, strolling along with her as we passed row after row of wide, shallow tanks.

Glancing in, I quickly looked away again. The foul mess before me bubbled as it was force-fed massive amounts of growth hormones. Its pale skin slowly shivered as pseudo-muscles shifted and massaged the slab, six meters on a side, ensuring an even distribution of the flavor.

I saw the marker, and instantly knew that my days of eating Royal Porkin' sandwiches were damn well over. The sight of that mass of flesh, like someone had skinned a whale, then set it to bobbing in a shallow tank, would never leave me.

"You looked in?" Reign asked me, and I nodded.

"Yeah, never again."

"That's what I said," she offered. "My kind, we're usually pretty easygoing with plant-based, you know?"

"Yeah?"

"Trust me. You don't want to see the fields of brocciflower." She shivered slightly. "Three days before I could bring myself to eat anything, and by that point? Fuck it. You learn to get over it. You want my advice? Whatever it was you saw, order some as soon as you're back to your digs tonight. Eat it, force it down, and you'll get over it. Otherwise it'll stick with you."

"I'll remember that," I muttered. "I thought nothing would put me off after eating army grub."

"Yeah, I bet." She laughed. "You've seen this stuff on 'casts, right?"

I nodded. "Yeah. Hell, at school we were taught where food comes from. It's just…"

"It didn't look or smell like that," she agreed. "Believe me, I know."

While we were talking, we passed a handful more of the vats. All of us made the point of not looking in. As Reign and the map led us to the far lift, the five of us stepped in and sent our idents and job details to the RI again.

This time, when the RI accepted the details, it unlocked a section of the lift, and a new pad slid forth.

> Please confirm acceptance that no injury, damage, nor loss of life sustained on these premises are legally the responsibility of Bio-Corp.

We all had to send a second indent confirmation and press a thumb to the scanner. But that done, the lift finally moved, passing down into the undercity.

"No offense, people, but I hope you're ready for this," Reign called out, moving to the back of the group and pulling a helmet over her head. Six separate lights triggered on the front, making it look as if she had glowing insect eyes watching us all. "As of now, recording date and time-stamped at twenty-one hundred and eleven minutes, sixteen seconds, I confirm assessor status has been logged for the guild Vigilant Heart."

That said, and with each of us getting a request from her RI to accept recording access to our senses, the fun really started.

"Begin."

CHAPTER TWENTY-TWO

"Okay, people, look sharp," I ordered. "Goggles on. Check your rifles. Check your ammo. Gessh, you're on the left. Luna, right. I lead, Reign in the middle. Hobbs, you're ass-end Charlie."

"Ready," Reign said, echoed quickly by the others.

"Got it," Hobbs agreed.

"Aye, sir."

"Aye, sir." The sisters replied almost as one.

As soon as the lift hit the first floor, the sealed barriers shuddered for a second, before sliding back in a slow release of chilled gasses.

We were off.

The lower floors of the bio-farm were massively different. Up above, the air had been sweltering, like the height of summer. But down here? We were surrounded by clouds of vapor. Our own breathing fogged up the air and made it hard to see.

The passage ahead of us led between massive storage tanks, making it narrow, but high. Coolant pipes covered in frost ran down either side, and the lights overhead here were spaced farther out. A low, blue light tinted the air and made the passages seem even colder.

There was metal everywhere, and frost, but inside my helmet, I grinned, thankful for the temperature regulation capability. I'd not expected to need it, certainly not this soon, but damn.

I led the way down the corridor, the five of us as silent as we could be. We came to an end and followed the indicator my RI flashed on my vision, taking a left at the end of the T junction. We continued down, then a second left, looping around coolant towers. We passed between old vats that were out of commission and undergoing repairs, or flavors that had been long since decommissioned. Fifty minutes later, we were approaching the lift from the right-hand side fork, having done a full loop of this level, and Reign spoke into her recorder.

"Full loop of level one complete. Assessment: solid run." With that, she clearly clicked it off as we approached the lift, speaking more normally. "Okay, guys, good one. Yeah, we didn't see anything, and that's totally fine. No, we don't get more than the basic rate for this mission if we don't actually kill any specters, but honestly, as a training and evaluation run, I'm fine with limited danger."

"Anything we missed?" I asked.

"Look up more," she said after a second, clearly considering whether she should say it. "Remember these aren't sane enemies. They don't feel pain, so they climb across areas that would be no-go areas to us."

"Shit, do we..."

She shook her head. "Don't worry. I kept checking. It's something loads of teams forget until the first time one falls on them."

"Okay, thanks." I sighed as we all piled into the lift, selecting the next floor and heading down.

Two more floors passed like this, before the fourth and final floor, the one that led to the tunnels, opened in a fresh cloud of vapor.

Instantly, we all knew the game had changed. For a start, the floors above had been covered in frost, with the floor covered in pristine whorls and ice crystals before we scuffed them, passing over.

The floor here was covered in meandering, overlapping footprints—dozens at least—and the walls were scraped and scuffed much the same.

The icy pipes that ran here and there had frozen bits clinging to them, and I uneasily suspected they were remnants of flesh.

I spoke quickly.

"Okay, people, game faces on. We've got roaming ones here."

I led the way out, the same layout as the floors above here, with a T junction ahead. I paused at the edge, looking left and right, then examining the floor.

This was the first realistic problem we had. If we move left, and they come along from behind us to the right? We might stroll around and miss each other all the way.

Alternately, if we split the team, we'd cover more ground, but massively up the risk.

My first instinct was to leave a drone here, to watch, or to set up overlapping fields of fire and make some noise, draw them to me. Neither was available, as we were required to patrol, and had no fucking drones.

"Keep on me. If we see lone stragglers? I'll direct Luna and Gessh to take them in melee. We do this as quiet as we can, for the first loop," I ordered.

"First loop?" Reign asked, and I smiled in my helmet, knowing this was being recorded.

"We do a full loop, eliminate anything we find, then set up here again, make some noise and wait. Anything that's here but that we've missed while wandering the corridors is drawn to us. We eliminate it and move on. If there's too many? A nest or whatever? We can fall back to the lift, rather than draw them deeper in."

"Logical. I like it," she admitted.

We were off then, taking the left as we had been. I moved with my rifle up, the others behind me with theirs down, apart from Hobbs, on the rear, rifle up and walking backward.

Two lefts, and we were passing a cooling tower, a mass of interconnected pipes that flooded in and out of a specialized super-cooler. The temperature dropped massively as we approached, and based on the levels above, we were used to passing through this section quickly.

As we closed on it, though? There were definite metallic *clunks* echoing ahead.

I took the corner slowly, edging around a set of outward-jutting pipes attached to the wall. And there she was, our first customer.

She'd been tall in life, clearly a party girl, judging from the remains of her outfit. It was too classy and expensive to be a hooker, yet showing about the same amount of flesh in clear advertising.

That she was tugging herself free of the pipes ahead, a ripping and cracking sound coming from the skin of her upper arm, and yet she wasn't making a sound beyond that?

Yeah, she was gone.

I moved closer, then stepped to the left, pressing myself against the wall, and gestured Luna closer, making an "off with her head" gesture, and getting a nod from the half-orc.

She slid the rifle over her shoulder and drew the sword from her back, the gentle hiss of steel leaving its sheath lost in the constant *thrummm* of the machinery all around us.

Stepping up, she hesitated, before looking back to me.

I cursed, seeing the look in her eyes. *Uncertainty. Was this definitely a specter, and not a woman lost, and somehow here, drugged up to the eyeballs?*

I paused and gave her a "wait" gesture. I slid around her again, moving up to the woman, then tapped her hard on the right shoulder, before darting to the left.

She turned slowly, staggering as she ripped herself free. The flesh and material left behind exposed blackened wiring and slowly moving pistons in her upper arm.

It wasn't the arm that got our attention, though, nor that set Luna swinging.

I'd guessed party girl—I didn't know what the others had guessed—but clearly something had happened when she was getting a facial reconstruction, or the faceplate had been ripped away since.

Her head had skin and hair from an inch below the hairline and running back, from just before the ears, and from below the chin. But the actual face? The eyes? All of it?

Totally *gone.*

In its place was a robotic visage. The plates of chrome that should have had the cheeks and muscles attached to individual sensors and hooks were bare. The eyes darted around, filmed in death with flickering, clearly damaged artificial eyelids still in place. And the mouth?

Damn.

Gleaming porcelain teeth gripped by steel reinforcement clacked and reflected the light.

Luna slammed her sword into her neck, the blade clearly a lot more advanced than simple shining steel, judging by the way it sheared through the composite plastic of her neck brace.

The body collapsed, falling sideways and clattering off the pipes. The head bounced, a fleshy *bump-bump* as it landed…before a loud *clang* as the faceplate connected with a pipe.

I moved quickly, leading the others forward, as Luna deactivated then wiped the blade, sliding it away and taking up position behind her sister in the line.

The path looped around the outside of a circular tower. All the pipes flew into the center, and as I led the way around it, feet crunching in the ice and general "bits" that were suddenly everywhere, cold-welded to the floor, the rest came into view as the room opened up into the central chamber.

At least a dozen of them were all gathered around a small section of a defunct tower, trying to open it. They'd been working at the metal, pawing and scratching. But now? The clang had alerted one or two at the back, and as soon as they saw us, they started to move.

Something about their movement alerted more and more, as they ran at us.

"Spread out, rifles up," I ordered, my voice adding to the draw.

"Remember, minimum collateral damage," Reign barked out, and I winced, remembering that from the contracts.

"Single-shot headshots," I called out. "If you're not confident, take them down with legs, then headshot when they're on the floor. Open fire in three…two…"

We all fired on one, a solid single roar as all five guns opened up. Reign took her targets down with military perfection: single shot, single kill.

I was less so, the rifle new to me, and although the distance wasn't huge, it was still thirty meters. And their staggering, swaying motion as they ran at us meant I missed as many as I got.

Hobbs was good—damn, he was good—single shots ringing out steadily, as more and more came from the sides where they'd been apparently swarmed around the tower, trying to get in.

As they closed on us, we switched from single shot to triple. The four of us did, anyway. Reign continued in single fire, and I moved steadily from one to another as more and more appeared.

"Okay, people!" I called into comms, my training keeping my voice steady as I spoke. "We've got more swinging in from the sides. Luna and Gessh, slide out to the left and right. I've got the center, Reign on my immediate right, Hobbs on the left. On two, rifles dip; three, you move. Got that?"

"Aye!" Four lots of agreement rang out, and I nodded, before speaking. "One, two…" I paused, giving time and lowering my rifle as the others did. "Three…" Luna and Gessh had previously been in the middle of the group, and as the melee experts they were, they were much more valuable on the outside when the numbers picked up like this.

"Okay, rifles up. Cut them down!" I barked, doing it myself as I opened fire.

More came from around the tower, but as the shots flew, they lessened, and I moved slowly, flicking back to single shot, aware I'd be running low on ammo. I lined up and fired, taking another in the head.

"I'm out!" Luna called, jerking her empty mag out and dumping it, reaching for another, swiftly echoed by her sister.

The specters were uniformly filthy and low level, battered and hungry, arms and teeth reaching as they sensed our nanites and mods, desperate for them. We fucking mowed them down, one after another. I sent a thought to the RI: *Track kills*.

In the corner of my vision, a number flashed up: fourteen. I fired and it shifted, blurring to fifteen, then sixteen. Over and over, we fired, and I cursed as my mag clicked, the gun ejecting it as I thumbed the release, catching the mag as it fell.

"Reloading!" I called, echoed a second later by Hobbs. Luna and Gessh were already back up and firing.

I rammed it down into the mag-grip on my back, designed for literally this: it'd hold the magazine, provided there wasn't a serious blow there or anything, until I had the time to grab it, reload, and put it away properly.

Almost as soon as I released it, I slid another from my chest rig, slapping it into place with a solid click as the latches engaged. I yanked the charging handle.

They were close, much closer than I liked. Raising the rifle, I opened fire, taking down the nearest.

Nineteen kills. Twenty, twenty-one, and…I switched aim, zeroing in on the last one, only to have it fall before I could fire.

"Mine," Reign said smugly.

"Good shot." I approved. "Okay, everyone, reload, check the area. Luna, Gessh, clear the bodies."

Agreement rang out, and then we were all moving. Those with low ammo replaced their magazine with a full one, just in case, and the sisters moved out.

"What's the rules on the bodies?" I said to Reign, and she paused, shifting to look at me.

"What do you mean?"

"I mean the salvage."

"Julius said sixty—" she started to say.

I nodded, cutting her off.

"I know for the normal stuff…I mean the mods."

"What about the mods?"

"Are we salvaging the mods?" I said clearly. "Like, do we get a portion of that? Who do they get sold to?"

"AH!" She grinned as she understood. "Sorry, totally confused me there. No. I mean, who'd use a mod from a specter? Sounds like a fast way to the grave to me. We have a team that comes along behind us. They clean up when it's in unowned areas and so on. In places like this? We take what we want and the owner of the building either contracts a cleanup crew, or they pay the extra and we dispose using our team."

"And today?"

"Best just to leave it. We check them and loot anything that's valuable, then we hand it in on return to the guild. It gets split up and paid out, less fees."

"Fees?"

"Cleaning, repairs, and guild membership." She sighed. "It's not that bad really, you know. There are days I'd rather not pay it, but…" She tapped a hand under her eye, or where her eyes were, considering her helmet.

I took the hint.

We'd all allowed access for recording and evaluation, and if there was a way around the taxes and so on, she wasn't going to say anything right now.

"No worries, just wanted to be sure." I forced a smile as I looked around, mentally cursing at the mods that were going to be lost.

I had no doubt that whoever the cleanup crew was, they'd be making a killing off this.

As soon as the sisters had confirmed the bodies were just that, and definitely dead, we fell to with a will, searching them and piling the loot in the middle of the room.

Everything from credit-chips and precious metals in the shape of rings, necklaces, and more were collected, along with a handful of tech items, busted datadecks and more.

I asked Reign to go over it, her having a lot more experience than the rest of us. She quickly sorted it all out, discarding a bunch of the crap before moving to the ammo and weapons.

Three knives, a small pistol, laser—which was nice, and clearly designed to be concealed, considering where Hobbs had found it on the first body.

He didn't elaborate, but the ladies looked at him a bit weirdly after that, and I chose not to ask.

There were also some shock knuckles—discharged—and a single high-power "assault alarm" that one of the bodies had on him. It was a semi-legal "defense tool."

Basically, you point it at the issue, and you press the button. At your end, it shook a little, and that was pretty much it. In the very specific cone of effect, you got hit with a sonic-based attack that although silent to the rest of the world, hit you with debilitating nausea, making the target lose all control of their balance and experiencing both explosive diarrhea *and* nausea.

Apparently, they were effective. No rapist was going to be up to doing the deed while crawling around on the floor, unable to stop shitting themselves and vomiting everywhere.

We bundled them all into a bag, Hobbs volunteering to carry it, and started off, heading back on patrol.

Or at least that was the intention.

CHAPTER TWENTY-THREE

We'd just started off, when Reign spun, dropping low and lifting her rifle, zeroing in on the derelict cooling tower the specters had been trying to get at, and from which she'd apparently heard a noise.

"Inside," she snapped, and I nodded, speaking quickly.

"Okay, people, spread out." I expected that we had either a specter stuck inside or some kind of vermin or something. "Luna, you see something?" I asked, as she started to move, then stepped back, squatting down.

"Liquid…" she said slowly. "Leaking from under a manifold."

"Liquid?"

"Piss," she corrected, sniffing, then sighing. "If it's strong enough I can smell it over all this shit in the air, there's only one fucking species it can be."

"Oh, for fuck's sake!" Reign growled. "They'd be how the specters got in! Fucking hell, that's all we need—a bloody infestation in the bowels of the building…"

"What?" I asked, seeing the others all grimacing or sighing.

"Goblins," Reign clarified. "Shit, you're really still stuck in 'soldier boy' mode, aren't you?"

"Ah, crap," I muttered, nodding. "Sorry. Of course, goblins!"

Goblins were regarded, depending on who was speaking, as anything from vermin that were slightly less welcome than ex-partners with a sexual disease to occasionally, if you were feeling generous, a highly unfortunate sapient species.

They were the most adaptogenic of the species living in the city, had both an extremely fast genetic adjustment period and were ferocious breeders. These traits meant that goblins, although rarely seen, were literally fucking everywhere.

They weren't the brightest, and although their bodies adapted to allow them to survive almost anywhere, their brains weren't in the same category. That was the only reason they weren't running the world right now.

Their minds moved more to cunning and manipulation, or insane weaponry and creations, rather than developing as a race, and there were as many theories about why as there were raindrops.

Most of the goblins in the city were baseline gobbos: short, around three feet tall, living on rats and other vermin, attempting to break into anywhere they could and steal anything not nailed down.

Shopkeepers had learned to their detriment that if you dealt with gobbos, it cost you. Buy stolen goods? Expect them to be casing your defenses as they sell you their loot.

Attack them? They'll target you, piss in your window, and rub shit on your walls all the way around, and you could expect mail with squishy additions at any time of the day or night.

No, the only way to deal with gobbos was acknowledged to be to make them someone else's problem. Leaving some meat outside a rival shop's garbage disposal or random bits of tech worked wonders, as did ignoring them—close up, seal the shop, have a long day off if they turn up.

You might as well; nobody was entering a shop with gobbos around it, and if you stayed open? They'd rob you blind.

No, best to close up and let them get bored and move on.

The other option, of course, was extermination.

Entire guilds were dedicated to goblin "issues," offering anything from "protection" packages to outright slaughtering the little bastards. The fun thing was, most of the top guilds offering this?

Run by half-breed goblins.

Higher and more intelligent versions, true, but there were a hell of a lot of different variants, and most of the half-goblin breeds weren't accepted the way the rest of the city was with the other races.

I'd dealt with them a lot growing up in the city, mainly placing bets on the various internecine conflicts as they sprang up, or hiring random gobbos to do "jobs" for me.

Things like sending them to deliver "gifts" to an ex, that kinda thing.

I'd viewed them as slightly brighter rodents, and that was it. I'd grown up in a military family, so they weren't really an issue for me. They tended not to fuck with the forces, because they got exterminated quickly when they did.

They were "experience" for green troops, after all.

Now, though? Now I was remembering the other side of dealing with the goblins, and fuck.

They tended to view it as anything they could grab was theirs by rights of conquest. And finding their way into here? The bottom of a literal bio-food factory?

This wouldn't be cheap to sort out...or it wouldn't if...

"How many?" I asked.

"Not sure," Luna admitted, before moving over and kicking the side of the tower. "Oi, you little shits! Get out!"

There was silence for a few seconds before the response came.

"We's not here!" a voice called out, and I facepalmed at the stupidity.

"Who's not there?" Luna asked.

"Us."

"Who's us?" she asked again, looking over at me and grinning.

"We grew up with gobbos in the block," Gessh whispered to me. "Give her a minute."

"We's us."

"No you're not."

"Yes we is!"

"No, you're not there. You already said."

"We is here!"

"I don't believe you!"

"We here!"

"Liar!"

"Me no liar!" A scuffle broke out and ten seconds later, five battered, filthy, and glowering goblins stood before us. One wore a hat that was…yeah, it was wearing a porta-potty seat as a hat.

It even had the image of a toddler shitting on it, albeit upside down at the minute.

"We's us!" the toilet seat-wearing idiot proudly proclaimed.

"No," Luna said flatly. "You said you weren't there, now you say you are. You're liars!"

"Me NEVER lie!" he growled, straightening up and glowering at us, while fingering a shitty hatchet with a cracked edge.

"Prove it."

"How?"

"How'd you get in here?"

"Tunnel," he declared happily. "Tunnel not locked."

"I don't believe you."

"We shows you! You have to 'pologise then!"

"Maybe." Luna stifled a smile as the little leader stormed off, the remains of his clan following him.

We followed as well, stepping over bodies as we went, passing the occasional specter, apparently gnawed, clawed, or stabbed to death, and dead goblins, literally dozens of them for each of the specters.

Ten minutes later, we found the tunnel entrance, propped open and with a veritable mound of the dead beyond it.

Seemingly, as Luna found out by questioning the gobbos, the noises that the bio-farm staff had been hearing filtering up and the weird sightings had been the gobbos and specters fighting it out.

Normally gobbos wouldn't bother the specters, as they had nothing worth stealing to make it worth the almost certain slaughter they'd get. And the specters didn't bother the gobbos, as they rarely had the mods that the specters wanted.

The only goblins that tended to have mods were the half-breeds, most often the dvar.

Dvar were much rarer than the other species, mainly because to breed a dvar, you needed a goblin and a dwarf to get it on—and dwarves were notoriously insular, or at least they were until recently. Unlike humans, of course, who demonstrably would fuck anything that moved. And if it didn't? It got fucked *twice*.

The dvar were insanely rare outside of dwarven territory, and, according to urban legend, only existed due to a particularly drunk dwarf one night who was so far gone in his cups, he didn't realize that not only had his wife left him—for having a shitty beard, so the story went—but that when he climbed into bed and tried "prodding her with it, to get her in the mood" failed to notice she was much smaller, greener, and apparently more willing than normal.

The next morning, he'd sobered up and been furious, kicking the goblin out. But in true hungover, morning-after-the-one-night-stand style, he decided that he might as well have one last go first.

The goblin was perfectly willing, totally ignoring him essentially as she ate everything on the table and he entertained himself.

Once the deed was done, she'd been evicted, and when he'd sobered up, he'd been furious and disgusted with himself.

After a hard week at work, though, and a lot to drink, the dwarf had "accidentally" left the window to his apartment open again, and sure enough, she "snuck" in.

That went on for weeks and then months, until suddenly, much to his horror, she presented him with a bouncing baby boy, the first dvar.

She'd buggered off, having found something shiny elsewhere, and he was left to raise the child. He kept it hidden, often leaving it to play with some of the simple machinery toys he'd learned with as a child.

When he returned home from work one day and actually paid attention, he'd been astounded to find the machinery correctly assembled.

He tried his son on a more complex issue, then another and another.

By the time the dvar child was ten, he had a grasp of mechanics and engineering that was so advanced that his father was forced to take him to the dwarven council and admit to the whole sordid story.

At first, they were disgusted, then intrigued. Ten more dwarves were picked out and ordered to breed with the goblins.

Six refused outright. Four agreed, with caveats and impressive advance payments. After the first four shared their first night's experiences with the other six—including that not only did the women in question *not have beards* but that they were exceedingly willing, rather than basically glaring at them and offering unhelpful comparisons and comments as encouragement—well, they promptly changed their minds and gave it a go as well.

The next generation of dvar grew up to be a problem. Naturally adaptive and engineering wonders, they were recognized as a potential threat to the dwarven race, as they could supplant them and literally breed them out of existence.

The dwarves solved the problem in their own, inimitable way. They declared goblins fair game, but only one per clan could breed with them, and by lottery only.

This eventually evolved, according to legend, into a game of bingo, and the dwarven taverns soon rang with the calls of "two fat ladies, eighty-eight" and so on, as dwarven clan leaders frantically dabbed out the numbers on their bingo cards.

The winner would be proclaimed with a great cheer, before the rest of the tavern would finally get drunk, drowning their sorrows over the lucky dwarf who was being mobbed by goblin ladies.

The dwarves, of course, denied this myth totally.

All of this went through my mind as I stared at the goblins before me, and a sneaking suspicion grew. It only took a minute to check the goblins over. It was blatantly obvious that none of them had anything that the specters would be interested in, until I focused on the abnormally large "hat" their leader wore.

"Your hat," I said slowly, as Luna and the goblin argued over whether he was a liar or not, and he tried to deny having ever met her before right this very second, in the tunnels outside of "his" factory.

"Family hat," he said. "Very old. Very important."

"Can I see it?" I asked.

"It invisible? You no see it?" he asked me, confused. "Me invisible?"

"No, I can see you, and the hat," I clarified. "Can I have a closer look at it?"

"What you got?" He smiled, looking me up and down. "Trade?"

"For a hat?" I asked him, reaching into a pocket and pulling out a dead credit-chip. "Depends. I'd need to look at the hat first."

"How much on this?"

"Lots," I assured him, and he nodded, slipping it into a pocket. "So?"

"So what?"

"So give me the damn hat!" I growled.

"No." He grinned. "You say closer look. You look." He leaned forward, angling it so I could see it clearer, but still leaving me utterly unable to tell whether there was anything inside.

"Listen here, you little shit!" I growled. "We just saved your fucking life from those specters! We spent all that ammo to save you and…"

"You save goblin?" he asked slowly, his smile widening as Luna frantically shook her head to me in warning.

"No…" I said slowly, confused.

"You liar!"

"No I'm not!" I growled, before shaking my head, realizing I was arguing with a goblin, that I'd just lied to, about whether I was a liar or not. "Ah, fuck it," I growled, shifting my rifle across my chest, and reaching for my handgun, about to "solve" the goblin issue permanently.

"Kabutt…" Reign said slowly, and I glanced at her, only to have her tap her eye again warningly.

"Fuck," I growled. "It was only a thought."

"I know," she agreed. "And I understand it, but obviously you wouldn't have been actually thinking of executing a sentient being here for annoying you, right?"

"No," I assured her from between gritted teeth. "Certainly not."

"Glad to hear it. Of course, should the owners of this property demand we do something, that would be different, as we'd be paid exterminators with a formal contract."

I couldn't help but grin, and then, taking the pretty unsubtle hint, I replied, "Reign, make the contract owners aware of the goblins in the basement, and that they *and* specters are down here. In fact…might want to mention that we've found…" I paused, quickly counting the overall numbers of specters and goblins—not the living numbers, just the overall. "At least twenty goblins and about fifty specters, with probably more in the tunnels outside."

"Will do." She released her rifle and casually fist-bumped me as she put the call through.

"What you do?" The goblin looked from one of us to the other.

"Nothing," I assured him. "She's talking to the person who owns this place, and who paid us to come here to kill the specters…"

"Me did it."

"What?"

"Me paid you," he declared, smiling grandly. "Me own this."

"You own it?"

"Me do."

"Then you owe us…ten thousand credits," I declared, picking the number at random.

"What!" He screeched. "No!"

"Each."

"Me no pay!"

"You see all of these?" I gestured to the specters. "We killed them. We need to be paid."

"Me no pay."

"Well, if that's how it's going to be…"

"Kabutt?" Reign called, and I nodded to her, looking away from the goblin for a minute, only to see a sudden sharp movement as he lunged in close.

I twisted, blocking on instinct. Long years of wearing armored suits came to the fore as I blocked the hatchet with my left forearm. Sparks flared to life from the metal on metal before I punched the little shit in the face with the right.

It staggered back, and the others lunged to attack my squad. Luna and Gessh, well versed in dealing with gobbos and their innate treachery, were already flicking blood off their blades. Hobbs had apparently punted his so hard in the crotch that even if it lived, it'd certainly never walk straight again, and Reign didn't bother with a bullet, flipping her rifle around and slamming it butt-first into the nearest one's head with a crunch.

That left only mine staggering, hands pressed to his face, as he snarled at me. Pulling them down, his long ears quivering in outrage and pointed nose blatantly broken, he screamed at me and leapt forward, hatchet swinging wildly.

I dragged the pistol out and shot him once in the chest. His little toast-rack of a rib cage barely slowed the bullet, before he collapsed, dead.

"Wait!" Reign called out as Luna went to behead Hobbs's opponent—who was clutching his family jewels and making sounds that only small dogs could hear—and we all looked to her.

"Accept the update…" she said to me, shooting the contract over.

I read it, seeing the amendment that had been added. It was outlined in red against the original version I'd seen, thanks to my RI.

I skimmed it, then nodded, approving it and grinning. An additional twenty credits would be added to the bill, per goblin killed.

As soon as I signed it, and approved, Reign nodded to Luna, who ended the little goblin's misery.

"Saw the way you marked it." I nodded to Reign in respect, and she grinned, before explaining for the others' benefit.

"Well, as you said, there *were* more than twenty goblins down here, so I got it phrased so we're paid for each goblin marked as dead."

I saw the understanding spreading. Sure, we might have killed five, but that didn't mean we were only getting paid for that.

Every single body dragged in, we'd get paid for.

We set about quickly, looting each one, and although there was little more to add to the pile, I thought I recognized the botched-together bit of kit I found, unsurprisingly, hidden in the leader's "hat."

I was also stunned that it was here, and seriously curious how a fucking goblin, of all creatures, had managed to get its filthy claws on it.

"What's that?" Reign asked.

I grinned as I checked it over.

"It's a bonus if I can get it working." I pointed to the damage that was clear for all to see. "It looks a bit like some of the tech I used to have to carry in the APS Corps. Might be able to fix it yet, but—"

"More specters, boss!" Hobbs called around the edge of the door, and I grunted, quickly dumping it into my bag, rather than the general one.

"Okay, people, game faces back on!" I ordered, stepping up and through the door, squinting down the tunnel that ran left and right from the entrance. "What are we dealing with, Reign?"

"We've got to get this door sealed to confirm the contract completed, but even if we could with them out here, they're determined to get inside. We need to wipe them all out."

"We've got more bodies out here to loot anyway!" Gessh added, making me grin.

I liked dealing with half-orcs. I sort of liked dealing with orcs as well. They were good soldiers, or they were once they survived long enough for the army to see past their species.

At first? They were generally used as cannon fodder. Sent out to catch a bullet so it didn't end up in someone the army had already spent money on training.

Half-orcs, though? People viewed them as they did the other half-breeds that made up a serious percentage of the city's population, as just another person, rather than the way that people crossed the street when an orc dared to walk down the sidewalk in the posher areas.

It was probably down to the way that just as in humans, a blonde and a brunette parent might have blonde, brunette, or redheaded kids, but you never knew. And some might have almost none of the parents' visible traits, and others would be carbon copies.

Well, half-breeds were the same. Half-orcs varied from just slightly denser muscles and bigger teeth, to looking like full-on orcs almost. Where people could pass as simply generic half-breeds? They did.

Half-orc mercs, though? Damn, they were *good*. As intelligent as any other, but stronger, faster, and when the shit hit the fan, they stood their ground. They also liked loot and partying as much as any other soldier I'd ever served with.

It was like being home.

The tunnel we'd stepped out into was one of the old mass transit ones from under the city—not a physical transport one, like the ones that carried trains and more. This was one of the additional foot traffic ones, running alongside and under the trains, letting people travel to work from the stations, without ever having to set foot above ground.

I'd heard that harked back to the days of the nukes and the wild nanite plagues, but who knew really.

It meant, though, that the entire undercity was riddled with tunnels, and although the city above had tried to close them all off, sealing sections as more and more goblins, specters, and undesirables were driven deeper, the tunnels were gradually opened by them as the new inhabitants took over new sections, fought hidden wars, and then vanished again.

These tunnels had been moved into at some point. Wooden barriers had been set up, forming hidden shacks, and then they'd been smashed down. Old blood stains covered the walls, and at least a dozen specter and goblin bodies were scattered around out here. Most of them had been hacked apart, making it clear that the goblins hadn't been happy to be driven back.

They were vicious little fuckers, and wherever they'd gotten their little artifact from, I didn't know, but the specters seriously wanted it back.

The route to the right was empty and silent, but at least a dozen of them staggered forward. The glowing red and blue of backlit optics made the tunnel look even weirder with my vision enhancements.

"Okay, people!" I called out. "Let's get some room first. Shoulder to shoulder, free fire—take them all down."

It only took a few seconds, maybe half a minute of careful fire, and they were dropped. In the distance, though, I could see more coming already, slowly appearing at the very limit of my range.

"Is that it?" Hobbs asked.

"Nope," Reign replied before I could. "Ten more I can see…nine."

She finished her words with a gunshot, and then another a few seconds later: "Eight."

"Reign, keep taking them down. I'll keep an eye on our rear. Luna, Geesh…loot the corpses. Hobbs, check that goddamn door. We need to seal it," I ordered.

They moved fast, the occasional curses rising as the girls searched the bodies, before Hobbs called over from the door.

"Boss, we've got a problem."

"What's that?"

"Goblins fucked the locking mechanism. No way we can seal this."

"What'd they do to it?" Luna asked in disbelief.

"Looks like a jury-rigged plasma torch. Literally carved the lock apart. The door won't stay closed, no way."

"Shit." I cursed. "Okay, so can we brace it? Or—"

"More coming!" Reign called, and I twisted around, moving to stand next to her, squinting.

"Too far," I said in a low voice. "I can't see anything."

"They're hanging back." She cursed. "Nothing behind us?"

"Nothing *I* can see. Take a minute and jog that way—you'll see farther than me. I'll shout if they reach my range here," I ordered after a second. "Luna, Geesh, with me." They moved in closer, and I spoke quickly. "The goblins had something that drew the specters, and—"

"That thing you grabbed?" Luna asked, and I paused, looking at her. My helm must have been intimidating in the dark, as she held one hand up in apology.

"I don't know. It could be, if it's what I think it is, but I don't know how they got one, and it's damaged."

"What is it?" Hobbs called, and I ignored him.

"So, we need to hold this line until Hobbs can fix—"

"I can't fix it," he said. "Not without some tools at the very least, and one of them better be an arc welder. That door is *fucked.*"

"Okay, we've got specters gathering at either end of the tunnel." Reign jogged back to us. "What's the plan, boss?" She grinned nervously.

"What happens if we can't seal the tunnel?" I asked her instead.

"If we leave?"

"No, I mean if we just can't seal it. The door's too damaged. They didn't send us with construction gear…"

"Ah." She hesitated, clearly giving me a chance to figure out a solution, before she had to mark me down for it.

I realized this was something that had to happen fairly regularly, so therefore…

"Reign, contact the client, request a team to seal the door?" I asked, and she grinned, nodding, as I let out a breath of relief.

Taking my question as an order, she got to work while I turned to the others.

"Okay, the doorway is our retreat point. If the shit hits the fan? We get inside. We're not losing people for the sake of the contract. That being said, we need to sort this clusterfuck out. If there's specters gathering, rather than just rushing us, we've got a ghoul at least somewhere. We hold the line here, kill the fuckers, and once they start shooting at us? We all focus fire on that fuck."

"Take him down, and the rest will revert," Hobbs agreed. "Ranged?"

"As much as we can," I said. "We take down all those we can at range. If they get in too close, melee if we have to. I'll switch to shotgun if they get in close. I've got a few 'fun' rounds loaded, so make sure you're not between me and them when I pull it."

"Oh gods…" Luna breathed, before grinning. "Well, at least there's gonna be plenty of loot, and if we're claiming for all the specters and all the gobbos?"

"Yeah." I grinned, even if they couldn't see it. "Payday."

CHAPTER TWENTY-FOUR

With specters alone, I was at twenty-nine now. If we counted all the dead ones, and the kills the rest of the team had gotten so far, we were over a hundred. And there'd been at least thirty gobbos. That brought us up to…

I stopped trying to work it out and sent the details to the RI, relieved as I did so that I could do this again.

Ten thousand minimum, split five ways, without including the split for the loot. Add in the goblins, and as there'd been at least thirty, at twenty credits each, we were at six hundred creds there…Two thousand, one hundred and twenty, plus any bonuses and the loot?

It was worth it.

"Okay, boss, we've got movement," Reign said after a few seconds, before turning and staring up the tunnel in the other direction. "Yeah, both sides…pincer movement."

"Hold your fire until you're sure you'll hit," I said firmly to the team. "We take as many down at range as we can, then we switch to melee. If it starts going to shit? We back up through the door, fight in there."

"Uh, why not fight in there anyway?" Hobbs asked. "I mean, we'd be able to slow them right down, catch them as they bunch up and…"

"And the team coming to seal the door wouldn't be able to do it," I said. "We stay out here, give them time to fix the door. Then, once they've fixed it, we retreat through it and seal it if they keep coming."

"Sounds good," Reign agreed. "Same as before. Luna and Gessh, ready to swap to melee?"

"Yeah, and we fight back-to-back. Any word on the team to fix that door?"

"Twenty minutes. Apparently there's a shortcut and they were expecting the call to seal somewhere after the goblins were mentioned."

"Joy," I growled.

"I can see them," Hobbs said.

I grunted. They were still out of range for the goggles, but Hobbs's rifle sight was dialed in a little more than mine, evidently.

Ten seconds later, and boom, there they were for me as well.

"Rifles up!" I barked, staring to the right—Luna at my side, and Reign, Hobbs, and Gessh behind us.

"Firing!" Reign called, and the solid thump of her high-powered rifle rang out.

I sighted in as well. A face popped up in my sights; two mechanical lenses glowed dully, before vanishing as I sent a round to punch through his forehead.

The body collapsed backward, lifeless truly, and I twitched to the right. Another head was already there, a mouth filled with glowing teeth for some reason, making this one look almost comical. Then my shot took him on the bridge of the nose, sending him to the next life, by express delivery.

Beside me, Luna opened fire finally, triple shot; then switched to single, the *crack-crack* of her firing and cursing loud in my ear.

"Slow is smooth," I told her. "Slow down. Smooth pulls…don't stress."

"They're getting closer," she growled, firing even faster.

"And you're missing as many as you hit. Stop, zero in, one shot, one…" Before I could finish the old phrase, a new sound rang out, and the battle changed again.

The figure reaching for me ahead and to my right practically disintegrated, flesh sloughing off as Hobbs screamed behind me, falling to the ground.

"Grazer!" I shouted in warning, frantically switching to full auto and mowing down the group ahead of me. Bullets took them in the head and upper chest, blasting many from their feet, only to have them rise again slowly.

"Hunting!" Reign called out, her barrel appearing over my right shoulder, hesitating only a second before barking out a response to the enemy fire. "Kabutt, take my six!"

I cursed, ducking down and lowering my rifle to avoid sweeping either her or Luna, and turned, seeing how close the other side was now.

I opened fire, still on full auto, driving them back, then cursed and dropped the rifle when I ran out of ammo, the oncoming horde too fucking close to have time to reload.

I snatched out my handgun. Five shots, five targets down…

"Got him!" Reign called out, just as a second grazer blast tore through the specters to my left, dropping three more of their own side.

Gessh screamed in fury and dropped her rifle as it clicked empty. The blade whistled from its sheath on her back and lopped off a reaching arm, before coming back for the head.

"They're still coming!" I shouted, sighting on the next in line and firing. The shotgun slug removed his head, as well as taking the figure behind down.

"Well, fuck!" Reign growled. The sound of her firing changed, as she lifted a submachine pistol and opened fire.

The blast that rang out lasted exactly two seconds; the banana magazine attached to it emptied in literally that little time, and yet…it punched a load back, giving Luna an opportunity to hit a few more, and get them some room.

"Luna!" Reign barked. "Get Hobbs inside!"

"Aye!" she responded, rifle dropping, sword whipping out and slicing a way through the bodies toward the door, grabbing him by the back of his armor.

That he was silent wasn't a good sign.

"Motherfuckers!" Gessh screamed, chopping and hacking as I pumped the shotgun and chambered one of the unknown rounds.

A figure appeared far too close, rising up, one of those I'd knocked down and not killed. I twisted it around, smacking him in the face with the butt of the rifle, before twisting back around and aiming into the gap, hesitating for a second before grunting.

"Fuck it!" I snarled and pulled the trigger.

The entire tunnel was suddenly lit to daytime brightness, as a magnesium and fuck-alone-knows-what Devil's Asshole shell was apparently one of the ones I'd gotten as a bonus.

The fire that ripped free of the barrel was hot enough to qualify as plasma, provided it also had the moniker "lost containment" added to it.

The blast was about two inches wide as it left the barrel, and was a good foot wide in a second, then meters wide.

The nearest ten or so of the specters simply stopped giving a shit about anything. Heads detonated as they were superheated; clothing burst into flames, bodies were blasted apart, and fuck yeah, we got some room again.

"What in the name of the god of chrome's *shiny fucking left fucking testicle was that!?*" Reign shouted in barely constrained panic, as I grinned uncontrollably.

"Devil's Asshole!" I called back, pumping the shotgun again and firing a slug into the face of a new figure that pushed his way through the staggering, burning bodies.

"Warn a girl!" Reign shouted, clicking a fresh mag into her sub and firing again, emptying it.

"What?" I shouted back, drunk on the insane level of destruction I'd unleashed, and having a pretty damn good idea that the other one was going to be the same. "Should I have asked first?"

"At least buy me a fucking drink!" She half laughed, a manic edge to her voice. "Or some lube!"

"You're all right—it was right in front of my face!" Gessh called out, only to let loose a giggle full of adrenaline as she went on. "I nearly went blind!"

"Should have closed your eyes!" Reign called back, before cursing. "Fuck's sake! Tell me you've got more of those!"

"One, and it's my last one in the shotgun."

"Need it on this side!" she called after a second. "Switch!"

We both dipped our weapons, barrels aimed at the ground as we passed each other. She opened fire at almost the same time as I did, and bodies flew back as I pumped and fired, pumped and fired, blasting back the fuckers.

"Got you!" Reign shouted, snatching her rifle back up, dumping the sub, and firing almost all in the same motion.

All at once, the massed specters sagged. Whatever control the ghoul had been exerting cut away; the sudden loss of command reduced them to mindless for long seconds as their instincts revived.

I fired once more. A slug punched through a head; I flipped it and smacked a body from its feet, ramming the shotgun home into its back sheath rather than waste the last shot. I popped the empty mag free of the rifle, slammed a fresh one home—two more left, that was it—and I fired again.

Luna and Gessh were everywhere, seemingly all at once, again and again. Reign and I jerked our rifles up at the last second, barely avoiding the half-orc women as they hacked and spun, kicking and punching to keep the specters back. There were fewer and fewer gunshots ringing out from us and more swords, when the sudden flare of a welding arc lit the tunnel.

"Engineers are here!" Reign called out.

"Keep them covered!" I barked. "Keep the specters back!"

We retreated toward the door, forming a defensive arc before it. After a few seconds, Reign swept up Hobbs's rifle, using it as she ran out of ammo and a last surge attempted to overrun us.

Two minutes later, and it was over. The last of the specters collapsed like a puppet with its strings cut as Luna stabbed it through the eye.

I hunched over, chest heaving, panting for breath, searching the darkness for any signs of enemy movement, only to nod as Reign spoke.

"The engineers say Hobbs is alive, but they used his medikit on him, and it's not working."

"Fuck, nanites don't work for him?" I grunted, straightening up and looking around.

"Genetic differences. It's something weird, I know. Who knows, maybe he's an alien spy," Reign joked tiredly. "Either way, they're taking him to the upper floors for the medivac."

"Medivac?" I asked, stunned. "Fuck, I *like* Vigilant Heart so much more—"

"Don't get your hopes up!" She snorted. "It's a personal insurance, kicked in as soon as he was seriously wounded. It was in the brief when he joined the team. I read it on the way over."

"Shit, where the hell did you read that?" I asked.

"Ah, advantages of being an assessor and being in the guild officially. Once you're approved, and a team lead, you'll be given access to the records. Sorry." She winced. "And I totally didn't mean to let that slip."

"Damn…" I groaned, straightening and reloading my guns. Reign was already finished doing hers, and Luna and Gessh were busy stabbing bodies, making damn sure of them.

"Okay, people, let's secure the area," I growled, dragging my vibro-blade free and starting by sawing its head off. Twenty minutes it took, for us to make sure of every single body; then we started looting.

"Any word on Hobbs?" I asked Reign after another half an hour.

She held up a hand flat, wiggling it from side to side, unsure.

"The nanites worked to repair some of the damage apparently, before breaking down. He's got a chance, but it's touch and go."

"At least he's got that." Luna sighed. "I liked him."

"Me too," I admitted, before whistling as I pulled out a seemingly intact datadeck from a backpack on a body, looking it over and grunting as it failed to power up. "Anyone any good with these?"

"What model is it?" Reign stepped over.

"Zentrades, Xz45," I read off the back. "It's a Black Cyber Widow."

"Damn." Reign grunted. "They're expensive. I mean, they're not 'we don't need to work again' expensive, but they're not cheap. Should get a decent price for one of these."

"If it works," Gessh added.

"Yeah, minor point," I agreed with a grunt. "Hey, what happened to the bag of loot?"

"Ah, fuck." Luna groaned. "Hobbs had it."

"No worries. Maybe it's by the door." Gessh clambered over a small pile of bodies, before heading back up the tunnel a little; we'd moved along it a little to get to the other gear. "I'll check it out."

"Thanks," I called, before stepping up next to Reign and staring down at the body of one of the ghouls. "What a waste."

"What's that?" she asked.

"I know someone who could have sold these mods," I said softly, and she shook her head, commenting loudly.

"Well, that's all kinds of wrong, but that's neither here nor there. I guess with the last of the specters dead and the patrol complete, I can confirm you all as more or less competent."

We could hear the smile in her voice as much as see it when I glanced at her, and she reached out to us all, requesting access to our recording for the job.

I approved; the RI accepted the request and sent it over, before confirming the recording was still running.

"The recording—" I started to say, and she cut me off.

"As per the contract, until we leave the client site, the recording is continuous, *but* the client only gets the highlight reel recorded from the bit they pay for. We've finished the patrol, so we're off their clock now," she said.

I grinned, popping my helmet off.

"So, you know someone who deals in specter mods?" she asked quietly.

"Yeah, but—"

"Uh, guys?" Gessh called, striding back toward us. "We've got a problem…"

"What's that?" I turned back to her.

"Well, you know the door?"

"Yeah?"

"They welded it *shut*."

"Well, fuck," I growled. "That's not happy making!"

"Two minutes. I'll call them." Reign sighed. "Fucking idiot engineers." She cursed, moving to lean against one wall, clearly making a call.

"So…" Luna whispered, moving up to stand nearby. "Specter mods?"

"I did a deal with a gang boss. I owe him the loot from a few runs to pay it off."

"So, what? You think you could dump some of this standard shit on him, and then sell him the good shit?" she asked carefully.

"Not sure." I rubbed my chin as I thought. Gessh moved over to join us. "Honestly, I think he's going to try to shaft me one way or another, but he'll at least take my portion of anything we take him as a group off my debt. So if we can get Reign to go along with it…"

"You think he'll pay us our share?" Luna asked, and I nodded.

"He's smart. He knows he could try to claim all of this and pay nothing, but that would kick things off early, and he wants me to do a few jobs for him. He's going to want them sorted before he stabs me in the back."

"Okay, good news, bad news." Reign ended her call and pushed off the wall. "Good news, Hobbs is alive."

"That's fucking great news," I said, surprised.

"It is, and it isn't. The grazer seriously fucked up his left side, and because he can't use mods? He's basically fucked as a merc now."

"Shit." I winced.

"Yeah, anyway, as I said, genetic differences. I wish I knew why, but it doesn't work for him, and frankly I'm not that interested as why, right now, because the *really* shitty news is that the engineers finished their shift when they took him up to the ground floor."

"What?" I asked coldly.

"They've gone home," she confirmed. "I've called Julius, and he's currently tearing the bosses of this place a new asshole—additional fees, danger bonuses, the works."

"That's great but how the fuck do we…" Luna groaned. "Oh, hell no!" She grunted, facepalming. "Seriously?"

"Yeah." Reign nodded. "We need to find another way out. On the upside, Julius said that he'd look the other way if you didn't hand everything over when we get back today. Sort of as an apology from him, and a welcome-on-board bonus."

"Welcome?" Luna asked, before grinning. "We made it into the guild?"

"Oh yeah." Reign laughed. "We've just taken down what was probably going to end up as a nest in a few days, easily two hundred specters and two ghouls. We're good with you joining."

"Well, that's something." I sighed. "So, we just need to—"

A distant scream rang out from somewhere deeper into the nest of forgotten tunnels, one filled with clear rage and a painful subsonic electrical screech, echoing toward us.

We looked at one another, eyes wide and seeing the same agreement in the entire group.

"We need to move," Reign said quickly to me, and I nodded.

"Grab anything we're taking," I ordered the others. "We've got thirty seconds, then we run like rabbits."

"Which way?" Luna asked.

"The fuck away from whatever made that scream," I said flatly.

CHAPTER TWENTY-FIVE

We didn't waste any time. The datadeck and various items we figured looked reasonably valuable were piled up already, and we moved as one, grabbing them and stashing them away.

The ghoul at this end, the left-most one of the two as we entered the tunnel, had a pretty standard rifle, good scope and in good condition, admittedly, but that was it, nothing special. We split the ammo between the four of us, adding in all of what we'd found so far, which wasn't much, unfortunately.

After we'd done that, I was left with a single full mag after the one I had in my rifle currently, a single goddamn shotgun cartridge—and that was the Devil's Asshole, which was both awesome and frankly terrifying—plenty of ammo for the handgun, which was shit, and my knife.

Oh, as well as the two frags and the two flash-bangs. But that wasn't the point. We were underground in tunnels that were a hair away from collapse; using a grenade when it wasn't an absolute "us or them" situation was plain stupid.

Thankfully, I still had the two hundred rounds that I'd bought earlier—I'd not dumped them back at the guild—and I pulled a full box out of my bag, offering handfuls of bullets around.

The others stuffed their pockets quickly rather than reload now. We could load on the way, after all, and every step down the path was one away from whatever made that noise.

"Dammit, shame about the mods," Reign snarled, shaking her head as she looked down at the ghoul. "I could have done with the creds."

"Didn't you do a load of missions already today?" I asked, and she nodded, clearly pissed.

"Mama has a way with cards," she admitted after a brief pause that screamed that she was hiding something. Then she was checking her nearest body, clearly as unhappy as I was to leave without looting the area bare. "Or, more accurately, I fucking don't."

"Debt?" I asked.

"Maybe I'll tell you one day, Kabutt." She shook her head. "For now? We've got enough to worry about."

"Okay, fuck it, move out," I ordered, gesturing up the tunnel away from the scream as another echoed toward us, seemingly much closer.

We set off jogging, passing the bodies quickly, most of which we'd checked. But we'd not had time to do them all, and that became seriously obvious when we reached the second, or more accurately, the first ghoul.

The one that Reign had killed first was slumped against the wall, head down, chin resting on its chest, rifle laid by its side.

"Fuck!" Reign grunted, quickly slapping her rifle onto her back. The mag clamps held it in place as she crouched by the body.

"Leave it!" I ordered, gesturing to her to move.

"No chance! It's a grazer!" she replied, reaching out and sweeping up the gun, checking it for damage.

"Fuck's sake! How much charge?" I asked quickly, skidding to a halt and moving in. I ripped my knife free and made goddamn sure of the ghoul, then hesitated, and sawed the rest of the way through its neck and lifted the head.

It was almost all cybernetic, and I glanced over it, before cursing and dumping it. *Was it worth something? Yeah, probably. Was it also fucked up? Most definitely.*

Reign's shot had entered just above the painted-on eyebrow on the left-hand side of the face. It'd blown half the back of the skull out.

It wasn't worth carrying something that size and heavy for a maybe, and I discarded it with a sigh. What was good, though, was when Reign searched the body and found three more batteries for the grazer.

"Got them. Fuck it, let's go!" She grunted, climbing to her feet and clinging onto the grazer like it was her first-born.

"You okay carrying that?" I asked. The damn thing was much bigger than a standard rifle, twice the size of a laser and easily three times its weight. But the wild grin she gave me made it clear how she felt about it.

"I've been saving up for one of these," she said breathlessly. "Or I was, you know, until…"

"Until the cards."

"Yeah. Anyway, look, we get back? I'll sign my share over to you fuckers if, you know…"

"That's worth a fuckload more than your share," Gessh said. "That's what, thirty thou?"

"Fifty, new." Reign sighed, shaking her head. "Okay, fine, but let me buy you guys out, all right? You wouldn't use this, would you?" she asked the girls.

Luna smiled and shook her head, while Gessh hesitated, frowning.

"No, we wouldn't," I answered for all of us, seeing the glare from Gessh. "It's a damn sniper's dream, Gessh, you know it, and you're a ground pounder all day long."

"Fuck you!" she growled at me.

"Gessh!" Luna snapped at her sister.

"What? The evaluation is over, and—"

"We'll let you buy us out," Luna said. "And Gessh—he's APS. He's a damn ground pounder like us. The only difference is he's in shinier armor."

"I wasn't dissing you," I said. "I was in the army as a soldier first."

"Yeah, well, it sounded like…" She paused, then shook her head. "Sorry, boss," she whispered, almost too low to catch over the sound of our running feet.

"Don't worry." I grinned, even though they couldn't see it. "Besides, what am I gonna do? Court-martial you?"

"Point." She grinned self-consciously. "Sorry, Reign," she apologized, and Luna spoke up as well.

"We're used to people trying to fuck us over."

"You're girls, you're half-orcs, and you're mercs." Reign laughed. "Believe me, I get it."

"Yeah, you're an elf, though…humans love you fuckers," Gessh said. "Spend all their time trying to get some elf ass. So do all the races."

"Yeah, there's a reason there's so much elf porn." Luna laughed over the sound of our feet, all four of us on the edge of hysteria from the adrenaline high, the fear, and the encroaching darkness.

I bit my tongue, not sure whether I wanted to agree, or stay the fuck outta this conversation, being the only male.

"What about you, Sarge?" Reign asked after a few seconds of silence. "You like elf ass?"

"Fuck's sake," I muttered under my breath, before shrugging. Might as well admit to it. It was too much to hope they'd have left me outta it. "Yup, what can I say? Elves have the best asses. Half-orcs have better tits, though."

Considering that was a minor detail that was well commented on, I knew it'd come up next, and just threw it under the bus as well.

"Really?" Luna gasped, pretending to be shocked. "I can't believe you've been looking! Shame on you, soldier!"

"Yeah, can we claim for workplace harassment?" Gessh joked.

"Maybe later," Reign said. "I think we're a bit too busy right now. And besides, who'd watch the tunnel if we all start harassing him? I mean, he's the only guy here…"

"I could go for some group 'her-ass-ment,'" I added in, grinning at the groans from the others.

"Oh damn, Sarge, that just killed the conversation!" Luna replied sadly after a few seconds.

"It was terrible," Reign agreed, glancing back behind us, then stumbling and screaming, "DOWN!" as she dove for the floor.

I did it instantly, without thinking, hitting the rough fractured stone of the old passageway and rolling as something whooshed overhead, striking the wall a dozen meters ahead where the passage took a turn to the left.

The wall exploded. A great gout of red and yellow flames washed over us. The sonic and pressure shock waves made the tunnel shake as Reign twisted around and fired.

"What the fuck?" I groaned, shaking my head, stunned. "RI, isolate attack!" The RI, used to working with me in my APS armor, responded as it'd been programmed.

> *Breaker-217 anti-personnel rocket identified, likely launched from a Pinnacle Assault Systems single-shot launch device. Est. location, 37m to the rear of formation.*

I rolled, blinking, my ears ringing as I locked in on the rough location my RI indicated.

"Ping!" I ordered, and it sent out a generalized identification ping. It was a seriously basic friend-or-foe identifier. But what the civilian world always forgot was that when you used military kit?

It came with military back doors.

The launcher responded instantly, pinging its location to the military request, and I zeroed in on it, sighting and opening fire with my rifle as I muttered under my breath to the RI.

"Share target location with local team!"

My vision telescoped for a second, then zoomed out, before zooming in and clearing up as the zoom settled. The glowing red eyes of a specter shifted from staring at us, to glance at the launcher on its shoulder, then focused in on me, presumably as it identified the source of the ping.

"Firing!" Reign shouted. The grazer rifle, a long and seriously heavy-duty bit of kit, hummed for a second, then fired again. Ports along its length opened to discharge the additional heat with a sudden wash of it into the tunnel.

"Switch!" I ordered Reign, staring at the specter that was right at the outer edge of my darkness-piercing vision. "It's a fucking specter! Use the solid shots!"

"Still got flesh," she disagreed, slapping the discharge ports closed and aiming again. The specter slowly drifted into clearer sight of us all. "Fuck! Switching!" Reign finally agreed as she took in the actual condition of the enemy before us.

Specters were rumored to come in different grades, like the ghoul did over the standard specter, growing more and more powerful as they evolved past the limitations of their humanity. But this?

It was horrifying, and utterly inhuman.

It floated along, lit by the ungentle light of repulsors, stuttering and flaring, barely keeping it aloft. It stared at us, the half skull and its glowing red eyes extended before it on a cantilever arm; its lower jaw was missing and the upper made even more terrible by the glowing eyes shining out from a skull that had an old national flag painted across it.

"Fuck me..." Reign gasped in horror. "We need to run!"

"Kill that fuck!" I countermanded, sighting down my rifle at it, and letting fly with a quick three-round burst.

As soon as I fired, though, the creature seemed to re-awaken, twisting and zeroing in on me. A second launcher cranked into position, rolling up from its back to lock into place over its shoulder, aligning on us.

"Move!" Reign bellowed, scrambling to her feet and turning tail, struggling with her massive rifle and her normal one as well.

"What the fuck!" I screamed at her, firing again. My bullets cracked the air between us and my target, before bouncing off. Bright flares of light from the ricochets added to the blue glow of the repulsors.

It reached out one hand; long arms that were never designed to be human, looking as though they'd been ripped from a robotic assembly plant, clacked and flexed.

"Trust me and run!" echoed back down the tunnel from Reign, and Luna's voice rang out next.

"Boss?" she shouted. "I can't even see the fucker!"

"Fuck!" I snarled. The red light of the targeting laser on the launcher blinked to life. "Run!" I roared, forcing myself up and turning. I ran as fast and as far as I could, but I'd barely made it a few meters before the rocket hit the floor behind me, and I screamed. The blast picked me up and hurled me through the air.

I crashed into the wall, then the floor, bouncing, rolling, and more than a little on-fucking-*fire* before a pair of hands, then another grabbed me and started dragging, as a high-powered shot rang out, then another from somewhere nearby.

"Fucking fuck!" I heard Reign screaming as she fired again and again. "Run, you idiots!"

"Wha…?" I mumbled, my bell well and truly rung. My helmet's faceplate spiderwebbed with cracks and symbols; warnings and the wraparound vision that was projected onto it flashed and flared as the basic systems tried to compensate for the damage.

I stumbled and pushed myself upright, clambering over a mass of rubble, dragged this way and that by the sisters as they ran, half carrying me.

"Move, move, move!" Reign bellowed, as they—and I—made it around the corner. The screech from our pursuer made it clear it wasn't happy. "Grenades!" she snapped, suddenly before me, and ripped them off my chest rig. "Gimme and fucking run!"

"Mine!" Gessh corrected her, snatching one of them and shoving at her shoulder. "I can run faster and throw harder than you, elf!"

"HALF-elf!" Reign grumbled, not that anyone was paying attention.

"What…the…" I tried, getting a foot under me to take my weight, before I was unceremoniously spun around and thrown over Luna's shoulder, hoisted in a fireman's carry as she started to run.

"Bundle them all up…" I heard from somewhere behind. A second later, as Luna was complaining in a determined voice about how "fucking heavy ass" I was, I heard the sound of running feet.

"Go, go, go!" Reign shouted as she passed us. Her longer legs made short work of the distance as I muzzily tried to make sense of the world.

The next thing I knew, I was dumped on the floor, rolling and shaking my head, trying to get back up as someone grabbed me and dragged me in close.

I blinked, confused to all hell, then winced as someone put a hand on the back of my head and tried to put my face down closer to my crotch than the gods ever intended I could go.

"Stay down!" Luna bellowed, before the world dissolved in light, fire, and sheer sensory overload.

CHAPTER TWENTY-SIX

I blinked, working my jaw as I tried to make the world resolve fully, then reached up and pulled off my helmet. Everything went dark, then brightened again as my internal visual augments took over from the helmet's fractured ones.

Luna leaned in close, frowning at me before peeling back an eyelid and nodding as she shone a light in.

I cursed as the world whited out. Safety cutouts came online to prevent damage from the sudden unexpected white glare.

"Sorry, boss!" She winced before she grinned. "You'll be all right. Looks like a concussion."

"Here." Reign leaned in and showed me a small medikit. "Use it."

I nodded my thanks, trying to ignore the way the tunnel spun and my stomach tried to demonstrate my breakfast to everyone from that simple movement.

"Thanks…" I mumbled, pressing the injector to my neck and grimacing as it hissed. The needle punched into my vein and poured icy-cold nanites directly in.

There were a few seconds of throbbing pressure as they swarmed my brain, then blessed relief as they broke down, spending themselves in an orgy of rebuilding and repair.

I sagged back, feeling the cold of stone under me, sharp and pointed fractured rocks and the seeping wetness of a puddle, but I was alive.

The seconds passed and everything seemed to change gradually, until, all at once, I was no longer watching uncaringly through my own eyes, like I was watching a vid-drama, and I was back in the world.

"What happened?" I gasped, sitting up and wiping away the water that ran down the side of my face.

"Fuck!" Luna grunted in surprise, her blade in her hand already, before she let out her breath in one long sigh, shaking her head. "Boss, don't do that! I nearly fucking stabbed you!"

"Luna?" I winced, wiping more water away and looking round. "Where are we? Where are the others?"

"Looking for a way out." Luna shrugged. "They told me to stay and watch over you."

"Where are we?"

"Still in the tunnels. Reign used your grenades and her own, tied them all together and set them off at once. Gessh tried for a bank shot, but they barely made it around the corner before they went off. Two flash-bangs, three incendiary, and three frags. Took the tunnel down and a load more besides. We barely made it out."

"And now?"

"We're in some old underground station," she said. "Most of the direction we came from collapsed, three tunnels currently, with a fuckload of rubble from higher up. Not sure if there was any damage on the surface or if it's all down here, but…"

"But we need to get the fuck outta here if we want to survive, and not be taken down by angry people, never mind the specters." I groaned as I twisted my neck and popped a joint.

"Yeah, basically." She grinned. "I managed to hold onto your loot, but it's a bit fucked." She offered a bag to me.

I took it, glancing inside and seeing a load of technical crap, as well as the more general stuff I'd been looting as I went. I nodded my thanks, putting it all away, and gathered up my weapons, settling everything back into place as I got myself ready.

"Which way did they go?" I asked Luna after a minute.

"That way." She pointed to a narrow stairway behind a grate that had been pulled out. "Both because it goes up and, if that fucker survived, it can't come after us."

"What the hell was it?" I glanced back toward the rubble. "I mean, I've heard of higher-grade specters before, but I thought things like that were urban myths?"

"Me too," Luna admitted, gathering her gear and pulling a handful of bullets out, pressing them one at a time into a magazine as she led the way to the stairs and I slipped my helmet back on. "You think I'd have come down here without a plasma cannon if I'd known they were real?"

"Heh, same." I grunted, shaking my head. "That would have gone massively different if I was in my suit."

"Why don't more APS do that then? I mean, you get out, you get your suit, and you get registered, and boom. You could make a fortune strolling around down here, hunting those fuckers."

"Because they get paid a lot more to sit on their asses in a pretty office," Reign called down from farther up the stairwell. "I was coming back for you. Come on, we're not far from a ladder up to the next level."

"Imagine it, though," Luna said after a few seconds as we climbed higher, moving out into a narrow corridor, then into a tunnel that appeared to have been for maintenance at some point. "You could have killed all of them, probably without needing ammo. Take down what, two hundred a day, on your own? Twenty thousand credits a *day*." She let out a long whistle and shook her head. "What I couldn't do with that kinda creds…"

"Same," I muttered, before sighing and nodding to Reign as we caught up to her. "Realistically, though? Most of the smaller tunnels I wouldn't be able to get into, not in my suit. And the bigger ones? I could march along them for days and see nothing, or I could have a ceiling collapse and be trapped forever. I might not see a single specter, or I might draw them like flies, in their thousands, and be torn apart. Who fucking knows."

"If you stay with us?" Reign said softly, moving in closer as we walked and trying to edge Luna out. "We could team up. That way, you'd have people to watch your back and draw them to you, or rescue you if that kinda shit happened."

"Yeah," Luna agreed, utterly ignoring the annoyed look Reign gave her when she joined a conversation that she wasn't wanted in. "How about it, boss? Are you going to stay with the guild after this? I know you said you were working to get your mods up to scratch to get your suit back online, but once you do that, are you staying or ditching us for a richer guild?"

"Fuck's sake, Luna," Gessh said from farther ahead where she leaned against the base of the ladder. "You're supposed to be subtle with this shit, remember? Make sure he likes us first, flash him your tits or something, *then* you ask him to form a permanent team."

"I can do that." Luna shrugged and grinned at me unrepentantly. "Remind me when we get back to safety and I can get a shower, though, right? I'm filthy right now."

"I'm amazed it's just you offering, Luna." Reign sighed. "I mean, if you really want to catch his attention, surely it should be you both, right?"

"Fuck it. After we get out of here, and provided we get paid like I think it should be? He can join us both in that shower." Gessh grunted. "But like I say, subtle, dammit!"

"Room for a third?" Reign asked casually, and I had to swallow my tongue to stop from blurting "fuck yes."

First of all, I was fairly sure it was just a wind-up. Second, I was tired, and despite the nanites' intervention, I still felt like shit. And third?

The most basic precept of all, in any squad, group, or friendship: Never shit on your own doorstep.

I was a serious believer in never fooling around with anyone I was too close to, as fighting and fucking, then going out and fighting properly? It never ended well.

I did, however, allow myself a moment or three of unsubtle reflection as we set off climbing the ladder, Reign's hot half-elven ass only a few rungs above me.

The thoughts of her, Luna, *and* Gessh all in the shower with just me?

It was the thing dreams and fantasies were made of.

A handful of minutes later, and Gessh, at the top of the ladder, clambered out into the next level, calling down that it was all clear.

"Now what?" Reign asked me as I scrambled out and stood next to her, huffing with the exertion.

"Now, we find a fucking way out." I looked at the hatch as Luna climbed out, then closed it behind her.

This level was a lot better. Hell, it looked as if it'd been maintained recently. And besides the lack of piled bodies, mold, various shattered sections of tunnel, and the general shit that was piled everywhere below? There was even a light in the distance.

We set off in that direction, hurrying along the tunnel, passing recessed sections every twenty meters or so, which looked vaguely familiar.

Ten seconds later, the noise that filtered back to us had us running like fuck back to the last recess. Gessh barely made it into the gap behind us in time, as an automated goods transfer train roared past.

A good thirty individual sections, like vertebrae in a snake, flowed along, dragged behind the mag-lev engines. We pressed ourselves deeper into the recess, staring wide-eyed at the containers passing before us.

A matter of seconds, and it was gone. The tunnel echoed with the sounds of its passage, and I practically collapsed.

"Uh, boss?" Gessh said after a few seconds.

"Yeah?" I muttered.

"I think I'm gonna pass on that group shower this time. I really need to get clean in private after that."

There were a few seconds of silence, before we all started to laugh at the sheer ridiculousness of that comment before I replied.

"Honestly, given the stress and sheer state of me right now? I doubt I could summon the energy anyway."

"Next time, though, yeah?" Reign asked.

I glanced at her. The emotionless façade of her goggles watched me, and her lips were drawn together, either in disappointment or amusement. I wasn't sure which.

"Next time..." I agreed, uncertainly, playing along. That uncertainty only grew when she nodded and smiled.

"Right then, ladies, time we got our tired boy toy back home. Otherwise, no shower fun for us in the future!"

"Whoo." Luna yawned. "I can hardly contain my excitement."

"Meh, he's not much to look at," agreed Gessh. "But you never know, maybe he tries hard?"

"He's got a nice ass," Reign pointed out.

I shook my head, listening and making sure there was nothing else coming, before stalking out of the recess and leading them down the tunnel toward the dubious safety of the light.

An hour passed, then two. In that time searching for a way out, forty-seven goods transports and a single black, heavily armed and armored transport passed by, each doing their damn best to make me shit myself or simply kill me.

By the time we found the exit, climbing up onto a low platform that led to an emergency exit, and from there directly out into the city, we were well and truly knackered.

"Reign?" I looked around the alleyway we found ourselves in, and a handful of goblins peeked out from a pile of rubbish.

"Yeah, boss?"

"We're in the guild now, right?"

"Oh yeah."

"Fancy booking us a taxi and billing it to them?" I suggested, and she grinned.

"I think that the least we can do is bill the client for that," she said. "Give me a few minutes."

I nodded, kicking a pallet over, so that it fell from upright and braced against the wall—apparently sheltering a goblin I'd had no idea was there as it screeched at me and bolted for cover—and I laid down with my back on it, staring up at the sky above, letting the softly falling rain wash some of the funk of the tunnels away.

I closed my eyes, and relaxed, before marking myself as "safe."

It was a stupid thing, a little thing, but something that a training sarge had drilled into us all years ago, when we graduated from being a "normal" soldier and into an elite APS operative.

RIs are wonderful machines, but unless you wanted to spend literally years and decades of your wages on buying a high-tier one, they were fairly simple systems.

That didn't mean they were dumb—just that they wouldn't do anything unless they were told to do it.

Soldiers and engineers being what we are, the forces started tinkering with the RIs as soon as the first ones were handed over, much to their creators' chagrin.

One of the simple things that came out of it was the custom programs.

Tens of thousands were created, most basic as all hell, but when taken the right way? They could elevate a lowly RI to almost the same level as an AI in many ways.

I'd never bothered with a lot of the programs. Richie was always espousing the benefits of some new one, but for me, a few dozen made my RI much, much more useful.

One of them was given to us all by that first training sarge.

"Safe" and "On Mission" were two settings, fairly self-explanatory. But when you were on mission? The RI would filter things out. Social messages, calls, asshole officers who asked for status reports with pretty graphs that they could understand in their nice safe bunkers, while we were under fucking fire. Those little details were all culled and set aside, while the RI returned an "unable to connect" message or some such.

It saved careers, as well as lives.

Now, as I marked myself as "safe," I got hit by three messages.

The first was a nice simple one from Lucky. A location for the first of the targets he wanted me to kill. Apparently she'd stuck her head up and was with a group of muscle, dealing drugs in an area that Lucky considered his.

The message was blunt, rude, and demanding, basically telling me to go kill the fucker right now.

I closed it and moved on.

The second was a video recording from Julius of the Vigilant Heart, who I guessed was apparently now my new guild leader and boss.

"Hey, Kabutt," he said tiredly, rubbing at his cheek and forcing a smile. "Look, I know you're gonna be pissed at me about this mission, but it was supposed to be a simple one. Perfect for a training run. Well, you and I both know no plan survives contact with the enemy, but this one? I swear we're fucking cursed.

"So. It went badly, and I understand if you're pissed. Do one thing for me, though, and come see me after you hand in the mission or first thing tomorrow. That's all I ask." He sat back, his eyes bloodshot as he rubbed at the bridge of his nose.

"Hobbs...he didn't make it. I'm sorry. Last-minute complication with his biology, no clue how or why, but the nanites just didn't work in him. They died off too quick, formed a clot, and then hit his brain, starving it of oxygen. By the time the doctors saw it? It was too late. He was gone.

"His medical form stated if he was unable to be revived after two attempts, he was to be let go. His family are heading to Sacred Soul in the 34th District. They'll take care of him, and we, as 'the bastards who let him die,' aren't welcome. Sorry, man, but I'd rather tell you myself than let you read it in a bulletin. I'll send the others messages with the details as well. His body is being collected tonight at 2100 if you need to go, but honestly, we're not welcome, so be warned."

I glanced at the time, groaning aloud: 2317. Even if I'd *wanted* to pay my respects? I couldn't have now.

It brought Fergie and the others crashing back, and I cursed, pausing the message and sending off another through "correct channels" to the army, demanding access to their records so that I could create their reels.

That done, I went back to the recording, starting it and snorting as the damn thing ended a second later.

I shrugged and opened the third in line. A second message from Lucky, clearly not fucking happy at getting an "unavailable" when he sent another message.

"Kabutt, you better not be fucking with me..." He glared at me from the recording. "If you've taken my credits and run? You're in for a *big* surprise!"

That was it, and although I seriously wasn't in the mood? Fuck it. Best not to take his money then end up at war with him in the same day.

That could wait till tomorrow.

CHAPTER TWENTY-SEVEN

"Lucky," I greeted the half-orc as my call and remote VR invite went through. My avatar appeared, as did his, as if we were both actually in a bar, as I'd mentally selected. Just for shits and giggles.

He appeared on the far side of a table from me, digital, and unfortunately non-refreshing beers sat on the table between us, adding to the ambiance, and I desperately wished they were fucking real right now.

"Kabutt," he replied grimly, looking around, clearly not recognizing the bar—it was a forces-only one from near the base, and somewhere I'd spent a lot of time. "So. Where the fuck are you, and why is Lilith still breathing my fucking air!"

"Who's Lilith?" I grunted and nodded as Luna crouched next to me in the real world—invisible to Lucky, of course—and whispered in my ear that the cab was two minutes out.

"The fucking shitbird I told you to kill!" he snarled, furious. "Listen, you arrogant little fuck, when I say kill, you kill and—"

"Shut the fuck up," I said flatly. "Lucky, I'm only going to say this once, so listen, because if this is how things are going to be? We can move straight along to where you try to kill me, and I get annoyed and slaughter you and your fucking gang."

"You think…" he growled, leaning forward. His massive knuckles rested on the table between us as he stood.

"I know," I said flatly. "Now shut the fuck up. You asked where I was? I was doing a specter hunt, deep under-fucking-ground with a merc company, proving myself to them, so I can go on recons where we know there's likely specter activity and actually kill some to loot, rather than wandering the undercity fucking blindly, all right?"

"You get anything?" His demeanor changed instantly as he no doubt matched up the details he clearly had from the tracker he'd had implanted in me.

"Nope. First gig. I'm being assessed, and the guild have scavengers that sell it all for scrap."

"Bullshit," he growled.

"Lucky, I don't give two shits about you beyond your usefulness to me, so believe this—I don't view you as important enough to lie to," I said grimly. "Now, I'm on my way back to the guild. I've had a shitty day and I'm not really in the mood for this, so, send me an update in an hour or two as to this Lilith. If they're not out of my way on the way back, I *might* take care of it. Or, you know? Maybe I fucking won't. I'll see how I feel. This, though?"

I gestured to him and me, flicking a finger back and forth.

"This is a partnership. That was the deal. Now that might not matter to you—you might think I'm an employee—but believe me, try giving me shit like this again? I'll be dissolving the partnership, and you can try to get your creds from me."

"I'll rip the fucking mods out by hand," he growled. "You talk to me like this? I'll skull-fuck your head and use it as a fucking goblet! I'll—"

"You'd spill your drink," I said, and he glared at me, chest heaving as he clearly tried to restrain himself. "You take my skull for a goblet—okay, you can try, but let's say you succeed? First, you're saying you're gonna skull-fuck me. I'm guessing unless you're going for my nose, there's gonna be some damage. You crack it, your drink leaks out. I mean, yeah, you could repair it after, or fill bits in, but then nobody's going to recognize me, surely, and that's the point of this, I'm guessing."

"You'll regret this, Kabutt," he growled.

"No, Lucky, I fucking won't. You know why? Because it's been a long-ass day, and I'm still considering helping you out, despite you being a dick. So, what's going to happen is this. You're gonna seethe a bit, then calm the fuck down, because we both know you only get a real return on investment if you put your big-boy pants on and carry on. Secondly, I'm doing exactly as I fucking told you I'd be doing—getting my mods done and hunting. I'm working. And because you couldn't figure out where I was? You're throwing a fit right now. When you calm down? You'll see that the only one with an issue here is you, so fucking get over it."

He stood there, glaring at me, and I smiled.

"Or, you wait until I get back tonight, and we sort this out between us. I win, and you're no longer a problem. You win, and I won't give a shit anymore. But you'll have to go to Oshbob and explain that you lost the new supplier of primo mods you'd gotten. I'd imagine that won't go down well."

My boot was kicked, and I forced myself to my feet. The image before me separated as I willed normal vision to return in my left eye only.

"Now, I'm heading to a taxi. Do you want me to divert and head to you right now? We can kill each other, and there's a chance I don't need to spend the time cleaning my gear, so, you know, be honest here."

"The partnership stands…" he growled. "But you'll be hitting Lilith today, and her partner tomorrow, or I'll—"

"Yeah, okay, we'll see." I nodded. "Good talk." I cut the line and climbed into the transport with the girls, sighing as, unsurprisingly, as soon as my ass hit the seat, I got a warning for "fouling" the taxi, as well as a notification that the charge had been added to the bill.

"Fuck's sake." I sighed, pulling my helmet off and dumping it on my knee as I settled back. "Tell me the guild's picking that up?" I blinked as the real world swam before me again and the bar vanished.

"They damn well are," Reign agreed, sighing as the pseudo-leather of the seat adjusted, settling her in comfortably. "An advantage of being an assessor is I get access to some of the advantages of the team lead as well, when it's not being used. This is one of the bonuses. Essentially, if you decide your team deserves a little treat after a nightmare of a mission? You have a discretionary slush fund to pay for things like this. This is coming out of *your* fund, by the way."

"Nice…" Luna groaned. "I needed this."

"What?" I asked, confused and looking around, noticing for the first time that while I was still in my armor, the rest of the team had shucked out of theirs while I was on the call.

"Johnny Air-Cab," Reign pointed out, grinning. "I paid the extra to have the massage seats an' shit."

"Motherfucker." I groaned. "I didn't realize, and I can't feel a damn thing through this!"

"That'll teach you to take a call when we're all recovering," Luna said with a smile.

"Yeah, well, it was the ganger I'm dealing with. He wasn't happy."

"What you gonna do?" she asked. "I mean, you going to see him or…?"

"I'm going to clean my gear, reload and repair, as well as have a damn meal," I said. "Then, and fucking *only* then, I'll look at the details of the job he's got for me. If it's a simple one? Fair enough. No need to make things worse yet."

"Yet?" Reign shot me a look, and I hesitated, before shrugging and going on.

"It'll happen sooner or later. He's setting me up for a large bounty as the last job in our deal. It's blatantly a case of I do the hit, then he hits me and claims the bounty."

"You sure?" Gessh asked. "I mean, he might be honest…"

I looked across at her, and she sighed and nodded her acceptance of how fucking likely that was.

The four of us sat facing one another in the back of the cab, the windows darkened to prevent outside observation, and I grinned, realizing that when Reign had picked this company—for the seats as she'd admitted—she'd also unthinkingly made things worse in some ways.

The light for "privacy and comfort" was lit overhead; a single red blinking dot that was there to make sure we all knew that. It was an additional touch to ensure we enjoyed the relaxation the cab offered. Essentially, unless we connected to the cab and deactivated it, we'd not be pestered with calls and so on as the cab had a blocker active.

That was fine; it'd gone live as soon as I'd finished my call presumably. But now? That tracker would be registering as gone again, and I had to think Lucky would be going apeshit about me vanishing again.

So, in conclusion, I was getting fucked by Reign twice over. First, she was using my discretionary fund as a team leader to pay for the upgrade from a standard cab to this cab with the massage and so on that I couldn't enjoy because of my armor. Second? She'd just made it look to that half-orc prick that I knew about the tracker—I did, but that wasn't the point—and that I was deliberately goading him.

I was getting fucked twice without getting fucked. *Great. Story of my life.*

"So, you said there's a bounty?" Reign asked into the silence. Her eyes cracked only slightly, and I snorted when Luna groaned.

"Fuck's sake, Reign! First we get him to formally invite us to the team, *then* we complain about how poor we all are, *then* we ask about the bounty!"

"Yeah, unless you're actually giving up that elf ass for real, try some subtlety," Gessh added, not even opening her eyes.

"Yeah." I smiled, shaking my head as I realized how much I'd missed the solidarity that you got from fights like this. "Wait till you're asked." I winked.

"Well, just letting you know that if you need a sniper, I'm available."

"And muscle, if we're throwing all subtlety out the window," Luna said, echoed by a grunt from Gessh.

"If I need backup, I'll call," I assured them. "Honestly, I don't know what's happening with it all yet, just that he has a line on a target. He agreed straightaway to me keeping the bounty, no argument. So, either he doesn't believe I can do it, and that's why it's the last job on the list, or, as I say, he's planning on hitting me once I take the target down. Then he gets the jobs done he wants, he strips my corpse, and sells my parts, and he claims the bounty. Win-win."

"Well, he'll be in for a hell of a surprise if he tries that shit and we're there." Reign snorted.

"Damn right," I agreed.

Silence fell after that, the girls clearly curious but not wanting to push any harder, and preoccupied with their own lives as they did whatever they were doing.

The cab ride across the city wasn't a short one. Where we'd come out, we were on the wrong side of the main freeways, and to get onto them, across to the guild and then back off, took forty minutes.

By the time we pulled out, the gentle rain of earlier had turned into a solid downpour. The drops hammered off the roof of the cab and sent up a steady haze of broken water.

The neon signs all around us reflected off the sidewalk, and I dragged my helmet back on, ignoring the cracks as I splashed through the puddles to the front door of the guild.

Reign had approved the cab fare—including the fouling charge. She and the others were getting soaked as they unloaded their gear from the trunk.

I'd clung onto mine, not being able to take it off in the confines of the cab, and I grinned upon hearing curses as they got soaked all over again.

The guild was much as I'd left it earlier, just a little darker and quieter, considering it was after midnight now.

A single counter was open. A bored-looking assistant sat behind the desk, eyes lit from within as he watched something. The few couches and random seats scattered around the room were filled by sleeping noobs, hoping for a rush, last-minute job.

I shook myself, water cascading off my gear as I strode deeper in. The assistant canceled whatever show he was watching, sitting up and scanning us quickly.

"Team-17," he said in greeting. "Uh…Sergeant Kabutt, welcome back from your mission. Do you have any loot that you need assessing?"

"Wait one." I turned and looked at the doors as the others crowded in. "Reign, you want to deal with this?"

"Not really," she said, before grinning tiredly. "But, hey, I guess it's part of the fun. Okay, guys, first mission is done, so this is how it works now…"

Reign walked us through the steps we needed to take, including tagging our personal feeds that had been recorded and uploading them to the guild AI for assessment. Our gear was gathered up, and the bags were turned out for the assistant to evaluate and log.

A handful of guns, credit-chips, some jewelry, and a load of random shit was assigned to the team's account.

Notably, three things stood out. First of all, the grazer rifle and its batteries weren't mentioned, and judging from the way Reign was clutching it, anyone who tried to take it had better be ready to pry it from her cold, dead hands.

Secondly, the datadeck that we'd found and that was in my bag was totally ignored, and I mentally tagged that as our bonus from Julius when he'd said that not everything needed to be reported this once.

The last thing was the mass of electronics and shit that I'd taken from the goblin's hat. It was assessed as "random mod, damaged beyond recognition," and assigned a value of five credits.

I tagged it and deducted the five credits for it from my pot, deciding I wanted to have a look at it. And if all else failed, I'd palm it off on Lucky for a laugh.

Once that was done, and things like the recovery and cleaning team had been confirmed as on sight and working, we were led out through the main public areas, and into the back.

I'd been taken into a ready room before, where I'd first met Reign, but here? This was the guild proper.

Away from the bits the uninitiated got to see, the building changed drastically. Everything was clean and well maintained, but military in design and Spartan.

No frills, no soft cushioned seats; instead, back here were workstations, locker rooms, and more. There were machines that were stocked with all the parts you could possibly need for standard weapon maintenance, from oils and tools to crystals and springs, all loaded into a vending machine that charged only a slight markup.

"It's one of the best bonuses of the guild," Reign said. "Everywhere I've worked besides here? You need a single crystal or a screw and you don't have it? You need to buy a full maintenance kit. And you know how those work—you always end up with a dozen of one part you don't fucking need, and never enough of the ones you do."

"So where does it all come from?" I glanced over the catalog.

"Loot, mostly," she admitted, shrugging. "The gear that we bring back, the guns that we don't want, and that the guild has a load of, but that the price on the open market is crap? They're broken down by the guild gunsmiths and stripped for parts. If it's less than eighty-percent durability on assessment? The parts are sold on the net. Someone always needs something, after all. If it's over eighty? It goes in here for cost plus ten percent."

"Damn." I approved, already thinking of my guns. "I like it. What about upgrades?"

"Physical or weapons mods?" she asked.

I hesitated. "You've got a carver?"

"Nah." She shook her head. "We have some mods, though. Ones that are recovered from dead people—or looted uninstalled occasionally, uncontaminated and not claimed by the recovering team—are put into the catalog for us all, then you can take them to a carver yourself. Weapon mods are a bit more common."

"Do we get a discount?" Luna asked, and Reign smiled, leading us down another corridor and into a small room.

"We do and we don't." She moved across to a wall of lockers that were clearly attached to a storage area and laid a hand on the reader on the side and presumably sent a code from her ident, as the lockers sprang to life. "So first of all, these lockers." She nodded to the wall; noises rang out from somewhere behind, as the storage area was accessed and things moved around internally.

"You have your own personal storage space here, if you want it. Anything in there is locked to you, and you alone. Nobody else can access it, unless the guild master, Julius, or the quartermaster, Bento, registers you as dead. Once you're dead, and the system queries your ident, getting either a full offline signal, or confirmation of death from the central government, the locker is opened and the contents sold to the guild. Any profits are given to your registered next of kin, or go toward any guild debts you've run up."

She pulled out a change of clothes, and grinned around as she held them up.

"Believe me, it's well worth keeping a few changes of clothes in here. The guild has a cleaning service, and it's not bad, but it's not cheap either, if you need it straight back."

"How much?" Luna glanced down at her gear.

"It's generally a credit per small item of clothing, two to five per large, and depending on how bad? It can be an additional charge. You want it back in an hour? Triple it."

"Triple!" Gessh growled, and I winced, already knowing I was going to be paying it.

"It's because the kid who runs it needs to drag in more help." She shrugged. "Honestly, I think it's weird that Julius had street rats working on shit like this, but it works."

"An hour you say?" I looked down at my gear, and she nodded.

"There's a clothing dispenser out with the other machines. Last thing we all need is you walking around naked."

"First you want me naked, then you don't." I sighed. "Story of my fucking life."

"So, as I was saying," Reign started up again, grinning at me. "Keep a change of clothing here. There're shower stalls in the bathrooms on the next level up, and despite the jokes earlier, sorry to say there's no way we're all fitting in one—certainly not if you want to actually enjoy anything—so wipe your mind of that for now."

I snorted, seeing amused smiles on the others' faces.

"Julius is of the opinion that if we can get all our 'work' jobs done here, and for reasonable prices if we want to farm them out? Then we'll spend more time here. Then not only does the guild become 'home' and covers its own upkeep, it also means that we're likely to be here when the shit hits that fan, and he can send us out to take nests down. It's a little cold and calculating, but it's really not that bad."

"That why you were here earlier?" Luna asked Reign, and she laughed.

"I'd fallen asleep after a job," she said after a second's hesitation. "Pinot, a friend of mine, was going home. I didn't have any plans, and my apartment's...it's on the other side of the city, so I crashed here. I've got debts to pay as well, so, you know."

"So the weapon mods...?" I asked after a few seconds.

"Right! Yes, that's what we were talking about. Come on..."

She led the way out and down the corridor to another section, this one with several large tables set up, some seats in the middle of the room, overflowing trashcans, and more vending machines along the wall.

"So, you need mods? The machines hold them. Basically, just like the parts, they're salvaged from the various guns and gear, repaired, and if they're worth it, they're stored here. The guild takes forty percent of the value on the sale. The rest goes to the team that took it down, split up by standard salvage rules."

"Which are?" Luna asked quickly.

"Twenty to the team lead." Reign nodded to me. "The rest split between surviving team members."

"So he gets twenty, and we get, what? Thirteen?" Luna said, nodding as she confirmed her math. "Close enough, anyway. That's fine."

"I was expecting you to have a problem with the split," Reign admitted, as I stayed silent.

"Nah, he's all right, and he did pick us outta the mass. I suppose we owe him a little respect." Luna shrugged, nudging me with a shoulder, and I nudged her back.

"Besides, you didn't try to kill or fuck us," Gessh, always subtle, added.

"There is that," Luna agreed, grinning, and I smiled despite myself.

"So! Repairs and upgrades." Reign went back to the tour. "Basically, you need gear? We strip what comes in, and we sell to our own first. If it doesn't sell, it goes onto the net for sale by the guild. Any prices offered in here are generally cost plus ten percent. When the same shit is offered outside? It's at least double that, so don't be too surprised if someone isn't happy when you buy a mod or whatever. They'll get over it, though, because as much as we all like a payday, we also like to replace our fucked gear for cheap."

She led us back out into the corridor, and to a set of stairs, leading up to the next floor, pausing before going up.

"If you want any clean clothes for after your shower, the vending machines are there." She pointed back behind us, and Gessh, Luna, and I all headed back in that direction. The sound of Reign's laughter followed us as we hurried to find clean clothing.

CHAPTER TWENTY-EIGHT

It was cheap, and yeah, pretty shit. I bought a top and pants, setting me back twenty credits, but knowing that I'd actually be in clean gear soon was a massive incentive. The three of us rejoined Reign on the next level, and she led us through the rest of the brief tour.

We saw shower areas, as well as small private rooms if we needed to just crash, and I grunted at the familiar layout that reminded me of barracks housing. There were a couple of additional hanging out and team areas, as well as a larger room with a map of the city on one wall, hundreds of markers on it at any time.

"What is that?" I looked it over, seeing the flashing markers and tags moving.

"Mission board." Reign nodded to it. "Basically, as soon as we accept a job and start recording, our ident is tagged to the location. That way, another guild member knows not to head there and do the job, as someone's already on it.

"The colors of the jobs are fairly clear. Green is available, blue is taken. If there's a team tag there, then it's taken and the team is working it. If it's not? It's available. So if you know you're going to be there later today? Tag it. You've got twenty-four hours before the tag auto-releases, and if someone else clears it first, you'll get a notification. Stops you getting pestered with updates for places you're not interested in."

"What's red?" I asked.

"Depends," she said. "Red and yellow flashing? Emergency. That's a request to drop your shit and go help. We'll all get messages if that happens. As to a solid red tag? It's based on your registered experience with the guild, so it's recommended you don't take a red tag."

"There's a lot of them," Gessh said softly.

I looked at the map to check the number, guessing that she saw a very different sight than I did, and grunted as I wondered whether she and the others had their aug on.

I always forgot about that shit with city dwellers. From as soon as you joined the army, you learned to do without Aug-World a lot. It took months to wean you off it, but once you'd learned? It was terrifying to walk around the city with it on, seeing the things you'd missed before.

Not everyone could do it. Most people needed that shit, just to get through their days. But when you realized how much it hid?

Aug-World was the corporate and governmental overlay that they sold you of the city. Everywhere you went, the adverts, and hell, the reality, was tailored to you.

They used it to control us, making it so we saw what they wanted, and damn, we helped them to do it. Things like the homeless who were laid in alleys, and bodies of those who'd been mugged, stripped for their mods or had just given up, were subtly blended out of your vision, and instead bright, cheerful colors were enhanced.

For kids, it had things like their favorite cartoon characters dancing around, doing things and helping our corpo overlords pass their message on, as they bought expensive shit that nobody needed and they played at being good little worker bees.

For the rest of us? It was everything from directions to wherever we were going, to hiding the cracks in the sidewalk. Muggings were blurred out, bums begging vanished, and all you ever saw of things like that were a blank automaton with a warning symbol if they moved too close. It was all aimed supposedly at protecting the user from seeing the real world and improving our lives.

In reality, it was control.

They controlled what we saw, what we heard, and even what we smelled, meaning they controlled us.

When we went on dates, the shitty restaurant that was all most of us could afford was suddenly a seven-star place at the top of a tower. The assholes around us, clad in shitty overalls and stinking of sweat, were suddenly beautiful people, dressed and primped.

All of this came at a cost, though.

The basic packages? Yeah, they were free, but you want the good shit? You want the world-altering wonder? You pay for the next level up.

It wasn't hugely expensive, but it was enough. We'd all done it, and once you saw the "beauty" of city life? You paid for the better package.

You did, at least, until you joined the army, the mercs, or you fell foul of the gangs.

For most people, as long as you avoided the gangs, you were all right, and if they ran your area? Most of the gang lords ran a very reasonable "protection" racket, and you got a simple tag that kept gangers from fucking with you.

If you didn't have that, though? You never saw them coming. Augmented as your vision was, you'd get no warning, and suddenly you were being fucked up by faceless automatons. They used blockers, meaning that reprisals didn't work, as there was no recording of their faces or idents.

When you entered the area next? You damn well paid a fee to pass through gang territory, or you stayed to the heavily trafficked and "safe" areas.

The army drove this home, though, and heavily. The paranoia that any good soldier developed was massively enhanced by Aug-World. Because if you had it active? You couldn't see shit. You missed the threats around you, and although, yeah, some soldiers left the service and were totally fine with that, wanting to forget the shit that lay beneath the sugar-coated version of reality that most saw, for the rest of us?

We just couldn't.

I had my Aug-World dialed down to the absolute minimum, allowing only the smallest personal changes, and my RI had comprehensive filters to make sure that I saw what was really there, only adding in the occasional enhancements, like the coding system, rather than making me think I was surrounded by fucking magical giraffes or whatever.

Either way, that was something I'd need to bring up. Luna and Gessh were both ex-army, so they'd have been broken of the aug addiction. Reign, I thought, probably was as well, but couldn't remember off the top of my head, and we'd need to be assigned a replacement for Hobbs, so best to discuss this once they were picked as well.

"So, that's it!" Reign shrugged. "That door over there is to the upper floors, and you'll note the locks on it, as well as the distinctive 'fashion' additions...?"

"Yeah, I noticed." I snorted, looking at the door at the end of the hall.

It was fairly heavy-duty, and yeah, a palm and code lock. Nothing that excessive, but solid security that'd take a minute or so for a decent hacker to beat.

It was also, however, bracketed on either side by heavy auto-cannons—large turrets that looked lethal as fuck were watching us all with unblinking red sensors.

"That's the guild master and upper guild private area. Don't ask me what's up there, because I've no fucking clue. Julius prefers to be down here with us all, so why he's got a private area? I'd recommend you don't get too curious, though."

"Armory?" I asked, already dismissing her recommendation.

"Nope. Damn, sorry, should have covered that. There's an armory and general outfitting area in the basement."

"So..." I said after a few seconds. "The showers?"

"Fuck's sake, boss." Luna sighed. "She already said there's no room in there for us all..."

"Men," Gessh agreed, shaking her head in feigned disgust. "One-track minds."

"Oh, fuck off," I said to the general laughter of the others.

Reign led us back to the showers, and where she'd just jerked her thumb at the door before, she led us all in there now.

It was a narrow room, square with lockers on the sides for us to deposit clothes, as well as a chute marked For Cleaning with a bag to dump everything in, as well as a towel dispenser.

There was an awkward moment where we all sort of looked at one another, waiting for someone else to start, before Reign pushed past and went into the first cubicle.

The shower system itself was a standard one: a good dozen tube-like cubicles standing in a ring, with the water cleaning, containment, and heating equipment in the center.

Each cubicle stood eight feet tall, with a door that closed across the front; the top of the door came to mid-chest. A secondary door could be drawn down from above and sealed to the bottom half, creating an enclosed and private tube. Or, if you wanted to talk or whatever, the upper tube could be left off. As there was a partition wall between each, you had reasonable privacy, and considering the place and those who were likely using the equipment?

As mercs, most of us weren't overburdened with modesty issues, scruples, or any form of morality, admittedly, but what we did tend to have were a *lot* of guns.

That meant that if someone left a tube open for a conversation, you better either keep yourself to yourself and respect their privacy, or be damn sure they didn't mind if you looked in on them, because a bullet to the face often offends.

Reign walked into hers, closed the lower door, and started stripping. We all took the hint, moving into our own.

Everything that I took off—from guns to gear, pants and boots, socks to my goddamn helmet—all of it was filthy, and I sighed, looking at myself before wrapping the towel around me.

I didn't like dirtying the towel I was about to use to dry my clean body. Alternatively, I could either put my clean pants on and do that to them, or walk around naked.

I'd only met the girls a few hours ago, and although we all joked about it, there really wasn't a real bond between us yet.

There was also a little unresolved sexual tension. A few of the comments? I wasn't entirely sure they were jokes. Not totally, and yeah, it'd been awhile.

With that in mind, I wrapped the towel a little tighter, and gathered everything up, carrying it out and setting it on the tables to the side. Guns and gear went into a locker that was keyed to me—although it'd only stay that way for an hour, I was warned, so they didn't get locked and forgotten. Clothing and armor was bundled up in a special bag, and the Emergency Clean chute was used.

I also did my damn best to keep my eyes front and center, as although Reign's towel covered her from chest to knees, Gessh and Luna had tied theirs around their waist.

I moved quickly, minimizing my accidental views, and reminding myself that I was their team lead and there was nothing sexual about this. There was the beginning of a bond of trust between us, and that was all. I also reminded myself that Luna and Gessh were sisters, with an evil sense of humor from what I'd seen, and were probably deliberately doing this to get a rise out of me—in any way possible.

Reign I was less sure of, and I sighed with relief once I was in the cubicle again, towel hanging in a recessed—and safe from the spray—section.

The water, when it hit me, was a little cold—more than a little, really. But it soon heated up, and I gloried in a full-on, hot water bombardment, scrubbing the filth from my body, making good use of the soap dispensers and plastic scrubbers.

This was something I'd need to invest in, I decided, head down at the end, enjoying the water pounding on the back of my neck.

A decent shower and a scrubber seemed like luxuries to most people, but to someone who spent half their lives in armor, or fighting in the shit?

You got *stuff* everywhere.

Filth, dried blood, literal shit, and hair—hell, I swore at one point, I'd seen a goddamn fingertip when I'd been scrubbing. It didn't bear thinking about which crevice had been sheltering that.

I turned it off, wiping the water from my face and sighing. The conversation of the others was low as they assumedly got ready, the sounds of running water dying away as my own finished.

I straightened, feeling a hell of a lot better, and grabbed the towel out of the recess, drying myself quickly, before tying it around my waist and stepping out.

"Well, there he is!" Reign called, clapping her hands slowly as if in appreciation. "You see, ladies? I told you he scrubbed up okay!"

"Love you too," I growled, trying to hide the smile as I moved over to join them, grabbing my new clothes from my locker and dressing quickly.

"Spoilsport."

Luna coughed, unsubtly, when I pulled my pants on under the towel, before tossing it into the chute for cleaning.

They were all dressed, more or less, and I snorted as I grabbed my guns and gear, looking at the chute, then turning to Reign.

"So, where do we get it all back?" I asked. "I mean, we don't wait here, right?"

"No, it'll be delivered downstairs," she assured me. "At the front desk, or if you have a locker…"

"It gets put there for you?"

"Yup."

I sighed. "I need a damn locker."

"Us too," Luna said, Gessh nodding along.

"Well, you're officially guild members now, so no stress there. Let's go sort it, then I'm heading for my rack."

"Uh…" Gessh clearly wanted to say something but decided against it.

"Yeah?" Reign asked, as if clueless, before grinning. "Don't worry, I know." She nodded. "I'll get the grazer evaluated, then I'll sort out some kind of payment plan for you all to consider later today. That okay?"

"Deal," I said firmly. "You didn't name it as loot, though. How does that work? It's clearly the most valuable shit we found."

"It is. But that was supposed to be a cakewalk, and we nearly got ass-fucked. The guild owes us, and well…Julius owes me a favor. I'll let him know, so it's all aboveboard, don't worry."

"I need to have a word with him as well," I said. "Any idea when he'll be around?"

"He's generally here. The guild's his life, so he's probably asleep upstairs. It's late, after all. Anything important?" Reign asked a little too casually.

"He asked me to meet him after the job, that's all." I smiled. "Don't worry. And we need to do something with the datadeck too."

"Fair enough." She grinned tiredly. "In that case, I'd say message him, then do whatever you're doing next. If he's up, he'll come see you, and if not? When you're around next will do."

I took her advice, messaging him, and then trooped along with the others, getting a locker assigned to me, then getting my payout, thirteen thousand and twenty credits.

Apparently one reason for the recording wasn't just to make sure we weren't fucking each other over. When it was uploaded to the guild AI, it scanned the recording and confirmed the deaths, then provided a report to Julius.

The note that was attached to the payout came from him directly.

Kabutt, I'm impressed. Reign clearly taught you well. That or you're a natural. And yeah, all those dead are being credited to your team, so congratulations! A nice little payday indeed for your first day.

Again, my apologies for the shit hitting the fan. Unfortunately, there's realistically no way to guarantee that your missions will be whatever we're told they are, so although I strive to be honest with all my guild members, when it drops in the pot? There's not much I can do beyond praise you for surviving, and commiserate on the loss of Hobbs.

Reign has informed me about the random mod you got. Apparently it's damaged and needs work. If you want help with it, we'll cover the cost as a welcome bonus.

If not, you're welcome to it.

As to the grazer and the datadeck? Yeah, she's told me about them, and I officially don't know about any of it. You split the value internally, and that's a line under this all.

Hopefully you'll be back tomorrow, as I've a use for an additional steady team. If not? Well, good luck with whatever you're searching for.

-Julius.

I read it twice, as the others celebrated their windfall, before deleting the message and turning to the others.

"So, you got paid?" I asked, getting disbelieving grins from Luna and Gessh, and a smug one from Reign. Clearly she was used to the level of payout being better in this guild than the girls were from their last.

"Damn right! Fuck it, you guys up for a club?" Luna asked, and I shook my head, smiling but determined.

"I'm cleaning and repairing my gear," I said. "You do what you want, but tomorrow? I'll be here."

"So will we," Gessh said. "You want us on your team or not, Kabutt? I know we've been joking about it, but…"

"I do. I'll ask for you to be assigned to me, if that's good with you?" I looked from Luna and Gessh to Reign, getting smiles from the first two, and then a slow nod from Reign.

"What's up?" Luna asked, and Reign paused before answering, clearly thinking about her response.

"I need to earn a lot," she said eventually. "Look, I had a lot of fun with you guys, and yeah, we mesh well, but I spend a lot of time here, because I've got a fuckload of debt. So if there's a mission that needs me, and you're not here? Don't be offended if I'm gone, all right?"

"I understand," I said into the sudden silence. "I need the money too, so how about this? We invest in *us*. As in, we invest in our gear, and in making damn sure we survive the missions. Keep the team small, maybe one or two more members, but that's it, and we start doing as many jobs as we can? Hit them over and over, and yeah, I know someone who'll buy specter parts. We grab any decent mods…they're just scrap value to the guild because of where they come from, after all."

"Then what?" Reign asked.

"Then we upgrade our gear again and again—mods, weapons, the lot. We make damn sure we survive the missions over and over, and as soon as I can afford my mods? We start clearing the tunnels with me in my suit."

"You think it'll work?" Luna asked. "I mean, the suit underground? Like you said, those are tight spaces, and the place isn't exactly stable…"

"We'll look at it." I shrugged. "It's the best I can suggest, but for now? It's good to have a plan."

"So…" Luna sighed, looking at her sister. "No club?"

"Weapons and gear maintenance," I said firmly. "You do what you want, but I'm doing that now."

"Fuck." Gessh groaned, rubbing at the side of her face. "We left the fucking army to get away from shit like that…"

"Well, I've got good news," I offered.

"Really?" She perked up.

"Yeah! We've got loads of gear and it's fucking filthy, so the sooner it's done, the sooner you get to use it to shoot someone in the face."

"That's it?" she asked flatly.

"That's the good news?" Luna complained.

"You don't want to shoot someone in the face?" I asked.

"Oh, well, yeah, obviously I do, but…you know? I was hoping for more." She sighed.

"Well, you'll get to shower with us all again sometime soon?" I joked, and Reign laughed.

"You did agree he's got a nice butt," she said to Luna. "That's a plus point?"

"We looked," Gessh admitted, nodding as she looked over at me, utterly unrepentant. "You do, boss."

"Uh…thanks?" I forced a smile, inside snarling over the unfairness. Had I been the one staring in at them? I'd be on charges right now.

Then again, I wasn't in the army anymore, and turnabout was fair play. If they were checking me out? I'd at the very least start damn well teasing them.

"Right. Clean your gear, then hit the rack. Tomorrow's gonna be a hard day," I said. "We've got a long way to go to make it to the top, so no time to fuck about. We've got specters to fucking kill."

I grinned at them, unwilling to even hint at what I suspected we had. But if it was what I thought? No wonder the specters had wanted it back.

If I could get it working?

Fuck. Yes.

CHAPTER TWENTY-NINE

The sisters came with me, and eventually, after a lot of complaining, so did Reign.

All four of us took desks in the workshop, stripping and cleaning our guns, our knives, swords, and the rest. Once I'd finished my rifle, shitty handgun, and knife, though, I *really* got to work.

The shotgun was next. Most of the issues with it were minor. A rusted spring here, some grit that I had to work out of the magazine with a fucking tweezer— that required disassembling the entire magazine, screw by fucking screw of course, because you know, nothing's ever easy and it slipped deeper every time I tried to grab it.

By the time the mechanical issues were resolved, though? It was time to start the complicated shit.

The electrical systems in the shotgun were fucked. Entire sections were burnt out, relays were dead, and as to the fiddly bits?

They were blackened remnants.

There was, however, a lovely shiny new stock in the spare parts catalog for only eighty credits. Why replace individual electrical components one at a time, when I could simply unscrew, disconnect, and reconnect?

The old stock had a lot of the internal parts that were damaged, including the transmission, comms, and tracking data. I replaced it, then a few sections of the receiver, namely the charging handle, the loading port and finally, when I couldn't get it to power up, and I damn well knew it should have, I swapped out the safety cutout as well.

As soon as I thumbed the switch this time, the shotgun powered up and registered in my HUD. My RI activated it and registered it as an owned weapon.

I loaded the magazine, buying a full second mag from the armory—again, discounted and at guild rates, which made me happy—and a full spread of twenty solid slugs for it. There weren't many "fun" rounds for the shotty available, only three, and they were all bolo, so I picked up another ten regular slugs and six fléchettes, then filled the second mag with them and the "fun" ones.

The shotgun was decent. In the receiver, which was one reason I'd had to spend so long on it, was an identification and transmission system, that connected with the stock and then to me.

Basically, it'd register in my HUD what ammo I had in the shotty, and how many rounds I had left.

There was also the option, should I pump it again, when the magazine was powered, to swap the shell out. That way, if it was close quarters, I'd not kill everyone on my side with the blowback from a Devil's Asshole.

It took me way longer than I wanted to spend on doing this job; I'd been trained in field repairs for my suit, after all, and any and all of my weapons. But generally? That was what the armorers were for. They were dedicated, skilled, and experienced at working literal magic to repair the APS systems.

I just marched in, parked the suit, and fucked off for a shower, usually.

That wasn't to say that I and the other APS operators were too good for that kind of work. Fuck no. It was simply that we'd sometimes spent days fighting and living in those things.

When we got back? We needed to rest, before we could work on shit.

In older times, the first thing you did as a soldier, much as I had tonight, was to check and clean your gear. You never knew when you'd need it next.

With the APS systems, though, they might take hours or days to remove a single section and replace it. Even reloading could take hours if you got a round jammed and had to strip the system.

That meant that you needed dedicated people looking after them. Much as a fighter pilot didn't do all the maintenance themselves, but they damn well checked their shit over before they climbed aboard, because out there? It was their ass that was lost if someone fucked up.

That was how it was as an APS operator. We didn't do the grunt work ourselves, *but we could.*

Richie could write programs in his sleep—that was why we had him as tech support—but in a pinch? We could all do a little of it.

We had masses of training; downloads of specs, complicated as shit, were stored in our RIs, ready for the day when we needed them.

For some APS operators, the first thing they did when they left the corps was delete all that shit. It took up space, and sometimes we damn well wanted to have some distance from the things we'd done in the corps.

I'd not done that, though, because I was going to get my damn suit back, and soon.

That meant that as soon as the rest of my gear was done, I pulled up the specs for the system I thought I needed, smiling to myself when I dismissed the Classified markers, and finding the similarities I thought I'd recognized.

Hell yes.

I had clearance—copies I had for a legal reason—so fuck them if they saw my marker accessing the file.

I still didn't dare hesitate, though, skipping to the relevant "field expedient repairs" section, and taking totally unauthorized screen shots as fast as I could.

Just in case.

Seven minutes of access I enjoyed, knowing that retrieving this file would have triggered a monitor program. I was fast, skipping through the boring crap, before a sudden message popped up.

Authorized access revoked.
Please contact your line manager if you believe you should still have access to these files.
Note: APS Server access revoked. APS Access to Ident 99238657543, Harry James Kabutt, blocked.

We were told that any and all our files, once they were unlocked to us, were available for access at any time. Primarily because a lot of the APS Corps ended up working for the corpos after retirement. As a bodyguard, we needed to be able to keep it going in the field when we were protecting their asses or using that particular equipment, and they had their fingers in writing the contracts.

That I'd been revoked, without it requiring a full court-martial, meant that Tyrannus was fucking with me again.

That was fine, though, because given that he'd actually been stupid enough to blacklist me from the server? All living APS personnel were permitted access for life, as most of the upgrades and tweaks were done by retired specialists, the forces being what they were now. This meant that officially, I had no access, and the walking turd had ensured, in cutting off the APS Corps' last official connection to me, that they in turn couldn't access *my* gear, should they have a need.

I checked the shots I'd taken, and yeah. They'd do.

Comparing them to the device spread out before me, damaged, I nodded, spreading it out further, and mentally marking up and identifying the connective systems.

It looked as though it'd been built around something originally, something oval shaped when I tried to reassemble it, and I grinned when I spotted the likely shape.

A hand.

The goblins had probably dumped the hand after looting the system.

I paused, rethinking that. The gobbos wouldn't have taken this; they'd have no reason to. Why fight a specter and steal this, then dump its fucking hand? They were fighting specters down in the depths on occasion, and if they knew what this was, they'd know why the specters would keep coming after it. If they didn't?

Why carry it?

Why choose to take what looked to the untrained eye like scrap?

No, they'd not done this, I decided, looking it over. "They stole it from someone else," I muttered, nodding to myself. It made sense. Someone else had been down there, either to steal this or trying to use it, and that had drawn the specters.

They'd locked in on it, and they'd gone mad trying to get the fucker; then the gobbos had seen something shiny and grabbed it. Probably shanking the original thief as part of the deal. That was why the specters had followed us. And if I took this back down there? They'd come for it again.

That…could be useful, though. Use it, maybe figure out a way to shield it or to hide it. Some kind of armoring maybe? Then when we'd gotten all we could carry, and we were ready, set up a trap. Uncover it, and draw the specters in. Slaughter them over and over, strip the mods. Rinse and repeat.

Could it be that simple?

Could I really do this?

I'd definitely need a team if this was what I thought it was. I couldn't do this alone, and there was no fucking way I was going to try. Realistically, neither was there any chance I was going to tell Lucky about this and let him "help" with his gangbangers.

I didn't know Julius, and despite the good feeling from the last few hours, and the offer I'd made Reign, Luna, and Gessh, I sure as shit didn't trust them with *this* either.

Not yet.

No, I needed to test this, and I damn well needed to make sure that it actually worked. I needed credits. I needed to earn as much as I could, upgrade my gear, and I'd keep the team together for now. We worked well so far, after all.

I'd test them, one by one, somehow, and if they passed? Well. We had a chance to really make some serious credits.

By the time I'd finished connecting the various systems, and I was ready to try powering it, the others were long gone. The sisters had gone home, promising to be back at the guild for noon—it was getting light outside already—and Reign had done some maintenance, then got up as if she were going to the toilet, and just never came back.

I was at fifty-fifty currently whether she'd pawn the grazer or use it in a card game straightaway, or if she'd deal with her demons on her own and keep it.

I know which I'd prefer, as a grazer was a hell of a weapon. And for a sniper? I'd definitely prefer her to be there by my side. What would be, would be though.

Dressing quickly in my now-clean armor, I nodded my appreciation of a job well done. They'd even polished the helmet, and considering how many cracks ran through that right now, that couldn't have been easy.

I needed to replace it, realistically, as it wasn't much use as it was, but it'd do until I could find another. As well as hiding my face, it kept the rain off.

Settling back in the cab, I watched the city roll past. The rain streaked down the side of the glass, and the lights beyond flared and blurred.

It was a waste to spend so much on a cab, it really was, but I needed to get some sleep, and if I'd stayed in a guild rack, after ignoring Lucky so much, it'd look like I was avoiding him, if not full-on running.

As if the thought of him was a talisman, a fresh message dropped to me from him, along with an image.

Lilith better be dead and soon.

That was it, along with a set of coordinates. I groaned, pulling the image up: a smiling woman, deep-purple hair, impressive cleavage, and glowing purple nails. It'd been taken while she was talking to someone. The image zoomed in to show her leaning on the shoulder of a massively modded man. The arms looked to be tier two at the minimum, maybe three. Chrome all the way, artistically layered with "muscle."

He was clearly armed to the teeth, mostly standard-issue crap, but a nice-looking HK-TT slug thrower on his hip. I could see a few others to the sides, laughing, and…

I checked the image, finding it was zoomed in, but not locked. I rolled the point of view back a little, seeing a dozen idiots with her. Most were like Lucky's lot, gangbangers who thought that a willingness to use uber violence was the same as being lethal adversaries.

It wasn't, and the condition of their guns when I zoomed in on them made it clear they were amateurs. Most of them were filthy, and a few even had the red warning light of low-zero ammo blinking.

They were walking round with empty or low weapons, and didn't do anything about it. Idiots.

Most of their weapons were melee, as near as I could see—electro-shock knuckles, batons, blades—and the bodyguard had discharge plates on his knuckles when I zoomed in on them as well.

Yeah, that was a *nice* set of arms.

I was ready to ignore it, to head straight back to the apartment, until I saw the last figure.

It was an older man, one who wore the same tattoos as some of Lucky's gang, and he was laid on the floor to one side. A trail of blood led from him to the bodyguard, while another ganger counted out credit-chips.

They'd moved into Lucky's territory, he'd said, and I guessed this image was supposed to make me believe they were the aggressor, and that they were attacking the innocent?

No. They were selling drugs and stims, I betted, zooming in and out of the image at different points to confirm. They were the same level of scum that Lucky and his people were, but they also had credits, and I had slightly more reason to kill these people.

Besides, it'd be a shame if someone else got those arms.

Send me the job details...

I sent the message to Lucky, and a few seconds later, a new message popped up, making me sigh as I read over it, nodding and confirming the coordinates attached.

JOB: UPDATE!

Kabutt will carry out five [5] contract hits for Lucky, including and limited to the following:
- 2 x Standard Assassinations:
  - [Lilith, Floor 72 – Market District – Location attached]
  - [Unconfirmed]
- 2 x Chemist lab raids
- 1 x Assassination of [Stinger]

Supplemental:
- 1 x Recover 100,000 credits worth of Specter Mods

In exchange, Kabutt will receive:
- 47,500 x direct credit transfer
- 30,000 x store credit for Lion's Chop Shop
- ? x Additional bounties
- 4 x gang members will be dispatched to Kabutt's choice of location to act as a distraction

Job Accepted

I ordered the cab to divert to the current coordinates, and three minutes later, I was pulling up to the south entrance of my accommodation block.

"Huh?" I mumbled, climbing out of the cab and yawning as I looked around. The locals glared as they saw someone rich enough to afford a cab, and I saw the convenience of having my target in my damn building.

I could go straight to bed afterward.

The glares vanished as soon as I popped the trunk on the cab and dragged out my shotty, slotting it into the sheath on my back, then the rifle, connecting up the restraining harness and double-checking my gear.

I nodded after a few seconds and closed the cab's doors, before setting off.

No real grenades. A man just felt plain naked without at least one decent grenade on him, and here I was, without any. I shrugged, resolving to buy some more, as I slid my helmet on, and walked in the nearest entrance.

This entrance was slightly nicer than mine—less piss in the corners, and the crazed old lady was noticeably missing, which was also a bonus. The lift had a guy passed out in the corner, though, and I activated the code that Reign had given me yesterday. It changed the assault on my olfactory senses to a pleasant vanilla and coconut mix and I relaxed, smiling to myself.

Why the hell had I never thought to ask Richie for a damn code like that before now?

The lift doors opened a few floors up and the family who stood waiting took one look at me, heavily armed, assault rifle held ready and with my face hidden behind a black, glossy and clearly cracked helmet.

"We'll get the next one," the dad, presumably, said, frantically stabbing a finger at the Close Doors symbol on his side.

"Good choice," I agreed, as the doors closed again, and I whooshed upward.

This goddamn lift even started to play music, for fuck's sake, and I shook my head in disgust. It was terrible music, admittedly, and I was fairly sure that it was actually law somewhere that all lift music must make you want to gouge your ears out with rusty spoons, but still.

That wasn't the point.

The lift paused again, and a pair of drugged-up gangers stared at me in confusion.

"You here for Jenny?" one asked after a minute, fingering his gun.

"No."

"Cool."

That was it. The doors shut, and I was whisked higher. Minutes passed, until finally the relevant floor dinged, and the lift slowed again.

This time when the doors opened, I was hit by a wave of music, laughter, and smells, as the entire floor was revealed to be a single huge market.

I stepped out. The throng of people moved this way and that, quickly enveloping me as I moved deeper. The coordinates clearly updated as a directional marker appeared on my HUD.

Hundreds of people surrounded me; meals were cooked in woks and on grills, self-heating trays of food were bought up at counters, and arguments raged as people jostled each other, fighting to get through the madhouse.

I felt a hand trying my pocket and I slapped it hard. My metal left hand registered a crack of bone as I beat it aside; a shriek echoed from someone unseen in the mass.

Moving deeper and deeper, I passed counters and seating areas, tables and bars. There were bands playing music, dancers and lights, screens showing various sports being played—mostly fights—and people begging or stealing.

I saw people passed out in corners—some clearly still breathing, others whose condition was less certain. One body was slumped half behind a curtain; a leg stuck out, twitching over and over as they accessed something, a thick cable plugged into the side of their neck.

It was a mess, a madhouse, and it was like every other slum market in the city: a mix of screaming lunatics, laughter, and an attempt to get through the goddamn day.

I moved through the mess slowly, stunned that this was even here.

My shitty apartment was a handful of floors below this level, and although I knew intellectually that these places were in the arcology, I'd not been here until now.

I noted a few places in passing, bars that looked like they might be actually all right, and a place selling noodles that looked and smelled amazing. The only thing that put me off? A sign outside that proudly proclaimed they served "real meat."

Real fucking meat? I'd had it once, and that was in a posh restaurant on a date. With the amount of stims the meal was laced with? If they'd served up a block of cardboard, I'd have been none the wiser.

For this place to be advertising it? There was no way they were getting supplied by the people who sold the real meat; it was for corpo scum only.

That meant they were catching something themselves—probably rats, but who knew—and serving it to people who were paying good credits.

Fucking low-life scum.

I kept moving, catching a second pickpocket a few meters farther on. I clamped my metal hand on his wrist, hauling him out of the stream of citizens, and glared down into his single eye.

"Please sir…I'm just hungry…" he started, dangling from his left wrist. His right reached up behind his back for something.

"Try using whatever weapon that is, and I'll rip your hand off," I said flatly, getting a glare of hatred back from him.

"Lemme go!" he snarled, twisting and trying to yank his hand free.

"What gang controls this floor?" I asked, only to grunt in pain, dropping him and spinning as someone darted out of the crowd to my rear and stabbed me, a tiny scalpel in hand.

I had to play it back to even see it, they were that fast, but a tousle-haired mop of a child—perhaps seven or eight years old—had sprinted out of the uncaring press of people, stabbed me in a joint between my body armor and lower back, then vanished again, as another figure dragged the attempted pickpocket away.

It was done in seconds, and I was left snarling, reaching back and pressing a hand to the wound. Little shit had only made a minor wound, but still.

It damn well hurt!

I glared after them. The direction they'd taken off in was the same one my HUD was showing me, and I sighed, knowing damn well what was coming.

I checked my gear, making sure, and grunted as I found a "safe" trigger clip had been pressed into both my handgun's trigger *and* my fucking shotgun.

How the hell had some little bastard managed that?

I plucked it free and slipped it into a pocket, torn between annoyance and admiration. The sheer skill and outright brass-fucking-balls it took to do that?

Moving through the crowd, I cursed and activated my RI with a counter-insurgent "identify and assess" package. It was overkill for the situation, or so I had believed, and it took most of the operating cycles I had available for the RI. But when it kicked in after thirty seconds?

Fuck my life.

The program washed the colors out of my vision, muting the vast majority, and enhanced the colors of those it identified, using a complex mix of tracking algorithms, data and transmission hacks, and a load of code I really couldn't be arsed to figure out.

The basic premise, though, was that it made those it identified as following or paying excessive attention to me *much* more identifiable—without slapping a massive flashing marker over them and making it obvious when the eye was naturally drawn to the change.

What concerned me, though, was that six figures were picked out immediately, and two of them weren't with the other three gangbangers. The last? I mentally marked as neutral and to be watched.

I mentally tagged them, focusing on their faces, and a second later, the three were picked out as idiots who worked for, or at least had been around, Lucky.

They were moving through the crowd, following me, and the other two were doing the same thing.

It was almost comical that there were two groups, utterly unaware of the other, trying to sneak up on me. It probably would have been hilarious, if they weren't all heavily armed.

As it was? I sent Lucky a message.

> Scouting target. Tell your monkeys to fuck off before they ruin it.

There was a long pause. Then, predictably, he denied all knowledge of them.

> You need to do as you're told, Kabutt. You were supposed to kill her last night, and my people are nowhere near you.

I snorted and sent him images of the three, deliberately picking out the most stupid stills I could get as I paused and leaned against a wall, letting the RI examine the crowd.

> Really? Then these three just happen to be right behind me? Also, how do you know where I am? To be able to say that they're nowhere near me? Is there something you want to tell me, Lucky?

A few seconds passed before all three turned heel and headed off.

> Good boy. Now, you try that shit again? I'll not be happy. I put up with it on the train and since then because you're an idiot, and you needed to be sure I wasn't running away. Right now? I'm too tired for this shit, Lucky. I don't run, and I don't backstab. Remember that. I *judge*.

I set off again, pushing through the crowd, coming to a wider section around a set of ornamental outdoor tables, the ceiling painted and implanted with tiny lights that were supposed to resemble the night sky, and dozens of concentric low walls with space in the top for drinks and so on to be placed.

If it was anything like the versions I'd seen growing up, it was vandalized probably inside of the first hour that people moved in, and had never been fixed since.

> Watch yourself, Kabutt. Keep this shit up, and I'll cut my losses…and your throat.

"Promises, promises." I sighed, dismissing his message as I strode into the middle of the mosaic, noting the attempts to improve it over the years by people signing it, and replacing entire sections with new lights, ones that proclaimed that such and such was a stud, or a gonk or whatever.

The location marker pinged to say I was at the target, and I sighed. The kid from before darted out of a small building and ran for it, having clearly passed word on of my arrival, even if the others tailing me hadn't.

I focused on the buildings, checking them out. A half dozen of them were in the concentric rings, made to look like old-style houses: all white plaster and curved windows around the center, doors opening this way and that.

In other versions of this I'd seen elsewhere, this was used as a market, one that people claimed a spot in for a day or two; as soon as they moved, another took their place. Here, though? They were all empty, making it clear that this was a forbidden area, considering how everyone on the rest of the floor was pressed cheek by jowl.

A handful of figures sat around on the seats, including a couple of the gang I recognized from the photo earlier. They all turned to me as I walked into their midst.

"Stop right there." One of them sighed, shaking his head and holding up a hand. "What, you thought you could just rock right up? That we'd not know you were coming?"

"Where's Lilith?" I moved across to a chair that had a seemingly solid stone low wall right behind it. The figure in it glared up at me, and I grinned, already in a shitty mood, and seeing only one way that this was going to go. "Move, or be hurt," I said softly.

"Get fucked, you—" He reached for his drink, and I grabbed him by the back of the head, slamming his face into the table with an audible crack of breaking bones.

He managed to get out one scream—a truncated, pain-filled thing—then I did it again. The second impact rendered him unable to add anything more to the conversation.

CHAPTER THIRTY

I tipped him sideways out of the seat and onto the floor. His body convulsed as I sat on the newly vacated seat and laid my rifle before me, reaching up and drawing the shotgun, and adding that to the table as well.

As soon as I'd attacked him, the others had leapt to their feet and jerked their weapons out. Now they were staring from the body to me, then back again, armed, ready, and totally confused.

"Lilith!" I bellowed. "For fuck's sake, get your ass out here."

"You're very confident," a new voice said, sounding both husky and annoyed, as she moved out of one of the small white buildings that ringed the fanciful plaza.

"Best way to be." I smiled, even though she couldn't see it through my helmet. "After all, I hold most of the cards here, and creeping in and out like an assassin? Not my style."

"You hold no cards," she said grimly, sitting down at a table two over from me, and gesturing to her people to sit again. The massive chrome-armed bodyguard stood behind her and glared at me.

"Really?" I asked conversationally. "Seems we're at an impasse."

"Standoff," she corrected. "You're armed. We're armed. Nobody needs to die, though. You walked right in like you own the place, so tell me why."

"I wanted to meet you," I said honestly.

"Now you've met me." She nodded, then shrugged, smiling widely. "So tell me why, and why I should let you leave here alive."

"First, because you can't stop me leaving." I ignored most of the people there. "But as to why? I wanted to know who you were, and why someone wants you dead."

"Because Lucky wants my turf," she said. "He thinks he's got a disposable soldier to take me down, APS no less, but it's bullshit."

"What makes you think that?" I settled back, ignoring the creak of the old chair under me.

"What, that it was Lucky, or that it's bullshit?"

"Both."

"You think I don't have my people in his gang?" She snorted. "I knew you were coming for me before you did, Kabutt."

"And the bullshit?"

"No real APS operative would have come here. Not in a million years. You'd be up in corpo-town, choking on a cock, living it up. So you're not an elite soldier, just an arrogant fuck stain that thinks he can walk in and out of here. So come on, what makes you different?" She sneered.

"Two things." I nodded. "But we'll get to those in a minute. Tell me, why you? Why's Lucky after you specifically?"

"I'm the boss. This is my floor, and Lucky knows I'll be taking his soon. My people already control the chemists here, and these useless fucks pay for my protection, or they have 'accidents.'"

"Okay, standard low-level gang shit." I shrugged. "Nothing special then. But why you? I mean, the job wasn't to kill your gang, but you, specifically."

"He thinks if he takes me down, he can move in and my people will accept him," she guessed. "Fuck knows, really."

"And Maribeth," one of the idiots around the group said.

I pointed my left hand at him.

"Maribeth?" I said. "Tell me about that."

"Fuck off." He swallowed hard as everyone stared at him. "What? I thought maybe it's—"

"Come on then, Lilith. Let's not leave me hanging." I had my right hand on the stock of the shotgun, and I turned it to point at her, smiling as I did so. "I'm asking so nicely as well."

The big fucker with the chrome arms growled, his voice a synthesized snarl, and I cocked my head to one side in question.

"Why should I care what you ask?" She smiled. "My people have you covered. One signal, and your spine is fried. I'll have all the time I want to play with you then."

"Two reasons. First, though…a dead man's switch. You shoot me, I fire. Ah-ah!" I growled as she started to stand. "You stay right fucking there. You move again, and I fire."

"So you get one shot off. That's it," she snapped. "You die as soon as you fire, and your chance of taking me out? What, fifty-fifty? Most likely, I end up with a new mod. Shit happens."

"That's how we get to the second point," I said. "My shotgun is an automatic, and it's loaded with Devil's Asshole rounds. I unload this thing? Nobody on this *floor* walks away."

There was a pause of several seconds as she clearly assessed the threat, then the shotgun's magazine.

"Twenty shots," I confirmed. "Want to think about the chances of anything surviving that? I could entirely miss you, and the heat alone will render you down to a smear of melted fats."

"You're bluffing."

"You willing to risk it all on that guess?" I asked. "You think me marching up here and just sitting down suggests I'm a stable man?"

"So what do you want?" she asked after a brief pause for thought where most of her people changed their point of aim. Locking onto my shotgun now.

"Maribeth."

"She was a whore lower down the tower. I bought her, brought her up here." She shrugged. "She didn't want to be a whore after a few months, thought she could quit, and she'd not paid off my investment yet, so I sold her for parts."

"Parts?" I asked coldly.

"To a carver," she confirmed. "What? You think corpo scum all look so young and healthy by magic? Most corpos spend half the year recovering from surgery. I sell them stripped primo 'parts,' and they've got no idea their new lips have been hammered more than an anvil."

"And Lucky?"

"He's no white knight in search of love, if that's what you're asking." She snorted. "He had a buyer for her as well, so don't go thinking he's a hero trying to free her."

"That's fine," I said after a few seconds. "I guess I just wanted to be sure of who I was working with." I sent the message to the sixth observer who I'd been toying with for a while, figuring it was time to find out what the hell was going on.

"And now?" she purred, sitting forward. "You know, you've got some balls, boy. Why don't you tell Lucky to fuck right off and—"

Lilith's head exploded as a hypersonic round passed straight through it, hitting her in the right temple and exiting midway on the far side with a loud crack.

With blood and brains spraying in all directions, I pulled the trigger on the shotgun, then ducked to the side. My fléchette's round shredded most of the bodyguard's upper torso, as I rolled out of sight.

The shock of a hidden sniper distracted them enough that they were slow to fire on me, and I hit the ground behind the low wall with only two actual hits. Five more were absorbed by my armor as it solidified.

I hissed in pain. Both fucking shots had hit me in the left leg, calf, and the thick muscle at the back of my upper leg, passing between two armor plates.

Sod's fucking Law.

I yanked the handgun free and fired three shots blindly over the top of the wall, keeping them interested, then swapped the handgun to my left hand and pulled out a medikit.

I bit down on the covering on one end, yanking it off and spitting it out, before priming and stabbing it into my lower thigh.

The nanites weren't enough to fully regenerate the wounds, not a single small medikit and certainly not two wounds. But they were enough to break the bullets down, or push them out, and slow the bleeding at least.

With that done, I pointed the handgun over the top and fired off a few more rounds, as I dragged the shotgun closer, and decided the next step.

Was this really what you came here to do?

The response to my message came through despite the usual blocks in combat, because, for now at least, she was registered as part of my team, and I grinned manically.

I came to check things out, but seeing you were here anyway? I'm improvising.

There was a brief pause as the wall I was sheltering behind was hammered over and over with bullets, and I sighed, waiting.

> Should have known you saw me. So, what's the plan? That wall won't hold much longer, you know.

I winced as plaster exploded nearby, and I was covered in a dusting of white.

> Give me a distraction and damn well help then!

There was a brief pause before the answer came back.

> Fine. You owe me half the bounty. Deal?

I sighed, then grinned as a thought occurred to me.

> Half of the bounty I get for this single job.

I got a single goddamn smiling face as my response, then the heavy *crack, crack* of a high-powered sniper rifle filled the air. I rolled to my feet, shotgun in my right hand, handgun in the left.

I fired the handgun first—three shots at a wall on the far side as people dove out of sight—then I dumped it, switching to both hands on the shotty and firing a single solid slug into the nearest wall of the little "house."

The solid metal slug tore through the wall, barely slowing. A man dove out, hands over his head as I pumped the shotgun, firing and taking him in the side, sending him flying.

I flicked it to full auto, and fired: three slugs, then a second fléchette round, the first having done so well that…I glanced from the figures running and diving out of my way, looking for the bodyguard's body.

Gone.

Fuck!

I was hit from the side at almost the same time that I saw the fucker was gone, my shotgun torn from my grip and two ribs on the right side cracking even through my armoring.

The suit hardened, cushioning the blow, but it still fucking hurt. I hit a second low wall. It caught me behind my left leg, on the far side of the knee, and sent me tipping over it to fall onto my head.

I rolled, training raising to the fore, and I twisted. A blur resolved into a boot as it slapped down next to my face. I grabbed it, left-handed, and clamped down with maximum pressure, even as I reached for my blade with my right hand.

I didn't get it.

My left hand squeezed and squeezed, and I heard the sound of metal under pressure, slowly buckling. But the right hook that took me in the face sent the world spinning as first my already damaged helmet, and then my jaw, broke.

Next thing I knew, I was being dragged upward. One hand gripped me by the front of my armor, left hand drawing back and punching me in the gut.

I coughed and wheezed. The motion and the sheer force, not to mention my own cough, sent my broken jaw into paroxysms of agony, the world full of bright lights and spinning.

"CEASE FIRE!" the idiot holding me screamed out at my ally, shaking me. "Cease fire or I kill him!" he roared, using me as a living shield.

There was a brief pause as he waited for a response, and I made the most of it, clapping both hands over his ears as hard as I could, bursting his eardrums and making him drop me. He screeched, then threw himself sideways as a sniper round hammered through the air where he'd stood. I coughed, groaning in pain.

My second medikit was out...and was grabbed and dragged sideways. The medikit dropped from my hands as the asshole I was fighting lunged atop me, scrabbling for it as well.

I saw him properly for the first time, and fuck me sideways with a double-ended dildo, he looked like shit.

It was the bodyguard, and for a second we were face-to-face as we both struggled to get the medikit.

My fléchettes round had done a number on him, but what I'd not realized was the sheer fucking level of work he'd had.

He was well on the way to full cyborg status. The fléchettes—which were essentially several dozen carbon-steel darts packed close together—had shredded his chest and head. But fuck.

Under the layer of clothing and skin was a layer of subdermal armoring. What looked to be tens of thousands of tiny scales, laid overlapping, had been exposed on his chest and neck, with a cranial cover on his head. It was a solid-looking skull coating that, again, went under the skin and over the bone.

Right now, he looked like a half-stripped skeleton. Both eyes were cybernetic, and the front of his head was a tattered mess of torn flesh and muscle, occasional darts embedded here and there.

That my cupped hands had worked at all on his was a relief, and as I frantically kept from screaming, my face flexing as muscles moved and bones failed to brace them, I realized *why* it'd worked.

It was a covering.

I could see the white of bone around his eyes, the edges of the armoring, and I saw the desperation in his fixation on the medikit, rather than killing me, which he probably could have done with those arms if he'd kept trying.

At first, I'd thought cyborg, replacing all his human bits as he could afford them.

Some with a high enough score could do it and not go mad, provided they were careful and did it gradually.

I was wrong, though.

He'd gone for the arms, that was clear, and the eyes. But the way he moved? The way he hissed and frantically grappled for the medikit?

It was just the armoring beyond that, I was betting.

I let go of the kit, wrapping my left arm around his neck and dragging him closer against every instinct and going for the knife again. He went for the medikit, grabbing it and desperately dragging the rubberized plug off the end, to expose the injector.

He flipped it around, trying to get it back over his shoulder, and I did the same. His desperation had exposed the weakness, as my knife flared to life.

His armoring was on the front only.

He couldn't stab himself with the injector anywhere on the front, as they'd just pour over the armor and try to integrate into it, instead of fixing the flesh, so he had to get them into an unarmored area.

Before the injector could stab in, though, my blade did, sinking into the back of his spine, right between the shoulder blades, tearing deep and severing the spinal cord.

At the sudden look of panic on his face, I dragged the blade upward, carving deeper and doing catastrophic damage. His arm holding the injector sagged.

I grabbed it, twisting and stabbing it into the side of my neck, whimpering, as much as I'd never admit it, with the pain as it triggered.

We stared at each other from a distance of a few inches. His eyes flared, the lenses twitching and zooming, before relaxing in death, the light deep within them fading.

His body sagged atop me, making me groan even more as his weight settled. The fucker must have had bones replaced, he was so goddamn heavy!

I dumped the medikit. My head sagged back, the shattered helmet clanging against the stone behind my head, and more parts fracturing off.

It *might* have taken the blow before it'd been so fucked up, but the condition my helmet was in when I walked into this fight, it was half hanging off now, broken beyond belief.

I reached up, wincing, pulled it free and tossed it aside. Then, coughing and spitting something out—hoping it wasn't a goddamn tooth—I forced the dead bodyguard off me.

I grabbed my shotty and pumped it, getting a notification the chambered round was a bolo. I stood, squinting around at the madness.

There were a dozen dead gangers, Lilith was slumped half on and half off the table she'd been leaning on for our conversation, and the formerly white buildings were covered in bright arterial splashes. People were screaming, running and hiding; alarms were going off and a loudspeaker blared the same message that was being pushed out to all Keystones in range.

> Illegal Activity Detected: ACE have been requested. Do not attempt to leave the area. All visual systems are recording, and idents have been registered.

As usual, everyone absolutely fucking ignored it. There wasn't a cat in hell's chance that anyone was staying here. And that the idents had been recorded? Good luck with that. One of the first things that anyone with a Keystone did as soon as they could afford it was get the fucker hacked.

Mine spoofed a secondary ident for a corpo scumbag when it was pinged by a recorder whenever I was doing something that was even slightly dodgy.

It meant that the ACE, who everyone knew were notorious cowards and thieves, had the choice of attempting to arrest and question a corpo suit, when they damn well knew that'd end badly for them, or just ignore my ident on whatever shitty list they ended up with.

That it was a common way of doing business these days? It meant that the only chance the ACE had was if there were actual visual recording and decent scanners live, as everyone else would have been doing exactly the same.

Add in that the corpos didn't give a shit and actively dissuaded anyone from solving this little loophole? It meant that they could do what they wanted and then deny it, so fuck no.

So yeah, scanners and recording devices…considering it was a territory actively being ruled over by a gang? Uh…no.

That left witnesses, and anyone who came somewhere like this knew what happened to witnesses who helped ACE.

I snorted at the mere thought, then groaned at the pain in my face, before grabbing the remains of my helmet, dumping it into my bag and roughly searching the bodyguard.

I ripped the blade free of his spine as the crunch of boots on broken plaster and glass rang out, and Reign moved in closer as I started cutting.

"What now?" she asked me, and I nodded to the bodies.

"We've got about two minutes. After that, we might actually be inside ACE's net, if they bother to come. Unlikely but hey, strip the fuckers for anything valuable—guns, gear, weapons. And grab her head."

"Her head?" She sighed. "Really?"

"It's proof." The pain of speaking as the nanites fixed my jaw made tears blur my vision. "Just do it, Reign. We need to get out of here."

CHAPTER THIRTY-ONE

Two and a half minutes later, and we were off, running past faces that deliberately looked in any direction but ours. A new waypoint plotted by my RI guided us to the lift we needed, and after a few minutes of running?

We were reduced to walking again and dealing with pickpockets, obnoxious salesmen, and people trying to hawk us shitty knockoffs that they swore were real.

"Oberyn Systems datadecks!"

"Nemesis upgrades! Two for one!"

"Corpo meat! Feed your family the best!"

"Tits and ass! Cheap and tasty!"

That last one made me smile despite the pain as I passed the caller, a whore leaning against the wall nearby obviously deciding that if you can't beat the shitty salesmen, you might as well join them. "Seriously, I wash and everything!" she announced to general laughter.

"So," Reign said as we entered the lift, ignoring the gang signs that glowed here and there on it, warning others off. "What the hell was that?"

"You tell me." I shrugged. "You followed me."

"I wanted to see what you were doing."

"You could have fucking asked."

"And you'd have told me?"

"Yeah," I said, deciding honesty was the best policy here. "Seriously, Reign, I told you I was going to go to bed after fixing my gear, and..."

"And instead you went bounty hunting," she pointed out with a smile.

"Nope," I corrected. "I went to do a job. You remember what I said? Five jobs I've got for the gang—two outright hits on gang leaders, after them, take down two chemists, then a bounty. The bounty is the last of all."

"You..." She paused, looking at me, then grinned. "Are you registered as a bounty hunter?"

"No." I shrugged. "It's on my list of shit to sort but..."

She smiled happily. "I am."

"And...?" I asked after a few floors of silence, as the lift slowed.

"And I got paid the bounty on her head," she admitted, hefting the bag.

"I'm not getting paid a bounty," I said slowly. I swore as suddenly it all made sense. "Fuck's sake. She had a bounty off someone else?"

"Three people." Reign grinned at me. "ACE, some corpo scumbag, *and* a private citizen. Payment for each was lodged with the Armed Brigade, so I just made...yup. Seven hundred and forty creds."

"Motherfuckers." I groaned. "I need to add that to tomorrow's jobs."

"Today," she corrected. "It's nearly seven."

"For fuck's—"

"Hey!" She cut me off, staring into the distance. "Some fucker just contested my kill! They're trying to claim the bounty!"

The doors opened on the lift, and she blinked, clearly filing a counter-claim from the notification as she stared fixedly ahead into the gloom.

"What the hell is this?" She blinked one eye free and stared around confusedly.

I grunted, stepping forward, looking around and seeing only one of the gang passed out on the floor nearby.

"This is the wonderful floor I live on." I spread my hands in welcome, before walking over and prodding the unconscious figure with a foot. "Hey—hey, dickhead!"

He groaned and rolled over, trying to ignore me, and I sighed, turning to Reign. "Give me the head."

She pulled it out, glancing at it and clearly taking a visual shot of it, just in case, before handing it over. I crouched down and set it and the arms and so on right before the idiot on the floor, before pressing my rifle barrel to the side of his head.

That woke him up. And the first thing he saw when his eyes opened? What was left of Lilith's head and the collection of looted body parts I'd grabbed behind it.

He screamed, frantically trying to get away and I stood, letting him scrabble away on all fours.

"Oi!" I called after him. "Give those to Lucky." For good measure, I sent the shot I'd taken of him staring at the head and arms on the floor to Lucky directly, then turned and headed for my apartment.

"So," Reign said after a few seconds, catching up to me and striding along, her long legs easily keeping pace with me. "You've really not registered with any merc bounty hunter guilds?"

"Nope." I sighed. The crash from the adrenaline surge hit me hard. "Fuck, I need some sleep."

"You and me both," she admitted. "You know how long I was watching for you?"

"Hours?"

"Literally!" she growled. "I thought you'd be like half an hour polishing your barrel, at most!"

"Well, I'm terribly sorry I dared to disappoint," I muttered, unable to stop from quirking a smile as she mumbled, almost too low for me to hear.

"You haven't...*yet...*"

We walked in companionable silence until we made it to my apartment, and I hesitated, before sending the code to the door.

"Look, Reign—"

She snorted, reaching out and putting her hand over my mouth. "Don't get your hopes up. I'll crash on your couch. I need sleep, and I can't be bothered to head anywhere else. That's all that's happening here."

"Couch?" I laughed, only to cut off as the door opened, and I looked inside. A small, admittedly shitty couch had indeed appeared from somewhere—presumably Lucky—as well as a handful of other luxuries, like chairs that didn't look to have been designed to punish you for sitting on them.

"Yeah." She strode past me, peering around in disgust. "Damn, Kabutt, I know you said it was shit, but still..."

"You've got no idea." I grunted, moving in after her and keying the door to close. I sat on one of the chairs while Reign used the bathroom, the sound of her arguing with someone over the bounty clearly audible. Seconds later, my comm chimed.

I looked at it, seeing a request from Lucky, and I sighed, accepting it.

"So," he said as a greeting.

"So."

"So Lilith's dead."

"Yeah."

"Most of her gang too, I hear."

"That a problem?"

"Not really. I'd planned on absorbing them into mine, but you know, it depended on how many survived when you hit the chemist. I guess you made that easier for yourself, but…" He paused, dragging the word out, and I groaned.

"Fuck's sake, Lucky, I'm not in the mood for this shit. Say what you want to say and fuck off."

"Fine," he snapped, sitting forward. "You hit the gang hard, too fucking hard maybe, as the other floors know whoever's left and tries to take over from Lilith has got a damn good chemist, and fuck all security now."

"So?"

"So they'll all go for the chemist."

"And?"

"And I need that fuckin' chemist, Kabutt. That's the second job! I'm warning you here, because if you take them now? It'll be an easy fight. You wait? Chances are you'll be fighting another entire fucking gang to get them!"

"You want them right now?"

"Yes!" he snarled, sending an updated job's notification along with the demand.

JOB: UPDATE!

Kabutt will carry out five [5] contract hits for Lucky, including and limited to the following:

- 2 x Standard Assassinations:
  - [~~Lilith, Floor 72 — Terminated~~]
  - [Unconfirmed]
- 2 x Chemist lab raids
  - [Lilith's Lab – Location attached]
  - [Unconfirmed]
- 1 x Assassination of [Stinger]

Supplemental:

- 1 x Recover 100,000 credits worth of Specter Mods

In exchange, Kabutt has received:

- 47,500 x direct credit transfer
- 30,000 x store credit for Lion's Chop Shop
- ? x Additional bounties
- 4 x gang members will be dispatched to Kabutt's choice of location to act as a distraction

---

Job Accepted

"You fucking go get them then," I grunted, before closing the connection, then locking it into Privacy and Do Not Disturb mode.

Fuck that asshole, trying to send me on jobs after all that shit.

Reign came out of the bathroom a few minutes later, and I froze, staring unconsciously as she walked past, her gear bundled up in her arms.

She'd stripped out of most of her clothes, wearing only her under armor top and shorts, with her hair loose, and I couldn't help but stare. I knew she was pretty—she had great bone structure, at least—but as she yawned and stretched, deliberately I bet, then threw herself onto the couch, I had to force myself not to look.

Reign was a half-elf, half a race known far and wide as being both unbelievably shitty if they wanted something from you, seemingly believing that you owed them whatever it was simply for being permitted to breathe their air, and simultaneously unreliable in the extreme.

The entire race would be viewed much as we did the goblins: untrustworthy shifty little fucks who stole anything not nailed down, if not for two minor details.

Firstly, the elves were, as a race, chemists and farmers extraordinaire. They had an almost innate skill to make anything grow, and they could coax individual genes to dominance with little more than whispers and a wink, as well as manipulating nanites with a grace the other races desperately tried to emulate, as well as being rumored to be magicians or some shit.

The second reason? They were, as a race, fucking gorgeous. The women were all stunningly beautiful. And the men? They were renowned for fucking anything and everything, taking what they wanted and sodding off with zero fucks given.

Elves were slimmer than humans, and longer of limb generally, but everything from their smiles to their fucking carefully cultivated pheromones screamed sex appeal.

That meant that loads of people who had much to do with male elves generally ended up loathing them. After all, a species with sexual morals that made an alley cat look uptight got a lot of attention, but when they had that many "friends," it pissed others off.

The dwarves hated them, banning them outright from their sectors. Humans, equally willing to fuck anything, were constantly oscillating between hatred when their lover wandered off and screwed another family member, and frantic lust, chasing them.

That wasn't to say that all elves were like that. For some reason, it was the pure-blooded males who were the worst, and by a massive degree. It didn't help that the attitude was actively encouraged by the Living Earth corporation, which was in turn one of the "big four" that pretty much ruled the city in all but name.

They got other races pregnant, then discarded them, moving onto the next and the next. The result was that elven women really disliked the men, while simultaneously looking down on all of us "lesser species," and doing absolutely nothing to curb their appetites.

That, in turn, meant that the half-elves were everywhere. It wasn't just human and elven mixes; it was orcs, goblins, and dwarves. Hell, it was anyone and everyone they could get their hands on, and then they kicked them out the next day, strolling on.

There were a lot of the "gorgeous" people in other races who had always done the same as well, but they didn't specifically tailor their pheromones to have that effect. And they generally at least pretended not to be fucking dickheads.

I'd known people who swore blind it was all part of an attempt to take over the city, that the plan was that all elves would report to the corporation, and all half-elves to their parents, etc.

Personally, I decided it was more likely that most elves were dirty bastards who liked fucking and moving on.

Reign had a lot of her elven parent in her, that was clear: long legs, hair like spun gold, now that she had it down, and yeah, very pretty, as well as being a hell of a shot with her rifle.

The issue I saw with having Reign in my team wasn't the unresolved sexual tension.

I could live with that. I'd served with plenty of women I'd been attracted to—some over me, some under me—and they were out of bounds both times. Sadly, there were never many at the same rank, but again, that's life.

No, the issue was that she damn well knew it, and was using it. She'd decided she could sponge off me, getting access to my kills and bounties. She'd seen that I had a plan and access to a good bounty, and rather than back off when I asked her and the others to, she'd pretended to leave, then tracked and followed me.

She made it clear that either I shared with her, or she'd help herself. My options were down to telling her to fuck off and deal with whatever the following fallout from that would be with the guild and her, or accept it and use her.

And not in the fun way.

She lay there, deliberately showing a fuckload of leg, pretending to get comfortable and waiting for an invite to share the bed.

Not to fuck as well, I was betting. No, just to share the bed, leaving me unable to sleep while she relaxed. I didn't know what she had planned with all of this shit, but I was damn sure there was an angle there somewhere.

I hit the shower, deciding that I'd play her at her own game, popping out my last medikit from the emergency slot in my arm, then injecting myself with it in the shower, replacing the used cylinder in my arm with a mental note to get some more.

By the time I was out of the shower, I felt a lot more sanguine about Reign being there, having decided, again, to play her at her own game. And rather than fuck about with things, I simply walked out of the shower, and through to the bed, naked and unconcerned.

I knew I'd scored a point when, despite ostensibly being asleep, she jerked slightly and shifted. I deliberately ignored her, climbing into bed and pretending to sleep.

After twenty minutes, I gave in and activated the RI, requesting a somnolence routine, and a careful automated monitoring of the room.

If Reign moved from the couch? I wanted to be woken up before she could stab me or whatever.

Eventually, though, the routine kicked in, and I fell asleep.

Four hours later, the RI triggered a growing pulse of lights and sounds in my mind, rousing me slowly. I fought against it, before eventually giving in and opening my eyes.

Turning over on the bed, I stared across the darkened room at Reign, sprawled on the couch, legs over one end, head barely on the other, and I laid there, listening to her snoring, as I tried to figure this shit out again. There needed to be a better way to deal with her than giving in and letting her have what she wanted.

Ten minutes later, alternately annoyed and frustrated as I tried to come up with ways to respond to Reign, I finally got up and got damn well dressed, before kicking her foot.

"Huh?" she mumbled, waving a hand at me, eyes closed. "C'm back later. Pay you then…"

"Reign!" I called, and she wrapped her arm over her eyes and held a finger up in salute.

"Laaaterrr!" she called, twisting round and snuggling in to the shitty couch.

I hesitated, partly because I really didn't know her that well, and partly because I hadn't realized just how amazing her ass looked until right now. Then I shook myself out of it.

Reaching out, I laid a hand on her shoulder. The transformation was instant and terrifying.

A half second before, she'd been starting to slip back to sleep, or so it'd seemed, stretched out in skintight shorts and a tiny top. Now, though? I stared down the barrel of a gun I'd not even seen.

Where the hell did she have this? And that it was ready, and right now, pressed to my fucking eyeball?

"I SAID NO!" she screamed at me, and I stared into her eyes, seeing the barely constrained madness, the lack of any kind of recognition and the willingness to pull that trigger.

"Reign," I said slowly and clearly. "If you want to stay in my team, you get that fucking thing out of my eye right now. Otherwise, I set off the explosives in the couch, and we see who lives."

"What?" she hissed, eyes darting this way and that as she tried to make sense of my words.

"You notice how lumpy and uncomfortable the couch is?" I asked. "That's explosives. Three frag grenades and a fuckload of high ex, all wired to a dead man's switch. You take the gun away, or you use it and we both die."

"What?" she repeated.

I blinked, looking into her eyes, and seeing…seeing a lot of things actually, which confused the fuck out of me. She was scared, I was guessing, borderline terrified, and…and she seemed ready as well, like she was ready to go, to set the totally bullshit explosives off and end it all, simply because I'd made her wake up early.

She'd not woken up like this yesterday, though.

"Reign," I said slowly, forcing calmness into my voice as much as I could. "Come on. It's Kabutt. Calm down."

She stared at me for a few seconds, before jerking the gun away from my eye and smiling widely, pushing past me and sashaying into the bathroom, throwing a comment over her shoulder as she went.

"I know you're watching my ass!" she called, before closing the door.

I collapsed on the floor. A cold sweat covered me as I realized how close I'd come to being blown away. *Reign was fucking certifiably crazy!*

Forty minutes later, she was showered, redressed, and walking alongside me as we strode to the lift, all chirpy good nature and flirtatious again.

She'd spent long enough in the shower, that I was torn between thinking she was deliberately using all my water ration for a laugh—thank fuck for Lucky—and that she was deliberately waiting in there to see whether I was going to follow her and try for something.

I heard the snick of the latch as she left the bathroom, and I'd definitely not heard it on the way in, making me think she'd locked it very carefully, which made my mind whirl.

Had she locked it carefully to make sure it was locked, out of fear and uncertainty, or had she done it silently so that I'd think it wasn't locked, and would try something?

I shook my head and glanced at her out of the corner of my eye as we walked, realizing finally that, as fucked up as the rest of us were? She was on a whole different level.

Lucky was sitting with some of his crew as we reached the lift, ostensibly holding court. He opened his mouth as we passed, clearly thinking to say something, then thought better of it, turning away and speaking to someone else.

We entered the lift, only having to wait a handful of seconds for it; the two people inside were on their way down from higher up the megastructure. They looked terrified as Reign and I stepped in, and I forced myself to nod to them, deliberately not being rude or intimidating.

Reign really helped with that, of course.

"You know he was ordering a watch, don't you?" she asked after a few seconds, and I shrugged. "A watch on you and me, right?"

"Nope."

"You don't believe me?"

I snorted, looking her in the eyes for the first time since she'd put a gun to my head. "Reign, you invited yourself along on this ride. One minute, you've got my back and you're taking down anyone who fucks with us. The next? You're fucking insane and putting a gun to *my* head. Honestly? No fucking clue what we're doing right now."

"I..." She clammed up, saying nothing.

The rest of the trip to ground level was in silence. The nearby screens on the wall warned of a heavy storm-front incoming and some asshole presenter complaining about how much the weather had changed of late. The atmosphere was certainly uneasy between us, that was for sure, and probably terrifying for the others, but when it was over, and the two of us were in a cab—paid for and summoned by Reign, without so much as a mention—she eventually started to speak again, and this time, it was from the heart.

CHAPTER THIRTY-TWO

"So, about earlier," she said, and I sat silent, waiting and sure as shit without a clue where this was going to go. "Ummm, look. I'll just ask outright, and then it saves us both the awkwardness, okay?"

"Okay?"

"Am I out of the team?" she asked, watching me.

"I don't know," I said after a few seconds of careful thought, tamping down the first instinct, which was to scream, "Of fucking course you are, you batshit fucker."

"Because you don't want me out or because you want to know what's going on or…"

"A bit of all of those," I admitted. "You want to be open about this? Fine. I like simple and straightforward. You're a hell of a shot, great sniper, steady under fire, good at pointing out the things I miss without being a dick about it. You could also cause me some serious issues with the guild if I boot you, and—"

"Don't worry about that." She shook her head and looked away, glancing out of the window. "I've been booted from a lot of teams. Julius will understand just fine."

"Then why'd he send you with us?" I asked. "If he thinks you'd get booted anyway?"

"He didn't want to." She shrugged. "He was looking for Pinot."

"Who's Pinot?" I asked after a few seconds. "You said that he's a friend, so you have friends in the guild, and Julius seems to trust you."

"He's a friend." She shrugged. "Julius has been around a long time—he's used to me. Pinot? He was in one of my old teams, way back."

"And now?"

"Now he does assessments and fills in the gaps, like I do."

"All right, what the fuck is the deal here?" I asked after a few seconds of silence. "You're a damn good soldier, and clearly they trust you, but when I woke you? You were ready to fucking shoot me."

"I…ah, fuck it." She groaned, twisting around to look at me, straight on. "Fine, it's not like you won't hear soon enough from someone else. Look, I told you I have debts, right?"

"Yeah?"

"Well, I didn't just 'get into' debt. I lost everything. My home, my friends. All of it. I stole from my team, and the shit I stole? Medikits."

"Why?" I asked.

"I sold them," she admitted, tears in her eyes. "I fucking sold them for a couple of fixes of angel dust, and I was off my tits on the job. It went sideways and they needed the medikits, and I…I'd *sold them*. I didn't know what to do.

Seeing the way it was all going wrong, I thought we were going to die, and I..."
She shook her head, looking back out of the window.

"I took the rest of the angel dust, all of it in one go, went off the rails, and I
just went mad. Shot the shit outta our enemies, but..."

"Your people died?" I guessed after she trailed off.

"Two of them. Sinas and Kerin. Kerin was my partner."

"You shot...?"

"No!" she groaned. "I never shot my own fucking side. Hell, man, what the
fuck do you think of me?"

"I think you were off your tits on drugs!" I snapped back. "You admitted you
stole from your own fucking team, *and* it wasn't something like loot or creds,
which would be shitty but understandable. It was the medikits! Something that
when you need it, you *really* need it!"

"Well, I wasn't thinking, all right?" she shot back. "I was in need. I was
addicted, and I goddamn wouldn't have done the medikits if I didn't think we
were safe!"

"What do you mean, safe? You were on a mission!"

"One that was supposed to be a cakewalk!"

"You don't hire mercs for cakewalks!" I snarled. "You hire fucking ACE or
whatever to do that shit, or idiots, or you just don't do it!"

"I KNOW, ALL RIGHT?" she yelled at me, the tears there and clear. For a
few seconds, we glared at each other, until she sagged back again, shaking her
head and drawing down a deep breath, clearly struggling to get her words out.
"Look, I...ah, fuck it, it doesn't matter. We're nearly at the guild. I'll make it easy,
and I'll quit on you. You just...you fuck off and find some replacements for me
and Hobbs, and you're fine, okay?"

I stared at her for a long few seconds, and she sighed.

"I know what you're thinking," she whispered. "I left the grazer in my locker.
I'll hand it in to Julius, and you'll all get your cut, then you're free of me."

"Why'd you follow me last night?" I asked, troubled but still annoyed.

"I...Look, I'm clean, all right?" she explained. "That wasn't cheap, though.
I lost everything, and now my debts?"

"Cards?"

She snorted. "Wouldn't that just be perfect, if I was a gambling addict as
well?" she mocked herself. "No, I just...it sounds a bit more acceptable than 'I'm
a junkie who couch surfs because I can't afford my own place.'"

"So when you woke up and had the gun on me?"

"I..." She took a deep breath and let it out, putting on a brittle smile. "Some
guys don't like to be told no, or that I'm not interested in more than the couch. Some
don't take no for an answer. I learned to make sure I'm always armed, that's all."

"And the whole walking around in your fucking underwear thing? Because I
gotta say, you're sending some seriously confusing signals."

"Yeah." She winced. "Look, I'm a half-elf—"

"Really?" I said sarcastically. "Damn, you know you should hint about that
maybe?"

"Shut the fuck up, Kabutt. I'm trying here, okay?" she snapped.

"Yeah, I—" I broke off, took a deep breath, and nodded. "You know what, fair point. Sorry."

"Right, well, I'm a half-elf, and people expect me to act a certain way. But they're also scared of us—elves, I mean. Nobody's ever sure if what they feel is real, or we're doing it deliberately, or…"

"Uh-huh."

"So when I stay quiet and understated, people try to take advantage, all right? When I act like I don't give a fuck, it's a lot less frequent."

"So it's all an act?" I asked, surprised. "You gamble that guys aren't going to try it on if you wave it in their face?"

"You think I've got a choice?" she snapped. "Julius lets me crash a few nights a week in the guild for free, but he's bound by the rules, and his shareholders! He needs to charge me, and I can barely afford my interest payments as it is!"

"Interest?"

"To get clean, I needed a full cleanse, all right? Not just a wipe. I mean a full nanite cleanse, to get my body clean and fit, and then two weeks in a corpo clinic."

"Right?" My stomach clenched.

I'd heard of them—"health and wellness" clinics, places that took in those who were seriously fucked up with drugs or drink or whatever. They didn't accept many, though, and those they did? Their victims paid through the nose for it.

A permanent lock on your credit account, they took anywhere from ten to seventy percent of everything that you earned, depending on the level of addiction. And unless you could somehow buy your way out? They did it for life. *Your* life, anyway.

Take the interest charges, and that you were being charged what they decided was "*fair*," for essentially hitting you with a single large medikit and locking you in a room to go cold turkey?

The only good bit was at the end, when they injected you with a mod, a tiny one that interacted with the pleasure centers of the brain. You have a good day, or great sex? Supposedly no effect. You have a sudden chemical high?

Seriously, seriously ill for about a week or two afterward. It was designed to make sure you learned to never, ever touch shit like that again.

The minor issue that all emotions were verifiable by chemical markers had been brought up by some do-gooder, and that same person went missing and was found three days later. Nailed to the underside of a bridge with spikes through their hands and feet. Their tongue was apparently ripped out and they were left to die when the tide rose.

The message was clear.

Keep your mouth shut about our business.

Now that I looked at Reign, like really *looked*, I got it a lot more. She was damn good at what she did, but that was why she was always on the move. If she was that deep in debt? And that the survivors of her old team split up, thanks to her, then word would spread…

"What's the deal with Julius and Pinot?" I asked.

"My partner Kerin…he was Julius's brother."

"Seriously?" I grunted, shocked. "I'd expect him to hate you more."

"So did I." She looked down at her hands as she toyed with the stitching along the back of one glove. "He's a good guy, though. That's why he has the guild doing this shit, instead of more profitable missions. He thinks we should be better than we are, and he, well, he gave me a chance."

"And Pinot?"

"We've been friends awhile." She shrugged. "Pinot lost his whole team. Now he doesn't like getting close to people, so he does assessments and fills in when people need a tech type."

"And you're in debt up to your eyeballs," I finished.

"Pretty much."

"How much do you owe?"

"Two thousand credits a month, or forty percent of all my creds earned—whichever is the greater, of course—until I pay off the outstanding balance, which is a hundred and ninety-seven thousand credits." Her voice dropped as if sick to her stomach as she went on. "Each time I miss a payment? Five percent added onto the balance."

"Fuck me," I whispered.

"I'm fine, thanks." She smiled, looking defeated. "The aftermath isn't worth it."

"So, if you—" I broke off as I thought about how to phrase it.

"If I orgasm, I'm ill for about two weeks," she confirmed, dejected. "Try earning enough to pay for the payments, rent, food and all the rest when you've only got two weeks in the month to work." She quirked her lips. "Puts a bit of a strain on a relationship."

"I don't know…" I tried to joke. "Sounds like you'd be fine with most guys?"

"Ha. Well, yeah, not so much with girls, but that's not really here nor there now. I gave up on it all."

"And when you've been sleeping on couches, just trying to make the payments…" I groaned, shaking my head.

"Yeah," she admitted grimly. "People tend to take my being there as permission."

"The way you acted, I was torn all night, thinking you were playing games." I felt ashamed of myself. "But you can't afford to crash at the guild all the time, can you?"

"No chance."

"And this cab ride?"

"It's…it was an apology," she whispered, smiling brittlely. "I led you on and took advantage, and then I claimed the bounty when you didn't know about it. I'm sorry. I was going to split it, but as soon as it hit my account? The clinic took their forty percent, then the bounty guild reversed the payment, saying that someone else claimed the kill. That pushed me into negatives, and incurred a hundred cred fine. The guild accepted the proof I sent, a clip of my staring down my scope and the slug taking them down, but when they sent it again?"

"The clinic took another forty percent?" I groaned, knowing what was coming.

"Yeah." She nodded, closing her eyes and slowly banging her head on the back of her headrest. "So out of the bounty of seven hundred and forty, they took two-ninety-six. That put me down to four hundred and forty-four. Then, when they reversed the transaction, I was under the minimum, so I was fined a hundred.

Then it went back in and I'm left with three hundred and forty-four…and a claim on that of another two ninety-six…"

"Which leaves you with?"

"The cab fare, and lunch."

"Fuck my life." I groaned. "And none of it's even your fault."

"Think they care?" she asked, and I shook my head.

"Not at all," I agreed. "So, you basically couch surf because you can't afford an apartment, you spend all your time at the guild waiting on jobs because you desperately need to hit them to keep your payments going and…" I winced. "And you need to also pay for the ammo and expendables and so on. Shit."

"And the payout yesterday?" she said. "Most of it was sent to pay off another debt."

"Fuck."

"So yeah, I'm tragically poor." She finished with a little laugh. "But at least I'm clean! There's that, right?"

"I don't know how the fuck you've not ended it all." I stared at her with new respect.

"You think I wouldn't if I could?" She shook her head. "Behavioral mod is part of the deal. I think about seriously self-harming? Same as an orgasm, or drugs. I get fucked up. I've thought about it in the middle of a fight before, but I can't. I keep fighting and then, at the end? Somehow I'm still alive, despite myself."

We pulled up at the guild, and I tried to knock on the cab, finding it had, as she said, already been paid for.

Reign shrugged as we unloaded our gear, speaking softly as we headed toward the doors.

"Now you know."

"Now I know," I agreed. "Okay, so if they take forty percent each time you get paid anything, how the fuck are you expected to pay them off?"

"I'm not."

"Not at all?"

"Well, there's an anti-slavery clause in the city charter, so it's not literal slavery, just, you know, economic."

"So even if I transferred you the two hundred grand or so you owed—I don't have it, so don't get your hopes up; I'm just trying to understand—but even if I did that, they'd take the forty percent, and they won't accept anything less than the full amount off your debt?"

"Exactly."

"Can someone else pay it off?" I asked. "Like if we earned that money in the team and we paid it off between us?"

"No. They won't accept a payment from another account. 'It's for your safety,'" she mimicked in a high-pitched, syrupy-sweet voice. "And even if they would? No offense, but I don't see anyone paying that off for me, not for anything I'm willing to do."

She quirked a sad smile, then shook her head.

"Don't go getting any ideas of your own personal half-elf sex slave. I have it on very good authority I'm shit at blowjobs as well, so just…" She shrugged.

"Who told you that?" I asked, unable to help myself.

"I tried to have a relationship once." She glared straight ahead. "Even knowing that I couldn't, *you know*, I tried."

"And he said that?" I asked, confused.

"Yeah."

"Okay, either you really don't understand the concept and you tried to blow him up like a fucking balloon, or he was lying, because I saw you going to town on a ration bar yesterday," I joked, trying to make her smile. "There's no way that woman I saw with that bar is crap at blowjobs."

"Oh, fuck off," she said, but the change in tone told me I'd cheered her up a little at least. "Look, I'll go see Julius. It'll not be held against you, okay?"

"Is that a threat or a promise?" I tried again, before sighing. "Look, Reign, honestly? I'm willing to give this a try, if you are."

"Seriously?" she asked, surprised. "Even after all this shit?"

"Yeah," I said. "I'm not gonna lie. I'm uncomfortable knowing what you did, but I understand it as well. Add on now I know that you're really trying to put me off by acting like the crazy elf, rather than actually trying to get me into bed? Yeah, I feel a little better about this all."

"Kabutt…" She hesitated and blew out a breath. "Thank you."

"Hey, don't thank me yet. That means we need to get ready and go hunting more fucking specters, as well as you talking me through the byzantine fucking rules of registering as a bounty hunter."

"Ah, shit."

"Yeah, bureaucracy!" I made a little "jazz hands" wave as best I could, armed and loaded as I was.

"Well, I suppose after that, at least I'll be ready to shoot some fucker in the face."

CHAPTER THIRTY-THREE

As we entered the guild, the overcast sky darkening as we switched into the bright artificial lighting, it was much like it was yesterday, packed with hopefuls.

Dozens of people stood around, reading markers for jobs, filling out applications, trying to bargain with the staff and making it blatantly clear they had no clue what they were doing.

"Is it like this all the time?" I asked. "Seriously, I mean, they hang around, hoping to get picked for a random mission?"

"Yeah, but not just that," she said. "They're recon as well."

"What?"

"If we get a report of a specter roaming, you know, somewhere it shouldn't be, but it's not confirmed? It goes on the board there." She nodded to a much smaller and less comprehensive map compared to the one upstairs. "They can pick the location and go check it out. If they find it, and update the location with real-time tracking? They get a credit."

"That's it?"

"That's it," she agreed. "That being said, there's a dozen guilds that deal with specters, so these guys?" She nodded at the small group gathered around the board. "They're spotters. Probably working in a team. They keep an eye on the board, send some street rat to confirm the location, and then they pass on the video feed. A single credit isn't much, I know, but these are live, and they get updated and paid out on the hour, every hour. If you've got a spotter here, and a team working with them? They might earn a couple dozen credits an hour reporting and tracking."

"Yeah, but then they pay the street kids and…?"

"It's a shitty wage. But it's a wage."

"Fair enough." I sighed, before frowning. "You think we could get them searching for decent mods?"

"What, then hit and loot for your friend?" She slowed her stride as she thought. "It'd probably work, yeah."

"Want to bet we're not the first to consider it?" I grunted, looking at the figures again, and she grimaced.

"Yeah, that makes sense, actually." She nodded. "I always wondered why they'd keep doing it."

"Still, if we could get to them first…?"

"Probably worth it, if we're in that area to begin with. But unless we're there? A single kill isn't worth the effort."

"True."

We walked through the back doors, Reign nodding to the occasional desk worker she knew or merc, and we headed up to the main jobs board upstairs. I diverted as I saw Julius talking to someone in a side room.

"Go ahead," I told Reign, nodding toward the board. "Pick us up something decent, and then we'll go speak to the spotters, and try to find the girls."

"What about a fifth for the team? Or a sixth?" she suggested.

"We could probably do with two. But I want people with military experience, or it's not worth it, as well as decent gear."

She winced. "Slim pickings out there."

"Exactly. I'd rather do it with just us than needlessly get idiots killed."

"Or let them fuck it up and get us killed," she agreed, nodding. "Okay, I'll check it out and see if there's anything we can make use of, boss."

With that, she was gone, and Julius nodded to me, finishing his conversation and heading over.

"Kabutt," he greeted me, offering a fist.

"Julius," I replied, bumping fists and looking around. "Anywhere we can talk?"

"In here." He gestured to another room and led the way.

It was a bunkroom, small with a bed, and that was pretty much it, but when he swiped his hand across the door sensor, it closed and outside sound cut off.

"Privacy field," he explained with a wry smile. "You try sleeping in one of these rooms without it…it won't happen, believe me."

"Good point." I grunted, having not even thought about it. But with the sheer number of people moving back and forth, clattering up and down stairs, dealing with their gear and so on? It wouldn't have been cheap, but it was worth it, I bet. "So, you wanted to talk to me?"

"Yeah." Julius drew the word out. "So, first of all, again, sorry about Hobbs. From what I saw on the recordings, he did well. It was a plain shitty lucky shot that did him in. That grazer could have taken any of you. That it was him was just the luck of the draw."

"It was," I agreed, hating that it was true, but also glad it'd not been me. "By the time we got out of the undercity, it was too late to pay my respects. You said his family took him?"

"Mother and a sister." He nodded. "They sent me some fantastic messages last night, screaming eternal vengeance and so on. Apparently, he'd not told them he was specter hunting. They thought he was a wall guard or some shit."

"And it's you who gets the blame?" I guessed.

"Every time." He grunted. "Most wouldn't even bother to contact them and tell them what happened, but for the extra effort? That's what I get. Shoot the messenger."

"Well, I appreciate it," I said. "Look on the bright side. For me, there's nobody to contact."

"Well, hopefully that'll change." He sighed. "No man is an island, Kabutt. No point in living if there's not someone there for you."

"Whatever," I said, not willing to elaborate on Richie and Sync. "So, anything else?"

"Yeah, two things. First, you did well. I watched the recordings, and yeah, I don't mind about the datadeck and the grazer, but it's a one-time thing. You pocket shit normally? You'll be out, all right?"

"Right. That brings up a point, as you'll be recording us. Mods."

"What about them? Guns?"

"No. Specter mods," I said, and he shook his head.

"Don't do it, Kabutt," he said seriously. "I know a guy who chipped one once. He's a specter now, or he was the last I heard about him. Don't risk using them."

"I'm not. I owe a gang, and they want specter mods. I want to harvest them as I go."

"They want them?" He looked disgusted. "Fuck, that's all we need, more powerfully modded gangs…"

"Think of it as a natural cycle, if it helps," I suggested. "We kill the specters, get the mods. I give the mods to the gangs; they chip the mods; they become specters, and we kill the specters. It's that whole circle of life thing."

"With innocents getting caught in the crossfire, no doubt."

"I don't think so. If anything? The more gangs that do this, the more it'll convince people that being in a gang is bad for your health. Let's face it, if all the gang leaders use the mods and we get paid to kill them? It'll wipe a lot of the gangs out."

"Or they'll kill a load of innocents as they turn." He shook his head. "That's why you joined us?" he asked. "To harvest the specters?"

"Yeah. Normally I'd not admit to it, but you know, recording and all that."

"Yeah," he said slowly. "Look, I don't like it, okay? But…look, your team…"

"Yeah?"

"How'd Reign do? And the girls?"

"The sisters were fine. Little mad, happiest in the fight, but that's the orc blood in them."

"And Reign?"

"Any reason you're asking?" I countered.

"She's…she's a friend, but she has a few issues." He sighed. "I'm not going to betray her trust, but I need to look after my guild, so here's the deal. You want to loot specter mods, you do it quiet, and you keep her in your team. She's a damn good sniper, and she's more or less stable, but—"

I nodded.

"But if she had nostrils atop her head, she'd still drown…she's that deep in the shit with debt," I finished for him.

"Yeah."

"And don't trust her with medikits."

"Ah, fuck."

"Yeah, I know," I admitted. "I've agreed to give her a chance, and she gave me a medikit of hers last night, so I owe her for that. Actually, now that I think about it, dammit, I'd forgotten about it."

"Well, you keep her." He nodded as he leaned back on the bed, bracing himself against the wall and looking at me. "You're all right with me. Harvest the mods, but don't let anyone outside of the team know. And if it's reported to me, we'll have to reevaluate. I'll probably have to order you to stop, publicly, so don't bring them in here either."

"You don't see it, you don't care." I nodded. "Gotcha."

"Exactly," he agreed. "Well, it was Reign and the mission I needed to talk to you about, so yeah, we're good here. I am sorry about the way it went sideways, and I've demanded compensation for those stupid fucks locking you out of the bio-farms as well…"

"Shit. I just remembered—the loot!"

"What loot?"

"Hobbs was carrying all the loot we'd gotten up until that point," I explained. "It wasn't much—a handful of guns, some random jewelry and some credit-chips, that kinda shit, a couple of trashed personal cyber-ware…"

"Two minutes." He sighed, one eye lighting from the inside as he accessed something, then he was sub-vocalizing, before cursing and cutting the line off. "The cleanup crew claim it wasn't there when they arrived. I've ordered the AI to review their recordings. It's not something we generally do—the first team picks anything valuable, after all—but if they get the loot, I'll make sure you get your share."

"And if not?" I asked, fairly sure which shifty fucks had done away with our loot, right after locking us out.

"Then I'll make a formal complaint to the client, demand the full value of everything we can prove was in the bag is paid to us, and you'll get that instead." He sighed. "It'll take time, though, and until they pay it…

"You think they'll pay it?" I asked disbelievingly.

"Oh, they will," he assured me with a wry smile. "The bio-farms are shitholes, but they're profitable ones. They'd have to reinvest massively to seal the lower floors away properly, as well as stop production for a few days. Or, they can pay us. Failing that? I was thinking we needed to get rid of a few contracts anyway, as busy as we are, so they'll have to replace us with a new guild, and the others are as stretched as we are."

"Fair enough." I grunted. "Anything else?"

"Just an honest question," he said after a few seconds. "Now we know why you're with us, and that you'll be harvesting as you go, I at least know why you're stooping to specter hunting rather than anything else, so…"

"So?"

"Welcome to the team. And as much as I don't like what you're doing? I damn well need you, and it gets Reign back in the game, so thank you."

"Thanks, Julius, and you're welcome," I replied sardonically. "So, any jobs in particular you got for me?"

"The jobs board is upstairs. Did Reign…?"

"She showed us."

"Then that's it." He nodded. "Go pick your jobs and get to work. Do as many as you can."

"Will do, mate."

With that, the discussion was over, and I was back out in the hall, Julius moving on to look for someone else for whatever reason, and me looking for Reign and the girls.

I eventually found them in the ready room that I'd been taken to originally, and as I approached, they were arguing good-naturedly about the contracts.

"I still say the waterfront is the best," Luna grumbled, as Gessh sighed and shook her head.

"No chance. Industrial all the way."

"What's that?" I slid into a seat next to them.

"Luna wants to hit the sightings along the waterfront, specifically the pleasure beach at Rodman's Throat." Reign sighed. "Gessh, on the other hand, wants to hit the industrial zones, as there's a lot more confirmed sightings down there."

"So why the beach?" I asked Luna.

"Because it's a beach," she explained. "Clean sand, water, all that shit."

"It's supposed to piss down all day," I pointed out as a distant rumble of thunder rang out, and I winced. "And there's a storm incoming."

"Beach still," Luna said quickly, and I looked at her in confusion.

"It's going to be pissing down," I repeated.

"With rain," she said, slowly and clearly. "We go into the tunnels? They'll be filled with the same rain, but there's also the wonders of floating shit, literal piss, and more. Given the choice, I'd rather have rain on my body than…"

"Yeah, baby," Reign muttered in a low voice, and Gessh snorted a laugh.

"Fuck's sake!" Luna barked a laugh as well before shrugging. "Hey, I'm game for that too. We could just get a room and work tomorrow. That was a good payday, after all. And after a few drinks, maybe a club or two…?" She bounced her eyebrows suggestively, and I grinned at her.

"Appreciate the offer," I said into the pregnant silence. "But unlike you lazy fuckers, I need to earn some creds. Gessh? Why the industrial zones?"

"There's a reasonable amount of sightings near a memory farm, probably high-tech enough it's drawing them, without it earning enough that it's able to afford gear to slaughter them all. We're talking hundreds of people sitting there all day getting mind fucked, and drawing the specters. Not only are we killing specters, we're protecting people."

"I didn't know you were so sensitive." Reign frowned at Gessh.

"We spent long enough working in places like that." Gessh glared at Luna. "And unlike *some*, I remember how fucking terrifying it was when you knew that specters might be nearby. Counting your mods and comparing them to others nearby, hoping that if a specter found its way in, they'd draw it instead of you…"

"I remember." Luna hung her head. "I just don't want anything to do with the fucking places, all right? Too many memories."

"Then it's time we got some good fucking memories of them in their place!" Gessh snapped. "Think about it! There's bound to be some of those asshole 'security' guards around! If we catch them being dicks? We can cut them off!"

"Cut them off?" I asked.

"Their dicks." Luna nodded. "Seriously, you don't want to know what happens in those places."

"I really don't," I agreed, wincing.

"I've heard," Reign said. "Okay, look, how about we check the specters that have been seen there. If there's a decent amount? We hit them, then go onto the next?"

"See if we can hit a few places?" Luna suggested. "Get the memory farm done fast and move on, maybe hit a handful of places?"

"Definitely." I nodded. "And, uh…" I looked around, noting the others in the room, and sent a message to the team instead.

> *Julius said as long as we're not caught, we can harvest the specters. He doesn't care. If we're caught? We stop or we're out of the guild, I think…*

The others read the message and nodded, smiles lighting their faces.

"So," I said aloud. "We do this, hit as many places as we can, then we dispose of any loot, less the guild fees of course, and later?"

"Yeah?" Reign asked, hesitantly.

"I've got a private job," I said, looking around. "It doesn't pay, okay? And we don't get to take the salvage unless it's a mod we can use or a gun we need. The…stock? Well, the stuff at the target is to be left behind, but…there might be some decent mods and some decent guns for loot, and it'd be gangers, not specters."

"You want us to help?" Luna asked slowly.

"I helped him out last night," Reign said, winking to her. "It was well worth it."

"Yeah…" I sighed. "Fuck's sake, Reign, you're just so subtle, but go on, tell them what happened."

"Well, after I got back to his place…" she started, leaning forward as if to tell some deep dark secret, before dropping her voice and sending a message to us all, even as she started spinning aloud some bullshit about sex that nearly broke the apartment block.

> *We didn't fuck or anything like that. That's just to confuse anyone listening. I followed Kabutt, and he got into a fight. The target he had? She had bounties on her already. I'll help you register with the bounty guilds, and we share any bounty, getting Kabutt's jobs done.*

"So yeah, I think that's enough spilling my secrets!" I said loudly, red-faced for real as she described the things I could do with my tongue. "Fuck's sake, Reign!"

"Hey, skill like that deserves to be praised." She grinned. "I knew you were the team lead for me when you winked at me and licked your eyebrows!"

> *I told you about some guys not taking no for an answer? One of them is in this room. The sex story was more to fuck him off than anything else, so don't get your hopes up.*

I read the message, knowing it was sent to me only, and I slowly looked around the room, seeing a half dozen guys pretending not to be listening, and three of them staring at me.

None of them looked happy. That could be because I was new, because Reign was attractive, because she was waxing lyrical about me being able to "fuck her through the headboard" or even just over how utterly unprofessional all of it was.

When Luna asked if she could have a go next, and Gessh joined in loudly saying that she wanted a go, too? The looks I was getting were fucking terrible.

No matter whether any of these guys had a history with Reign or not—right now, I was getting eye-fucked…and not in a good way.

I coughed and said something about "Later" and "If you impress me" before dropping my voice.

"Fuck's sake, you lot!" I snapped. "Professionalism!"

"Oh, bless him!" Luna sniggered. "He's such a pretty shade of red!"

"You do blush well," Gessh agreed. "Virgin?"

"Are you seriously asking me that?" I groaned.

"Well, you know, a little joke about sex and you're blushing this much?" Luna shook her head. "Wait, have you actually seen a real boob before? Do I get a bonus if I give you a little look…?"

"I'm not saying what I'd do for a decent slice of the bounty," Gessh said in a low voice, "but it rhymes with 'duck' and…"

"Is it really too late to trade you all in for a new team?" I hissed, before standing and shaking my head. "Enough. Come on!" I strode toward the exit, head spinning and cheeks flaming.

The laughter that followed made me sigh as I led the way out of the room. The four of us slid through the mass of people as I moved toward the door.

"Wait up," Reign said quickly, holding a hand up. "Sorry, seriously, guys, but I need some ammo and new gloves, so give me a few minutes, okay?"

"Fuck," I growled, before nodding. "I need grenades and a helmet, as well as more ammo." I followed her to the back of the building, and through the doors again, this time headed to the catalog for the armory.

Linking to it with my Keystone, I sighed. I'd not trusted myself to have a little look last night, not properly. I'd looked for just those clothes, and the bits I'd needed to fix the shotgun.

Now, though?

Now I started to search for some new toys, as well as ammo for the nice HK-TT slug thrower I'd liberated from the bodyguard this morning, and that now hung on my hip.

CHAPTER THIRTY-FOUR

The helmet was a decent upgrade, I decided a few minutes later, and at five thousand creds, it damn well better be. But between the all-round vision it provided, the additional processing power it made available for my RI, and the ability to link to a tacnet?

Hopefully this one would last a little longer than the last.

Again, it was a full-face model, gunmetal-grey and metal, with a neck that linked with my existing armor smoothly. It was also air-cooled, capable of being sealed from the outside environment, and had a layered titanium outer skin.

Most people disliked this kind of helmet. The fully enclosed design made it hard for anyone without the necessary training or mindset to wear it for long.

They got claustrophobia.

But for an APS operative? This was home.

It was also much, much more resistant to impacts. I could get shot in the head and survive most calibers with this on. And the way my days were going of late? That was a wonderful thing.

I got two frags as well, one flash-bang, and sighing, I paid the three thousand for an EMP as well. Between that, the medikits—four small and one medium—ammo—I got a *lot* of ammo—and the hatchet I decided to treat myself to, just in case, I was pretty much on the road to being poor again, down to three thousand and seventy-two creds.

It was worth it, though, as I felt like I was fucking loaded for monster hunting now.

The others were much the same. Reign apparently had some kind of a deal with the guild whereby half of her creds were kept for "incidentals" and the rest she'd earned yesterday, she explained, had been split between her various debtors, so she, too, was now broke again.

If she hadn't had the deal where the guild kept half of her money? She'd have been fucked when it came to resupply as well.

The sisters were looking at us funny as they realized that far from being the poorest in any team, as they were used to, they were currently the richest.

Luna laughed her ass off when she realized, and Gessh, who often acted the brute in public, insisted she would cover the cab costs to the first target site.

Reign smiled, thanking her for the offer before I could, but explained that now that we were all guild members? We could use the transport tab.

Fifteen minutes later, we were stuck in traffic, as Reign—after several messages between us about everything, asking my advice—filled the sisters in on her real issues.

"Medikits?" Gessh growled, and before she could say anything else I cursed, fishing one out of my pocket and tossing it to Reign.

She caught it, just, fumbled it and then made an awkward grab, accidentally flinging it across the cab to bounce off the back of the partition between the cattle section—where the client sat—and the automated driver.

Please confirm your intent: assault/accident?

We all got the message at once, and the general laughter that rang out defused the growing tension, as Reign confirmed the mistake to the cab.

"Sorry," I said after a few seconds. "I forgot until just then that you'd given me one of your medikits in the tunnels last night. That's why I threw it over. I got it to replace yours." I reached into the recess in my left arm and popped the dead medikit out, putting it in a pocket and placing one of the others into the small space.

"I forgot about it," Reign admitted. "Thanks, Kabutt. Okay, so after that…" She went on with her explanation, and by the time we reached the target site, all of us trooping out and getting ready, gearing up to get hunting, the others were up to date properly.

"I'm not happy about this," Luna said flatly. "Look, Reign, I understand you were on drugs then, and yeah, you're not now, but fuck's sake. You were screwing one of those guys, right?"

"Not just stealing their medikits, but draining his balls, she means," Gessh added in helpfully.

"Yeah, I got that, Gessh," Reign replied calmly. "Thanks for the clarification. Yes, I was."

"And you still fucked them over," Luna pointed out. "You met us yesterday, and we're half-orcs."

"Right," Reign growled. "Look, I was fucked up then with drugs. I'm not now, but you need to make a decision. Either you trust me or you don't, because you can't be behind me with a fucking gun if you don't."

"It's a fair point." I agreed with all of them. "Look, Reign told you because she'd rather we were all honest with each other, and the shit you're going to be seeing over the next few days? It's not gonna be fun. Either you're in or out—and I'll be clear, I'm giving Reign a chance. Partly because yes, she has that damn nice elf ass…"

"Asshole," Reign shot at me, her eyes twinkling.

"I've not seen that, but I'm sure that's as nice as one can be too," I agreed, not even pausing. "But that's not the point, okay? She could have not told us. She needs a team she can trust, and she's learned from her mistakes. I've made mistakes too, serious fucking ones, but I'm here. I don't doubt you have too. Give it till the end of today."

"What changes then?" Luna asked.

"Then if you don't want in anymore? At least you've had hopefully another good payday," I pointed out. "I'll sort it with Julius so nothing is held against you."

"You trust her?" Gessh asked.

I looked over at Reign, then Luna, before sighing and pulling my helmet off so they could see my face clearly.

"Yes," I said. "She's a dick, but she's earned a little trust, I think. Add in that she's a hell of a sniper? I think she's worth the risk."

"And you're watching her," Luna added shrewdly.

"Oh, I'm fucking watching her. But then, I'm watching you all. Aren't you?"

"Yeah, we are," Luna admitted, and Gessh laughed.

"Cool." I smiled. "Now, how about we leave all the bullshit out here, because as soon as we cross that threshold, there's just our team, and all the rest of the fucking world against us, all right?" I gestured to a marker, denoting the beginning of Aramicorp's legal boundaries.

"Fine," Gessh growled after sharing a long silent look with her sister. "But if you steal from me, bitch, I'll cut your fucking tits off," she warned Reign, and she snorted.

"Fuck's sake, make it my head. My tits are too small as it is."

"Hey, don't stress. They're not that bad." Luna grinned, patting her on the shoulder as she moved around Reign. "Mine used to be like that."

"Yeah?"

"Yeah," Luna said. "Then I hit puberty."

"Oh, fuck off," Reign groaned, but the edges of a smile tugged at her lips.

The four of us pulled on whatever armor and gear we needed, before striding over the line. An automated message was sent to us all.

> *You have entered Aramicorp's legal territory and are now bound by Aramicorp's rules. All weapons must be relinquished to...*

I dismissed it, looking around at the sorry state of the place. It was an old factory complex, literally a hundred meters by three hundred, and maybe five stories high, each floor filled with the slumped forms of the poor.

"I hate these places," Luna muttered, even as Reign jogged ahead to introduce us—at my request—to the local security forces as they stepped out of the building, having clearly been waiting by the door.

It was a single older man who looked as though he'd never heard of soap, with a grimy optical mod that tracked us all. Behind him were two automated drones—blocky, graceless, and old, clearly ex-military models that should have been stripped for parts. One floated on a constant circuit around the building, while the other hovered protectively behind his left shoulder.

I shook my head, looking from the three to the literal hundreds of people in the building. They sat side by side on long benches, a narrow table before them, barely big enough to lean on. They wore full head immersion helmets, helping them to create the mem-cores. Their physical bodies slumped while their minds were put through the wringer for scumbags to be entertained.

My disgust rose as I looked at those poor people. Not at them, but at the city that forced them into this, for the few creds they got paid by the hour.

Some, like the sisters apparently once had been, were there to fight, their minds piloting simulacrums of themselves in a pit, facing the others, beating them to death, or in turn being beaten and killed.

Some faced monsters, while others were forced to endure adverts, one after another for AI training algorithms. More were used in virtual whorehouses—cam-girls and cam-boys they'd been in the past, exposing themselves and performing acts for their audiences, while they planned their weekends, or mentally shopped or whatever.

Now that little escape was gone, as they were forced into sexual servitude, producing mem-cores that allowed perverts to spend their time riding their senses, their bodies, or joining them in more intimate ways.

Friends sat side by side; people who had never been attracted to each other outside of the net were forced to perform acts of degradation on each other inside. And when they left the memory farms—if they ever managed to—those friendships were, more often than not, destroyed by the things that they'd been forced to do.

Some earned higher rates, allowing their bodies to be used for tortures or worse, while more were hooked up to be used in complex quantum processing situations, literally providing overflow brain matter to the AIs.

Places like this were horrific dens of slavery, no matter what anyone said. Staring at it now, seeing the hundreds of people slumped side by side inside?

I wanted to burn it all down.

I desperately wanted to set them all free, and I damn well knew there was no way to do it. They were coming here because it was all they had. They were paid an utter pittance to perform for the amusement of others. And if I did burn the place down? If I tore the Aramicorp servers apart and killed every single one of their shit-eating corpo scumbag bosses?

These people would starve instead.

Their kids would starve; they would be thrown from their shitty apartments and left on the streets. They'd be bought for real by the fleshpots and worse. Not only their minds would be broken by what they were forced to do, but their bodies as well.

I swallowed hard, forcing myself to look away. The need for violence rose in me as I tried to control the shaking of my fists.

"Fine…I'll let you in," the old man sighed eventually. "But don't disturb my pets…They break off? They lose their hour's cred. Ain't none of them who can afford that."

"Your pets?" I growled, only to have Gessh grab my arm and squeeze.

The old man shrugged. "I walk my rounds and I watch over them, make sure they're safe and alive, as well as dispose of those who die. That makes them mine, I guess."

With that, he set off, trudging around the outside of the building, and we followed. "The noises come from underneath, in the old sections."

"Are they open still?" Reign asked, and he shook his head.

"There was a fire a few years back," he said, sadly. "A whole floor of my pets were lost…"

"Where were you?" I growled.

"Here," he admitted. "I was asleep. Some kids threw something in the window, some kind of a firebomb, and it took the south wing out…" He pointed to the remains of a building next to the one we were circling. "The fire suppression systems kicked in, and I left these ones working. Their building was fine, after all."

"But?" Luna swallowed hard.

"But there was a tunnel between the buildings that I didn't know about." His head bobbed on his scrawny neck as he shuffled along. "The south building was empty, just being set up and ready to serve the area, so there was nobody in there. But the fire? It went through the tunnel, and as the lower levels were sealed to keep them warm? We didn't know until it was too late."

"So…" I was sick to my stomach. "You had a few hundred people under the building, and because you didn't pay attention, they all burned to death?"

"One hundred and seventy-three," he corrected grimly. "Cost me three years' bonuses, and I'm still paying off the fines, so don't try lecturing me, murderer!"

"Mur—"

"You, with your guns and the blood on your hands! Just you wait!" he hissed, jabbing one arthritis-riddled finger at me accusingly. "It'll all come around. It always does! I was supposed to be with the Keeper by now!"

"We can find our way from here!" Reign stepped between us, as Gessh and Luna moved, one on either side of me, to guide me around the old shit.

"Door's at the far end," he called after us. "Lock it after you. Code's seven-seven-oh-nine." With that, he walked off, and I turned to the others, who were all glaring at me for some reason.

"What the fuck!" I snapped. "That old prick—"

"He's a watchman, that's it…security patrol. If he disconnected those people, they'd have lost their wages, and he'd lose his job. As soon as they said that the fire was next door? They'd have jacked back in themselves, and you know it."

"But…"

"Kabutt," Luna growled, grabbing me by the shoulders and forcing me to stare into her eyes. "You're angry because that old fuck is here still, but he's done nothing wrong. Was he stupid and missed that there was a risk? Yes. Could he have known, though? Probably not. So let it go."

"Let it fucking—"

"Fine, don't!" Luna snapped at me. "But aim it at the fucking corpos! Not him, and not us! You're army through and through, right? Grew up in the barracks?"

"Depending on the posting for the family, sometimes we were in the city as well, but yeah, mainly the barracks," I admitted.

"Then you hardly saw the real life of the city. Yeah, you were probably dirt poor like we fucking were, but you had the entire army as a family to look out for you. Here? Inside the city slums? If you've got a sister, you're lucky. Having parents who give a shit? That's insanely lucky! You won the fucking genetic lottery just by being born a fucking human!"

"Point there." Reign sighed. "You don't know what it's like when you're half and half. We're not trusted by one race because of the other half, and the same the other way around. My parents were human and elf, not that I knew my dad, but growing up? Nobody trusts the elf."

"*You* think it's bad?" Gessh laughed. "They send full-blooded orcs out to clear the fucking minefields around the city with nothing but a few tools! They treat most orcs as animals, and half-orcs? We're treated better than that, but we're not as good as pure anything, in the eyes of the city."

"Parents?" Reign asked, and Gessh snorted.

"Human and an orc," she said. "He was into fucking 'beasts,' apparently. Got Mum pregnant and fucked off. We were three when she sold us to the Ravagers Guild to use as monster bait."

"Fuck me," I gasped. "Are you for fucking real?"

"Bait," Luna confirmed. "We were starved and taught that food was at the flare. The faster we could get to it, the more we could eat. Then they took us to a monster site, fired the flare and set us loose. We'd run, while our friends, brothers, and sisters were picked off, and the guild would follow, shooting the monsters."

"We escaped when we were five," Gessh added, pausing at the door to the basement of the building and keying in the code we'd been given. "Next ten years? Well, let's say we earned our scars."

"Fuck me," I said again, before shaking my head. "I…I'm sorry."

"Why?" Gessh asked. "You didn't do any of it."

"No, but I thought I had it bad."

"Ah, it wasn't that bad." Luna sighed. "We got to hurt a lot of people, made some good friends, had some good sex when we grew up. There was a lot that, while it was shit, was great as well. Besides, as half-orcs we get Keystones. They don't waste them on full-bloods."

"Uh, on that note." I shook my head. "How much of it are you using?"

"The Key?"

"Yeah."

"Uh, no clue. Why?"

"Aug-World…" I started, only to get laughs from the sisters.

"You're worried about that?" Luna asked, and I nodded.

"Yeah, we barely use it," Gessh admitted. "Too many attacks, and when we grew these?" She tapped one finger to a breast, covered in body armor, admittedly, but still clearly there.

"You learn not to let your guard down as a woman," Reign added, getting nods from the other two.

"We disable most of the Aug-World 'improvements,' so we know exactly who's around us," Luna said. "But I know what you were thinking. When we joined the army, they had to break a lot of the recruits of it."

"Exactly," I said. "Well, that's a relief—"

I broke off as the stench of the lower floors rolled up the stairs, and we all looked at one another. All conversation broke off as we hefted our guns.

"Time to get busy," Reign announced cheerfully. "Last to get a kill buys the beers tonight!"

"Oh, you fuckers!" I growled, having been standing at the rear of our little group as they raced ahead of me. "I'll damn well get you for that!"

The doors started to close, and I ran after them. A boom announced the arrival of Luna or Gessh to the party, as one of their new shotguns introduced itself.

CHAPTER THIRTY-FIVE

Some two hours later, we were sitting and standing around, waiting for the cab to take us to our next target, a suspected nest, as Reign argued with the half-goblin in charge of the cleanup crew.

He was apparently both the leader of the crew that had cleaned up after us at the bio-farm, and wore a bag that looked suspiciously like the one that had gone missing from the fight, after Hobbs had vanished.

He was denying everything though, and as his crew were mainly goblins, not all of them had Keystones or any other implants. That meant that there were no recordings to act as evidence.

That, in turn, meant that they were in a sort of standoff, as both sides were well aware of the thefts. We knew they'd stolen our gear and were keeping it, and in turn, they were *very* unhappy about the bag full of mods I had next to me on the floor.

That they were paid to dispose of the mods and the bodies, for the price of the scrap, not the actual value of the mods on the market, meant that they would all be dirt poor, as they were required to hand in any weapons, etc., much as we were.

As it was, though, they all wore better clothes than any of us were and most of them had custom weapons. They could probably clear the specters better than we could.

The end result when Reign finished arguing with them was that a "we didn't see you, and you didn't see us" deal was struck. Specifically, it came about when I accidentally let slip that Oshbob character's name, and suddenly the atmosphere changed.

Apparently, the goblins knew not to fuck with him, and if we knew and "worked for" him "too," then we were suddenly all friends.

As much as anyone could be with a fucking *goblin*.

We agreed that we'd hit one more probable specter point, do some cleanup there, then we'd send the recordings of the mission to the guild, and head back to my apartment block. We'd drop off the mods with Lucky, and then we'd go scope out the chemist.

While we'd been waiting for the cleanup crew and the cab to arrive, Reign had walked us through the signup for the bounty guilds, making us all laugh as she pointed out that to sign up to be a bounty hunter, you had to be "of outstanding moral character," which apparently also counted pretty much the entirety of the fucking city out.

We unloaded our gear into the trunk of the cab, having picked an actual ground cab for this journey as it meant it'd take longer and be cheaper. We were all settling in for an hour or so's nap when I received a message.

I almost refused it, on the edge of sleep as I was, and seeing the army decals on the identifier, until the rank and name registered.

Major Marcial.

I triggered the accept, then went through the rigmarole of verification, allowing both internal verification through my Keystone, digital through my ident, and finally, only possible because of the gear I was wearing thankfully, my helmet triggered to send a facial scan to the system as well.

Once all of that was done?

The message began to play.

"Kabutt," the major began, fixing the camera with a solid glare. "I've been informed about the actions taken against you, both by Tyrannus and the corpos, since you left the service. I was ready to reach out and offer my assistance, until a quick search verified that not only had you already begun to replace your equipment, but that you were making a name for yourself in the criminal underbelly of the city..."

How the fuck did he know that? I wondered blankly, but I shook the thought free as the recording continued to play.

"You also triggered the watch protocol by checking classified docs after leaving the service. While this is normally permitted, approved of even, as the fixes that 'private contractors' come up with always find their way back to us, it provided a flimsy reason that passed enough of a test that Tyrannus got you barred from the system."

He shook his head as he went on.

"It'd be a hell of a lot easier if that little prick hadn't done that, but we need to work with what we have, not what we wish we had."

He sighed, flicking his hands forward, and my RI informed me that several files had been attached to the communication, as he spoke again.

"So far, three of my investigators have turned up dead. The two remaining have found remarkably little on Tyrannus and his friends, but they have found a significant windfall of credits in their accounts. As much as I detest that they've been bought out, it appears the choices were to have their accounts stuffed with credits or suffer 'accidents,' along with their families.

"I've deliberately left you for a few days to get your feet under you, but it seems that after the 'accident' in the Fingers, Tyrannus has taken the opportunity to claim 'trauma,' and is currently recuperating in the city. You'll note that he's on full pay, and despite his time in the forces remaining being less than yours, there's been no talk of cutting him loose."

"Motherfucker..." I breathed.

"However, this provides us with an opportunity," the major went on. "I cannot be involved in the situation you find yourself in, for obvious reasons but, should you go looking, I think you'd find that a slight change was made to the requisition and final disposition for your suit..."

My blood turned cold at the look on his face.

"It was seemingly 'misplaced,' and sent to be smelted along with the remains of the rest of your team. A little digging, however, has identified that something matching the weight and dimensions of your suit was transferred from the reclamation site before destruction. That container is currently making its way through the clearing process, before being sent on to a *corporate* trans-shipping address. You have at most fourteen hours before that suit is gone for good, I'm afraid, operator.

"I'd suggest that a personal visit to Tyrannus, along with a hacker who can check such things out, might be in your—*and our investigation's*—best interests, as this is looking like a string to pull, one that might lead to whoever's behind the shit that happened. Last of all? There's some hints that there might be an actual Black Team out there, so watch your back.

"Find him, question him, and find out who he's working for and what the fuck he's been up to, and maybe there's still time to fuck that little shit's retirement plans up.

"Major Marcial, out."

I sat back, staring at the freeze-framed image, before banishing it, ignoring the low-level banter of the others, staring straight ahead as my mind scrambled from detail to detail.

That little fucker Tyrannus.

I kept coming back to that arrogant motherfucker, thinking he had the right to…thinking he could…

He'd tried to steal my suit.

That was why he'd gotten me out of the system, I realized. It wasn't just the usual shitty tricks; getting me blacklisted from the system meant I couldn't chase up my suit.

I'd not done it yet because I couldn't bring myself to. To be in such a mess physically and then to tease myself with the unmatched sheer magnificence of the APS?

To know that it'd be weeks if *everything* went well before I could order the delivery, and most likely months? I'd left it alone. Not least because if I got in touch with the APS armorers and didn't provide them with a delivery address, I'd get a load of shit from people I knew.

There was never enough room in the armories. That was part of the nature of the world—big tech required big parts and maintenance equipment. For them to keep my suit there while I got myself together, for a year possibly?

They'd be going apeshit.

There'd be a new Red Team, and they'd need the slots my old team—and my armor—was taking up.

They'd be desperate to get it out of the way, and once it left them? I'd need to either provide it a safe area for storage—which I couldn't afford, not at all—or be wearing the fucker all the time. And I couldn't do that either, not without the correct mods.

No, my armor being delivered to me would set every fucking gangbanger, merc, and corpo team on notice. It'd be a bloodbath as they tried to take it from me.

It didn't matter that thanks to the sheer complexity of the system, nobody untrained with it could so much as lift a hand in the suit. It didn't matter that the number of nanites needed to provide the full bonding process meant that it was cheaper and more efficient to melt the armor down when its operator died.

No, not at all, because the suits were tightly controlled and tracked!

The corpos were only permitted five of the suits each. That was it. Yeah, they had more than that in the real world; they got around the limit by hiring APS operators out of the army as guards…Hell, there were rumors that entire teams were sponsored through the program!

But the one point there was that all the APS suits were fitted with trackers. Back-hardpoint perma-sealed fucking thermite explosives, to make sure that if we went off the rails? We could be taken down before we took half the city out.

They were determined that it be that way "for public safety," but really? It was because if an APS operator went fucking nuts and started to really go for it? We could do serious damage to the city, and who knew what else.

There'd always been rumors of APS that made it out without being tracked. That were "lost" and that formed black teams of ghost operatives.

They were joked about, and we all talked constantly about ways to get around the trackers and so on so that we could join—or if there wasn't such a team in reality, so that we could be the first—and to create a real Black Team.

Nanites were expensive, but the thought that you could get a suit out, get it around the registration and tracking requirements, and then get it wiped, use a fresh batch of 'nites to bond some other fucker to *my* suit?

It'd be horrifically expensive, but it could be done. And once it was? You could send your APS operative out on assassinations, hit enemy corpos, trash depots, and raid research sites…

There was nothing you couldn't do, and every single APS that existed would be a suspect because…

No.

The government wouldn't permit that, because they'd invested so much in the myth that we were impossible to capture. That our suits were impossible to steal. No matter the reality, if word got out that one of the suits was off the rails and couldn't be identified, the other cities would inundate us with their operatives trying to grab it.

It'd start another arms race.

My mind spiraled around and around, seeing the possibilities, some realistic, some fucking insane—entire wars starting all over again, all for some corpo little fuck who'd seen a chance to make some scratch and had taken it.

Regardless of anything else, that's what this came back to. I didn't know whether Tyrannus was involved in the shit that happened in the Fingers or whether he was just incompetent. I didn't know whether the AROC or the scavs and that fucking mech were involved in the theft of my suit, or whether Tyrannus thought he could steal *ten-fucking-years* of my hard work and planning, to pad his account out. And right now? I didn't care.

His incompetence had led to Scott and Fergie's deaths. His greed had made things far harder than they needed to be. And his being a little shit had even blocked me from creating the reels for their families when he'd booted me from the system.

He'd done that, at the very least, and that was more than enough for me to take his fucking balls and grind them to an atomic level of dust below my boots.

I realized suddenly that I'd gone straight through irritated, passed through anger, and out into cold rage, then I'd blown the fucking doors off nuclear fury, and I was out into the far side, skating across the frozen surface of hell as all emotion compressed into a tiny box and was put away, ready for when I needed it.

The cab had grown slowly quieter as the others realized that there was something wrong, and Reign was the first to speak.

"Uh, Kabutt, are you okay?" she tried, looking at the cold titanium of my helmet.

I shifted, turning to stare at her like my head was on rails, all smooth movement.

"No," I said flatly. "No, I'm fucking not, and I need to kill something, right now."

"We're close to the next site," she said slowly, clearly trying to figure out what she or the others had done to cause offense.

"Tell me when I can kill something. Till then, leave me alone, please." I forced the words out, trying to keep my calm. The compressed marble of my emotions shook inside me, the glass that held them in check a hair's breadth from shattering.

"Okay." She sat back as she shared a look with the girls.

I couldn't bring myself to speak to them, and started to search instead.

Richie had given me the details of that hacker. I couldn't remember his name, but he'd said he was good…and I needed to get in touch with him anyway, so fuck it.

I found the contact details after a few seconds, and I grimaced, already hating dealing with fucking hackers. Connecting up, I put the call through to Bowdoin.

CHAPTER THIRTY-SIX

"Thirty fucking *thousand...*" I hissed as I ended the call, staring ahead, sitting on the second from bottom stair of an old concrete loading bay. "I'll kill him!"

"Who?" Luna asked, and I flinched, having totally forgotten about her and her sister.

"It...it doesn't matter," I snapped, straightening up and looking around the shitty area we were in.

We were never called to fucking nice areas, of course—oh no, not to hunt fucking specters. This was the "pleasure beach" that Luna had wanted to visit, but it wasn't a fucking "beach" area, not anymore.

The specters had been sighted around there, and then had wandered off, apparently leading the locals to believe they were forming a nest in the sewage pipes, and had headed into an abandoned reclamation plant, one that specialized in metal.

That meant that although the outside looked much like any other industrial building on the edge of the zone—tall stone walls, shitty, filthy windows that hadn't been opened or cleaned by anything bar the rain in at least fifty years, and blocked and covered fire exits—it was also topped by great chimneys that belched soot-laden particulate matter into the sky.

"You sure?" Luna asked carefully. "Look, boss, you gave us a chance, all right? If we can help, we will, okay?"

"You've no idea what you'd be getting into," I said grimly. "Seriously, you don't want any part of this."

"You don't know what we've done over the years," Luna said softly. "Look, boss, I'm not offering to go out and do murders for you, nor suck your dick, despite the joking around, but we're mercs at the end of the day. You need us? We're there. And if there's some creds to cover the incidentals and maybe something more? Great."

"Luna, I..." I nodded. "Thank you." I left it at that, unable to do more at the minute, and desperately in need of getting things moving.

I needed time to plan, I needed to figure this shit out, and I damn well needed to earn an absolute fuckload of credits, because that little shit Bowdoin was charging me thirty fucking thousand creds for his part in hitting Tyrannus!

Plus he'd tried to claim half of whatever we recovered!

I'd told him to go fuck himself if he thought he was getting anything from my suit, that it was personal, and not to take the piss, and he'd accepted that after a few grisly threats.

I had a rough location in a corpo "pleasure estate" for Tyrannus as he "recovered," and Bowdoin was going to narrow it down, find the little shit and find out what security was involved. It'd cost me my last three thousand creds, as a deposit, but I'd made it clear to the little turd that, if he didn't do the job? I'd be visiting him personally to beat my credits' worth out of him.

The armor was already on the move, though, and Tyrannus was my only contact to it. If it got into a corpo hub? I was never getting it back. That meant I had no goddamn time to fuck about. I needed to get to him tonight, and before I could do that? Well.

I needed thirty thousand credits.

Twenty-seven thousand really, after the deposit was taken off, but I'd no doubt need more goddamn ammo as well, so fuck it.

Just thinking about that made my fists shake again, and I had to clench them tight to stop from holding my rifle grip.

"Okay!" Reign called, jogging over, and I shot to my feet, ready. "So, there's three specters been seen here. They think there's more, but they're not sure, and—"

"Three," I growled. "Fucking *three?*"

"They apparently claimed there were more because they didn't want to wait for a team to get around to them." She forced a smile, clearly not happy either.

"Where are they?" I asked grimly.

"The specters are—"

"Not them. The lying fucking shitbags!"

"The manager is in there." She pointed to a door with sections of grey showing through the peeling paint. "Kabutt!" She grabbed me as I started past her. "This is a client. No fucking him up," she warned me. "Julius will boot you from the guild, and us as well."

"I'll just have a little word," I promised, before walking up to the door.

The manager evidently saw me coming, probably on the camera above the door, as a hand reached out and grabbed the edge of the door, dragging it closed. As I reached it, the heavy clunk of locking bars slid into place.

"Reign, grazer," I ordered, and she winced, but handed it over. "Thank you." I spoke with forced politeness, before turning to look at the door.

"I have reason to believe there's a specter inside that room," I called out loudly. "If there's any living being inside, open the door now. If not? On three, I fire this grazer, full beam, full power, and drain the battery. One. Two..."

"Don't fire!" a panicked scream rang out. The door was unlocked and the duty manager, a scruffy bearded little bastard in striped pink and white, held his hands up, shaking his head. "Don't shoot! There's no specters here!"

"Thank you, Reign," I said through gritted teeth, chucking the grazer to her and nearly knocking her off her feet, before striding forward. "Now, you fucking streak of piss, why the FUCK am I here?" I screamed into his face at half an inch's distance.

"Sp...sp...specters...?" he stuttered.

"A NEST!" I roared into his face. "We clear out infections of specters at *nest* levels!"

He closed his eyes, panicking as he tried to get a breath.

I held onto the collar of his shirt, shaking him like a mastiff shakes a kitten.

"We're here, wasting our fucking time with *three specters* when people are being eaten, they're being dragged into the depths and torn apart, and you *lied to us?!*"

He promptly pissed himself, and I dropped him on the floor, disgusted.

"We'll be back in an hour," I told him coldly. "The site will be billed for a full fucking nest, and you'll approve it, or so fucking help me. I swear by the gods of blood and chrome, I'll drag you down into the deepest part of the city and I'll nail you to the fucking wall for the specters to come for real."

With that, I spun on my heel and marched out of the room. "Reign!" I barked.

"Yes, Sarge!" she responded, stiffening automatically.

"Lead the way. I need to fucking kill something!"

"This way…" She set off running; Luna and Gessh fell in behind me as we ran for the nearest grate. She sent it a code, unlocking it, then jammed a crowbar into the gap at the edge as the bolts retracted with a heavy *clunk*, levering it open.

The ladder inside, old rungs literally welded to the wall, was just visible with the heavy cloud cover overhead and the rain that hammered down. I started in without pause, my helmet illuminating the darkness below me after only a brief flicker.

I climbed down. The rusted rungs took my weight without so much as a groan, and at the bottom, I dropped the last few feet, landing lightly and bringing my rifle up, ready.

I swept left and right, checking out the tunnels that ran in either direction. Faint light filtered down from above here and there, as well as dripping water.

Beyond that, there was fuck all signs of life.

The rain was heavy enough and the openings frequent enough that the bottom of the tunnel—a literal overflow drainage pipe that was three meters high and circular—was a few inches deep with running water.

I splashed through it, heading to the left at Reign's recommendation. Despite knowing how fucking stupid it was, I didn't wait for the others, either.

I was too angry, I was too furious, both with that asshole above us, figuring that why should he wait, why should he have to put up with anything, when he wanted it dealt with straightaway, and with Tyrannus.

He, like that dick above, said only what he wanted, not what it'd cost anyone else, and I was incensed by the fucking arrogance.

Tyrannus was trying to profit by stealing ten fucking years of my hard work. He was fucking me over, and in the process, making it so that I couldn't even make the death reels for my friends, just because it was convenient for him.

I reached the end of the tunnel, taking a left at the T junction, but finding nothing at the end of that line. Then I took a right, striding on as the others exchanged worried glances with one another behind me.

Reaching the far end of this passage, I found a sealed grate, heavily slotted to permit water egress, but to prevent anyone else. Reign slipped around me, punching in the code, and then stepped back.

I entered, taking point, and quickly found the source of the sightings.

A single specter.

"Are you fucking kidding me?" I hissed, staring at the specter before us, hanging suspended over the storm drain.

It was tightly bound, shaking and trying to get free, while all around it, draukka roamed.

We'd found a fucking nest all right, but it was a *spider* nest, one that, although it might cause serious issues for the locals and end up requiring a visit from an exterminator, was absolutely fuck all use to us!

The single specter was being examined by a dozen draukka, long-legged spiders with thick bodies. They'd mutated back in the uncontrolled nanite expansions, their life cycle massively expanded from that of a "normal" spider. They now bit and injected their young into their victims, using a nanite charge—how the fuck it worked, I didn't know, but it did—to force massive cellular replication in a short time. The spider's eggs were incubated and brought from microscopic size in the mother's bite to almost the size of my pinky nail in the victim in about four hours.

The area around the bite was totally numb as they spread, feeding on their host, and it wasn't until they broke through the walls of their tiny little replication prison that the host would truly feel them.

They'd damn well feel it for a short time, though, as they burrowed through and out of the victim's flesh, eating and growing all the while.

A single spider could become twenty full-size adults inside of a day, and from there? Their spread was exponential. They should have been ruling the city, killing and eating everything in sight, except for the fact that they were only *one* of the fuckers down here, and everything else, especially fucking goblins, loved the taste of spider meat.

I hissed at the sight of the spiders, then backed up, lifting my rifle. My single round took the weakly struggling specter in the head, ending it all.

It collapsed backward onto the web, and the spiders hissed and scattered, darting for hiding places.

Luna grunted, looking in and shaking her head.

"What a waste," she said sadly. "A few hours' work, and it'd be spider kabobs for us all weekend."

I ignored her, stalking back and looking left and right, mentally reconstructing the route, trying to make sure there was nowhere we could have missed anything.

"Kabutt." Reign stepped up to my shoulder and waited.

"What?" I snapped a few seconds later, as I mentally came up empty.

"Calm down. Look, these things happen, all right? Some missions are just a waste of time. Our run through the bio-farm should have been for like three or four, that's it. That's the normal."

"No," I snapped. "No, it can't be! I need a fucking nest!"

"A nest? Kabutt, we barely survived yesterday. We were hunted by something that has to be higher up the food chain than the ghouls, and we were lucky. We got away. Some days it's like that. Some days, it's all bullets and blood, and the next, you're sitting, sewing up the rips in your armor—"

"Fuck's sake, Reign!" I snarled, turning to face her. "I've not got time for this shit!"

"You think I have?" Her voice dropped. "You know what I'm living with, what my debt's like! You think I'm happy about this? I hate fucking around down here. You think I want to spend my life in the sewers!"

"You don't?"

"Of fucking course I don't!" she shouted, waving her arms around as if to say, *Look at this place*. "I'm here because there's always more missions! You know how many normal merc missions a single, female half-elf gets that don't involve me somehow ending up in my underwear, or being railed by the entire team? The decent merc outfits won't take me with my past—the shitty ones? I'll be stripped, used, abused, and disposed of!"

"It's true," Luna said; Gessh nodded. "We tried other merc bands before, and it's not just that we'd be used as bait, just like she would be. She'd be sent into places to get attention, unarmed, half naked, then the 'real' mercs storm the place, and she'd be getting a little cut of the profits. That's why we don't want to work with the shitty guilds."

"The shitty guilds…" I growled, shaking my head as I remembered how bad the shitty guilds were. The way I'd been jumped and dumped, my gun stolen, and…

"You want to make some money?" I spoke before I could think better of it. "Fuck it, I've not got the time to be careful, not now, so fine!"

I turned to face them all, noting that Gessh was sealing the door back up and that it was locked before she turned to me.

"I need thirty thousand credits by tonight," I said, noting the winces and the way the others looked at one another. "Don't worry, I'm not going to ask you for donations." I snorted.

"Glad to hear it." Reign shrugged. "Because being offered a credit if you'll do a dance often offends…"

"You hate the shitty guilds?" I asked, getting nods. "Any of you ever dealt with a guild called Errant Mergers?"

"Once," Gessh growled. "Never again."

"I've not dealt with them, but I've heard shit," Reign admitted, and Luna just grunted, making it clear that her sister and she had been in whatever issue they'd had with the guild together.

"Well, last chance to back out," I offered. "Because they fucked with me, and I need money, so I'm going to pay them a visit."

"A visit?" Reign asked slowly. "What kind of a visit?"

"The kind where I burn their guild house down around their ears, and we fucking loot them," I said. "You do this with me, you do my jobs?" I looked from one to the other of them. "Then we're in this together. I'm offering you a chance here, as part of my team."

"What's that worth?" Reign quirked an eyebrow. "No offense, boss, but the bounties? That's one reason I'm in on the jobs you have. Most likely, if that bitch had a bounty, the others will too. The merc guild, though? If they had a bounty on their heads, their guild would be broken up. You're asking us to help settle personal scores, to make you money to do something that you're not sharing. If we're in, we're in all the way, or I'm out."

"You two feel the same way?" I asked, and Luna and Gessh glanced at each other before answering.

"More or less," Gessh said with a groan, scratching the underside of her chin as she spoke. "Look. I hate those Errant Merger assholes, so yeah, I'm up for pissing on their parade, but you're talking about assaulting a guild. There's four of us."

"It's a pissing contest where they've got a machine gun, and you've just got your dick," Reign said subtly. "It's not a good idea."

"You're out then?"

"I didn't say that," Reign said with a sudden quirk of her lips. "I just asked what's in it for us, considering the risks."

"What's in it for you is that we slaughter the top nutters in the guild. Then we strip them, and we armor up from their armory."

"They've got shit in the armory," Gessh said. "Sorry, boss, but we were there a week ago. Lasted an afternoon before quitting and walking out. They claim fifty percent of everything you loot, and they get to pick the bits, they keep all the good shit, but where it goes, nobody knows."

"They'll be keeping it private, or selling it," I said. "Either way, we hit them hard, and we fucking take it all."

"And then?" Gessh frowned. "I mean, look, no offense, but you do this, and they're going to pull all their guild in to kill us. Even if you take the fuckers down, getting away? It's not gonna be easy."

"It wouldn't be," I agreed. "Except for a minor detail."

"Oh?"

"There's an entrance to the undercity in their guild hall." I smiled. "They tried to kill me and dumped me through it."

"Okay…"

"I escaped and killed a few specters on the way out. That's how I ended up EMP'd."

"So there's a way out, and I'm betting that there's a way in that's not too hard. I mean, they want people in off the street to join them, so we can march in through the front door and order every fucker out maybe?" Reign said musingly.

"But then what?" Luna said. "No offense, boss, you're a nice guy and all, but we're basically risking our lives to help you get even. Sure, we might get some creds out of this, but I doubt it'll be that many, and even if we do? It's an insane risk."

"It is," I agreed. "But the point here? Is that my suit is actively being stolen right now."

"The APS?" Gessh asked. "I thought they couldn't be stolen? That only their operator can use them?"

"Exactly," I growled. "There's a way around that, though, if you're corpo scum, and they've taken it. They're stealing my gear, and I need to find out where it is, then get it diverted somewhere safe. That's the thirty thou I need, and why I need it tonight."

"So…if you don't get it tonight, it's gone? Like in a corpo vault?" Reign asked, and I nodded. "Shit."

"Exactly. So, here it is, I'll lay it all out. You told me the truth, so I'll do the same. You help me do this?" I looked at them one by one. "We hit the guild, yeah, we cover some personal debts there. Gessh and Luna, you like them about as much as I do, so we all get something out of burning the place down, regardless of the loot. But…"

"But?"

"But we also get *gear*. We kill the guild leadership. They're assholes who were apparently a gang at first, then they went legit and started a guild, but they still have a gang mentality. They keep their shit in tight, and they fuck over anyone they think they can get away with. I'm betting they'll have some good gear. We hit them fast and hard. Kill them, seal the place up, loot it to the fucking ground. Then we blow a hole through the sealed air lock underneath, and we escape through the undercity.

"ACE turns up, finds that we're gone, and that because we can't take everything, there'll be plenty of loot left around?" I grinned.

"They won't even chase us." Reign grunted. "They'll pocket what they can first, then call in for backup once they've got theirs…"

"Then we hit the jobs that Lucky has for me. All of them."

"In a single day?" Luna asked. "All of them? Boss, it's like, mid-afternoon!"

"Yeah, and we're wasting time," I growled. "We hit the targets, and we pay off my hacker. We get the job done? And I share the bounty with you all, all four of us, even split."

"That bounty had better be—" Reign started to say, until I cut her off.

"It's for Stinger, and it's a quarter-mil bounty," I finished. "Sixty-two thousand, five hundred credits each."

"That's…that's a hell of a bounty," Gessh gasped.

I nodded, turning to look at Reign directly, knowing that the sisters were almost certainly in, but that she was the one I really needed.

"It is, but, if you'll help me with this? I'll help you. All of you. You'll be in my team for good, and that means real bounties, and real bonuses. You're being fucked over, day by day, Reign, by that chip in your head and by the corpos. Well, I'll help you pay that off. In an APS, the bounties we can get? Much higher, not to mention that I've got a way to draw the specters. We get it working and we can draw them to us, set up traps and slaughter them in their hundreds."

"The tech you grabbed?" Reign guessed, and I nodded. "What is it?"

"It's classified, but it's not like I give a fuck about that anymore. It's a way to strip nanites from a corpse."

"Right?" Luna said, unimpressed.

"*Pure* nanites," I said, louder and slower. "Not the corrupt shit, the actual good stuff. We can strip the nanites from the specters and anything else we kill. You know the harvesting teams? The specialist monster hunting guilds that take down the big shit? They don't just bring back meat. When it's a *big* one? They call in the APS Corps and we help out. Using that tech, we strip the corpse of nanites, and we all get a portion of the salvage."

"Pure nanites," Gessh said slowly. "Like really pure? The stuff that the government produces, that there's never enough of?"

"Yeah," I agreed with a grim smile. "We do this, and I get that working? We can strip the nanites from the specters, as well as the mods. I know Lucky will be planning on hitting me as soon as I take down Stinger, so when he tries? We take him and his gang down as well."

"Then what?" Luna asked, her sister nodding that she was thinking the same thing.

"Then we go directly to an orc called Oshbob," I said. "Apparently he hates humans, but he's a crime lord, and we need one of those to move this level of shit. He's also who we're dealing with for it all already…ultimately, I mean."

"He hates humans?" Reign asked, then she nodded. "Ah, he's not going to work with you…" She turned to look at the sisters. "But he might with you?"

"We've heard of him," Luna admitted, glancing at her sister for support.

"We have, but you know…dealing with him, once you do a deal with *the* Orc, you're never free again. You know that, right?"

"He's a ganger, just like any other," I said firmly. "He fucks with APS operators, he ends up a smear on the floor."

I saw the wince on the girls' faces, and I shook my head. "Look, I'm doing this, with or without you. I've got friends who need me. Once this is over? I'll explain it—you'll have earned that. But for now? Either you're in or out."

I stood there, watching them, my heart sinking as they looked at one another, and I waited for the inevitable refusal.

"I'm in," Reign said suddenly, and I jerked, looking at her.

"What?"

"I'm in." She shrugged. "Look. You say you'll help me get out of this? I can trust you, or I could not. Regardless, the one thing that's changed for me from yesterday? Today, I've got a chance. That's it. It might be a shitty chance, and it might be an insane plan, but you know? I've been waiting for the end anyway. I wake up every morning and wish I was dead, so fuck it. We do this? Either I wake up tomorrow with some hope, or I don't wake up tomorrow. Either way, it's better than I've had for a long time."

"Luna? Gessh?" I looked at the sisters, seeing the way they stood. The pair of them subtly mirrored each other as they always did, their matching armor with the paint splash running down it. They'd added to their loadout with new shotguns each—a rifle was over each shoulder, a shotgun in their arms—and their swords standing out over their opposite shoulder, at the ready.

Their gear was simple, the swords easily the best of it, but it was all well maintained, black and grey, apart from their characteristic red and blue stripes to identify the identical twins.

They seemed to communicate silently, not with digital means, but that special way that siblings always did.

"We're in," Luna said after a few seconds, nodding to me.

"But…" Gessh drew the word out.

"Yeah?"

"We're a team?"

"Yeah," I agreed.

"Then there's something we want," she said quickly. "That we've wanted for ages."

"Go on…"

"We want out of the arcology."

"What?"

"Look, you're APS—you fuckers live in the military zones. We live in an arcology surrounded by goddamn gobbos, and we want out. You think you can swing us a decent place? We'll pay the rent, not asking you to do that, but you know? Maybe you know someone who might rent to us?"

I looked from the sisters to Reign, seeing the honest-to-God dream reflected in her eyes of not being a homeless vagabond, couch surfing and always at risk, of waiting to see who's going to claim more than she was willing to give.

"I'm in a shitty apartment as well," I admitted. "Reign's seen it, but at the end of the month my lease is up. So how about this? We do this, and we get the armor? We pool our money and get somewhere decent, the four of us? Try it for a month, see how it works out?"

"I'm in," Gessh said quickly.

"Me too," Luna agreed.

"You guys know I'm up for it, but I'm losing half my money every time I'm paid," Reign said slowly. "I want to, but I might not be able to pay it."

"We'll make it work," I said firmly. "We might all be dead tomorrow, but if we're not? We'll be set up to earn a fuckload more than any of us ever have."

"Then let's do it," Reign said with a genuine smile. "So…there a plan for the guild house?"

"Oh, you'll like this…" I said with an evil smile.

CHAPTER THIRTY-SEVEN

The girls *hadn't* liked my plan, not really, and they'd spent some time reworking it, as we waited on the cab, breaking off only when struck by some new level of perverse madness. I stuck my head in to remind the lying dickhead in the office that "client reviews are important to us, so please, be sure to mark down how you felt my team did."

Lucky hadn't been happy when I'd called him from the cab either, having expected me to be telling him I was going after one of his targets, and when I told him that I would be, just not until I'd done one more job?

Not a happy bunny.

Or, you know, giant grumpy half-orc gang leader.

When his four people showed up? I was sitting on a bench across from the guild house, well aware I was being watched, and having already fended off several pings and identity grabbers.

Something about the kind of group the guild was meant that when a totally innocent guy sat on a bench across from their guild house and just waited, they got worried for some reason.

It might have been because I was concealing my identity, or possibly because I was heavily armed. It also might have been because I was holding Reign's grazer, fully loaded, charged and ready.

But whatever the reason was, the two orcs on door duty were pulled in and replaced by a pair of meatheads I recognized.

The one on the left was particularly memorable, as that fucker had booted me in the balls at one point, and I really needed to reply in kind to him.

Regardless, though, while I sat there, they practically ignored everyone else.

That included Reign as she walked up and in, pausing as the guards asked her a few questions, before waving her in as business as usual.

Once the four gangbangers showed up, clearly high as hell on something, and at least partly drunk, I settled back, waiting.

The guards on the door watched me, then the gang members, then back to me, clearly seeing the change in my attitude, and they geared up, ready.

The first of Lucky's gang members—an utterly terrible actor, even by the standards I'd been expecting—stopped and asked about joining up. Then, when he was, surprise, surprise, told to fuck off, he acted about as predictably as possible.

He tried to stab the guard, who was in full body armor.

The knife hit his abdomen, and they all stared at it, then the ganger, then the knife, then the ganger…before all hell broke loose.

They knew something was going on, they *knew* it, but they were gangers themselves not that long ago, and they still had the scars to show it.

That these fucks actually dared to stab them? Worse, that the level of stupidity shown was so fucking insane?

Best of all, as far as they were concerned, was that I stood…and got into a cab at that point.

That changed the dynamic totally. I'd hyped the guild up, expecting that something, probably a rival guild, was about to attack them, then I fucked off? That I got them all hyped and ready for a fight, then I left?

That just sent them off the deep end.

The gangers were dragged inside. One was dead already, having been fed his own knife. The other three had pulled a variety of weapons ranging from shock knuckles—useless against someone in armor—another knife—yup, still useless—to a low-caliber handgun—practically useless. And last of all?

A length of lead piping.

As I'd left, the guards told anyone nearby to fuck off, and locked the doors, activating the heavy-duty protective grates over the door.

The end result, as I got the cab to stop out of sight around the corner and got back out, was that the people already inside were hurried out of the back door and shoved into the street, along with the cashiers and general staff.

That last group, used to this kind of thing, were ordered to wait.

Reign, being—as mentioned a time or two—a highly attractive half-elf, had struck up a conversation with one of the staff, and was told to "wait right there," while he sent the others away. He apparently thought he was about to get a blow in the alley in exchange for a preferential chance at any high-earning jobs.

I jogged back to the building. A message from the girls showed on my Key as I got closer.

> *Sounds like a bad day to be in a gang. We're in place.*

I almost felt bad for the four thugs I'd sent in, but I reminded myself that they were scum as well, and given half the chance, they'd be on the giving side of the attack, with absolutely no qualms.

Getting closer, I looped around to the rear entrance just as Reign gave up on trying to persuade the object of her affections to open the door for her to "use the loo."

Instead, she sighed, smiled, and kneed him in the balls. That action rammed his face into the scanner and pressed her handgun into the back of his head, and she whispered that all she needed was his ident.

He apparently decided that he'd like to keep his head attached, and provided the necessary details that the hacker Bowdoin requested.

Entering the guild house had been the weakest part of my plan, I freely admitted that, and the girls had essentially torn me a new asshole over the plan I'd had.

Another call to the hacker, a quick meetup, and the Zentrades, Xz45 Black Cyber Widow datadeck we'd gotten in the depths of the bio-farm had a new owner.

We, in turn, had remote access to the door here, and a small plugin each—one that, as long as we plugged it into the main servers for the guild, would end a great many of our troubles.

Reign led the way inside, taking her grazer from me, and I nodded to her, more than ready for what was to come.

"Girls are ready," I said.

She lifted her head in acknowledgment.

"I got the message too," she reminded me.

I nodded again, my heart hammering.

"You ready for this?"

"Fuck, no." She grinned, pulling her mask down to cover her face and making sure her spoofed corpo ident was broadcasting. "Shall we?"

"Let's!" I agreed, before moving.

The alley had led into a simple backroom. It had once been a kitchen from the look of the place, but it'd been long since stripped of any cooking equipment; the fire door and old brackets and so on gave away its original use.

The next door led to a corridor, one that ran around the back of the building, and we moved quickly, not taking the easy exit into the main room—oh no, not yet.

This was a gang that'd had access to a fuckload of money of late, and as such—the paranoid bastards that they were—they'd bought turrets and more into the main area of the guild, set up ready to take out any threat.

Reign and I split up, me moving through the side rooms for a quick search, and her darting up the stairs, starting to search the second floor.

The screams and pleading from the gangers out in the main area were dying off, and I knew we didn't have long.

"It'll be a decent bank of servers, I'd think. Nobody's going to put their security systems on the web without corpo cybersec, not anyone who knows that they're doing anyway," Bowdoin had babbled earlier, unable to take his eyes off the deck.

I'd waved it back and forth, watching the way his eyes moved, tracking it.

"You need to be fucking sure about this," I'd growled at him. "This will give me control of their security systems? All of them?"

"I think so," he'd hedged. "Look, all I can do is tell you what *should* happen, okay? *If* they have their security systems hardwired into a central server? And *if* you plug this in—direct, mind you, not into a secondary system or a firewalled network slot, but directly into the server? Yeah, it should accept you as the registered keeper. That's if they don't have a dedicated defensive RI or an AI. If they do? You're fucked. Sorry, but it's that simple."

"There's nothing you can do?" I'd asked, and he'd shaken his head.

"Look, if I was there? Ready and waiting? I might be able to get you around an RI, if I get lucky and it's a low-tier one. As it is, by remote using a cracker and just programming in a brute force attack? Nope."

"We could take him with us," Reign had suggested.

"Not if you want me to sort that address and the details out for you tonight." Bowdoin had shaken his head. "You want me doing this or that? I can't do both…and I'm already not happy about the possibilities of turning their own security against them."

"Why not?" Reign had asked, leaning against the wall and looking him over, letting loose a little smile that utterly failed to work on him.

"Don't even bother." He flicked his hood back to show his ears.

"Another fucking half-elf," I groaned.

"Hey, you want my help or not?" he snapped.

"If you can keep from fucking someone long enough, yeah," I grumbled, watching him.

"Right. Look, the security system here is going to be yours *if* this works, but it's not going to just open fire on the guild or whatever. It'll only do that if you're attacked, or if you order it to, so that's all on you, okay? I'm not setting this to kill anyone, but what you do with it? That's your business."

"Works for me." Reign stepped forward and took the datadeck from me, handing it to him and taking the two small devices, passing one to me and pocketing the other.

"If we live? We'll be in touch," she promised.

"And if you don't?" he'd called after us as we walked away.

"Well, clearly we fucking won't!" I'd called back, shaking my head at Reign. "Fucking hackers. I swear, they live in a different world from the rest of us."

Now, with us running from room to room, frantically searching for what some idiot hacker had described they'd *probably* have somewhere?

It wasn't going well.

I skidded to a halt, eyes darting back and forth as I tried to pick out anything that looked like a server rack.

I had a mental image of those massive machines in vids that ran the defensive city AIs and so on, or the old-school machines in vids of the past.

A modern "defensive security system server"?

It could be anything, he'd said, showing us a variety of machines quickly.

Some had looked like old computers, all flashing lights and cabling, others were practically organic, and nowhere I looked was there fuckin' anything like the shit that pointy-eared bastard had shown me.

Reign was up on the next level, and I raced back to the stairs, sprinting up them after her as the first of the bodies was dragged to the concealed air lock in the floor.

I took the steps two at a time, leaping from the landing to the next set and skidding. I bounced off the wall, heard a scuffle ahead and saw Reign staggering sideways as a man in full stealth gear grappled with her.

I cursed as shouts rang out from below, and the sound of running feet, even as I yanked the HK-TT slug thrower out of its holster.

It was one of those insane guns that you saw from time to time, designed more for overt threat than actual utility. Pulling the trigger, I was damn glad I'd set my wrist and had been expecting the recoil, as otherwise?

It'd have snapped my damn wrist.

The slug that it fired, from a handgun no less, was bigger than most heavy-duty breeching shotguns could manage, and the hole that appeared in the side of the stealth idiot's head made it clear that it packed a punch.

It also sent his corpse flying, hands releasing the garrote that he'd been using on her. She collapsed to the floor, clutching at her throat and gasping, even as I turned, cursing.

"You motherfuckers don't know who you're messing with! Fucking trying to rob *us*!" a voice screamed up from below, and I cursed again, longer and louder this time.

They weren't just aware we were there; they had control of the security systems as well. I twisted and searched the ceiling and walls quickly, yanking the gun around and firing once, destroying the camera on the wall to my left as it swiveled.

The turret that slid out of the ceiling farther down the corridor, I missed with the first shot, but the second took it in the barrel, causing it to explode when it tried to fire. I spun, looking hurriedly for any others.

I relaxed for a half second when I couldn't see them, then grabbed a soft drink can from the side, tossing it down the stairs with a bank shot that sent it clattering off the walls, even as I shouted, "Frag out!" after it.

Screams and shouts rose below, quickly followed by cursing as they realized that the item they'd all shit themselves over, and that had caused them to go running…was a synth-cola can.

The clattering of feet on the stairs paused as I threw another can, shouting the same again. I grabbed Reign and dragged her to her feet, snagging one of her actual grenades—she wasn't using it, after all—and pulling the activation ring on it.

This one I rolled down the corridor, shouting after it, "Grenade! Honest!"

This time, they kept coming as we darted into a room. I had to imagine there was a hell of a look on the guy's face who was first to find out that it was an actual grenade.

I missed it, just hearing the muffled explosion, the sounds of sharpened fragments slamming into reinforced walls and screams of pain.

"Fucking told you so!" I bellowed down the corridor, before grabbing someone's lunch container and closing it, then flinging that around the corner into the corridor. "Probably not a grenade!" I shouted, before flinching as a boom rang out next to me.

"Tur…ret…" Reign croaked, rubbing at her throat. "Keep…'em…busy…" I nodded, and she did something to her headgear, starting to search, even as she jabbed herself in the throat with a medikit dispenser.

I frowned, thinking it was a waste to use it for such a minor wound, then shrugged. It wasn't my kit, so fuck it. I promptly angled the handgun around the edge of the door and fired three rounds before jerking back as armor-piercing rounds punched into the doorframe where I'd been standing.

I moved quickly as more bullets slammed into the wall, making me curse.

Reign spoke up, the medikit having helped already, I guessed.

"All the cables lead into the next room," she told me, making me glare at her, unseen in my helmet.

"Are you fucking kidding me?" I asked her.

"Electromagnetic and fiber-optic cabling. It's running from the turrets to the wall there." She pointed. "If it was going into a different part of the building? It'd be easier to run through the ceiling gaps."

"So the server…"

"Next door." She nodded. "Bowdoin told us to watch for that, remember?"

"Nope." I bit my lip. Running into the corridor was a sure way to get a bullet in the back of the head, but something she'd said…

"Wait…ceiling gaps?" I looked up.

"The armoring only goes so high. You need cables, ventilation, and so on, it goes through the walls and ceiling."

"Get ready to run," I told her, nodding to the door and the next room, even as I stood on a desk, using my shotgun to smash the ceiling tiles loose.

As soon as I did? I grinned. There were long rows of cross posts for the piping to be attached to, and it took literally a couple of steps and a jump, kicking off the wall while Reign threw a flash-bang out into the corridor as a distraction, banking it off the door.

I dragged myself upward. The bracing creaked and groaned under my weight, making me move as fast as I could, expecting at any second to crash back down.

There were shouts from the corridor, threats, and some reference to my ancestors' preference for sexual encounters with goblins and farm animals. After ten years in the APS, though, their attempts were, frankly, terrible.

I moved quickly, not bothering with stealth, as I ran, leaping from bracing to bracing, grinning over the fact that these cheap assholes had been so stupid as to armor only the lower sections, and leave what'd clearly been a high-vaulted ceiling as hidden.

I leapt onto the last section, judging that I was nearly there to the assholes, shotgun at the ready…and totally misjudged it. Crashing through the ceiling on the far side, I hit the far wall and bounced off, not even facing the right direction. I appeared behind the assholes, hit the wall…and fell down the stairwell.

"Fuuuuuck!" I screamed, pulling the trigger as I frantically twisted, firing the shotgun once and terminally injuring a defenseless poster on the subject of checking your nuts.

I hit the landing halfway down the stairs and rolled to absorb the impact, as I'd been trained.

That, of course, sent me bouncing down the second set of stairs, and the idiot above took off after me, as I screamed and swore.

I hit the wall at the bottom of the stairs. The world spun, and I forced myself to my feet, running straight ahead, trying to get to the nearest room and out of sight…

Only for my inner ear to inform me that left was actually straight ahead.

I crashed through the doors and into the main area of the guild, barely keeping my balance as my upgrades and training corrected my balance. Then I went ass over tit, tripping over one of the dead gangers.

I landed, rolled, and came to a stop under a table, which, when I tried to stand…ably that it was made of metal, and was bolted to the floor.

I barely got my shotgun poked out from the legs in time to take the first of the running figures in the face. The bolo round opened out to spin end over end.

It impacted in the lower right of his jaw, and practically decapitated the top half of his head. Blood sprayed up the walls as his body went from running with a purpose to sliding across the floor, pumping blood everywhere.

Others were right behind him, and I fired again and again. The dozen or so figures ran this way and that while firing back at me.

Bullets hit the table, the floor, and my armor. The automatic stiffening of it deflected the impact, but weakened the overall integrity each time.

I rolled, or tried to, hitting the leg on either side, before I got a message. A second later, a voice called out and silence fell.

"That's it, dickhead!" the voice said, and I recognized it as belonging to the fucker who'd not only stolen my handgun but had pissed on me. "Turrets are all activated. They're holding fire, waiting on my command, but there's no way you walk out of here."

"Wanna bet?" I grinned inside my helm. "I've done it before—I'll do it again!"

"Who the fuck are you?" he called back after a second. "Get out, leave your gun down there, and take that fucking helmet off!"

"You don't remember, eh?" I slowly dragged myself out from under the table, laying the shotgun on the top. I winced, rolling my shoulder. A round had hit there right atop another, and although the armor had held, it was gonna leave a hell of a bruise.

"Helmet!" the pisser screamed. "Take it off!"

"All right," I agreed, reaching up to my helmet as I accessed the new options that unfurled before me, mentally designating and approving as I went. "Look, I'm a generous guy," I lied. "I'm going to give you a chance to transfer any and all your creds to me right now. You do that, you leave your guns where they are, and maybe I'll let you live."

"Get fucked," the woman with the grazer rifle, a much smaller version than Reign's, but still nice, said with a vicious curl of the lip.

"Well, you can't say I didn't give you a chance," I said philosophically, before tossing my helmet aside, and smiling at them all. "Bang, bang, motherfuckers." I made finger-guns and pointed at the figures that half ringed the room.

There was a half second of frozen disbelief, and then the turrets, all eight of them, opened fire.

CHAPTER THIRTY-EIGHT

That was a memory I'd keep with me 'til the day I died.

The look of utter disbelief as their own turrets opened fire, every single one locked on a head; the armor-piercing, heavy rounds that they'd loaded the turrets with to protect them instead turned their brains to literal mince.

I sagged, allowing myself to sit on the edge of the nearby table and mentally reached out to the air lock, now available to me as the master of the security system. I triggered the emergency door and grinned as Gessh and Luna crawled up and out a few seconds later, guns at the ready, only to find me sitting, exhausted, surrounded by the dead.

"How's Reign?" Luna asked straightaway.

"I'm fine, thanks. How're you?" I muttered under my breath.

"I'm fine!" Reign called down from the stairwell, limping down it and looking around at us. The walls and ceiling literally dripped with blood as we looked at one another, unable to believe that not only had that crazy, shitty plan worked, but that we were still alive.

I queried the security system. The cameras outside showed two cashiers currently looting the unconscious figure of their boss in the alley behind the building. But besides that? No apparent interest from the outside world.

"We need to move fast," I said, categorically unable to accept that it'd worked as well as it had. "Something has to have gone wrong, so let's loot the fucking place, and get out."

"I'll take this floor…but not in here," Gessh said, and I snorted, looking over at the bodies.

"Yeah, fair point," I acknowledged. "I'll take in here."

"I've got the next floor," Luna said, tearing out after Reign, who'd called out that she'd get the armory.

I shook my head, not knowing nor caring who got where, just hoping that they'd not rip me off too badly, considering how new our little alliance was.

Instead, I set to with a will. My vibro-blade made quick work of the flesh that any decent mod was attached to, even as I set their guns, credit-chips, and more aside.

In ten minutes, I was done. My bag and a spare I'd looted from one of the bodies—collapsible, which was nice—were full of expensive replacement body parts. I'd dumped my shitty rifle, replacing it with a Centronics Five: solid, dependable, and with the capacity to fire mission-dependent rounds.

Anything from incendiary to high explosive, trackers, armor-piercing and smart rounds joined the standard old-fashioned slugs, and I loved it. It just "fit" me, looking pretty fucking evil and sleek.

The shotgun I kept. My old handgun was back on my hip, and I nodded to myself in satisfaction over that, mentally making a memo to recharge the damn grip later.

Beyond that? I had a couple of new toys: grenades, sticky-bombs, and that old favorite, the MADD grenade.

Monomolecular Area Denial Device – [MADD]	Tier: Three
The Monomolecular Area Denial Device, also referred to by its more familiar name of the MADD grenade, is both beloved of the deployer, and an unrivaled nightmare for those at the "business end."	
Upon deployment, the MADD grenade fires two hundred and thirty monomolecular wires in all directions. The maximum range of said wires is 20m, and each wire ends with a single expandable anchor. While powered (Mk1 MADD holds a maximum charge of 230A), the molecular wires give off a faintly discernable shimmer.	
This is the only warning your enemies will receive.	
Any contact with the wires by any form of flesh or any armor under a tier three minimum, is expected to be fatal. The MADD grenade has been banned in seven of the twelve states, and earned confirmed kill-counts of over one hundred and seventeen armored and enraged orcs in the Pelosian Conflict per grenade.	
Five more states have embraced the MADD and as such, supplies are highly limited, so purchase additional supplies as soon as possible using this link: [Redacted] and quote code [slaughter117] to receive a one-off discount of 0.3% against cases of 12 or more.	
Durability: 100/100	**Credit Cost**: 150

I held it uncertainly in my right hand, staring at it and trying to decide whether I wanted this fucking insane thing anywhere near me, or whether I should try to get more.

They'd been banned in more than the seven states that the company crap claimed. At last count, it was banned by anyone who had any fucking sense, after a faulty sensor batch resulted in over three hundred of these little darlings detonating after so much as a loud noise was made near them.

The monomolecular wires deployed via an explosive charge, firing in all directions and punching into the walls, floors, and people that were nearby on each occasion, killing thousands of people.

It wasn't the explosion that was the issue, although I'd imagine having one in your trouser pocket didn't feel that way.

It was that the wires were almost invisible, able to cut through tier one through three body armor and literal steel. *And,* as if those details weren't insane enough, for so long as the charge lasted, it was also electrified.

So much as touching a wire resulted in you shaking uncontrollably, which basically ensured you ended up shredded into tiny ribbons.

The original designer of the MADD grenade was brutally murdered by the relatives of the orcs he hired for "testing," and he'd damn well deserved it.

Not even goblins deserved that shit.

I'd pocketed it—gingerly, to be sure—but the way my life was? It was a hell of a weapon of last resort, and I'd damn well keep it for that just in case.

Besides, if it went off accidentally? I'd never know.

After twenty goddamn minutes, I rounded the others up. Reign was easy to find, wailing on a recessed safe, and screaming abuse.

She'd apparently tried to open it quietly, then loudly. Then she'd gathered some high explosives from the armory, and was making goddamn sure that it was pressed into each and every corner, nook, and cranny it could be.

I paused, staring at the utter mess of plastique, the wildly grinning Reign, and was about to point out that the way she'd done it? It wasn't going to work the way she wanted…when she winked at me and set it off.

Luna dragged me out from under the table a few minutes later, dusting me off and nodding, apparently pleased that I was intact—more or less—while I tried to speak through shock and apoplectic rage.

It was made worse by the minor detail that not only had Reign's jury-rigged explosives utterly failed to free the door, they had set off the booby trap that was waiting for anyone who tried to pick the lock.

That was what had picked me up and thrown me across the room. The backs of my legs had hit the front of a desk and flipped me over it, before it rolled atop me.

Whatever was stored in the "safe" was beyond looting now. Fuck, it was practically atomized. And where the firefights, the hacking, and frankly, the full-scale assault on the guild headquarters had gone unnoticed by the outside world pretty much?

The attempt at opening that fucking safe didn't.

Reign was being dusted down and having a medikit applied to the nape of her neck, as well as being handed towels to wipe the blood from her ears, nose, and mouth.

I was reminded of dealing with the idiots who had first graduated from basic training in the army, or worse, those goddamn first-week-out-of-training second lieutenants.

The utter idiots who didn't realize that, as they were right now? After completing the "training" modules that were literally designed by other officers? They had the real-world survivability and common sense of a baby duck, and one at that, that had already plucked itself, rolled in the marinade, and was contemplating the nice warm oven as somewhere for a lovely nap.

I glared at her, torn between the absolute desire to just up and shoot her, the need to keep her—because like it or not, I needed, and even liked her—and worst of all?

Knowing that she had potential, and I was now stuck with breaking her in.

At least now I knew one thing for sure that I'd meant to ask.

She was most likely a career merc, *not* ex-army.

Only one ex-army member in the known universe was suicidal enough to play with explosives like that, and thank the gods Michael Head wasn't here right now.

That fucker, I'd have had to shoot out of self-preservation, if he hadn't already proved himself to be nigh-on unkillable.

I shook myself, realizing that I was drifting and probably had my second concussion of the week, or a good dazing at least, and I forced myself to my feet.

"Okay…everyone okay?" I asked, getting nods from Luna and Gessh, and a confused look from Reign. "Fuck it, good enough."

"We got the upstairs sorted out, more or less," Luna told me, with Gessh nodding to a pair of bags by the door.

"We got some more mods and gear that was in a private safe upstairs, as well as tearing the back of the locker system. Idiots armored the front, then left it against a standard stone wall. Crowbar in, and boom, the lockers were free to loot." Gessh nodded in satisfaction. "You'd be amazed how many items of lacy underwear we found."

"And who was apparently wearing them," Luna added. "We're not judging, though. I mean, if the least likely guy in the room wants to wear lacy G-strings, more power to them."

"I don't want to know." I held up a hand as my mind filled with the images from a particular party we'd attended once.

Fergie's giant, red-bearded goliath of a frame squeezed into a latex dress was enough to have me needing therapy. Add in G-strings, and I'd rather shoot myself now than go on.

"You got everything then?" I asked, and Gessh nodded.

"Literally anything I could find. Left the shitty guns, took the good stuff. Got some specialist ammo as well. Couldn't carry everything, so just grabbed the best I could. Then I heard the explosion, so…" She shrugged, and I winced as a direct feed demand came through.

I pulled up the request, seeing it was from ACE, and I dismissed it, turning to the others. "Luna, anything we can salvage?" I nodded to the remains of the safe.

"Fuck all," she said disgustedly. "Must have been some serious explosives in there." She held up a handful of shattered and burned electronics and tossed them on the floor. "Judging from the sheer fucking number of these? At least fifty cred-chips as well as whatever else was in there."

"Fuck's sake, Reign!" I growled, looking at the dazed half-elf, before shaking my head. "Fuck it. Time to run. Grab what you got and let's get out of here."

"I'll bring Reign." Luna grunted, ducking under an outstretched arm and tossing the blonde woman over one shoulder with ease, as the rest of us started gathering her—and our—gear and loot.

A minute later, the demands for digital camera feed access became more strident by the second. ACE was attempting to insinuate a worm into the security system, and of course, some of the guild who had been out on jobs were banging on the front door, or contemplating the windows higher in the structure for access points.

We raced for the main room. The still-open air lock leading to the level below was obvious enough that if anyone did a real search, they'd find it. So instead of trying to hide it, I dragged the bodies over and pitched them through it unceremoniously.

They fell, crashing and splatting into the ground far below, before we started down the ropes that Gessh and Luna had put into place. The growls from whatever beast lived down here normally echoed around in warning as we appeared.

We ignored it, and I ordered the air lock to seal, then stopped it halfway, before setting the turrets to fire on anyone who arrived as an enemy. I triggered the "wipe" that Bowdoin had given me, removing all trace of us from the system, and we started to run.

The plan wasn't to conceal that we'd been there—there was no way that'd work. The building was on fire in places, the entire upper management had been slaughtered, the vault destroyed and the armory raided.

Most telling of all, the various assholes had not only had their weapons nicked, but they'd been stripped for parts.

In dumping their bodies through the air lock into the undercity, though, it exposed that they'd been disposing bodies that way for simply forever. Add in that the undercity was full of specters? Well. The mods being stripped gave a nice, simple explanation for the ACE, should they want it.

Asshole mercs disposed of people into the undercity; one day they opened the hole, and something came up instead of going down. They got slaughtered, specters killed everyone and set off the explosives; they took the weapons and mods, and fucked off.

It was a shitty explanation. It really was. My intention had been that I'd hide the air lock as much as possible, and hide the bodies down here still, then open the back door, and leave them to make their own decisions.

ACE would have turned up, found the staff wandering around trying to make sense of things, and they'd have promptly arrested them all on the grounds that the best police work involved the least effort on their part.

As it was, that would result in the staff being slaughtered by their own automated turrets, so I left the doors locked, leaving that surprise for the ACE assholes, as they'd no doubt break in as soon as they could, intending to loot the place while "securing the evidence."

One good turn deserves another, after all, and ACE members deserved summary judgment in a way few others did, in my experience.

Now they'd have to fight their way past the turrets and so on, then find that "something" came up from beneath, then probably fucked off that way again.

They'd have to decide whether they wanted to go searching in the depths themselves or whether they wanted to close the case.

I bet on the latter.

Either way, though, we hurried along the narrow passages, clambering up and down where we needed to, and essentially followed the same path I'd followed days earlier, and that Luna and Gessh had traveled to get here, using my RI to produce a map.

"I still say you got it easy," I grunted to Luna as I helped her up onto a platform a few minutes later.

She laughed, clapping me on the shoulder.

"We did, more or less. A handful of specters were wandering about and we hit them, then dumped them underneath the opening, scaring off the cave dragon and..."

"The what?"

"Cave dragon," she repeated. "Ah, crap, I've got no idea what they're really called, but we always called them cave dragons. They're big damn lizards with pointy teeth that live in a cave. What else would I call it?"

"Point." I shrugged, not really interested enough to give a fuck beyond that it wasn't chasing us. We'd moved around it, then fucked off as it jealously guarded its pile of bodies, making sure there was even less evidence to tie us to this, as it feasted.

The trip to the surface took over an hour, made insanely easier by the combination—once Reign was on her feet—of none of us being injured seriously, all being able to see, and all being healthy and heavily armed.

The few specters, creatures, and random vagrants we bumped into either ran for it, attacked and were mowed down, or backed away slowly.

By the time we got out of the undercity, we were all a lot happier, and a short while later, we were in the lift at my apartment block.

"Why here, though?" Luna squinted out over the city as the lift rose. "I mean, why'd the army put you up here?"

"That captain I need to go see later?" I tried to keep the bitterness out of my voice.

"Yeah?"

"Well, he fucked me over, massively. He's why my friends died, and I got so badly fucked up. Then he pulled a fast one and charged me for the loss of the suit, the helo, everything, right the fuck up to the maximum."

"What do you mean, charged you?"

"Corpos brought it in three years back," I explained. "You do something that fucks the mission up, like massively so? They can charge you a percentage of the cost of the losses. It's never really used, as all you do is counter the claim with your records, and if you weren't in the wrong? The cost of the claim is added to the accusing officer."

"So why'd he do it?"

"He knew that I had classified shit on my recording, and that I'd wiped all other sources of evidence—on orders—and that the only version of it was being given to his boss, so I couldn't appeal it, not without sharing classified recordings."

"And if you did that?"

"Then all earnings, etc., while in service would be deducted from my balance, and I'd have been sold as an indentured soldier to the regular army, used on the front lines, serving a life sentence."

I growled that last bit out, having only realized this afternoon just how neatly I'd been stitched up, and having gone even deeper into my hatred for Tyrannus than before.

That fucker's last hours were going to be painful.

"He did all of that because he gained twenty percent of the creds recovered from me, and then he basically sold my fucking suit out from under me. That I had a month's rent agreed to be paid somewhere by some corpo scumbag? He picked the shittiest and cheapest place possible. Believe me, that shitbird is going to pay for this."

"Glad to hear it," she replied, nodding. "I'd hate to think you let that kind of thing slide."

"Oh, don't worry," I said with a cold smile. "By tomorrow, you're going to know exactly who and what I am, as well as what I'm capable of."

"Yeah, or we're all gonna be dead," Reign offered, getting a snort from Gessh.

"Sister, you nearly killed us all with your stupidity back there, not to mention fucking us over for the creds…"

"Hey, how the hell was I supposed to know that they had the safe booby-trapped?" Reign growled, and I shook my head as the pair of them launched into an argument over "common sense" and "limited time" and more.

I stared out the window, watching the pounding rain, the dark skies and wondering whether we could really, genuinely do everything we needed to in a day.

We had until tonight to get the armor rerouted, the major had said. Literally tonight. *Was that midnight? Was that by sunrise?* Fuck, I didn't know. I just— *Wait, he'd said fourteen hours, right?* Fuck it.

I needed to do it. I needed to get the thirty thousand, and the only way I was going to do that was by doing the jobs for Lucky, sell the mods, and the spare guns, and claim the bounties.

Most likely, the only way we'd get the thirty thousand that Bowdoin was demanding was by killing Stinger. That was worth two-fifty, after all.

The only way we'd take down a professional assassin? Superior firepower and equipment, not to mention surprise.

The only way to get those? We needed to hit the merc guild for decent gear, then we needed Lucky to share the target location with us. He would only do that when his other jobs were done, so we were down to running around like our asses were on fire as we tried to fit everything in.

The lift made its strangled attempt at a *ding* as we reached our destination. The ancient speakers, long since defaced, let loose that classic fart note that hung in the air longer than anything not related to a dodgy meal possibly could.

"Oh, this is such a classy place." Luna groaned, disgusted, as the doors opened, the music of yet another party washing over us all.

"Urgh!" some dumb socialite complained as the smell rolled off the four of us—we had been traveling through abandoned sewers and worse, not to mention some of us being covered in blood and burnt by explosions—and I snorted my disgust in turn at the creature before me.

They'd gone in heavily for the body mods: feline ears atop their head, three tits—because hey, like any guy needs three hands—and judging from the literally sprayed-on glitter and lack of any clothing, they'd given themselves a full hermaphrodite workover.

I didn't care what sexuality they were: male, female, they, them, toaster oven—people could literally be whatever gender or identity they wanted these days. It made no difference to me. What I didn't like?

That they were standing in high heels that must be twenty centimeters high, naked apart from glitter, and they were swinging a goddamn horse-cock around directly in front of me.

"More fucking orcs! That's it. We're leaving this party," the dumbass snapped, bouncing before us and deliberately drawing the eye.

Gessh took it worse than I did, though. Apparently that the disgust was in part due to her and her sister being half-orcs, she made her feelings known.

That she made it known by punting the fucker between the legs as hard as possible? Well. They were lifted a good half meter off the ground. And when they landed?

The only sound they made was clearly filled with pain.

"Let's go see Lucky!" I smiled, deliberately ignoring Luna squatting down to have a "little conversation" with the downed partygoer, one foot on the tip of their cock.

People got the fuck out of our way quickly.

Possibly due to the furious look on Gessh's face. Or possibly because we were armed to the fucking teeth, and she'd just punted someone into the middle of next week.

Either way, when we met Lucky on the far side, sprawled on a new, larger, and clearly more expensive couch, he nodded in greeting, paying markedly more attention to Reign, Luna, and Gessh than I was used to getting from him.

"So…you ladies here to join the party?" he asked, and Gessh snorted.

"We're half-orcs, we're not welcome," she said, getting a frown from Lucky, who finally turned to me, one eyebrow raised in question, his own lantern jaw and parentage clear.

"One of your guests made their revulsion clear at our species," Luna said flatly, rejoining us.

"They still alive?" Lucky's brow lowered as he peered around us.

"For now." Gessh shrugged. "They'll not be fucking for a while, though."

"Fucking?"

"They had a horse-cock and—"

"Calos," Lucky growled. "Fucking Calos!" He gestured and two of the gangers were moving already, before he turned back to the group. "My apologies, ladies…and Kabutt. Here, beers are on me…" He gestured to a couch to one side; a few others already sitting there got up hurriedly and moved, and I snorted, recognizing it as his old one.

"We're not here for the party." I pulled one of the bags out, then dumped it on the floor before him, getting a glare from Lucky as I did. "That's the debt square."

He snorted. "I say when the debt's done, Kabutt," he growled, going from inviting to aggressive in a heartbeat. "You still owe me for—"

"One more hit and two chemists," I agreed, nodding to him. "Send me the details now, and anything you have on the final hit."

"You'll get that when you're done with—"

I cut him off, as one of his partners, the woman who had checked the drugs, slid the bag aside, looking in.

"Send me everything, Lucky. You've got six hours. Then I'm leaving the city. You want the job done before I go? Send it to me."

"The fuck you are. You owe me—" he snarled.

I nodded to the bag.

"I owe you a hundred grand in mods. There's twice that there. Consider the rest a deposit for when I return. I'll be gone about three weeks…" I was making it all up on the spot, but I'd just realized that if I didn't give him a reason to, when I tried to get the info off him later? He could be drugged up to the eyeballs and unable to share it.

"But when I come back? That's when this little deal gets renegotiated."

"Uh-huh." He sneered, glancing to the side and doing a double take as his partner pulled one of the four arms that I'd put in his bag out.

It was a standard Nemesis #5, nicer than the one I had in place, but of fucking course, it was a right arm again, and I didn't feel like losing my own for shits and giggles just to chip that.

The girls had agreed that any mods we ripped were to go toward paying off my debts, and all the weapons, armor, and ammo were to be sorted out between us fairly.

I had no doubt that they'd each pocketed a little something, at the least. I'd said nothing about the replacement of their personal guns with much better ones, and that when we quickly sorted shit out in the car, none of those guns were put in the loot "to be shared" pile.

That was fine, though; we still had plenty, and I'd done the same.

The Nemesis #5 was, obviously, several versions higher than the basic model I had on my arm, incorporating some seriously shit-hot autotargeting and integration options that I just didn't have.

It was also a tier-three mod, as were the forearm replacement and the eyepiece.

Just those three when I'd checked them out, I was confident would be over a hundred grand in any chop shop. Add in the full set of synth organs, the lower legs—short-range jump-jets included—and the integrated deck in the left forearm?

Two hundred was achievable, if at a push.

That wasn't my problem, though. I was heavily armed, and clearly about to kill people if this went badly, and so were my friends.

That gave Lucky enough of a reason to pause. And when he checked the gear? It was clear that it was more than he'd invested in me by a good ways.

I'd kept a few mods back, and they were going to go to Lion, if I could get things sorted later. But for now? Lucky was left with two choices.

He could get pissy, and we possibly start the fight a little early. Or he could play nice, get me to do the jobs he wanted doing, and then kill us, as I was betting he'd always intended on doing.

As soon as he smiled widely, spreading his hands in a "well, what can I do" gesture, I knew I was on the money.

"Fine. We're partners here, after all, Kabutt. No reason to be like that! Here…"

He sent me a datafile, and my RI checked it for viruses and so on, before running it.

Three locations popped up, one on the floor a few above the one we were on, deep in the market level again. The other two were higher, just over a dozen floors higher, and all three came with images, letting me be very sure of the target.

JOB: UPDATE!

Kabutt will carry out five [5] contract hits for Lucky, including and limited to the following:
- 2 x Standard Assassinations:
  - [~~Lilith, Floor 72 — Terminated~~]
  - [Sirisena, Floor 85 – Location attached]
- 2 x Chemist lab raids
  - [Lilith's Lab – Location attached]
  - [Sirisena's Lab – Location attached]
- 1 x Assassination of [Stinger]

Supplemental:
1 x Recover 100,000 credits worth of Specter Mods

In exchange Kabutt has received:
- 47,500 x direct credit transfer
- 30,000 x store credit for Lion's Chop Shop
- ? x Additional bounties
- 4 x gang members will be dispatched to Kabutt's choice of location to act as a distraction

---

Job Accepted

"It's the lab you want—the physical location, or the chemist?" I asked, and he snorted, shaking his head and looking at me like I was an idiot.

"The chemist, obviously," he said flatly.

The data before me updated as he said it to reflect that.

"You fucking said the lab." I shrugged, uncaring, before storing them and setting waypoints, before speaking.

"And the last one?"

"You do those first, and then I'll send it to you," he promised. "But six hours? You'll never get it all done in that time. And Kabutt? I may be pretty as an angel, but I ain't one. You try skipping out without doing those jobs…"

"I'll hit your fucking jobs, don't worry." I turned and led the others through the darkness of the floor toward my apartment.

CHAPTER THIRTY-NINE

"So…this is the little love nest, eh?" Gessh muttered, looking around my tiny, shitty apartment, and I snorted.

"Yeah. It's just wonderful, isn't it."

"It's…memorable." Luna kicked at the end of the couch. "I don't think I've ever been somewhere that made our place look like a step up, not that still had four walls *and* a roof, anyway."

"Don't ask about the stains on the couch." Reign sighed. "He insisted I was on it, and you know, when one thing led to another…"

She broke off, bouncing her eyebrows a little, and Luna and Gessh looked at the couch, noting various stains I'd ignored, having never paid that much attention to it.

"It's true," I agreed, picking my bag up and dumping it on the couch. "Those stains are from last night…from where Reign drooled and farted all night long. Now, if you're all done with slagging my place off, how about we sort this gear?"

"I guess I see why you were so happy to agree to us all getting a place somewhere now," Gessh muttered, and I sighed, mumbling that they weren't supposed to figure that shit out yet, playing along.

There was a general low level of snorts and laughter, and that quickly broke up when I pulled out the guns.

"We've got three targets to hit, each of which is likely to have a little loot as well, but the good gear? It'll be with the assassin, I bet."

"Everything from mines to turrets, sniping gear and stealth suits," Reign agreed, all business again. "He's a legend, and there's no way he'd have shitty gear."

"So we sort ourselves out now, gear up as if we're not coming back here. We take them down, and any loot we take? If it's worth stashing, then we can come back. If not, we've got a lot to do tonight, and we return here before going after the assassin."

"So load up, but keep it light," Luna quipped, nodding.

"Basically," I agreed. "I'd suggest we collect like equipment together first, then kit up…it'll make it easier."

"Shotguns on the bed." Gessh pulled three out of her bag and dumped them on the bed, passing an assault rifle to Luna, who dumped it on the couch, as we emptied bags.

It only took a few minutes, most of which was spent sorting ammo out as much as anything else, as we'd grabbed a shitload of magazines as well as the actual weapons, and they'd all gotten jumbled up together.

In the end, though, the loadout was good for all of us.

I had my MADD grenade, which the others had stared at in horror as I explained about it, taking it out to show them. They'd all backed the fuck up at that point, despite my protestations that they were safe, as it was either from a "decent" batch, or we'd already all be dead.

That wasn't apparently happy making, though, so I moved straight along.

I had two flash-bangs, two frags, and a sticky, as well as the MADD, and the others all had roughly the same. Luna and Gessh went for a single flash, but three frags each, and Reign went for the single recon grenade, the EMP, and the last two flashes.

We also had an incendiary. But on closer inspection, the damn seal on it was rusty as fuck, and we decided to leave that alone, putting it in the gun cabinet. My spare ammo and the other shotgun and shitty rifle came out as well, and were added to the mix.

My automatic shotgun—it could be fired on full auto or single shot, and I loved it—stayed with me, with a few more fléchettes and slug rounds taking me back up to full on both magazines for it.

Gessh and Luna had both bought shotguns yesterday, and they kept those, along with their swords—I had my vibro-blade as well as the hatchet—and all three of us had rifles as well.

For me, it wasn't so bad. The assault rifle was a bullpup design, compact and fucking lethal, but being a Centronics Five, it was fucking beautiful as well. There were a dozen aftermarket mods for it: the stock could be lengthened, the barrel replaced, and the receiver upgraded, then a new set of optics and you had anything from a machine gun to a fucking sniper rifle, all off the same base model.

I'd used them in the army before I qualified for APS, and it'd only been the Centronics Two we'd had. We'd loved them, though, and I made it clear as I set it down by my side—not with the other guns—that it was *mine*.

Luna had taken a pair of submachine guns, both with great long banana mags in them, a nice chest rig that held four more mags, and her shotty cradled in her arms, with the subs going one under each arm.

Gessh went for the grazer rifle, much to Reign's disappointment, but it was only fair really. It only had a single reload for the grazer, but with two hundred shots per mag, that was fine.

She also took the unsubtle hand cannon I'd looted from Lilith's bodyguard, and I nodded my blessing for it.

I had my own hurricane revolver back again after all, and it was currently plugged into the wall, merrily charging.

Last but not least was Reign. Her dual sniper rifles—the grazer and her original slug—were insane enough on the slim half-elf, but the chest rig with the grenades hanging from it made it clear she was all business, as did the twin Styx suppressed auto pistols.

They were fléchette pistols, crap for any long-range targets, but she had the rifles for that, admittedly. The fléchettes magazines each held a hundred individual darts, short steel fuckers that were fired at a horrific speed.

They were useless at anything over about twenty meters, their stabilizing fins being susceptible to wind, magnetism, and more. But if you were up close and someone unloaded one of those fuckers? They'd clear a room.

All in all, we were armed to the teeth. We had some spare ammo—not much, but enough, we agreed, considering we were after gangers.

The armor we'd looted was less impressive. I'd improved on my gloves, replacing my main body armor that was starting to give out with a full front and back dragon-scale design that ran halfway down my arms, ending at the elbows for some reason, and a long, cool as fuck-looking laser-resistant trench coat.

The mirrored finish it needed for that was less impressive, making me look like I might be on my way to a fucking party, rather than a slaughter, but hey.

The girls upgraded to full-face helmets with integrated optics, and new boots that they'd liked. And Reign…well, she swore blind that she was happy with her current gear. That might have been something to do with the armored chainmail top that Gessh was trying to get her to try on, but the comment that there was no way it could defend, while covering basically her nipples only, was a fair one.

Upon closer examination, it was found to be a shield projector, so it was actually a damn good bit of armor, all things considered. But because of the way these things worked, anything that broke the field would drain the battery, therefore, yeah, it needed to be set against bare flesh.

I actually considered it when she offered it to me, thinking that if I wore it under my armor, and powered it only at the worst part of the fight, it might last long enough to do some good.

Then I reconsidered, based purely on the suggestion from Luna that she was sure there was a matching thong option. I'd never live it down, going into battle in essentially a chainmail bikini, regardless of how effective or useful it might be.

We looked at one another, and there was silence for a long few seconds, before I spoke.

"Look, seriously, I know this isn't what you signed up for," I said. "You've all got your own shit, and yeah, while this helps us all? It's me who gains the most from it, and I can't even promise you my share of the creds, as I damn well need them for the last stage tonight.

"I guess…I guess what I'm trying to say is that if you want to walk away now? No hard feelings. I totally understand." I paused, and all three kept staring at me, as I smiled ruefully.

"Well, thank you," I said. "We're a team—you're all risking your asses for me, and I'll do the same for you."

"Well, look, boss, you're making it sound like it's all altruism here, but let's be honest," Reign said with a faint quirk of her lips. "I'm a homeless bum, with little chance of a normal team. Since I joined you, I got my grazer, which I wanted for like *foreverrrr*." She drew the last word out long, and batted her eyelashes, fanning herself with one hand while the others laughed. "I mean, be still my beating heart! If this thing had a vibrator optional attachment? I'd marry it."

"And we're…well." Luna grunted, shrugging.

"You've never been a dick about who and what we are," Gessh said. "You gave us a chance, and yeah, this isn't what the damn guild was advertising the job as, but we're mercs. You're offering us what could be a serious payday. That it might not come off and we might all die? That's kinda part of the territory."

"Thank you all." I nodded to them, then gathered up the guns that were left over and stacked them as well as I could in the gun safe.

It said a lot that although the apartment came with fuck all furnishings, it'd come with a built-in gun safe, and that after less than a week of living here, the one thing that was getting real use wasn't the shower—it'd had normal use, but you know—nor the bed. It was the gun safe.

It was also full, and I left a handful of rifles on the bed, along with some ammo, and took the last of the mods—ones I wasn't giving to Lucky but taking direct to Lion as soon as I could—into a bag, before forcing the safe's lock to engage.

That done, I turned to the others again.

"Okay then." I grinned. "Only a few floors up, and we get to go shoot some drug dealers in the face."

"Ah, the simple pleasures in life!" Reign quipped, before bowing low and gesturing to the door. "Lead on, good sir!"

"Fucking elves…" I muttered, deliberately loud enough for the others to hear it. "Dramatic to the end…"

"Your end certainly," Reign joked, eyeing my ass, and I groaned, popping the door and walking out without another word.

The trip along the corridors was silent. As much as the joking had made us all feel a little less on edge, the reality was that we were walking into a firefight, and that there was a good chance some, if not all of us, would die tonight.

We'd done all we could, in terms of gear, planning, and mental readiness, to mitigate that risk, but when all we had was a random location tag, there wasn't much we could do with planning.

We were in the lift, when the first bit of good news I'd had in literally ages dropped into my lap, followed by some bad.

"Kabutt," Lucky said, the call having come literally seconds after the doors to the lift closed. The fucker laid there, sprawled across his couch, a blanket draped over him as he relaxed, ignoring us. The crossed legs that peeked out of the bottom of the blanket suggested that he was doing anything but "relaxing."

I'd seen it, seen the way he was laying, with his eyes almost—but not quite—shut and I'd known damn well he wanted us to interrupt, to ask a question, anything, just so he could tell us to fuck off.

Instead, we'd treated him with the respect he deserved, and totally ignored him, marching past the few people still hanging around, and dragging a pair of doped-up idiots out of the lift and tossing them onto the floor as we climbed in.

"What do you want?" I asked Lucky, glancing at his image, and getting a hurt look from him.

"I bring news, and I wanted to wish you good luck, that's all."

"Go," I replied flatly.

"Sirisena, your second target, is involved in the supply of drugs for five floors…" He paused, and when I said nothing, he shrugged and moved on. "He's currently attacking the last of Lilith's guards on the market floor, and it looks like he's going to take the chemist. If you're quick, you can take him from behind."

"Not my favorite, but serviceable," I admitted. "Question."

"Yeah?"

"What'll he do with the chemist?"

"What?"

"The chemist, their kit and all that shit—what'll they do with them?"

"He'll take them back to the eighty-fifth floor and add them to his team, take the gear, set it all up and make them start producing. Why?"

"Will they go straight there after taking the guards out?"

"Probably…They'll not know who to trust, so rather than watch over the entire floor, they'll have some gonk ready to load it all up, then they'll run back to their base. They'll be expecting you or someone else to hit them, so you better move fast…"

"Nope," I said firmly, as the lift farted and slowed. The doors started to open. On the other side, I could see dozens, if not hundreds, of people sprinting for the doors. The reaction when they started to open, to show a bunch of heavily armed and armored mercs?

People tried to go from full forward sprint to backward in the same second, with the result that dozens of them simply hit the floor, bouncing, tripping, and screaming.

Distant echoing gunfire could be heard, and I surprised the others by reaching out and pressing the button for the eighty-fifth floor instead.

"I thought…" started Reign, only for Lucky to speak over her, his voice in my ear thanks to the call, and so I responded to them all at once.

"Look, they're here, taking all the shit they want, which is great. But that means they're not where their chemist is. They've split their forces, and they're out in the open.

"We need to get their chemist and the one from this floor, then Saracen…?"

"Sirisena." Lucky corrected with a growl.

"Yeah, fine. *Sirisena* is going to return home soon. No point in fighting them here, then going for their base, and having to make two trips with everything. Far better we hit their base, secure their chemist and all their shit, as well as their supplies, then we kill them when they come back."

"You're evil," Reign said after a few seconds. "You know it won't be that easy. They'll warn Sirisena as soon as we attack them."

"They will," I agreed. "The difference is that Sirisena will have to either abandon the new chemist and gear, which they probably won't want to risk, or they'll bring them along. We let them bring them—we get all the loot, we get the chemist brought to us, and we save time overall."

"It's…it's ballsy, but it's a sound plan," Luna said, and the others agreed, smiles all around.

"So…you said there was news. That it?" I asked Lucky, only to get a shake of the head.

"Not all of it. I sent the details for the gear you brought tonight to Oshbob. He wants to meet you."

"That's nice," I said, having no interest in meeting him at the minute. I needed this deal with Lucky to be well and truly dealt with first, and to approach the orc from a position of strength.

"Ten tomorrow morning at his place. I'm to take you," he said, and I glared at him.

"I leave in six hours."

"You said that an hour ago."

"I meant five."

"Bullshit."

"Watch me be gone in six hours."

"You better not be," Lucky growled, and I smiled at him.

"Tell you what?" I purred. "I'll stay for the meeting…"

"That's be—"

"As long as we survive the encounter with Stinger anyway."

"Fuck…No, that's not gonna work."

I snorted. "Lucky, I'm doing that job, or I leave tonight. Your options are you risk Oshbob being pissed because I leave and he can take that out on you, or being really happy because I take down Stinger."

"Kabutt…" Lucky growled.

I forced myself not to laugh, knowing the position he was in right now. He either accepted me claiming that bounty and then going to see Oshbob, who was almost certainly going to cut Lucky out of the deal from now on, or he hit me after all and let Oshbob be pissed.

"I'll make it easier for you…*partner*," I said, drawing the word out. "I'm going after that bounty tonight because I need a hundred thousand in creds. If you want me to not go after Stinger? You transfer that over, and you can explain why later. If not? Then I'm going after Stinger, and when I kill him, I'll have extra mods to sell to Oshbob, as we agreed the rifle and his head was yours, nothing else. So tomorrow, either I'll be there with Stinger's mods for Oshbob, or I'll be dead, or I'll be gone. You pick. Now I need to go, so make your mind up fast."

I cut the connection, the last sight of Lucky the rage in his eyes, and I nodded, speaking to the girls quietly.

"I'm betting he's going to—" A final datapacket came through from Lucky. Stinger's location, under the fucking arcology, six floors down by the main reactor. "Well," I said slowly, sharing the details with the others. "I guess that means no explosives then, and it's game on."

JOB: UPDATE!

Kabutt will carry out five [5] contract hits for Lucky, including and limited to the following:

- 2 x Standard Assassinations:
  - [~~Lilith, Floor 72 – Terminated~~]
  - [Sirisena, Floor 85 – Location attached]
- 2 x Chemist lab raids
  - [Lilith's Lab – Location attached]
  - [Sirisena's Lab – Location attached]
- 1 x Assassination of [Stinger – Location attached]

Supplemental:

~~1 x Recover 100,000 credits worth of Specter Mods~~

In exchange Kabutt has received:

- ~~47,500 x direct credit transfer~~
- ~~30,000 x store credit for Lion's Chop Shop~~
- ? x Additional bounties
- ~~4 x gang members will be dispatched to Kabutt's choice of location to act as a distraction~~

Job Accepted

"All the way, boss," Luna said.
I looked at her, only to hear the strangled attempt at a fart ring out again.
"I swear, if that's the last sound I hear, I'm coming back to haunt you all."
Luna growled, and I grinned, unseen in my helmet.
"Okay, kids." I took a deep breath. "Game faces on."

CHAPTER FORTY

The doors opened onto a surprisingly pleasant floor, clearly better maintained than those lower, and even well lit, with signs showing the location of the various important locations—security offices, the floor's single shop and the delivery room, as well as laundry and the "management suite"—all clear on the map.

"Where we going, boss?" Reign asked, and I grunted.

"Reign, you've got the rear. Luna left. Gessh right. I lead." I stepped out into the hallway, noting the subtle dome that twitched in the corner.

I tagged it mentally and sent it to the others. My RI took the photo, classing it as a "Rover-16 perimeter defense model" of recessed turret.

There were others as we started to walk, and I got an uncontrollable urge to grin.

"Try not to take out too many of the turrets if we have to," I said quietly.

"You crazy, boss?" Luna asked, and I reached into a pocket, pulling free the little hacking tool that Bowdoin had given us earlier.

They were single-use devices, each keyed to my ID, and once they were triggered, they were wiped. The ID that this and the guild hall one used was my fake corpo ID, making it even more amusing as I imagined ACE arguing over whether they dared to pester a corpo over such a thing.

Yeah, some guild had been wiped out, and probably some ACE as well, but this was a *corpo*. They'd know it almost certainly wasn't that person who was involved, but hopefully that'd be their only lead. And I loved the thought of those assholes shitting themselves over who'd be sent to ask the questions.

"Oh, that's just evil." Reign laughed, and I nodded, slipping it back into a pocket.

"So, security office it is," Luna commented, pausing and checking the map on one wall. "It's here…Does that match your location?"

I paused, checking my internal map and using the RI to overlay it on the map, before grunting. "Manager's office," I replied. "It's the room next to it."

"Probably keeps it nice and close," Reign agreed.

A ping sounded, and I glanced at an unknown connection request.

I almost refused it. My RI was set to refuse them generally, unless it came from a military ID, a locally geo-locked ID—so it was tagged as coming from somebody next to me; that way, if it was a shitty sales call, I could smash their face in—or answer if I was clearly expecting a call.

Otherwise, if I didn't know the ID, it was automatically refused. No need to permit spam about my car's extended warranty, after all.

This one, though…it showed as a restricted ID, so someone was hiding their identity, and yet was close enough to bypass my settings.

I opened it.

A middle-aged man glared at me, speaking quickly. "Listen, fuckface, turn around, and get off my floor." Sirisena—presumably—snarled. "I won't tell you again."

"That's not very friendly." I nodded to the others and walked toward the security office.

"Fuck your friendly shit," he growled. "I know who you are."

"And who am I?"

"You're the orc's new hitman."

"Uh…no," I said firmly.

"Really? So you didn't kill Lilith?" he asked sarcastically.

"Technically? No, I didn't."

"So you didn't have your pet sniper—who's that elf, I'm betting—do it then?"

"Oh, my sniper totally shot her in the head," I admitted. "She was a bitch, though. I went to ask her some questions, and she threatened me. Guess how that ended for her?"

"You think you can do the same to me, boy? You think I'm as dumb as Lilith? You're in the crosshairs of five turrets right now. One word from me, and you're all dead."

"Give it then."

"You think I won't?" he growled. "Get the fuck off my floor!"

"I think if you had five turrets, you'd have already opened up, not the three I've seen so far," I pointed out. "I think you're running, desperate to get here before I burn your lab down and kill your chemist."

"Don't you fucking dare!" Sirisena snarled, practically frothing at the mouth. "You fucking know what I'll do to you if you touch him?"

"I'm hoping your threats will be better than Lucky's were, but feel free to go for it."

There was a pause as he tried to make sense of that, before he responded a few seconds later.

"You're not working for the orc?"

"Which one?" I asked. "I mean, I know a lot of orcs…"

"You're working for Lucky?"

"Not so much," I hedged. "I occasionally take a contract for him, if that's what you mean."

"A hundred meters, boss," Luna said softly. "Next intersection, we take a right, then the next left…that's the security office."

"Well, I'd love to stay on the line and chat, but there's a problem with that."

"Which is?"

"You're boring me. Run, little man, run." I cut him off and blacklisted the local node he'd called through. My RI identified the ID that had been relaying the signal, and I blocked that as well. Then I cursed.

The RI had linked to the local subnet to ID them, and it picked up more IDs, a *lot* more.

"Boss…" Reign called out as doors opened farther down the corridor, both behind and ahead of us.

"Fuck! RUN!" I barked, seeing the turret on the wall ahead shudder then spin up, a small dome atop a cylinder that slid half a meter out of the wall. A pair of gun barrels extended and swiveled toward us.

"Lucky, you asshole!" I shouted, unthinkingly, as dozens of people stepped into view, guns tracking.

Reign had her sniper rifle over her shoulder, with the grazer in her arms, and faced back down the corridor. She dragged the rifle from left to right slowly, trigger held down, burning through half the battery loadout in a single evil crackle of energy. But the effect?

Grazers, or gamma-ray lasers, destroyed unshielded flesh and electronics alike. The solid beam that she dragged across the corridor at roughly chest height killed easily seven people, and it could have been several times that, considering that the walls in here barely attenuated the beam.

Screams rose, even as I locked in on the turret, firing off three armor-piercing rounds, shredding the dome and camera. The gun got off only a single shot that staggered me slightly. The dragon scale of my left shoulder armor—under the laser reflective trench coat—was damaged, but besides a curse dragged from my lips, I was all right.

Gessh let rip with the grazer assault rifle. The crackle of atomic reactions as she fired off thirty shots into the corridor in half a second was enough to make her grunt in surprise.

Luna pumped her shotgun and filled the air with fléchettes, making people scream—those who Gessh hadn't literally fried—and we raced forward, the corridor blurring as the fight began.

The corridor itself was nothing special: shitty plastic linoleum or fake stone or whatever it was covered the ground, and raised up the wall a few centimeters, with the wall from there a solid grey color. Doors stood offset from each other— one on the left, then the right, then the left—and every twenty meters or so, another turret.

I could see that next one drawing a bead now, and I raised my rifle. The targeting suite in the rifle—fuck, I loved Centronics gear—was already linked automatically to my eyes, providing a slightly disorienting, but damn useful third point of perspective.

If I'd never worked with anything like this? It'd probably have thrown me off. I'd used them before, though, for years at a time, and to make sure I got used to it, I'd been using the scope in the lift to check out Reign's ass.

Life was all about the little bonuses, after all.

Right now, I zeroed in and fired again, single shot this time, one hitting after the other. *Slow is smooth; smooth is fast.*

The bullets slammed into the delicate housing for the electronics in the next turret, punching clear through. Then the point of aim adjusted, sliding down as a bearded face appeared around the corner ahead, shotgun raised and trigger pulled already.

Fléchettes sliced the air, passing each other in a blur as both he and Luna fired. My rifle barked; the armor-piercing round took him in the right cheek and exited the back of his head, sending him spinning in a shriek of blood and shattered bone.

Others appeared, left and right, and I sprinted, skidding, and kicked off, jumping and planting one foot on the wall. I leapt; two bullets passed by my right, missing entirely, before a third hit someone following me. I heard a strangled curse from Luna or Gessh, and then the crackle of the grazer and screams, followed by the painful electrical hum of Reign firing on full beam again.

More screams rose, and I sighted. Two half-goblin-looking fuckers raced out of a room with knives…I fired and moved on.

To stay still here was to invite death—there was no two ways about it. We were in the corridors, with almost no cover, and a fuckload of people we weren't expecting coming for us.

The next left was only a dozen meters away, and I yanked one of my flash-bangs free of my chest, ripping the restraining bolt free in one smooth motion and bank-shotting it off the edge of the adjoining corridor, headed in the opposite direction. It clattered, bouncing out of sight and to the right, even as I continued to slide my rifle right, lining up on the next figure in line: a screaming drug addict, most of his teeth missing as he sprinted at me, right hand held behind his back.

I pulled the trigger, almost without thinking, my natural—well, augmented, but fuck it—eyes tracking to the next in line even as the gun sight remained on him, making sure he was hit before moving. I crashed to the floor, taking two quick strides before throwing myself onto my back as the door to my right opened and a shotgun swung out.

It fired. The boom of a scattershot filled the air as a thousand tiny pellets took the already dead and tumbling back druggie in the side, hurling him into the far wall.

I rolled, trusting those behind me to get the fucker with the shotgun as I popped back to my feet, presenting my back to the door. My skin crawled and the hairs on the back of my neck lifted in terror as I forced myself to stay on target.

I fired twice more at the fuckers who appeared around the corner. The one on the left's black body armor caught and stopped my shots, but sent him staggering.

Cursing, I fired again, this time flicking the selector to triple shot, and took him in the shoulder, upper chest, and neck.

He flew sideways, blood spraying as his friend leveled a rifle at me and opened fire. The bullets were standard, not armor-piercing, but fuck they hurt as he took me in the chest on full auto.

I dove sideways, hitting the floor and rolling, releasing my new rifle on instinct, the roll pressing the rifle flat against me on the floor as I ripped my handgun free.

I came to my feet, handgun booming, even as the flash-bang went off. The massive sensory overload package was deafening and blinding anyone without protection.

That was most of them.

The floor seemed to be full of gangers. Not like Lucky's floor that had a few dozen—here it seemed like fucking hundreds were coming from all sides. But what they gained in enthusiasm and apparent crack and angel dust addiction, they lost in skill and equipment.

People staggered this way and that, screaming as I lined up and shot them. The fire from behind me went from frantic overlapping sprays of gamma rays, slug throwers, pistols, and shotguns to screams. Suddenly, the gunfire was steady, the screams ending abruptly as the screamers were taken down.

I took the corner, seeing the security office ahead and the ready and deployed heavily armored turrets. As soon as I glanced around the corner, they opened fire. I leaned back, bullets chewing up the edge of the wall.

"Well, fuck," I growled, trying to think about the best way around this. I'd have preferred the turrets intact, but…I jerked back again, then backed up a half meter as the bullets continued chewing through the walls, getting closer.

I grinned, querying the RI for the building layout.

"Boss, we need to move!" Luna called. The gunfire got louder again as people from the corridors who hadn't been affected by the flash-bang started to show up.

"Gimme a fucking minute!" I snapped back, searching the public domain building plans and trying to find another way around the turrets.

"We don't have a minute!" Gessh snapped back. "MOVE!"

"Fuck's sake!" I snarled, before holstering the handgun, grabbing my rifle again and stepping out. I sprayed fire at the turrets, then dove back, cursing as two of the turret's shots hit me, and my own armor-piercing rounds sparked off them.

One tore through the skin at the top of my right shoulder, the dragon scale already weakened. The other hit the stock of my rifle and ricocheted off, cracking it, though.

I cursed, glancing up the corridor in the direction we'd come, as Gessh fired past me at a form moving around the corner, out of my sight.

There were literally dozens of bodies strewn around. The once calm and reasonably clean corridors were a mess. Shattered turrets hung from walls, light fittings swayed and shattered, sparking electrics, and there was some seriously fucked-up Pollock-style repainting going on.

I focused on one wall, seeing the damage that shotgun blast had done, the tiny pellets having trashed it, and the damage the turrets had done to the edge of the corner I'd been hiding behind, and I grinned evilly.

I released my rifle; the strap auto-retracted and dragged it back against my chest as I stooped and tore the shotgun from the dead fucker's hands.

"Boss?" Gessh called, rifle held in one hand, a medikit in the other, the needle already exposed as she spat the cover aside. "We really need some cover!"

She stabbed herself in the stomach with it. Blood ran down her side as she hissed in pain, the nanites deploying.

"Follow me!" I shouted, booting the door behind her open and running into the apartment, gun at the ready. There was nobody inside, fortunately, but the back wall that held the shower was dead ahead. I ran at it, pumping the shotgun and firing, once, twice, then the third time. The plastic coating shredded as hundreds of pellets tore through it, and the wall behind.

I ducked, running on, and charged through into the next apartment. The door on the far side was closed and it, too, was empty. I turned right, realigning against the map and, grinning, fired the rest of the shotgun's magazine into the next wall.

The wall held out for a few seconds, but that was all as Luna, seeing what I was doing, shouldered me aside when I ran out of ammo.

I dumped the looted shotgun onto the floor, and she opened fire, full auto ripping through her magazine in a matter of heartbeats, but the reinforced wall of the security station was breached.

She dumped the magazine, and Gessh rammed her grazer through the hole, firing off a quick burst to screams from inside.

I dragged myself through, widening the hole as my armor took a couple of hits. My rifle replied to the sporadic bursts of fire as someone on the far side of the security station shared their displeasure with my method of entry.

Most of the hits so far had been minor, glancing blows mostly. We'd been that fast and unexpected. But now? I got another burst of gunfire out, mostly hitting the fucking expensive-looking chair he was hiding behind. But his return fire?

It was well aimed, and lucky.

I hissed, falling out of his sight behind a chair. My left arm, the fucking cybernetic one, twitched and shook as a flurry of pain signals overwhelmed it.

The armor-piercing bullets had hit me high on the left side. Three of them punched through my armor and out the far side in sprays of blood. Two got stuck inside me, one breaking my clavicle and one lodging in the bone where the cybernetic shoulder joint met my biological one.

The result was a serious level of pain. The weight of the artificial arm caused the shattered clavicle to split, pulling apart even more. The holes that had run through and through shattered my shoulder blade as well, and badly fucked up the top of my lung.

I slumped down, hissing in pain.

Gessh shoved through behind me, taking out the security guard who was fixated on me, and screaming back over her shoulder,

"The boss is hit!"

CHAPTER FORTY-ONE

"Incoming!" Luna barked back, following her in and dropping to her knees by my side, checking me over. "Medikits!" she yelled at me, and I patted my right thigh pocket that I'd been fumbling with.

She tore the medium medikit out. Twin injection ports on the bottom sparkled as she uncovered them, then stabbed it into my upper chest like she was staking a fucking vampire, just with shitty aim.

The injector hissed and the nanites boiled out of the end, hitting the wounds and expanding. The pain was horrific, even more so when Luna dug a finger into one of the wounds, then another, checking them, before grabbing my shoulder and straightening it up, holding it more or less in place for the nanites to start work.

Reign backed through the hole, her rifle booming as she took down people trying to follow her.

"H…here!" I grunted, then coughed blood, shaking with the pain as I pressed the hacker into Luna's palm. "Get it done!"

She nodded, twisting and searching the room quickly. She was up and running a few seconds later, sprinting to the far end where a massive server rack stood, the door ajar, fortunately for us. I assumed that they'd been in the process of doing something when we'd come through the wall, as the explosives dotted around couldn't be good. But even as I stared, Gessh yanked detonators out of the mass, tossing them into a secure explosives drawer.

It might not be enough, but considering they'd clearly been rigging the server stack? It might yet work. Either way, though, as Gessh yanked the explosives free, she uncovered a small port in the side of the server, and Luna plugged the cracker in.

As Bowdoin had warned us when he coded it, it *should* work, but it was also written on the fly, by a hacker without access to the target, and so it had a lot of IF/THEN written into it, and warnings that although it might work, it also might fucking not at all.

It'd been a seriously warning-laden deal as he handed the crackers over, basically saying that he'd done his best and if it didn't work, it wasn't his fault.

Now, though, as the server went into overdrive and the lights across the entire floor flickered and went dim, I cursed. The turrets outside had ceased firing, true, but that might be because they were programmed to fire only on assholes without a certain ID or because nobody was in their line of sight right now.

I didn't know, and I wasn't going to stand in front of them to find out.

"How you doing, boss?" Reign called down to me.

I snarled as I forced myself to my feet. My left arm lifted and locked onto the strap of the rifle, rolling over from my right.

"I'm functional," I forced out through clenched teeth. The arm held itself as still as possible as I moved, drawing my handgun and hefting that as Reign grunted in response.

"Well, we're getting hit a lot here. Gotta admit, didn't expect this many assholes!" she snapped, and I nodded unthinkingly.

"Me neither." I pulled up the breakdown of the floor and noted that the door in the back of the security office, that apparently led into the management offices, wasn't on the map. "That way," I ordered, nodding to the door, and Luna led the way.

The security office was a good one. The approaches leading up to it had the turrets in place and additional armoring, besides. But the walls?

Nobody ever thought about the walls.

As an APS operator, I was used to that. We ran through them a lot, plowing down buildings that annoyed us, out in the field, on a regular basis. Now, as we moved into the plush management suite, I whistled.

The interior here was nice—like, seriously so. Three apartments rolled into one, with a massive bed, a tall armory with security features that screamed it'd be a bitch to get past, and of course, a shower that looked like it'd been designed to shoot pornos in.

Hell, it probably *had*.

That wasn't important, though. What was? The door on the far side that led into the lab. Luna took it at a run, bursting through and swearing as shots sparked off her armor, a low-caliber handgun apparently all the three workers in there had been left with.

A second later, though, she was rolling back through the door. A massive figure pinned her down as metal teeth flashed for her throat.

She braced her arm under their throat, then heaved, barely keeping the creature back. She yanked her submachine gun out again, pressing it to their stomach and firing on full auto.

The noise was horrific. The bullets impacted some kind of interwoven body armor, as the ceiling of the bedroom opened, and three more of the twisted semi-humanoid creatures were dumped in.

I barely had time to register it, the slight whirr of the ceiling opening all the warning that I got before the nearest one hit me, sending me rolling and onto my back. Screams rose as my upper chest and shoulder—still being repaired by the nanites—was broken again.

I lifted my left arm in time. Fortunately, it was faster than my natural one was, and unhindered by pain. I grabbed onto the snout of the creature, twisting sideways as I brought my handgun up, ramming it into the underside of one ear, then pulling the trigger.

Whatever armoring the fuckers had implanted, there wasn't any there at least, and the high-caliber handgun round shredded its brain, before impacting the wall on the far side.

I tossed the body off me with another scream of pain, before twisting and lining up on the one that had Gessh's leg in its mouth.

I hesitated, aiming as she moved, and in that time, her blade was out and its head was severed, blood fountaining free. Reign had hit hers with a round from the sniper rifle. And regardless of the armoring, a high-powered sniper rifle at a range of a few meters wasn't being stopped by anything like that.

Luna was the only one still fighting. Her arm was a mess now, as the fucker chewed on it, until she twisted, driving her fist down its throat.

It bucked, writhing, teeth sunk into her heavily bleeding forearm as she shook it around. But once her fist was closed in there? It was only a matter of time.

The creature's struggles grew weaker and more panicked as she twisted, then forced herself to her feet, her chest heaving. The massive musculature of the orc side of her genes made itself known, as did the insane levels of ferocity, as she marched through the door and back into the lab.

I could see her through the open door, as she stared at someone, the choking creature still dangling from her arm. Then she grabbed onto the top of the snout and pulled.

The cracks of bones as she slowly and deliberately tore the upper half of its skull free were savage, and the hiss of pain was lost under the roar of triumph as she killed the creature.

I slumped back, glancing around. The others looked just as fucked as I felt. The security system finally pinged, opening itself up to me.

I grinned, sagging as my head banged off the floor—actual carpet and everything—and I got to work. All the turrets were loaded with mine and the team's images; the security system went from friend to foe with the idents programmed in so far, every one of those marked as "safe" now being marked as a target.

I loaded in a pause authorization and watched as my target walked out of the lift. Two dozen gangers, all in decent armor and armed to the teeth, accompanied him. In the middle was the chemist Lucky had wanted me to get, along with a pair of large boxes that hovered along on drone repulsors, presumably filled with his equipment.

I removed the block on the chief asshole's comm, and a second later, it chimed as he registered the change, and called me.

"So," he said coldly, even as I watched him through a camera. "If you've made a mess in my quarters, I'll make your death painful."

"Meh, define 'mess,'" I replied. "Seriously, what the fuck were those things?"

"My pets?" he said, a sneer clear on his face. "Goblin and orc hybrids, wet-wired for enhanced aggression and kitted with subdermal armor, as well as replacement jaws. How many did they kill?"

"Kill?" I asked with a snort. "None. They fucking slobbered all over us, though."

I deliberately didn't mention the injuries, and when I sensed the access request to the cameras in here, I permitted it, watching his face as he saw his trashed room.

"You'll pay for that," he swore, as Luna strode in, dragging the chemists, shoving them into the corner, and I added them to the "safe" list for the security system.

"Well, that's the point," I said slowly. "Will I pay, or will I be paid?"

"You'll fucking pay!" he snarled, turning in to the corridor that led toward the one his apartment was on, and moving closer and closer to the security office.

I grinned, my helmet and my mental avatar both hiding that as I spoke. "So, here's the deal. You transfer me all your creds, and we don't kill them."

"You kill them, and I've a new chemist right here—"

"True, but you could have four chemists, rather than just the one. Surely that'd be better, right? I mean, you did just fight to get him."

"And let's say I play along," he said. "What's to stop you from killing them once you have my creds?"

"Enlightened self-interest." I took Gessh's hand and clambered to my feet. "I mean, I'd much rather we all got along," I lied. The passages to the apartment flickered up one by one as I changed the camera's views, showing me dozens of thugs standing there, armed to the teeth. Most had no armor, but those who did? They were loaded for bear.

"Tell you what," he replied. "You shoot your team, right now, and then you surrender. I'll make it quick."

"Or, I could not." I snorted.

"Fine." He accessed the speakers, and I approved it, keeping the illusion intact as he started to speak. "To all of you. One of you gets to walk out of here, and it's not that fuck that led you in. Whoever shoots the others first? You go free. You've got till the count of five."

"I'll make it easy on you," I said loudly, to him, but still playing the game. "I'll kill all your guards on three, and if I don't get a fuckload of credits when I hit five? I'll let you join them."

"I'm holding all the cards here, asshole. One." He sneered, stepping into the corridor that held the security station front entrance, as well as the entrance to his room.

"Two," I replied, smiling, and connecting to the speaker system all around him. "When we hit three, you all die. Anyone who drops their weapons before they get shot? There's a chance for you."

"Three," he said.

"Your choice," I agreed. "Fire."

The heavy turrets and the wall-mounted ones that had been such a nightmare for me jerked into life, their targets already locked in. They opened fire, as I zoomed in on my target's face.

"Checkmate, motherfucker," I purred.

That the same trick had worked twice was awesome, and I made a mental note to buy some more of those fuckers from Bowdoin when I got the chance.

Sure, yeah, they were limited use. They worked only if you could get past all the security, past the firewalls, and literally had to be plugged directly into the security server. But the effect?

Especially on assholes who thought they were safe?

It was just plain wonderful.

The heavy turrets spat out rounds that tore through the armored bodies in the lead, deliberately excluding the boss and the chemist, but taking down the rest of his closest security team. As the wall-mounted smaller turrets spun to life, the guards who were used to being protected by the hardware were the first to fall.

Then we opened fire, doors opening and fire filling the corridors.

When I say "we," obviously I meant the others, as I sat on a rather nice chair, making a mental note to take the fucker with me, as I sent a mental knock with my Keystone to Sirisena, grinning as I spoke into the sudden silence. The air filled with the echo of heavy fire, the slowly rising screams and groans as the realizations kicked in.

"Four…" I said slowly, drawing the word out, as those few who were both still armed, and still capable of using those weapons, dumped them *fast*. "F—" I started, only to receive a response, and a credit transfer.

I stared at it, long seconds passing, as I considered my next move.

"Luna, grab that fucker and the chemist." I nodded to the door, knowing that although her arm was a mess, I'd seen her use a medikit, and right now, she was still on the ragged edge, making her even more terrifying.

"Reign," I said softly, "get bags ready. Gessh, get out there and loot the team around that dickbag. Make it fast. You've got two minutes."

They moved. Whether it was the strain in my voice or the ingrained response to orders, or even that they trusted me, I didn't know. But what I did know?

We'd just won.

CHAPTER FORTY-TWO

Luna dragged the pair into the room. Sirisena, the gang boss, went to his knees when she stomped on the back of his calf, driving him down, and the chemist staggered toward the others, heading to the corner at her shove.

I smiled down at the fucker on the floor, all friendly-like, as I nodded to the armory door.

"Open it," I ordered.

He glared at me, before spitting on the floor.

"What's to stop you shooting me then?"

"I only kill when I've been paid to," I said. "I had a job to recover your chemists, and that one." I nodded to the one who was moving to the others, joining them in the corner.

"So you've—" he started to say, and I lifted my hand cannon, the comforting weight of the hurricane revolver sitting nicely in my hand as I leveled it at his crotch.

"You'll live so long as you're useful," I explained. "Those guns and that gear? Useful. Your crotch? Not useful to me. One."

"But I—"

"Two…" I aimed and sent a mental order to my RI to record this, just in case I needed it for Lucky. "Th—"

"Okay!" he snarled, as the armory door clicked, unlocking with a hiss.

"Good boy!" I grabbed him by the back of the left shoulder, the barrel of the revolver jammed into the rear of his skull. "Now, let's go have a look, and see what we have, shall we?"

"I'll find you after this," he assured me in a low voice. "You fucking little shit, I'll find you and I'll…"

I jabbed the gun in hard to the back of his head.

"You know, I've got to wonder," I said thoughtfully. "You think you've suddenly got a chance of surviving, and you immediately start threatening me with the consequences of letting you do so. Is it suicide, or death by gobshite that I should put this down to?"

"Gobshite?"

"Yeah, army term," I explained, watching him carefully, waiting for the move I was sure was coming. "It means to run your mouth uncontrollably and fucking stupidly."

He didn't wait long. As soon as my hand left his left shoulder, he darted forward, reaching for the armory door with his right, even as he swung his left up and around, hoping to slap the gun off its aim.

It ended badly, because I'd released him to grab my vibro-blade, and the arm that went for my gun met it in midair, shearing through it nicely.

He laid his hand on the edge of the armory door as the pain hit and he started to scream. That was when I shot him in the back of the right leg, sending him crashing to the floor.

Being the trusting person I am, I stepped to the left of the door, so I was behind it as it opened, and he in front of it, and I made sure there was nobody else in the line of fire.

The boom of a directional fragmentation grenade was loud and permanently ruined his face, as well as keeping him interested for the rest of his life. I winced, the door suddenly covered in dozens of pockmarks and ripples, and I hesitated a few seconds, before opening the door fully, and risking a glance inside.

"Holy mother of Sam, son of Jack!" I cursed, invoking the patron saint of mercenaries as I stared at the racks of high-quality weaponry, nestled undamaged and comfortable behind the directional booby trap. Sure, they weren't insanely expensive, but they were good, solid weapons: A handgun with what looked like pearl-encrusted grips. Grenades by the box. Ammo on racks. Rifles with a dozen mods—yeah, they looked fucking stupid, there was that much aftermarket work done—as well as gold chasing added to it, probably reducing the actual usability of the rifle. But still!

"Yeah, we're having these," I declared to Reign, who darted in and started looting as the far door opened.

This time, it was Gessh leading the transport cases, and grinning at me as she came.

"Anything good in there?" I asked, and she shrugged.

"Fuckload of drugs, some equipment to make more, but I dumped it on the floor, and filled it with the guns from out there."

"Nice," I agreed, grinning.

"What...what do we do?" a call came from the corner, and I looked over, seeing one chemist standing hesitantly. "Do we owe you for our freedom or..."

I hesitated, then cursed, and shook my head. "You're not free," I said between clenched teeth. "Not yet, anyway. For now, you work for Lucky."

"You're Lucky?" the speaker questioned, and I snorted.

"I'm feeling insanely lucky right now, but no. Lucky will be on his way." I turned to the girls. "You all okay?"

"Not really." Gessh grunted, indicating her side. "You?"

"Same," I admitted, glancing at my fucked-up left side. The nanites had stopped the pain and sealed the leak in my lung. They'd also started to form a bridge of bone to cover the fucked-up clavicle. But that'd not last long and although nanites could replace the bone, they weren't magic.

There'd be fragments left over—there'd be issues. No, I needed a decent doc, or better yet, a chop shop. We had shit we needed to sell anyway, and our only chance against Stinger was if we were loaded for bear and on the ball.

Add to that, I was certain that Lion had inserted a tracker into me. If he'd done that, it was fifty-fifty that he'd rammed in an explosive charge as well. And if that was there? I needed it out.

Best person to remove it was the man who'd put it in, and I had the girls to watch over him as he worked this time.

"Okay, load up, and get ready. We leave as soon as you're done."

Reign grinned like a lunatic, grabbing more shit and dumping it into the transport crate.

I pulled up the comm log and started the call as I regarded the fucker, speaking quickly before the link connected. "And get us a cab that can take the crate!" I ordered Reign, who paused, then nodded.

"Kabutt," Lucky greeted me a few seconds later, and I forced a smile.

"Lucky," I replied. "The floor is yours."

"The floor?" He sat up and stared at me.

"We took the entire floor—the security station and labs and so on. I think about ninety percent of their troops are dead, and all four chemists are standing ready to do a deal with you."

"A deal?" He scoffed. "They're mine. There's no deal to be had here…"

"They're people, Lucky," I said coldly. "Not slaves, not—"

"Your job was to take them. Now they're mine," he snapped back. "They're what I tell them they are."

"Okay, let me save you some time, Lucky." I forced another smile. "They're employees, not slaves. You treat them as slaves? That makes you a slaver scumbag. I spent ten years in the wilds judging and killing slavers. You don't want to end up on that fucking list, do you, *partner*?"

"I think you and me are gonna have a little talk about our 'partnership' real soon, boy," he hissed, and I nodded.

"Yeah, I think after the jobs are done, we are. For now, though? We're going to rearm and grab some new gear, then we'll be back for Stinger."

"Don't forget him," he agreed with a final smile, before cutting the connection.

I stared at the End Call symbol, knowing, just fucking knowing what was to come, and that in giving him time to prepare, we were making a mistake.

The truth was, though, if we didn't get fixed up, and especially get that bomb out—if I wasn't just being a paranoid fucker—I'd definitely be dead in an hour, one way or another.

"Boss?" Reign asked, and I jumped, having been miles away. "You all right?" she asked, noting my grimace as my wounds made their presence known.

"Nope," I admitted. "You got that cab sorted?"

"Aircab." She grinned and gestured upward. "It'll land on the roof, figured it was closer, and that way it can fit the case. It's more expensive, though, and I'm broke now."

"I'll sort it." I glanced at my bank balance and shook my head in momentary disbelief.

"Let's go," Luna said, and I nodded, looking over the battered team before me.

"We're headed to get fixed up, then replace any gear we need, and the hit," I explained. "Once we're alone, we can talk."

"Johnny Air-Cab?" Gessh asked hopefully, and I glanced at Reign, who hesitated.

"I can if you want, but it's a hundred creds more, and…"

"Do it," I said.

Gessh nodded to the pile of unlocked cred-chips in the case.

"I used their thumbs," she admitted. "Transferred them all."

A second later, a new knock went through, and we were all four thousand and change richer from her.

"Thank you." I smiled, then nodded to the door. "Let's get moving."

The trip up to the roof wasn't long, and the four of us, even wounded as we were, enjoyed staring out the window as more and more of the city became clear.

It wasn't the first time I'd been up so high. Hell, I'd done it a load of times. I'd walked the wall on occasion in training with the army, and I'd been on helos aplenty, passing up and over the city.

It just wasn't normal, though.

We weren't meant to be so high in the sky, no matter what those batshit bastard flyboys claimed, and as I stared out over the city, watching the ground vanish so far below, I gritted my teeth.

The lift farted again, and we slowed to a gentle stop. The doors opened after a second round of beeps sounded, and we all had to approve the warning that was sent to us.

> *Please be aware, Dayocare Corporation accepts no responsibility for lives lost from this, or any other platform within any of Dayocare's arcologies. Due to a recent increase in the loss of lives from this location, please confirm that you accept that Dayocare is not responsible for your safety, and that you accept full responsibility.*

We all accepted and affixed our idents to the warning, and the slow opening doors suddenly jerked as the wind up here yanked at them.

The wind that whistled around the upper floor was insane, and we all grabbed the transport crate as it drifted, having to fight with it to cross the short distance to the central landing field.

The roof was a massive square, tapering inward to the central landing area, with four lifts spaced around the outside edges, and ornamental walkways that led from the center to them.

There were also nice benches and more around the outside, proving once and for all that no amount of AI assistance could overcome good old human stupidity. The arcology rooftop was two and a half kilometers up, or thereabouts, meaning that the wind was fucking constant on a normal day.

Add in the storm that was currently soaking the city?

The fucking planters that made up the lines of the walkways had ornamental hedges and shit in them once upon a time, and despite the sheer stupidity of that, when they'd been building this place, they'd been able to feel the damn winds, and they'd still put them in.

Madness.

The route we ran to the cab was short, and the winds blew all four of us left and right as we got to it. As soon as the storage area had accepted the crate and sealed again, we all piled inside, dripping wet and stunned by the ferocity of the world up so high.

I stared out the window, all four of us dismissing the "fouling charge" warning we received, all of us bleeding as we were. I confirmed the destination, as well as calling ahead to Lion, warning him we were coming and to be ready.

As we arced around, most of the special features of the Johnny Air-Cab—the massage seats and so on—were all ignored in favor of the privacy field as we talked quickly, knowing that, for now at least, we were safe from eavesdroppers.

"What now?" Luna asked, and I smiled.

"We've got options," I said. "I got the gang boss to transfer me his creds and—"

"Did you claim the bounty?" Reign asked, and I paused.

"Fuck, I forgot all about that!" I snarled to myself.

"Idiot," she growled, shaking her head. "I've found him. Give me a minute, and…There! Accept the invite and attach your ident at the bottom."

I paused, a knock on my Keystone letting me know what she'd done. I moved quickly, affixing my ident and approving the short declaration that was outlined, confirming that the four of us were claiming the kill equally, and splitting the bounty.

"Another thousand, two-fifty, nice!" I nodded my thanks to Reign, as she grinned.

"Now what were you saying?" she asked.

"I got the asshole to transfer his creds," I repeated. "A hundred and fifty-seven thousand and eleven creds."

"Holy shit!"

That was the consensus around the cab, and I pulled my helmet off, nodding as I looked at them all.

"Exactly. That gives us two choices," I explained, setting up the split between us all and hesitating before transferring it, seeing the looks on the faces of Luna and Gessh, and the sudden concern on Reign's.

"First of all, with your situation, Reign…" I paused, then pulled out a credit-chip, holding it up. "Do you want me to put it on the chip, so that they can't claim their cut, or do the transfer?"

The relief on her face was touching, as well as slightly concerning. She'd clearly thought we were about to rip her off.

"I'll take the transfer." She smiled sadly. "If I use a cred-chip? It alerts the corpo anyway, but thank you."

I nodded and transferred the money over to each of them, splitting it equally, seeing the way she relaxed marginally once it was in her account.

"Right," I started again. "So we've got two choices. First, we all need fixing up. That's something any chop shop can do, but Lion seems reasonably trustworthy, for all he's in Lucky's pocket."

"So we get fixed up here?" Luna asked, and I nodded.

"Gods, we need it." Gessh lifted a hand away from her side and a trickle of fresh blood leaked free.

"You need a medikit?" I asked, and she forced a smile, shaking her head.

"Used one. Not using another. Not when I need some work doing anyway."

"Fair enough," I said softly, looking her over. "Seriously, though, if you need one, just say."

"Options?" Reign reminded me.

"Yes, fuck's sake, sorry." I grunted. "Okay, I'm pretty sure that Lion put a tracker and maybe a bomb in me the last time I visited, and—"

"And this is the guy you think we should visit?" Luna shook her head. "Fuck's sake, Kabutt, you've got some weird friends."

"Yeah, well, he didn't try to kill me outright." I shrugged. "Believe me, that's rare enough I'm giving him extra points. He gave me a note, warning me about the tracker. He didn't need to do that. I think he only installed it because Lucky sent some gangers to make sure he did. We're going to get him to take it out, as well as fix any issues. Once he's done that? We're off, and we need to decide where we go."

"What's the options?" Luna asked, and I shot her a glare.

"Stop fucking interrupting and I'll damn well tell you, fuck's sake," I groused, ignoring the smile on her face. "Right, I'm going to send Bowdoin half of the fee now. That gets us the location, I hope, and the rest on completion of the job. But regardless, we don't need that bounty now, so…"

"I still want it," Reign said. The other two nodded quickly.

"You sure?" I asked. "I mean, we can do the bounty another time. We're almost certain to be hit as soon as we complete it, so that we can't claim the payout."

"I need the fucking money," Reign said. "If you guys don't want to risk it, I do, still. Even alone."

"I need it as well," I admitted, and as I looked around the group, I saw the others were in, too.

"Okay, so we still do it. The only point is, do we do it now? I mean, we could tell Lucky that the deal's off, do it tomorrow or another day, give him the chance to be elsewhere, and maybe we don't get stabbed in the back."

"Call Bowdoin," Gessh suggested after a few seconds' thought. "If he's not ready yet, and we've got time? Honestly, I say do it—hit the fuckers and hit them hard. Claim the bounty. He'll think you're rigged to blow, and when he tries it? It'll end badly for him."

"Or someone else, depending on where the bomb is…" I grunted, then nodded. "Fine, I'll call Bowdoin. Might as well sit back and relax. We're nearly there." I turned away and looked out to the window as I put the call through, hoping the flakey fucking hacker answered.

CHAPTER FORTY-THREE

Bowdoin, it turned out, was as good as his word. He'd not only found the location, but he'd verified the target was there—currently with a couple of high-priced whores, although their booking was only valid for another two hours—and he'd even cased the security system, more or less.

He'd tell me nothing else, not yet, and I transferred the first fifteen thousand credits to him, enjoying the slight break in his composure as the creds registered with him as being delivered.

I'd also pointed out that if he ran, and didn't do the job I'd hired him for, I'd hunt him down and murder him in a variety of different, painful, and interesting ways.

I didn't know whether he was honorable, whether it was the allure of another twelve thousand creds, or the threats and knowing that although Richie wasn't about right now, I'd told him he would be soon—but whatever the reason, he assured me he was good for it, and he'd be in touch in about three hours, as it'd take him that long to reach the target site.

He'd also given me the rough area, so I could be there. But without access codes for the corpo zone, I wasn't getting in there easily, even to look around.

"Well, look what the cat dragged in," Lion said a few minutes later, when I'd finished the call and we were unloading the cab, directing the container into his shop. "So…to what do I owe the pleasure?" He shook his head at the state of the four of us. "No docs or carvers wherever you were?" He got Gessh and Luna scanned, while Reign looked at a catalog of upgrades.

"Plenty." I pulled the top off the container and let him look inside, seeing the dozen or so tier-three mods laid atop the piles of guns. "We needed to see someone we could trust, though, and I think I need some internal work done."

"Internal?" he asked slowly, and I nodded, fixing him with a glare.

"Yeah, one of the shots hit something, and I keep feeling a reverberation, almost like a signal, but it cuts off. Something's clearly broken."

"Yeah…" He watched my eyes. After a couple of seconds, he glanced to the side at some papers, and I moved to them, picking up a pencil and awkwardly forming the letters while he snorted, and pretended to show me something on the datadeck next to it.

> *I know what you put in me. Get it the fuck out.*

The glare he gave me was priceless, but he still drew an eye on the paper and tapped it.

"It's in my eyes?" I asked, getting a long-suffering stare from him before he gestured behind him.

"Cameras?" I whispered, and he nodded, tapping the paper again, and taking a pencil from me and speaking aloud.

"Okay, the injury could be here…the organelles might do what you're saying if…" He went on talking utter bollocks as he scrawled a note.

> *Asshole in the room behind, watching on camera. Works for the gang.*

"Lucky?" I whispered, and he shook his head.

"Luckier than you've a right to be, if that's the extent of the damage done to you," he said loudly, before muttering, "Works for him, yeah."

"Chest as well, right here," I pointed out, getting a sigh as he got scanners and more and checked me over. It took a few minutes for him to scan all of me, and by the end of it, I was handed a very simple note again.

> *Not my choice to add it in. I can take it out, but need an excuse for Lucky.*

"All of it," I said aloud. "Replace it all—the damaged organelles and the clavicle and the rest. Fix me up, carver. Make me better than before."

"I can, but you might be better off upgrading the internals. Let's see what you've brought me, and we can talk a price…They're not specter parts, right?"

"No, all genuine living donors," I grunted, as he shot me a look.

"Willing donors?" he asked. "Am I going to have pissed-off people knocking on my door searching for their loved ones?"

"Do you normally?" I countered.

"Normally I'm buying from the Orc. Nobody comes knocking for those he's pissed at."

"Believe me, nobody's left alive who fucked with us," I said. "Those who started this one? This is all that's left of them."

"Well…" He paused, looking it over, then shook his head. "I can't."

"What?"

"I can't take them."

"The fuck you can't," I snapped. "They're right there and you've got—"

"I can't buy them," he hissed, glaring at me. "First, I can't fucking afford it. You think I'd agree to deals like that with Lucky if I had a choice? I don't. Second, I can't buy these from you, not without Oshbob's okay."

"Are you fucking kidding me?" I snarled. "He's a fucking orc, that's all!"

"There a problem?" Luna called over, and I shook my head, realizing how that might have sounded to a half-orc.

"No, don't worry!" I called back, before turning to Lion. "Listen, dickhead, you're acting like he's some corpo head and you're sucking his balls for a raise! He's a fucking gang lord, that's all!"

"He's *the* Orc, not *an* orc." Lion scratched the back of his head and gestured at the guns and mods. "Look, all of this? He'll be selling this kinda shit. I buy from a competitor of his? I might be getting a few pointed questions, or I might be getting my head handed to me, my family liquidated, literally."

"I'm not a fucking competitor, all right? I sold him some through Lucky. Now I need to move some more. We need repairs and the girls need upgrades. I need fixing up and…" I paused, then nodded as a thought occurred to me. "It's not Lucky that's the issue here, right? It's this Oshbob?"

"Damn right. Lucky is a punk. Sure, he thinks he's a gang boss, but he's nothing, just another floor boss in some arcology. Although, he's got some muscle behind him. He turns up missing? Nobody's going to give a fuck. You fuck with the Orc? That's different."

"Fine. Look, we need fixed up and now. You say you can't buy these, okay. How about a loan?"

"I'm broke, you asshole. I'm not taking some goddamn deal that puts me in your pocket as well as Lucky's…" Lion growled.

"No, you dick," I snapped, glaring at him. "What I'm saying is you take these, you clean them up, put them on the walls, do whatever you do with them, and we take half. No cost upfront."

"I'm listening," he said, after pausing.

"I've got a meeting with Oshbob tomorrow. Might be that we make a deal, might be that we fucking shoot each other—no idea yet. But, as part of a deal— *if* we make one—I'll make sure I can sell parts to you, or trade or whatever. Sound good?"

"And the rest of this?" He gestured to the guns and weapon mods. "I can't take that, man. I don't deal in that shit, and before you ask, no, you can't leave them here. Word gets out, I'll be hit inside the hour."

"Fuck…Fine!" I snarled. "Look, fix up the girls, whatever they want, and take it off the trade value of these…" I gestured to the pile. "Then fix my guts— *and give me it to take with me*—and my chest, that'll do for now."

"And you'll trust me with these mods?" He frowned. "No offense, Kabutt, you've met me once. You're either a trusting fool or…"

"I'm a good judge of character," I said, with a wide smile. "Also, if you fuck with me? I'll come torture you to death. I should be getting my armor back in the next day or two, and I need the spinal mod. You'll need to order one in, and the only way you can do that?"

"Is if I'm alive and I've got the creds," he agreed, sighing. "Fine, get your ass in the chair and let's get you sorted first. It'll not take long."

"How long?"

"An hour?" He shrugged. "The mods need time to settle, even with nanites."

"Fuck, we need to be out of here in an hour. We need a cab and…" I bit my tongue, then nodded, heading inside. "Okay, people, got a plan." I grinned.

~~~

"Deal, I guess," Julius said an hour and a half later, standing in the chop shop over the box of guns, now severely depleted, as we bumped fists.

"Glad to hear it, mate. I'd hate to do this without you," I admitted.

The older merc grinned, then shrugged.

"For this? It's enough to get my little guild rolling nicely back on track, and a deal with a carver of our own? Definitely worth it."

"Yeah, well, it's only if he can get the Orc to sign off on it," Lion growled, sounding more and more like his namesake as I loaded more and more onto our fragile relationship.
~~~

"I'd say that's his problem, carver." Julius shrugged. "Ours are the mods. If we bring our wounded to you, and only you, you give us a twenty percent discount, and we provide any mods we get, living only, obviously—"

Julius frowned at me. "It's not like anyone would traffic in specter mods, but you'd be surprised how many people we end up in fights with, even with the aim of our guild. Those mods come to you, you hold a line of credit for us, and we call on it when we need it. Something for everyone."

"Especially me." I clapped Julius on the shoulder and took the small package from Lion. "I'll see you later tonight, if not before."

"Definitely before," Julius grunted. "You know the old adage— no plan survives contact with the enemy."

"Well, just keep that fucking line free, I guess." I grinned, before turning and walking back to the aircab that was waiting patiently. "See you!" I called, climbing in, and for the first time in ages, not getting a warning that I'd fouled the cab on entry.

"We all ready?" I asked the others, with Luna, holding up her formerly chewed left arm—now a tier-three mod replacement from the elbow down—to demonstrate just how ready she was.

"You have no idea," Luna said softly, her fingers extruding long bladed claws as she waved the hand, before retracting them and closing it again.

"Good to go," Gessh agreed, shifting uncomfortably as she tried to get used to the new layout. Several of her organs had been replaced with organelles by Lion, as it was apparently cheaper than digging around inside her and "fucking with the balance of your guts."

Her intestines had been nicked, and the bowel had been slowly leaking literal shit into her abdominal cavity, while the nanites had been struggling to make headway against what had turned out to be a necrotic poison loadout on the bullets.

That had pissed Lion off no end, as the combination of that, her high pain threshold, and her "not wanting to be a bother" had meant that by the time he found the actual real level of the damage, she needed a lot more work than he'd been expecting.

Reign was the best off out of all of us. All of her injuries were minor and easily solved with a dose of 'nites, so she spent her time ostensibly watching Lion to make sure he did the job right.

I was trusting him a lot, but not that fucking much.

I'd had a little additional work, nothing fully cybernetic that required integration, just an additional load-bearing bone augmentation across my upper left side, literally a replacement for the collarbone, and some armoring on the back to repair the shoulder blade.

It didn't count against my cybernetic total, I was damn pleased to hear, and the end result was that I was ready, should I decide to go for a full subdermal armoring next.

Regardless of anything else, though, I was back in the game, as were the others. We were armed for bear, complete with a tiny, and *very* old-school drone, now loaded with my tracker, and the fucking bomb that Lion had removed at my demand.

It was time to take down Stinger. And then? We were ready to face whatever happened with Lucky.

CHAPTER FORTY-FOUR

Watching the arcology growing larger in the distance, I sat back and sighed. "You know what?"

"What?" Reign asked tiredly, passing around a handful of stims that we'd bought from Lion, along with the replacement medikits.

"I fucking hate this place."

"The cab?" Luna popped the top off the injector and pressed it to the side of her neck, wincing as the needle punched through, releasing a heavy dose of Superbull. *"Guaranteed to give you the stamina you require."*

"No, for fuck's sake, why would I hate the cab?" I asked, confused, peeling down my armor around the neck as I pressed my own injector into place and triggered it. "Ahhhh, fuck that stings…No, I mean that goddamn arcology!"

"That makes a little more sense then," Reign said as I caught my breath.

The drug hit my system at seeming light speed, banishing tiredness and providing a general surge of confidence, as well as a general feeling that if I needed to flap my arms and fly? I fucking well could.

This was always the risk with stims like these: a general feeling that you were bulletproof. But considering the other choice was the adrenal crash we were all experiencing?

Nope. The surges and dumps of adrenaline came with a massive cost, namely slower reactions, blurred vision, and more. If the option was that, or hopped up on stims? Stims it was.

"Fuck, I hate these…" Luna muttered, shaking her head and blowing her cheeks out. "I wish we didn't have to take them."

"Look on the bright side. At least you can have them!" Reign lifted her coffee and wiggled the cup slightly. "I'm on the fucking brown bean of the gods, and that's it."

"Shit, your chemical checks…" I winced, and she nodded, glumly.

"Exactly. So, keep me awake, boss. Explain why you hate the arcology." She forced a smile, sipping on the coffee. "This is even worse, because I fucking *hate* coffee."

"Shit." I grunted, then snorted. "Just feels like we're always going back and forth to the place, that's all." I shrugged. "It wouldn't be so bad, but knowing that the gangs are all worked up in there? And after doing those jobs for Lucky, who's clearly spread the fucking word on who we are, and that it was all for him? It means any time we pass through any floor, the local gang bosses are going to think we're there for them."

"And then they'll hit us." Gessh nodded. "Well, we were going to get a new place anyway." She shrugged, getting back to work on the drone we'd bought from Lion, playing with its payload.

"Anyway." I shifted in my seat. "I hate the fucking arcology, so how about at the end of this, if the job goes well, we raid the room, grab my gear, and not come back? I don't see the gangers letting us leave easily after we've killed three gang bosses…I'm betting some asshole will get the great idea of banding together and fucking slaughtering us."

"Sounds good," Reign said. "As long as we can get somewhere easily. But let's be serious here. Even with the drone, and the help you brought in with those guns, you think we're just walking in and doing this?"

"Right," I agreed, pulling up the map and the insanely sparse fucking details Lucky had given us earlier. We'd essentially been going by the seat of our pants so far today, running from fire to fire, but it'd worked—more or less—and we were still alive.

This was where it got tricky, though. We'd pulled in a few favors for the exit, knowing that Lucky was likely to have his own plans for us, but that was all we'd been able to do.

Well, besides removing the tracker and the bomb that cheeky fucker Lion had installed—yes, the bastard—in my fucking guts. The bomb was now mounted on the drone, and Gessh was busily sticking a fuckload more of the high ex that she'd apparently grabbed from the last job all around it.

Looking at the map of the lower floor that Stinger had made his home on, we were grimly sure that it was going to be a nightmare to assault.

First and foremost, the section he was holed up in was alongside the archology's supplemental reactor. The way that the city was run meant that there were massive primary reactors, as well as solar and nuclear plants, fission and more, all that good—possibly about to blow if you looked at it wrong—fun and *safe* technology.

Because of the inherent risks involved in such a huge city being run by both governmental politicians and corporations that liked to cut every single possible corner on quality control and more, it meant that no reactor was supposed to run close to redline, simply because if one went kaboom, the whole city was fucked.

Because of that, the main, huge fucking reactors that were the primary suppliers of the city were supplemented by smaller, individual reactors, like the arcology ones.

They didn't produce all the power the arcology needed, but they produced a lot of it. They were also buried underneath the arcology, presumably in an effort to see how high they could fling the poor if they ever exploded.

That this fucker had snuggled in close to the reactor? He knew people would be hunting him. His last target, some corpo asswipe high up the ladder, had been a success, and—so the rumor went—the corpo who hired him put a bounty on his head rather than paying.

He'd killed that corpo, only to find that the fucker had prepaid the bounty, and it couldn't be canceled. He'd been in hiding ever since, as every hunter in the city was after that payday.

According to Lucky, he'd brought a fuckload of turrets and automated defenses, and was hiding up against the reactor, secure in the knowledge that if anyone tried to get past his various toys with an EMP? They'd seal their own doom.

The arcology reactor would go into meltdown without the delicate systems that protected and regulated it, and no matter how fast you ran, you'd be a dead man.

If you got away before the explosion took out a serious chunk of the city? You'd have a bounty put on your head as the claimant, and obvious destroyer of the arcology. No chance that'd be a small one, so the EMPs were out.

That meant the drones, turrets, and more that he used to protect his home needed to be taken down "old school."

I'd considered getting Bowdoin in on this, see whether there was a way to turn the turrets against their boss for the third time, and I'd been assured, when I talked to Reign about it, that we'd be wasting our time, and needlessly delaying Bowdoin's job on Tyrannus at the same time.

We'd talked before now, in the cab earlier, in the chop shop and in free minutes here and there since we got the info, but it came down to this.

There was no sneaky, cunning, and manipulative way of getting around this. It was a straight-up fight. The cunning shit would come afterward.

The only entrance to the underground was through the security offices at ground level, followed by passes that required access verification codes for each door. Lucky had somehow arranged that, but I didn't like that we were essentially going to be letting him know exactly where we were at each checkpoint.

Once on his level? Well.

Lucky's information only went so far, and most of it came from a wounded janitor with a very distinctive injury. He'd been given a chance to live by the assassin, provided he kept his mouth shut, and he'd taken it.

Then he'd promptly gone to his local gang boss and had tried to sell the information.

Lucky had apparently not wanted anyone else to get the info, so he'd broken the old man's neck as soon as he had it.

"This fucking city," Luna growled, looking over those details and shaking her head. "So Stinger gave the janitor a chance, having accidentally shot him already for daring to do his job. Then the janitor promises to not tell anyone, and goes straight to his local gang boss, and tries to sell it..."

"And the gang boss hires us to do the job because, and I quote, he wants the 'merc dead, and his head and his gun' for sentimental reasons apparently." I paused, looking around at the snorts of disgust and disbelief.

"Exactly," I agreed. "After he's dead, there's no chance we won't get hit, so we've traded most of those guns to the guild, and Julius is bringing in the cavalry to help us escape. We get hit by that asshole? All we have to do is make it outside. Lucky'll be in for a hell of a surprise."

"That's a relief." Luna laughed. "Imagine his fucking face when he comes for us, and finds out about the others outside?"

"We'll need to get to them, though," Gessh pointed out. "So come on, boss. Give me good news."

"Here." I sent them all an image of the reactor, and its layout. "Secondary emergency steam vents." I smiled. "They're supposed to be maintained by the staff, and this dick killed them, or moved them on or whatever. I'm betting he's not sealed them up, as that'd make his new home horrifically hot, which means he's going to be letting them vent regularly."

I spun the image around, showing the vent climbing upward and to the first floor, then opening out to spew the hot gasses into the air.

"It's a steam vent, non-harmful, but…"

"Steam is boiling hot," Luna broke in. "Seriously, boss, that's not 'non-harmful.'"

"I mean it's not fucking radioactive or whatever," I corrected. "We shut down the vent leading to it—it's something that they have to do for maintenance anyway—we fight our way in, kill Stinger, then escape up the vents. Jump down to the ground floor from that point, walk off with the rest of the guild around us."

"What makes you think Stinger won't just do that themself?" Reign asked after considering it. "And failing that, what stops Lucky from following us, or hell, killing us when we go to meet Oshbob tomorrow?"

"Stinger apparently went in with a fuckload of gear," I pointed out, showing the shipping manifests that Lucky had gathered for "reactor parts". There was a fuckload of them, and he'd needed special transport containers for them.

"He'd have the option of abandoning all the shit he brought with him and running, or he fights his way out. He gave the janitor a chance to run, and he's apparently still down there. That says to me he's protecting something."

"Like what?"

"Fuck knows," I said. "It could be loot, it could be a family, it could be his favorite sex doll and his best guns. I don't know, but we're gonna find out."

"You're sure Lucky isn't sending us in as sacrificial lambs?" Gessh asked, and I shook my head.

"Not at all. He gains nothing by killing us at this point beyond personal satisfaction, which yeah, he's a ganger, so that's possible enough. If he waits, though? He could not only claim the bounty if he could kill us, but Oshbob wants to meet us as well. I'm thinking him killing us before that meeting is going to go down badly with the Orc, and from what I can tell? He's some kind of a crime lord, not the kinda guy you fuck with."

"He could still be following us with a wave of his own people, kill Stinger himself once we're all dead and claim our gear too?" Reign suggested.

"Possible," I agreed. "But frankly, if that's his plan? We'll have died in the assault, and we won't care anymore."

"Wow." Gessh groaned. "I'm so filled with confidence right now."

"Feel free to back out." I smiled. "I mean, it's only a quarter of a million credits, so rather than a four-way split, a three-, or two-way even would be nice…" I suggested, rubbing my chin.

"Fuck you very much," Gessh growled. "I've got plans for that money, and they involve men and women with, what did you call them the other day, Reign? 'Questionable morals, and a lot of skill.'"

"Mercs?" I suggested.

"Fuck, no. I want a team of hookers." Gessh grinned. "A full day and night of living it up like a corpo, a gang of hotties all dedicated to just doing me over and over again!"

"Ah, priorities!" Luna laughed. "I'll go half with you!" she told Gessh, who shrugged.

"Damn, now I need a camera and sensory inputs," I muttered. "Reign, don't suppose I can convince you to get in there with them while I film it and make a fortune?"

"Pay my debts off, and hell yes." She snorted. "As it is? I'm closed for business."

"That's insane." Gessh shook her head. "That even sex breaks you for weeks? And not in the fun way? It's just wrong."

"Well, if you ever want to help me torture the owner of the 'health and wellness clinic' to death? I think I could make some room on the roster." Reign snorted. "Believe me, I'm thinking that the job will take awhile—a year, maybe? Two?"

"It'd be well earned." I grunted as the cab descended. The storm around us was still blowing heavy, the rain hammering like it'd grown disgusted with the city and planned to wash it all away.

The doors opened, along with a warning about the ground level being sent to each of us.

> *Warning: This area is considered unsafe by the regular users of Johnny Air-Cab. Please, honored client, be wary...*

I cursed as a sudden gust of wind brought the pouring rain into the cab. I pulled my helmet on as I stepped out, blinking as the neck plates sealed together.

The blackness of the helmet's interior flickered for a second, before the cameras linked to my mods. I stared around, the metal of my helmet appearing as perfectly clear glass to me.

"Kabutt!" Reign called from the trunk.

I twisted, catching the rifle as she threw it to me, nodding my thanks, and strode around to join her, checking it and attaching the sling to my rig, while peering into the storage hold.

We worked quickly as the main doors closed and locked. The cab waited patiently, a marked difference from most of the cabs we used. But when the cab cost this much? A little patience was expected.

We loaded up our gear, checking one another over, making sure we were ready, before heading for the entrance. We were carrying much the same loadout as the last mission, except that I'd pulled in a few favors with Julius—part of the deal for handing over so many decent goddamn guns to him—and I'd got some mission-specific ammo for my new Centronics rifle.

Five additional magazines clung to the magnetic loading points on my harness, and I was awash with minor fears that a single badly aimed, or incredibly lucky, shot would kill us all.

I had gas-tipped rounds—hallucinogenic, not knock-out as I'd requested, but it was a case of what he had, really—high explosive, corrosive acid-tipped, regular armor-piercing, and of course, that old favorite, thermobaric.

The thermobaric magazine was firmly on my ass, separated from the others, just in case, as a weapon of last resort.

Each bullet as it hit would crumple, releasing the liquid chlorine trifluoride mix, which would then revert to its gaseous form, along with a small piece of flint or powdered phosphorus, depending whether it was loaded in the even or odd configuration.

The combination of the expanding gasses, the flint shattering on impact and ricocheting off things, and the powdered phosphorus basically resulted in an assault rifle capable delivery system that was both terrifying and glorious.

It was both a fantastically lethal option, and one that required balls of steel. Not just for the risk of someone shooting the magazine and sending me to hell via the express "my pants are *literally* on fire" route, but also because I'd be firing them at or around a live fusion reactor.

Between our insane quantities of ammo, our masses of guns, the medikits, and the replacement armor we'd been forced to order from the guild stores, we looked exactly like what we were.

Trouble, looking for a roost.

CHAPTER FORTY-FIVE

We headed for the entrance—weirdly, the one that I'd used first and most frequently ended up being the one we needed—and motion caught my eye as we piled in.

We were heading directly for the security office, and for the first time, as I saw the old lady who stank the place out and was so weird and crazy, she neither attempted to accost any of us—common sense really, all things considered—nor did she move beyond watching us across the room, curled around whatever was in her corner.

"Reign…" I said softly, mentally tagging the old woman with the help of my RI and sending it to her in the team chat.

"What's up?" she asked, apparently glancing at the picture I'd sent, then nodding. "Gotcha." She watched the old lady as I led the way across the far side of the foyer, and deeper into the building.

I'd never bothered with the lower floors before—hell, given the choice, I'd have never gone anywhere beyond my damn room, and that was only if I'd absolutely had to come here—so it was no surprise that the floor was an utter unknown to me.

The corridor that led deeper into the structure passed abandoned and closed shops, their glass and steel facades covered by old security meshes.

The deeper we marched, the more the filth piled up, and it wasn't just general wind-blown filth from the outside, either.

Piles of cardboard, plastic packing sheets, and more narrowed the pathway. And as we navigated it, on all sides we heard the scratching and shifting of movement.

"Guns up and ready," I ordered my little team, flicking the safety off my rifle, as I heard safeties being disengaged on shotguns behind me.

"She's following," Reign sent, accompanying her words with an image. In the very corner, close to the bottom of a stack of abandoned packaging, I could see wild hair and a single eye peering out.

"Yeah, that's something seriously wrong there." Luna shook her head and spoke quietly into the team comms. "She looks like a bum, but I can smell chemicals…"

"There's a lot of chemicals here," I replied, kicking a used set of injectors aside as we continued.

"No, I mean…ah, fuck it, I hate this shit. Kabutt, what do you smell?" she asked, and I paused, not smelling anything through the filters of my helmet.

I told her as much, getting a low growl as my only response. I reached up, one-handed, and unsealed the bottom of my helmet, taking a deep sniff, then gagging, quickly resealing the bottom of my helmet to the neck of my armoring.

"Fuck's sake, you could have warned me!" I coughed. "I'll be tasting that shit all day."

"That's the point," she growled. "What did you smell and taste?"

"Piss, shit, and, fuck knows…probably dead bodies," I said, disgusted, and brought up the scent receptor alteration script that Reign had given me before, ready to wipe the smells out and replace them with—

"It's chemical," Luna said. "It's not a natural scent."

"Right?"

"It's a chemical scent to drive you away," she continued. "The passageways aren't as messed up as they seem. They've been treated to keep people out." She tapped her nose. "Orc nose. We're sensitive to chemicals, and nobody really gives a shit about the orcs, so nobody plans for them for shit like this."

"It's true," Gessh agreed. "We might be twins, but her sense of smell is *waaaaay* more 'orc-y' than mine. I got the human version, and it fucking reeks to me."

"Fuck," I growled. "Chances Stinger knows we're coming?"

"Oh, I'd say good."

"Fuck."

"Boss…" Gessh whispered into the commlink.

"Yeah?"

"You know there's more of them, right?"

"People?"

"Goblins."

"Around us?"

"On all sides," she confirmed.

I nodded slowly, taking the next right and pausing as I saw a half-hidden map on the wall. A quick double-check confirmed that yeah, it was unreadable.

Someone had smeared something brown that I didn't want to focus on too much all over the map.

I sighed, reaching out and permitting my RI to pull up the local Aug-World overlay, frantically enforcing the directions-only demands on it that I normally used, only to find the images around me subtly changing as I did it.

Packing crates faded, dying away. The path glowed, highlighted as images in the very corner of my vision shifted.

> *Warning: Intrusive local Aug-World manipulation detected. Recommend disconnection.*

I cursed, annoyed at first and trying to wipe the access, before becoming seriously concerned as my RI had to devote serious cycles to expunging it, cutting it out and blocking it before the damn thing could sink any deeper into my kit.

"Boss…"

"Yeah?" I snapped, glaring as my RI flashed up warnings, requests, then settled on a full reboot of the Aug-World protocols as the best—and fastest—solution.

"Are you seeing this shit?" Reign asked slowly. The disbelief in her voice made it clear she didn't trust her eyes right now.

"No," I said. "I'm rebooting my Aug-World protocols. Give me thirty seconds, then each of you do it. Cut off the local server."

I got firm approvals from Luna and Gessh, and a grumble from Reign. But when my systems came back up, this time with the local servers firmly locked out, the world was different.

Some of the filth we'd been stepping around was gone for a start, and in its place, cleared sections of corridors that looked concerningly like fucking firing ports. I outlined them with a thought to my RI and sent a warning to the others on silent.

The more I looked, the more I saw the tiny signs. I cursed, long and harsh, before turning to the defaced map nearby. But I remembered enough of it from the last time I'd tried reading it, and the overlaid version I'd had before, to make some fast comparisons.

They were totally different.

The security office was scrubbed out, as were the local emergency exits. And with Aug-World's subtle twisting? This was looking like a shitload more of a nightmare than we had any business being involved in.

That there were goblins here, hidden on all sides but not attacking? That the stinking woman I'd taken for a lunatic and homeless bum was now following us, and the corridors were treated with some kind of chemical to drive people away, as well as goddamn firing ports installed in the walls?

I hesitated, then cursed, before speaking to the team on comms, dropping my voice as low as possible to fuck with any listening devices. My next investment, I swore, would be a decent secure tac-com for us all.

"Anyone think we have a chance of pulling this off?" I asked.

"No chance," Reign said. "I'm seeing movement at the firing ports…now that I can fucking see them. Damn, that was good manipulation. AI, you think?"

"Probably," I said. "To spoof the local Aug-World overlays, and blend it in so that it looked that seamless? Yeah."

"We gonna try a tactical retreat, boss?" Luna asked, and I hesitated, gritting my teeth.

"He'll take us all down, I think. We're witnesses now."

"Shit, yeah. He's got to be watching us," Gessh agreed.

"Fuck it, let's try this," I grunted, reaching up and flicking the safety on, then making the point of stepping out into the middle of the corridor, lifting my hands away from my rifle and holding them out in the air.

"Stinger!" I called. "I want to talk, that's all."

Silence fell after I'd said that, broken only by the rustling of the occasional goblin or whatever was behind the various piles of rubbish.

"Fuck's sake, we were hired to clear the place out. We're happy to back away, but you need to know that word's out on where you are, and who knows. So you going to talk, or do we all go out in a blaze of glory?" I called.

A new voice replied, coming from behind the group.

"You've got some balls, boy." The scratchy voice of the crazy old woman carried down to us, as she shuffled out into the corridor, watching us.

"Just born stupid, I guess."

"Well, speak up. Whatcha think ya know?" she asked, and I hesitated. "There's nobody else listening," she assured me, reading my hesitation. "Your keys are communicating through a mirror network. Nothing gets off this floor that we don't approve."

"There's an orc here, Lucky…"

"Gang boss, sixty-fifth floor," she replied, nodding. "Making inroads into controlling the forty-second through seventieth, and trying his damn best to seal up the higher ones as well. Floors you just wiped out to help him, if we're not mistaken."

"Well, yeah," I admitted. "We…*I* was dragged into helping him. Took a couple of jobs I shouldn't have."

"And this 'Stinger'?" she asked. "What makes you think they're here?"

"Besides the fucking security?" I shook my head. "Look, can we talk?"

"Seems to me we are, boy. You rather we took the other option?"

"No, I'd rather talk somewhere private, somewhere with a beer and a damn seat if possible."

"Open a channel," she said after a couple of seconds. "Accept the invite."

I felt the knock on my Key, and I hesitated, then cursed, knowing that there really wasn't an option here, not at all. If they started shooting out of the firing ports, we were fucked.

I thought about what I'd have done in his place, and then looked at the floor, staring a bit more carefully, until the old woman called out again.

"They're in the ceiling," she said, clearly growing tired of the conversation. "Last chance, boy."

I glanced up, seeing the outlines of fire suppression devices, and for the first time I realized how similar they were in size to the shredder mines I'd seen deployed around army bases.

"Okay, give me a minute," I called to her, moving to sit down against the wall on one side.

"You sure about this, boss?" Luna asked. "We know what their AI managed before…"

"If they wanted us dead, we'd be dead already," I countered. "This way, we've at least got a chance."

"Well, try not to fuck them all off, okay?" Reign said in a low voice. "I'd really like a chance at a decent life after this shit."

I grunted, sitting on the floor and resting my back against the wall. The various weapons and magazines shifted so that, as was tradition, I had something jabbing me as uncomfortably as possible.

As soon as I was settled, I accepted the knock, and felt the world around me disintegrate. I was dragged elsewhere; the blur of pixels and sensations made me feel like I was falling down a tunnel. Fragments of the world blurred past me for a split second, until I reformed, sitting across the table from…

From a *hell* of a creature.

"Stinger, I presume?" I guessed.

The figure nodded at me, slowly, stepping away from the wall it'd been leaning against and turning to a small heating module.

As it moved, pulling out a pot and filling it with water from a faucet that appeared in thin air, before vanishing, I watched it, trying to make sense of what I was seeing, even as I noticed I was in loose pants and a cloth top, unarmored. The control they had over this setup was frankly terrifying.

"It's an old trick," Stinger said into the uncomfortable silence. "Not used much these days. Too much effort for the current generation. You all seem to like just marching up the front steps and opening fire instead."

"I've never seen anything like it," I admitted, and Stinger turned, setting a pair of cups down before me and pouring for us both.

Stinger was an amalgamation of at least a hundred people, and with every movement, a section of them changed, blurring and becoming different. Their skin was pale white, golden tanned, and black as I'd ever seen, all on one hand. They had elven fingers, long and delicate, matched with orcish hands that became dwarven halfway across.

Ears that started as a goblin's ended as rounded human; a beard fought with a clean shaved face, and more. Every aspect of them shifted as I looked on in wonder.

"Now, you came here to kill me, so before I deal with that, you wanted to talk, I think?" Stinger asked. Even the voice blurred as it changed, rising to pre-teen adolescence then dropping to scratchy fifty-a-day habit in a handful of words.

"Yeah…" I admitted, before trying the digital tea and finding not only had it been coded in as drinkable—a major improvement over the bar I'd used for the call with Lucky—but it was actually seriously refreshing.

I knew that outside of here, I'd be just as thirsty as I had been before the drink, but right now? Despite my brain confirming it wasn't real, it damn well felt it.

"So, you've got sixty seconds, then I kill you," Stinger said conversationally, twisting their hand in midair and catching a small old-school hourglass as it tumbled out of the air, setting it down flat. Sand ran from the top bulb into the bottom.

"Right…" I grunted. "Ah…"

"Articulate, aren't you?"

"Fuck's sake." I grunted. "Fine." I sat back, the feeling on the wooden chair holding me comfortably as I started to speak.

"I got badly injured in the army, mustered out with only tier one's as replacements for all my good shit, thanks to someone else playing silly fuckers. I got a place here paid for as a sort of apology from the army, and that was it. On arriving, I knew I needed to make as much money as possible to get somewhere half decent, and I went to register with a merc guild…"

"Fairly standard," Stinger commented, sipping from their own cup, and I glared at them, going on.

"Yeah, well. I got fucked over by the guild and dumped into the undercity, my guns stolen and a damn good kicking besides." I glowered at them. "I ended up setting off an EMP grenade I got from a specter down there, frying my mods, my gear, all of it. Only things I had going for me was the salvage I walked out with."

"Sounds terrible," Stinger agreed, uncaring, and sipping at their tea, watching me.

"Yeah, well, that's when Lucky comes into it, with an offer I literally can't refuse. He comes into my apartment, and offers me a choice: I do a few jobs for him, or he kills me and takes the little gear I've got there. I've got one working arm and a few shots in a shotgun I've looted from the undercity. No idea if the fucker will fire safely or not…I'm at that kind of a position."

"Uh-huh."

"That's when he agrees to pay for my mods, to repair them, and tells me I need to hit *you*. He sells it as my final job, to hit you, and claims he wants no part of the bounty…it's a personal honor thing for him."

"A gang boss who doesn't want the creds?" Stinger asked disbelievingly, and I nodded.

"Exactly," I agreed. "The plan was blatantly that he gets me to hit you, then he hits me, before I can claim the bounty."

"And how does he do that?"

"A tracker and a bomb. Implanted as part of my repairs and upgrades, though I wasn't supposed to know."

"And you found out how?"

"The carver," I admitted, laying it all out. "He's in debt and was forced to operate on me."

"Sounds like a terrible situation," Stinger agreed. "Now, which part of this am I supposed to care about?"

"Lucky is the one who knows about you. I thought, going off the details he provided, you were a hermit hiding in the basement."

"And an easy target." Stinger nodded. "That's what you're supposed to think."

"Yeah, but you've turned the ground floor into a death trap. You've invested in this, seriously so. Lucky claims he was going to sell your location but decided to give me a chance at you first. Now, as near as I can tell? His ideal scenario is that I kill you, he kills me, he claims the bounty, and wins."

"Uh-huh."

"If not? If you kill me? He'll sell the location and cut his losses. Then the bounty hunters descend on you here, and boom, all your work is wasted."

"Unless I trust you, I bet." Stinger snorted. "I trusted a janitor who trespassed when he shouldn't have. I gave him a chance, and now here we are. First thing he did was sell that information. I won't make the same mistake again."

"That's because he saw a gain out of the situation," I countered. "He saw selling your location as a way to win. My win? No offense, but I don't give two shits about you. I want Lucky dead, so that I'm not having to deal with his shit, and I want out of here to get on with killing the people who've fucked me over."

"You think I'm a carver to take the tracker and bomb out?" Stinger asked, and I shook my head.

"Fuck no, I already got them out. No, what's going to happen is this. Lucky will be on his way down here now. I was in a Johnny Air-Cab on the way over, blocking the signal on the tracker, so he'll have gotten no warning before I arrived. But he knew I was coming, so he'll not be long. All I ask is that you let me use an area to kill him. Then we leave, and the slate's wiped clean. I don't give a damn about you, and you don't give a damn about me."

"And I have to trust that you won't just tell someone about my location? I think not."

"I was APS, a judge for the wasteland. I have no authority in the city, but yeah, I'll admit, as I go, I've been generally improving the place, eliminating the guilty as I can. It's not just what I was trained to do, it's also my calling."

"And? You think you'll judge me?"

"No, frankly." I shook my head. "From what I heard about you, you're an assassin, but no evidence I could see points to you being a wanton murderer. You killed mainly criminals, scum. Some of the hits you did? Yeah, that'd get you on my radar in better times, and frankly, again, it was enough that I made my peace with hitting you. Now, though? I have no issue with walking away, provided you're really retired, as you seem to be?"

"I am on a…sabbatical," Stinger replied with a smile, before shrugging. "But I admit, I don't hunt the innocent."

"Then, for now at least, we've got no interest in each other. This place is a fucking death trap," I repeated. "Seriously, you'll slaughter whoever comes for you. No doubt, you've got a bolt hole out of here. Let's say I sell your location? You kill the fuckers when they come for you, and then escape. Now I'd got what? Twenty thou for your location, and only if they kill you?"

"Fifty, but yeah, it's on a successful hit only," Stinger agreed.

"Right, so I've gained fuck all, but pissed you off. They don't kill you, I don't get the fifty thousand but I do get to spend the rest of my life watching over my shoulder for a pissed-off master assassin." I shook my head, taking a swig of my tea. "I don't see my life being worth shit at that point."

"You'd be dead inside of the day, two if you really go to ground," Stinger admitted, watching me. "So what you're asking is what? That I turn a blind eye to the fact you came to kill me, and I let you use my traps to kill your boss?"

"Ideally, yeah." I shrugged. "Look, he's not going to sell your location, not until he's sure I'm dead. After all, why give up any of the bounty? He's planning on killing me and claiming it, so why allow the competition to his payday? This way, you're safe. No muss, no fuss."

"Except I'm left relying on you not selling that information."

"Yeah, well, the other option is that you kill us, all of us."

"I'm fine with that. Assassin by trade, remember?"

"Yeah, but your cover is blown if you do that shit. We've got backup coming to help us shoot our way out, expecting to have to help with a gang fight. You kill us, they're going to come looking, thinking that Lucky managed to do us over. They'll come looking for him, find our bodies and whatever damage we managed to do to the area, then they'll find Lucky."

I shrugged. "That's a lot of bodies and damage to hide. I seriously doubt you can do it. You're *hiding*, not standing atop a mountain of the dead and daring people to come at you. I'm betting you need this to go quiet-like, and that's what I'm offering here."

Silence fell, and the pair of us sat for a long while watching each other, before I reached out—feeling like I was dancing along the edge of a razor blade—as I tapped the hourglass on the top.

"Running out of time here," I pointed out.

"You're trying to hurry me along, when you know that one of my options, frankly my preferred one, right now, is to kill you all and deal with the fallout?"

"Yeah." I shrugged. "You kill me? I'm gonna be pissed, but frankly, my troubles are over. You take your time, and there's going to be a full gang presence here soon. Maybe we end up shooting it out and trash the place—that draws attention to exactly where you don't want it. Maybe, just maybe? Our only other option is to use the gangers as shields? Once the lead is flying, who knows what happens. And if you try to kill us, you better believe I won't walk away."

"So what are you offering?" Stinger asked me again, and I shrugged.

"I'm betting this isn't your last line of defense," I pointed out, and the figure across from me snorted, shaking his head.

"Not even close."

"So let us in and let us set up. Lucky and his lot come in. We kill them; you let us back out. Problem solved."

"And you think I'll just let you walk?"

"I think that if you won't, the EMPs we set off will fuck your hiding place up."

"The reactor explosion will take you out as well."

"Nope," I replied cheerfully. "The EMPs won't reach that far. They'll fuck all your defenses up, then you'll know that you're back to the beginning. Except, rather than packing all your shit up if you decide to move on? You'll be stuck leaving most of it as it's all fucked."

"And if I let you use my outermost defenses against Lucky and his gang?"

"Yeah?"

"What do I get?"

"Besides not being exposed and being able to relax again?"

"I could blend into the city with ease," Stinger said with utter confidence. "So here's the deal." He leaned forward on the table between us, fixing me with a glare, watching my eyes as he spoke. "You use my outer defenses, kill Lucky, and his gang, and then you instead owe *me* a favor. A job—"

"Fuck," I groaned, as he kept talking.

"In exchange for you killing Lucky and his gang, using my defenses, you cause as little damage to the floor as possible, then you'll do a job for me."

"Listen, no offense but..."

"I'll pay you the quarter of a million bounty that's outstanding on my head."

"I'm listening."

CHAPTER FORTY-SIX

The chamber that Stinger allowed us to use was both bigger than I expected it to be, and fucking dangerous. He'd clearly designed it for two forces to take each other out. Presumably for him to hold off attackers, but who knew really.

Either way, we'd barely made it down the ladder to the next floor and into this room, when the door at the far end sealed and the handful of small barriers rose.

"You'll not be permitted to leave the room," Stinger had told me before we entered. "Not until either Lucky and his people are dead, or you are. Whoever survives, I will deal with as I see fit, be that by permitting you and your people to leave by the small emergency exit, or by flooding the room with gas."

"Lucky and the others might have masks on," I pointed out.

"I intend to set fire to the gas."

"Okay, yeah, that'll probably work," I agreed, wincing and moving swiftly on. "Still, you're asking for a lot of trust from us."

"I'm giving you a chance," Stinger corrected. "I don't know you, and of the two of us, which one came to kill the other? Prove you can be trusted by doing as you've said you will, and I'll permit you to leave. Attempt to backstab me? You'll find that my paranoia is a tool not to be underestimated."

"That's…not filling me with confidence."

"Tough," he said. "Take the ladder down and face your foe, or try to run and all deals are off. Whatever happens, happens."

With that, the conversation had ended, and I'd been booted back to my body, blinking and disoriented. I'd forced myself to my feet and filled the others in quickly on the plan, as well as the deal that Stinger had offered.

There'd been some grumbling, some outright cursing and name-calling. But after thirty seconds or so, they'd all agreed that when you had the choices we had, it was the best we were likely to get, especially with the two additions I'd gotten Stinger to agree to.

First and foremost was to prove to ourselves and him that Lucky was just that much of a shitbag, and second was to make sure that when the end came, it was poetic.

Now, we were trapped in the room, waiting, along with a dead body on the floor—we asked no questions about where the body appeared from so quickly—and even though we damn well knew it wasn't Stinger, our mods were identifying it as him, thanks to some Aug-World trickery.

"I swear, I don't know how the hell this works, but…could we claim it as a kill?" Luna asked, and even Reign seemed to consider it.

"Probably not…" Reign said after a brief pause. "I mean, maybe? It might work. After all, the system queries the net address and Keystone for the user. And if there's no answer, and there's proof of death, then maybe. But when they tried to use their augs next? To, I don't know, buy a coffee?" She shook her head, and I nodded slowly.

First of all, the bounty would be taken back and we'd be marked as attempting to fuck over the bounty system. They'd request the recordings of the fight, etc., and when we couldn't provide them? They'd know we'd attempted to rip them off.

The bounty on our heads would be *insane*. The banks and more would all chip in, and we'd be dead in a matter of minutes.

No, the best choice here was to stay as we were, follow the plan, and hopefully, fucking hopefully, it'd all turn out well in the end.

The room was narrower than it was long, sort of squarish, and tapering in slightly at the end we stood at, around the body, with the ladder that led in at the far end of the room, leading to a hatch which, in turn, led to the next level.

At our end of the room were several low walls, clearly movable, and locked into place currently as if after a hard firefight. We'd contributed to that look by firing a handful of rounds each into the barriers. Reign had taken the rifle we'd found with the body, and she'd fired several of the specialist needles downrange, letting them hammer into the ladder and around it, raining shattered sections free to add to the illusion of a close fight.

I took a deep breath, and made the call, even as Gessh climbed onto Luna's shoulders, sliding the drone we'd gotten from Lion—covered as it was in explosives—into a small cavity in the ceiling, hidden among the pipes and ducts right next to the only barrier on the far side of the room.

The plan was complicated, and yet as simple as we could make it. No matter what we planned for, the fuckers would do something else.

Once the drone was in place, the girls were backing away and Reign had finished drooling over the loaned rifle, I put the call through, the connection deliberately cutting out and losing visuals.

"Kabutt?" came Lucky's voice. "That you? Where you at?"

"Under the security center," I replied in a curt voice. "It was a bastard of a fight. He nearly got away."

"Who?" Lucky asked grimly. "Stinger? Where the hell are you, Kabutt? How do I get down there?"

"In the corner of the security office," I told him. "There's a storage unit. The hatch is in there."

"Hold right where you are. I'm coming," he snapped. "Don't report the kill yet…"

"Why not?" A little knot in my stomach uncurled slightly as he went on.

"He uses body doubles. You report the death and claim that bounty, and it's not him? You don't need that shit."

"And you never thought to goddamn mention that before! You better not be fucking with me, Lucky," I growled. "He had the rifle and everything…"

"Send me an image," he ordered.

"Fuck, no. What's to stop you claiming the bounty?"

"Idiot. If I did that, you'd send the recording of your kill and then the bounty guild will hunt *me*. I'm not that dumb…"

"Yeah, well, you can wait," I said, getting a grunt as the image dropped out again.

"I'm on my way. Just hold off until I get there," he demanded, before cutting the connection, and I grinned, wondering how pissed he'd been getting, trying to figure out where I was when the tracker must have been giving him a general location and that's all.

Two minutes later, the hatch opened at the far end of the room, and I waved to the others to assume their places.

"Kabutt?" a voice called down, notably not Lucky.

"Yeah, who's that?" I called back.

"Irena."

"Irena who?"

"You want my bio?"

"Not really."

"Then shut the fuck up with the stupid questions!" she snapped. "Is it safe?"

"It's a lunatic assassin's home—of course it's not fucking safe!" I called back. "He's got the far end of the room locked off. We're trying to figure it out."

"You've got his body?" Lucky's voice echoed down.

"Yeah, it's here." I kicked the body in the middle of the room, as Irena— apparently one of the girls who was usually sprawled across him—climbed down the ladder, looking around the room.

"Bring it here," Irena ordered, and I snorted.

"Fuck, no. I'll loot it once we're done here. You want to look at it? You can come down here." I turned and walked away.

Luna and Gessh sat by a barrier at the end farthest from the ladder, with Luna supposedly injured, and Gessh tending to her.

We'd actually taken some of Stinger's distinctive rounds, the armor-piercing ones, and had attached them to Luna's armor, making it look as if she'd basically been riddled.

Reign was at the far end of the room, Stinger's rifle now leaned against the wall as she supposedly attempted to bypass the lock into the next area.

I turned my back and walked over to her, paying apparently far more attention to the lock than Lucky and Irena.

We stood there, Reign playing with a handful of wires, as we argued about the inner working of the doors. Both of us watched through the link that Stinger had shared as Lucky and his people slowly made their way inside.

That they were there to take advantage was never in doubt, but that Lucky brought seventeen people with him, on top of himself and Irena? That wasn't just overkill; that was a blatant fucking execution party.

I turned, seeing the group and the way they spread out, guns not pointing directly at us, but damn close, and I made a point of hesitating.

"Lucky, what the fuck is this?" I asked. "This doesn't look like you're coming to help a partner, not even close."

"You're really that dumb then?" He sneered and stood straighter. "You just wandered into my territory, and you looked down your nose, sneering at us poor dumb gangs, acting like you were so different, so smart. Well, you ain't."

"You fucker," I growled, acting as outraged as I could. Inside? I was filled with relief! This had been the worst part of all of it, for me at least. The worry that the army had driven me to seeing bad guys in every shadow.

I liked being an APS operator, because I didn't need to worry about the details: I got to plow straight in and fuck people up. If they tried to backstab—which they inevitably did—we replied with superior firepower.

For me, the situation with Lucky had been made far more irritating because although I thought I knew what was coming, that he'd betray me, I also hadn't known.

I didn't know for sure that civilian life was going to be like that, and of all the goddamn doubts I had racing around in my mind, the biggest was simple:

Was I going mad and paranoid?

After the shark had taken our helo down, after the guild had beaten and disposed of me—hell, after that motherfucker had literally mugged me on the way out of the goddamn clinic?

I felt like the whole world was out to get me, and I'd caught myself watching Reign and the others. Even now, Julius could be waiting outside to fucking mow us down. I'd been expecting Lucky to try to get me on the way out, and when Julius said that he'd bring the guild to protect one of his own in public, he wasn't going to be rooting around in an arcology to lose people to friendly fire, I'd agreed.

I didn't blame him. We barely knew each other, and me selling him a fuckload of guns in exchange for a few boxes of ammo, some replacement gear, and a favor was a hell of an ask.

I was grinning inside my helmet as I lifted my rifle. Luna got dragged behind cover by Gessh, and Reign moved up to stand next to me as Lucky smirked at us all.

"Now, that's hardly friendly," Lucky said. "I'm just renegotiating our deal, based on the new situation."

"Which is?"

"That you're all fucked, and I've got the guns." He shrugged, tucking his thumbs behind his belt. An off-white T-shirt strained to contain his muscles as he rolled his shoulders. "So, this is how it is, people. You now work for me. You're used to being hired muscle—you're mercs, after all—so nothing changes. You go where I say, and when, and you all get to live."

"And if we tell you to go fuck yourself?" Reign asked conversationally, her grazer out of sight behind a nearby barrier, but Stinger's special rifle, loaded with armor-piercing darts, held ready.

"You could, but you see, Kabutt has a secret, one that even he doesn't know about."

"Hell of a secret, that," I replied laconically.

"You see, you arrogant little bastard, I sent you to *my* chop shop for a reason!" Lucky snarled. "You've got a tracker and a bomb installed, and it's enough to seriously fuck up your day!"

"Bullshit." I scoffed, and he lifted one hand, apparently sending a signal as he gestured. I felt the tracker—actually in my pocket now, as we'd confirmed it was literally just a tracker and not a bomb—vibrate.

"You feel that, Kabutt?" He grinned. "You do, I can see it."

"That something you regularly have to ask your partners?" I asked. "If they can feel you trying to fuck them?"

"It's a bomb, in your guts, and when I send the signal, you're fucked," Lucky growled. "And you still mouth off?"

"What can I say? I think you've not got the balls for it." I snorted. "So come on then, what's this new deal? Any other minor details you've forgotten to mention?"

"No, you little fuck," Lucky jeered. "You all work for me now. You're gonna do the jobs I tell you to do, including bringing back my fucking armory that you looted!"

"What armory?"

"Sirisena's fucking armory!"

"Oh, I sold that." I laughed.

"The credits then," he hissed.

"Spent them." I shrugged. "Got some new mods and—"

"You dumb fuck," Lucky huffed. "This is your last chance. You give me your credits, you drop your guns, and you fucking pray I'm feeling generous with your jobs from now on. Otherwise, you're—"

"So you always intended on this?" I cut him off. "You always planned on claiming the bounty on Stinger, and making us either serve you, or killing us?"

"No," he admitted. "I never expected you to kill Stinger, and I didn't expect the rest of your team, but that's fine. I'm claiming the bounty, and you'll be killing my rivals and hunting specters for me."

"And what makes you think that's gonna work?" I asked. "I mean, we walk out of here…sure, you've got a bomb in me, but my team? We met a few days back. They'll just go work with some other asshole."

"We'll take you all to the carver," he corrected. "You'll all have bombs installed, or you'll not leave here alive."

"I'll say it again." I smiled. "You've not got the balls for this, Lucky, so here's my counteroffer. You and your little fucking gang surrender. From now on, you work for me, and maybe I'll negotiate a rate with Oshbob to sell you all back. You drop your guns, you transfer all your creds to me, and maybe, just maybe, we'll leave some of you intact after this."

"Intact?" Irena asked, and I nodded.

"Yeah, regardless of the outcome here, I'll be gelding Lucky. The world is fucked up enough—we don't need more honorless fucking assholes running around."

"You brought this on yourself, Kabutt," Lucky hissed. "Say goodbye, asshole!"

"Bye, asshole!" I grinned at him, as he apparently triggered the bomb, and a massive section of the room vanished in the detonation.

CHAPTER FORTY-SEVEN

The bomb that Gessh had attached to the drone, and had then had a fuckload of the high explosive shit that we'd stolen from Sirisena's place added to it, was right where we wanted it by that point.

As soon as Lucky had kicked off his little speech, and Luna and Gessh had got safely out of sight, Gessh had started to control the little drone.

It was old, like seriously old, some kind of a pipe-cleaning model, with six legs, each with a cushioned magnet at the end that left it more or less silent—a must in the sewers, or it'd be eaten by something—and it'd crawled along the pipes until it was almost directly above the group.

When Lucky detonated the bomb, small as the original had been, it in turn triggered the rest of the high ex. The fragments of metal and more that went flying from the remnants of the pipes it'd been atop of, were, in my opinion, overkill.

As soon as Lucky had gestured, we'd dove out of sight, more or less, hiding behind the barriers as the explosion scythed through Lucky's team.

Five were killed outright. Lucky himself, by dint of being directly underneath the largest of the pipes, was shielded from some of the explosion, and was merely smashed to the ground and pinned there, as half the section of roof collapsed on him. Those around him were blasted from their feet, shredded by sections of destroyed pipe, and, in one unlucky fucker's case, steam-broiled by a damaged coolant pipe that had apparently been in mid-vent.

Most of the gangers, though, were both armored and had been expecting trouble. That didn't mean to say they reacted well, but they also weren't taken down easily.

Of the nineteen who walked in, including Lucky and Irena, ten were still combat capable, against our four, and the air was thick with flying slugs, flames, coherent light, and worse.

I hit the inside of the barrier I was hiding behind, whipped my rifle over the top and opened fire, the optics relaying the sight as gangers sprinted for cover.

People were running in all directions, and as two of the fuckers actually ran directly at us, Luna stood, firing off a half dozen rounds from her shotgun on full auto.

The closest figure to her was picked up as if by a giant hand and thrown backward. Slugs punched through him and out the far side, even as she switched aim to the second, then hammered a handful of shots directly into one of the barriers opposite us as idiots dove behind it.

Gessh had rolled to the side and was sighting down the room, grazer assault rifle humming and crackling as she sprayed the room with destructive energies.

Reign had dived behind her own barrier, and then leaned around it, aiming carefully, before letting loose a single dart from Stinger's gun.

It hurtled downrange, hitting the barrier and punching straight through it. The scream that rose on the far side made it clear that someone had been highly unfortunate.

I jerked my gun back down, dumping the depleted mag as slugs hit the barrier where my gun had been. I slotted a second mag with speed born of practice, then sighted carefully around the edge, firing three shots into an ankle and foot I could see peeking out from cover on the far side.

There was a scream, and the figure jerked up…only to take another hit to the face as Gessh ended her target's issues.

I grinned…until a well-placed smoke grenade exploded nearby, and the room vanished. Sneering, I flicked to heat vision, then moved on, the still-venting steam pipe making that useless. Two more modes activated then vanished, before I got a grainy motion tracker working, and I swore, bursting from behind cover to vault to the far side, as a frag landed next to me.

It went off as I cleared the barrier. A single shard caught my boot and tugged me into a roll. And then I started to really swear, as I slid out of the smoke and into the main room again.

I shifted, firing, then rolled to my right as a figure sprinted at me, gun swinging around. I fired again, taking him in the knee, then hip, and then the upper chest and head, sending him tumbling past, reduced to sliding meat.

A blur appeared to my left, and I was rolling again. The world spun as someone hit me with something from stealth; a hand yanked my rifle aside, as another grabbed onto my throat, squeezing hard.

"Call them off!" I heard Irena's voice demanding, and I grabbed her wrist with my left, squeezing with all the augmented strength that hand could bring to bear.

I heard creaks, but it was me who was up shit creek. My armoring for my throat, being dragon scale, resisted blunt-force impacts, like fucking bullets, not enhanced fingers!

I gasped as she squeezed harder. My armor held her at bay for a second or two, then started to compress and added to the pain.

"Last chance!" she snarled, twisting my rifle and forcing me to release it, or have my fingers, and probably my right arm, broken. Then she rolled free, blood and some kind of augmentation fluid spraying across my helmet.

Luna was there, sword blurring as Irena leapt backward. Her right arm now ended in a stump at the elbow, even as augments cut in, sealing the wound and tamping down on the blood loss.

"Bitch!" Irena snarled, the party girl and druggie that I'd seen draped across Lucky no longer anywhere in evidence as she flipped my rifle around, catching it in her left hand and opening fire on Luna.

Luna was fast, though, and fucking hell she was good. The flat of her blade slapped the rifle aside—bullets hammered into the floor near my head as I cursed and coughed, rolling to my knees—and then she was in close.

Her blade sliced the inside of Irena's left thigh on the downswing; then, a roll of her wrist and the blade rose again, hacking through the back of the right knee and out.

Irena screamed, crashing to the ground, and a second figure hit Luna from the side. The pair of them fell and rolled, blades flashing as they fought.

Bullets flew overhead, as well as the crackles and ear-tearing screams of grazer beams. I snarled, shoving myself to my feet, yanking the shotgun off my shoulder and firing three fast shots into Irena, who'd been bringing my rifle to bear on me.

The first hit, a solid slug, hit her in the chest, slamming her back into the ground. The slug punched through her cleanly, hitting the metal floor and ricocheting back up, tearing a second wound in her shoulder blade.

My second and third shots were to the upper chest and her chin. Honestly, they were probably overkill, but that bitch deserved it. I could barely breathe, and I coughed and hacked as I struggled back into cover, dragging a medikit from my belt. I grabbed the covering and yanked it off, only to have someone rip it from my hand, claws leaving deep gashes in my hand.

I hissed in pain, then grunted. The world exploded in stars as someone hit me in the side of the head next, sending me to the floor, spitting blood through a broken jaw and cheek, my helmet dented and cracked.

They clearly thought they'd killed me, turning their back and running.

I grabbed the shotgun and dragged it around, aiming for a second blur in the air, noticeable only by the way the smoke eddied and swirled.

I fired, three shots, then switched to full auto, spraying and praying. One of the last shots hit a sprinting figure in the back as they dove from sight around a fallen pipe, even as a hit to the barrel smashed my shotgun out of my injured hand.

The shotgun hit the floor and I abandoned it, instead yanking the next medikit out, a medium, and tore the plugs free, stabbing it into my throat and discarding it as soon as it hissed empty.

I clawed at my helmet, crying out in pain as the dented-in metal took skin and hair with it as I tore it free, and then again as the nanites got to work, repairing and restructuring my throat and cheek. My hand itched like crazy as a veritable stream was redirected to focus on the gouges suffered.

I was up and moving, though. Gunfire still rang out, and I could see Luna and someone fighting nearby, rolling over and over, blades glinting in the light.

I dragged my hatchet free. It was nothing special, no vibrating wonder of modern technology. No, it was a fucking short axe with a wicked edge, and I hammered it into the back of the figure atop Luna, as they tried to drive a blade into her throat.

They screamed, and I dragged the axe free, as Luna shoved the dagger to the side and grabbed her foe's chin, yanking it sideways and filling the air with the snap of breaking bone.

"Behind you!" Luna shouted, and I spun, axe whipping sideways to take a ganger in the chest as he launched himself at me. The two of us staggered as he coughed blood all over.

His eyes widened, my axe buried up to the head in his side. A cascade of blood fountained out of his mouth, as I got a sudden connection request.

"What!" I snarled into the commlink.

"Five more figures have entered the room. Assumedly, they were alerted by another. They're in full stealth gear, and are clearly here for me. Take them down in the next thirty seconds, or I activate the gas," Stinger said.

"Fuck's sake!" I snarled. "You're a dick, Stinger!" I roared, reaching into my pocket and dragging the MADD free, depressing the trigger and underarm flinging it toward the entrance, before grabbing Luna and dragging her to her feet.

"MADD OUT!" I bellowed into the commlink. "Get down!"

We hobbled and staggered; bullets hit our armor as we ran, counting down the steps.

We almost didn't make it, diving behind a barrier and crashing to the ground, Luna's breathing loud in my ear as she spoke.

"What the hell was—"

The MADD exploded. Hundreds of tiny monomolecular wires burst free in all directions. The explosive charge sent them rocketing outward. Their anchors punched holes into everything around them, then fired the second phase. Tiny posts drove out, securing the anchors to whatever they'd hammered into.

Two hundred and thirty monomolecular wires, literally finer than a hair and sharper than a scalpel, deployed to convert the fair end of the chamber into a spider's web of fucking terror.

The wires could cut steel like butter, and as for flesh?

The five stealthed assassins who had been sneaking through the room, presumably intent on making sure Stinger was dead and then claiming the bounty—or, for all I knew, intent on making me dinner and giving me the best blowjob of my life—were rendered down to collapsing threads of meat and technology. Blood sprayed from their severed remains like a giant's hand had crushed an invisible cranberry juice container.

The remainder of Lucky's forces at that end of the room were reduced to cascading kibble. The single fighter still standing—a ganger of surprisingly little situational awareness—screamed "Follow me!" and raced out of cover, running toward our end of the room and the dissipating smoke.

He managed a half dozen steps, before the sudden silence, as all his allies stopped firing, reduced as they were, finally got through to him.

There was a confused call of "Uh…guys?"

Then Reign shot him in the chest. The dart lifted him from his feet and sent him flying backward in a mist of blood.

Silence fell, broken only by our heavy breathing as we peered over the barriers at the drifting smoke, the devastation, and the glittering strands that dripped blood.

"You didn't tell me you had a MADD grenade," came the complaint from Stinger.

"You didn't tell me there were so fucking many of them, or that there were five fucking stealth assholes," I countered.

"There were nine," he admitted after a second. "Four were with your friends. The other five were more professional."

"How'd you know they were there?"

"A scanner on the hatch and pressure plates on the floor. Any movement alerted me."

"And you didn't think to fucking share that?" I growled, sagging back down and pressing my back to the barrier, glaring at the locked door at the far end of the room. "So…you gonna try to kill us, or you gonna stick to your word?"

"Try?" Stinger said, as if amused.

"You've seen four of us take out what, twenty?"

"Twenty-eight."

"Fuck's sake. So, you gonna honor the deal?"

"I will," Stinger said after a few seconds, having clearly thought about fucking us over. "But only once the deal is done. You have two survivors."

"Fucking hell, really?" I looked over the top of the barrier. "Who?"

"Lucky and a companion."

"Heh. Maybe there are gods after all." I grunted, pushing to my feet and looking the others over.

We were all injured, I saw straightaway, scratching at the itching on the back of my right hand as the nanites worked to seal the wound fully.

"Are you okay?" I asked the others, glancing from Luna with her cuts—the blade fight at close quarters had left a pair of long cuts that exposed bone on the right side of her face—and a bullet wound to her right leg, to Gessh who, frankly, looked awful.

"Contagion grenade," she said. "Fuck. I didn't know anyone still used them."

I winced, taking an automatic step back, despite the obvious fact that she was still breathing making it clear the grenade hadn't been a powerful one.

They ranged in strength from a plague-like effect, covering anyone who breathed in the spores in painful lesions and coughing blood, to essentially the flu, all aches and pains.

The spores were time sensitive, though—something about the deployment, activation, and the original loading of the grenades meant that the most powerful and virial pathogen they carried might give you a weak cold when it was finally used. As such, the contagion grenades were scrapped from military use, and then from corpo officially.

I'd heard that the last supplies of them were being used to clear areas out for urban redevelopment, but that might have just been a rumor.

Either way, Gessh was injecting herself with a small medikit and waving to us all that she'd be fine in a few minutes.

Reign was rubbing at her tit, and we all spent a few seconds watching, before Luna spoke up.

"Look, if you want some private time to take care of your needs, we can respect that. Just, you know, warn us next time. Poor Kabutt here is drooling."

"No I'm not!" I snapped.

"Touched a nerve there." Luna laughed, and I growled at her, before looking back at Reign.

"You okay?"

"Crowd-suppressant round," she explained. "Direct hit to my goddamn nipple."

Crowd-suppressant rounds dealt with rioters in basic body armor but without killing them. Simply put, they were a kind of rubber round that expanded on impact, then released a flash electrical charge.

We all winced, knowing that right now, her tit was literally turning black and blue with bruises. For the next few days, she was going to be insanely sore, but equally, it'd be a hell of a waste to use a medikit on it.

"Besides that and this…" She indicated a small chunk taken out of her upper left shoulder and shrugged. "I'm good."

"Then let's go fucking kill Lucky," I suggested, getting smiles and nods from the others.

CHAPTER FORTY-EIGHT

We stumbled, staggered, and wandered around the barriers, with Reign waving to us to wait a minute, before slipping around the back of the pipe.

We paused. I leaned my head around the corner, and jerked back as a shotgun loaded with fléchettes went off. The blast tore past me and into the roof, ricocheting deeper into the room.

"Now, now, Lucky, that's not very friendly!"

"Fuck you, Kabutt!" Lucky hissed, and I grinned at the pain in his voice.

"You know, it sounds like you're stuck," I called back. "Maybe you and your friend should toss your guns out, and we can talk about your options…"

"I've called Oshbob!" he shouted. "He's sending reinforcements!"

"He tried to place three calls," Stinger said a second later on a direct call to me. "Two were to the same location, and the third was to ACE. He also tried to send a compressed datapacket. I intercepted all attempts."

"Really?" I called to him. "You hear back from them?"

"They're gonna be here any second…" he tried, and I snorted.

"I don't think so. And just so you know? Calling fucking *ACE*, of all people? I mean, that's low, dude. The compressed data file is interesting as well…"

Silence for a few seconds.

"What do you want, Kabutt?" Lucky called back grimly.

"What do any of us want, Lucky?" I replied philosophically. "A home, somewhere to call our own? Friends?"

"Fucking stop playing with me, you asshole! What do you want?"

"I want to renegotiate our partnership, Lucky," I said. "I want a fuckload of credits, and I want an apology."

"An…apology?" he hissed, his companion still silent.

"And the credits," I replied. "You've cost me credits here, and frankly, you hurt my feelings. Credits first, then the apology."

I gestured to the others and spoke in a low voice. "Search the bodies and get ready to move. Stay away from the far end of the room."

I got nods, and while they started to move, I leaned on the pipe and the pile of debris from the fallen section of the roof, making sure I was close enough they could do nothing as I edged my rifle around the edge, connecting to it and watching the fucker as one of Lucky's assholes tried to keep the big orc alive.

There was a section of the roof atop the end of the pipe that held Lucky down, and the big half-orc's skin looked even greyer than normal thanks to the blood loss that I could see adding to the gradually spreading puddle by his side.

"So…" I watched Lucky trying to get free, and the ganger, a familiar and young ganger of indeterminate gender who glanced from him to the door in the distance as he pulled futilely. "Last chance for the creds," I said.

"Fucking give me an account then!" they snarled, and I hesitated, before sending both them and Lucky my account with a knock.

"Throw the guns out!"

I'd not actually expected them to do anything, and their identity finally clicked with me, as they sent over…thirteen thousand credits and change. They'd been the one who'd looked down on me as I'd gotten off the lift that time a day or two back, and who apparently hated orcs, from what they'd said to Luna.

As it was?

"Calos!" Lucky snarled at them, and they sneered, before dragging Lucky's shotgun free and tossing it aside where he couldn't reach it.

"Sorry, hun, end of the road!" they said, before calling out to us. "Can I go?"

"Sure." I shook my head at how fucking easily they'd betrayed Lucky, and the way they were trying to hide a gun down by their side. "One coming out, people."

Calos was up and running in a flash, sprinting for the entrance they'd come by, and I spoke quickly, but not quick enough. "I wouldn't go that…Ouch."

They ran headlong into the remnants of the MADD grenade. Their scream barely started before they collapsed into minced shreds of flesh, bouncing and dicing themselves with their momentum.

"Damn." I shrugged, turning back to Lucky and watching him through the scope. "Ah, well. Last chance, Lucky."

"You killed them?" He panted in pain as he tried to pull himself free.

"They concealed a gun, then ran straight into a monomolecular wire. That was all on them." I smiled. "Let's face it, I think I'm being pretty patient here. Last chance, though, before I shoot you in the fucking face. Credits or bullets. Your choice."

He finally saw the rifle and froze, then snarled and responded to the knock, with a grand total of twenty-seven credits.

I started to laugh, then stepped around the corner and pointed the gun at his face.

"Lucky, you sure as shit weren't named for your brains, that's obvious."

"I spent it all!" he snarled. "I had to restock, to get people moving, to—"

I shot him in the knee, making him scream. He let go of the pipe, the weight settling even more, and he screamed again.

"Count to three, Lucky, and you might as well close your eyes."

"No, wait! Look, I have more credits! They're invested, that's all, and…"

"One."

"What the hell do you want!" he half screamed. "You want a fucking apology? Fine! I'm sorry! You happy now?!"

"Two." I settled comfortably on the pipe, making him hiss in pain as I aimed at the bridge of his nose. "Close your eyes, Lucky. You don't want to see this coming."

"Fine!" he surrendered. "FINE! My apartment…it's got everything in there, just…you need me, remember? You're meeting Oshbob tomorrow, and he hates humans!"

I received a data code for access to his quarters as well as a locational marker.

"I've got two half-orcs on my team," I pointed out in a low purr. "They're both prettier *and* smarter than you."

"I…I…"

"Goodbye, Lucky," I said conversationally, shifting to get more comfortable, before pulling the trigger.

The bullet hit Lucky above the nose, punching through the skull and out the far side in a spray of fluid, cranial gloop, and Lucky's innermost personal thoughts.

"You're not very honorable," Stinger said after a few seconds, calling me directly again.

"I am, actually," I corrected him. "What I'm not is very *patient*. That dickbag…" I gestured off toward the pile of shredded meat that had formerly been known as Calos. "Was damn rude to me on the other occasion we met, and despite being told to leave their weapons behind, tried to run with a gun.

"Lucky, on the other hand, had betrayed me already, and no offense, but you do that once, I'm not giving you a second chance to do it again. The fact the fucker had me tagged with a tracker and a fucking bomb? That's not a 'maybe' he was planning on offing me later—that's a 'when.'"

"And now we come to our particular situation," Stinger said, and I nodded.

"Very true."

"What to do…" he mumbled, as if thinking aloud.

"Well, consider it carefully," I said clearly. "You know what happens if you try to kill me, and frankly, I'm ready to EMP the shit outta you if I have to."

"Now, now, Kabutt." Stinger sighed. "There's no need for that."

"You're considering betraying me…"

There was a sudden laugh, before the voice changed. "No, actually, dear boy, I'm not." Stinger's voice changed from the obviously synthesized amalgamation of voices to that of an older woman and settled there.

I hesitated for a second. "So, what are you considering?"

"Exactly as Reign suggested, actually," Stinger said. The door at the end of the room opened smoothly, showing a small, older woman in smart body armor who gestured at us to come to her. "Deactivate the MADD, and get anything you need from their corpses, then come this way."

I winced. "Deactivate…?"

"Send the code to the grenade," she repeated, then sighed. "Save me from working with amateurs. Here, send this code to the grenade's processor core."

I received a complex code, and I squinted at the blur from the monomolecular wires, ordering my RI to scan for a processor core. It found a dozen, mainly remnants of people, but after a second, it'd narrowed it down to two, and I sent the code to both.

There was response from one, and a faint blurring of the air, followed by a gentle clang.

"You think the designer of the MADD wanted people to never be able to use the area again?" Stinger asked me, sounding disappointed. "All MADD grenades are set with a default activation and deactivation code. Sending the code results in either deployment or retraction, so be damn careful when you're carrying one, and always change the code on it!"

"How?" I asked, confused.

"You bought it or looted it?" she asked.

"Looted."

"That explains it." She sighed. "Any proper sale comes with the activation, editing, and deactivation codes."

"They're banned, aren't they?" I asked, and she snorted.

"Of course they are. You remember the mess those defective ones made, don't you?"

"Well, yeah. So…?"

"Oh, lad." Stinger snorted. "You've so much to learn yet. If you want to become a real bounty hunter and assassin, you've not even touched the surface yet!"

"You offering to teach us?" Reign asked, hopeful, and the older woman shook her head.

"Retirement time for me. But, you can still do nicely out of this, I think, provided you're at least a little smarter than you act."

"Me or her?" I asked.

"Definitely you." Stinger snorted. "She's plenty bright enough."

"You'd be surprised." Reign snickered, glancing at Luna and Gessh, who grinned at her.

"So, you want to loot those bodies or not?" Stinger asked, and Luna straightened.

"I'll do the far end," she said. "If she can switch the grenade off, she can probably switch them back on again, so you all stay back…"

We nodded, spreading out and looting as well, watching Luna as she demonstrated insane bravery, considering what we'd just seen. After a few seconds of clearing the stuff closest to us, she bit the bullet and walked straight into the middle of it all, feeling around and occasionally cursing over how messy it all was.

I turned back to Stinger, having looted the space around me quickly, taking only credit-chips, guns, ammo, and the occasional explosive, until I finally stood on something I couldn't quite see. I grinned as I realized I'd found the fucker.

Squatting, I ran my hands over the still form, half rolling them until I could see the hole in the suit, that I'd blown through with the shotgun. The adaptive camouflage made the bloody mess of the body underneath twist and warp as I felt for the seams.

It was a camosuit.

I checked for the seals, finding them after half a minute of swearing, and running my fingers down the material, splitting the edge to reveal the idiot inside.

It was another of the women who had worked with Lucky, apparently unarmed. But remembering the blow she'd landed on me, denting the titanium of my helm and breaking bones through it? She'd clearly not needed the weapons. I rolled her out of it, seeing it had only a few minutes of charge left. I connected to it and shut it down, putting my prize in my bag for later.

Clearly this was why I'd only ever seen her once, and when I did, the other one, Irena, had been missing. I was betting the pair, as bodyguards, had taken turns wearing this fucker, ready to slaughter anyone who attacked the boss.

Sudden comments by Lucky, like when he was in my apartment, made a lot more sense when I considered there could have been a stealthed bodyguard there watching over him.

I stood again and moved back to stand by Stinger. "Is that possible?" I asked, the thought having rolled around my head as Luna looted the bodies. "To reactivate the grenades, I mean?"

"Yes and no." Stinger shrugged. "The wires and anchors deploy using an explosive charge. No explosive, no deployment. When it's unlocked, it is possible to tease the cables out, but dangerous."

"You've done it?"

"Kabutt, I was acknowledged as a master assassin before you were born. Believe me, I've done almost everything."

"So what now?" I moved over to stand closer, shaking my head as I recognized her as the stinky crazy lady I'd met on my first day. "And what the hell were you doing out in the entrance? I mean, any ganger could have attacked you at any minute."

"It'd have been the last thing they did." She snorted. "I'm far from defenseless, boy, and I like to see who enters and leaves my building."

"Your—" I frowned. "You own the building?"

"Ha!" She snorted. "Gods, no, but I do have, shall we say, a vested interest in it. The lower floors are mine, and have been for many years. Others…?" She shrugged. "Perhaps I'll send one of my people to replace the floor bosses you took out so happily. Or perhaps not."

"So…" I looked at her expectantly, and she huffed.

Luna rejoined us, her arms full of gear that she quickly passed around. The rest of us packed shit into our bags, intending to check on them later.

"Fine." She waved for us to follow, leading the way into the next corridor and down to a second ladder, then from there to a hatch, and finally…into a fucking luxurious apartment.

Looking around, I was stunned. It was easily ten times the size of mine, if not more, and the layout? It looked like something in a corpo vid, the ones where they tried to convince you if you were a good little drone, you could one day earn something like this.

It was bullshit, there was no way anyone not of the corps got something so sweet, but here?

"Goddamn," I muttered, and saw several others standing around, each wearing masks. "Are they…?"

"They're Stinger."

"They're…then who the fuck are you?" I asked.

She smiled. "I'm Stinger."

"And they're…?"

"Also Stinger."

"Explain that please," I asked softly, my mind racing.

"I'm a master assassin, but no assassin lives free, boy. We're always hunted, we're always on the edge, and the retirement package? Not the best," she admitted. "So we decided some time ago that the best way to do this was to create a fictional identity. We were all assassins already, you understand. We'd reached about as high as it was possible to go, and we had some impressive bounties on our heads, but…"

"But we were tired of being hunted," another voice, this time a man's, rang out. "Every time we finished a job, no matter the scumbags we were removing from society, we were hunted by more and more. Their friends, family who refused to see what they'd been, their replacements who wanted to make sure they didn't meet the same fate…all of them."

"So we created Stinger," another voice said from the side, and a young woman, judging by the long hair and elfin figure, replied, also hiding her face. "A master assassin from another city. Between us all, we could perform any hit we needed to easily, and our team gradually grew."

"We went from a handful of assassins who were sick of the business, to ten in less than a year, and we rediscovered the joy of the challenge." The old woman made us all tea, setting the cups before each of us.

I glanced at the tea suspiciously, and she laughed.

"Kabutt, if we wanted you dead, you'd be dead. There's nothing dangerous in the tea. Drink up." She took my cup and set her own before me, sipping from it and smiling.

I shrugged, knowing that she was damn well right. I took a drink of the goddamn tea, before regarding her as a faintly familiar taste registered on my tongue.

"That's drugged," I said softly, and she nodded.

"Yes, and you're far too trusting," she agreed with a little shake of her head.

CHAPTER FORTY-NINE

"What the…" Reign was rising to her feet as I reached out, grabbing her arm and stopping her, even as I called for the others.

"Stop!" I ordered.

"Wise." The old woman smiled.

"You said she's drugged…"

"Sodium pentothal." I stared at the older woman. "I recognize the fucking taste of that one. They dosed us with it in training so that we'd know."

"Ah, the joys of the APS operatives. It's one of over three dozen chemicals used in our particular creation, but it's very effective, nevertheless."

"So, truth serum?" I asked, and she nodded, reaching out and taking my cup, then taking a long draught from it herself.

"This way we both know where we stand," she explained. "Finish the tea, boy, and we can get this over with."

I nodded, knocking back the hot tea and wincing as my mouth was burned.

"Damn…that's hot. You mind if I…"

"You can have water after this. I know that trick as well, boy, flushing the substance as quickly as possible." The old woman smiled, and I grinned ruefully at her.

"So, ask away," I suggested, smacking my lips and pulling them back, before running my tongue across my teeth. "Tingles…"

"First of all, are you looking to betray us and claim the bounty by killing us or selling our location?" the old woman asked, and I answered before I thought about it.

"No. Provided you don't try to hurt me or my team, we're fine with leaving you be."

"Good." The woman smiled, then gestured to me. "Your turn, boy."

"Are you intending to kill us?"

"Not at this time," she said. "If you keep faith with us? Not at all. If you become a danger? Then yes."

"Okay, about all I can expect." I grunted, gesturing for her to ask the next question.

"What will you do if we let you leave?"

"Go to kill Tyrannus."

"Who…" She hesitated, then cursed, gesturing for me to go next.

"What do you intend to do with us if you decide to trust us?"

"We'll offer you occasional contracts, as well as some training, and the benefit of our experience, as well as introducing you to certain markets that aren't available to the usual grade of merc and assassin."

"Why…dammit," I growled, having to wait for my "turn" again.

"Who is Tyrannus?"

"An ex-army corporate stooge who I think is involved in the deaths of my old team, and who fucked me over, stealing my suit and emptying my cred account."

"Fair enough…" She nodded, clearly respecting the reasoning.

"Okay, why would you offer us contracts and help?"

"We're old—most of us, anyway—and we're tired. With your help, we could officially die off. We've got more than enough credits to last us the rest of our lives. We were assassins for years before we became Stinger, and we commanded high fees until the end." She shrugged.

"While we don't need the creds, we'd like the peace and quiet. One of us could claim the bounty on our head, but it's only two hundred and fifty thousand, and then that one is back out in public, a target again. If they 'retire' publicly? They'll be hunted by up-and-comers who want to say they killed us. We've no interest in that."

"Also, we'd like to occasionally go out and kill some fuckers who need killing," another voice called out from the back of the room, and I grinned.

"So—" I bit my tongue.

"It's okay. Speak."

"Okay, so you want us to claim your death?" I asked. "We get paid, you publicly die, and we all move on with our lives, except that on occasion you'll have jobs for us?"

"Assassin and bounty hunting jobs," she confirmed. "Very well-paid ones. You'll take your own, of course, from time to time no doubt, and you'll make a good name for yourselves, as we'll help you, if we feel like it."

"Why?"

"Because while some of us are happy to retire, others are goddamn bored to shit and have a list of motherfuckers who need to be shot in the face," another voice called.

"And if we don't want to do the job?" I asked the one who seemed like their leader, as she poured us both a coffee this time.

"Depends on the job," she admitted, passing one over to me. "Most of the time? We'd be annoyed but that's it. Now and then, though, there's a few motherfuckers who have crossed lines, corpos who have executed families for being in the wrong place at the wrong time. We're the only consequence most corpos ever come across…So, believe me, there's a list."

"And we'll be paid for this?" Luna asked.

"Highly."

"I'm in, boss," Reign said softly. "If you are, I mean?"

"Us too, you know, if…" Gessh added.

"I've got a mission already." I held my hand up to forestall them. "I'm not discussing it, so don't fucking ask if you want this to end well. It has no real bearing on you fuckers and this deal, and will probably help massively further down the line. But it's to do with friends of mine, and their lives are at risk, so *do not* push."

"Very well." The old woman settled back and crossed her arms. "I will not pry, except to ask, will your mission be likely to prevent any jobs we request you do?"

"No," I said. "It was always my intention to do other jobs as well, build my reputation and grow as a merc. This fits well with that. Bounty hunting and assassination doesn't concern me. But I have a few house rules."

"Go on."

"I won't hunt innocents, nor children," I said. "If I'm going to kill some fucker like Lucky? No issue. I don't give a damn about species or whatever, but some scumbag? Yeah, fine. You want me to kill some kid to teach their parents a lesson? I'm out. I'm APS. We bring judgment—we don't break it…at least, not those of us with any self-respect."

"That…is more than acceptable. It would have been a condition of ours as well, had we not already been observing you." She smiled.

"Joy! Anything I should be aware of?" I asked.

"Not that we wish to raise now. Suffice to say that we'd been considering this as an option before this, although, I'll admit, the current situation has moved our timeline up."

The older woman sighed, then gestured vaguely above us.

"The stealthed assassins make it clear that another knows we exist, and our probable location, therefore, it is time." She stood, gesturing for us to stay put as she called out in a loud voice, "I call for a quorum and a vote!"

Others appeared from all around the massive apartment, and we looked at one another in shock, seeing how many there were, and how heavily armed they all were.

"Twelve are here…" the woman said after a few seconds. "Twelve of the thirteen is acceptable. I call for the death of Stinger, and our retirement, with these four as our successors. Do we have any who dissent?"

"I do," a large figure growled, stepping forward. "For years, I've been stuck down here with you fuckers. I want to be free!"

"Any others?"

Silence reigned.

"I call for a vote. All those who agree, raise your hand and send me approval."

Eleven of the twelve did so, and the twelfth cursed.

"You all know why I say we should still work, but that's fine! I retire as Stinger!" he said. "I quit, although I'll be bound by the rules we agreed, and I have no issue with these claiming the bounty—"

"Very well…"

"Provided they agree to a single job for me." He stood straighter. A massive gamma cannon rested against his shoulder as he reached up, pulling off his mask, and revealed a horrifically scarred face. "They're to kill Anthos Black, with no help from any of us. Once that's done? Aye, I'll agree that we can be called upon for training."

I cursed as a new job was sent to me, and I hesitated before reading it.

"This Anthos Black…does that job stop us claiming the bounty here? Because that's gonna add to the time that fucker's come looking for you. You know that, right?" I asked.

"No, that job, while deserved, as he's a scumbag flesh peddler and war criminal, is separate," the old lady said. "I'll agree that you should be made to prove your competence beyond basic thuggery. Kill Anthos Black, and we will agree to train and adopt you as our successors. We'll guide and act as your handlers, taking a percentage of the jobs we choose for you.

"You'll have the option to take or refuse any of the jobs—save that of Anthos—and regardless, you can claim Stinger's head. The only difference is that we will not train you, nor offer any advice and access to the advanced markets, until this job is done. Do we have consensus?" The old lady looked around, and this time even the scarred man nodded.

"Then it's up to you. You may leave here now, no hard feelings, but you leave without the bounty, or you accept our offer, and the game begins."

"The game?" I asked.

"All of life is a game, boy, the greatest game of all. Take it from a master assassin—nobody ever wins. It's all just about accruing points and shiny achievements until you lose." The scarred man grunted, and I nodded to him in understanding, before looking to the other three.

Luna and Gessh were clearly uncomfortable with the situation, but the opportunities this represented? Hell, yes.

Reign practically vibrated with excitement, and she shot me puppy-dog eyes as soon as I looked to her, making me snort in amusement, before I pulled up the job notification and read it over.

Job Offer

Kabutt and his team will carry out the assassination/execution of the war criminal Anthos Black without assistance or advice from the Stinger collective.

- 1 x Assassination of [Anthos Black – Location attached].

In exchange, Kabutt and team will receive upon completion:

- Access to the Assassins Jobs list.
- Access to Advanced and Master level training.
- Access to Advanced, Specialist, and Master equipment and artifact markets.

Accept	Refuse

"Well, looks like we're in business together then," I agreed, seeing massive potential for my little corpo scumbag hunting intentions, when combined with the training on offer here.

Then I accepted the offer.

We were permitted to grab a drink—not drugged, thank fuck—and I quickly downed mine, ordering the others to keep any questions to themselves for the next half an hour or so.

That order was—of course—utterly ignored, as they amused themselves by questioning me when I couldn't help the responses.

Questions like "What do you *really* think of Reign's ass?" and "How often do men really think about sex?" were the tip of the iceberg. Although, thankfully, they were respectful of my privacy enough to not pry on certain topics.

They focused on anything they thought might make me blush, including asking whether I wanted a foursome with them, and whether I'd actually do it, if I thought they were offering.

They waited until I admitted that yes, I'd love to have all four of us in a bed, before the sisters admitted that it'd never happen and they only liked me as a friend.

I knew that. Fuck's sake, I was *ninety-nine percent sure* that Reign felt the same, especially considering she couldn't physically have any "fun" and I had my own damn rules about not shitting where I ate. That wasn't the point, though. Because when highly attractive ladies offer basically a gang-bang just to see whether you'd be interested, and you're under the influence of psychoactive truth serums?

You say the absolute truth and curse your goddamn tongue the entire time it betrays you.

By the time the girls had their fun, and I'd flushed my system of the drug, the oldest of the Stinger collective was back, and I accepted a transmitted recording of someone dressed as Stinger being shot, falling to the ground and dying.

"Who was that?" I asked in a low voice, hoping they'd not just killed one of their group to mock this up.

"A criminal," the woman said. "He lived on the seventeenth floor, but four days ago he beat his partner half to death in the lift. When it opened on the lobby, I was there, observing as usual, and I decided the world would be a better place without him in it.

"We had been contemplating this path before now, and had intended that we would hire someone to hit him, as we released them. That would have addressed the immediate issue, of course, but there would have been loose ends to tie up. This way, you may address any you find yourself."

"Such as?"

"Such as the fact that many upcoming assassins will seek to raise their own profile by eliminating the upstart who killed Stinger."

"We're going to be drawing a target on our backs, aren't we?" I asked, getting chuckles and nods from the other Stingers around the room.

"Get used to it, kid," said the unmasked man, shaking his head. "Believe me, I didn't sleep deep for at least ten years, and it wasn't from nightmares. The worlds of assassins and bounty hunters are fun, but not for the faint of heart."

"Well, thank you so much for that inspirational speech," Reign replied brightly. "Now, is there anything else? We've still got a job left to do tonight before we can sleep."

"Yeah," I agreed. "Let's go pay that pig-fucker Tyrannus a visit."

CHAPTER FIFTY

It wasn't that easy, of course. First of all, it wasn't like we could just get an aircab to the target. That fucker was hiding out in a corpo pleasure retreat, and they screened to stop "undesirables" from entering.

No, we'd need Bowdoin's help to deal with the security and get in there. But regardless of that, first we had a bounty to claim—a quarter of a million credits was very nice, after all—and even once it'd been split four ways, it was still sixty-two thousand, five hundred credits each.

I saw the wince on Reign's face as we left the sub-levels of the arcology using Stinger's security lift, and I knew that the scumbags had taken "their" forty percent off her earnings already.

The bounty wasn't disputed this time, making me think that it'd probably been Lucky playing silly fuckers before. I let out a long sigh of relief, seeing that finally, *finally*, I had enough in my account to pay for the mods I needed to operate my damn suit again.

Leaving the building, I couldn't help but smile, despite everything, as I saw Julius, standing where I'd asked him to be, waiting patiently with thirty plus guild members, all loaded for bear. I marched up and offered a fist to bump, getting a solid jolt as he replied in kind, before speaking.

"So, I take it we're not needed?" he called over the rain and the wind as I approached him. The damn weather sent literal sheets washing across the open space out here.

"No, but thank you. It was touch and go a few times, though."

"I can see that." He nodded to the battered state of my armor, and I glanced at it, before shrugging. "Well, no offense, Kabutt, but we're keeping the guns. The deal was we come and be ready to back you up if it goes badly. It didn't, but we're all fucking soaked and tired, so the deal's done, all right?"

"Yeah, yeah," I grumbled, having expected that and already having written the deal off. It was better to have had the backup and not need it, than need it and not have it. Same principle as a prophylactic, really. And add in the shitty weather that a load of the guild had mustered up to stand around in? I sure as shit couldn't blame them for wanting to leave as sharp as possible.

The rest of the guild moved as soon as Julius gave them the all clear, mounting up on their personal transports. Others called cabs or set off walking, vanishing in all directions as I put the call through to Bowdoin.

"Hey, Kabutt," the hacker greeted distractedly. "What's up?"

"What's up?" I repeated. "Fuck's sake, Bowdoin, what's happening with the job? Have you definitely found him?"

"Hmm? Oh, yeah! Sorry, weird data architecture here. Yeah, found him. He's still there, so…"

"So…?"

He smiled. "So when I get paid, I'll give you the location."

"And what exactly is to stop you from fucking off to some bar as soon as the creds are handed over?"

"Uh, nothing?" he replied, seeming confused.

"Exactly!" I snarled. "Fuck's sake, Bowdoin, you agreed to get me in there and help me with the hack. So you get paid at the end, once it's all done, like everyone else!"

"Yeah, about that…" He grimaced. "Look, no offense, pal, but I don't need to be there. In fact, there's no good reason for me to be there at all. If I'm there, it's extra risk for me. You might decide to off me rather than pay me, after all, and it's a risk for my team as well. They'd be watching you…you'd be watching them. I'd be creeping around, trying to get into places to do hacks, when, seriously? All I need is access to their gear.

"I'll walk you through the things you need to do to open the backdoors for me, and I'll remote in. That way, there's no risk to me that you decide to save on my wage, and less risk to you that you'll get caught out by my team accidentally tripping something."

"Fuck's sake, Bowdoin!" I snarled. "What if I damn well need you on the ground?"

"Why the hell would you?" He seemed genuinely confused. "No offense, but you know fuck all about hacking. You're going to a corpo site. It's literally a pleasure park for them. *Everything* is remote capable—how else would they record everything to use as blackmail later?"

"I…" I paused, thinking about it, and really considering it, and winced. "Fuck, I need to go into that."

"Exactly. And while you're there? Every single movement needs to be cloaked by me. Like seriously, man. I not only need to spoof the security systems to ignore you physically, I need the digital ones to erase your presence. They need to see you, to approve you as being permitted, and then be wiped, one at a time, to make sure they don't report you. On top of that, I'll have no fucking clue when the systems are backed up, if they have random security checks or manual eyes on it."

"Can't you, I don't know, give me a fake ID? Make them think I'm supposed to be there?" I asked.

"Yeah, yeah, I could, if I was a fucking idiot." A long-suffering sigh filled the link as Bowdoin buried his head in his hands. "Let's just think about this, okay? You're a corpo drone, and you're trying to climb the greasy ladder. You've got a little hacking experience under your belt, what are you going to do?"

"No fucking clue," I said grimly. "Seriously, is this necessary?"

"Just…just trust me, okay?" He fixed me with a glare, then forced a smile. "So, I want to get promoted, and I know the only way to the top isn't by being a good little drone, it's by backstabbery, buggering up others and basically being a proper corpo scumbag, right?"

"Yeah."

"So, do I stay at work an extra hour on this day, whatever day this is? Do I do my job right and hope for a little recognition, or do I trawl places like this, looking for anything I can use for blackmail?"

"Shit."

"So, let's take it a step further, because, you know, this is important to make sure you understand. Do we then let 'Bob,' the career corpo asshole, sit in his shitty apartment, waiting, then get a ping that he's set to alert to *any* corpos moving around the grounds, or do we let him get a ping that shows nothing, simply a blank, erased passage log? Something that, when he goes looking for it, looks like it was triggered by a pest, instead of, you know, exactly the thing he's going to be desperately watching for?"

"Fuck you, Bowdoin. I can take a hint," I growled.

"You sure?" he asked sarcastically. "You don't need me to send you a drawing, maybe take all the long words out? Get some dancing cartoon characters to act it out for you?"

"Do you want me to come fuck you up?" I growled.

"Hey, I'm trying to educate you here, Kabutt, and I'm only doing that because you're Richie's friend. Where is he, anyway? You said he was still 'in' but I'm getting returned pings…"

"He can't comm from where he is," I whispered, truthfully.

"He…is he dead?" His voice changed to one with a little more concern.

"Honestly, I can't say," I said hollowly. "He told me to contact you, though, for a few jobs. So, when I can explain more? I will, all right?" I hoped that anyone who might be monitoring this—I didn't think anyone was, but that touch of paranoia was back—would assume I was just lying to Bowdoin and myself.

"All right…" he said, although it was clear he wasn't happy. "Look, you want the location and my help, or not?"

"Yeah, I do." I took a deep breath and blew it out. "Okay, how do we get in?"

"There's three methods I can fix up for you on short notice, but for something like this? And as short notice as it is? None of them are perfect, and there's risks with them all."

"Story of my life. Hit me," I said flatly.

"Okay, option one. Corpos do the absolute bare minimum they can themselves. That means there's a constant stream of bots moving around the area. They're delivering everything from food to hookers, and disposing of garbage, like the remains of the food, and for what looks to be a very sick fucking party in number seventeen, the remains of the hookers as well."

"Shit."

"Yeah, well, the option there is, we can get you into a van as 'entertainment' and send you direct to the tower. Then you wear a mask and run for his floor and apartment."

"That…sounds okay?"

"It is, except he'd need to approve it, and he's already had such entertainment leave for the night. On top of that, no offense, but you look like a bunch of scavs took a dump and shaped it into a human. Besides, any transport directly sent to a property sends a dual ping—as it's en route, and on arrival—to the local security forces, and to the target location.

"If the target location doesn't approve it? Security takes it down. The ping is sent at the same time to both locations, but at a random point in the journey, over the few minutes that takes. That means we can't guarantee that we can intercept it, and for the entire journey I need to be laser focused to hack both locations at once, so anything else that comes along? I can't help. Someone decides to have a look inside? You're boned."

"Can't you control the transport? Make it not send that ping?"

"Ah, you're learning! No."

"But—"

"If the transport doesn't send the ping, it's automatically viewed as a suspect vehicle, and terminated."

"Terminated?"

"Gamma cannons on the roof," he clarified. "They take their security really fucking seriously, okay, Kabutt?"

"Shit."

"Well, let's face it, if the transport doesn't ID itself, they're losing nothing. It's the transport company's problem that their machine is wiped, not the corpo's."

"And if it's a signal issue, then it's only a bunch of hookers…is that it?"

"Basically, yeah." Bowdoin frowned. "I don't fucking like it either, but that's these assholes all over."

"Okay, so what's option two?"

"Option two is a fast, hard hit. Basically, I'll take down a section of the security wall, the sensors and everything, on the opposite side of the compound to you…"

"The…?"

"Just hold the questions, okay?" he growled. "The opposite side of the compound to you goes down, then I spoof a dozen attacks, all rolling over the walls. Make it look like some third-rate hacker is fucking with them, send all their alarms wild. Then you get your ass over the wall as far from the point of the original interest as possible.

"Then you run like fuck to the tower. I'll take down anything that sees you, as fast as I can, but again, no promises. And it'll get the security teams out and running, so you'd need to avoid them.

"Then you get inside, and, I don't know, charm your way to the target's location, floor thirteen, apartment four."

"Don't like that one," I admitted, and he nodded.

"Fair enough. That leaves option three."

"What's option three?" I asked.

"That's…that's the problem." He sighed. "Look, Kabutt, and all threats and shit aside—yes, you're a scary motherfucker, so you don't need to make threats and so on. I've not found a third option that I like, not a viable one anyway, not yet. I'm still working on it, though, so, I don't know…head there and we'll start as soon as I can come up with a plan?"

"That's not good enough," I growled.

"Which part of you don't need to make threats and shit is confusing you?" he snapped. "You gave me a matter of hours to find this dickhead, and you hired me to find you a way through security, and to be ready to hack some asshole corpo cocksucker. I'm doing my fucking best, okay? I've found you two ways through security. It's not my fault they're shit! And corpo security isn't something you break easily without corpo resources. So either you accept those facts, hand me those resources or I walk my merry way."

"Shit…" I muttered, gritting my teeth. "You said there was a third option, you just didn't like it?"

"Yeah." He snorted. "You'd go in underground, like through the sewers. But it's not specters and shit you'd be dealing with. Well, it's probably shit, yeah, but you know, still…"

"Just fucking tell me!" I snapped.

"There's a high-security zone down there. Something's drawing a lot of power, but it's not on any of the records. Some serious heat releases—I'm betting some kind of heavy-duty reactor or heat sinks. Definitely something hidden, either way. They won't be leaving that kind of shit open to intrusion, either. They'll have sealed it off fully from the undercity."

"We could probably blow through though, right?" I scratched at my chin. "Use stealth in the sewers, then a breaching charge, rush them through the lower levels, take out—"

"Have you heard yourself?" Bowdoin asked disgustedly, shaking his head. "What the hell kind of stealth are you thinking of using with a breaching explosion? Heavy stealth? Nobody can report you if they're all dead? Fuck's sake, do you even understand the concept?"

"You got a better plan?"

"I could eat the alphabet and *shit* a better plan than that!"

"Which one has the better chance of success?" I asked caustically. "Your ones where we all hide in a fucking box, hoping nobody scans us, *you know, like they'll do for every goddamn package*? Or where we bum-rush the tower and hope that nobody is looking in our direction?"

"Fuck's sake, Kabutt, a shitty plan isn't made better by comparing it with other shitty plans!"

"Which one?" I asked again.

"Not yours, dimwit!" he snarled. "That's the kinda shit that gets all the alarm bells ringing, even for the shittiest kind of cyber security! There's something hidden in the goddamn basement, something that they're keeping off the grid, and you're suggesting you blow up a goddamn wall to 'sneak' past it. Do you know what sneak means, Kabutt? Because I'm thinking you fucking don't!"

"Then pick another!" I snapped.

Suddenly the feed filled with an image of a man banging his head on the desk, repeatedly, while a prerecorded track played repeatedly: "Why me? For fuck's sake, I'm surrounded by idiots…"

It was a scene from a vid from a few years back, and it'd become iconic for the sheer fucking stupidity of the people the hero had to deal with.

It was something that we sent each other as NCOs, when dealing with officers. And to have it sent at me, clearly viewing me as the fucking idiot? I snarled, determined to find this little fucker and—

"WAIT!" he barked, suddenly back, eyes flickering as he did whatever hacker mumbo-jumbo voodoo shit he did. "Yes!" he crowed. "Oh yeah, I'm a fucking genius!"

"What?"

"Oh, don't you worry, Kabutt. You wouldn't get it, anyway. You just accept that I'm amazing, and, uh…can you get to this location in, oh, say the next five minutes?"

I got a location ping, and I checked it, frowning and spinning it around, making sense of where it was.

"Maybe ten minutes…?" I replied, confused.

"Too much. I can probably stall him for a few minutes more, but that's it. Look, just get there, and take the guy out, or down, or whatever you do, then we have our ticket in. Are you with me?"

"You want me to kill him?" I asked, confused, sending the location to Reign and a quick text file saying we needed to be there *right fucking now*.

"Keeper, help me!" Bowdoin snapped. "For fuck's sake, what is it with you people? Let me be clear here. Go knock him out, and be stealthy…Don't fuck him up too much! And to clarify, Kabutt? Stealthy means nobody sees you—not you blowing up a building, playing a fucking trumpet as you go, all right? Awesome! It's a pleasure working with you, mate, and this'll totally mean you owe me a bonus. Bye-bye!"

The link cut off, and I was left blinking, trying to make sense of that last barrage of shit from the hacker. I shook my head. Clearly, I wasn't going to get anything else, yet.

"Reign?" I snapped, turning to her, and she smiled, nodding as the pair of us fell into our accustomed roles easily again: me as senior NCO, and her as my second, ready to make shit happen.

I guessed this was how it was supposed to be for officers and senior NCOs as well, minus the frontal lobotomy they apparently had as standard.

"Aircab is incoming. ETA less than a minute," she replied. "Paid the extra for an emergency pickup."

"Thank you," I said, relieved. "Send me the tab, and I'll sort it."

"No worries. Luna! Gessh!" she bellowed to the other two, who'd drifted off to one side and were chatting happily with someone they apparently knew from the guild.

They broke off, waved, then quickly made their goodbyes and hurried over.

"You know him?" Reign nodded after the sole figure who was even now running after his departing team in the distance.

"Yeah. Santos. Insanely talented mechanic! We used to date his brother."

"You…both of you?" I looked from one to the other, and the pair nodded. "Wow, okay." I shrugged.

"What's wrong with that?" Gessh frowned.

"Nothing's wrong with it," I said quickly, glancing around to spot the incoming aircab. "He's just…"

"The brother you were talking to is half your size." Reign said it for both of us. "If the guy you were dating is anything like him? You'd have killed him in the sack."

"Ah!" Gessh grinned as Luna started to laugh.

"No, no, don't worry. Min and Santos are half-brothers. Min is, well, he's…" Luna hesitated.

"He's like some genetic freak," Gessh finished for her. "He's a man mountain—half-elf, half-orc, and he's…Usually half-bloods are smaller than full-blooded orcs, and less pretty than full elves, right? He's the opposite. He's some poster boy for corpo security forces recruitment now."

"Corpo, eh?" I winced.

"Security gig." She nodded. "He's too pretty to be a merc, I guess. Spends all his time 'protecting' corpo women…probably from their beds, if we know him."

"So, just to be clear, if we meet him in a fight here? I reserve the right to shoot him in the dick," Luna said.

"Luna liked him a lot more than I did," Gessh admitted, smiling fondly at her sister. "Believe me, he'll deserve the shot if we get the chance."

"Okay…" I winced, before Reign saved us all.

"Cab!" she called.

I twisted around, grunting as I saw it coming to land behind us, and reflected—as I grabbed my gear, chucking it in the transport trunk—that no matter what direction you watched for the damn things from, they were always unpredictable.

"Load up!" I grabbed the door and climbed in, flicking on the optional privacy setup and acknowledging the charge for it.

"What's the plan, boss?" Luna clambered in across from me. The other two joined us a few seconds later, with Reign complaining about the size of the trunk.

"Hey, you're the one with insane length guns," Gessh said as the cab confirmed we were all seated, the doors locking and the privacy light activating to show we were safe from outside contact or recording.

The cab lifted into the air, jinking to one side and making us all grab the restraints as something small and fast enough to trigger my instinctive missile trauma tore past.

"Goddamn delivery drones!" Luna snarled, catching the image on the side of it. "I swear, they try to hit things!"

"Probably," I agreed, sighing and sending them all a datapacket. "Okay, here we go, people…"

CHAPTER FIFTY-ONE

The packet I sent to them was the one that Bowdoin had sent to me, and as well as the overall layout of the building, it covered some of the security details.

"Boss, that's not where we're headed…" Reign was the first to interrupt, seeing the location, and I nodded.

"I know. Don't worry. Apparently the site is secure, but our hacker friend found this guy"—I pinged out another file to them—"and he's our ticket in."

"Okay, what's the plan?" Reign asked.

"First, we take this guy down…"

"Lethal or non-lethal?" Luna asked, apparently looking at the mug shot of him. "He's kinda cute, in a dorky way."

"Non-lethal," I said quickly. "We need him alive, and apparently not too messed up. Like I said, he's our ticket in. No clue how or why yet—hacker is working on that, but he's in the wind at literally any minute. Hence, we need to get there and grab the fucker fast."

"Right," Reign agreed, checking the feed from the cab. "Two minutes out, boss. We'll be landing on the roof. He's on the sixty-fifth floor. I'm calling the lift now."

"Nice." I approved. "Okay, we grab him, as he's apparently going to get us into…here." The image I pulled up and sent around was of the target building, and we all paused, assessing it.

"You know, when you said he was in a corpo pleasure place, I definitely didn't imagine that," Luna said after a few seconds, and I nodded, totally agreeing with her.

Bowdoin had gotten us the blueprints already, and the damn place was scary. The building itself was fifty stories high, five sided, with five apartments per floor, a goddamn pool area in the middle of each floor, with little swim-up areas leading from the center to each of the apartments. Here and there, little ornamental bridges crossed the swimming areas, and every five floors was an entire floor dedicated to restaurants or entertainment centers.

The place looked like pictures I'd seen of the old world resorts, all palm trees and bright sunlight, beaches covered in golden sand and more.

The few pictures Bowdoin had managed to get of the inside were apparently from some corpo reel, and it showed families laid out on the sand, kids playing in the water, and all that wholesome family shit that was lost to everyone else hundreds of years ago.

I noted that it also showed, between the floors dedicated to various food styles and massages, manicures, and fuck knew what else, two floors that were dedicated to hedonistic pleasures I probably couldn't even imagine. One was all sultry lighting and beautiful people, with the corpos wearing ornate little masks—presumably so nothing they did could be held against them later—while the other one?

Fuck, the other one was as far from sexy as it could get, all black leather and whips and shit. And the masks there? Not for me. Although I wasn't bothered about the various kinks most people had—in the army, I'd probably seen all the range—I knew these corpos wouldn't be satisfied with consensual kinks. Full head helmets were worn in the pictures to make damn sure that nobody could press charges or blackmail the scum that got off on that kind of shit.

Suddenly the comment from Bowdoin about "disposing of the remains of used hookers" made my stomach churn, and I had an urgent need to set off a MADD grenade on that fucking floor.

I pulled back, looking at the overall view of the tower, noting that I'd seen these places before with their enforced "no-fly" zones around them, and assumed that, like so many places, they were corpo research or something, never guessing there was an entire floor there devoted to torture and worse.

Looking at the tower itself, I shook my head at it. It was a good size, not insane, but large enough, five sided, with each of the faces of the tower about a hundred meters on a side. That gave each of the apartments about five hundred square meters, which I was betting was a "small" space for a corpo to relax in.

Fucking scumbags. My entire apartment was less than twenty square meters, and that was including the fucking shower and the bed!

Regardless, that meant that although the outside of the tower looked almost utilitarian, with its reflective plates over the sides to absorb the light, the inside was anything but.

There were also gamma cannons on the roof on each fucking side of the tower, to ensure that no horrible poor people dared to get too close to their betters.

Add to that, the lowest level was surrounded by a perimeter wall with its own security systems that flashed red as I looked at them. The entire building was suddenly blanketed in yellow dots as I switched to the warning sensors.

"Damn," Reign said in a low voice, clearly seeing the security systems as I was. "Can we actually do this, boss?" she asked, even as the chime sounded to let us know we were landing. "I mean, security at the gates, sensors on the perimeter wall, sensors on the ground, the walls. Hell, you see this section?"

She flicked a file to me, and I checked it as I released my harness, shifting to grab the door release, waiting as the cab dropped the last few meters to the rooftop.

The file had the "guest personal security" tag on it, and I winced as I pulled up the details.

"Wearable security sensors to monitor heart rate, health, and wellness," I read aloud. "Shit, if he's wearing one of these, even if we get to him, as soon as I start to 'chat' about things, that's the security office going nuts!"

"That hacker better have a good plan, boss," Luna said as I opened the door, leading the way around the side of the cab and to the trunk that opened as we approached it.

The rain was finally slackening off, of course, as we'd probably need it to cover our approach or something. So as we grabbed our gear out of the trunk, Luna already running to the lift, Bowdoin called me again.

"Seriously, Kabutt, what the hell are you doing?" he snapped as soon as the connection was accepted. "Did you stop for coffee and a hand job? You don't get this is the only way—"

"We're on the roof, getting into the lift now," I snapped at the little turd, and he let out a long-suffering sigh.

"Dammit, seriously? Fine, time for this to go nuclear."

"What's that supposed to mean?" I asked.

"Look, we need him to stay there, and he's already called a lift to his floor, all right? He's sent the start-up sequence to his car, and he's heading for his coffee machine. That leaves me one option, and I need you to understand that this is a last resort for me."

"What is?" I asked, as a grainy image appeared in my vision, sent from Bowdoin.

"This is." He sighed. "Man, messing with someone's morning coffee is just *wrong.*"

The image resolved into that of a man hurrying about a small—although much larger and nicer than mine—apartment, tucking a shirt into trousers, waving his arms as he gesticulated wildly about something, then reaching out to a coffee machine on the wall, grabbing a cup as he headed for the apartment door.

The cup was empty, and the figure paused, frowning at the cup, then took a step back, looking at the coffee machine, putting the cup back under the nozzle and jabbing at the buttons.

Nothing happened, and he started to hit the machine, doing a little "why do the gods hate me so" dance, before clearly giving up and heading to the door.

Presumably the machine made a noise, as he jerked around and ran back to it, grabbing another cup—the original having been dislodged when he was hitting the machine—and rammed it into place.

Nothing happened.

Cue more dancing and a few kicks. The guy spun around, and started heading for the door…

The machine spewed liquid into the cup, which was released by the automated grippers—presumably by Bowdoin. The figure frantically tried to get the cup back into place.

By this point, we were rocketing toward his floor, Luna counting them down as we went.

"Four…three…Oh, fucking come on!" she snarled as the lift stopped on the floor above our target's floor, and a woman got on. She looked to be a typical low-end manager with a short haircut and a sneer set as standard as she looked us all over.

"Idents!" she snapped at Gessh, clicking her fingers.

"What?"

"The security lift is on the other side of the building! Your sort aren't permitted in these sections! Idents, now!"

"Ma'am…" Reign interrupted, forcing a respectful smile. "Our apologies. We've been summoned to a report of a corporate employee being harassed…"

"And why would you be sent? You're no corporate team!" She sneered. "That's it, I'm reporting th—*urk!*"

Luna grabbed her by the throat and closed her fist, at the same time ramming something into her stomach that crackled to life, making her victim hiss and tense up.

"Taser," Gessh announced casually as the lift moved again. "Hands down the best way to deal with someone like this."

"Fuck's sake, Kabutt! You stop for lunch or something..." Bowdoin started up again, and I spoke quickly.

"We've got a passenger, Bowdoin. Need to make sure she didn't send any alerts or anything."

"A passenger? What? Show me!" he snapped, and I focused, seeing that Luna was still frying her captive.

I winced. "Might want to hold off on that..." I suggested. "That's got to be doing serious damage by now?"

"Kabutt, as long as the charge is going through her, she can't send a request for help. Tell her to keep it up until you've made damn sure she's out cold. I've seen people wake from stronger charges." Bowdoin cursed, apparently doing something else. "No security alerts marked for your area. But if she's mid-level, she'll have private security cover. Might want to make sure she's out...you know, soon?"

Before I could speak, Reign had punched the woman in the side of the head, knocking her out, before grabbing her bag and searching through it as the lift slowed again.

"Here we go!" Reign said cheerfully, lifting up a small cylinder.

"What's that?" I asked.

"Angel dust," Reign announced, pressing a lever on the side and checking the canister's contents. "Good shit, no doubt. Give her a good toot on this."

The doors opened and we all froze, before seeing nobody waiting, and moved quickly. I blocked the doors open as Luna released the taser. Reign helped to pose the woman, laying her slumped on the floor. Before I could ask, she put a similar taser from the woman's bag into her hand, then the cylinder in her other hand, and gestured for us all to leave the lift.

"Bowdoin, can you...?" I gestured at the lift and the woman, as he watched the event from my eyes.

"Hmmmm?" he asked, then appeared to wake up. "Oh! Yeah, sorry, I'll erase the lift footage...No, wait, using a vid-generator here...There! Made it look like she walked on, deleted the surveillance feed herself and decided to have a little dust for the trip. She's done it all herself now."

"Fuck, that's scary," Reign muttered as we backed away. The lift doors closed, and I explained to the others what he'd done. "Just like that, she's done it to herself..."

"That's what you set it up to look like?" I said, and she shrugged. "Yeah, but a hacker who's that fast with that shit? That's impressive, boss."

"I'm the best," Bowdoin said through the link. "That you know of, at least. Now, I don't want to rush you, but our target is about to fuck off, and you're not even at the closest lift to his apartment..."

"Fuck!" I snapped, turning and running down the hall. The system picked up on my desire and plastered an arrow on my HUD, as well as a range finder as it counted down the distance.

A dozen lefts and rights flashed past as we ran. Occasional potted plastic plants and benches, and the utter lack of broken lights, passed out or dead gangers, and piss in the hallways made it clear that this was low-level corpo housing as opposed to anywhere the likes of us should be.

"We need to keep him quiet. I don't know if we need him unconscious or…"

"Get the elf to shake her booty!" Luna suggested, and Reign growled at her, making me grin through my panic.

Thirty seconds later, we took the last left, running past another lift, one that was marked for the parking garage. The door up ahead flashed as our destination, even as it started to open.

The face of a harried, exhausted, and seriously confused man appeared. Coffee stained the left sleeve of his shirt, as behind him I could see the coffee machine spraying jets across the remains of an apartment that looked like a bomb had gone off.

"Uh…" he started, eyes widening, and before I could speak, Reign was.

"Sir, get back inside!" she called.

He frowned, glancing over his shoulder at the mess.

"The coffee, my shower…" he mumbled, and then we were there.

I grabbed him under one arm, Reign the other as we bodily lifted him back inside.

"Hey! You can't…"

"Assassination attempt," Reign said quickly. "We're undercover. Someone's targeted you, sir. Has anything unusual happened?"

"*Yes*!" He practically wept, all confusion vanishing from his face, replaced with desperate thanks that he wasn't going mad. "Yes, all of it!" He gestured behind him, and I paused, looking around the room.

"Okay, sir, I'm going to need you to stay absolutely silent. Do not, I repeat, do *not*, under any circumstances, send any messages or accept anything, until I tell you to."

"What's going on?" he blubbered. "You don't understand. I'm late! I'm so fucking late! I should be there by now. The boss is gonna fucking frag my ass for this!"

I glanced at Reign and jerked my head at the idiot we'd dumped into a seat, and she talked quickly.

"We're a specialist undercover security team, sir. You've been targeted by someone who's trying to get into the pleasure complex you work in. They've been attempting to hack your implants, but—"

"My implants!" he squawked, hands going to both his head…and his crotch. "Shit, I knew it!" He groaned. "She told me not to go to that chop shop! I should have gone to the company sculptor, not some fucking cheap-ass carver. Oh God, she's gonna kill me…"

He went off on a tirade about some woman who had convinced him to get his dick augmented, and how she'd ruined everything for him, and everything was her fault.

I snorted, then turned away, reconnecting the call to Bowdoin. "You ready to do whatever?" I asked him under my breath.

"You got him?" he asked.

"Yeah, we've got him." I snorted, looking around the room. Everything from a massage bed to his toothbrush was going mad, and the floor was already a good inch deep in simmering coffee. "Want to turn the coffee machine off?"

"I can reset it," he assured me. "Is it important, though? I mean…"

"It's going to flood the apartment, then soak through no doubt, so…"

"So someone will notice. Gotcha. Two minutes," he replied, distracted for a second before nodding as the coffee machine shut off, then beeped as it started to reboot. "There you go. Plain black, extra sweetener, because you're clearly not sweet enough."

I grunted at his little joke as a fresh cup dropped and the machine beeped, before starting to pour again.

"How…how'd you do that?" the target asked, stunned, breaking off from his diatribe against some apparently blameless woman, as he watched me reach out to the coffee machine and snag a cup.

"We have our ways, sir," I said formally, sipping from the cup and nodding, impressed despite myself. It was actually tasty. "Okay, I'm going to need you to do exactly as we say, sir…"

"But the security at the site—"

"Compromised," I said. "One of them is the mole, and they've marked you as the target. We can't let them know you know, and that we're onto them. That's why we're dressed like this."

"Oh…okay?" He licked his lips nervously. "I mean, they say that they can't be—"

"Which they would," I agreed, nodding. "Listen, sir, this is how it is. One of them is compromised. There's a team on their way to kill you, do you understand? All of this was their hacker deliberately making you late. Our hacker is in the system now, which he just demonstrated by making me a coffee. You think a hit squad is going to stop for coffee?"

"Well…no?"

"Exactly," I continued. "Listen, this is how it is. Either you keep quiet, and we wait here and hope the squad comes. We'll kill them, and then you can go to work, but you'll be late—"

"I'm *already* late! Look, can we—"

"You can't report in," I said. "If you do that, they'll know and they'll vanish. Then we'll have to report that you fucked this operation up…You think your boss…" I paused.

"Michaels! Bartholomew Michaels!" he supplied helpfully.

"Exactly. You think he'll care that you're late when *my* boss, who's a hell of a lot higher, is praising you for helping to catch these fuckers? No."

"Can't he just tell my boss it's okay or whatever?" he tried hesitantly.

"And let the hit team know that we know that they're coming?" Reign snapped. "Come on, sir, we let them know we're here, they'll just vanish, probably come for you when you're alone."

"And if you fuck this up, next time, corporate won't dispatch us, sir. They'll have us watch and wait, instead of risk you screwing that up again."

"You know what the survival rate will be if we're told to hold back?" Reign asked him, speaking before he replied, shaking her head.

"It's not good," I agreed. "No need to scare him though, operative. He's not going to screw this up for us. He's going to help, isn't that right?" I sipped from my coffee again.

"Yes?" he whispered, clearly unsure.

"Excellent. I'd hate to have to abandon you here when we know they're coming for you, after all."

"What?" he squeaked.

"We're not going to do that though, not now," I assured him. "Not now that you're going to do exactly as we say."

"Yes, sir!" he agreed, wide-eyed.

"Hacker?" I looked off to one side as I triggered the link to Bowdoin again. "Are we clear?" I asked, acting for the idiot who was watching.

"Clear? Clear as day that he's an idiot, yeah," Bowdoin said, my overlay showing me his image as he shook his head in disbelief. "Okay, look, we're gonna need him to fly us in the front door, but he's going to need to give me root access to his mods. That way, I can spoof the internal cameras and make his vision match if they remote into him to check."

"Root access. Got it."

"You really don't, do you?" He sighed. "Root access doesn't mean grasping your damn pocket weasel. Okay, I'm totally doubling my prices for any jobs we do together in the future, for the teachable moments if nothing else."

"I'll remember that," I said, before forcing a smile for the idiot before me. "Sorry, sir, getting advice on the enemy, and their attempts to hack you."

"They're trying it right now?"

"Definitely," I replied, before turning away as I spoke, as though not wanting him to hear it. "If they get control, do we terminate?"

"No!" he squeaked in terror. "No, I'm good!"

"Tell him to accept the ping I'm sending via you. He's to approve all access, even the sections that he gets warnings about," Bowdoin said distractedly.

"Okay, sir, I'm relaying a ping from our hacker. The enemy are already past your basic defenses, and if they get full access to your mods, they'll see us all. That leaves us with two choices. Are you ready?"

"Yeah?" he asked nervously, hunching down even lower in his seat.

"First, they got access, apparently from a repeating link that was installed recently, a physical link that was installed and wet-wired into you, do you understand?"

"N...no...?"

"Really?" I glanced down at his crotch and then back up. "I think you do."

"Oh..." He covered his face with his hands. "Oh, God, I can't fucking believe this..."

"So, they're already in your system. Basic firewalls and security are being breached, and frankly, thanks to your sheer stupidity in allowing yourself to be fooled like this, I'm of the opinion that the best choice we've got is to remove their hack at the source."

"The..." He pointed at his crotch.

"We've got no time for surgery here, no time to bring in a carver, or anesthetic, so as I say, we've got two choices. First is we remove their physical link to you. We do that here and now—"

"No offense, sir, but I'm not using my personal vibro-blade on that," Reign said, instead picking up something from his counter that looked as though it'd have difficulty cutting warm butter. "I'd never be able to look at it again. I'll be using this on you instead."

"Fuck no!" he half screamed, crossing his legs and contorting to protect his crown jewels. "Please! What the hell is the other option! I want the other option!"

"It's dangerous…" I growled.

"More dangerous than having my dick cut off?!" He whimpered.

"Dangerous for our team!" I snapped. "My hacker would have to fight them on their own ground, fight them in Aug-World, in the code itself! He could be killed, all because you don't want to risk your dick!"

"I've got credits!" he tried, thinking he'd found a lever, and I snorted.

"You think your credits matter? We're professionals, son. We earn your annual wage most days! No, there's only one way that he can do this, and that's from inside. If he has to waste time attacking your firewalls and security, they'll see him. They'll kill him while he's distracted, and our entire operation is a bust!"

"What do I do!" he begged. "Fuck's sake! Just tell me!"

"The ping," I said. "You'll need to approve him for full access, all the way. It's the only option here. You give him access, or we remove the link…And even then…" I shook my head.

"Sir, maybe we should leave. They're going to guess there's a problem soon. They'll call off the job—"

"Then they'll come when we're not ready." I nodded. "Good point."

"What…?" he hissed.

"You think we should just leave them to hack him?" Luna asked, getting in on the fun. "Draw back and take them down when they attack him?"

"Possibly…" I muttered, rubbing at my chin.

"He'd be dead in ten minutes, boss." Reign shook her head. "Remember, it's his implants and ident they need. They'll just kill him and puppet him, like the rest of the specters."

"Specters?!" he whispered, eyes widening to almost comical levels. "You mean…they're really…oh my God…"

"I think the best option is the blade," I said firmly, standing and resting my hand on my handgun. "Sorry, sir, I'd have shot you, and made it fast, and relatively painless, but the noise…"

"He's accepted it," Bowdoin told me at the same time as the guy started to frantically babble that he'd done it. "Holy shit, he actually did it, full root access to his Keystone…I can't believe this monkey's going to…never mind that."

"You've got it?" I asked Bowdoin, and he nodded, clearly busy elsewhere.

"Yeah. Okay, get moving. Get him to the parking garage. You'll need to give me access to the vehicle once you're there. I'll spoof the camera and his optics to show the same, and then we're on our way!"

"We still need to discuss that," I pointed out. "Fucking urgently."

"Yeah, good point. Look, no offense, but the deal was I get you in, and when you get to the target, I help you hack his shit. I can't do everything, all right? From here till you reach the target, you're gonna have to put your big-boy pants on and sort it yourself. You need help? I'll do my best, but planning it? All my time was spent in getting you this far, and I'll be erasing signs of you as you move around. That's literally all I can do, and anybody who is going to look at this afterward *is* going to notice somebody's messed with things, all right?"

"Bowdoin—"

"I'm serious! I'm not fucking with you, okay? I—"

"Thank you," I finished, walking away from our confused corpo prisoner.

"Would if I…Oh." He paused, then scratched the back of his neck and nodded. "Yeah, no worries. You, uh, you paid for the full service, okay? Friend of Richie's and all."

"We'll head straight for the garage, and as soon as we're in the vehicle, we'll work on the next section. Do you need his help still?"

"Well, yeah, I need him to like walk and talk if they call him, and to fly the car, but beyond that? Wait…shit, yeah, get him to take a data cable as well, you know, a physical data access cable? If he can plug in using that to anything with access, we can use him as a walking datalink!"

"Okay." I turned back to the figure as Bowdoin got back to work. "We're in, and congratulations, dickhead, you just became an accessory," I informed him with a grin, searching around and quickly finding a datalink cable in a drawer, tossing it to our target.

"Wha…?" the idiot whimpered.

"You just gave my hacker full root access to your systems. He can not only transfer every cred you have to us, he can puppet you into the garbage disposal after if you piss us off. So here's where it gets really *fun*."

CHAPTER FIFTY-TWO

The idiot—Kal Trentini—was only too happy to help, once he understood that we were going to pay a visit to the pleasure site, then fuck off as silently as possible. Apparently his position in the catering section meant he got to deal with corpos all day long, and as the complaints manager, he was both slightly more trusted than the average—which was why Bowdoin had picked him—and slightly dumber than the average potato.

Well, "happy" was a description that fit only compared to the state he was in when he found out that we had full control over all his systems and could literally do anything from send ourselves every credit he had, and run up huge debts at insane rates, to sending pictures he'd taken and stored of himself naked— apparently they were from his "dating profile"—to the head of the corporation he worked for.

That was the fun bits, I explained, because the other part, was that as our hacker was already in the corpo retreat's systems, using Kal's ident, so if we got caught? He was as guilty as we were, given that he'd willingly given us root access.

So his best chance? To help us get in and out, and cover our tracks.

Now, fifteen minutes later, we were listening to Kal practically screaming blue murder at some security operative at the main entrance over a secure link. That he was so late for his shift had prompted a security call, and we were braced, ready for a firefight, as they threatened to check the van using high-powered scanners.

They'd see through anything that Bowdoin could do, and at best we'd be left shooting our way out. Most likely, they'd use the gamma cannons on us, and we'd all be toast.

"Listen! You fucking use those scanners on me and my van and you fuck me over? I'll make it goddamn clear why I was late was because you're fucking incompetent! You've remoted in—you've seen there's fuck all in my van but me. You searched it *yesterday*, for the love of blood and chrome! If you make me even later than I already am? I'll get fired. I get fired? I've got nothing to fucking lose! I'll make sure you go down with me, so help me, you goddamn mother fucking piece of…!!!!!!"

We waited a moment.

"Oh, right, well…yeah, thank you, you too!" he snapped.

I let out a long breath as Reign stifled a fit of the giggles over the stress as we started to move again.

"Fuck that was close," I muttered, shaking my head. We'd spent the very limited time we had on the way over here examining the situation from every angle, and we'd come up with two solutions.

First, and definitely not the way we wanted to do it, was that we landed, and then went in on brass balls. Essentially, we march in and brazen it out to the suite we needed with Tyrannus, bluff and distract all the way, shoot any fucker who got in the way, the full works.

Option two, while far less insane, I liked even less.

It was me. Alone, making use of the stealth suit we'd looted, the one with a nearly depleted goddamn battery. We'd gotten another of them as well when we'd compared our loot on the way over, thankfully. We'd ended up having to bodge things together to cover the gunshot wound in one's back, and the slice across the chest of the other that had killed its owner.

But, after some seriously last-minute work with some glue that'd probably never last, we were ready.

Basically, the best plan we had was that we use our friendly little idiot to get us all into the maintenance section and get admin access to the systems, then we head for the security office, and we put me in the system. I dress in their uniform, march through the place—on my fucking lonesome—and my team basically hide in the security office while I do it, giving Bowdoin access to the security systems.

Then I do everything, and they essentially watch me, probably while eating popcorn, before setting off the alarms in the farthest section of the site, and we all fuck off quietly. No muss, no fuss.

We all knew what we were going to do, but I hated every goddamn second of it as he landed, despising how everything that I was doing was so last second.

I was used to the army's way of doing things. Ten planning meetings by senior officers, all tugging each other off. Then the congealed mess of their plans would be given to us as NCOs, and we'd spend a few days hosing them down and burning anything they'd touched, before redoing the entire thing so it made sense.

Then, and only then, once all the plans were properly made, would we present them back to the officers, pat them on the head and tell them they'd done a good job.

They'd look over the notes, and the plan, and most of them would know that they were nothing like what they'd put together. They'd keep their goddamn mouths shut, though, and they'd accept that the plan now worked.

The dumber among them, usually also the highest ranks, would nod and claim credit, not knowing any different, and the job got done.

It took a little while, but at least everything was planned properly.

The other side to that was when we were given last-minute objectives like "take that building."

Then NCOs did what we did best, and liked least—besides dealing with officers, of course—as we improvised all the livelong day.

Since I'd gotten out of the fucking army, I felt like that was all I'd done: racing from one disaster to another, constantly firefighting.

When I flexed my left arm, though, and considered my credit account? It seemed to be working out okay so far actually, despite every goddamn instinct.

We landed, and Kal banged on the side of his van, moving slowly along it as he went, before opening the door and peering in at us.

"Are you ready?" he asked.

"Fucking of course we are!" I hissed back. "What the hell was the banging for?"

"Oh…Well, anyway. So the sensors here are every few meters in the lower areas. Can your hacker…" He paused, then looked to me as Bowdoin clearly asked him a question, answering, then waiting. Ten seconds or so later, and Bowdoin was on with me.

"Okay, Kabutt, good news, bad news time."

"Bad news first," I said instinctively.

"We're now inside the perimeter, and I've got access to a lot more of the system. There's a shift change on the site. Looks like security is swapping over, so there's more around than we hoped. I'd suggest you leave the others in the van until we've got control of the security office. If you take it by stealth? You can probably do it alone. Still, if you try to take it by force, as it is now? No fucking chance."

"Shit. Fine. Okay, great. What's the good news?"

"I lied."

"About there being load of security?" I sagged with relief. "You utter bastard. I'll get you for…"

"No, I lied about the good news, bad news thing. There's no good news."

"Bowdoin…" I growled.

"Also, they've brought in security turrets since the copy of the plans I managed to get. If they see you? You're fucked. And honestly, I don't see that stealth suit lasting till you get to them."

"When the hell did you find that out?"

"On the flight over here. I've got Kal's access, so I've been going over the recordings of the site when he's been wandering around. Let me tell you, Kabutt, he's a fucking pervert. I mean, yeah, I can be a bit of a perv at times, but this guy? Nope, total different league."

"Fine," I growled, before turning to the others. "There's a security shift change going on, lots of people in and out. Best if you all stay here. I'll send a message when the route is clear."

"Think you can make it all the way to maintenance and then security?" Reign asked, and I checked the battery on the suit.

Seven percent.

"No, I guess not," I growled, looking around the parking garage for inspiration.

"There's spare clothes in the locker room, if that helps?" Kal suggested diffidently, and I fixed on him.

"How far and where?" I asked.

"The next floor down," he said quickly. "We're on sub-three, the third level below ground. This is the better parking one. There's a smaller space on sub-five as well. The security forces sectioned off sub-six through ten, and we were warned that if we go anywhere near it, we'd be shot, no warning."

"What's above us?" I asked, not trusting the maps we'd gotten now we knew there'd been changes. "Sub-one and two?"

"Sub-one is for the corpo parking, like the higher ranks and customers, and sub-two is maintenance and security."

"Maintenance, that's where we need to be."

"Really? But that's just where all the bots and stuff goes, and the maintenance types do, you know, whatever they do."

"You're just a font of knowledge, you know that?" I said grimly. "Okay, get me to the locker room below us. I'll swipe some clothing, then we can check the maintenance area. Maybe they'll have a compatible battery I can use as well."

I'd already taken most of my gear off in the small van, quickly stripping down to my plain black under armoring, glad that I was wearing that at least; then I'd redressed in the stealth suit. I'd also stashed my hurricane revolver into one of the pockets of the suit, long narrow things that were sealed up.

It was a last resort, as me holding a goddamn gun when in the suit was a blatant giveaway; it'd not be covered by it, and would instead be floating along. I also had the vibro-blade strapped to the inside of my right wrist instead of to my chest.

I felt naked—and not in a good way—as the girls wished me luck. Reign smacked my ass as I stoop-walked past her out of the back of the transport, triggering the suit just before I stepped out.

"So," Kal whispered after a few seconds, as the pair of us walked across the parking garage, with Bowdoin apparently using every trick in the book to hide me from local systems as my stealth suit flickered and lagged.

"Yeah?"

"Ummmm, this job you're doing?"

"Yeah?"

"Does it pay well?" he asked after another brief pause.

"What?"

"You think I want to be in catering?" he asked me suddenly. "No, okay? I *really* don't! I have to put up with people telling me all day that their food isn't right, or their bed was lumpy, or that the cleaner they fucking ordered beaten black and blue yesterday for interrupting them? Well, surprise, surprise, that cleaner didn't go to their room today and they need their sheets changing or they've ran out of lube and they need a new jar, but only lingonberry flavor will do…"

He paused, shaking his head, and I realized that as furious as he was? He wasn't actually furious at *us*, the people who were risking his life. He was furious at the corpos, despite being a low-level one of those fuckers.

I nodded to him. "Yeah, it fucking does."

"How much?"

"How much do you earn?"

"A hundred thousand a year," he said, and I looked at him in shock. "I know, I know, it's a shitty wage but…"

I tuned out the rest of what he was saying, stunned.

A hundred thousand credits a year.

I'd earned *half* that as an elite operator in the army. I'd sacrificed half of everything I earned to paying off the suit. And even if I'd not done that, I'd not have fucking earned that much in a year, and I was an elite frontline fighter risking my life every goddamn day.

That some asshole who stood there, letting corpo dickheads complain about shit to them all day earned more than me? I buried the indignation and moved on. Yeah, he earned more; of course he did. He was a corpo himself, and the fucker had to deal with corpos all day and not shoot them in the face. That had to be harder than I could believe. I'd barely been around this guy half an hour or so, and I desperately wanted to shoot *him*, never mind the others.

We trooped down a set of stairs, him pointing out that, first of all, the lifts were all security controlled, and second, they were always on the go, meaning that we were likely to bump into someone if we used them.

It was quicker to use the stairs.

They were old-school, narrow steel steps, guaranteed to do a number on bare feet if anyone was ever dumb enough to try walking on them without shoes. I shrugged, not really interested as Kal started on about the reason that the head office preferred some dickhead over him for the better shifts.

I occasionally interjected with a "uh-huh" and even more rarely "shame that," and it seemed to keep him happy until we reached the next floor, then passed along a corridor to the service staff section of the lockers.

"There's security team gear down here?" I asked after a few seconds, catching a random word in the dross he was spouting, and he nodded.

"Yeah, did I not say? This entire section is theirs, but, you know, there's a shift change going on, so there's going to be people in there?"

"Bowdoin?" I said, the hacker having left a line open to me.

"Yeah?" He popped back up in my vision and blinked.

"Were you having a fucking nap?" I hissed, and he grinned.

"No, just relaxing. You know how boring that fucker is. So, what's up?"

"Are there security staff in the lockers?"

"Two minutes." He checked something, then clearly asked Kal something, as he got him to move closer and plug in the direct data access cable from his Key to a port in the wall.

"Time's important here, Bowdoin!" I snarled after a few minutes, flattening myself against the wall as people passed by the bottom of the corridor we stood in.

"Patience is a virtue," he replied, unconcerned, still fucking around with something.

"I swear, I'm going to get a fucking ulcer working with you," I growled, before being cut off as he came back.

"Okay, yeah, three people in the locker area. Two finishing their shift, one starting. Two cameras…I can loop them though, and…done!"

"Anyone we can use?" I asked.

"The guy who's starting is big enough, maybe. If you can take him and the others down without raising an alarm, then you can stash their bodies somewhere…Garbage chute!" He said that last bit with a laugh.

"What?" I hissed.

"Garbage chute. On the far side of the lockers, there's a chute. Leads down to the sixth floor. It's a laundry room, closed off since they started doing whatever below."

"Will they survive?" I asked.

"When you're the one attacking? Probably not." He laughed again. "Yeah, no worries there. Looks like people have been using the laundry chute to sneakily dump anything they don't want to deal with. There's like a *mountain* of filthy clothes down there. All the shit-stained sheets and so on are being chucked down there as well, so yeah, a soft-ish landing!"

"Perfect place for corpo-sec then," I agreed. "Okay, give me a heads-up view of the room, and pop the door when I say."

"Sending!"

A new link opened in my vision; Bowdoin's image reduced to a tiny block as I mentally reorganized my HUD. I shifted the new one to the top right and studied it for a minute, seeing the helpful tag that Bowdoin had attached with "you are here" at the top.

The locker room ahead of me was roughly square, slightly narrower at the top and bottom, with doors at the center south position, and the showers taking up the middle of the room.

Lockers stood along the outer wall, tall and narrow, with changing rooms on the inner wall, ringing the shower section. I gritted my teeth, seeing the two at the bottom left, joking and flirting. Their body language suggested a recently begun relationship, judging from the fact that they both wore a towel around the waist and nothing more, and them being a man and a woman in rather close proximity.

They glanced over at the guy undressing slowly in the middle of the left section, going as slow as possible as he got ready for his shift.

I couldn't tell whether that was because he was trying to get a better look at the admittedly impressive tits of the female security, or whether I was totally misjudging it and he was just desperate not to start his shift.

Either way, it was time to play the game.

"Pop the door," I ordered.

CHAPTER FIFTY-THREE

I crept inside, moving as silently as possible. My heart raced in a way that it'd not in sodding years, and a smile tugged at the edges of my lips.

I'd joined the forces, aiming to be an APS operator, but they didn't just say "Yeah, sure, kid" and boot you straight into the seat of a multi-million-cred machine of death and destruction.

They trained you first. They picked you up and they beat you down. They sent you on missions, both alone and as teams in training. They made us into animals, and they trained us to bite everyone but the hand that fed us, all the while ridding us of any reluctance to kill and sending us after those who did what we did, but without official permission.

Now, feeling more like my old self than I had in ages, I knew that the doubts that had assailed me on my release from the army were just that.

Doubts.

Meaningless and fucking unhelpful in the greater scheme of things, especially when I had a fuckload of people around who needed judging.

The locker room was reasonably narrow, made so by the changing booths, the toilets, the lockers, and the showers that stood in the very center of the hollow square shaped by the rest.

The floor, like the walls, was white and tiled, with a ceiling of dull nonreflective plastic, dotted here and there with lights. The walls, where they weren't covered by lockers and cubicles, had narrow mirrors, clearly there to make sure the staff took the time to be properly presented for their corpo overlords.

Well, the entrance I'd used was at the top left of the square, and I crept down that side, moving as close behind the single slowly dressing figure as I could, waiting both for his lack of attention to reach the right point, and the other two to either get sick of him ogling them, or to fuck off somewhere else.

I laid each foot slowly, being as careful as possible to be silent, feeling the full body suit stretching as I reached out…

And the fucker twisted around and full-on faced the pair, calling out in a clear voice filled with frustration.

"Fuck's sake, Amanda!" he snarled. "A week!"

"Oh, fuck off, Blythe!" the woman snarled back, clearly more than ready for the conversation.

"A fucking week!" he repeated even louder, striding forward.

I cursed and slipped into the cubicle next to me. The half-open door provided cover as I moved out of sight and turned the stealth suit off, the battery now at four percent. I waited, as the situation developed.

"We're supposed to be on a break, and you waited a single goddamn week before fucking him!"

"You moved out. You've got no right to question me." She stepped up and got in his face, as I watched on the camera.

"I've every fucking right! We were supposed to be getting married!"

"You left me!"

"You changed the fucking door codes!"

"Hey, look, man, no offense but—" The blatant third wheel in all of this started to interrupt, only to have them both turn on him.

"Fuck off!"

"Shut it, Steve!"

"Whoa, look, you've both got some serious fucking issues here. You need to—"

"Steve!" the woman hissed in warning. "You want to fuck me again? Shut it and go wait in the car!"

"I…I…"

"Get outta here, Steve, and if you hang around, I'll smash your skull in!" My target—Blythe, apparently—shoved the smaller man.

Steve grabbed Blythe's hand and twisted it back, punching the larger man in the stomach once, twice, then a third time…while Blythe just stared at him.

The camera angle wasn't great, not for seeing his expression, but Steve clearly hadn't been expecting that. And Blythe?

Well, there was an animalistic sound from him, followed by a single, damn hard punch to the smaller man's face.

His head rebounded off the tiled wall behind him. The white tiles suddenly spattered with blood, and then Blythe was a blur. Punches flew, and so did more blood.

"Fuck, Blythe!" Amanda snarled. "You…he's just…ah, fuck!"

"Motherfucker!" Blythe screamed, grabbing Steve by the throat and punching him again and again, smashing him barely conscious to the floor before kicking him in the gut, over and over.

"Blythe!" Amanda screamed, shoving at her larger, apparent ex, and screaming his name. "Fucking hell, man! Blythe!"

"WHAT!" he screamed into her face. The pair of them were centimeters from each other, chests heaving in rage and…and she fucking threw herself at him, kissing him with a frenzied passion.

He hesitated. Then her towel was torn off, thrown aside, and he was yanking at his uniform, even as she desperately tore at his trousers.

"Well, I didn't expect that…This is better than a fucking docu-drama!"

Bowdoin's voice made me jump, then curse as silently as I could, as the apparently reunited couple started fucking on a bench that was half covered in Steve's blood. The loser dragged himself out of the way and crawled toward the exit.

"You guys are insane. Pass the popcorn!" Bowdoin chortled.

"Fuck's sake," I growled, shaking my head. "Warn Kal that the loser is coming out. He better hide."

I paused a minute. Bowdoin was back in my vision, nodding, apparently eating something and presumably still watching the couple fucking. It was brutal, animalistic, and apparently exactly what they both needed, judging from the groans and cries.

"He's hiding," Bowdoin assured me, and I snorted.

"Fucking perfect. A guy who's about the right goddamn size and his uniform's fucking torn now," I pointed out as Amanda ripped his shirt.

"Well, put it this way—would you have really interrupted this pair? I mean, she'd shank you, and then probably jump you if you beat him down…"

"Point," I grumbled. "Well, they're still in sight, but they're sure as shit not paying attention. Can you pop his locker for me?"

"I probably couldn't have. I've got the lowest level of security access to the cameras and so on right now, and to open locked doors remotely without a physical hack would be beyond me for now. *But…*" He drew the word out as he replayed Blythe storming away from his locker.

"It's not locked, is it?" I asked, and he shook his head.

"Not as near as I can tell. The door's closed, but not quite…"

"Fantastic. Watch those fuckers."

"Oh no, whatever will I do? Oh wait, record this shit, that's what." Bowdoin snorted, apparently getting another handful of something and munching on it while I reactivated my suit.

I snuck out of the cubicle and headed over to the locker, opening it again—checking that the others weren't watching—and quickly grabbed his spare uniform, even taking a gun belt and a rather nice little handgun out, then ducking into the next cubicle to change.

I was as fast as I could be, figuring that, first of all, he was clearly late for work, and that was unlikely to go down well here. Secondly, judging from the sounds echoing around the locker area, they'd not be distracted for much longer.

I was right, buttoning up my shirt to the neck—and hating it…goddamn white shirts! Who the hell makes staff wear a tight white shirt?—and as I tucked the shirt into my trousers, the last cries died away. I finished dressing, making sure my holster was on straight and I was as tidy as I could make myself look.

Blythe was bigger than me, both in muscle and in physical size, which was a blessing, meaning that as long as I flattened my hood down the back of my neck as far as I could, I could wear his uniform over my own clothes.

I looked rumpled and scruffy, like my clothes didn't fit well, and I was generally unkept, but better that than leave my gear behind.

The pair gathered up their clothes, several protestations of eternal love were exchanged, and then cursing rang out as Blythe realized his clothes and gun were missing.

"Fucking Steve!" he snarled. "The bastard must have nicked them!"

"Shit, you'll get fired!" Amanda snapped. "You can't get fired! We need to pay the rent!"

"We…there's enough in the cred account, right?"

"No…Look, we can talk later. Let's get your fucking uniform from Steve, all right?" She groaned. "I'll explain later, just…come on!"

She dressed quickly in street clothes, then tore out of the bottom doors following Blythe, who was cursing Steve and swearing he'd kill the fucker.

I shrugged and strolled out of the room behind them, finding Kal hiding behind a support beam, and gestured for him to join me.

"What happened in there?" he asked, wide-eyed. "I thought I heard…?"

"Fucking?" I asked.

"Yeah!"

"It's all part of the job," I assured him. "Sometimes you need to do whatever you have to, to get the job done."

"You…Wait, you mean…?" He pointed after the other two. "What the hell happened in there?"

"Best not to worry about it," I said. "Right, maintenance office…"

"It's down here. But why?"

"First, I need a spare fucking battery for the stealth suit, if possible. Secondly, even you have to realize that for the maintenance team to do their fucking job, they need access to the servers, right?"

"So?"

"Just…shut the fuck up and stay out of the way," I growled, as Bowdoin spoke up in my ear.

"End of the corridor, take a left. The right leads to the stairs. You want the third door along. Only one technician in there, and he's watching a couple of young corpos banging in the pool."

"Great," I muttered. "Another fucking pervert."

"World's full of them," Bowdoin agreed happily. "Only difference is that some admit it, and some lie."

"Whatever," I growled.

"Look…I'm late, like *really* late now, and if I don't get there soon…"

"You need to go?" I asked, and he nodded emphatically. "Okay, well, you got us this far. Don't forget that my hacker is still riding your implants, so no fucking us over. But once we're done? He'll leave you be, all right?"

"Okay, just…um…?"

"Spit it out," I ordered, marching along the corridor toward the lift and stairwell to the next floor.

"Can…I have a job?"

I stared at him in disbelief.

"What?"

"A job," he repeated. "Seriously, you guys, the stuff you just did, and then fucking that security guard…I mean, the guy who dragged himself out all covered in blood, then you have like a threesome with Amanda—she's only the hottest of all the security staff—and a few minutes later, you're strolling around, armed and dressed like a security guard…"

I looked at him in confusion before Bowdoin saved me.

"I told him to hide himself because you'd kicked a guy's ass and were having a threesome with his girlfriend, and he bought it."

"Why…?" I hissed to Bowdoin, only for Kal to think it was meant for him.

"Look, I know, but you can trust me, right? You know who I am. You've seen my background and you know I hate the bastards, and—"

"All right," I said, more to shut him up than anything.

"All right?" he squeaked. "Like, you mean yes? I can join you?"

"Yeah…sure,'" I lied with a straight face. "Let's view this as a test. Go to your normal job, get on and make sure nobody suspects anything, okay? If the shit hits the fan, try to distract people. My hacker will be watching and evaluating, and when we're done, he'll leave you, but he'll give me a report. You do well? We'll be in touch."

"Grab his fucking connection cable!" Bowdoin interrupted, and I grabbed it quick, nodding my thanks as I pocketed it.

"Thank you!" He practically hugged himself to death, squeezing that hard, before coughing and remembering what, and who, he was. He quickly let go of himself, straightened his clothes as best he could, and nodded to me, before tearing off in the opposite direction, calling something about "getting ready."

"You really giving him a chance to join you?" Bowdoin asked, and I snorted.

"Fuck, no. He's a corpo. Given half a chance, he'll sell us out. No, I just don't want him thinking about selling us out. This way, he's going to cover for us instead."

"Sneaky," he replied, and I nodded.

"Anything I need to know, you know, before I reach the next level?" I jogged down the corridor.

"Not really…The new shift is mainly going out. Last shift is riding the lift down…There's gonna be some questions raised about the blood in the changing rooms, I bet."

"Yeah, so nothing on the floor above?" I asked.

"Corpo parking," Bowdoin said. "Some nice rides, but that's it. There's also a security bay for their armed wagons, a damn nice Cryson high-speed interceptor in there at the minute, well-armed—got the passes for weapons deployment and everything. Nice option if you need to shoot your way out later."

"If we get to that point, then we're fucked either way."

"True. Be a hell of a show for me, though, which brings me to the next bit of bad news."

"Which is?" I went up the stairs to the next floor, and hesitated outside the door of the maintenance section as he looped the relevant camera for me.

"Fuck, I'm good!" Bowdoin grunted.

"And the bad news?" I prompted.

"Oh shit, yeah. Well, you just sent our remote access point away."

"Uh-huh?"

"So…guess who gets to be my next ride?"

"Oh, fuck no," I said. "Not a fucking chance."

"You want me to hack this shit to get us to the security office?" he asked. "I can't *do* that by a remote link. I need to be plugged into it, to bypass most of that shit. This is a corpo site, remember? They'll have patrolling AIs and everything roaming their corpo Aug-World. The only chance we've got? Is if I'm able to hit hard and fast enough that when the AIs come looking, they believe that there's nothing wrong."

"And how the hell does that mean you need to ride me?" I growled.

"First off, that phrasing means I'm going to take a razor to my brain to cleanse it. Urgh. Second, I need you to literally plug me the fuck in as soon as you get there. If I'm just riding a relay link between here, there and you? Too much that can go wrong. Trust me, this is not going to end well if I don't have that."

"Fuck no." I growled, "It's not happening."

"Add in that you need me to hack this guy's augs when you reach him? I mean, you're gonna need me to hack not just normal augs, but corpo and army level shit, remotely. Even with me having a direct connection, that's a tall fucking order. Anything that slows down my link? We need it out of the way."

"You better not be fucking me here, Bowdoin," I swore under my breath, reaching out for the door handle.

"If I am? We lose the payday, right? No offense, Kabutt, but fucking with you, an APS operator, and both losing fifteen fucking thousand creds and then being a target for the rest of my life, not to mention having Richie fucking gunning for me?" He shook his head. "That Richie was insane. As much as yeah, I'd fuck you around for a laugh usually, I'm not that stupid, all right?"

"You better not be," I whispered. My stomach dropped out as I offered him the top-level access to my system.

"Yeah, that's not gonna cut it, mate. No chance."

"You better not fuck me here, you little shit!" I snarled, hating it even as I was accepting the spate of access requests he made. "Seriously, fuck me over here and I'll hunt you down and murder you and anyone you've even so much as looked at sideways."

"Sure...sure..." he agreed. The video feed of him faded away and a replacement feed of the corridor on the other side of the door popped up.

"Two minutes. There, you're good to go."

I opened the door slowly, peering around the corner, and trying to spot any possible threat...before swearing under my breath and standing up, slipping into the room and closing the door softly behind me.

The maintenance tech in the room was clearly too busy to care about us being there, judging from the cable he had plugged in already and the frantically moving forearm.

I moved around him, trying not to be too much in the "line of fire" just in case, as I reached the server the filthy bastard was physically jacked into.

"Just plug me in there. Second spot, right above his cable..." Bowdoin whispered, and I shook my head at his instinctive whispering.

Ten seconds later, the pervert next to me finished with his business and sagged back, sighing, then pulled his jack free, only to blink the real world back into his vision...and find both a recording of him doing what he'd been doing, and what he'd been watching, in his public access, sent by Bowdoin, and my handgun an inch from his eyeball, as I slid a nice pair of pliers I'd spotted into a pocket for later.

"Uh...how can I help?" he asked, his voice full of panic. Even if I let him live, he knew his career and life was over, unless he was very, *very* lucky.

Minutes later, I was calmly walking up the stairs to the ground floor, my access as a network administrator in place, meaning that I had the authority to both insert and remove lower ranked system users at will.

Amusingly, that included the head of security and all his staff. Or it would, once I was approved by the current security network override, in the security office.

Bowdoin had taken the time to downgrade all the other maintenance and tech team by one level to ensure that should this guy develop a set of brass balls after I left?

He'd be able to do fuck all about the whole situation.

I took the last few steps and paused at the door. No need to be cocky about things, after all.

There were a handful of security officers about, some staff, and…yeah, they moved off as a group, heading to a second corridor that branched off the main one.

"Okay, go now. There's two corpo types coming past, but that's the quietest this section gets for a while," Bowdoin said.

I moved, trusting that either he was on the level, or I was utterly fucked and I might as well get it over with.

I got out into the corridor and all of three feet, before one of the pair of passersby, a corporate scumbag and his wife, fresh on their way back from presumably a spa session, stepped in front of me, looking outraged.

CHAPTER FIFTY-FOUR

"You!" the man snapped, looking me over. "You're security?"

"Ah…" I hesitated, and he stepped in front of me, glaring. My instinct was to shoot the obnoxious little bastard, or at least take him none-too-gently by the throat and shake some sense into him—he literally topped out with his chin about nipple height on me—but still. "Yes sir, of course. How can I help?" I replied, forcing a smile to my face.

"It's disgraceful!" his wife agreed, also glaring at me. Where he was short and wide, dark, pockmarked skin drenched in sweat, and a bathrobe barely containing the apparent ocean of oil he was covered in, she was the opposite in almost every way.

Tall, so buxom that she clearly wouldn't fit into a normal robe, and so had left it open at the front, her hair was piled atop her head in something that resembled a drunken builder's attempt at a skyscraper. And for all her processed beauty, it was clear the soul beneath was anything but.

She was also *heavily* upgraded, everything from eyelids that reflected the lights overhead in special patterns, to her porcelain teeth, sharp cheekbones and of course eyes with feline slitted pupils as had been the rage…*ten years ago*.

Everything about her, from the slightly sagging skin to the crow's feet at the corners of the eyes—smoothed, but still starting to show—screamed "danger" to me.

Too poor to be kept perfect, too stupid to save up or accept that aging happened to us all.

She—and by extension, he—were the worst type of corpo for most people to interact with. Petty, with just enough power to be on the ladder, without enough power to be rich, and without enough brains to know they should be happy with their place. Instead, they'd be constantly blaming anyone they could, and picking fault to make themselves feel superior.

I lumped them in with the same crowd as Captain Tyrannus: powerful enough to be a nightmare to anyone below, vicious to anyone on the same level, and with tongues worn to a goddamn stump from licking the assholes of those above them.

Fucking *great*. Just my luck to run into them, and presumably why the other security staff had vanished.

"The spa!" the short ass snapped; his wife nodded so viciously she seemed in danger of breaking her neck. "I made a *perfectly* reasonable request to the massage assistant, and they thought I was ordering them to 'service' me! It's a disgrace!"

"I'm very sorry…" I kept that polite smile plastered to my face. "So, she refused?"

"No, he didn't!" he snapped. "He dared to touch me, and there I was, stunned, shocked at the effrontery, and totally unable to stop him, I was in so much shock, when my wife walked in..."

"Disgraceful!" she cried, voice rising even higher.

"I dread to think how it looked..." Dickhead frantically babbled on and on about how it was all a misunderstanding, and he wanted that staff member fired, etc.

"I'm sorry, sir. A regrettable misunderstanding," I assured him, years of dealing with officers' bullshit coming to the fore as I forced a sad look onto my face. "I'll see to it that they're disciplined."

"Fired, I said! I want them...Wait, why are you blocked out?" He froze, staring at me, clearly expecting to see my personal details, which we'd set to "private" on the local Aug-World relay. "All the local staff are *required* to be..."

Bowdoin swore in my ear. "Better shut this down. He's pinging the local node for confirmation..."

"Sir, I'm here from the head office, dealing with a security matter. As you'll see, my uniform is hardly up to the standards of such an important location, but needs must," I lied, glancing up and down the corridor. "But, perhaps, you and your wife could follow me into the security office? You could make your complaint to one of the local staff?" I nodded to the door a few steps behind them that, according to the floating Aug-World signs, and subtle wall-mounted ones, led to the main security area.

"What?" he snapped, frowning.

"The office, sir. I'm happy to provide identification, but we need to be in a secure area," I said firmly. "Sir, I was sent here by..." I hesitated, my on-the-spot-bullshitting skills only getting me so far, before Bowdoin interrupted me, pulling up the corpo organizational chart.

"Hinto, Security Commander Hinto," he told me.

"Hinto!" I repeated quickly. "I was sent by Security Commander Hinto, and I'm afraid his orders take precedence. I'm sure you understand?"

"Who?" The woman's nose wrinkled in confusion.

"*Jared* Hinto?" The man frowned.

"Sir, either you can come right now, or I'm leaving you here," I said firmly. "Commander Hinto ordered me to make it to the office as fast as I could, forcing me to grab another's uniform to blend in—"

"You didn't do that very well," she sneered, and I glared at her.

"Ma'am, I'm wearing full body armor under this suit," I pointed out. "Why do you think that is?"

"I'm sure I don't know!" she replied haughtily, before looking at her husband, and freezing at the sudden look on his face. "D...darling?"

"Jared Hinto is the head of security for the corporation," he hissed at her. "If he's sent this, this..."

"Operative," I said quickly. "Last chance offered, sir. Either come now, or hold your complaint until tomorrow."

I stepped past them, opening the door with a quick knock from my fake ID, before closing the door behind me. The pair started to move, clearly unwilling to give up on a perfectly good opportunity to complain about something. I didn't give a shit. When we'd been in the maintenance section, I'd checked the turrets out, and having these idiots with their guest IDs between them and me? I was all in favor of, just in case.

I should be fine. My new permissions and authorizations *should* be more than I needed, but trust was thin when dealing with fucking turrets.

"I don't understand!" she snapped at him, and then me. Her voice changed as a hint of fear crept in, the demand becoming a whine. "What's going on?"

"Commander Hinto is afraid there are spies here. Heavily armed ones. And I need to get to the security office and make sure the site is secure," I lied to the pair grimly, standing just inside the door, the corridor leading away from us to the security office. "I was ordered to terminate any possible threats…" I set my hand on my handgun, and the shock and horror on their faces was fucking comical. "But…"

"But?" she asked. Her husband stared at my half-drawn gun, his jaw sagging.

"But, if you could prove that you're not a spy?" I suggested.

"I-I've no weapon…" the man stuttered, starting to open his robe, and I shook my head, not needing to fucking see that.

"You could have concealed mods, sir. I'm going to ask you to lead the way to the office. We'll scan you, and when it's confirmed that you're clean? Well, I'll include your helpfulness in my report to the commander, and you can make your own report. You see? Everyone wins."

"To Commander Hinto?" the man questioned, sounding unsure.

"The report? Yes, sir. I know he's reviewing the current upper echelon for loyalty, so there may be…opportunities coming. Although that's not something for the likes of me to be concerned with."

"No, no, it's certainly not. But I take your hint. And yes, I'll be sure to remember you, should things work out…" he assured me. The look in his eye said he'd already forgotten what I looked like, and was counting the credits his new—totally imaginary—promotion would earn him.

"It'd mean you'd be in my report to the head office as helping me," I repeated and the woman, clearly the faster on the uptake of the pair, nodded quickly.

"Of course!" She smiled. "And you'd be including my name as helping?"

"Certainly," I agreed. "Provided you move along quickly."

"Oh, of course!" She sneered. "Follow me!"

With that, she was off. Her husband and I stared after her for a few seconds, before we both hurried to catch up. Her husband ran a few steps to get ahead of me, speaking to her in what he clearly thought was a low voice.

"I don't know about this…It's all very susp—"

"Be quiet!" she snapped. "A report in the right ear, and we're climbing the ladder again. No more sitting still! We've got that file, but we need to get access to them to use it, so…"

I strode along behind them, doing my best to look as though I was escorting them, as they blatantly discussed what sounded like blackmail material on a superior.

"Man, I know I don't see them up close that often, but I fucking hate the rich. Almost more than elves," Bowdoin muttered in my ear. "I mean seriously, how dumb, shitty, and backstabbing can you get?"

"I know," I murmured.

"No, I mean, that was some amazingly shitty acting on your part, there's no way that should have worked, but you know why it did?"

"No?"

"Because Barabbas, that's the short asshole, and Tartaglia, that's his wife, are such obscene pieces of shit, that they'd take any opportunity to fuck someone else over. I'm in the local node and monitoring them. They've both opened up recording. Heh, they tried to connect to a remote facility, that's how badly they want to get evidence of whatever happens next. They've no idea they're backing their shit up to me."

"Shit…"

"Oh yeah, I mean, without me you'd be seriously boned here, unless you could get them to stop recording and backing up their blackmail material. I seriously doubt you'd be getting out of this without them having shit on you.

"These people are idiots. That they really think this is going to get their names known by higher-ups? I mean, it will, just not in the way they're hoping. But still! Then they get access to someone they've got shit on—which I mean, surely that's fucking unlikely. If they try something like that, I'm betting an AI gets sent after them and erases everything digital, then a hit erases them—or they get to hand you in if it's bullshit. She's already tried sending a message to a friend of hers…Basically, everything they send will show as sent, but it's all going out into the great wide nothing…Yeah, she's gonna try to get you in the recording, so watch it. She won't be able to send it out, but if she keeps it…" His voice trailed off.

"Be aware, any attempt to capture me on a recording will be grounds for its server's erasure by military-grade AI," I said quickly, stepping up close to the pair. "At the end of this operation, you'll have your implants examined, so please, be aware of the risk."

"Of course!" Tartaglia lied, angling around and trying to see me anyway, until she felt the gun I rammed into her spine through the bathrobe.

"That was your only warning," I said. "Commander Hinto authorized the execution of any threats to my mission…"

"Uh…of course!" she agreed, going back to staring straight ahead.

"Fuck. I don't know what she just did. I'm dipping the feed. She's sent something encrypted—can't crack the code, not anytime soon, so I've locked it."

I shook my head, having no clue what the fucking hacker was up to, and leaving it be.

This wasn't going well, but as we approached the security office at the end of the corridor, I saw the turrets clearly, and I swallowed hard.

Those fuckers, I'd have had serious problems with.

I recognized them, and all my suspicions were proved right. Whatever was going on here wasn't fucking small scale. Bowdoin's guess that my stealth suit might not have worked was an understatement. Last time I'd seen these kind of turrets, I was in the army and they'd been deployed outside one of our armories.

Seeing them here, I suddenly realized how fucking lucky I'd been to get into the maintenance area. If I'd tried sneaking in here directly, I'd have been seen instantly, and I'd have been fucking shredded a quarter second later.

Now? Marching along the corridor behind Tweedle-dim and Tweedle-fuckwit? I stood a chance. I had to hope that whoever had set this up was cheap and dumb. If these mil-spec turrets were backed up by a mil-spec AI in the security office?

We could still be utterly fucking hosed.

> Bowdoin?

I sent the message, getting a frown as he popped up in my feed again, nodding for me to speak.

"Don't worry, I'm deep enough in your system architecture nobody is going to be able to read me. What's up?" he asked.

> Mil-spec turrets. I recognize the model. Stealth suits definitely wouldn't have worked. If we can't get control in the office, I need you to get the girls out, and fucking fast. There's a LOT more creds been spent here than there should be.

"Uh…" He paused, then nodded. I guessed he was taking an image from my augs and running it for a match against some database. "I'm not seeing anything special…"

> Check Takemoto mil-contracts, perimeter defense, autonomous and net sharing.

"Shit," he grunted, and I tensed involuntarily as we stepped out of the end of the corridor into a waiting area. One that was entirely covered by the two turrets.

> Gotta go. Watch over me, and DO NOT try to hack them. If we can't get into the security office? We're fucked and I'll let myself out, don't worry.

"What do you mean, you'll…Oh." He winced as I sent him an image I had stored in my RI's memory. It was another we used to use when speaking to officers, one that I or another of the NCOs would send to each other.

The image was of a soldier lifting his handgun to his head and taking the express route out of the army.

Bowdoin took the hint, going silent as I stepped around the pair who were hesitating by the security office's reinforced glass. There were two figures inside I could see dimly. The glass was deliberately tinted so that you'd see if there was movement, but nothing clear. Assumedly it was so that if you were a threat…or more likely, an asshole corpo complaining that your latest maid wasn't friendly enough…they could get rid of you without being unduly bullied.

It was fine for the lower ranks to be bullied, but the actual management of the place didn't need that shit.

> Will my pass definitely get me in there?

"Uh…should do, double-checking…" Bowdoin started, even as the woman stepped up and glared at the reflective glass, before snapping—fuck knows why she thought that was appropriate—at me that she'd "done her part."

She also deliberately fixed on my face, and I saw the triumphant gleam in her eye as she made sure she had my face recorded. Her husband spoke up, asking whether he could still make his complaint, then directing a repeat of his bullshittery at the shadowed figures on the other side of the glass.

For fuck's sake.

I shook my head, knocking on the system architecture and feeling a massive upswelling of relief as the door into the security office accepted my ident, and the pair of turrets continued to track from side to side, utterly uninterested in me.

The door next to me clunked as the lock released, and I was moving before even I knew what I was doing, stepping into the room, and bringing my gun around.

I didn't hesitate, viewing it as the only fucking chance I had, and I fired twice, one shot taking the man at the desk in the forehead. He'd been looking at me in confusion—I was wearing one of their uniforms, after all. The second shot took his friend who'd been standing behind him, only half listening to tweedle-dim, in the meat of his neck.

He crashed to the floor even as his friend collapsed dead. He was frantically trying to stanch the bleeding. Two quick steps took me to the server stack. A sealed door kept it hermetically sealed, and I pointed the gun at the panicking, heavily bleeding figure on the ground.

"Open it, and you get a medikit. Don't, and you get a bullet. Three seconds. One, two…" I snarled, and before I could get to three, the door popped.

"Good choice." I took a step and plugged the cable into the server stack.

"Working," Bowdoin said distractedly. "You might want to give him that medikit. We're going to need him."

"Here." I plucked the spare I kept in my left arm free and tossed it to the figure on the ground, who frantically uncovered the injector module and jabbed it into his shoulder, close to the neck.

"This is how this is going to work," I told him. "You're going to give my hacker root access to your Keystone. He's going to verify all your details and transfer all authority to me. I'll do the job I'm here to do, and then I'll ghost."

"N…no…" He started to refuse, and I shot him in the kneecap, spreading blood and bone fragments everywhere as he screamed.

"Wrong answer," I said. "Now, look, there's one outcome here where you don't die. Unless, of course, you *want* to die? Do you? Is that it?"

He shook his head frantically, and I nodded.

"Okay, so we've got control of the system—"

"No, we fucking don't," Bowdoin snapped at me. "Incoming security RI— this isn't fucking good!"

"Give me your access, or I kill you." I pressed the gun to the wounded corposec officer's head. "Seriously, you give me access? They might kill you later. They might just fire you. I, on the other hand, will definitely fucking kill you *right goddamn now!*"

I dragged the gun across and shot him in the other knee, before ramming it against his crotch.

"NOW!" I roared in his face, only to sense a sudden connection form as Bowdoin sent out a ping to him, via me, and he accepted it, transferring the details over.

"I've got root access, authorizing us, patching…RI has accepted…I'm linking through him, it'll be quicker…Be back soon."

"Bowdoin?" I snarled, gritting my teeth, as the pair outside the security office got my attention again.

"Fuck's sake, what?" he snarled. "Do you have any idea how much I'm fucking doing right now?"

"No clue. Do we have control of the turrets?"

"Yes!"

"And there's no signals getting out?"

"Do you think I'm a fucking idiot?" he raged. "Of course not!"

"And those two?" I peered through the security glass at the now-silent idiots who I'd used as a distraction.

"They're broadcasting to a spoof address. Now, can I fucking go before this RI figures out what we're doing and kills us both? Huh? You mind?"

"Go." I unplugged the data access cable from my Keystone, and forced the bleeding man on the ground to let me plug it into him instead. That done, and with the pair of corpo idiots on the other side of the glass, I tipped the corpse of the first man out of his seat, and pulled his belt off, rolling the other man facedown—with some screams of pain on his side—and binding him tightly, before I broke the emergency seal on a pair of large medikits stored by the side of the desk.

I put them both onto the desk next to me, and smiled at the pair squinting through the reflective glass, trying to make out what was happening.

The computer was open to me thanks to the access authorization I had locked in earlier, now approved by the local on the floor, and I connected to it. My own RI bridged the gap between the system architecture and my wishes, showing me the paths I needed to take.

In less than ten seconds, just enough time for the fucking idiots before me to notice that they weren't actually getting the feedback they wanted, I'd removed them from the "guest" list and instead put them in the "ex-employee, security risk" group.

Both turrets reacted immediately.

CHAPTER FIFTY-FIVE

The pair froze as both turrets spun to face them, heavy caliber slug throwers locked onto them, and smaller, short-range grazers deployed from a shielded side section.

"Uh…Officer?" the woman, Tartaglia, called hesitantly, and I flicked the control, speaking up.

"Yes?" I asked distractedly.

"The…the turrets—" she tried to explain, and I cut her off.

"You were being monitored as we walked down the corridor by one of our AIs. You attempted to make a call, then you started recording the event, including my face, despite being warned not to."

"N…no—"

"You were under observation," I continued. "Your transmissions were rerouted to a secure server, and you've been offline since you entered the security section. We have a full recording of you, of the warnings I gave you, and your attempts to circumvent them, as well as your comments about the blackmail you have stored. Your guest status here has been revoked, and the turrets are set to terminate you if you attempt to leave the area or access this office. Sit down in the corner and be quiet. The commander will be here to speak with you shortly."

With that, I cut the speakers and shifted to Bowdoin.

"How we looking, Bowdoin?" I muttered.

"Not good, very busy…" he grunted. "System has accepted you. You now have full auth, and the security RI believes you're here on top-level corpo-sec business."

"That good?" I asked.

"It means I don't have to delete your images from the servers. The RI is doing it for us. As soon as we leave the site, it'll perform a full security wipe as well. Currently, I've got it believing that there's been a breach and we're here to remove the evidence before there's an audit." He chuckled. "I can't believe the corpos had that contingency in place. Must have happened before."

"An audit?"

"Governmental oversight, Kabutt. The corpos let them watch over them all, and they pretend to play along, but fuck, that there's an actual position in the system architecture for a corporate evidence eraser? Makes a joke of that oversight, doesn't it. I mean, hell, they didn't even hide the role!"

"You complaining?" I asked, vaguely amused by the offended tone in his voice.

"Listen, I've just hacked my way into a corpo system. I've diverted RIs, I've convinced security turrets that not only should they not shoot you, but that you're God as far as they're concerned. I've done all of this, and right at the end, you know what I found?"

"No."

"An AI."

"What?!"

"It's watching us, and it's not fucking interested," Bowdoin growled. "Seriously, I found the limits for it. It's watching the security system, and as long as we're not going near the lower floors? The cut-off high-security areas? It doesn't give a shit."

"That's good, right?"

"It's a newly awakened AI, Kabutt. It's got the processing power to go through everything we've done so far like a fucking nuke, and it doesn't care. It looks like it's been told where its borders are, and it's not aware enough to care beyond that. This…it's the equivalent of you strolling up to the armory door and finding it's unlocked and everyone went out to lunch. It fucking offends me, all right?"

"It offends you?" I smiled, checking the last of the details over and making sure we had complete control.

"There's a right way to do things, all right?"

"You'd rather we were all dead?"

"Well, no…"

"Then shut the fuck up, Bowdoin, and stay the hell away from that thing and the lower floors!" I snorted. "Right. Do we need the girls in here?"

"Rather than leave them in the car, you mean? I guess it could be funny, but…"

"Is there a reason to march them through the building to here, or should we just leave you in charge of this, I mean?" I asked him.

"Better they're here," he admitted. "If anything happens and I get cut off? We're fucked if we don't have a physical ass in the seat."

"Can you route them through to here?" I asked, and he nodded.

"I'll divert them around people and get them up. I've got full control of security now."

"Glad to hear it. Have we got anything interesting in here?" I looked around the large office, noting the row of narrow but tall lockers on the far side.

"No clue. Let's find out," Bowdoin said distractedly. "Locks, locks, locks…here we go! Thank the Keeper for orderly file administration!"

The locks on the doors popped as I walked over and glanced inside. I couldn't help but fucking smile.

The first one was clearly in case of riots or something—why they needed riot gear in a pleasure tower, I don't fucking know; maybe they'd run out of flavored lube or something—but as well as the corpo-sec equivalent of body armor, there was also a full riot loadout.

"Mine!" I proclaimed loudly, grinning and pulling a weapon I'd rarely seen in the real world but had *always* wanted to try.

Well, to try using on someone else, anyway.

The Riot Suppression [Non-Lethal] Electro-Impact Lance, or RSEIL, also known as the arse-lance, was the kind of a weapon that could only be dreamed up by a truly sadistic bastard.

It was as long as a rifle and offered three settings:

First, Ranged.

It fired a riot suppression round, much the same as the one that had hit Reign in the tit earlier, just more powerful. It was a rubberized, electrified mass that when it hit—with the force of a pissed-off orc's best punch—it spread out and released a high-powered electrical shock to the victim.

It was powerful enough to knock most people out with a single hit, and the magazine carried thirty shots.

Ranged Suppression setting was much the same, except that it was the fully automatic version, and it'd fucking kill anyone who took more than two or three hits, I had no doubt.

Last, and arguably the most fun, was Impact.

The arse-lance was basically a stub-barreled rifle in the first two settings, but in the third, the additional four prongs that laid flat to the barrel in the first settings, slid out and into place, forming a four-pronged, and highly electrified impact weapon that now resembled a long-barreled rifle or lance.

The original version also came with an attachment that basically turned the end into a flanged, electrified mace, but that'd been removed from the market after excess deaths.

Something about it being made of steel and having sharpened points that you were encouraged to use to hit people made it difficult to market as a "non-lethal" riot suppression device.

I searched the locker quickly, and to my disappointment found that they'd not stocked the attachment.

On the upside, I now had a wonderful toy to help Tyrannus talk.

There were also three boxes of grenades, helpfully marked as To Suppress Riots Only. What kind of riots needed three boxes of thirty grenades—namely sticky, flash-bang and fragmentation—to "suppress," I didn't know, but by the time the girls made it to the security office, I was feeling *much* more cheerful.

I dressed in the full security riot suppression gear, and as the girls walked in, staring open-mouthed at me, I grinned and waved to the four remaining suits in invitation.

They didn't waste any time, grabbing them and stripping their old gear off, replacing it in favor of the new, much more expensive mil-spec gear.

"Pervert," Bowdoin muttered into my ear at one point, and I jerked, twisting away from the view of Reign bent over at the waist, struggling to pull the armor into place.

"Your ass is fantastic," Luna, ever the example of subtlety, complimented Reign.

"Thank you." She grinned back. "It's home grown…"

"So are these," Luna agreed, squeezing a tit then laughing as I abruptly about-faced, trying not to choke on my damn tongue.

"Fuck's sake, you two, get a room!" I groaned, before moving over and checking on the figure on the floor. My shot to the neck had been more in the muscle than the bone and windpipe, but still, it'd been damn near to the artery, and it'd clearly been enough to scare the shit out of him.

He'd stayed where he was since being moved aside, and had basically been laid with his face pressed to the floor, muttering prayers.

Now, the nanites having sealed the wounds in his neck and slowed the bleeding in both knees, he was woozy, suggestable, and weak. Perfect.

"Bowdoin, keep yourself in his implants, just in case, and monitor things here," I ordered, tugging my armor straight. "Reign, keep control of this place as long as possible. Use that guy to route the local security on constant patrols or whatever. Hold this place as long as you can, then use the turrets to cover your retreat. Get to the armored car in…"

"Bay S-01," Bowdoin said into our comms. "I've set it to open to one of you four only, and got you all in the system the same as Kabutt—anything you do, the security system RI will erase, which I'm starting to love, by the way."

"How long do you think we have?" I asked him.

"Maybe an hour, two at most?" he admitted. "The security team are used to being sent on bogus patrols if there's a 'visitor' to the security office. Feel free to add in whatever kind you want, but they'll get suspicious eventually. Either they'll come to check what's going on, or they'll come expecting their 'turn'. Either way, that's when all hell breaks loose. Of course, any outsider could crash the party any second. *So* glad I'm doing this remotely."

"When that happens, you use the full riot gear, helmets down, the works. Bowdoin, is there a general 'get the fuck outta our way' code?"

"Uh…not really, not in the security lexicon…Although…"

"Yeah?"

"You could take him with you?" he suggested. "I mean, he's a security guard—pretend he's injured and carry him out?"

"Security guards wouldn't be a good enough reason for people to get out of the way," Reign pointed out, before nodding at the pair on the other side of the security glass out the front. "Maybe one of those, though?"

"What do we do with them afterward?" Luna asked.

"Open the doors as we're flying away, give them a flying lesson," Gessh suggested. "They're corpo fuckheads."

"Sounds good to me," I said. "Fine, you guys get to the car if you get into trouble, then come to me. I'll find a way to the ground floor or the roof, depending—"

"That's a point…the gamma cannons?" Reign pointed out. "They'd slow us down?"

"Nope. Authorized vehicle, authorized crew—they'll protect you," Bowdoin corrected.

"Damn, you are useful." Reign smiled.

"You have no idea." He grinned, his vid-link bouncing his eyebrows suggestively. "Anyway, I'd love to chat, but I'm already fending off curious security staff, so…maybe move your ass, Kabutt?"

"I'm gone." I pocketed a last few of the grenades and another spare magazine.

That was four I had now, all stashed about my person, with three sticky, three frag, and six flash-bang grenades, my handgun, the standard-issue handgun, both my two small and the new two large medikits, the arse-lance, and my vibro-blade.

Add to that, I was now in full riot suppression mil-spec gear, which was awesome. It wasn't up to my usual APS level of gear of course, but nothing was.

It was good gear, though: heavy armoring on the torso, upper legs and shoulders, less so on the arms and lower legs, as well as the crotch. It was flame resistant, treated to make sure liquid rolled straight off in case of firebombs, and powered, although only minorly.

The battery was good for about ten uses, and the augments in the arms and legs could either make you run fast for about thirty seconds, punch like a piledriver, or lift a metric ton plus for a few seconds before draining.

It was as much smoke and mirrors as it was effective realistic gear. After all, rioters who saw you blurring across the road to them in this gear, killing their friends with a single punch, and lifting a car weren't going to hang around long enough to make sure you had enough of a charge for round two.

The helmet was shitty, really. Yes, it was a full-face helm as I liked, but it connected to the upper armor and seriously limited mobility.

It looked awesome, though, and seriously intimidating.

The only problem with it all? I still had to wear my stolen security gear under it, so that I looked the part, unlike the girls. I was going to be walking through the center, after all; they would only be running to the car.

Add to that I was wearing my stealth gear underneath, as I might need it and didn't want to just dump it, and under that? My normal clothes.

I was sweating like a corpo getting audited, and that was before I started waddling—walking was seriously starting to chafe now—toward the door.

"You shit yourself, Sarge?" Reign called to me.

I shot her the finger as they all laughed, before forcing myself to move as naturally as possible. I paused between the turrets as I faced the corpo pair who had accosted me earlier.

"Stay here," I ordered them. "My team may decide to separate you. If that happens, do as you're told and you might live through this. As it is? You're on borrowed time."

"I've got credits!" the man, Barabbas, quickly declared, only to have his wife speak over him.

"I'll make it worth your while to let me go!" Tartaglia said. "Blackmail, secrets, credits…I've got access to it all. You could be rich."

I ignored them, snorting in amusement as the pair bickered.

The trip to Tyrannus's floor didn't take long. Reign watched me on the map and routed me around the occasional security guard or upper staff member as they patrolled, and once in the lift, she blocked it stopping for anyone else, using the security override.

When the doors opened on the floor I needed—Bowdoin had confirmed that Tyrannus was in his room, alone—I wasn't sure what I'd been expecting, but the sight and sounds that greeted me sure as shit weren't it.

The lower floors were standard apartment or office block in design, concrete in most places and marble wherever a corpo toe may fall.

There were nice touches, subtle lighting and shit, but that was it. Here though?

Fuck me sideways.

The lift doors opened onto a scene of chaos. At least a dozen young men and women of several races, but all fucking *stunning* and fully naked, frolicked in a massive pool. A handful of older, considerably uglier and fatter men and women lounged about on luxury recliners, watching the younger models at play with avaricious eyes.

I stepped out onto the floor. A veritable wave of warm salty air hit me, like the heat of summer in the slums, but without the oppressive stench that inevitably came with it.

Instead, there was a scent of salt water, coconuts and vanilla, fruity drinks, and yeah, sex.

The entrances to the apartments on this floor were around the outside, dotted here and there among palm trees that swayed in generated breezes. The five massive apartments cut into the floor space, but still left a damn good-sized area for the pool, one that had little bridges crisscrossing narrow "rivers" and leading to the rooms.

I started around to the left, heading to the second apartment, eyes locked on the door like a fucking homing missile. The pleasant wrap of ivy that encircled it and swung in that same breeze only served to piss me off even more.

That these corpo fucks got to play in places like this? That Tyrannus, a fucking turd-swallowing little slimy bastard who'd fucked his own operators over, to earn a measly few credits, got to come here and play as well?

It was more than I could bear.

My fists were clenched so hard in my reinforced armored gloves that I could hear the creaking, and I just plain couldn't wait to wrap them around his fucking neck.

Ten meters from the door, and my righteous vengeance.

Nine.

Eight, and I could practically taste that excuse for a human being's cheap aftershave.

Seven.

Six.

I could envisage his face, that little self-satisfied sneer that he always wore.

Five.

The way that he looked down on each and every one of us, those who actually had to work for a living.

Four.

That he'd risked us, our lives, while he sat in his corpo bribing-earned office, while better men and women died in the dirt, and he ate fucking canapes.

Three.

He'd known what was going on.

Two.

He'd known that we were going to be hit by the shark, and he made fucking sure that Blue Team was gone, so that he could kill us.

One.

He gave us no notice—not for the job, and not before blowing us out of the sky.

Zero.

He was responsible for the deaths of Fergie and Scott; he raped my fucking bank account, and now he was stealing my suit.

Just fucking *no*.

I reached out with my RI and Key combined, using my wonderful new authority as a company man. I popped the door open and stepped inside, closing the door behind me gently with shaking hands.

My eyes adjusted to the darkness of the room, seeing the strewn empty bottles of booze I'd never been able to afford, seeing the spilled liquids, food trays, and more, dumped wherever, uncaring.

I heard the steady snoring from the bedroom ahead, and I strode across the marble floor, glass crunching underfoot.

The bedroom door was slightly ajar, and I pushed it open with the tip of the arse-lance, taking in the room beyond.

The rear wall was all glass, showing the city in all her neon glory. The left side of the room was covered in closets, seating areas, and an entrance to what appeared to be a dressing room. A fucking sex swing hung limp in the middle of the room.

To the right was a bathroom, the door open, fan still running as it struggled to pull the scent of shit from the air. And straight ahead, between me and the windows?

Three marble steps that rose to a massive bed that could have comfortably slept ten fucking people.

I strode silently up the steps, coming to a halt over Tyrannus, seeing the scrawny little bastard laid there. A line of drool ran from the edge of his mouth. He had thinning, greasy hair and a scraggly few days' growth covering his cheeks. And somehow, in one of those ways that only the scummiest pretend soldiers could manage, he was both clearly too unfit to pass even the most basic of the exercise requirements for the army, and managed to have a fucking pot belly.

The state of the little shit offended me in every way, and I reached out with my RI.

Privacy Mode: Engaged. All sounds will be suppressed.

The message from the building RI was simple, but broadcast as it was to any inside the marked zone, it woke Tyrannus, who blinked muzzily, trying to figure out what was going on.

"He's cut off from the network," Bowdoin assured me, his voice hesitant, as Tyrannus squinted up at me.

I fucking smiled. Reaching up with my right thumb, I flicked the lever, and the lance deployed the impact prongs. My fist tightened around the grip and sent the activation code to the onboard processor.

The room lit with crackling blue electrical discharge, and I stared down at Tyrannus, seeing the confusion morph unto unbridled terror on the little bastard's face.

Then I hit him.

CHAPTER FIFTY-SIX

The first blow was my fist—it couldn't be anything else. I swung down hard and fast with my left, refraining from activating the powered exoskeleton only at the last second and snapping his face sideways in a spray of blood as his nose broke.

I rammed the lance into his stomach and triggered it.

He'd lost a bit of the air in his lungs at the blow to his face, but he managed a respectable scream of pain before his body locked up and he chewed on his own tongue.

I pulled the lance back a few seconds later, grabbing him by the hair and dragging him from the bed, throwing him down the three marble steps to smack face-first into the floor.

He shook and whimpered, trying to get one arm under him as he coughed and squealed. The blood spurting from his tongue made it clear he'd really done a number on it.

Well, he wasn't getting off that easy. *Oh fuck no.* I kicked him in the face, then dropped the first of my two small medikits on the floor in front of him. I rested my new toy on the wooden table and checked the bedside storage, finding a snub-nosed slug thrower that looked more like it should be riding in a hidden thigh holster under a dress than a real weapon, but hey.

I pocketed it, watching him, as he frantically activated the medikit, stabbing it directly into his tongue and screaming as it went to work, repairing the damage and keeping him alive, as well as able to answer my questions.

I checked the other side of the bed, finding a large hunting style knife, heavily worn, and clearly valuable for its age, if nothing else.

I took it and walked around the bed as he tried to make it to the lance before me, clearly in shock and not considering that it was a security weapon, and therefore auto-locked to the user.

Rather than deactivate it, and ruin that particular surprise too soon, I kicked his foot out from under him, sending him crashing to the floor. Then I took a good windup and punted him as hard as I could in the side, hearing ribs break.

He collapsed, wheezing and crying out, blubbering, trying to get out that he didn't know who I was, that I had the wrong room.

I knew better. I waited, seeing the way he braced one arm under himself and shifted. My fucking *years* of training, of fighting and killing on the front lines made his intentions as clear as if he'd written me a fucking love note and sent it in triplicate.

He lunged for the weapon. The cry of pain as his freshly broken ribs shifted almost made the entire fucking day worth it, as I dragged the weapon out of reach, and slammed the blade down, driving it through his hand and into the counter, nailing him in place.

He screamed. He fucking screamed so loud I knew that Fergie and Scott would hear it in the next fucking life, and I booted him in the face hard enough he fell sideways and half cut his hand free.

"Kabutt," Bowdoin whispered, clearly in shock.

"Stay the fuck out of this!" I snarled, furious that he even dared interrupt this most sacred of times.

"You…you need information…?" he pointed out, and I growled, hating that I did, and couldn't torture the fuck to death.

No, I needed to get that information *first*.

"Fine." I squatted across from Tyrannus, staring into his eyes, seeing the open fear and confusion, smelling the rank, stale booze on his breath, and listening to him babble that I had the wrong person, and that he'd never tell anyone, just to go, to leave him.

I reached up and flicked the latches, releasing my riot helmet, then dragged it off, tossing it toward the door for later, and waited.

Tyrannus's voice trailed off as his eyes widened. Fear became bowel-loosening terror, as he realized that not only did I *not* have the wrong room, but I was there most definitely for *him*.

"Kabutt," he whispered, eyes like fucking saucers. "You don't under—"

I hit him, a straight right, snapping his head back and making him shriek as the blade cut even further through his hand. His voice rose in another scream, before I grabbed him around the throat with my left hand and *squeezed*.

The scream died before it got really started. My left thumb laid flat against his windpipe, and I increased the pressure over and over, slowly crushing it.

I stopped long before I wanted to. Fuck, I wanted to watch his eyes pop out of his face, but I needed him alive. For now.

"Tyrannus, you traitorous piece of shit, I'm going to give you a single fucking chance to live, before I go all out and do what I really, *really* want to do, and torture you to death. Blink once if you understand," I said softly. My voice shook with suppressed emotion.

He blinked, quickly.

"You sent us to that site to fuck us over. It was deliberate, wasn't it?"

He stared at me, face purple as he tried to speak, and I hesitated before I relaxed the pressure slightly, letting him breathe.

"Was told…*cough*…to send…"

"Who by?"

"Corp."

"I fucking know that, you little shit!" I snarled. "They paid the fucking bill and dropped creds in your account, and you danced to their tune. That's how you ended up here. But WHY!" I roared into his face.

"You killed my team, you ruined my fucking life and saddled me with shitty mods, all because you could. Then you fucking stole my suit! Oh, I fucking know you took it…" I assured him, seeing the terror in his eyes. "The only thing I don't know is *why*! If you'd planned that shit better, you'd have taken us all down, you'd have stolen our suits…But is that it? You were just too fucking incompetent to do it?" I shook him as he tried to speak, babbling something incomprehensible.

"What?"

"Didn't know!" He swore. "Corium, that's all I knew about!"

"Bullshit!"

"No!" he managed to get out, his eyes filled with terror, and I let the pressure off a bit more. "My *cough* handler! He paid me to send the team for the rod…Blue Team was headed for a different mission. I diverted them, got them there ahead of schedule, and he wanted to make sure we got it back, that's all. So he paid me to make sure you went as well!"

"So, what? You fucked it all up? You got us and Blue there before they were ready? The scavs were being lazy and it all went tits up?"

I scoffed.

"Didn't know!" he begged. "We didn't know about the scavs. Not straightaway! We thought it was a system failure that caused it to crash. Then, when it was taken to the site, maybe scavs—we didn't care! You were supposed to kill them all and get the Corium back. It was part of the Sentinel Project!"

I stared at him, having no clue about any project, and not liking that he was adamant that he didn't know what happened.

"Bullshit!" I snapped. "You'd not be here, you'd not be getting made a fucking corpo for fucking that up!"

"No!" he gasped. "No, the sentinel was fine, as long as it was covered up, all good!"

"What was covered up?" I snarled.

"The Corium—it was rigged with the rest of the satellite as an orbital weapon. The scavs hit the satellite with a missile, that was a fucker, but the Corium could be used again. It's too valuable to waste, so they wanted you to recover it!"

"And my suit?!" I snarled, and he flinched. "Where the fuck is my suit, you little shit…" I punched him in the stomach, then again, and again.

"Don't know…" He wheezed. "Melted…"

"Melted? Fine!" I roared, hitting him again and again, then pausing as he tried to speak. "No, no, you don't need to fucking try that shit anymore!" I snarled. "You had your chance!"

I stood, dragging him upright and triggering one of my stored charges to rip his hand free of the embedded knife. He screamed, and I carried him to a chair, an old-looking one, all carved wood and shit.

I slammed him into it, then took a few quick steps, grabbed the lance and triggered it, extending it slowly upward as he squirmed, trying to avoid it.

The tip touched the underside of his chin, and I pressed harder. The prongs slid further open to the sides to sit over his lower jaw and cheeks, even as smoke curled up from their contact points and he shrieked over and over.

"Kabutt…if you keep going, you'll fry his Key. We won't get anything else from him!" Bowdoin shouted. "Fuck, man, your suit! You'll not get your suit!"

That made it through my rage.

I needed my suit, or I'd never be able to find Richie and Sync. Without the suit, they died, and this shit got off too easy!

I pulled it back, staring at him as he shook and quivered in the seat, blood and piss running down his legs.

Then I tossed the lance aside and moved.

I levered the blade free of the table, and used it to cut the sex swing down, then stripped it into long cables. Those cables I used to bind him to the chair, before grabbing my second small medikit. I injected him with it, grabbing another chair and dragging it over to stare into his eyes as he slowly recovered.

When he focused on me again, he jerked his hands and legs, trying to get free, until he realized that I'd tied him to it well, and he started to babble some shit about having nothing to do with my suit.

I knew better.

"You see this?" I picked up a large medikit and set it on the floor to my side, then the second one. "And these?" I pulled the pliers I'd swiped from the maintenance office earlier free. "I'm going to torture you," I told him, watching his expression.

"I've had you cut off from the net, and we've set this room to block all sounds. I've got about six hours before the next shift change, so we've got at least that long here. I'm going to torture you to the edge of death, then use these medikits." I nodded to them, and he stared at me, one eye wide with disbelief, the other swelling shut.

"I'm going to wait until you recover…then I'm going to start again," I said. "I wanted my suit back. I need my suit, but you don't have it, and you don't know where it is. That was your *only* bargaining chip. I've lost my suit? Fuck it then. All of this?" I gestured around the room we were in.

"I'll never get out of here, not alive, not after what I did to get in here. So this is how it ends." I smiled. "You killed my team, and I'm going to make your death fucking terrible. Then, when they come for me? I'll go happy."

"You…you *can't!*" he half begged and half wept.

"Oh, I can, and I fucking will. So, tell me, dickhead, which is your favorite finger?" I grinned at him deliberately as I reached for his hand, the pliers gripped tight.

"NOOOO!" he screamed. The words fell out in a desperate rush. "Transport! It's in transport! It was repaired. Someone fucked up…It should have been melted, but it was marked for repairs…You couldn't use it, so I…I…"

"Yes?" I hissed, slowly increasing the pressure on the pliers.

"I sold it to M-Corp!" he screamed. "Please! I sold it to M-Corp. It's why I'm here!"

"They made you corpo and gave you enough money to sit here, all for my fucking suit?" I snarled.

"No! It's not…They didn't pay me, not yet!"

"Then why the fuck…It's here?" I asked, suddenly connecting the dots. "It's fucking *here*?"

"Not yet." He wept. "It's on its way. I'm supposed to be here to confirm it's intact and to go over the next stage."

"Which is?"

"It's going to the Ghost Squad, M-Corp's Ghost Squad…They're corpo black ops, deniable…" He shook his head. "They'll fucking kill us both for this. Nobody knows…"

"They'll have to find us first." I snorted, seeing it as another fucking addition on the list of people who wanted me dead these days. I stood and moved to the nearest closet, searching it quickly as he sat there, weeping.

"We're dead...we're so dead! They'll never believe I didn't tell you," he blubbered, and I ignored him.

Nothing in the first one, nothing in the second—nothing of use anyway. But the third? That was it. A small shelf held his datadeck, as well as all the various crap that anyone who was serious about that shit always seemed to have. Special gloves, cables, fucking random clips and shit: I didn't care about most of it, but I grabbed the deck and the cable, plugging the cable in and stepping up to stare into his one open eye. I rammed the other end of the cable into his Keystone, forcing the link between him and it, then sent a connection request, one that he accepted instantly.

He was broken, and he knew the only way he died fast now was by doing what I wanted. It was that, or die fucking *slowly*, a digit or a tooth at a time.

"Sending the request to pair...Got it, got root...Fuck's sake, you people..." I saw Bowdoin shaking his head in my HUD as I waited. "Okay, he's transferring all his backups to the deck..."

"My credits," I snapped at him. "Give me my fucking credits back, and the routing details for my suit!"

"I've already got them," Bowdoin said. "Give me a minute, maybe two, and we'll have everything from him on the deck...Shit, there's some serious corpo-sec shit on here...He's auth'd us, but..."

"Can you divert my suit?" I snapped at him.

"It's not that fucking simple. It's in a specialized transporter...I'm having to work around the security lockouts. Right, right, where the hell do you want me to send this when I get there?"

"Where?"

"Through the lockouts!" he snapped. "Fuck's sake, I'm trying to divert a private transport for mil-spec gear, stuff that shouldn't be anywhere outside of the army or the highest corpo armories, and it's being monitored by M-Corp! You think I'm a fucking god?"

"Shit..." I growled, trying to think. I should have thought about this. I'd known I couldn't have it delivered to my fucking apartment like a pizza, I just...with everything that was going on, I'd not had time to think about this shit again. I was going to get Lucky to stash it somewhere, then he'd proved fucking unreliable...And it wasn't like I could ask Gunther to hold it for me. He'd either sell it, or be raided for it and murdered!

"I..." I racked my brain, trying to think of where the hell I could send it, when Bowdoin spoke up.

"Look, I've done some work with a smuggler now and then. He's an orc, and an absolute dick, but..."

"Oshbob?" I asked, and he hesitated, nodding.

"Yeah, you know him?"

"Fuck's sake, he's like a rash! Everywhere I go, some fucker works for, or with him!"

"He's a fucking crime lord, what the hell do you expect!" Bowdoin snorted. "Look, can he use it?"

"No, nobody but me can pilot it," I assured him.

"Fine, I'll divert it to him, get him to stash it in a warehouse. Then you can arrange to collect it, all right? He's got a load of warehouses—smuggler, after all—so he'll probably never even check it, just overcharge you for accepting the package and holding it, all right?"

"Yeah, fuck it, I've got a meeting with him tomo—today, I guess, anyway."

"Well, that's good. Look, this is gonna take some time, and…I'm just gonna say it. I don't need this shit. I don't want to see what you're gonna fucking do to that guy."

"He deserves it," I growled, and Bowdoin nodded.

"Maybe, yeah. He's a fucking dickhead, and you said he killed your team. Richie?"

"Yeah," I lied. "It's complicated, but yeah."

"Then fine. I'm fine with him dying, and fucking painfully, but I don't need to fucking see it, all right? I'm going to have nightmares as it is! You're…yeah, I'm opting out."

"Can you patch me through to someone, before you go?" I asked, and he nodded.

"I'll keep a line open for now. Just, you know, send a message if you need me. But right now, I don't need to be here, not for this, and I think I earned my creds, right?"

"And more," I agreed, a little deflated as I queued up first the remaining twelve thousand credits I owed the hacker, and then another ten thousand on top, sending it over.

"Thanks, Kabutt," Bowdoin said after a few seconds, clearly struggling with something, before he leaned forward, and stared at the pickup. "Look, I know you're a good guy and all…"

We both snorted at that, before he went on.

"All right, a guy, one who pays what he agrees and gives bonuses, even if not a good guy, but seriously? Listen here, you moron. Richie treated me fair. Now, you've done me a good turn, so I'm about to do you one. When you deal with hackers, you need to fucking *read what you're giving them access to*. With the permissions you granted me? I could have fucking made you my toy."

"You'd have regretted it…" I said after a second's thought, and he laughed.

"Root access, Kabutt. Root fucking access. I could have shut all your mods down, including your eyes and your organelles, or set them to reverse. I could have transferred all your money to me…Incidentally, what are we doing with dickhead's creds?"

"How much is there?"

"Over two hundred grand…He's been a busy boy, considering he had nearly double that a week ago."

"Transfer it to mine. He can help pay off Reign's debt."

"Done. Okay, I've set you to be able to send out, nobody else can, and I've locked all of his shit down. Anything else?"

"No, I can sort most of it—wait! Can you separate out his conversations with his handler at M-Corp, and—"

"Already done. I set the datadeck to back up everything in his Keystone. Give it, five, maybe ten minutes and you'll have it all to look over whenever you want. Looks like he was blackmailing someone and—"

"Thanks, Bowdoin…seriously." I watched as the messages popped up, each confirming that he'd relinquished the access levels I'd allowed him. A trickle of cold sweat rolled down my back at his admission of the power I'd unthinkingly given him in my distracted and desperate state.

Once I was sure he was gone, I sent the major a call request and moved back, sitting down across from the weeping Tyrannus and regarding him, waiting.

There was so much I wanted to do, to say, but most of it came down to releasing my boiling hatred on him, screaming and beating him to death.

His entire defense was basically claiming that he was incompetent, and a backstabbing shit, but he didn't mean for the team to die.

That was it.

"This—this won't be over quickly," I assured him, my anger rising again, and he surprised me with a sob that became a laugh.

"You think?" he asked me. "Whoever you're talking to, they've diverted the suit? Once that's gone, when it doesn't turn up here…? When they realize that they can't contact me anymore?"

"What the fuck are you talking about?" I growled.

"You think your suit's the only one?" he cried. "Fuck, no wonder your team died. You're as dumb as I thought you were! They've been collecting them!"

"Eh?"

"Why do you think I'm *here*!" he shouted. Tears streamed down his face, blood still dripping from dozens of minor wounds that the small medikits hadn't been enough to seal. "They're fucking here, Kabutt! The Ghost Squad! It's under the fucking pleasure tower! I'm a guest…but I'm also a fucking *prisoner*!"

I stared at him, as the call to the location the major gave me connected.

"Kabutt?" he asked grimly, face and voice scrambled. "You have the data from Tyrannus?"

"I do, sir," I assured him, uploading the data I'd gotten from Tyrannus, all his comm logs between him and the corp specifically, as well as all his comms over the last two years. "He admitted that M-Corp has a Ghost Squad, sir, black ops, and they're housed here."

"They're there?" he asked, sounding disbelieving. "Their squad is in that fucking building, right now?"

"Apparently so, sir, under the building."

"Evidence?"

"Just his word, but they have significant security here, sir. Not in the main building, but under it? They've separated off the area. No access to the lower sub-basements, and the only details I can find show heavy weapons emplacements. My hacker found evidence of an RI in the building, a security one—"

"That's common enough."

"Yes sir, but there's a newly awakened AI as well, apparently. He found evidence of it watching him, but as long as he stayed away from the lower areas, it didn't give a shit about him."

"Defenses?" he asked, and I paused before going on.

"I encountered military-grade turrets outside the main security office. Beyond that, nothing really. But we were moving in the opposite direction all the time, so if that AI is really defending the lower levels?"

"They'd not waste an AI unless there was something there, that's for sure," he agreed, clearly thinking hard. "This could work, this could really—" He broke off again, then came back.

"Kabutt, I need you to be clear now. Does Tyrannus have access to the net? Is there anyone who can get these details, any other sources of the data?"

"The data…no, sir," I said. "I've uploaded from him to me, and then to you…"

"And your hacker. I need locational data…he's there with you? He's close by?"

"Uh…" I started to get a bad feeling about this, and decided that he didn't need the whole truth, and certainly not about where Bowdoin was. "We've got the areas we needed to locked down, sir. Anything that gets sent from those we've interacted with is being stopped at the local node."

"And your call to me?"

"It's a single broadcast, sir. Routed through…I don't entirely understand it. My hacker is…in the security office. I told him to set me up with a single-use message to contact you. Once I'm done here? I'll return to the office, and we'll erase our presence from the system, then leave."

"Excellent," he approved. "It's a corpo site with stolen military technology that they're hiding, though, Sergeant. I'll need you to stay on site. Keep your entire team there for now. I'll send Blue Team to extract you."

"Thank you, sir," I replied, feeling less and less sure about this. *Blue Team?* They were good, sure, but if there was a corpo ghost team below us, as soon as they saw the helos incoming…not to mention the gamma cannons on the roof? Blue Team would be taken out, and…

"Sir, there's gamma cannons on the roof, but if we take them out, it might trigger the AI's protocols…"

"Don't you worry about that, son. Just listen to me. This is an order, all right?"

"Yes sir."

"Kill that shit Tyrannus," he ordered. "Make it fast. I need to know that he's dead. Do it now."

"Sir…" I hesitated, and he spoke again.

"Dammit, soldier, I need to know his evidence is gone. Do that now. Your revenge isn't a fucking priority, not here!"

"Yes sir," I agreed, hating it, but trained over years to obey. I dragged the handgun out and turned to face Tyrannus, who sneered at me.

"Huh, hiding the evidence, eh?"

"Shut the fuck up, Tyrannus," I snapped, then shook my head. "Any last words?"

"You told me to shut up."

"Good words," I approved, aiming at the point just above the bridge of his nose.

"Make sure you erase his Key as well," the major ordered. "Is it done?"

"We didn't send the sharks," Tyrannus said suddenly. "Don't get me wrong. If I could have killed you all and stolen the suits? I'd have done it, but it never occurred to me," he admitted, all fear gone as he saw his inevitable death coming. "It wasn't me or my liaison who set this shit up. I just sold them your suit and some secrets they couldn't get otherwise. Think about it, Kabutt! You interrupted them before they were ready. If I'd sent you to have the suits taken out by the AROC? I'd have sent just you, not Blue Team as well."

"Sir…" I paused. "I haven't located my suit, not yet. He could have it anywhere. We need to—"

"Kill him! Fuck's sake, Kabutt, kill him NOW! That's an order, soldier!" the major roared.

I stared at the little shit before me. I hated him—fuck, I hated him—but I shifted my aim to the right slightly and pulled the trigger.

"He's dead." I stared into the stunned eyes of Tyrannus, the bullet having missed him by an inch, if that.

"And the Keystone?" the major asked.

"I put the bullet through it, sir."

"Again. Make fucking sure!"

I fired again, shooting his bed twice more, then holstered the gun.

"It's destroyed, sir."

"And your copy?" he asked.

"I just relayed it to you, sir. I'll delete my logs now…Done."

"Good. Good man, Kabutt. I'm going to send you a program, a little something to run. It's just a cleaner. We need to make sure those details don't make it out, you understand?"

"Yes, sir, but the link here is narrow, and goes through the security system. Anything you send—"

"Fuck!" he snarled. "Fine, fine! The security office…go there. I'll make sure Blue Team knows exactly where you are. Out."

With that, he was gone, and I was left with a shitty feeling in the pit of my stomach as I exchanged a long look with Tyrannus. Too many details that I'd ignored until now suddenly linked up.

The sharks that had hit us, the erasure of the files, the determination that I erase any hint of the AROC…supposedly all of this was to stop military tech from being misused. And yet, he'd not asked about my suit. As far as he knew, it was fucking lost, out there somewhere—some random fucker was shipping it back to one of the other cities.

"Reign?" I called, activating the link to her, and getting her face popping up. A smile started but vanished as she saw the look on my face.

"What's up, sir?"

"We might be about to get royally fucked," I warned her. "Set the security office to kill anyone who's not you three and move out. Get to the—"

That was as far as I got, before the window behind me detonated. The reinforced glass blew inward in a great wave that pockmarked my armor and rendered Tyrannus down to soup stock.

CHAPTER FIFTY-SEVEN

I dove for the lance instinctively, only starting to look toward the window as I hit the ground, sliding and…

A massive, and all-too-familiar foot crunched down on one end of it, reducing it to scrap.

I stared upward as a rifle, sized to fit the rest of the blitzkrieg loadout for the APS before me, moved over to a stop directly before my eyes.

"Don't fucking move," a voice rang out of the external speakers. "Remove the node lockouts on this floor, and remain absolutely still."

My brain raced, wondering first how the fuck Blue had made it so fast, then realized this was a member of the Ghost Squad. "I'd need my datadeck…" I whispered after a few seconds of silence, me staring into the barrel of a gun exactly like I'd carried for fucking years.

"Move slowly," came the response. "Try anything? A single round is all I'll need."

I moved, slowly, deliberately, knowing damn well that any hit from that rifle was me dead. If it hit my hand? It'd not be a hole in my hand; hydrostatic shock would propagate through the arm, and I'd be a pale-pink fucking mist.

Either way, though…I was massively outclassed by the suit behind me, and the way that he moved, the gun alone tracking me, showed that he knew it too.

I watched him in the mirror as I moved around and over to Tyrannus's body, disconnecting the wire from the remains of his neck, and rolling it up slowly.

"The lockouts—take them down NOW!" he ordered.

I nodded, lifting the deck in one hand to show I was doing as he asked, slowly turning back to him, as I dumped all but two of my flash-bangs' triggers.

I was counting down silently as I stepped toward him, holding the deck up as if to show I had it, and ripped a sticky grenade free.

"What the fuck do you think that's going to do?" he asked, the speakers carrying the obvious derision he felt.

I triggered the three-second countdown, and flung it at him.

He caught it with his left hand. Four of my flash-bangs went off all at once as I closed my eyes and dove to the left. My senses overloaded, but I was ready for it.

The sticky went off in his hand, gluing the fucker closed and shooting out to the left and right, covering the ground as I rolled and hissed in pain. The goddamn flash-bangs shredded half the riot armoring I was wearing, setting fire to more, but my second sticky was flying already, even if I couldn't see properly yet.

My eyes were enhanced, replaced with cybernetic ones, but like the visual systems in the APS suit, it took a few seconds to adjust.

He twisted and saw me, locking the rifle into place and apparently deciding I was more trouble than I was worth as he fired. Three shots, one after the other, hit dead center…in the *mirror.*

The sticky grenade went off, in midair, and while his servos were more than powerful enough to strip the shit off him, he had to see it first.

When it went off, the upper half of his armor was covered, literally fucking *covered* in glue, and he roared in frustration. Titanium alloys rubbed against each other as he tried to scrape it free. The rifle switched to full auto as he fired a full barrage, left to right; the backup ammo storage bin over his shoulder kept the gun going, and my eardrums were in danger of perforating.

I sprinted a handful of steps, then leapt, throwing myself through the fucking door and out onto the main floor.

Although the screams hadn't gotten through the blockers to disturb the revelers, the fucking heavy rifle's slugs certainly had, and the pleasant pool area was now filled with screaming people.

I ran a handful of steps, then stepped off the edge of the walkway into the water, my armor pulling me down.

I was struggling out of it already. The emergency release for the riot armor was a commonly needed thing—for some reason, people disliked seeing someone in this gear, and if they could kick the fuck outta you? Once that battery was drained, they were going to try. Best to be able to get out and run—and I triggered it. The straps and powered sections unfurled, opening up to free me.

I swam sideways, my lungs reminding me I couldn't stay down here forever, especially not when it was as shallow as it was, but…

I pulled the hood over my head as the water around me shivered. The stomping feet of the APS came closer, and I laid on my back, staring up.

Waiting.

The vibrations got stronger, the impacts hitting…and then the flare as the rifle opened fire, making me wince as I wondered what the fucker was firing on.

I waited until I couldn't hold my breath any longer, then I triggered the stealth suit, well aware that with the battery as drained as it was, that I'd get little fucking coverage.

I breached the surface. The slick material of the suit covered me head to toe, and I grinned at the APS facing the other way, scanning the room.

I dragged myself up, moving as slow as I could to minimize both sound and the effect of the water sluicing off me. I moved behind a tree, slipping around the edge of the pool, moving around the fucker as it stood half in and half out of the room I'd been in, swearing loudly as he tried to get around the lockout for the local area.

Without a connection to his commanders, he was left making decisions "in the field." And the scattered shredded bodies, both corpo and hired staff, suggested that wasn't his fucking strong suit.

It helped that he'd only uncovered two of his cameras, one on the front and one on the back. The scratches marring the surface of his suit made it clear how hard he'd had to drag his claws over the front to get that shit off.

Fucking amateur.

Sticky grenades were a problem just over a year ago. Word had gotten out to the scavs that it was one of the few things that worked against us, and they'd gone overboard.

We'd found, however, that the suits were great for thermal insulation, and the sticky shit burnt really well. Our solution? Set fire to each other. An incendiary grenade, or anything, really. Just make sure the gunk caught, and a minute later you were clean again.

Add in the psychological damage that seeing an APS suit, utterly unconcerned about the fact it was on fire, mowing down all your friends?

It was fine by us.

We solved the issue easily.

That this dickhead hadn't come across that problem, and its creative solution, was clear.

That made me think.

His suit was repainted, all black and grey, clearly meant to blend in, in the dark. His weapons? He had a blitzkrieg build, the plasma sword sheathed still, and the shield replaced with a heavier version…He did, however, the fucking idiot, have cluster bombs attached.

And they were the older, unbaffled design.

That dated his suit to a second generation for me, and I grinned.

The cluster bomb dispensers were replaced from the third gen onward. Mine, a fourth gen, was massively different internally, and as soon as I dated the model he was wearing, I was fucking moving.

He wasn't an APS operator.

The second gens were replaced better than thirty years ago, and he'd sounded like—and his actions proved—he was a dumb kid.

That meant he was a corpo fuckhead black ops soldier wannabe playing in one of our suits.

His front-facing camera gave good vision, as did his back, but he kept panning left and right, checking to make sure nothing was sneaking up on him.

I was in a current-gen stealth suit. Yeah, I had just over two percent of the charge left, but that wasn't the point. His systems were out of date and covered in fucking glue.

I sidled up to him—almost being crushed by his rifle when he pivoted suddenly—and waited until he started to pan in the other direction.

I stuck my last two flash-bangs to the glue right next to his rear camera easily, and I backed up, waiting to see whether he'd see them…

Nope! Great, phase two.

Frag grenades.

Three of them, all primed, pins pulled, and pressed into the armpit, nice and deep into the glue.

He clearly felt something, as he swung around. I tried to back up, but wasn't fast enough. The rifle smashed into my right forearm, snapping the bone and sending me flying. I hit the wall and slumped down, stunned, as he turned to see what the hell he'd just hit.

That's when the flash-bangs went off.

Both of them went off with an insane level of brightness. I was facing away, eyes closed, and it still fucking hurt them. As he was? With only two cameras working, he screamed, waving his arms.

The flare ignited the sticky shit, which roared across his frame.

The natural reaction, seeing flames licking across the cameras as they were uncovered, feeling the detonation, and seeing the light from behind?

He spun, gun coming around as he opened fire on the empty room behind him, convinced he was under fire.

Then the three frags went off.

Pressed in close into the armpit, they were in a point of weakness already. The multitude of frags were driven by the explosion through the limited underarm armor, and they fucking shredded the body inside like a smoothie machine set to fucking puree.

Well, I imagined that was what happened anyway.

What I saw was the armored figure stagger, then drop to its knees, before falling facedown.

I stood shakily. The sound of gunfire from outside finally made its way to me, and I shook my head, my senses overloaded from all the explosions and shit going on so close to me. I snarled in fury as I realized that I'd missed that my fight was only a tiny part of what was going on.

I also had a fuckload of notifications that the others were trying to call me, but they'd been suppressed by the RI through my danger settings and their lack of proximity.

"What happened?" I barked into the commlink, dragging the rubberized covers off the medikit and stabbing the large medikit full of nanites into my right arm.

"Fuck's sake, now? *NOW* you answer?" Reign screamed at me. "We're under fire! There's APS everywhere and we're getting our asses handed to us! Fucking HELP US!"

I ran around the side of the fallen suit, skidding to a halt as the gunfire echoed up—the crackle of lasers and grazers crossing, the boom of a turret going live—and I reached down.

The rifle the APS had been carrying was too big for a normal human to carry, but the plasma sword? I'd had some interior reinforcing done when my collarbone was smashed and my left arm upgraded; my right was healing at an insane rate, the bones snapped back into place. I felt the familiar weight as I hefted the weapon.

We trained with these—both in and out of the suits—mainly because it was the one weapon that you could still use, the hilt being the only physical component.

I triggered it. The whoosh of ionization and the crackle of contained sun burst to life in my hands as I turned and looked toward the broken window.

The plasma sword felt almost light in my hands as the years of training with them came back to me: the hours upon hours facing Fergie, Scott, Sync, and Richie in the dojo, the endless hours of forms we drilled in.

I remembered the clack of training blades as we fought mock battles, and the scarcely controlled fear when we faced the few captured enemy versions of the APS.

We trained to face them no matter what, to fight on foot, in APS and from vehicles.

The APS, both our versions—which were obviously the best in the world—and the inferior imitations of the other cities, were the kings and queens of the battlefield, beaten only by the great assault mechs that were kept hidden in readiness for the next war.

As such, we were both the lords of war, and the only realistic counters to other APS. We were trained to fight in them, and to face them, to never permit our suits to be taken. And if, for whatever reason, our suit failed? We were trained to take up our swords and finish the fight.

I unclipped the monofilament drag line from the back of the APS, used in case we needed to drag each other out of a ditch or whatever, and I wrapped the end around my left wrist, then stepped up to the broken window, staring down and out across the city.

It was time to go and fuck some shit up.

With that thought in mind, I leapt from the window and fell into the night.

CHAPTER FIFTY-EIGHT

I'd done jumps before, in training. We were taught to improvise, to always succeed, and basically to slaughter the fuck out of any problem we had. But where the night had been silent before? Now it was anything but.

I fell into a fucking war zone!

A second armored Cryson security vehicle, similar to the one I'd told the girls to take, had crashed into a barrier and had rolled onto its side. Currently, it was being stitched with heavy machine gun fire while its onboard cannons returned fire. But, honestly, it was a fuckin' sideshow compared to the real fight.

The road in and out of the tower had security barriers raised here and there, bollards more than anything else, and clearly designed to stop charging vehicles.

One of those had been hit by a truck that had apparently been transporting a full goddamn team of APS operators. The massive machines shredded the back of the truck to get out when the transport was trashed, and now four of them were staggered around the outermost edge of the compound in cover, firing great blasts at the defenders.

Six APS units, all in blacks and greys, faced off against the four blacks assaulting the tower. Despite the number difference, the sides seemed roughly equal, thanks to the firepower and skill levels.

The six were standing about, half in and out of cover, clearly used to being the biggest bastards on the battlefield and making use of that. The four they faced?

They advanced through cover, using the various barriers and low walls to absorb their enemies' incoming fire.

I scanned both sides quickly, looking at their loadouts, and triggered my comm to Reign and the others.

"Where the hell are you?"

"Parking garage. Pinned down by security, fucking heavily armed security! The APS all left and—"

"Get out!" I ordered. "Drop whatever the fuck you're doing and get the fuck out!"

"But—"

"NOW!" I sent her a link to my visuals, letting her see not only the two sides facing off against each other, but that the incoming side was loaded for fucking bear, and I was down to one percent of my stealth suit's battery. I set it to a strobe. Sections of the suit vanished intermittently to break up my outline. It wouldn't save much power, but it would a little, and anything that made it harder to get hit was worth it.

The defenders were using heavy machine guns, mainly. One had a pair of plasma casters, like a bombardment version of the standard plasma cannon, capable of firing a sustained barrage at a target until it was melted into slag, and his casters were warming up, ready to fire.

The attacking side, though…well, they were pros. Moving from cover to cover, they returned fire with the bare minimum of wasted shots, and from above, I could see the pincer as it was laid out.

I'd be sending the squad leader my fucking approval, if not for three minor details.

First, I was out of the loop, and didn't have access to the squad.

Secondly, I was approaching fast from above, and although I might like to stop and watch, it wasn't going to happen. The emergency unspooling of the drag line was slow enough that I'd land more or less intact, but it wasn't going to be fun, and it was going to be in the middle of the deployed enemy.

Third, and slightly more concerning…this wasn't Blue Team. In fact, they were showing absolutely none of the required identification. And the weapons?

I damn well knew that at least one of them wasn't permitted inside the city boundaries. I also saw what looked to be a transport helo moving into place in the distance, either ready to deploy another team, or ready to extract this one at high speed once they'd fired that missile on a timed fuse.

The incoming team deployed their shoulder-mounted rail cannons to suppress the locals; then the one loaded with the special weapon stood up and fucking sighted in on the building.

The missile he fired was a one-off. Nobody carried a reload for that kind of a weapon, not in a firefight. It was literally a level below a minimum-yield tactical nuke, designed to take out hardened bunkers in war zones.

That it was used by an unmarked APS team against another unmarked APS team, in the middle of the fucking city?

It was doing all sorts of terrible things to my asshole right now, not least that I was still rappelling down the outside of the target building.

As soon as the shot was away, the rest of the team were up and backing away, rail guns and grazers firing constantly to keep the defenders down.

I saw two of the suits taken out, high-power hits that pierced straight through the armor, and I screamed as the missile flashed past overhead, hitting the glass and punching through.

I released the cable, dropping two stories to the floor, landing hard and rolling to absorb the impact. The APS on either side of me turned to track the motion.

A massive foot came down next to my head, and I rolled behind another. The live plasma sword carved a trail of sparks and spit melted stone from the ground, as I came to my feet.

"Kabutt, we're pinned down—"

"REIGN!" I roared, cutting her off. "MISSILE!" I tagged the image and sent it, the RI responding to my unspoken wishes. I swung the sword across the back of the leg before me, spinning to the left and dragging the blade behind me.

"Fucking move!" she screamed at someone, before swearing again. "Kabutt, are you fucking insane?!"

"I'm a little busy right now!" I snapped back. The massive APS before me twisted, trying to rotate to the right and swinging an enormous arm out, before the right leg froze up.

I dragged the sword free. The spitting, flaring molten metal ran like butter as the torn section buckled. More of the leg collapsed and sent the inexperienced operator to the floor.

He tried to catch himself with his hands out before him, an instinctual thing, and one that was beaten out of us in training, making it even clearer that these were corpo goons.

In a suit that weighs multiple tons, trying to catch yourself with your hands would work fine, *if* your hands were free. If instead they're filled with weapons?

No.

His gun crumpled under the impact, sending him rolling in the other direction onto his back. A turtled APS was a fucked APS.

A supersonic rail gun round smashed through the armor before me, one of the attackers clearly seeing an opportunity for an easy kill. And if I'd not dragged my sword free and been moving already?

He'd have gotten two.

The defender with the plasma casters stood up and extended both barrels forward. His armored feet locked into place, the side flaps clanging down and firing as they drove stabilizing pins into the ground. The legs now secured, his shield crackled as it was hit repeatedly.

I ran, headed very much in the opposite direction from him, as the casters clanked up from their "rest" position on the back, pointing straight up, into "ready" position, extending over each shoulder and forward at a forty-five-degree angle.

The back of his armor opened in a dozen places as the emergency vents locked into place, ready to dissipate the horrific heat, and a dozen corpo-sec goons ran out of the building to my left, racing toward me and to presumably get into place to defend against the attack.

I didn't slow.

I fucking knew what was coming.

Running, blade crackling and lighting the way, I drew the eye, no doubt. But the plasma casters, behind me and so close to them? That was the issue.

The operator fired.

A full bombard, a *full fucking* bombard.

Ten shots from either caster were launched, literally emptying the plasma tanks as twenty miniature suns flashed forward. The retreating attackers pulling back hammered the shields, but they didn't take them down in time.

The rear plasma dissipation vents unleashed hell, literally roasting the corpo-sec idiots where they stood. It was like someone had opened the door to the deepest pit of hell, and it was confined into a single jet of discharge.

The majority were killed instantly, even as the plasma shots were still streaking toward their target. The rail gun rounds finally punched through the shields, killing the operator of the heavy APS. Holes were liberally punching through from front to back and kept going for the heavy sniper I knew was out there, hidden somewhere.

The smaller, dual shoulder-mounted projectiles hit a quarter second later—pockmarking, denting, then tearing through the titanium to shred the soft flesh inside.

Even as the heavy jerked back and forth, the legs locked into place and holding his shredded corpse in place, the plasma screamed through the air, landing in a concentrated area saturation that caught two of the retreating APS.

One was hit full-on, staggering as his shields overloaded. The plasma containment sphere dissolved and released temperatures as close to the surface of the sun as it was possible to get while planet bound.

He didn't even manage to scream. The shield popped like a soap bubble, the plasma eating into his armor, as other impacts landed all around him. The horrific heat rendered the armor to wisps of contaminated gasses.

The sidewalk ran, holes eating into the road and the sodden earth around it.

Moisture from the soaked ground was flash converted into a thick fog that rolled out. Flares of fire and glowing plasma lit it and turned the fog into a nightmare scene.

The second APS was on the outer ring of the impact. The nearest plasma landed a meter to the left and detonated. The explosion lifted the armored figure and sent them flying, burning, one leg and that side of the APS a literal melting wreck.

The others were far enough outside of the blast radius that they'd survive, merely being toasted—which again pointed to the amateur level of the operators in the defending suits—but they were still staggering here and there, lost in the sudden fog.

The temperature of that fog, which was even now rolling out on all sides, was high enough to cook an unarmored man, meaning that it was as good as a damn steel wall at blocking most of the visual systems on either side of the impact zone from seeing each other.

I saw a security transport rocket out of an entrance on the far side of the grassy area. The armored car I assumed held Reign and the others raced full bore away toward a second exit, presumably the employees' one, as the area I was in was far too nice to be the commoners' entrance.

The rest of the defenders should have been racing forward to counterattack, capitalizing on the situation and taking down the other side as they retreated. Instead, half stood around, waiting for orders; others stared in horrified amazement at the dozen flash-fried assholes. And the last few?

I dove to the right as a rifle swept me, a three-round burst punching through the wall of the tower as he missed. I rolled, popping to my feet. The movements of the kata were instinctive as I rotated my wrists, the flare of pain from my still healing right ignored as the blade flashed in an arc, severing the massive rifle halfway down the barrel.

I dropped one knee, the punch that flashed overhead easily enough to behead me…had it landed.

Instead, I rose again into "Kingfisher Launches", a form I'd hated when I first learned it, believing that I'd never be reduced to fighting on the ground, without my suit.

Now, the blade rose almost vertical, the tip punching through the elbow joint as I rose behind it. I swung my right foot around behind me, pivoting on the left, sliding the sword free of the suit; the burning, melted joint gave way as the forearm and hand fell free.

The sword came in closer to my chest, held at ninety degrees, as I flowed around, then swung to my right, still spinning.

"Holy fuck…" I distantly heard on the comm channel as the world around me vanished.

In my mind, nothing existed save the three figures: the wounded, staggering APS I fought, the second APS on the far side of him, turning to face us, and the sword.

I was the blade, and I danced through the forms like I'd never done in my life.

The blade slid into the small of the back of the APS, and I dragged it sideways, carving a shallow trench out of the sensitive systems below the armor, knowing, even as I came to a stop, facing the other APS, that the one behind me? That I'd just hit?

He was dead. All that was left was for his body to accept it.

The APS before me paused, his gun rising then hesitating as I ran at him, giving him the option of firing—and probably hitting his friend behind me—or holding fire to fight a lunatic with a stolen plasma sword.

I made it three steps. The barrel of the massive rifle right before me seemed to grow larger by the second. Determination filled me that I'd carve my way through him…until the building behind me exploded.

CHAPTER FIFTY-NINE

The missile that exploded behind me was designed to take out bunkers, heavily fortified military targets, places with unreasonable levels of interior reinforcement, which was probably all that saved us.

That and the fact that the explosion was so insanely powerful that it was entirely the wrong device for the job.

The building had a central spire that was load-bearing and interior walls, but most of the rest of the building was literally glass.

That meant that when the missile detonated, the force went outward and through the glass more than anywhere else. The upper floors of the building actually lifted off, radiating outward and shattering into a bomb blast that hurled wreckage into the buildings nearby.

The lower floors were much the same, but kicked downward. I was picked up and thrown through the air by the pressure wave from the blast front. I barely had the instinctual presence of mind to power down the plasma sword before it could cut me in two before I hit a parked vehicle and flipped ass over tit, hitting the ornamental grass and rolling to come up against the inside of the wall, dazed.

I shook my head, concentrating on my hand, the burnt ornamental grass below me, the dark torn loam…and the blood. I could see it smeared across my stealth suit, and I focused on it, quickly checking myself to make sure I wasn't bleeding that heavily…

Nope.

The large medikit I'd hit myself with earlier had been working hard to keep me in tip-top health, sure. Hell, I could feel it right now, literally, as bruises, aches, and more vanished like a popped joint, suddenly settling back into place. But this much blood?

I pushed myself up from my prone position on the grass to all fours, and turned, freezing as I came practically nose to nose with an APS.

As I blinked, the condition of the APS resolved at about the same time I barely managed to not load my pants. The shattered hulk that was literally inches from my face was half crushed on one side, a beam of interior reinforcing driven in one side and out of the other.

The beam had been driven into the ground, and the combination of that anchoring the fresh corpse and the security vehicle that had been overturned—and that I muzzily remembered my legs smashing into only recently—had formed a sheltered alcove.

Blood ran from the various cracks in the shell of the APS and dripped free, a veritable stream that was only picking up speed as I winced and dragged myself out from underneath. I paused and returned, searching around as quickly as I could.

My own new plasma sword was easy to find, but the armor that had nearly crushed me was set to carry one as well, and I wasn't damn well leaving without it. They were both insanely difficult to make and expensive as fuck.

Not to mention being a clear and valid counter against an APS by an unarmored man.

I found it after a few seconds. The hilt jutted from the storage pouch on the left hip—a bloody stupid place to keep it—along with a pair of additional batteries for the shield.

Well, that fucker was gone—who knew where and how—but I'd never have been able to control the shield anyway. The batteries, though? I hunched down in the lee of the corpse and frantically worked on the stealth suit.

It was torn in places, rips and stained, not to mention that I'd gotten fucking blood all over it, *but*…

Anything that could help was well worth it.

I stripped the original battery out, ripping the connectors and bypassing the safety cutouts, dragging my knife free and using it to strip cables down to the cores and then attach them to the battery.

It was a dirty botch job. The battery temperature jumped almost as soon as the connection was formed, making it clear that it was bleeding out at least as much power as it was using.

It worked, though. The suit blurred; looking down at my hands, they vanished, flickered, reappeared, and then vanished again.

I nodded to myself; it would do. It'd have to.

I was up and moving, a plasma sword in either hand, currently unpowered but ready to trigger at a second's notice as I started to run. The previously pristine ornamental lawn that had run from the edge of the poured plascrete driveway was now burned and torn, literally still alight in some places, with bodies and sections of the building strewn across it. Not to mention the damn fog was still dissipating, the high background heat of the moisture-laden air playing hell with scanners.

"Ka…t?" A fragmenting link established, then cut out again.

"Reign?" I sent.

"Kab…!" The relief in her voice was clear, then it broke into a high-pitched yowl of sonics.

"Send again?"

"…PS!…us…"

This time when the connection dropped, it didn't come back, and I swore, getting my bearings and running.

Where they'd driven through the barrier had been to my right as I faced the tower. The tower was mainly a pile of smoldering wreckage now, but the remains were just visible through the fog as a mess of shattered stone and flaring fire.

I leapt over gouges torn in the ground, and hurdled shredded supports, passing bloody and stunned figures that stumbled here and there. I heard distant screams, panicked cries, demands for help, and more.

Already, in the distance, I could hear the emergency transports incoming, a cacophony of sirens and warnings as insurance and body-loss transports raced against ACE. They and others fought to be the first on scene, to collect their subscriber and get them out ahead of the rest, probably in expectation of a fucking bonus.

I didn't care, leaping up from one fragment of wall to another, parkouring for all I was worth. I jumped, landing and sliding across a shattered section of stone. I slid to the ground on the far side of the wall. A couple of figures gawked at the destruction, presumably on their way back or to somewhere.

They screamed and ran. My suit flickered; the blood that covered me was clear in the air, seemingly outlining a bloody spirit racing from the building.

I sprinted down the alleyway, seeing the high-speed road at the end of it, running right to left. I skidded, turning out onto it, stumbling over debris and a random bloody hand, minus the rest of the fucking body.

It was disturbingly spongy as I stepped on it, gritting my teeth. I focused on the sight ahead: two APS, both all in black, facing the security car.

It was heavily armed: twin crowd suppression launchers on the roof, short-range dispersant taser projectors, the works, for the busy corpo shitbag who didn't want to wait for people who dared to cross the road before them.

None of it was any use against an APS, though.

I ran full speed at them. The nearest one stood by the driver side of the vehicle, rifle pointed in the window as they clearly checked the group. I saw the rifle shift, straightening as the operator presumably got the okay to eliminate the "loose ends," and I snarled in my suit. Both swords flared to life.

The effect was instantaneous.

Both APS twisted, their suits and operators trained and experienced, jerking around at clear movement, only to see the blades already in motion.

I hacked through the rifle, severing it halfway, leaving a glowing molten metal half in the suit's hands as they fired. The heat and the fucked weapon set the magazine off, exploding as I threw myself down, skidding, slashing across the backs of both the suit's legs.

The second APS was on the far side of the car from me, and they opened fire before I could close on them. I popped to my feet. The bullets tore through the air by the side of my head, then cut off as one hit their companion, who toppled backward, arms waving and his rifle reduced to scrap as his shoulder-mounted rail guns swiveled and opened fire.

I went down again, rolling, frantically dodging the fire as best I could…until the suppression launchers on the car opened fire.

They were basically more powerful versions of the arse-lance, firing a thousand rubberized and electrified bullets a minute from either barrel.

They slammed into the still-standing suit, shoving it sideways as they hit, unexpected. Then the car was moving, backing up. The fire was constant, and the APS spun, sighting on the car, and opened up. Twin rail guns, much smaller caliber than the sniper rifle one of their number had, but still powerful, sent the car's shields into overload. The bright blue of the shield appeared in the air. Sections appeared darker and darker as the rounds slammed into it, even as Reign spun the wheel and floored it, running directly over the downed suit.

I gritted my teeth, forcing myself to my feet and running, leaping through the air at the still-standing figure, triggering the swords as I flew.

The APS operator twisted at the hip, rifle coming up to block my swords, even as his rail guns continued to hammer the car, the shields running closer and closer to redline.

I speared both blades down. The tips punched through the rifle and into the armor, hissing and juddering as they skittered across the front, making me curse.

Then I was flying through the air, backhanded.

My ribs shattered; the world flipped over and over as I tumbled through it, before hitting the road. I bounced and rolled. My chest felt like a literal bag of broken glass and shattered ribs, before the APS appeared over me, rail guns swiveling down...

I was dead...I fucking knew I was...until her voice rang out.

"RECORDING!" Reign shouted. "I'm recording and backing up. If I cut out? The broadcast releases!"

"Recording!" Luna shouted, stepping out as well; Gessh joined her too, calling the same.

"You're black ops!" Reign called to the suit that had hesitated over me. "You can't stop me sending this, and that fucks your op! Look around. How many people are broadcasting you right now? WE KNOW who you are, though—they don't..."

There was a long silence as the APS operator checked the local area, seeing how many figures were in windows and more.

I tried to breathe, plasma swords clattering to the ground as I released the activation triggers. My left arm searched feebly for the last medikit, as my right arm...well. It flopped uselessly, pain radiating up and down it.

The knock that came through was from the major, and as soon as it appeared before me, I knew.

"Well...looks like an impasse," he said flatly.

"Y...yeah..."

"You don't seem like you're doing too well, but here's my offer, Kabutt. You've got some bright people working for you, and this operation's achieved what it needed to, even with our cover being blown. We'll spin it, make out it was a sanctioned team, throw some captain to the lantons for not reporting it...you know how it is."

"You..."

"My team's pulling back, and your team is going to keep their mouths shut. As it is? There's not much you can do. But I know you're a paranoid little fucker, even if you are easily manipulated, so here it is. You survive this? Scurry off and hide in a hole somewhere. If you cross my path again? I'll nuke you, like I did that building."

"Bast...ard..." I forced out, as my suit tore, the robotic left arm dragging the large medikit free. Gessh was there a second later, pulling it from my grip and uncovering it, priming, and then apologizing as she stabbed it into my upper chest above the impact point.

The medikit plungers activated, driving a mass of nanites into me, the horrible feeling of an alien mass snapping bones into place and restructuring things as I screamed in pain.

"Remember, Kabutt. Run and hide. Show up on my radar again? I'll level an arcology to squash you." The major sneered, before cutting the connection.

"A...PS?" I gasped to Gessh, who shook her head.

"Retreating." She winced as cracks echoed, and my chest sagged on one side. "Shit, boss, we need to get you to a carver!"

"Fuck!" Luna gasped, appearing next to me, then calling out as Reign backed the car up. "We need to get him outta here!"

The next few hours descended into a blur of screams, blood, and worse. Somehow they manhandled me into the back of the car, and from there to a carver.

I was too out of it to make choices, and my next of kin? Well. Long gone. The world spiraled away from me. Blood sprayed as the carver frantically cut my chest open; a saw ran down my chest to split the partially rebuilt rib cage.

I remember faces, and voices…garbled. Hands gripping me. And pain.

So. Much. Pain.

CHAPTER SIXTY

It was three days before I was well enough to move on my own again.

Nanites are so good they're practically magic, able to rebuild the body from so little it's insane, and, provided the brain was kept alive and *functional*, they could literally rebuild the body from scratch to the peak of fitness.

The only issue? For each nanite, they needed a building block.

They could convert themselves to that block, and they usually did, with others nearby using that block as building materials, then converting themselves. The only issue with that, though?

Cost.

To create a single human cell, you needed a single nanite. If they didn't have building blocks to use? They converted their own kind. That meant to rebuild a human body, you needed a comparable mass of nanites. And to rebuild my shattered chest?

At least ten times the number of nanites I had to hand.

That wasn't to say that they were useless, though. They kept me alive as the girls took me to Lion, and—joy—they worked to purge my body of any toxins and poisons as he worked.

Unfortunately, due to the level of damage?

He couldn't use the normal neural blockers. Instead, he was forced to rely on chemical suppressors. Chemical suppressors, it turned out, were remarkably like poisons.

That meant that the nanites worked to make sure I felt everything, as he cut and sawed at me, as he rooted around in my chest, dragging masses of shattered bone free, cartilage, and general crap.

It took him hours, and my own systems constantly bullied me into screaming sentience as he worked. In the end, when it was finally over, and I was able to sleep? I was a shadow of who I'd been, and my friends were broken as well, mainly by the things they'd seen and done.

The carver had forced them to help, to work with him in dragging sections of pulverized...well, *me*...free. Now, I was laid on my back, staring out the one window in the small apartment we had between us all.

Luna and Gessh had taken us in. I was in no fit state to be alone, and my apartment was even smaller than theirs. Reign didn't have an apartment, so...

Well.

I stared out the window, my mind slowly seeming to cycle up from the depths, unsure how long I'd been laid there like this, as I thought.

It'd been the major all along. Or, at least, that's what I believed now. Sure, the damn asshole Tyrannus had taken advantage as well, but as near as I could figure out, what had happened, was this.

The major was involved with the black ops APS team. Him and some corpo scumbags who I didn't know about yet. He'd arranged for a team to be sent to the mech assembly site, expecting that with the jammer and so on, we'd be easy meat. Our suits would be captured, we'd be reduced to jam, and the corpos could strip and reuse our suits.

The suits were insanely controlled, because the only counter to them, realistically, beyond an assault mech, was a lunatic with a plasma sword up close and personal.

So, the suits were strictly regulated, and to make sure that the corps didn't grow too powerful, only a limited number could be owned by any corp at any one time.

They could hire contractors, who had their own suits, but they had bombs installed by the government, and if they stepped out of line and tried to carry out a coup?

Kaboom.

No more suits.

Those suits were coded to their wearers as well, so the army wasn't that concerned about the suits once they got them back for destruction, as long as they were recovered, because the suits would be insanely expensive to recode.

However, for a corporation? That was only nanites. To spend a fuckload of nanites to get a functional APS that wasn't on the government's register? Hell yes.

So.

He'd arranged for us, or Blue Team, to go to the site, and then Tyrannus had taken a bribe from some other corpo fuckhead to send the other of us.

We'd gotten there ahead of his people being ready, and the whole thing had gone to shit.

Then, presumably when I'd been a dumb fuck and come to him, he couldn't believe his luck. I'd given him an opportunity to hide almost everything and to launch a counter investigation where he would be in full control of the only evidence.

By me gathering up all the files, the visuals and shit like that? Taking them with me after sending a copy direct to him? I'd basically set my fucking team up.

I wasn't sure how he'd done it, but clearly he set up the hit on us. I was guessing that Tyrannus was blackmailing him, and then he sent me to wipe the fucker out and to get my suit back. No doubt once I told him where my suit was, his hit squad would have come for me and would have taken it.

Finding out that the asshole corpos had their own black ops team directly under me? It must have seemed like all his wishes had come true.

Wipe me and Tyrannus out, remove the evidence against him, then wipe the corpo team out, and suddenly he's got no competition.

I didn't know what his next step was going to be, but I fucking well knew mine.

I'd get my suit, I'd get my upgrades, and I'd train my team. We'd earn some cash and get the guild up to speed on fighting APS as well as the fucking specters. Then I'd be setting a trap for that rat bastard.

When he came for me? He'd find me ready, and Richie and Sync ready to fuck his team up as well as Reign, Luna, and Gessh.

I blinked. The boiling core of fury that'd been growing in me for days seethed as I tamped it down, feeling almost drunk and unsteady, it was that all-consuming.

I forced my hands to stillness, as I looked around, seeing Reign, predictably, in the corner of the room, watching me.

"What's up?" I asked her, and she smiled.

"I wasn't sure if you were awake."

"My eyes are open," I said. "It's generally a hint."

"Not the last few days," she disagreed. "Seriously, boss. You've been…I don't know. Broken. I was wondering if you'd pull through or not."

"I'm here." I slowly forced my legs to work as I got to my feet.

A second later, she was there, catching me under one arm and helping me to stand. She shrugged under my arm, making me rest on her shoulder as she held me, making sure I was okay, and that I wasn't about to collapse.

As she did, and as soon as I could make my legs stable enough, I wasn't worried I'd fall.

It was a frozen moment, the pair of us almost nose to nose, as I stared in her eyes, remembering the last few days all over again. The way she'd cared for me.

She'd been there around the clock, literally. The others had taken shifts, but Reign? She'd refused to leave for more than the time it took to catch a little sleep, to eat, or take care of her own needs.

"I…" I whispered, breaking off as I swallowed, not sure where to go with the words that rose, not sure they'd be welcome. "Thank you…for looking after me."

"You needed me," she replied in an equally soft voice. "I, well, you know, you saved *me*, so it only seemed fair."

"Did I?" I asked, unsure, gaze flicking from one deep pool to the other. Her eyes.

They were blue, green, and more; the innermost point, where the black took over, had a ring of green, and they faded to a vibrant blue at the outmost part. I couldn't seem to stop staring into them.

"Careful," she whispered, and I could taste cinnamon on her breath. "Keep looking at me like that…I'll think you're going to kiss me."

I opened my mouth. I had no idea what I was going to say, or do. Hell, I *wanted* to kiss her. I wanted to kiss her insanely badly, and sure, I'd always thought she was pretty. But I'd never realized how deep this need was, until right now.

My right arm was around her shoulders; my left slid down to wrap around her waist, and she mirrored me, no longer supporting so much as just holding onto each other.

She pulled gently on me, and our bodies molded against each other. My need pressed against her, and by the quirked eyebrow, I knew she felt it.

Our heads angled slightly, sliding more and more as we moved in closer, and…

"Hey! You want breakfast?" Luna called, almost kicking the door off its hinges as she barged in, a tray in one hand, a pair of mugs held in the other. "I hope the boss's awake, because…"

She broke off, eyes going wide, and a sudden grin split her face in two as she took the scene in.

We almost leapt apart, or we tried to. I staggered backward, the bed right behind me, and I collapsed with a surprised yell, even as Reign jumped back, then reached out, trying to catch me.

The result was me hitting the bed and sprawling, her reaching for me, overbalancing and landing atop me, the pair of us sprawled on the bed, and Luna bursting out laughing.

"Oh, Gessh is gonna go mad! I win the sweepstake!" she crowed, dumping the tray of food on the chair and the two mugs with it, as we tried to protest our innocence. "Oh, you can lie all you like to yourselves and each other! But I got it all!" She tapped the side of her head, and I blinked, seeing a new prosthetic eye gleaming at us.

"Now look…" Reign said quickly, still half atop me.

"Nope!" Luna chortled. "An hour, then we need to be gone. Gessh is getting our ride sorted out. Lo-jackers are off and the trackers burned. Then we're off to meet with the Orc. You kids have till then, so have fun!"

With that, she was gone. The door banged shut, and the lock engaged with an audible clunk.

"I—" I started, only to be cut off as Reign shook her head.

"No, I'm sorry…" She apologized quickly. "I shouldn't have…Ah, fuck."

"No. It's *my* fault. You didn't—"

The pair of us broke off again as we spoke at once, then stopped, staring into each other's eyes, Reign supporting herself over me on all fours, me in just my shorts, laid on my back on the bed.

There was another long break as we tried to figure out what the hell we wanted, never mind what we should, or could, say.

"Fuck it!" Reign snapped, before leaning in and kissing me on the lips, hard.

It was a surprise, and when I froze, she mis-read it, pulling back. Her eyes filled with embarrassment and dismay, if not outright hurt, and I grabbed her arm as she tried to pull back.

She pulled again, and I twisted, right foot flat against the shitty mattress, arm around her shoulders, and I rolled to my left. She half fell, half flipped around, suddenly on her back between me and the wall, and I leaned down, kissing her.

This time, Reign hesitated; then her arms were around my back and pulling me down atop her.

The world vanished for us as we kissed, arms holding each other. Then I was moving down, planting kisses down her neck and my hands pushing her top up.

She slid her fingers under the material and wriggled out of it, pulling it up and over her head, exposing her chest. I trailed kisses down from her neck, tasting the salt of her sweat as I slid down one small breast, flicking the hardening bud of her nipple with the tip of my tongue, before…

"Kabutt…" she groaned, her voice full of lust.

I looked up at her. My right hand slid down the firm muscle of her stomach, fingers curling into the band at the top of her pants, slowly tugging them down, as my left, cybernetic hand, caressed her right breast.

"We can't…" she whispered, frustration rising in her voice, along with her need. "Ah, fuck!"

"We…oh." I winced. The reality of our situation came back to me—her implant, the effect that the release of the dopamine and serotonins would have on her if I did "my job" right.

She'd be incapacitated for days. Well, *weeks*, actually.

I moved up her body, my raging need still filling me. The knowledge that we couldn't, and why, *really* did not help.

"I'm sorry," she whispered, turning her face aside, and I reached up, laying a finger on her chin and turning her back.

"It's okay," I assured her.

"No." She snorted. "No, it *really* fucking isn't!"

"No," I agreed, grinning and shaking my head ruefully. "It's not...but it is. We can figure this out."

"It's pretty simple." She sighed, turning to look at me fully. "Basically, I can't, *you know*, fuck. Not properly anyway. And even now, as happy as I was? I feel sick."

"Even though we didn't...?" I frowned.

"Even though we didn't, I was still happy, so yeah, I feel sick. Not as bad as I could if we'd been fucking. Believe me, nothing ruins the moment like having an orgasm and then puking on your partner."

She sighed, shaking her head. "Basically, because we stopped and I didn't get that much of a 'high'? I'll be feeling shitty for the next day or two, but I can still function."

"Okay, well..." I broke off, then grinned. "All we have to do is pay off that debt, right? Or could another carver...?"

"Nobody else can remove them—complicated shit and booby-trapped to make sure of it," she said. "And no offense, Kabutt, but I need to pay off that debt with them taking forty percent of anything in my account, so I'd need like half a million creds. If you're willing to spend half a million creds just to get laid? Well..."

She tried to make it into a joke, but I saw the fear and the desperate hope in her eyes.

"We were going to pay it off anyway, remember? It's not just because, yeah, all right, I do want to fuck you," I admitted, before glancing down.

We both looked at the very obvious sign of my interest that was pressed against her stomach. After a second, she slid her hand down, running her fingers along me, before gripping it and pumping her hand down and up slowly.

"Well," she said seriously, her voice dropping lower, and growing more husky. "I suppose it's not *your* fault we can't, so maybe I could be nice to you..." She licked her lips, pushing me backward, and shuffling down the bed as she uncovered me.

"Reign..." I gasped, feeling the slow, steady pumping of her hand wrapped around me. "You don't have to..."

"I know," she whispered, moving up and kissing me again, before slowly picking up speed. "But I *want* to."

"But..."

"Kabutt?" she said, and I looked into her beautiful eyes.

"Yeah...?" I managed.

"Shut the fuck up."

I lay back, pushed into place as I stared at her, not really wanting to tell her to stop under any circumstances, but feeling like I'd had to try.

I did learn one thing, though.

Whoever had told her she was shit at this? They'd been fucking *lying*.

EPILOGUE

"Motherfucking, ass-fingering, goat-blowing sons of a turd sandwich!" I roared, staring at the APS before me in disbelief.

"He seems annoyed," Oshbob commented to Luna.

"He gets that way when people play with his toys," she said. "It came in like this?"

"It did," the Orc—Oshbob, boss of the orc crime syndicate, smuggler, thug, merchant, and general lord of the underworld—assured her. "I had it opened as I'm not handling something that heavy and with those warnings on the crate, when I don't know what it is. Beyond opening the transport crate, it's as it was when it arrived.

"It can't be!" I snarled, spinning and glaring at him. "The major...he...*Tyrannus!*" I screamed the name to the overhead girders, sending goblins and fuck knew what else scattering as I fought to control myself.

"What you see is what I've got, human. Now, you want it, you pay for it, or I sell it for scrap."

"Pay!" I snarled.

"The hacker...Bowdoin? He arranged for me to hold it, that's all. You want to remove it? You pay the storage fee." Oshbob grunted, folding his arms.

I glared at him, seeing the heavy muscles, the cybernetic and the shift in the background as his people moved, getting ready.

"How much?" I spat at him.

"For you?" He pretended to consider it. "Fifty thousand a week, for storage."

"You..." I hissed, hands coming up as I fought to restrain myself from going for the fucker's throat.

"We can make it seventy-five," he growled back.

I fought down to urge to fucking punch him. Then I saw the way his eyes moved to my hip.

I looked down, seeing the plasma sword's hilt in my hands. I'd not even realized I'd drawn it, and it was a hell of an effort to put it back in the loop on my belt.

"Boss..." Luna warned, and I felt Reign's hand on my shoulder, squeezing gently, even as in the darkness behind the fucking orc something moved, paused, then vanished.

I turned, tracking it, trying to find them again, glimpsing massive eyes, and maybe grey skin? All I knew was that I caught a glimpse, and then they were gone. And if they could vanish that easily?

Showing themselves had been a warning.

"So," I forced out. "You wanted me to come meet you. What was that all about?"

"I heard about Lucky," Oshbob said.

"And?" I waited for the whole "he was like a son to me…" bullshit I was sure was coming.

"Never liked him much," he said, making me blink in surprise. "But he had one thing going for him."

"What's that?"

"He was…lucky." Oshbob's lip curled in amusement as I tried to decide whether the massive fucking orc had made a pun.

"He wasn't that lucky."

"Oh, he was. I never said if it was good or bad luck…"

"So…he was still alive at that point, right?" I asked, trying to figure the big bastard's angle.

"He brought me mods that weren't as shitty as the normal ones I'm offered, so I wanted to see where they came from, and make you an offer."

"And that is?"

"Work for me. Find me those mods, and more. Luna tells me you're going into bounty hunting? Great. Strip those you kill, bring me the mods, and I'll pay a fair price, or…"

"Or?" I asked, ready to tell him to go fuck himself, angry at the world.

"Or, I'll reach out to some contacts I've got, and I'll arrange replacement parts for this," he suggested, crossing his arms and watching my face as I struggled with the deal.

"You—" I swallowed hard against the surge of hope. "You think you can find parts for *this?*"

The APS, *my* APS—the suit I'd goddamn worn for ten years, a suit I'd rebuilt a hundred times a hundred different ways, making modifications to, adding in everything from extra padding to a better storage for the memory core for movies and shit—sat before me, suspended in its transport harness.

The suit, when ready to go, was just over three meters tall. The transport container was four, by the time you included the support structure, the cushioning, and the general security sealed around it.

As it was, the suit sat comfortably in the harness, the support posts holding it under the chest and along each limb. Or they would…*if the rest of the goddamn suit was there.*

It'd been repaired, and had apparently been in the process of rebuilding when Tyrannus had diverted it and got it out. So, currently, the main frame was intact, the arms and legs were there…but they were skeletal, literally the internals and the connections.

But the main parts?

The weapons? The sensor pods, the short-range jump-jets, the exterior armoring, and the interior shielding? All of it was missing.

I had a skeleton of my fucking suit—it was even missing the goddamn power cell—a fusion storage cell, for fuck's sake! Where the hell I'd…

"You can get them?" I asked him slowly, barely daring to let myself hope. "You can get the parts?"

"Do arseholes stink?"

"How much?" The costs would be in the millions, if this was legit.

"Not sure…Maybe a few hundred thousand credits per unit…" He shrugged. "I'd have to have them stolen. Nobody's going to sell parts for these on the open markets, probably not even the smugglers' markets, not after that fight."

It was true as well. The knowledge that there were APS black ops roaming in the city, and that a corpo had managed to get a full squad?

M-Corp had denied all liability, needless to say, pointing to their publicly owned suits and their contractors and that there was just no need for the hidden group.

Some lower-leveled dickhead had been marched out; he'd confessed to trying to impress his superiors, and running the whole thing without their knowledge. Fines had been offered—and no doubt bribes—and a criminal trial was in progress.

He'd be found guilty and probably told he was a very naughty boy and serve a month in a luxury corpo prison, if he wasn't just put under house arrest for the damn weekend.

No doubt he'd serve his time in a more junior role in the corpo, being visibly "punished"…then he'd be promoted a few ranks higher as soon as everyone forgot his name.

Everything would go back to normal, and nobody gave a shit about the poor bastards who died.

"It'd need its weapons as well," I pointed out.

He nodded.

"And three plasma swords."

"Three?"

"They're the only effective counter to an APS, and my team will be damn well trained to use them," I told him. "Once we start using my suit, word will get out. There's no way it can't. The black ops team will be sent after me, and we'll take them down."

"Then what?" Luna asked.

I looked down at the stripped suit, for the first time seeing it without rage at the condition it was in. I paused, my mind whirring.

"Then, we get more parts, and we repair the suits."

"What's the point?" Oshbob asked. "Nobody can use them."

"Let me worry about that." I smiled, turning back to Oshbob. "So, you want me to bring you harvested mods…and you'll repair this? Okay. You take half the value of the mods we bring you off the debt for this, and you pay us the rest."

"I'll pay you what the mods are worth to me, that's it," he warned. "You take the offer or you leave it, and I'll be damn well charging your ass for the storage."

"No," I countered, smiling. "No, you won't. Tell me, Oshbob…what if I could bring you pure nanites? Containers full of them."

"Pure?" The orc blinked, clearly surprised. "How?"

"You don't need to know. I'm APS. We have our ways," I assured him. "You buy the parts, and I'll bring you the nanites as well. Those you get a sample of, to make sure they're good. Test them however you want, but after that? You pay for them, twenty percent under market value."

"I'll pay twenty percent *of* market value," the orc snapped, and I snorted.

"The most valuable resource in the world, one that's tightly controlled by those corpo fuckheads and the government, and I'm offering you a separate, private pipeline…"

"Thirty-five percent," he muttered grudgingly.

"Let's cut the crap. I don't fucking haggle well," I said. "I'll say thirty-five under market, you'll go forty of the market; I go forty under it; we meet in the middle at fifty percent. Let's save ourselves the fucking effort, all right? Fifty percent, and I sell them to you direct."

"You sell them to me or mine only. I tell you to deliver it to a chop shop? You do it."

"I deliver to a chop shop, I get discounts on the mods they have."

"Ten percent," he grunted.

"Fifty."

"Don't push it, Kabutt. I don't like you already."

"Boo-fucking hoo. I'll survive."

"No, you won't," Oshbob snapped, unfolding his arms. "Fine. *Twenty* percent discount at any of *my* chop shops, you deliver the nanites where I say, and I pay fifty percent of market on them. Mods will be individually valued, and you can take the offer or you can fuck off."

"This warehouse…you got many like it?" I asked, and he shrugged.

"A few."

"Got any with rooms?"

"They've all got rooms. What fucking use is a warehouse without space to store shit?"

"I mean living areas," I snapped. "Running water, toilets, beds, fucking walls and windows, doors that lock, all that shit."

"Maybe." He grunted. "I've got one, but I don't need you fuckers sleeping in the corners and shitting on my stuff."

"How big is it?"

"Smaller than this."

I looked around at the massive warehouse, the crisscrossing girders that held the weight of the building overhead and the thick walls that kept everything from specters to thieving gobbos out, and I nodded.

This place was far bigger than we needed, but the place we were all staying currently? It was two rooms. That was it. The shower was built into the bigger of the two, meaning that we'd need to all be traipsing back and forth, and there wasn't going to be much in the way of privacy either.

"Is it secure?"

"More or less."

"How much?"

"For the four of you?"

"Aye, and power, water, and all that shit…no whacking that on top," Luna interjected, and the big orc grinned at her.

"To you, girl? A thousand credits a month."

"And to me?" I muttered.

"To you, you human cockroach? Ten thousand."

She laughed. "We'll take it at a thousand."

I hesitated, then nodded, reaching out a fist and wincing when his massive one slammed into mine, almost breaking my fucking wrist.

"Done."

"You have bin." The big orc chuckled. "A month upfront, and a deposit, then you get to lug that shit there."

"We...fuck." I groaned. "How much to..."

"A thousand." He grinned. "Upfront. It'd need to be smuggled there."

"How soon can you get it there?"

"Oh...not long," he admitted. "You want it?"

"It's got rooms?"

"Here."

The file that Oshbob sent to me was devoid of locational tags, but beyond that, it was fairly well laid out. The structure was split over two levels: the lower floor and half of the upper as storage; the second half of the upper floor split into eight rooms, four of which had bathrooms. The others were set out as a kitchen, a main gathering room, and two empty areas, presumably for food or other storage.

"Yeah." I sighed, looking at the others first for confirmation, and getting enthusiastic nods. "We'll take it. Two thousand, yeah?"

"For the rent and deposit. Another thousand if you want this transported there. My people'll remove our gear. What's left, you dispose of. And you keep it clean—no trashing it. It's an investment o' mine," he warned us with a growl.

I glared at him, before nodding and transferring the credits. The four of us were led out of the warehouse as some of his people—goblins...he was letting fucking *goblins* handle *my* suit—sealed the transport container up.

"You going there now?" he asked us, and I glanced at the others, gauging their reactions.

"Should we?"

"We'll need to buy cleaning supplies and get our shit from our apartments," Luna said, and I nodded.

"I'll need to grab my stuff too," I said, having not thought about the apartment before now, and accepting the data transfer, along with the keycode, and finally finding out the location of the warehouse. "Fuck's sake!" I snapped. "A *thousand* credits, a fucking *thousand* credits you charged me?"

"It's a big crate." He grinned, before nodding toward the building directly across the street he'd just made me pay a thousand credits for his goblins to carry my shit to. "Remember, I expect to see it's looked after..."

With that, the big bastard strolled off, chuckling to himself as I stared after him disbelievingly. I didn't know whether I was impressed, or whether I was about to stab the fucker with the plasma sword that'd somehow made its way into my hand again.

"Kabutt?" Reign said softly, and I turned to her, seeing those beautiful eyes as she smiled at me, standing close to my shoulder. "Did you really just buy us all a home?"

I grinned back at her. "Rented, but yeah."

"Thank you," she whispered, her hand slipping into mine and squeezing tight.

"It's gonna be a bomb site, you know that, right?" Gessh asked, laconically, and I nodded.

"Probably." I led the way across the cracked and broken asphalt. "But you know, I've got a good feeling about this place..."

The building before us was squat and ugly. A chain-link fence encircled it, and a large garage door led into the warehouse. A small door in the side to let us in on foot, and a few little grimy windows, deliberately too small even for gobbos to get in, or at least, in and out with anything.

The walls were rusted and dented, occasional bullet damage showed here and there, and the far corner looked to have been set on fire at one point, the anti-rust paint having melted away and the entire section the red of dying metal now.

It was a mess. What looked like years of crap and general litter, abandoned rubbish and more was blown from side to side inside the perimeter fence. But inside?

Once we were in, the door closing with a solid clunk of a good lock behind us?

It wasn't that bad.

The warehouse had a collection of tables on one side, clearly from something that had been made in here at one point, and the other side held the remains of storage cradles, presumably for loading goods for shipping.

That was fine. My suit would go in one of them, stored and safe, except when we were working on it, and there'd be room for more in the future.

There was space to build a proper armory, and there were rooms for each of us, water, warmth, and safety.

We could order food in for now. Hell, we needed to sit down and plan, sort all this shit out, not least the whole thing between me and Reign that was now out in the open.

My cheeks colored as she crouched, checking a low cupboard, and then looked up at me, the similarity to earlier, as she stared up into my eyes, literally drinking me down, coming strongly back to the fore.

She blushed a little too, then grinned, and I grinned back.

Luna was already heading for the rooms, with Gessh jogging to catch up, loudly commenting that as the biggest, she needed the biggest room.

It was like being surrounded by a squad again: the jokes, the horseplay. Well, the only difference with the sexual tension in the air was that it wasn't Sync and Richie this time, but me and Reign...Also, to the best of my knowledge, unlike those two, Reign hadn't just teased me and wandered off.

No, this was good, I decided. Here we could grow. Here we could get ready, prepare for the future, and get things back on the right path.

Finally, we had a home again.

THE END

REVIEWS

Hey! Well, I hope you enjoyed the book? If so, please, please remember to leave a review, its massively important, as not only does it let others know about the book, it also tells Amazon that the book is worth promoting, and makes it more likely that more people will see it.

That in turn will hopefully keep me able to keep writing full time, while listening to crazy German bands screaming in my ears, and frankly, I kinda really like that!

If you want to spread the good word, that'd be amazing, and if you know of anyone that might be interested in stocking my books, I'm happy to reach out and send them samples, but honestly, if you enjoy my madness, that's massive for me.

Thank you.

ARTEM 2: VENGEANCE

By Jez Cajiao

Warfare below the streets, backstabbing and brutality.

Kabutt is out. Out of the army, out of patience and out of control, he's found a home, people to fight for, and once again, the city seems determined to screw that up for him.

He's got backstabbing elves trying to rip him off, corpos forcing him and his team into unsanctioned deathmatches for live broadcasts, and of course, the usual skulduggery, not to mention more goddamn goblins.

He's got his suit though, it might be stripped, but he's got it, he's got hope, he's got heavy firepower and hell, he might even get laid.

All things are possible…provided you've got enough high explosive, anyway.

It's time to start evening the odds…

ARTEM

Okay everyone! So, if you've just finished my own story of Artem, then you'll know by now that this is only part of the story! There are three other authors sharing this world with me (at present) and each of us agreed some year and a half ago, to write two books in it.

Essentially, some of our characters cross over each other, others don't, some of the areas are explained, others are left to the imagination, but the world itself? Its one that we all worked on.

Those authors are Kevin Sinclair, Lars Machmüller, and Dawn Chapman, and these are their stories:

THE RISE OF OSHBOB

By Kevin Sinclair

The thing about Artem, it's a damn hard city to live in if you haven't got creds, and for creds you need opportunities.

The thing about opportunities is that they're thin on the ground for Orcs. One of the most reviled races in the sprawling city. And if you happen to be an Orc, stranded outside of the immense city walls, left for dead on the front lines of Artem's roving monster problem, then you're doubly screwed.

Like Oshbob.

The thing about Oshbob, he's tough and he's pissed! Missing a couple of important appendages, but with a will to survive like few others, if he can make it back to the city, he's determined never to be subject to the whims of the elite ever again.

He's gonna make something of himself, no matter the cost to those around him.

ARTEM: UNDERDOG

By Lars Machmüller

Start from behind? Cheat the system!

Out of credits, with trash-tier mods and no hope, Bowdoin Katamari resides at the bottom of the pile in the city of Artem.

A place where megacorporations, merc guilds and inner city pricks live like royalty while the rest suffer.

In spite of his poor prospects, this self-taught hacker does have a few things left. A seething hatred for the upper castes, a mind bursting with plots, and a like-minded crew determined to get ahead.

Down with the corpos—let the towers burn!

ARTEM: TAILSPIN

By Dawn Chapman

To save his family, Ruslan will risk it all…

Ruslan is determined to get his family out of debt by taking part in a dangerous race. With dreams of being a pilot, he is quickly brought back down to earth when he crashes and almost dies.

Now homeless and close to death, Ruslan's future is in peril. Abandoned by his family and friends, Ruslan agrees to risky cybernetic surgery to save his life. Unaware of the implications, Ruslan soon learns that the procedure is more experimental than he thought, but it could lead him to finally becoming a pilot.

After being enrolled in M-Corps hottest flight school, Ruslan makes some friends and more than a few enemies. Pushing himself to the limits, he knows it is only a matter of time before his new tech fails him completely, but he is determined to fight for as long as possible.

When a mutated abomination attacks the city of Artem, Ruslan and his comrades are deployed to take it down. A fight they must win, or the city will fall.

Does Ruslan have what it takes? Or will his body give out before he gets the chance to be the hero he always dreamed of being?

FACEBOOK AND SOCIAL MEDIA

If you want to reach out, chat or shoot the shit, you can always find me on either my author page here:

www.facebook.com/JezCajiaoAuthor

_OR_

We've recently set up a new Facebook group to spread the word about cool LitRPG books. It's dedicated to two very simple rules;

1; Lets spread the word about new and old brilliant LitRPG books.
2: Don't be a Dick!

They sound like really simple rules, but you'd be amazed…
Come join us!

https://www.facebook.com/groups/litrpglegion

I'm also on Discord here: **https://discord.gg/u5JYHscCEH**

Or I'm reaching out on other forms of social media atm, I'm just spread a little thin that's all!

You're most likely to find me on Discord, but please, don't be offended when I don't approve friend requests on my personal Facebook pages. I did originally, and several people abused that, sending messages to my family and being generally unpleasant, hence, the author page:

https://www.facebook.com/JezCajiaoAuthor

I hope you understand.

PATREON!

Okay then, now for those of you that don't know about Patreon, its essentially a way to support your favorite nutcases, you can sign up for a day or a month or a year, and you get various benefits for it, ranging from my heartfelt thanks, to advance access to the books, to me sending them books, naming characters and more.

At the time of me writing this, the advanced Patreon readers are finishing up Artem 2: Vengeance, and they're also getting access to Arise: Reclaimer, book 3 in that series. By the time this launches? I *think* they'll have access to Arise 4 as well, so yeah, you get plenty for the support!

There's one of my wonderful supporters out there that I have to thank personally as well; ASeaInStorm, you utter legend you. Thank you for sticking with it mate.

http://www.patreon.com/Jezcajiao

LEGION

Okay everybody, if you've not yet seen or heard, well, the secret is out! My wife Chrissy, and our friend Geneva and I have launched the Legion Publishers! We're taking on new authors, as well as experienced ones, focusing primarily on the LitRPG side of things, but we're open to anything really, with one very clear rule that guides our company:

Don't be a dick.

That's it. Our contracts aren't hidden behind layers of legalese, you can find them here:

https://www.legionpublishers.com/legioncontract

If you want to reach out and ask any questions, get an idea of the support we offer, and possibly become part of the family? We'd love to hear from you, just go to the link and fill in the form:

https://www.legionpublishers.com/contact-and-submissions

Hope you're having a good one!

-Jez, Chrissy and Geneva

RECOMMENDATIONS

I'm often asked for personal recommendations, so if this book has whetted your appetite for more LitRPG, please have a look at the following, these are brilliant series by brilliant authors!

Ascend Online by Luke Chmilenko

The Land by Aleron Kong

Challengers Call by Nathan A Thompson

SoulShip also by Nathan

Endless Online by M H Johnson

Silver Fox and the Western Hero, also by M H Johnson

The Good Guys/Bad Guys by Eric Ugland

Condition: Evolution by Kevin Sinclair

Space Seasons by Dawn Chapman

The Wayward Bard by Lars M

LITRPG!

To learn more about LitRPG, talk to other authors including myself, and to just have an awesome time, please join the LitRPG Group

www.facebook.com/groups/LitRPGGroup

FACEBOOK

There's also a few really active Facebook groups I'd recommend you join, as you'll get to hear about great new books, new releases and interact with all your (new) favorite authors! (I may also be there, skulking at the back and enjoying the memes…)

www.facebook.com/groups/LitRPGsociety/

www.facebook.com/groups/LitRPG.books/

www.facebook.com/groups/LitRPGforum/

www.facebook.com/groups/gamelitsociety/

www.ingramcontent.com/pod-product-compliance
Lightning Source LLC
Chambersburg PA
CBHW072006180726
48291CB00001BA/156